P9-CAD-523

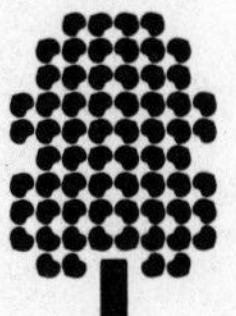

ALSO BY T. R. PEARSON

A Short History of a Small Place
Off for the Sweet Hereafter
The Last of How It Was

T. R. PEARSON

Call and Response

LINDEN PRESS/SIMON & SCHUSTER
New York London Toronto Sydney Tokyo

Linden Press
Simon & Schuster Building
Rockefeller Center
1230 Avenue of the Americas
New York, New York 10020

This book is a work of fiction. Names, characters, places and incidents are either the product of the author's imagination or are used fictitiously. Any resemblance to actual events or locales or persons, living or dead, is entirely coincidental.

Designed by Liney Li
Manufactured in the United States of America

1 3 5 7 9 10 8 6 4 2

Library of Congress Cataloging-in-Publication Data
Pearson, T. R., date
Call and response / T. R. Pearson.
p. cm.
I. Title.
PS3566.E235C55 1989
813'.54—dc 20 89-2627
ISBN 0-671-63992-7 CIP

For Mr. and Mrs. Lonnie J. Betts

Call and Response

One

IT had come to him from his daddy by way of his daddy's brother Tyler Lamont who'd wrapped it in a rag and laid it for safekeeping in the back of his uppermost bureau drawer which was for socks chiefly and cotton briefs and ribbed sleeveless undershirts as well and not heirlooms ever but this once which was probably how come Tyler Lamont forgot presently that back of his socks and his briefs and his undershirts was an item in a rag he'd been charged to pass on and bequeath. He did not, in fact, begin even to remember what precisely he'd been charged to do until purely years afterwards once he'd come to be widowed and alone and had failed somehow to cultivate the gumption for laundry his wife had possessed which left him soon enough undergarmentless entirely but for the clump of rag he discovered that he'd hoped, as he drew it out, was briefs.

They'd gone off outside Draper to the county fair in Tyler Lamont's secondhand Whippet which would be his daddy that was Nestor Tudor too and his daddy's brother Tyler Lamont that drove and George Wilmer from up the road and Eddie who had married one time George Wilmer's wife's sister but had gotten shortly shed of her, and they'd let on how it was Mr. Horace Bullins chiefly they'd developed an urge to see, Mr. Horace Bullins the man with three noses who for a solitary nickel displayed his six noseholes and for a pair of nickels together drove gutternails up through them like Eddie could have stood to look at, like Eddie most especially had a yen to watch that he told to George Wilmer and Tyler Lamont and Nestor's daddy that was Nestor too he did. But they didn't see Mr. Horace Bullins and didn't see the bigfooted colored woman with toenails like windowpanes or the midget horse or the tinyheaded man or the girl that turned every now and again into a writhing serpent or the rubbery boy or Amos the sizeable black bear that people paid to tussle and wrestle with but mostly got sat on by instead. They just passed altogether down the midway to the far end of it and stood for a time before a pair of timber posts with a square of canvas lashed and knotted between them, a square of canvas that moved and shifted and swelled on the breeze frontwards some and swelled on the breeze backwards some too and every once in a while just hung dead still like Eddie and George Wilmer and Nestor's daddy Nestor and Tyler Lamont with them could best peruse and ponder it, could best peruse and ponder anyhow the whole gaggle of women painted on the frontside of it in slick, lively colors, shapely women, bosomy shapely women in glittery underclothes and each of them bent and stooped so as to hold to their kneecaps which tended, Tyler Lamont pointed out, to enhance most especially the bosomy in particular that Eddie and George Wilmer and Nestor's daddy Nestor, who'd left inadvertently their chins upon their shirtfronts, failed somehow to dispute.

A squat bald man in a striped coat took the money and gave the tickets and held while he did it a Pall Mall between his lips that he squinted on account of and snorted on account of too and shortly plain spat out onto the packed dirt prior to picking fuzzy bits of rolling paper out from the corners of his mouth. Eddie wanted to know about the women, wanted to know from the squat bald man were they comely as he'd seen naked already in a tent show a woman one time, a woman he guessed had been beaten near about to death with the ugly stick like he didn't much want to pay money to see a whole pack of since there were evermore ugly women naked somewhere for nothing that the squat bald man in the striped coat figured was purely the truth of it and told to Eddie and George Wilmer and Tyler Lamont and Nestor's daddy Nestor how he figured himself it was after which he spread and laid back his lips and thereby displayed what sizeable teeth he had along with the sizeable socket he'd lost one from that he stuck his tongue into like he could not seem to help but stick it. He didn't take on himself any ugly women. He didn't take on himself but the manner of girls a man could carry home to his momma were he disposed for it. "Sweetest woman in the world," he said, "and handsome too," and he wiggled the fingers of his one hand after such a fashion as to suggest most especially to Eddie grace and elegance and breasts like honeydews all at the same time that somehow Eddie took the wiggly fingers to mean and so laid wide his own lips and displayed at the squat bald man his full entire set of sizeable teeth back.

Tyler Lamont wanted to sit down at the front just shy of the plankstage which most particularly Eddie and George Wilmer together were of a sudden emphatic about as they'd have shortly before them, they figured, an exposed gland to lay back and ponder which down at the front just shy of the plankstage seemed to them precisely the spot for. Tyler Lamont, however, wasn't the sort to do much gland pondering himself that he told to Eddie and George Wilmer he wasn't and explained how instead he intended to get chiefly wafted at like he felt obliged to sit just shy of the plankstage for as the sorts of things that did in fact waft, your perfumy scents and such as them, did not most times waft any ways to speak of. For his part, Nestor's daddy Nestor could not see the harm in getting, while he pondered what glands got brought out and uncovered, wafted at which, upon deliberation, Eddie and George Wilmer could not hardly see the harm in either, so they let themselves get led by Tyler Lamont not just down to the very front but to the middle of the very front too where Tyler Lamont figured the ventilation from the lefthand flap and the ventilation from the righthand flap, in conjunction with the rising air from the tallow lamps, would meet and mingle like struck him as propitious which Nestor's daddy Nestor and Eddie and George Wilmer told to him, "Fine," on account of and dropped down together onto their seats so as to try to discover could they, if they slouched and laid back, see plain where it was they all three figured a naked gland would shortly come to be.

George Wilmer spied back a row off to the one side a pair of Stoneville Gillespies he'd lately run up on elsewhere and he raised at them his fingers and told to them, "Hey boys," and fielded in return an inquiry from the lefthand Stoneville Gillespie who'd gotten encouraged by the righthand one to find out did George Wilmer intend to raise up shortly and bite that thing that George Wilmer guessed back he might if he didn't just wear it for a time like a hat instead clean down to the earlobes which both Gillespies together felt of a sudden obliged to uncross their legs at the thought of. A string of Wentworth Duprees came in to fill the seats back of Eddie and Tyler Lamont and George Wilmer and Nestor's daddy Nestor and brought with them their usual Wentworth Dupree pungent stink like illustrated in a dramatic sort of a way various of your wafting principles that Nestor's daddy Nestor and George Wilmer and Eddie too leaned in at Tyler Lamont to tell to him it did, and Eddie who had not ever cultivated much patience for a troublesome scent in other people, most especially other people like Duprees who did not just plain emanate but were as well the sort to belch and break wind and snort up phlegm and spit it as a kind of a sideline, turned near about full around and showed to the four Duprees his altogether icy indignant face that two Duprees in particular let on to him they'd be willing to alter and transform in an everlasting kind of a way. Consequently, Eddie just sat for a spell frontwards and slid his eyes from side to side so as to see maybe behind himself a little and he pressed every once in a while Tyler Lamont to tell to him what it was the Wentworth Duprees were up to which turned out chiefly to be just belching and farting and snorting and wafting with, at length, some noticeable fidgeting thrown in as well that went shortly to hollering instead, went shortly to yelping and hooting and stomping and whistling too by all four Duprees at the same time who appeared to be a little anxious to ponder an organ themselves.

The squat bald man in the striped coat only presently tied shut the front flaps and advanced towards the stage through the uproar that had spread and risen to a pitch. He took up off one end of the stagefloor a squeezebox and played straightaway on it a manner of squeezebox flourish that everybody fell silent on account of but for the Wentworth Duprees who left off with their hooting and stomping and such but persisted most especially with their snorting and phlegmdredging and occasional windbreaking too. They were desirous, they told to the squat bald man in the striped coat, desirous near about as acutely as they'd ever previously between them been desirous before to see shortly ahead of them on the plankstage an assortment of chesty women with their crucial parts exposed like the Duprees between them could not arrive at a consensus about and so announced by turns those particular parts that seemed to the each of them most especially crucial somehow which naturally was straightoff your pendulous glands followed by your chief nether one with your thick nappy growth atop it and your upended posterior breech as well along with that tiny white patch of skin back of the anklebone which the Dupree on the nearend had a passion for and told outright he did like Eddie felt obliged to turn around and pull at him a face on account of that he got, by the nearend Dupree, advised about.

The squat bald man in the striped coat was not, however, disposed to call out a chesty woman straightaway and undertook instead to tell a yarn about a dirtfarmer and his daughter Darla with lengthsome black lustrous locks who took up with a tinker that had come roundabout to sell to the dirtfarmer a skillet if he could, and they got together in the hayloft, which would be the tinker and would be Darla with him, engaged like they stayed for a spell until the dirtfarmer found them out when they got of a sudden disengaged instead and the tinker was fairly well set to explain to the dirtfarmer what just lately he'd likely figured he'd seen which probably wasn't hardly what it was he'd seen in fact when the two middle Duprees interrupted the squat bald man in the striped coat who possessed, they suspected, his own upended posterior breech that he was in some true and verifiable danger of viewing for himself the inside of like they let on to him he was. So the squat bald man pumped his squeezebox two times and showed primarily to the Duprees his toothgap with his wrinkly pink tonguend stuck in it, and once his flourish had died partly away he swept his arm towards the far wing and intoned most especially at the four Duprees together, "I give you the rapturous Sally," and then he raised with a cord the red velvety curtain back of him.

However, Sally did not straightaway slink out onto the stage so Tyler Lamont and George Wilmer and Eddie and Nestor's daddy Nestor studied for a time instead of her the canvas backdrop which had gotten painted to look like Egypt that Tyler Lamont, who guessed he'd been places and guessed he'd seen things, told to most everybody otherwise it had. He pointed out for George Wilmer in particular the pyramids and the oasis and the spotted venomous snake and the camel train along with the assorted Nubian dogheaded slaves that struck George Wilmer as homelier even than Rothrocks whom he had not previously suspected had much Nubian to them but just chiefly Turner somewhat and Lumly somewhat too. Presently Sally, once she was fixed and situated and rapturous enough for it, signaled the squat bald man from off out of sight and he struck up on his squeezebox a manner of melody like seemed to Tyler Lamont a touch Egyptian itself and he hummed at George Wilmer and Eddie as well as Nestor's daddy Nestor ever so hardly at all what parts seemed chiefly Egyptian to him which George Wilmer begged to differ on account of as the entire item sounded pretty completely a polka instead which Tyler Lamont, who'd been places and seen things, leaned forward and informed George Wilmer had come first off from Egyptian Nubian dogheaded slaves like he'd guessed George Wilmer knew already that George Wilmer straightaway recollected he'd just forgotten he had.

Sally slipped mostly sideways out onto the stage into the yellow lamplight and commenced directly to lurch and gyrate. She had on a manner of gauzy outfit with loose billowy legs to it and a loose billowy top and a scrap of gauzy cloth that hung suspended down across the most of her face like was enticing and exotic most especially once she'd reached up and snatched it off and said in a squeally kind of a voice, "Hey." They guessed she'd been willowy one time and handsome with it but had gotten lately puffy mostly all over and so had surrendered considerable of the willowy and noticeable of the handsome too and showed instead an inclination to be inordinately jiggly like Eddie and Tyler Lamont and George Wilmer and Nestor's daddy Nestor could see her at even under her loose billowy bottom and her loose billowy top as well that after a spell of twirling and darting and lurching she began to slip out of and thereby revealed a pink satiny brassiere with here and there some baubles to it. She seemed to have intended to slip out of her billowy pants near about the same way as she'd just lately gotten shed of her billowy top but she caught a jagged piece of a toenail in the gauzy cloth and so hopped for a while on her free foot like might have seemed altogether graceless but for the squeezebox polka that fairly cried out for a bout of one-footed hopping to go with the twirling and darting and lurching and such.

Sally's lacy panties had probably been one time white but had taken some noticeable abuse and so were not purely white any longer and had begun at the crotch to fray and tear that two of the Duprees together informed Sally about and announced what item they could see some of which seemed to them cause for whooping and stomping and yelping and phlegmdredging that they got by the remaining Duprees joined at. For her part, Sally just mostly bobbed and gyrated back and displayed for a spell her posterior which was itself of such a shape and magnitude as to dwell for the most part altogether outside the variety of lacy panties Sally had undertaken to contain and cover it with, and she swung it to the left and then back to the right prior to loosing it to circulate just by itself all roundabout which enthralled most especially the Duprees who inadvertently broke wind that way they tended to once they'd come to be enthralled like could not be taken for regular purposeful windbreaking when the Duprees were usually inclined to raise up both their legs and every now and again strike a match.

Presently, Sally reached with both hands behind herself and unhooked her pink satiny brassiere clasp and uncovered her pendulous bosoms one at the time that all four Duprees together vented themselves on account of every way possible they could while Eddie, for his part, praised God as God seemed to him at the sight of Sally's naked breasts pertinent somehow, or at the sight of Sally's primarily naked breasts anyway that were not full out to the very tipends naked entirely due to the sparkly discs she'd stuck one way or another where Eddie had not ever previously seen on a woman sparkly discs that Nestor's daddy Nestor admitted to him once he'd gotten asked it he'd not ever previously seen on a woman himself. "When Momma goes naked," he told to Eddie and told to George Wilmer too who at the sound of Momma and naked together had grown inspired of a sudden to pitch and lean, "she don't go but naked entirely," that Eddie recollected George Wilmer's wife's sister he'd come to be shed of had gone like herself whenever naked was how she went which George Wilmer wished Eddie had not made just presently mention of since he was not much pleased to think on his wife's sister all bare and uncovered as it put him in mind chiefly of his wife that way too like did not seem to him timely what with Sally's glands and such where just lately they'd come to be, or Sally's sparkly discs anyhow that were not just plain and unadorned sparkly discs but had dangling from them what appeared most especially to George Wilmer curtain pulls, or scant pieces anyway of curtain pulls like the ones in his front room back of his speckledy drapes.

Tyler Lamont himself had seen curtain pulls once previously on a woman's otherwise naked breasts that he told to Eddie and George Wilmer and Nestor's daddy Nestor he had and undertook to explain in a mathematical sort of way how it was Sally would probably twitch and sway just shortly though for her part Sally only stood a spell and announced in her squealy voice that she'd been born and raised in Talladega and was pleased to be where it was she'd arrived at which she could not recall straightoff the name of most probably due to the Duprees who were announcing to Sally back where precisely they wished to press their faces and what exactly they wished to mash their fleshy ears against that Sally shut at the Duprees a purply eyelid on account of. She did, however, endeavor after a spell to twitch and sway both like Tyler Lamont reminded Eddie and George Wilmer and Nestor's daddy Nestor he'd told to them already she would, and the pulls swung together the one way and swung together the other and then orbited directly full roundabout like they accelerated at until everybody could see where it was they were and where it was they'd been and where it was they were going all at once at the same time just precisely.

Eddie found he far and away preferred the stomping and the lurching and the twirling to just the standing and the bobbing no matter how Sally rotated her pulls roundabout which was clockwise there at the outset and counterclockwise behind it followed by a spell of both directions at the same time like seemed to the Duprees altogether confounding and they vented and grunted and snorted and spat and invited Sally by turns to draw up their bony noses and have atop them a seat that struck the Duprees as the hospitable thing to invite Sally to draw up their noses and do seeing as how lately she'd stomped and lurched and twirled and bobbed and so was likely purely frazzled and could stand to loll a time. But Sally from Talladega just exhibited once further her purply eyelid and at length, to the accompaniment of an elaborate squeezebox flourish, threw wide her arms and dipped and squatted ever so briefly after what fashion could not seem hardly stately and regal in sparkly discs and pulls and frayed lacy panties like maybe in regular clothes it would have, and Sally took up her brassiere from the stagefloor and her gauzy billowy outfit too and said all squealy as she raised up her fingers, "Bye," after which she trotted across the plankstage and wiggled one time her jiggly posterior prior to stepping entirely out of sight.

Straightoff the squat bald man was anxious to find out if hadn't Sally gotten taken to be wholly rapturous the way he'd let on previously she was and he inquired two times about it before the Duprees in the middle of the second row, who had not themselves joined in the general ovation, informed the squat bald man how they'd driven over clear from Wentworth to see chiefly some undiluted fully exposed snatch like they'd been told out front when they bought their tickets they would as they'd made it a point to find out would they since they'd driven anyhow clear from Wentworth most specifically for it, and the nearend Dupree wondered in a semirhetorical sort of a way if they'd any of them seen just lately naked uncloaked snatch like they'd driven clear from Wentworth for that the three remaining Duprees alone hollered, "Hell no," at since they did not between them have much grasp of the rhetorical. From atop the plankstage the squat bald man laid back his head for the Duprees and opened for them his mouth so as to indicate how he was himself fairly amused with the recent spate of naked snatch talk that he let on put him in mind of a tale about a man whose organ had gone altogether rigid and upright on him and had stayed for a considerable spell rigid and upright both, had stayed in fact swollen and extended so awful long that he'd carried it to his doctor so as to find out could he cause it again to droop and dangle like most times previously it had, and the squat bald man was set to reveal most especially to the Duprees what cure it was the doctor had advised for the man with the rigid upright organ when the four Duprees together commenced to tell the squat bald man instead how shortly they might come to be inclined to separate from him his own undoubtedly droopy dangling item which they intended to introduce entirely up into that part of himself where they assured him they still meant to stick his head firstoff as they had not forgotten how they'd promised already they would.

Naturally, then, the squat bald man left off his therapeutic talk straightaway like Eddie grew perturbed on account of as he'd been lately plagued himself with a rigid upright organ and figured he could stand some doctorly advice which was how come he said out into the general air at nobody in particular, "Hey!" when the squat bald man got interrupted by the Duprees and which was how come he said out into the general air, "Hey!" another time when he heard instead of therapeutic talk a squeezebox flourish. And Eddie said at Nestor's daddy Nestor and George Wilmer together, "Well shit," and he let on how he needed every now and again himself to get organ relief as he was the bulk of the time steely like women all over had told him the bulk of the time he was that he let on could be a plague and a bother as he tugged with his thumbs at his front beltloops, and George Wilmer, who was not often anymore steely himself, guessed if Eddie would just marry his wife's sister one time further he'd be after a fashion healed and mended which Eddie straightaway purely goddamned about.

The squat bald man did not call Laura Marie rapturous, Laura Marie whom he'd flourished on account of, but just waved his arm instead and then set in on a Nubian dogheaded manner of thing with some jump and lilt to it both and noticeable unpolkalike pretensions that got soon enough vanquished and done in. Laura Marie did not show much disposition to twirl and lurch and such but walked chiefly out across the plankstage and drew up dead still in the middle of it where she failed to say even the first squealy thing but just for a time stood and looked out past and overtop everybody to the back tentwall. She was scrawny and slight and pointyjointed and horsefaced that most especially the four Duprees noticed straightoff and announced to each other they'd noticed it prior to informing the squat bald man together about the scrawny and the slight and the pointyjointed and the horsefaced too in case they'd all somehow escaped him. She had on a kind of a satiny green thing over her upper parts that was not much in the way of a brassiere which George Wilmer, who'd been swept into the Dupree announcing glut, announced himself it was not much in the way of that Tyler Lamont announced to him back he'd noticed as well. Eddie, who'd not paid truly much mind to the brassiere, had recognized straightaway how Laura Marie's panties were not themselves satiny green like he intoned chiefly to Nestor's daddy Nestor they weren't that Nestor's daddy Nestor had on his own figured he might shortly speak of. Him and Eddie agreed the panties seemed to them instead your ordinary cotton lowrise sort and did not strike them as much in the way of showpanties as they lacked the glamour that maybe green and satiny would have lent them, and they told what they'd arrived at to George Wilmer and Tyler Lamont both who had just lately dropped down from the brassiere and so had not yet assessed the panties themselves.

The Duprees felt obliged to inquire was there pieces of their particular persons Laura Marie might be disposed to perch atop of as they'd asked Sally from Talladega ahead of her and did not want Laura Marie to feel slighted. If she wanted to perch a spell, though, she did not let on one way or another about it and instead stepped and kicked a time or two to the squeezebox beat and turned herself sideways so as to display in profile her upper scrawny parts and her lower scrawny parts and her shiny black spike heels with the straps roundabout the ankles. For a time, Laura Marie kicked her feet and twisted some and spun round ever so slowly as she entertained advice from the Duprees on the subject of her satiny brassiere and her regular lowrise panties that they were hopeful and desirous of seeing both of elsewhere and shortly too since they'd come, they told to her, clear from Wentworth where they guessed they could see if they wanted to underwear aplenty. But Laura Marie didn't appear disposed to go naked straightaway and she just kicked and just twisted and just spun round and made every now and again out past the plankstage a face like she'd lately swallowed a spoonful of earwax which seemed meant to be cheery but did not look at all cheery truly, and just when the Duprees most especially had begun to suspect she would not go naked presently even either she reached of a sudden back behind herself and loosed her satiny green top that she dropped to the floor prior to stepping fairly altogether free of her cotton panties and launching them off her left foot out beyond the Duprees, who had jumped and reached to catch them, and clean to the Stoneville Gillespies instead who tussled for a time on account of them until the lefthand Stoneville Gillespie had successfully wrenched them loose from the righthand Stoneville Gillespie's fingers so as to swab with them pretty much his entire face and wear them at last on his head with his ears out the legholes.

Laura Marie wasn't bedecked with pulls and discs and such and she was not ample anywhere at all like Sally from Talladega had been ample and so didn't shake and quiver on her entire person but at the bosom somewhat though not awful much truly at the bosom even like the Duprees felt pressed to announce, given their druthers, they preferred for a woman at the bosom to do. She was blessed, however, otherwise in the form of rubbery joints like seemed just your regular pointy sort until she all at once contorted, until she all at once bent full over and reached with her arms where arms generally don't and raised up her one leg to lay it where most legs never would and then situated her face so as to look out backwards and upside down at especially the Duprees who'd driven clear from Wentworth to see what item she was looking backwards and upside down over. Eddie, who had not anticipated he would have all at once and straightaway cause to, leapt bolt upright out from his seat so as to shift and situate his private organ that had gone on him steelier even than he'd so much as figured and speculated your private sort of organ could go like he was just undertaking to tell to Nestor's daddy Nestor the news of when the Dupree behind him reared up so far as to take hold of Eddie at the shoulders and cause him to sit of a sudden back down, cause him to sit in fact so directly back down as to snap, Eddie feared, his steely organ clean in two that he wanted to inform Nestor's daddy Nestor about as well but could not somehow collect the breath for it.

The Duprees as a group were feeling fairly redundant since Laura Marie did not look to require but her own nose to perch atop of like reduced appreciably their usefulness and they sulked awhile which meant they hooted and stomped and dredged and snorted but broke only dire occasional wind until at last they perked up once Laura Marie had lowered her naked backside to the plankstage and raised high her legs and crossed her feet behind her head where her spiked heels stood up like antlers. Naturally, it was a queer and remarkable sight already before she got, aside from plain contorted, pendulous too. Naturally it was already strange and already wondrous together even for the Duprees who'd probably struck out previously from Wentworth and seen all manner of snatches before without coming across one quite so upended and laid wide like George Wilmer told to Tyler Lamont put him in mind of throwing open the kitchen cabinet and pondering the sinktrap which Tyler Lamont undertook to hone and improve but could not truly since he found himself put fairly much in mind of pondering a sinktrap as well. They simply had not suspected pendulous was what Laura Marie would bother to get after she'd gotten already contorted prior to it and once she lifted herself off the planking on the palms of her hands until she swung free at the armsockets everybody altogether, which would be your Duprees and your Gillespies and your Suggs back of them and your adjacent Clodfelters along with an assortment of what George Wilmer took for Truaxes chiefly like had seemed to Tyler Lamont doubtful as they'd looked to him fairly Greerish instead, exclaimed in a breathy appreciative sort of a way that did not have to it words much but did not have to it truly call for them.

The squat bald man undertook to render on his squeezebox a spell of pendulous upended gland music that had some appreciable jump to it and fairly much suited, it seemed to Tyler Lamont, the feat which Laura Marie persisted at longer than the Duprees most especially could believe she was able to persist at it, longer than the Duprees figured they could likely persist at it themselves if they could get in the first place contorted. But she left off just up and of a sudden, dropped all at once her posterior to the planking and loosed her feet from back of her head and stood upright where she looked once more just scrawny and slight and pointyjointed and horsefaced like she had not as a sheepshank looked, and she kicked a little in her spiked heels and turned round ever so slowly and twitched and jerked every now and again pieces of herself to the squeezebox beat that had gone just lately altogether Nubian and dogheaded once more. The Duprees had managed to get steely items themselves that they spoke of together to Laura Marie who showed to them back her squinty earwax face and just kicked and just twitched and just jerked and jiggled at her bosomy parts though did not jiggle much truly like the Duprees, once they'd done with their steely items, spoke of as well while Laura Marie bent and stooped and looked set maybe to contort again but merely took up her satiny brassiere off the plankstage and requested from the lefthand Gillespie her cotton panties that the righthand Gillespie reached over and yanked off his head for her and tossed to the stage along with the moderate clump of hair he'd yanked as well that the lefthand Gillespie impressed upon him he had, and Laura Marie waved her hand one time with the brassiere in it and got by the squat bald man flourished on out of sight after which he dropped and let dangle his arms so as to send blood places it hadn't lately been.

There spread among the Duprees the notion that the squat bald man might attempt to speak, might set out to tell a pointless thing like previously he'd exhibited an inclination for which was how come the Duprees grew of a sudden preemptive and identified which parts they'd wrench and loose and spoke of what place they'd put them once they had like the squat bald man let on he took the gist of, or anyhow raised again his arms and worked again his squeezebox that he played a low moody scrap of music on prior to telling most especially to the Duprees how they were just before getting stunned and overwhelmed by Glenola and not just Glenola plain and alone but Glenola along with her jangly bells of desire that Glenola from off beyond the stage set to working so that they did in fact jangle a little and tinkle some too but purely clanged mostly and sounded for all the world like a dozen milkcows at a dead run. And Nestor's daddy Nestor looked past George Wilmer and Eddie at Tyler Lamont and told him, "Christ," and Tyler Lamont looked past Eddie and George Wilmer at Nestor's daddy Nestor and told him, "Glenola," back.

She pretty much bounded into view and struck most especially

George Wilmer straightoff as the manner of woman who'd not been built for bounding truly due to what heft and girth she had to raise up and float in order in the first place to bound like seemed to George Wilmer appreciable, like seemed to George Wilmer altogether more appreciable in fact than was worth so much as attempting even to raise up or float either one. But she went ahead and bounded nonetheless, bounded sideways the full breadth of the plankstage and sideways partly back beating the planking with the balls of her naked feet and causing noticeable grit and dirt to spring up from it like George Wilmer said suggested a thing about the heft and the girth that Tyler Lamont agreed with him it after a fashion did while Eddie wanted to know from Nestor's daddy Nestor had he ever previously seen such a sizeable woman leap and travel so that Nestor's daddy Nestor managed to say one time more Christ at.

She had on a kind of a leathery getup most especially along about her upper parts which were contained in a scant and ever so tentative sort of a way by what looked to be a pair of barber strops that had gotten looped and hung each one from her shoulder to her opposite hip and so crossed and intersected along about her bellybutton which needed itself to get contained some as well as it was purely in the midst of where her girth and her heft both had come to be most noticeably concentrated. Her lower parts were covered there at the first by a manner of tiny skirt that looked to have been once a dust ruffle but she straightaway freed herself from it and slung it for a spell roundabout her head prior to loosing it to sail out overtop of Eddie who could not, on account of his steeliness, jump and reach like in his regular loose rubbery state he could, and out overtop the Duprees too who did jump and did reach but failed nonetheless to take hold of the tiny ruffly skirt that sailed on back to one of the Greerish Truaxes who lifted up his fingers to maybe grab it with but caught instead chiefly the metal clasp of it against his flat bony forehead like stunned him a little and got him directly abused and ridiculed by all four Duprees together who let it be known in a widespread sort of a way how, had they gotten the ruffly skirt thrown to them, they'd not have been just hit on the forehead by it.

Glenola wore on her lower parts under where her skirt had been a pair of speckledy briefs she'd come upon some time back before she'd learned to use a fork with what thoroughgoing success she'd apparently learned lately to use one. Consequently, she looked constricted roundabout the hipjoints like Tyler Lamont announced she did that got him grunted at by George Wilmer and Eddie and Nestor's daddy Nestor and got him told by the Duprees back of him a bilious thing similar to the bilious thing they'd recently told to the Truax as the Duprees were not the sort to squander a vile abusive mood once they'd found cause to settle into one. They had an observation to make as well on the squat bald man's latest Nubian dogheaded polka which sounded to the Duprees remarkably like his previous Nubian dogheaded polka that they informed him they knew themselves it did and they went on to speak to the squat bald man of what particular orifice they'd previously spoken of with him which they figured they might slip a strop and some jangly bells up into if Glenola ever decided to go on and loose her upper parts from the strop off her one shoulder and the strop off her other shoulder with it like the Duprees were beginning to suspect she never would that they looked together set to tell to even Glenola maybe a moderately bilious thing on account of but got prevented from it by Glenola herself who stuck her thick meaty tongue out from her mouth and touched, after some fairly aimless wiggling and jabbing and poking, the tipend of her nose with it.

And the nearend Dupree told to her, "Babydoll," in an emphatic sort of a way and showed her his own tongue back that was not itself especially meaty and wouldn't hardly reach the tipend of the Dupree's nose but would trough up like the Dupree showed to Glenola it would prior to blowing for her a spit bubble off the end of it that was a gift he figured he'd been born with which he told to Glenola was how precisely he figured he'd come by it. The farend Dupree opposite to him guessed he'd been born with a gift himself that he unfastened his trousers and displayed the entire length of clean down to the wrinkly sack and Glenola touched for him the tipend of her nose another time like produced on the farend Dupree's exposed gift a palpable effect that the farend Dupree whooped on account of and lurched and jumped too and inadvertently touched with his affected item the Dupree alongside him who whooped and lurched and jumped some himself and vented at length towards the farend Dupree near about the identical manner of bilious thing that previously had twice already been vented which the farend Dupree replied to by touching not so inadvertently one time more with his agitated organ the Dupree down from him who whooped and lurched and jumped again and rose to altogether new heights of biliousness.

At length Glenola commenced to work free from her jangly strops, stuck anyhow her thumb under the one of them and made like to take it off and then quit at it prior to making like to take it off some more what way was meant to be tantalizing that Tyler Lamont explained it was meant to be most especially to Eddie who'd grown lately unbearably steely and was laid anymore against his chair like a stick of wood so that he touched just the front of the seat and the top of the back and figured he was sufficiently afflicted without getting tantalized too. She did, however, actually slip off over her head an entire jangly strop after a considerable spell of appearing about to, and consequently Glenola uncovered and made entirely naked a solitary bosom that the Duprees in particular grew straightaway transported by the sight of and so told to Glenola your enraptured variety of things and announced to her where their fleshy ears needed shortly to get laid that Glenola let on she was herself diverted to hear, or anyhow poked and jabbed and wiggled her tongue in what Tyler Lamont took for amusement that he explained to Eddie he'd taken it. George Wilmer was curious to find out from Nestor's daddy Nestor if he'd ever previously seen on a woman such purely expansive solitary pink bumpy parts, or such a purely expansive solitary pink bumpy part anyway like he guess suggested and implied how the remaining stropped over pink bumpy part was probably purely expansive itself though maybe not so utterly purely expansive as the uncovered one appeared to him to be since he knew for a fact that pink bumpy parts on the same exact woman did not have to be themselves identical as he'd seen with his very eyes evidence to the contrary, but before Nestor's daddy Nestor could tell to him his own particular opinion back Glenola tantalized her way clean out of her remaining jangly strop thereby revealing a pink bumpy part measurably more purely expansive than the pink bumpy part she'd just previously revealed that George Wilmer had taken already for likely the biggest pink bumpy part roundabout which of a sudden it just plain wasn't anymore.

"Sweet Jesus," George Wilmer told to Nestor's daddy Nestor with an evangelical manner of lilt to it and he butted up together his thumbends and his foremost fingerends so as to approximate and display the circumference as he took it to be that he squirted breath at the sight of and wondered at Nestor's daddy Nestor of didn't it seem to him the size of a jarlid, didn't it seem to him the size of a jarlid near about just precisely that Nestor's daddy Nestor couldn't say rightoff it did as a general sort of a thing since he'd seen previously your big jarlids and your middling jarlids and your tiny jarlids too. He admitted, however, he'd not seen any time before that he knew tell of such a massive pink bumpy part on a woman, a massive pink bumpy part that struck him, once he thought on it, as maybe near about jarlid size, and he butted his own fingers and thumbs like George Wilmer had just lately left off at.

"Quart?" George Wilmer wanted to know.

"Quart," Nestor's daddy Nestor told to him back and displayed again the empty air he'd shaped his fingers around.

The sight of Glenola altogether barechested and lurching and bobbing and bouncing and flopping and such had produced in the Duprees some fairly advanced frothiness like Tyler Lamont told to Eddie he did not find much surprising though he'd come to be a little astounded at how it was the Gillespies back of them were hooting and wailing and yipping and suggesting every now and again to Glenola applications for their own stiff extended organs which they insisted they each had one of. Tyler Lamont had simply not ever before heard such talk from a Gillespie as best as he could recollect and he inquired of Eddie had he ever before heard from a Gillespie such talk himself that Eddie, laid full out against his chairedges with the most of his spit gone dry and pasty, made a kind of a noise at that did not sound to Tyler Lamont much like a yes or much like a no either one which he told to Eddie straightoff it didn't. Eddie had to his own organ, which was well past stiff and well past extended, an extraordinary ache that he found he could not any longer just lay against his chairedges and tolerate and so he pitched forward and stood himself upright where he was just beginning to find out he could not hardly tolerate his extraordinary ache either when Glenola, who'd twirled and pranced to the lip of the plankstage, told to him, "Hey sugar," and stooped so as to press for a moment Eddie's face tight up against her cleavage where Eddie did not truly realize his face had gotten put until after it had been removed already when he could see plain where he'd just lately come from, and Eddie watched Glenola raise back up and twirl and prance off elsewhere like he grew captivated and fairly enchanted by the sight of and consequently failed to notice what ire the Duprees had just lately undertaken to lavish him with, failed to notice it anyhow until the Dupree that had creased and situated Eddie previously creased and situated him again like Eddie would have shrieked on account of had his spit not gone dry and pasty already.

George Wilmer had come to figure Glenola would likely just twirl and prance and bob and flop and lurch as it seemed to him enough that she could considering how she was inordinately bosomy and quite sufficiently thick and sizeable elsewhere to render just twirling and prancing and bobbing and flopping and lurching into a manner of accomplishment. She possessed, however, an additional talent that she had to get altogether out from her speckledy panties to display and she unconstricted her thighs like the Duprees let on they approved of and exposed her creamy bare backside which was itself of an altogether appreciable magnitude. Free from her various constraints, Glenola bounded all loose and jiggly up to the front of the plankstage and requested from a particular Clodfelter his eyeglasses that a middle Dupree did Glenola the service of snatching off the Clodfelter's face for her which the Clodfelter said Hey! at in an irate sort of a way that just slipped out like he explained to the middle Dupree once he'd been quizzed about it your irate manner of things sometimes do. They were little round gold wire glasses with earhooks and a crack in the left lens and Glenola dragged them up the length of herself as she made most particularly at the Clodfelter, who could not but remotely see her make them, low moanful breathy noises which Eddie bowed up his back between his chairedges and wished at Tyler Lamont he was stone deaf on account of as low moanful breathy noises seemed to him the last thing he had just presently call for. She put the Clodfelter's eyeglasses in her cleavage for a time and they stayed all by themselves suspended there while the Duprees wished aloud in a prayerful fashion they had astigmatisms of their own which they grew fairly impassioned about once Glenola had stuck the Clodfelter's eyeglasses near about altogether into her mouth where she slobbered them up pretty completely and then drew them out so as to stick them instead elsewhere, stick them instead elsewhere entirely that she dragged them back down the bulk of herself to do and she just plain spread out her legs and squatted and introduced into her exposed gland the Clodfelter's eyeglasses earhooks and all like had not even the Duprees, who'd in their day struck out from Wentworth to see naked a snatch or two, hardly anticipated she would. And the Clodfelter said, "What?" once most everybody otherwise had grown gaspy like he could hear they had. "What!" he said another time to chiefly the Clodfelter next to him who did not himself have call for eyeglasses but every now and again to read tiny print when he usually held up before his face his wife's pair to see through, but the sighted Clodfelter could manage only a Biblical manner of thing back like failed to clarify for the moderately blind one the general gaspiness which had not seemed to him much in the way of your Biblical sort of gaspiness though it had sounded to have a touch of the miraculous to it like presently the second bout of gaspiness had as well when Glenola spread and squatted and drew back out of herself between her foremost finger and her thumb the little round gold wire eyeglasses with the earhooks and the cracked lens that she gave over straightaway to Tyler Lamont who'd been convenient to give them over straightaway to but he got directly relieved of them by the farend Dupree who laid to his nose the Clodfelter's eyeglasses and sniffed them with the sort of zeal and fervor George Wilmer most especially had not ever previously seen a man sniff eyeglasses with that he felt obliged to announce and proclaim the news of.

On his squeezebox the squat bald man struck up for Glenola a slow sultry kind of a number that did not seem to have a trace of a polka about it but ever so hardly at all, and Glenola sidled and gyrated chiefly and held her bosoms for a time in her cupped hands, or as much of her bosoms as she could hold in them like was not truly considerable of either, and she displayed her meaty tongue that she laid sometimes to the tipend of her nose but mostly just poked and jabbed and wiggled instead. The Duprees, who were curious to discover what precisely Glenola's nether gland could tolerate, offered up an assortment of loose items they figured for likely and which for the most part were maybe likely even excepting the solitary brogan which the Duprees who had not taken it off wanted the Dupree who had to stick his foot back into and thereby stifle what aroma he'd loosed that could not even the Duprees otherwise much abide. Glenola, however, did not appear inclined to introduce any additional items into her gland and just lurched and bobbed and bounced and jiggled and pranced and twirled for a time until she swept at last along the frontedge of the plankstage and took from the nearend Dupree's outstretched hand his pocketcomb which did not look to George Wilmer to be packed and clogged with near so much scalp sludge as he'd anticipated judging from who it was that sometimes maybe put the thing through his hair in the first place. She got offered as well the farend Dupree's agitated organ clean down to the wrinkly sack but took instead a hinged Barlow from the middle Dupree next to him, a hinged Barlow with a fat long blade and a fat stubby blade too that she held together with the pocketcomb as she told to the farend Dupree, or told anyhow chiefly to the farend Dupree's exhibited organ, how she saw every now and again night crawlers roundabout that would shame it which produced on the Dupree's organ an altogether instantaneous and belittling effect.

Straightaway Glenola spread and squatted like previously she had and laid up into herself the comb rightoff followed by the Barlow all shut up and folded after which she stood back upright and pranced and gyrated pretty much like a regular unfreighted manner of woman might prance and might gyrate as best as Tyler Lamont could tell, and he guessed if he had the occasion and the orifice as well to shove up inside himself a hinged knife and a pocketcomb both he would not likely prance and gyrate afterwards, would not likely, Tyler Lamont admitted, be in much of a mood for it. And she bent even some too and twitched her expansive posterior from side to side prior to dropping once more into her squat and fetching out from her interior the Barlow and the comb both that she gave back over to the Duprees to inhale like they all four took turns at. Glenola wondered just out at everybody all at once after she'd gotten shed of the comb and after she'd gotten shed of the Barlow if wouldn't a cigarette sit just right that the Gillespies most especially felt a cigarette would and offered to her a Chesterfield King, offered to her in fact an entire pack of Chesterfield Kings which they hoped she would cart for a time roundabout, but Glenola stepped instead over to the squat bald man who left off with his squeezebox so as to give to her a Pall Mall and a match to light it, and she smoked it for a time just in her mouth but presently assumed on the stagelip her squat and smoked for a time her Pall Mall elsewhere entirely.

George Wilmer had not supposed she'd have the draw for it. George Wilmer had not guessed she could pull and toke so that he admitted to Tyler Lamont he hadn't and to Nestor's daddy Nestor and to Eddie too who moaned from his chairedges back at him. But the firecoal glowed and the ash grew and the smoke squirted and rose and the Duprees that had not in a great while dredged phlegm, dredged of a sudden considerable of it and spat and whooped and snorted and broke such a load of thunderous inadvertent wind as to only begin to suggest their awe and wonder. Eddie was himself a trifle fearful of a fire since he had to him a cautious streak and could not hardly approve of how Glenola pulled and toked in amongst her bushy hair that he figured could just go up, could just suddenly combust which Eddie from his chairedges endeavored to let on he was fearful about and so moaned in a grim anxious sort of a way that Glenola took for chiefly your regular steely-achy-extended-organ-in-the-pants manner of moaning and consequently showed to Eddie her lengthsome meaty tongue back.

Glenola flicked her Pall Mall off the plankstage before the coal of it was quite dead and done with and the Clodfelter that reached up his naked hand and caught it shrieked not near so straightaway as maybe under regular circumstances he would have. He did, however, loose fairly directly the buttend to drop onto the dirtfloor where the Duprees and the Gillespies too contested over it and stomped and picked at it and pulled it at last entirely apart which the Duprees as a group were inclined to murder and do in at least one Gillespie on account of and beat and pummel the other one into a pulpy mass which they informed the Gillespies about and jabbed at them their foremost fingers and showed to them their assorted Pall Mall scraps like hardly seemed worth holding to their noses and inhaling about. And maybe the Gillespies would have gotten a little beat and killed if Glenola hadn't fetched from the squat bald man's trouser pocket a half dozen walnuts that she piled atop the plankstage right there at the lip of it, and George Wilmer who looked from the nuts to Glenola and back to the nuts again wondered at Nestor's daddy Nestor would he tell to him please what it was precisely that Glenola intended with a half dozen walnuts to do and Nestor's daddy Nestor looked himself from the walnuts to most particularly Glenola's nether gland and back to the walnuts again prior to telling to George Wilmer, "Bust them open I guess," which seemed to him after the Pall Mall and the Barlow and the comb and the eyeglasses an altogether distinct possibility.

But the walnuts did not get busted open truly, did not get anyhow busted open by Glenola's gland, but got instead projected chiefly, got instead shot and propelled with the sort of velocity most people would not anticipate a nut and a gland in combination could produce. Certainly George Wilmer hadn't expected any velocity to speak of once he'd watched Glenola squat and insert into the breech her initial nut that he'd guessed would get cracked and get busted open and that he'd held even his breath to listen for the sound of and pitched sideways ever so slightly his head which was how come he did not with his own eyes see it, did not for himself watch Glenola lurch and thrust of a sudden in a pelvic sort of a way that caused her walnut to discharge and make as it departed a phfft like did not sound to George Wilmer much in the way of a busting shell, not even a busting shell all highly muffled and insulated, that he intended to speak directly to Nestor's daddy Nestor of but got told when he turned and raised up, "Sweet Jesus," by Nestor's daddy Nestor instead who elevated his head all over again and looked primarily above and behind himself like he'd left off at only so long to say to George Wilmer Sweet Jesus in the first place.

"What?" George Wilmer wanted to know by which he intended the phfft somewhat and the Sweet Jesus somewhat and the headlaying and elevating somewhat too, but Nestor's daddy Nestor could not seem to manage beyond Sweet Jesus to tell George Wilmer anything hardly except for the Christ he told to him instead which struck George Wilmer as so much in the vein of a Sweet Jesus as to be near about indistinguishable from one. Consequently, he turned and shifted and intended to inquire of Tyler Lamont about the phfft chiefly that he was fairly completely set to do when Glenola showed most specifically to him, as best as he could determine, her meaty tongue that she poked and jabbed and wiggled like George Wilmer found entrancing and so could not truly vent at Tyler Lamont his inquiry what way he'd meant to and told to him instead just, "Hey!" that Tyler Lamont would likely have said at least a What? at back if he hadn't figured he was specifically himself having showed at him Glenola's meaty tongue too that he found a little entrancing as well and so did not manage straightaway a reply and did not manage presently a reply either but just discharged air out his mouth like made a wheezy sort of a noise.

Eddie guessed he would shortly expire which he informed from his chairedges Nestor's daddy Nestor and George Wilmer and Tyler Lamont he was commencing to guess he shortly would that they all three failed to console him about as they had instead Glenola to watch and ponder, and she stooped before them on the lip of the plankstage that she took up a nut from and displayed it between her fingerends while the squat bald man pumped a march on his squeezebox with considerable thump to it that Glenola got all caught up in the beat of and so twitched and jerked and wiggled and stuffed presently her walnut into her gland with noticeable syncopation and lurched and twirled and pranced for a time with it prior to lighting at the stage edge and thrusting after what pelvic fashion she'd previously thrusted. It near about hit the tent roof and Nestor's daddy Nestor and George Wilmer and Eddie and Tyler Lamont laid back their heads and watched it sail towards the far wall where the Gillespies and the Clodfelters and the Greerish Truaxes and a couple of Duprees as well scratched and scrambled for it while Tyler Lamont undertook to explain to Eddie and George Wilmer and Nestor's daddy Nestor just what mathematical manner of thing they'd lately witnessed that had to it noticeable thrust and acceleration as well as some maybe not so noticeable imparted spin which he felt obliged to illustrate with a piece of stubby pencil out from his coatpocket like he was with his own fingers imparting spin on that he'd begun to disclose to Nestor's daddy Nestor and Eddie and George Wilmer too the significance of when the righthand middle Dupree squeezed for a moment Tyler Lamont's bulby shoulderjoint from behind and advised Tyler Lamont in a frank sort of a way, "Shut up," like Eddie and George Wilmer and Nestor's daddy Nestor had been wishing maybe a Dupree would.

They all of them anticipated the third nut together, some of them anticipating it from the back where it would likely fall and land and the most of the rest of them anticipating it from up where it would get shot out in the first place. While those in back pushed and swore and scrabbled, George Wilmer and Eddie and Tyler Lamont and Nestor's daddy Nestor along with the pair of Duprees packed in tight against the stage edge so as to study for themselves the mysterious workings of the mechanism. And in this particular instance, the workings of the mechanism were truly mysterious even to Glenola on account of how, for her part, she squatted and loaded up and pranced some and twirled and lurched and bounded even a while upon the balls of her feet prior to returning to the stage edge and drawing back in her customary pelvic sort of a way and jerking as well in her customary pelvic sort of a way forward like usually did in fact impart spin and induce loft and velocity all at the same time but neglected somehow on this occasion the loft alone and so only imparted the spin and induced the velocity and fired the sizeable third nut straight out and utterly loftless to where it bounced almost instantaneously off Nestor's daddy Nestor's forehead and made a manner of noise that sounded to George Wilmer like two cowstaubs beat of a purpose together which George Wilmer spoke of to Nestor's daddy Nestor once later on they'd managed to revive him.

He pitched directly over onto the dirtfloor and broke his fall with his noseridge chiefly and George Wilmer and Eddie and Tyler Lamont and Glenola too watched him straightaway just lay sprawled and then watched ever so briefly each other prior to watching him for a spell lay sprawled some more. Glenola had not any time ever fired her gland in anger that she announced most especially towards Nestor's daddy Nestor she had not any time ever done, and she told how she'd lost somehow her usual grip like she could not presently explain the reasons for which Tyler Lamont told to her back he had formulated already a theory about that he felt inclined to propound and had even drawn off a deep and thoroughgoing breath to propound with when the pair of Duprees persuaded him to reconsider using various of his organs and appendages as leverage like they'd demonstrated previously a talent for. Glenola climbed down herself off the plankstage and onto the dirtfloor and stood all naked and uncovered between Eddie and Tyler Lamont which was chiefly how come George Wilmer alone squatted down to roll Nestor's daddy Nestor off his noseridge and onto his posterior as Eddie and Tyler Lamont had become of a sudden undisposed to squat what with Glenola all naked and uncovered between them. She presently squatted herself, however, presently hunkered clean down alongside Nestor's daddy Nestor and so grew straightaway dangly after what fashion Eddie had not ever seen a woman grow dangly previously as he'd not ever before gotten to look up close at a woman that could, all of which he grew slightly moanful on account of once he'd found out how fullblown upright with a steely item did not hardly improve on chairedges like he'd thought maybe fullblown upright might.

There'd already raised up on Nestor's daddy Nestor's forehead a purply welt that Glenola licked a fingerend and touched as she'd heard how mouthspit had on purply welts an effect if applied most especially in conjunction with a stream of light breathy air that Glenola drew up her lips and provided some of which in the hypothetical, Tyler Lamont explained, cooled the mouthspit and so shrunk up most times the welt that Eddie exhaled ponderously at the news of as he watched Glenola squat and dangle and blow out her pucker at the same time. And presently Nestor's daddy Nestor did in fact open up his eyes a little and he touched straightoff his noseridge and touched after it his purply welt prior to scratching for a time the side of his head in an aimless sort of a way and Glenola, who was squatted all dangly overtop him, left off with her pucker so as to say, "Hey sugar," and so as to say, "Momma didn't mean no harm," that Nestor's daddy Nestor told to her at length a gurgly sort of a thing about.

"Like cowstaubs," George Wilmer said and held up where Nestor's daddy Nestor could see it the offending nut. "Like cowstaubs beat of a purpose together," and he made with his tongue a manner of noise that Nestor's daddy Nestor told to him at length a gurgly sort of a thing on account of too while Tyler Lamont, who had a theory, set to propounding it and Eddie, who had a steely organ, set to adjusting it and the nearend Dupree, who had five unemployed fingers, reached roundabout George Wilmer and took up with them Glenola's lefthand dangly breast which pretty directly got his fingers bent and laid ways they'd not been truly made for.

As Nestor's daddy Nestor couldn't seem to be but gurgly chiefly and only remotely articulate, his brother Tyler Lamont determined that they'd best carry him from the tent and cart him on home, and they tried to stretch him flatout in the backseat of Tyler Lamont's secondhand Whippet sedan but Nestor's daddy Nestor could not himself see the call for it and insisted on sitting upright since he'd gotten after all just a purply welt that he licked his fingerends and touched while George Wilmer approximated from over the seatback the path of the nut that he held between his fingers and guided while he whistled through his teeth so as to suggest pure velocity all bald and unvarnished, so as to suggest maybe altogether more bald and unvarnished velocity than the nut had truly sailed at that Tyler Lamont told to him the toothgap whistling was in fact suggesting which George Wilmer begged rightoff to differ on account of while Eddie situated himself at a diagonal across the back seatedges with his head in the rear window well and Nestor's daddy Nestor just sat chiefly looking off nowhere much and touched every now and again his purply welt and touched every now and again his tender noseridge and dragged every now and again his open hand down across his mouth and off the tipend of his chin.

He shortly relieved George Wilmer of the nut, Nestor's daddy Nestor did, and held it before himself between his own fingers where he could look upon it in just primarily the wan pale moonlight that filtered in through the back glass like was not truly good nut-studying illumination, but Nestor's daddy Nestor was not studying in fact the nut itself, was considering chiefly instead the mystifying and altogether beguiling organ that had somehow dispatched the nut at him, the nut that seemed to Nestor's daddy Nestor to coagulate and distill the mystification and the beguilement both and so became for him not just a nut but a token, a relic, an artifact of deeply profound and near about religious significance. And he gazed upon the nut and touched briefly his own welt that had risen from it prior to expostulating in a general sort of a way how it seemed to him that a woman was in fact a wonderful variety of item which induced Eddie, laid upon the seatedges with his head in the window well, to tell to Nestor's daddy Nestor, "Purely wonderful," back.

They put him out alongside the ditch before his house and pointed the way up the drive for him, but Nestor's daddy Nestor had come by then to be reasonably steady and was sufficiently ungurgly to tell to the three of them, "Go on," and he made his own way undirected and unadvised up through the yard and around the house to the back porch where his boy Edgar lay upon his cot and made to be deep under, sprawled there with his eyes shut and his mouth dropped open like he persevered at until his daddy had passed on into the mudroom and through it to the kitchen where he felt about the stovetop for the dishtowel with the biscuits beneath it that he ate one of just cold and unadorned. Nestor's daddy Nestor stepped up the back hall so far as to look in on his girl, Grace Anne, who lay in fact deep under in some actual slumber and then returned through the kitchen and up past the larder to his own bedroom doorway where he lingered and gazed a little as well that his boy Edgar, who failed of a sudden to hear the floorboards pop and check, took even for lingering that he was full in the midst speculating and theorizing about when he heard his daddy say a thing that he could not straightoff make out and so caught his breath and stilled himself and heard presently his daddy speak again.

"Babydoll," he said and out on the porch atop his cot Edgar Tudor could not help somehow but say, "Babydoll?" himself which drowned out for him the first "Nestor?" his momma said back like preceded a low throaty indecipherable manner of thing from his daddy that his momma could not seem to say but "Nestor?" at again which itself served as preamble to some inordinate popping and checking and creaking and rustling that Edgar, atop his cot on the porch, lacked the powers to speculate and theorize with much success about.

He just lay, then, and listened at the racket from up past the larder which was shortly not floorboards anymore at all but was chiefly steel bedsprings instead that twanged and squeaked and got joined soon enough by the headboard that rattled and thumped which, all taken together, was a source of supreme puzzlement for Edgar Tudor who lay still speculating as long as he could bear it before he rose and passed through the mudroom into the kitchen himself and slinked on by the larder to peek around the bedroom doorframe and so discover in the wan moonlight his daddy and his momma caught up and entangled together after a fashion he had not yet found cause to become personally acquainted with. His daddy had near about gotten out of his trousers entirely, was anyway one foot shy of it, and his momma's nightdress had ridden all the way up to her armpits like allowed his daddy to lay his naked stomach upon his momma's naked stomach and work and wriggle and thrust and humph which rose altogether to a pitch and culminated in what struck Edgar Tudor as a pretty elaborate shuddery sort of a display, most especially from his own momma and his own daddy who did not usually in the course of a day even shake hands.

And Edgar Tudor, who guessed he was entitled to an explanation, inquired through the doorway, "Daddy?" and thereby induced one additional uproar further which culminated itself in the general banishment of Edgar Tudor who got taken up like a fencepost and hauled back out to his cot.

So it was meant to be Nestor's nut, his relic, his artifact, the actual token of his own personal conception which had itself been touched off by a faulty glandular discharge and attended by his momma and his daddy under the watchful scrutiny of his brother Edgar like, in conjunction, had rendered it fairly memorable and significant as far as your basic Tudor conceptions went. And it came to be in fact Nestor's nut presently once his daddy's brother Tyler Lamont had taken it for briefs and so had found himself pressed to suffer a fairly acute disappointment when it turned out to be just the nut instead that he did at last bequeath and pass on to his brother's boy Nestor who bored it and lacquered it and ran through it a length of chain on which he strung his doorkeys and his Fairlane keys and his lockbox key as well.

Of course Nestor was himself pretty well past conception by then and discovered, once he'd gotten the nut, that the nut mostly was what anymore he had. His daddy and his momma were already reposing together under a cedar tree in the churchyard alongside their girl Grace

Anne who'd passed at the sanatorium in Black Mountain of consumption. Nestor's brother Edgar, who'd married an Averill from Rome, Georgia, had himself succumbed from a busted vein and been laid by that Averill in with the Baptists at Bethel as she was hopeful he might ascend on up into heaven like she figured he needed to lay in with the Baptists to do. Even Nestor Tudor's own wife Erlene had gone, as it were, to her maker on account of a surgical complication, or on account of a meager internal affliction anyway that had come to be complicated by a surgeon, and she laid in the churchyard herself up the slope from Nestor Tudor's momma and daddy and alongside her and Nestor's baby girl Rachel Anne who'd never even gotten started good and was anymore just the merest manner of dent in the ground.

Consequently, then, it was for a while him and his daddy's brother Tyler Lamont until it was, presently, just him alone once Tyler Lamont, who'd cultivated no gumption for laundry, had squandered as well his gumption for everything otherwise. So Nestor Tudor's people pretty much all lay in the churchyard while Nestor Tudor himself approached retirement from the highway department where his duties had come to consist primarily of sitting along the roadside in a dump truck watching a white man named Stumpy Tate and a black man named Harold Lister shovel asphalt into holes and cracks and wonder every now and again might Nestor Tudor ease the truck up or ease the truck back provided of course he did not have a goddam thing else to do like they most times leaned upon their shovelhandles and insinuated in the sidemirror was evermore the case. Evenings chiefly Nestor Tudor just sat as well, sat out behind the house in his green twill highway department trousers and his green twill highway department shirt, sat upon his springy metal chair with his feet on an upended log and smoked his Old Gold filters and drank inordinately more of his Ancient Age than he ever intended of an evening to drink and chewed Maaloxes like mints and watched the sun drop back of the slash pines beyond the yard where it left for a time a gaudy streak of sky that flagged and faded and got shortly done in by the night, yielded to the darkness all pitchy and deep where Nestor Tudor sat and drank and chewed and smoked and guessed but for the liquor and the cigarettes and the Maaloxes too he could just as well be in the churchyard himself.

ii.

ALTHOUGH it was her he did see shortly it wasn't hardly her he saw straightoff on account of Dick Atwater's hairpart that he got instead taken with directly as it seemed to him Dick Atwater's hairpart had lately migrated, had lately traveled southward down the side of Dick Atwater's head like he inquired of Mr. Wyatt Benbow had it and got told by him, "Oh Christ yeah," back. They'd collected together along about the Number 2 shelter out at the reservoir on account of the Methodists from downtown at the main church as opposed to the colored Methodists off the Burlington Road or the white evangelical Methodists back of the hospital that ranted and carried on and pitched full over sometimes in the church aisle like the Methodists from downtown at the main church found unseemly as they preferred themselves to plain sit atop the pews and just doze every now and again in a prayerful sort of a way. The Methodists at the main church downtown had lately suffered to be rotated from them their preacher Mr. Grady Mott who'd told from the pulpit a joke about a proctologist that he'd let on had a thing to do with scripture, had a thing most specifically to do with Leviticus chapter 4, verses 3 to 12 about the bullock that gets hoisted on the door of the tabernacle and toted to the woods or something very near it that the widow Mrs. Askew in particular along with Mrs. Dwight Mobley and the organist Miss Fay Dull did not themselves find much in the way of proctological truly, did not themselves find much in the way of proctological at all and furthermore failed to see just in general and altogether how any little scrap of scripture whatsoever could get even scantly illuminated by your manner of episode that turned like the Reverend Mr. Grady Mott's did on a piece of wry therapeutic advice, turned on a fairly roguish nether gland observation that the widow Mrs. Askew, who'd visited previously a proctologist in Danville, found not just offensive but purely unlikely too which she'd communicated in the churchyard to Mrs. Dwight Mobley and Miss Fay Dull she'd found it after the sermon and the benediction and the last two verses of "Watchman Tell Us of the Night."

Consequently, a movement had gotten afoot to rotate Mr. Grady Mott elsewhere once Mrs. Askew had implied in the churchyard how, if she were Mrs. Dwight Mobley or Miss Fay Dull either one, she'd be offended too which they went ahead and decided they probably were as soon as they'd been told together they ought to be like Miss Fay Dull guessed she'd maybe been already disposed for due to the spring previous out on the ballfield at the middle school when she'd singled into the gap off third and gotten patted by the Reverend Mr. Mott on the backside for it what way seemed to her, the more she pondered it, fairly scandalous. So they undertook together to get afoot a movement and mustered a wholly sizeable assortment of moderately offended Methodists who shortly excused after a fashion the Reverend Mr. Grady Mott who rotated clean to Capella and got replaced in the pulpit in the church downtown by the Reverend Mr. Theodore J. Parnell who'd himself been mustered against in Charlotte.

The Reverend Mr. Theodore J. Parnell had to him appreciable refinement that the widow Mrs. Askew most especially, who guessed she could gauge refinement, let out he had, and he most times held his chin as he listened to people speak at him and sometimes said, "Quite," and sometimes said, "Rather much," when he found a gap to put a Quite or a Rather much in. He wore on his left pinky a gold ring with a big swirly P in the middle of it flanked either side by a tiny T and a tiny J that were moderately swirly themselves, and of a Sunday he evermore hung and dangled over the pulpitedge his entire left hand thereby displaying for the congregation his bauble like seemed most particularly to the women elegant and dignified and stately somehow too along with his silky spotted ties that wove one way or another into lengthsome slender neckknots unlike the Reverend Mr. Grady Mott who'd looked most Sundays to be wearing under his chin a folded flag. The Reverend Mr. Parnell was given chiefly to deep blue suits with ever so faint stripes up them and vests too, vests the same exact color as the suits even just precisely, and no piping anywhere on the vest or roundabout the jacket pockets or along the lapels either like the Reverend Mr. Grady Mott had possessed himself a taste for, not anything truly otherwise with the suit and the vest and the stiff white shirt and the silky necktie too but for the upright kerchief corner out the breastpocket that with the Reverend Mr. Theodore J. Parnell came attached to even the rest of the actual kerchief instead of the manner of white pasteboard square the Reverend Mr. Grady Mott used to evermore exhibit at least some of.

The truth of the thing was he didn't seem hardly much in the way of preacherly and not remotely like the Reverend Mr. Mott had not seemed himself much in the way of preacherly either but tasteful and stylish and near about as utterly and altogether distinguished as the widow Mrs. Askew in particular guessed a preacher could get. Primarily, though, he seemed to her serene like she hadn't in fact figured precisely he had seemed before he informed her out in the churchyard after a service how serene was what he'd come to be, and he took up the widow Mrs. Askew's fingers and gazed full upon her face as he said to her, "Doreen, we float upon a sea of tribulation and woe."

And the widow Mrs. Askew, who'd not truly thought much lately about the manner of sea she floated herself upon, said to the Reverend Mr. Parnell back, "We do?" and the Reverend Mr. Parnell held to his chin with his vacant hand for a time prior to assuring Mrs. Askew how, as far as the sea of tribulation and woe went, they rather much did in fact quite float upon it.

"I'll tell you a thing, Doreen," the Reverend Mr. Parnell said and displayed for the widow Mrs. Askew his upper teeth like seemed to her a little serene itself and not but a trifle smirky with it, "some of us, we ride high on the swell. Some of us, we don't."

"What now?" Mrs. Askew inquired back once she'd contemplated already a spell previous to it.

"Some of us," the Reverend Mr. Parnell told her, "we ride high on the swell. Some of us, we don't," and he gazed another time all toothsome upon her.

"Oh," she said to him and added behind it, "high on the swell," that the Reverend Mr. Parnell told to her, "Yes," on account of with just his breath almost exclusively and not but precious little actual throatnoise.

"Life," the Reverend Mr. Parnell said and raised up alone his foremost chinholding finger, "is like a pond all iced and frozen over that we skate, you and me, atop of. The trick is not to fall on our backsides," and he paused so that the notion might penetrate and settle before he told to the widow Mrs. Askew, "Emerson," which the widow Mrs. Askew made pretty much her sea-of-tribulation-and-woe face at. And the reverend said, "Ralph," and the reverend said, "Waldo," and the reverend said another time, "Emerson," too and assured the widow Mrs. Askew how she was certainly herself acquainted with him, how she'd probably run up on him somewhere even if she didn't know it was him she'd run up on like happened sometimes with Ralph, he told her, Waldo Emerson that the widow Mrs. Askew made just shortly an exclamation on account of, or squealed one time anyhow prior to informing the Reverend Mr. Theodore J. Parnell how she guessed she had after a fashion run up on Mr. Emerson before as she'd owned, just previous to her Zenith, one of his televisions, one of his televisions in the console box with the doors that swung shut, and she couldn't say why it was she'd bought a Zenith once it gave out as she'd been, she recalled, pleased with her Emerson right up to when it quit at last, right up to when the picture grew all squat and dingy until it wasn't but a streak across the screen. "Like this," the widow Mrs. Askew said and showed to the Reverend Mr. Parnell a piece of air between her thumb and forefinger that was not truly any broad and sizeable piece of air at all.

The thing of it was, the Reverend Mr. Theodore J. Parnell had gotten his consciousness raised previously in Charlotte like had rendered him serene which he told at last of a Sunday he'd been rendered to the widow Mrs. Askew along with the rest of the congregation otherwise who'd maybe not been so anxious to know of it. But they were told it anyhow by the Reverend Mr. Parnell who, like most people with elevated consciousnesses, could not stand to be all by himself alone elevated and so proposed to the Methodists from the pulpit between the doxology and Mr. Cecil Dutton's semiquarterly fiscal report how maybe they'd like to have their own consciousnesses lifted and raised up too, how maybe they'd like to come to be serene after the fashion the Reverend Mr. Theodore J. Parnell himself was quite apparently serene already that the widow Mrs. Askew three pews back on the aisle where she most times sat and where she did not ever hardly speak up in the sanctuary from as she was not, after all, a Baptist figured just out loud of a sudden would be a fine thing, would be purely a benefit to everybody on account of life was chiefly a sea of tribulation and woe that they all of them had to skate on some time or another, and she inquired up towards the altar at the Reverend Mr. Parnell if didn't they all sometime or another have to skate on it, and the Reverend Mr. Parnell dangled for Mrs. Askew his gold swirly-lettered pinky ring and told to her, "Yes," with plain breath near about altogether entirely and a thoroughgoing upper tooth garnish.

The Reverend Mr. Theodore J. Parnell just happened to know a fellow, just happened to be acquainted with his daddy's brother's second wife's boy Dewey that, as a kind of a sideline, raised consciousnesses every now and again, had in fact come to be a doctor of consciousness raising like he'd not truly gone to school for but had visited instead the post office downtown in Gastonia where he'd mailed off to Bakersfield California a coupon he'd torn out from a magazine along with a money order and so had come to be, in four to six weeks just exactly, decreed and ordained and certified too and called himself anymore Dr. Dewey Lunt to people he'd not ever previously called himself but plain Dewey at. He drove a red Pontiac Ventura that had been his momma's but that his momma didn't have need to drive much herself any longer on account of the Reverend Mr. Parnell's daddy's brother Bud that did for Dr. Dewey Lunt's momma most everything and drove her all over the place in his Newport, or drove her eventually anyway once she'd let fall a strand of shiny blond hair and had picked with her nails and fingerends at Dr. Dewey Lunt's stepdaddy's shirtbuttons prior to saying at him, "Honeypot," with just what seemed evermore to Dr. Dewey Lunt's stepdaddy Bud her tongue chiefly like his first wife Irene hadn't said at him Honeypot even one time.

So the Reverend Mr. Theodore J. Parnell's cousin Dr. Dewey Lunt traveled roundabout in his momma's red Pontiac Ventura and raised consciousnesses for a fee like he'd found he had a talent for, like he'd found he could seem pretty completely a doctor at. And it was congregations mostly but not congregations all the time as it was every now and again garden societies instead and Mooses and Elks and Masons and Rotarians and Knights of Columbus and entire chambers sometimes of commerce like represented whole towns and cities and so could stand to have their consciousnesses honed and refined and made most especially altitudinous. Naturally the Reverend Mr. Parnell's cousin Dr. Dewey Lunt laid a few to his services that the Reverend Mr. Parnell spoke of from the pulpit and told the Methodists the figure and explained to them, by means of simple arithmetic, how they each might get the same thing and pay less for it if they brought in maybe Lutherans and Moravians and Episcopalians and Presbyterians and even Baptists from the church up by the FCX where they didn't screech and hardly yowled at all and so much as danced sometimes at the Christmas ball in the armory, and the Methodists pondered and considered and got wholly at last persuaded by the simple arithmetic primarily that Mr. Wyatt Banbow stood up midway back in the sanctuary to say a thing about as he'd run a business for a while now and guessed he knew how it was simple arithmetic didn't ever lie that the Reverend Mr. Theodore J. Parnell from up at the pulpit with his hand all dangly and his gold ring swirly on it vented towards Mr. Wyatt Benbow a breathy "Yes" at.

Consequently, then, they contracted with the Reverend Mr. Parnell's cousin Dr. Dewey Lunt for a course of study that would be altogether six multihour, Dr. Dewey Lunt in his letter told to them, intensive seminar sessions formulated and designed so as to inspire them to get in touch with various parts and pieces of their deepest innermost selves like they'd not probably been lately in touch with. Of course they'd relate and identify and interact too but just straightoff they'd delve on down to the very core of their beings that, as best as Dr. Dewey Lunt could tell, the bulk of people in this modern day and age in which we live didn't ever hardly set aside an occasion for. Now naturally there were Methodists who were not truly much interested in delving down to the very core of their beings most especially on a weeknight in the basement of the fellowship hall, but once word got put out to everybody otherwise there were plenty of Lutherans and Moravians and Episcopalians and Presbyterians and Baptists as well set to delve and relate and such along with Mrs. MacElrath's niece Judy who'd attended the university in Chapel Hill where she'd come to be Zenish though not purely Zenish entirely but Zenish enough anyhow to know a thing about delving already which left it just everybody otherwise and her, or everybody otherwise and her anyhow but for a Mormon named Bob who had undertaken to pass through town on his blue Huffy with the full fenders and the basket in the front but had gotten prevented from passing through town entirely by the firechief Mr. Pipkin's wife Dot that ran him down with her green Electra though not in any lethal sort of a way except for his Huffy that would not anymore ever be the same manner of Huffy again.

They settled firstoff on Wednesday nights all through July and partway through August but the Baptists could not see fit to miss their prayer meeting just to delve down to the core of their very beings so they settled on Thursday nights instead when the Baptists tended to collect together as well every now and again in the sanctuary up by the FCX so as to feel for Jesus, so as to switch off the lights and grope around for the Holy Savior that people said sometimes they'd found and sometimes they hadn't and that Angela Kirsten Little's boyfriend Ray Goolsby didn't ever bother even to feel for as he had other items entirely to blunder across with his fingers instead, but the Baptists had gotten lately fairly done in with feeling for Jesus as a manner of thing and so guessed they could stand for a while to delve and relate and identify and interact and probe as well their innermost selves with means other than their fingerends. Consequently, then, Thursday nights was what they settled on which would be your Baptists and your Lutherans and your Moravians and your Episcopalians and your Presbyterians and your Methodists too, your Methodists in particular who waited through May and through June for July and watched as they did it the Reverend Mr. Theodore J. Parnell with his swirly gold ring and his natty suit and his slender tieknot and his upright kerchief corner and his air most especially all easeful and calm and near about as flatout serene as anybody lately had seen an air be.

Now Mr. Phillip J. King, a lapsed Baptist himself, guessed straightoff when he heard from Mrs. Phillip J. King of the upcoming consciousness raising that he could already delve and relate and identify well enough on his own without taking instruction from a Methodist's stepcousin.

Consequently, he was not meaning to have his consciousness tampered with and announced as much in May but had by mid-June recanted due to Mrs. Phillip J. King's own personal condition that had worsened by mid-June severely. Mrs. Phillip J. King had begun to pass through the change of life that she would not have likely known even she was passing through but for Mr. Phillip J. King who got onto the cable when the cable came at last down the street and so exposed Mrs. Phillip J. King to thirty-three channels of television from most all over everywhere. Himself, he stuck fairly much entirely with the movie station that showed most nights people going naked, people going not usually wholly naked altogether but going naked somewhat anyhow like Mr. Phillip J. King had not previously ever seen people go on his TV. Mrs. Phillip J. King, however, watched mostly the news channel instead like was not itself entirely news but was news just somewhat and plain talk just somewhat too, plain talk by people that claimed to know a thing like the man who explained how to make mulch in a wire box and the woman who suggested how to give an Anacin to a cat when a cat had call for one and the scant little doctor with the pointy beard who informed Mrs. Phillip J. King how she was passing just presently through the change of life that he let on to her she had cause to be ill and sour about. So Mr. Phillip J. King and Mr. Phillip J. King's terrier Ittybit commenced to suffer with Mrs. Phillip J. King through her change of life and through as well her ultimate premenstrual syndrome like she'd never known previously was a syndrome until the little doctor with the pointy beard told to her it was. Consequently, she went for a time fullblown premenstrual and then lapsed out of it and grew ever so briefly sweet and kindly towards the dog in particular and Mr. Phillip J. King somewhat in a slight but measurable sort of a way as a preface and preamble to the flashes she came to be shortly afflicted with which were your hot variety straightoff that Mr. Phillip J. King undertook to remedy for her with an oscillating fan and did remedy in fact, transformed the flashes from hot ones to cold ones entirely like Mrs. Phillip J. King failed altogether to be the least little bit grateful about but just screeched and howled and snapped and hollered and wept and, presently, heated up all over again.

Ittybit stayed mostly in the spare room under the bed with Mrs. Phillip J. King's momma's octagonal hatboxes and came out only every now and again to wet the throwrug, but Mr. Phillip J. King couldn't himself straightoff find a spot to go and lay low and so grappled a spell with Mrs. Phillip J. King's affliction, watched one time anyhow on the news channel the doctor with the pointy beard who'd moved off the change of life entirely and had taken up cellulite instead of it that he explained could anymore get wholly sucked and vacuumed out from a woman's thighs and elsewhere even too, news of which prevented Mr. Phillip J. King from eating his supper with much noticeable relish that Mrs. Phillip J. King screeched and howled and snapped and hollered and wept and just generally grew snitty about and said at last to Mr. Phillip J. King all whiny and forlorn, "Oh, P.J.," that Mr. Phillip J. King said a little whiny and forlorn himself just "What?" at back.

Chiefly he was fearful she'd actually passed already through the change of life and come out the other side and so would stay evermore like she'd gotten to be which was ill and sullen and weepy too most all the time any longer that Mr. Phillip J. King attempted to improve and alter but could not much affect truly like he saw he couldn't which was how come he bought from Mr. Jackson P. Eaton jr. at the hardware store a rotary discsander and a pack of assorted rotary discsander pads along with a plastic particle mask that Mr. Jackson P. Eaton jr. assured Mr. Phillip J. King was, out of all the particle masks he carried, the foremost particle mask he had and he encouraged Mr. Phillip J. King to try it on that Mr. Phillip J. King did and got admired at it by Mr. Jackson P. Eaton jr. who'd not ever previously, as best as he could recollect, seen a particle mask sit and settle so against a man's jowls and he led Mr. Phillip J. King back along the aisle to the pipes and fittings and took up a chrome elbow for Mr. Phillip J. King to admire himself in.

"Like it's made for you," Mr. Jackson P. Eaton jr. told him.

And Mr. Phillip J. King pondered himself in the shiny chrome where he looked somehow infinitely more comely than he did most evenings on the back of his spoon even with the particle mask, maybe so much as on account of the particle mask truly that did seem to sit all flush and snug like Mr. Phillip J. King and Mr. Jackson P. Eaton jr. together agreed it did.

So he carried home his new discsander and his pads and his particle mask too and hunted out from a box under the basement steps his safety goggles that had gotten gouged and scratched across the lenses like Mr. Phillip J. King didn't hardly much care about as he didn't figure he needed to see but a little, didn't figure he needed to see but hardly at all. He found his Allis-Chalmers hat in the coat closet off the back hall and fished his orange dropcord out from behind the furnace where he'd piled it up once it had come to be all knotted and twisted round, and he worked it loose in the backyard and straightened it out across the lawn prior to plugging the one end into the outlet box alongside the doorjamb and joining the opposite end to his new discsander out at the carshed where he toted a three-legged stool to deposit his mask and his goggles and his hat atop of. And he didn't do anything straightoff, didn't do anything in the way of discsanding anyhow with his potent new discsander but just retired to the front room there in the shank of the day like it had come to be and sat for a spell on the settee with Mrs. Phillip J. King who'd tuned in a *Lost in Space* that Mr. Phillip J. King had just lately seen, or seemed to recollect he'd just lately seen anyway and inquired of Mrs. Phillip J. King if wasn't it the one where the little freckledy-faced boy and the wiry man with the beady eyes wander off with the robot that rolls somehow or another through the sand and over the rocks what way had never seemed to Mr. Phillip J. King likely and the three of them together come across an alien being that looks sort of like a big fruit salad, or looks laying down in the dirt like a fruit salad anyway but presently stands full up on his feet where he looks chiefly like an alien being instead and he takes out after the boy and the robot and the man with the beady eyes while June Allyson, back at the spaceship, steps every now and again outside to scan the horizon in a fretful sort of a way, and Mrs. Phillip J. King who let Mr. Phillip J. King get done and asked him even was he done in fact once he'd quit and left off, screeched presently at him, "It's just now started and you've gone and ruined it. Just 'cause you've seen it doesn't mean everybody has. Just 'cause you've done a thing doesn't mean everybody's done it. It hadn't but just this minute started," and Mrs. Phillip J. King wept and moaned a brief while that she'd almost left off entirely at when the wiry man with the beady eyes and the freckledy-faced boy and the robot came across what looked to be a heap of fruit salad which set off Mrs. Phillip J. King afresh with some weeping and some moaning and some additional screeching even that Mr. Phillip J. King just plain sat upon the settee and endured.

She changed over to a *Marcus Welby* that she'd seen herself already twice like didn't hardly matter as she wasn't in much of a mood for a *Marcus Welby* anyhow but had instead been looking forward the bulk of her adult life, she let on, to a *Lost in Space* that Mr. Phillip J. King had all by himself spoiled entirely like had tainted for her *Marcus Welby* too that she told to him it had as she got up and switched to the early news on the Greensboro station that she guessed Mr. Phillip J. King would have maybe done for her if he possessed any manners to speak of like she'd known for a spell he didn't, like her own dead momma had told to her he never would. The newsman at the Greensboro station was wearing, as best as Mrs. Phillip J. King could tell, an ugly tie that didn't remotely blend at all with his suitcoat that was ugly itself but different from how the tie was ugly that Mr. Phillip J. King agreed with her it was and got told straightoff by Mrs. Phillip J. King how she hadn't at all been looking to get agreed with like most people anymore do which was the trouble, she figured, with things, the trouble with things most all over in addition, she guessed, to the governor that was a Republican and so was the trouble with things himself too. And she looked like she might impart to Mr. Phillip J. King some manner of notion about the governor maybe or just people otherwise in general that agreed everywhere with each other when she grew instead mournful on account of the freckledy-faced boy that she could not bear the thought of all eaten up and devoured by an alien being, even an alien being that looked chiefly like an appetizer, but Mr. Phillip J. King assured her the freckledy-faced boy had not after all been eaten up and devoured and he told to Mrs. Phillip J. King how the whole thing turned out with everybody but the fruit salad safe and even June Allyson happy a little bit like Mrs. Phillip J. King grew briefly transported by the news of until she wished at Mr. Phillip J. King she'd seen it herself like she surely would have if he'd not come in to tell her all that happened before it ever did what way he'd done to her before, what way she recollected he did to her most all the time.

"Every waking minute," she told to him and slapped the settee cushion with her hand flat and open. "Every one," she said and Mrs. Phillip J. King showed to Mr. Phillip J. King a manner of pouty grimace he'd not ever known her to be partial to before the change of life when her pouty grimace got to be somehow her grimace of choice, and he said to her back of it, "But sugar," like he'd come lately to be partial to himself but she grew anyhow increasingly pouty until she displayed for him her upper teeth and her gums both just prior to wailing and weeping and telling through the tears and the gurgly spit a thing that sounded to near about have some actual words to it though not actual words entirely and outright.

And Mr. Phillip J. King said just, "Well," and stood up off the settee that he lingered for a time alongside while he retucked his shirttail and rehiked his trousers like he allowed himself to get done altogether with before he said to Mrs. Phillip J. King, "Well," again and left the frontroom for the dining room and left the dining room for the kitchen and passed on out the backdoor into the yard and across it directly to the carshed where he took up off the stoolseat his mask and his goggles and his Allis-Chalmers hat that he fixed on his face and the top of his head too prior to dropping and settling his backside and lifting up off the ground his new discsander that he squeezed the trigger of and applied to a piece of the carshed door. It screeched appreciably like he'd hoped it might, screeched and whined and fairly sang against the pitted paint and on through it clean down to the plain naked wood and it threw trash and raised a cloud of paintdust and wooddust too like pretty much swallowed up Mr. Phillip J. King and pretty much swallowed up back of him Mrs. Phillip J. King with him where she'd come to wail and holler and did wail and holler both but failed to get heard at it even by her own self that was doing the wailing and hollering too.

Two lots south down the street Mr. Grady Floars was kneeling in his periwinkle so as to thin and cull and root roundabout his wife Camille's cement gnome that was presently just plain cement-colored like had lately come to seem to Mr. Grady Floars's wife Camille pretty completely ungnomish which was how come she'd decided to lay some paint to the thing like would be blue paint for his trousers and red paint for his jacket and pretty peach paint for his face and green paint for his peaked cap and white paint for the tiny ball atop it that she figured would make him fairly jump out from the periwinkle which she'd asked "Wouldn't it?" to Mr. Grady Floars who'd guessed himself it would and so thinned and culled and rooted roundabout the gray cement gnome and raised up only presently at the sound of Mr. Phillip J. King's discsander two lots off, and Mr. Grady Floars watched what he could see of Mr. Phillip J. King in his pulverized paintcloud and watched what he could see of Mrs. Phillip J. King back of him where she seemed to him even from a distance irate, seemed to him even two lots off beyond irate somehow, looked to have ascended clean up into the ether of pure outright aggravation all stark and undiluted which was how come Mr. Grady Floars called out to his wife Camille and jerked his nose north towards Mrs. Phillip J. King who Mr. Grady Floars's wife Camille watched screech and holler and wail and weep like Mr. Grady Floars down in the periwinkle and his wife Camille alongside him grew nostalgic together about as Mr. Grady Floars's wife Camille had just lately passed through the change of life herself and Mr. Grady Floars had been obliged, of course, to pass through it with her.

As he couldn't see much at all and could hear even less, naturally Mr. Phillip J. King grew fairly enraptured with his discsander straightaway and made some considerable use of it most especially in the shank of the day when Mrs. Phillip J. King seemed prone in particular to fits and to spells, and shortly he'd rendered the one carshed door all slick and naked and wholly unpainted and had started in on the other one before he came to grief, or before he came anyhow to more grief than he'd undertaken with the discsander to escape in the first place from and, like is the case with grief most times, he'd not known he'd come to it until after it had fairly completely swallowed him up. He'd blown a fuse, hadn't much intended to blow a fuse but had blown one anyhow partly on account of the discsander that he'd run for a time flatout and partly on account of the chestfreezer that had kicked in and partly on account of Mrs. Phillip J. King's upright Hoover, maybe even chiefly on account of Mrs. Phillip J. King's upright Hoover as best as Mr. Phillip J. King could theorize in a hypothetical sort of a way as she'd been vacuuming in the living room upstairs at the time, had been bumping and barking the tablelegs and the feet of the chairs after the fashion she tended to with her upright Hoover like had come with a headlight on the front of it that she'd straightoff busted out against the sideboard. He figured she'd somehow with her circuit upstairs polluted his circuit downstairs, somehow caused his circuit to surge and such though he could not say surge and such how exactly as he was not much acquainted with electricity truly except for the way it came out from the plugholes most times he needed it to.

So he guessed it was partly her and her Hoover and sat on his three-legged stool and squeezed his trigger without any noticeable effect to speak of. He figured he'd burnt up a fuse, or figured anyway she'd somehow with her Hoover burnt up a fuse for him on account of some manner of surge, on account of some manner of wholly inordinate electrical impulse, and he struck out across the yard and into the basement and along the wall to the fusebox that he flung open and glared full into without truly much good effect as he could not hardly make out the fuseheads in the light from the solitary naked bulb up between the floorjoists and so took up instead the flashlight he kept in the basement to look in the fusebox with that didn't have a bulb in it anymore, not a whole bulb anyhow but just the threaded metal bulbend that screwed into the flashlight socket and had gotten cemented there by the insides of the batteries which seemed to have lately seeped to the outsides of them. So Mr. Phillip J. King hunted a match to fire and illuminate the fusebox with and found a pack in the bottom and back of his workbench drawer, found a red and orange Tampa Jewel matchpack that had maybe been washed or maybe been just sat on a while and was near about full of matches though was not any longer near about full of matchheads with them. But he got a spark anyhow and got even a kind of a flame too that he could fairly well see by until it went out when he got another spark and a kind of a flame again that endured a spell for him and allowed him to find in the tiny fuse windows the one burnt and severed item he'd guessed he'd find and he twisted loose the spent fuse and shut it in his hand and told himself, "Yep," that way he said Yep most times he'd solved and defeated a thing.

Mr. Phillip J. King generally kept a spare fuse somewhere and guessed he knew where until he looked there when he guessed he knew where again until he looked there too, so he supposed he'd buy one shortly, supposed he'd buy one altogether very soon and he set the spent fuse atop the fusebox where he found he could see it if he lifted up his chin and gazed towards the fusebox top like would remind him to step out and purchase a fuse like he'd told himself already shortly he would. He intended in the meanwhile to move a fuse instead, move in particular the back floodlight fuse on account of he never used hardly at all the back floodlight anyhow but sometimes late at night when he'd look to see were there any ne'er-do-wells out on the lawn or roundabout the carshed like there never so far had even one time been, so he studied the fusepanel and studied the list on the back of the fusepanel door that told him which fuse went with the range and the water heater and the washer and the dryer and the refrigerator but did not so much as indicate at all which fuse went with the floodlights under the back eave that he never hardly used which left him just to pick one like he did, which left him just to twist loose what fuse seemed maybe the floodlight fuse to him that he picked one of and twisted and so straightaway shut off Mrs. Phillip J. King's Hoover upstairs that struck Mrs. Phillip J. King as a curious thing there at the very first before it commenced to strike her as an irritating thing instead if not truly an altogether infuriating thing outright like she yelped and screeched and whined and wept on account of prior to taking up her Hoover, it sounded to Mr. Phillip J. King in the basement, and tossing it out the frontroom towards the kitchen where she bolted to take it up and toss it back.

So he figured straightaway on another fuse instead and replaced directly Mrs. Phillip J. King's Hoover fuse and loosed the one beneath it that he shut up in his hand and held as he caught his breath and listened to find out what had maybe quit and left off, what had maybe stopped altogether like Mrs. Phillip J. King might signify with a fit, but he didn't hear anything truly except for the Hoover afresh, didn't hear anything anyhow different from what already he'd heard before he'd loosed the fuse and held it and caught up his breath to listen like led him to figure he'd found in fact maybe the backlight fuse, or like didn't lead him anyhow to figure he hadn't. So he screwed it in the discsanding socket and eyed briefly atop the fusebox the spent discsanding fuse that reminded him how he intended still to buy a new fuse sometime what way he'd anticipated it would remind him of it, and he left the basement for the backyard and crossed it for the carshed where he took up his new discsander and squeezed the trigger of it like brought forth some whining and some whizzing roundabout and brought forth in addition, on the part of Mr. Phillip J. King, the manner of tingly flush he entertained most times he'd undertaken a manly useful thing and made a success of it like he figured he'd just lately in fact done and like he could not from out by the carshed truly know he had not done in fact after all as he could not from out by the carshed hear the noise in the basement he'd not just have needed to hear but needed to decipher too that wasn't anyway but a slight noise, wasn't but a tiny noise back of the chestfreezer, wasn't but a solitary click alone all by itself which most times it generally wasn't, which most times it never truly was.

So he didn't straightaway guess he'd done what he did but would have likely found it out altogether sooner than the gist of the thing at last came to him if Mrs. Phillip J. King hadn't the very afternoon it got done seen herself in the full-length mirror on the back of the bathroom door, seen herself stooped and bent and sideways all at the same time like she failed to look svelte and wispish at the way she'd cultivated somehow in her mind she was svelte and was wispish even stooped and bent and sideways all at one time together. She'd stepped into the full bath to run her Hoover over the nappy black rug before the sink and had scared up like usual a sizeable hairball that got loose somehow from her and led her a chase across the linoleum and back of the bathroom door that she probably wouldn't have shut and swept behind otherwise and so probably wouldn't have seen herself fairly bent and hunkered down that she watched herself at ever so briefly in the mirror until she got of a sudden all weepy and worked up and turned round so as to lay back her head and vent an assortment of pitiful noises, and she wondered just out into the air why it was she had not just to go through the change of life but had to go through the change of life and be chunky and puffy and swole up at the same time as if the change of life was not by itself enough that she told to the ceiling chiefly it was like she went ahead and assured after a spell the walljoint too. She supposed, however, once she'd gripped and collected herself she could come again to be svelte and come again to be wispish if she, which was in this particular case the collective She that took in naturally her own self but took in with it Mr. Phillip J. King as well, cut back on her starches and her fatty meats and such and ate mostly leafy greens and tubers and your occasional dried bean along with those brown crusty crackers that tasted like and squeaked like and seemed just generally to have probably one time previously been Styrofoam before they got broiled and got toasted, and Mrs. Phillip J.

King swore to herself an oath she would be shortly svelte and wispish and taut most everywhere she had not truly been taut lately and she went ahead and swore on behalf of Mr. Phillip J. King an oath too once she'd stepped on back to the kitchen door so as to watch Mr. Phillip J. King clean a clapboard while she swore it.

Consequently, then, neither him nor Mrs. Phillip J. King either one discovered straightoff what the click all by itself nobody'd heard anyway meant. Neither him nor Mrs. Phillip J. King discovered it even shortly in fact as they had no call between them to step into the basement, as they had no call between them to step most especially across the slab floor to the chestfreezer where Mrs. Phillip J. King kept her fatty meat and her Neapolitan icemilk and her nine-inch pie shells and her loafbread and her various unidentifiable icy items that had gotten sometime or another wrapped in foil and dropped down in the freezerbottom on the icy item pile. Instead they ate like sensible people, Mrs. Phillip J. King called it, called it from the first to Mr. Phillip J. King once he'd come in from the carshed to supper and seen on the kitchen table what looked to him undergrowth with a bowl of ditchwash on the side as Mrs. Phillip J. King had boiled a bone and a stick of celery and two whole entire carrots and a piece of an onion in a quart and a half of tapwater that she told to him was soup which Mr. Phillip J. King just up and contradicted her about as he'd seen soup previously and guessed he had a pretty good hold on what exactly soup was.

"Brothy soup," Mrs. Phillip J. King told to him.

"This here?" Mr. Phillip J. King inquired back and plunged his foremost finger down into the bowl and then drew it out so as to poke it into his mouth instead like Mrs. Phillip J. King found plain beastly that she informed directly Mr. Phillip J. King she did, informed him twice even and then exhaled pretty much all over him like indicated to Mr. Phillip J. King her thoroughgoing dismay and indicated with it how she'd probably eaten herself the piece of onion she'd failed to throw in with the bone and the carrots and the celery stick too.

Of course the brothy soup was just what they had on the side mostly as they had for the main item a leafy green salad with not just lettuce in it but raw leathery spinach in it as well that Mr. Phillip J. King, who did not take his spinach most times raw and leathery, felt obliged to pluck up a leaf of and taste like seemed to Mrs. Phillip J. King vaguely beastly itself and moderately dismaying which she went ahead and indicated about while Mr. Phillip J. King pondered the greens and the radishes in with them along with the four saltines that would be shortly, Mrs.

Phillip J. King explained, healthful brown squeaky crackers instead once she'd made time for herself to visit the Big Apple where she guessed they stocked brown squeaky crackers, where she guessed they stocked them in the international food aisle that was not exactly the international food aisle altogether but was instead the lightbulb and the motor oil and the antifreeze and the shoe polish and the floormop and the bugspray aisle primarily with a rack at the end towards the meat counter for food from elsewhere like was not always from elsewhere even but was sometimes from here too which seemed to Mrs. Phillip J. King just the very spot to seek out her brown squeaky crackers like she probably would have sought them out already had she not gotten all caught up cooking instead.

And Mr. Phillip J. King said to her, "Cooking," and Mr. Phillip J. King said to her, "This here," and pointed with the finger he'd just lately poked and licked both.

She found a book in the Rexall up by the front register with recipes in it for people that were looking to get svelte and not svelte just presently but svelte fairly completely straightaway, and it told how to make skimpy food, how to broil things and boil things and steam things and eat things just purely raw with maybe some dressing to dip and sop them in, special light skimpy healthful dressing made from water chiefly and vinegar somewhat and oil ever so hardly at all that Mrs. Phillip J. King mixed a dose of the night after the brothy soup and the green salad and tried out on Mr. Phillip J. King who got invited to go on and jab his finger in it and so did jab it and tasted off the end of it the special light skimpy healthful dressing which seemed to him very much in the manner of tapwater that had gotten maybe a skillet washed in it like he declined to let on it seemed to him and hummed instead through his shut lips, hummed with noticeable zeal and enthusiasm. They ate considerable tuna fish there at the first as Mrs. Phillip J. King's book from the Rexall was fairly tuna fish heavy, or anyhow Mrs. Phillip J. King ate considerable tuna fish while Mr. Phillip J. King just mostly pushed his tuna fish roundabout his plate and picked every now and again at it so as to find out had it gotten somehow untunafied that it never somehow had. They took salad greens with their tuna fish most nights and broccoli every now and again and cauliflower too and beets more often than Mr. Phillip J. King had ever in his lifetime eaten beets along with each night a solitary individual cheesefood slice like was meant to suggest and insinuate actual verifiable cheese and did seem even a little cheesy in the plastic wrap and cheesy as well ever so hardly at all unwrapped on the platerim, but it did not taste cheesy truly most especially atop the squeaky brown healthful crackers like seemed themselves to Mr. Phillip J. King wholly as savory as assorted boxflaps if not truly more savory even.

But he didn't much mind the crackers and the cheesefood, didn't much mind the greens and the broccoli and the cauliflower and the beets, didn't really much mind the tuna fish either that he only ever pushed round on account of Mr. Phillip J. King had taken to having lunch twice daily at the Dairy Queen out the Lawsonville Road where he ate at noon an outsized brazier burger with the pickles and the ketchup and the smear of chili along with the holster of fries instead of the sack of them and a turnover when they had turnovers like sometimes they didn't and a Pepsi-Cola and a quarter cantaloupe too that got sent with him every morning by Mrs. Phillip J. King and was meant to be his lunch near about all by itself but for maybe a trifling bit of salt and a solitary scoop of cottage cheese which Mr. Phillip J. King guessed was kin somehow to whipped cream that he finagled most days a squirt of on his cantaloupe slice along with usually a piece of a cherry like provided, as best as Mr. Phillip J. King could tell, a festive and jolly touch. Generally he could not much stand to eat lunch another time until roundabout four-thirty when he'd stop on his way home from the municipal building uptown at the Dairy Queen once more which was not ever so remotely on his way home at all until he'd struck out down 29 and then west towards Locust Hill like caused the Dairy Queen to be after a spell on his way home in fact. He settled late in day for a hotdog and the sack of fries along with a turnover if they had a turnover and a cone of soft swirly vanilla ice cream if they didn't followed by a Vick's throat lozenge that drowned out with its own stink most every stink otherwise and so allowed him to step on into the house and back to the kitchen and kiss Mrs. Phillip J. King on the cheek prior to standing with her before the window over the sink that they could see themselves all increasingly svelte in what way it seemed to Mrs. Phillip J. King most times they were except for when she found herself in the midst of a hot flash when it seemed instead to Mrs. Phillip J. King they weren't and likely never would come to be but would stay evermore blubbery like hogs which was good for some wailing and some weeping and some screeching even too.

Mr. Phillip J. King, then, was not truly suffering for his oncoming svelteness that was not itself truly oncoming but he was nonetheless afflicted in a sort of way on account of the grapefruits chiefly, on account of the grapefruits almost entirely in fact, the grapefruits him and Mrs. Phillip J. King both split every night one of once they'd finished with their greens and their tuna and their orange cheesefood. Now Mr. Phillip J. King was of a mind there was not much better in this life than most especially a pink grapefruit straight out from the icebox but he'd never previously had occasion to enjoy every single night of the week a pink grapefruit straight out from the icebox that he found had on him a particular effect, that he found disturbed his juices in a chemical sort of a way and produced, after his first week of steady pink grapefruits, inordinate vapors which were not hardly regular vapors like his normal vapors otherwise but were instead different vapors altogether, a strain of vapors unlike any vapors Mr. Phillip J. King had ever previously had cause to loose and vent. Chiefly, they were highpitched whiny vapors that introduced themselves into the atmosphere whenever it was they got the whim for it, whenever at all they wanted just to come out like Mr. Phillip J. King tried sometimes to forestall and tried sometimes to prevent outright and got routinely rewarded for it with a discharge more highpitched and more whiny than just the regular unobstructed sort. He was afflicted most acutely at night, afflicted most acutely late in the evening that he noticed firstoff one Tuesday evening Mrs. Phillip J. King had already Scotchtaped her hair and greased her face and climbed in the bed, and he lingered inordinately in the bathroom while he listened at his pulpy grapefruit and his natural juices mingling in his stomach sac where they churned and stewed and shortly dispatched gases along his tube that he undertook to expel the majority of in private so as to be polite and so as to be seemly, and he strained and he humphed and he blew breath and vaporized as best he could which resounded off the tile floor and the tile walls and the porcelain fixtures and the shiny enameled ceiling and arrived at Mrs. Phillip J. King, who'd drawn back the spread and slipped under the topsheet, like regular talk there at the outset, regular talk about her own momma's sister Elizabeth Marie in Burlington that Mr. Phillip J. King seemed to be asking after in a general sort of way and so got told by Mrs. Phillip J. King an episode she'd heard on the phone from her Aunt Elizabeth Marie just lately that Mr. Phillip J. King said a thing behind and then left off and then struck in again with his tone noticeably pitched up and his volume noticeably swelled like Mrs. Phillip J. King did not believe she approved of, like Mrs. Phillip J. King could not help but take as contrary that she told to Mr. Phillip J. King who fairly shrieked back at her and so set her off altogether. She insisted her Aunt Elizabeth Marie was a goodly woman and insisted how come and expressed to Mr. Phillip J. King her pure astonishment at him for telling to her such vile and hurtful things with no call much for it which she wondered the why of one time but did not get told the why of it straightoff and so wondered another time the why of it at Mr. Phillip J. King who made a brief and utterly glib reply.

He opened the bathroom door at length and stepped around the foot of the bed to his side of it and climbed in under the topsheet where he lay a time and listened to his gases yap and growl in his stomach sac and he breathed in through his mouth and out through his mouth both that way Mrs. Phillip J. King did not in the least approve of and so raised up and twisted round to show Mr. Phillip J. King her sharp peevish face prior to displaying for him her backside instead, and Mr. Phillip J. King told to her, "Night sugar," that did not get him told anything back and like usual he laid his nose ever so slightly against Mrs. Phillip J. King's greased and treated cheek and he said to her, "Night sugar," again near about directly into her elevated ear she'd taped a length of swirled hair under the lobe of and Mrs. Phillip J. King of a sudden moved her head just quick and hard enough to strike with the boniest part of it Mr. Phillip J. King's noseridge prior to speaking sternly to him of her dead momma's sister Elizabeth Marie who was likely the sweetest kindest woman on the face of the earth as best as she could tell.

"Who now?" Mr. Phillip J. King asked of her out from under his fingers he was feeling just presently his noseridge with.

"Nothing," Mrs. Phillip J. King told to him back and looked on him again all sharp and peevish just long enough to make sure he'd seen her look all sharp and peevish on him prior to lying full out another time so as to show to Mr. Phillip J. King her blank backside altogether by itself. But Mr. Phillip J. King didn't much notice Mrs. Phillip J. King's blank backside truly on account of his gases that were churning and simmering and coursing round through his ducts and tubes, coursing round mostly towards his nether gas vent that he lay stomach upwards and clinched and knotted and held tight as best as he could manage to clinch and knot and hold it and he pondered on the ceiling above him the light fixture that had pointy places chiefly all over and not but flat harmless places every now and again and he wondered what it might be like to get of a sudden projected towards and impaled upon the lightglobe in a pneumatic sort of a way like he feared he was in some verifiable danger of which was how come he went ahead and loosed what trifling vapor he guessed he'd better that Mrs. Phillip J. King took for a manner of rejoinder and so grew straightaway huffy about it.

And that was when she figured she smelled it firstoff, when she figured she'd received up through the floorboards a whiff of it that Mr. Phillip J. King did not trouble himself to tell her was him likely instead, was him probably instead for certain. She didn't, however, speak of how she'd smelled it until not the day beyond the Tuesday evening but two days beyond it and the most of another one when her and Mr. Phillip J. King sat together before the television after supper and watched a show on the Atlanta station about a lizard somewhere down the other side of the world that could walk on the water, or not walk on the water truly but kind of run for spell atop it before he went on ahead and sank clean beneath it instead like Mr. Phillip J. King guessed most of the rest of the lizards elsewhere did pretty much directly and straightaway but for this one lizard with the cowl around his neck and the big flat feet that he could run on the water with, and Mr. Phillip J. King had been just before inquiring if wasn't that lizard the damnedest manner of thing Mrs. Phillip J. King had seen lately when they showed instead a snake down the other side of the world itself that could fly or that actually could fall mostly, displayed anyhow a disposition for dropping off treelimbs and sailing fairly unsnakelike clear down to the ground like seemed to Mr. Phillip J. King far damneder a thing than the flatfooted lizard even which he intended to talk directly of when he got prevented from it by Mrs. Phillip J. King who wished to speak to Mr. Phillip J. King about his hygiene, his two feet in particular that had struck her lately as fairly aromatic.

Of course, like people will, Mr. Phillip J. King undertook to sniff his own feet for her and thereby lay to rest the notion that they'd come to be somehow tainted and odorous but he couldn't any longer sniff his own feet like he'd once been able to on account of his ripply chest that had lately gone altogether south to conspire with the lard back of his beltbuckle and thereby prevent him from bending and stooping and squatting and hunching over like he recollected once he could. So he did not lay his face near so snug up to his arches as he'd intended, did not lay his face even remotely so snug up to them as to satisfy Mrs. Phillip J. King who pointed down along the couch and beyond it to pretty much where the bathroom was and suggested to Mr. Phillip J. King how he might want to step on over to the lavatory and make some use of it, said to him anyway, "Go on," and would not hear from Mr. Phillip J. King talk of his Corfam shoes that possessed, he insisted, properties which had been engineered to thwart foot odor like was the beauty of Corfam, he told to her, like was the whole entire point of it which Mrs. Phillip J. King was not much disposed to listen just presently at.

So he went to the bathroom in just his gray socks that had gone at the heels a little blue and gauzy and he ran water and made what he figured for an assortment of footwashing noises while he groped a little blindly in the cabinet over the countertop for his Right Guard he never hardly lifted his arms and sprayed anymore since he'd gone to the waxy stick but that he had a can of anyway, knew he had a can of somewhere and so felt throughout the cabinet for it but came up instead with Mrs. Phillip J. King's Final Net that he squirted one time into the air and found to have a pleasing bouquet and so directed a dose on his one foot and his other as well where the spray, all misty and sweet, clung to Mr. Phillip J. King's gray socks like atomized woodglue. But it cured the stink, cured the stink enough anyway to satisfy Mrs. Phillip J. King, the stink that wasn't even feet but barely and a little bit like she failed straightoff to find out for certain it wasn't, like she failed to discover the day beyond the feet even too which was the Friday in fact she'd come to be taken with consciousness raising, the Friday she'd gotten caught up in the prospect of being serene on account of Mrs. MacElrath's niece Judy who'd seen Mrs. Phillip J. King Friday afternoon in the Big Apple and had waved at her a bunch of chicory and told to her, "Hey."

Since she'd managed to get Zenish at school in Chapel Hill, Mrs. MacElrath's niece Judy rarely ate but from the produce bin at the Big Apple where she bought up her greens to carry west on out 158 to her momma and daddy's house that she stayed just presently at like she felt obliged most times to let on she was staying at just presently after an altogether temporary sort of a fashion until she got, she called it, set up like being Zenish did not somehow much help her to get. For her part, Mrs. Phillip J. King had not ever eaten chicory but one time at the S&W in Greensboro in a mixed salad that she'd thought was just some Bibb lettuce and some leaf lettuce and some romaine lettuce too maybe like had been chicory itself instead that caused her face muscles to knot up when she bit it, and she figured there at the produce bin she'd just as soon gnaw a Bufferin as bite ever again a chicory leaf which Mrs. MacElrath's niece Judy told to her she understood on account of how chicory and such things as them were not just for any old body that came along with teeth. Naturally, Mrs. Phillip J. King did not much appreciate the implication that she had chiefly incisors to recommend her and plain told Judy to what degree precisely she did not appreciate it and then grew flashy for a spell that was a hot one firstoff with a cold one behind it which both together got punctuated and concluded by a kind of a general snit like seemed to Judy Mrs. MacElrath's niece a cry that she told to Mrs. Phillip J. King it did, like seemed to Judy Mrs. MacElrath's niece a kind of calling out in woe and anguishment primarily what way Judy had called out previously herself before she got to be transcendental like anymore Judy was. Now of course being transcendental is hardly the manner of thing that can get flatout explained but is instead sort of like getting saved by Jesus or becoming Republican which do not themselves show much in the way of knobs and edges to latch and grip onto, so Mrs. MacElrath's niece Judy could not full well convey to Mrs. Phillip J. King how just precisely it was she'd passed into an altogether higher consciousness and what exactly a higher consciousness might be in the first place good for though she let on as best she could how she felt improved and how she felt enlightened and how, as best as she could figure, Mrs. Phillip J. King could get herself improved and enlightened too and shortly at that with the Methodists downtown who'd arranged to have their consciousnesses refined and distilled and just generally tinkered with and attended to like consciousnesses evermore called for.

Naturally, Mrs. Phillip J. King found herself intrigued, or actually Mrs. Phillip J. King was irritated straightoff like was menopausal primarily and not transcendental any at all, but she calmed herself directly and came to be intrigued after a bit, somewhat intrigued at the prospect of hoisting her own consciousness that she figured needed mostly to get just refined and tinkered with and buffed up ever so hardly at all unlike Mr. Phillip J. King's consciousness that Mrs. Phillip J. King confided to Mrs. MacElrath's niece Judy had gotten somehow in a sorry state, had come to be all dull and lowly like Mrs. MacElrath's niece Judy seemed there at the produce bin purely appalled to hear, and she said to Mrs. Phillip J. King, "No!"

"Yes ma'm," Mrs. Phillip J. King told to her back. "Can't ever know what he's bound to just up and come out with. Can't ever know it," and Mrs. Phillip J. King and Mrs. MacElrath's niece Judy humphed together in their necks and wagged their heads at each other and Mrs. Phillip J. King took up from the produce bin a bunch of chicory that she let on looked comely to her, that she let on looked altogether comelier than the chicory she'd eaten one time at the S&W previously.

So she guessed she'd have her consciousness finagled with after all, guessed she'd have it raised and guessed she'd have it uplifted and guessed most especially Mr. Phillip J. King would have his own dull manner of thing fairly overhauled with her which she informed him come bedtime about and he held to the strap on the mattressedge like anymore he tended to and pondered most especially the pointy parts of the overhead light and listened at his grapefruit-induced gases churn about in his stomach sac and charge along his ducts and tubes and fairly much beat and hammer and prize their way out into the regular air that got fouled, he could tell, and tainted by his vapors, and Mrs. Phillip J.

King, with her face greased to near about iridescence and her hair curls Scotchtaped on her temples and back of her ears, told to him how she'd always wanted her consciousness lifted and refined by somebody that was trained for it and she guessed at him she'd most especially lately wanted his consciousness lifted and refined too that he broke by chance a snatch of wind in back of which she took for just precisely the manner of remark she'd told him already she was not hardly looking to hear and she said to him, "Hush," and he made with his backside chiefly a contentious reply which Mrs. Phillip J. King guessed she gathered the gist of well enough and so rolled over and carried like usual the topsheet with her.

Him and his duct, however, became shortly docile and agreeable on account of how Mrs. Phillip J. King saw fit at the top of the morning to visit the chestfreezer in the basement with the intention of fetching a piece of beef for her and Mr. Phillip J. King who seemed to have lost together their natural flush, had come somehow to be pale and waxy and so had noticeable call for a piece of red meat most especially before they took up with the Methodists whom Mrs. Phillip J. King was not much inclined to look pale and waxy in front of. And Mr. Phillip J. King might in fact have heard her even shriek straightoff but for his own personal circumstances that conspired to prevent him from hearing a shriek. He'd arrived lately at the dinette where Mrs. Phillip J. King had set out his bowl for him and his dry cereal and his thin cloudy skim milk that looked to have been drunk and passed once already, and he sat down in his cotton undershorts, tucked and situated his stomach roll, and doused his breakfast with the murky milk, his breakfast that was not remotely sweet and flaky but was wholesome and grainy instead with big chunks to it and little chunks to it and long spindly pieces and short squat pieces and even some nutty round pieces too that looked for all the world like assorted silage which had gotten maybe shoveled from a bin or swept off a barnfloor, and it tasted pretty much like Mr. Phillip J. King figured silage might taste and cracked and crunched between his teeth like Mr. Phillip J. King figured silage would probably crack and crunch both and like was how come Mr. Phillip J. King did not truly hear Mrs. Phillip J. King shriek straightaway since he heard exclusively instead himself chewing in both ears at once.

Of course, once Mrs. Phillip J. King had shrieked with no effect to speak of she yelped behind it but Mr. Phillip J. King, who was chewing and grinding and just generally pulverizing a mouthful of mixed grains, did not take notice of the yelp either which itself inspired a bout of hollering like Mr. Phillip J. King might certainly have detected some of had he not been just at that very moment considering his niacin as he chewed, considering his niacin with the manner of thoroughgoing attention he had to guess his niacin rated judging from how Mrs. Phillip J. King had spoken to him oftentimes of it. So he missed the yelping and the screeching and the hollering together and failed to get impressed and affected until the caterwauling set in once he'd fallen idle and was not chewing or considering either one, was not doing anything at all until he was levitating instead.

Straightoff he couldn't tell where precisely it had come from. Straightoff he didn't know what precisely it was as Mrs. Phillip J. King had not exhibited lately a disposition for caterwauling, had not caterwauled in fact since that time he'd backed their Monterey over her clutchpurse with the mother of pearl latch to it. Naturally, then, Mr. Phillip J. King could not have anticipated that she'd just up and cut loose like she did which was probably how come he merely levitated there straightaway, was probably how come he rose off his chairseat in a precipitous sort of a way and consequently beat most particularly his private organ on the table edge like induced in Mr. Phillip J. King an outburst that had itself some caterwauling to it, an outburst Mrs. Phillip J. King in the cellar took for a reply and so went straight ahead and caterwauled back. The trouble was he still didn't know just precisely where he'd been caterwauled at from, so he bolted up the hall to the front room and called out to Mrs. Phillip J. King who cut loose one time more with some yelping and some screeching and some hollering and some caterwauling too like sent Mr. Phillip J. King charging across the breadth of the house and off through the den and the dining room and back into the kitchen where he'd left from in the first place.

With what sweetness he could muster, Mr. Phillip J. King inquired from atop the linoleum, "Darling, where are you?" which Mrs. Phillip J. King heard him at through the floorboards and ever so sweetly informed him back how she was herself just presently in the cellar where she hoped he would shortly drag his sorry ass on down the steps to join her like incited Mr. Phillip J. King to charge another time up the back hall so far as the basement door that he flung open so as to call unobstructed down into the basement, "Darling?" that Mrs. Phillip J. King yelped and screeched and hollered and caterwauled a thing at.

Naturally, he meant that first time to go all the way down, meant to gain the slab floor and cross on over it to wherever precisely Mrs. Phillip J. King had come to be but he got prevented from it, got wholly and altogether interrupted in the very midst of it like he told to Mrs. Phillip J. King when later she gave him the opportunity to go on and try to explain to her just why exactly he'd done what he did. So he went down the steps, went down the steps more than halfway even and with some noticeable purpose and velocity both that he maintained and persisted at right up to that first whiff, right up to that first breath he drew off through his mouth a little but through his nose chiefly, that first breath that stopped and impressed him straightaway and caused him to wheel round and climb on back up the stairs with near about as much purpose and velocity as had carried him partway down them. He lingered in the backhall and breathed the air there for a spell while he listened at Mrs. Phillip J. King speak ever so sharply to him from down in the cellar next to the chestfreezer where he told to her, when later she gave him the opportunity for it, he meant to stop, meant to plain draw up and quit altogether that second time he set out down the steps and across the actual slab floor. He intended to find out from her just what precisely the trouble was, meant to inquire what manner of thing she'd yelped and screeched and hollered and caterwauled about but was not somehow able to stop and leave off once he'd started to run all full and flatout across the slab floor, was not somehow able but to bolt clean on out the basement into the backyard where he stood with his arms raised up and his hands laid atop his head like allowed his wind to best pass in and pass back out again, and he was standing there in the grass breathing the pure air with his hands atop his head and his undershorts a little lowslung on account of the sprinting and a little indecent on account of the poochy flap when Mr. Grady Floars's wife Camille and Mr. Jack Vestal's wife Virginia stepped together out Mrs. Grady Floars's back door so as to admire in amongst the periwinkle Mrs. Grady Floars's cement gnome that looked anymore as true to life a gnome as Mrs. Virginia Vestal admitted to Mr. Grady Floars's wife Camille she'd ever before seen anywhere, looked near about as true to actual life to her as Mr. Ira Penn's pickaninny, not the upright one in with the verbena but the one on the fencerail with the slice of watermelon and the pearly teeth.

"Like he might just say a thing," Mrs. Grady Floars suggested, "like he might just drop open that mouth of his and speak out it," which Mrs. Jack Vestal had been just before suggesting herself which she was right there on the verge of confessing when she got pretty completely prevented from it by Mrs. Phillip J. King two doors up in her basement alongside her chestfreezer where she loosed a manner of extravagant discharge which prompted Mrs. Virginia Vestal and Mrs. Grady Floars to raise up their heads and spy together Mr. Phillip J. King out in a patch of light with his hands atop his head and his speckledy undershorts riding low and indecent and his front flap pooched open near about as wide as Mrs. Grady Floars and Mrs. Jack Vestal had ever themselves seen a flap lay. Of course they couldn't make out plain Mr. Phillip J. King's uncovered organ but naturally they did not need to see it to be offended by it since they could make out well enough for themselves how there was them in Mrs. Grady Floars's yard and Mr. Phillip J. King a scant two lots off with his organ laid near about free and dangling for just the whole world to gawk at and not a thing between them but plain empty air like they felt obliged to let on to Mr. Phillip J. King they'd grown offended about and so undertook to display for him their backsides chiefly, jerked their noses anyhow and spun round like they figured they'd probably gotten seen at but that they hadn't gotten seen at truly on account of Mr. Phillip J. King's moderate compunction which prodded him on back across the yard towards the basement doorway and in through it where he did not intend to accelerate, where he did not mean to sprint another time across the slab floor but felt inspired once he'd smelled again the smell to dart chiefly on past Mrs. Phillip J. King alongside the chestfreezer and up the stairs into the backhall where he got straightaway yelped and screeched and hollered and caterwauled at prior to having loosed upon him a second extravagant discharge that sounded to him upstairs in the back hall all wild and beastly both.

He probably shouldn't have fetched her scarf, calculated how, if he had it to do all over again, he wouldn't have gone to the bureau and drawn it out on account of it was the silk one with the buttercups on it that Mrs. Phillip J. King treasured unduly, but he fetched it anyhow and folded it halfwise and laid it overtop his nose and his mouth and knotted the corners of it back of his head and then struck out again down the basement steps towards the slab floor that he did not anticipate he'd feel with the scarf much compelled to sprint another time the length of, but somehow the sour stink from the basement and the perfumy stink from the scarf mixed and blended into an altogether nauseating bouquet that Mr. Phillip J. King guessed he needed some air to remedy, most especially some air from the backyard out through the doorway which he was beginning to veer and aim towards and was even accelerating at as well when Mrs. Phillip J. King freed her near hand from the freezer doorhandle so as to take up with the fingers of it a sizeable hank of passing chesthair like maybe she would have let loose of directly but for the silk scarf with the buttercups on it that she'd not hardly bought so Mr. Phillip J. King could wear it across his face like a hoodlum that she told to him straightaway she hadn't.

Now of course chesthair on a moving man that gets itself just all at once interrupted and restrained gives rise to some factors and some complications that Mr. Phillip J. King, later on when he had the leisure for it, pieced together and theorized about and eventually spoke of out front of the Gulf station to Coley Britt and Mr. L. T. Chamblee and Mr. Bill Covington and his colored help Jump Garrison too once he'd shown to them just where it was precisely he'd been wounded and tormented and had suffered on his person his trauma, he called it. Chiefly, he told them, it was algebraical on account of you had your inert mass and your constant velocity and your variable forces otherwise all come together in a mathematical sort of way, and he explained to them what he called his direction across the slab floor that he said was *X* and what he called his constant speed that in combination with his general bulk made for his momentum which Coley Britt told him it didn't and got told himself by Mr. L. T. Chamblee it did too that Coley Britt told him it did not either and asked Mr. Bill Covington did it which Mr. Bill Covington appeared to ponder for a moment and then wondered back at him did it what, so Mr. Phillip J. King said you had your direction that was a big *X* and you had your momentum that was a big *M* and you had the pair of them together joined and multiplied by your big *F* that was itself two things, was itself your basic follicle uproar primarily, Mr. Phillip J. King explained, brought about by four fingers and a thumb closed up and held shut which could be closed up and held shut completely or could be closed up and held shut less somehow than completely as well like constituted what Mr. Phillip J. King called your variable grip that was your little *v* and your little *g* next to your big *F* that all got multiplied together and then added to whatever your big *X* and your big *M* had timesed out to which made there in conjunction a sum equal to your big *T*.

"Thrust," Mr. Phillip J. King told to the bunch of them and got told back chiefly by Coley Britt, "Thrust."

"Itself," Mr. Phillip J. King said and explained how his big *X* was straight and level and his big *M* was steady and flatout and his big *F* was altogether sizeable on account of Mrs. Phillip J. King's little *g* that hadn't had much *v* to it whatsoever and so had caused for him, with the *X* and with the *M* too, a fairly massive *T*, a bigger *T* than Mr. Phillip J. King guessed anybody who had not ever been *T*d like it could ever begin to imagine. "Boys," Mr. Phillip J. King said and touched ever so lightly through his open shirt his raw pectorals, "I got launched."

Mostly she meant just to grab him. Mostly she meant just to hold to him anywhere she could and had not meant to restrain his chesthair chiefly that, once he was heaped up on the slab floor, she assured him she hadn't. Of course, he'd wanted to stop cold where he was when she closed her fingers and her thumb on him together like she did but he was not sufficiently acquainted with his big *M* to realize how he couldn't, so in undertaking to arrest his big *M* entirely on account of the big *F*, which was sudden and inordinate follicle stress primarily from your near about utterly *v*-less little *g*, he mostly just altered his big *D* instead and consequently leapt direct up into the air and thereby deposited with Mrs. Phillip J. King the bulk of his restrained chesthair that she opened her hand and perused for a spell prior to suggesting to Mr. Phillip J. King, "Get on up," and she reached down with her grabbing hand to be what he figured for helpful but instead just snatched off his face her silk scarf with the buttercups on it and poked him with her left slippertoe and told to him, "Get on up," again fairly much like she'd told it to him previously though with hardly the same sweetness and charm to it.

Of course everything in the freezer was pretty completely ruined and done in as it had sat for almost a week unelectrified altogether and the butchered quarter cow and the battered fishsticks and the bagged turkey and the saturated loafbread and the seepy berries and the wilted pastry shells and the chopped barbecue in the pint tub that was meant to look wood grainy but did not look wood grainy even remotely along with an assortment of fist-sized items wrapped in dull crinkly foil were all stewing together in a manner of unspeakable gravy that had itself been made creamy by a half gallon of liquefied Neapolitan icemilk which had evacuated the carton entirely. It was just purely the manner of sight Mrs. Phillip J. King was anxious for Mr. Phillip J. King to look on with her though Mr. Phillip J. King himself was not much inclined for it and so loitered atop the slab floor all heaped and piled up and felt at his patch of slick naked skin that had not been slick or naked either only lately and so was a source of wonder to him along with the pain and along with the anguish it was a source of chiefly instead, and she suggested to Mr. Phillip J. King, "Get up," and encouraged him with her slippertoe and raised him only at last once she'd found some new follicles to reach down and stress and antagonize.

He guessed straightaway it was maybe the plug and so reached back of the freezer and fiddle some with it prior to guessing it was maybe instead the motor that thumped when he knocked on it what way seemed to him sound like he told to Mrs. Phillip J. King it seemed to him. So naturally, then, he turned to the fusebox and was just before guessing how it was in fact likely a fuse when he spied on the fusebox top the spent one he'd put there to do a thing for him like straightoff when he spied it it did. He said, "Yep," said to Mrs. Phillip J. King plain

Yep one time firm after he'd stepped on over to the fusebox and snatched up the spent fuse that he made like to unscrew from the vacant fuse socket and that he pondered the tiny window of in an altogether grand and elaborate sort of way prior to turning full around to Mrs. Phillip J. King and making at her his we-can-send-a-man-to-the-moon humph which he shook his head ever so extravagantly in back of and told at last to Mrs. Phillip J. King, "Surges," and told with it, "Humph," another time.

The trouble was, however, she told to him, "P.J." back and not P.J. all regular and flatout but P.J. on the incline, P.J. bent upwards like had to it an implication that Mr. Phillip J. King felt obliged to say, "What?" on account of like he evermore felt obliged in the face of a P.J. bent and inclined to say What? and he got just looked at for it, looked at like he'd figured and known already he would by Mrs. Phillip J. King with her lips pressed shut together and her head canted and dropped low like suggested fairly completely how dubious she'd come to be, and Mr. Phillip J. King told to her, "What?" another time and got for it looked on and got for it breathed at too.

So he cleaned it by himself in his hat and his goggles and his particle mask and his blue coveralls from the air corps that anymore climbed his crotch and pinched him, and he wore Mrs. Phillip J. King's pink rubber gloves that caused his hands to go slimy while he drew out the solid items from the freezerbottom with a fishnet he'd bought one time at the pier in Nag's Head when he'd anticipated a fishnet was a thing he'd need like it hadn't turned out to be until he reached with it down into the milky seepage and caught up straightoff in the netting a packet of dinner rolls that had gone larval from the damp. He stuffed two leafbags full up and stood with them at the curb where he waited for Walter and Evan Tuttle in their Ford truck that Jimmy Gerber rode the back of, and he flung the sacks in the bin himself and watched them get scooped and pushed and smelled them get compacted that Walter and Evan Tuttle and even Jimmy Gerber too had a thing to say about, an oathful profane manner of thing chiefly that Mr. Phillip J. King himself threw in with like Mrs. Phillip J. King from back of the front screen heard him do which she informed him from back of the front screen she had.

Understandably, then, since Mr. Phillip J. King found himself in a manner of domestic difficulty with Mrs. Phillip J. King who had, she let on, suspicions about the sander and the spent fuse and the subsequent seepage, he made himself quite thoroughly agreeable for a time and so did not hardly begin to object when she firstoff insinuated and shortly proclaimed outright that they would attend together the consciousness-raising sessions at the Methodist church downtown as she figured he had most especially cause to get his shabby and lowslung consciousness upraised which Mr. Phillip J. King found uncanny on the part of Mrs. Phillip J. King since he'd been right there on the verge of suggesting the identical item himself. So come the first Thursday in July him and Mrs. Phillip J. King took the dietetic supper at the Holiday Inn on the bypass, which would be a scoop of cottage cheese and a cling peach half and a helping of diced pineapple and some loose white grapes and some loose red grapes along with a lean beef patty fried on the griddle and mashed with the spatula and served up near about as succulent as a shoetongue, and then rode on around to the Methodist church where they ran up on Mr. and Mrs. Luther Teague who sat with them under the fellowship hall in the folding metal chairs, sat with them up front towards the podium though not right up front exactly but back a little truly from the very front as they were not looking to get quizzed straightaway on the state of their consciousnesses like Mr. Luther Teague guessed up at the very front they might.

Of course the widow Mrs. Askew did the bulk of the talking there at the first before the Reverend Mr. Parnell and his cousin Dr. Dewey Lunt had yet arrived and she spoke from back of the lectern in just a general sort of way about woe and turbulation and such as them followed by a manner of specific dirge on the topic of the late Mr. Askew who she became for a while fairly gurgly about but recovered presently from it and discovered pretty much extemporaneously how she had a thing to say about Mrs. Luther Teague's print dress with the dahlias on it that Mrs. Estelle Singletary back of Mrs. Luther Teague found herself obliged to say as well a thing on account of due to how Mrs. Luther Teague's dahlias looked to her pretty much some manner of beauty rose instead or if not some manner of beauty rose then begonias maybe that Mrs. Dwight Mobley down the row from Mrs. Estelle Singletary chortled about, or squirted anyway between her lips and roundabout her fingers a sort of a breath that proved to Mrs. Estelle Singletary fairly irksome, proved to Mrs. Estelle Singletary so irksome in fact that she laid her hands to her hips and inquired of Mrs. Dwight Mobley if maybe she wouldn't like to share with everybody otherwise whatever it was she'd gotten so jolly of a sudden on account of that Mrs. Dwight Mobley straightaway supposed she might and wondered at Mrs. Estelle Singletary how it was a thing could seem to her a beauty rose and a begonia both at the same time most especially when it was plainly a peony instead.

There was coming to be a real and imminent danger that palpable carnage would ensue before anybody's consciousness got hefted even a little and Mrs. Estelle Singletary glared significantly at Mrs. Dwight Mobley but was prevented from leaping over the chairback and thrashing her to pieces by the arrival of the Reverend Mr. Theodore J. Parnell along with his stepcousin Dr. Dewey Lunt who did not make, most especially upon Mrs. Phillip J. King, a very favorable impression there at the outset. For one thing, he had on a skyblue suit, a stretchy skyblue suit and brown shoes with it that grated, as best as Mrs. Phillip J. King could tell, each with the other, and she did not much care as well for his hair that was a streaky groundhog sort of a color and swept sideways chiefly across his forehead like Dr. Dewey Lunt was pressed to maintain as best he could with his fingertips that he dragged along his brow when he did not plain jerk his head instead and thereby throw his hair once it had sagged and crept down past where he figured it needed to lay. The Reverend Mr. Theodore J. Parnell managed a breathy and altogether sublime introduction prior to yielding the podium to Dr. Dewey Lunt who unbuttoned his skyblue coat and dangled over the podiumedge his own hand that had a ring to it all sparkly with gems and such, and suddenly Dr. Dewey Lunt did not appear truly the manner of man who might wear brown shoes with a blue suit or throw his hair with a headjerk, seemed instead altogether transformed, seemed instead pretty completely transmogrified even to Mrs. Phillip J. King once Mr. H. Monroe Aycock had told to her later what transmogrified in fact was that he'd seen from his own chair Dr. Dewey Lunt get. It was certainly the carriage and the posture partly but was undoubtedly primarily the talking with it, the talking all deep and smooth with gaps and pauses to it like made it sweet and like made it easeful, and he breathed in through his nose and he breathed out through his mouth and exhibited every now and again his upper teeth chiefly at most especially the ladies out before him who got somehow a little week and swoonish like usually from upper teeth they didn't ever hardly get but for the widow Mrs. Askew who was naturally disposed anyway towards weak and towards swoonish both.

He'd had, naturally, his own sensibilities heightened a while back and he told just precisely when and told just precisely how and indicated with his incisors primarily what tranquility his sensibilities all heightened and raised up had brought to him like he wanted everybody otherwise to share in, like he wanted everybody otherwise to know the undiluted pleasures of which was why he'd come in the first place, and Dr. Dewey Lunt turned round and drew on the green chalkboard behind him a manner of circle about the size of a pieplate that he tapped the middle of with the chalkend and identified as pretty much the sort of innermost self they'd all shortly delve down into once they'd gleaned from him the method for it that did not anybody say What? at until Mr. Wyatt Benbow said What? at it as he'd not himself lately had occasion to glean anything much, as he'd maybe not ever gleaned anything previously at all that he just went on ahead and admitted flatout like most especially Mrs. Estelle Singletary found disgraceful and her and Miss Bernice Fay Frazier next to her bemoaned together what trifling refinement people seemed anymore to possess.

Needless to say, they could not just all start in with delving down deep into their innermost selves but had straightoff to muck around in the shallow recesses for a while and relate and identify and get after a general fashion in touch with what parts and pieces of their personal sensibilities they probably did not much bother with in the usual course of things. Now Dr. Dewey Lunt, who'd been himself delving and relating and identifying and the like for a considerable stretch, was partial to sitting flush on the floor as it seemed to him conducive to sensibility raising in a general sort of a way, conducive after a fashion he could not truly explain but got excused from even so much as attempting to by the widow Mrs. Askew who told to him how she'd gleaned already what he meant like Mrs. Phillip J. King guessed she'd gleaned it too, guessed probably she'd finished even gleaning it before the widow Mrs. Askew had set in good as gleaning was just the kind of thing she'd evermore shown a talent for. So Mrs. Phillip J. King suggested, once she'd gleaned already how maybe she should, that everybody push their chairs back against the wall and sit on down atop the speckledy floortiles which most everybody looked beside themselves at each other on account of but for Miss Fay Dull who looked at Mrs. Phillip J. King instead and told presently to her how she, Miss Fay Dull, had worn her creamy skirt that she raised up a piece of between her fingers to display. Of course Miss Fay Dull was anticipating how Mrs. Phillip J. King might glean from just news of the creamy skirt the manner of grime and shoegrit a speckledy tile floor would likely put to it, but Mrs. Phillip J. King had apparently left off gleaning already like allowed Dr. Dewey Lunt to wonder himself if couldn't maybe Miss Fay Dull light atop a thing, a manner of spread or some such on the speckledy tile floor that Miss Fay Dull straightaway grew enchanted with the notion of and so her and Dr. Dewey Lunt aired together their bicuspids pretty much directly at each other.

The trouble was that nobody could find in the fellowship hall upstairs or downstairs either much in the way of a spread for the tile floor though

Mr. Sleepy Pitts did discover in the kitchen back of the serving window a sizeable stack of little square cocktail napkins with elegant crinkly edges and "Dwayne & Nancy" printed in the middle in graceful script under a pair of ribbonbearing doves, Nancy who Mrs. Estelle Singletary identified as that Pittman girl who'd run off with Dwayne's brother Earl once she'd found out precisely what Dwayne himself was like. So they were napkins with a history and a bit of a taint to them but they were sufficient nonetheless to cover the speckledy tile floor once they'd gotten opened and unfolded. Everybody stood and pushed back their chairs to the wall and Mr. Sleepy Pitts, who'd found the napkins in the first place, squatted back of Miss Fay Dull, who'd professed a need for them, and began to unfold them a napkin at a time and lay and lap them while pausing every now and again so as to raise up his head and reconnoiter. He took hers for a ten-napkin posterior and so laid out ten napkins precisely and continued even to believe they would be probably sufficient until the Reverend Mr. Parnell and Mr. H. Monroe Aycock together set to lowering Miss Fay Dull by the armpits and so placed her backside in such proximity to the open cocktail napkins as to persuade Mr. Sleepy Pitts how twelve would more likely suit and maybe even thirteen which he'd not so much as suspected even a little and so said, "Lord!" at, said Lord! not devotedly but chiefly with consternation instead that Mr. H. Monroe Aycock and Reverend Mr. Parnell were both curious to know the why of and that Miss Fay Dull was a little curious to know the why of herself.

And he said it wasn't anything, wasn't anything at all as he laid open the eleventh napkin and the twelfth napkin and the thirteenth napkin too that he pulled a face at Mrs. Sleepy Pitts on account of who said a thing behind her hand to Mrs. Cecil Dutton that said a thing behind her hand back and together they watched, along with everybody otherwise, Miss Fay Dull settle atop her cocktail napkins that she almost entirely obscured and covered over which Mr. Sleepy Pitts found himself inclined to say Lord! at another time and so said it. The widow Mrs. Askew, who'd not straightoff guessed she had much call for napkins herself, decided she'd go ahead and sit upon some after all that she let on was due to the floorgrit and was in fact due to the floorgrit a little but was due primarily to Miss Fay Dull's own thirteen napkins instead that the widow Mrs. Askew felt certain she could improve upon, felt certain she could better by two napkins anyhow and maybe even three as she could not believe, if she contracted and if she scrunched up, she'd have left to her much more than ten napkins' worth of backside which she was pretty much right about but for what piece of her left thigh Mr.

Sleepy Pitts saw fit to lay napkin eleven under that she sat on barely half of which she went ahead and made from the tile floor an announcement about.

Miss Bernice Fay Frazier who had on a semicreamy manner of dress herself guessed she could make maybe ten napkins too and so requested from Mr. Sleepy Pitts ten just precisely like she insisted was plenty even after they plainly weren't plenty hardly and weren't made plenty even until the fourteenth napkin got laid and situated which Miss Bernice Fay Frazier grew noticeably distraught about but got cheered shortly and comforted by her sister Mrs. Estelle Singletary who reminded Miss Bernice Fay Frazier what inordinately sizeable bones she had, bones all stout and girthsome like inflated probably her napkin count, bones with some heft and breadth to them, four full napkins probably worth of heft and worth of breadth both. "Surely," Mrs. Estelle Singletary said and Mrs. Phillip J. King told to her, "Surely," back and told to Miss Bernice Fay Frazier, "Surely," too though not either time near so grave and sober as Mrs. Estelle Singletary had herself in the first place said it.

Mrs. MacElrath's niece Judy guessed maybe she could stand some napkins as well that the ladies otherwise, which would be the ones on the tile floor already and the ones planning shortly to be themselves on the tile floor, grew straightaway disgruntled about on account of how Judy was not truly but a child that they told to each other she was and implied with their eyebrows chiefly what manner of napkin count a mere child's backside might call for which would, they figured, be scant and piddling, too altogether scant and piddling to tolerate with much grace truly, so they were planning to pretty completely loose their disgruntlement on Judy Mrs. MacElrath's niece with the juvenile backside when Bob the Mormon, who'd gotten his Huffy ruined by Mrs. Dot Pipkin in her green Electra, offered Judy his plastic rain jacket which he carried evermore roundabout in a tiny little packet, or offered to her anyhow his plastic rain jacket once he'd shown to her straightoff his various contusions by way of introduction. Consequently, then, Mrs. Dwight Mobley went on and took some napkins herself since Judy hadn't and she broke clean into the single digits with nine all laid and spread out that she didn't even entirely touch and cover the edges of like she proclaimed outright and made a manner of fuss about that Miss Bernice Fay Frazier in particular grew agitated on account of and communicated, as best she was able, her agitation to Miss Fay Dull and the widow Mrs. Askew both who got a little worked up themselves and seethed a spell at Mrs. Dwight Mobley like they would have probably persisted at if Mrs. Phillip J. King hadn't sat down on just seven napkins herself that she did not figure she needed, if the truth be known, so awful many of. Of course she had her legs all drawn up and was reclining on the pointiest piece of her behind that Mrs. Estelle Singletary made mention of to her sister Miss Bernice Fay Frazier who broadcast it a little herself and guessed if weren't her own bones so stout and girthsome she'd draw up her legs and perch on her pointy part too. But Mrs. Phillip J. King told how it was more than just spindly bones, admitted to Miss Bernice Fay Frazier and Miss Fay Dull and the widow Mrs. Askew and everybody otherwise who would hear her that yes, she'd come to be lately trim and svelte, gotten lately near about wiry she supposed and she wondered at Mr. Phillip J. King if hadn't he watched her dwindle away to hardly anything anymore that Mr. Phillip J. King confessed he had though without truly conviction enough to suit Mrs. Phillip J. King who wondered at him another time ever so sweetly if maybe he wouldn't confess it for her again.

Presently, they all got settled and circled round and the ones that could sit on their crossed legs did while everybody else just laid and propped as best they were able. Dr. Dewey Lunt and his cousin the Reverend Mr. Theodore J. Parnell sat side by side with their hands upturned on their knees and their eyes shut for a time and thereby induced Mr. H. Monroe Aycock in particular to upturn his own hands and shut his eyes too that Mrs. Phillip J. King watched him do and so upturned her hands and shut her eyes fairly completely but for the one she left squinty to watch Mr. Phillip J. King with, watch Mr. Phillip J. King just sit and poke his foremost finger deep down into his earchannel that she cleared her throat about, plain humphed four times on account of until she reached with one of her upturned hands and took hold between the fingers of it sufficient of Mr. Phillip J. King's loose armskin to persuade him to display his own palms and shut his own eyes and look somehow passably serene.

Dr. Dewey Lunt intended that the bunch of them would undertake there at the first some delving other than your deep profound manner of delving, undertake there at the first some skimpy delving truly that was likely more kin to a scant and shallow interact than a delve at all, and he inquired had anybody among them had occasion previously to partake of an interact that Mrs. MacElrath's niece Judy admitted she had at college in Chapel Hill which the ladies in particular told to each other they were not much surprised to find out. Judy revealed to Dr. Dewey Lunt how she'd come at college to be Zenish and so had found occasion to meditate after a delving and interactional sort of a fashion, and she was meaning to illuminate for Dr. Dewey Lunt the precise nature of her own particular brand of meditation which she'd embarked already upon when Dr. Dewey Lunt raised three fingers at her in a pontifical sort of a way and so blessed and interrupted her at the same time prior to raking his bangs as he was up anyhow in the vicinity of them. He wasn't himself hardly of the ilk that believed a man or a woman either one couldn't just up and get in touch straightoff with their own feelings the first time out, so it didn't truly matter to him that only Judy Mrs. MacElrath's niece had delved and interacted a little before, though Bob the Mormon did admit how he'd gone one time transcendental just of a sudden, how he'd gotten off his blue Huffy in Vesuvius Virginia and was sitting by the roadside chewing his fingerend that he'd draw every now and again out from his mouth to ponder as a prologue to chewing it some more, draw out and study the tip of for a spot to gnaw which he was right there in the midst of when things went kind of blurry on him and he couldn't for a spell see anything but light all radiant and golden and he heard what he took for angelic strains and felt his entire person bathed, he said, in pure contentment.

And Mr. Luther Teague inquired of Mrs. Luther Teague, "Who is that?"

"Bob," she told him.

"Bob who?" Mr. Luther Teague wanted to know.

"Bob somebody," Mrs. Luther Teague said. "Dot Pipkin run over him with her Buick."

"In Vesuvius Virginia?"

"No, Luther," Mrs. Luther Teague said. "He got transcendental in Vesuvius Virginia. He got run over up 87 outside the Shoetown."

"When?" Mr. Luther Teague wanted to know.

And Mrs. Luther Teague told him back all sharp and sudden, "Lately," which was partly on account of Mr. Luther Teague's near about interminable inquiries but which was partly as well on account of Mrs. Luther Teague's own personal backside that she'd been forced just recently to admit was your multinapkin variety of backside, probably your altogether more multinapkin variety than bore much thinking about like had made her ill and peevish to know of and fess up to which was how come she told to Mr. Luther Teague, "Hush now," before he'd said truly any additional thing to get hushed on account of like he endeavored to indicate to Mrs. Luther Teague he hadn't which she went on and took directly for the thing she'd hushed him just previously about that she told him it was.

Bob said he'd stayed transcendental there on the roadside, stayed all bathed for a time in contentment serenaded like he was by angelic strains until a man in the back of a Dodge truck heading west on the highway threw a Pepsi can at him and sloshed him with backwash which revived him and brought him around, and he'd undertaken subsequently to gnaw his fingerend in such a fashion as to go transcendental all over again but he'd not somehow succeeded at it except for that one time outside Vesuvius Virginia when he swore to Dr. Dewey Lunt he'd delved and probed and sunk clean out of sight that Dr. Dewey Lunt raised up his fingers pontifically about while Bob the Mormon turned sideways a little to eye Mrs. MacElrath's niece Judy atop his plastic rain jacket which he figured bound somehow and attached them together until, anyway, she got up.

Dr. Dewey Lunt guessed it was a fine thing how they would pretty much all of them set out from the same place and interact for the first time together that his cousin the Reverend Mr. Parnell threw in himself with prior to yielding entirely to Dr. Dewey Lunt who encouraged everybody that was fit for it to lay back their heads and roll them for a time roundabout from the front to the one side to the back to the side opposite and down to the front again and he advised them all to hang limp everywhere otherwise as they did it which was not awful much trouble for anybody but Mrs. Phillip J. King who could not hang limp and perch on the pointiest part of her backside both at the very same time, could not hardly plain roll her head and perch together, and so rolled just a little and perched somewhat and watched primarily Mrs. Cecil Dutton directly across from her who quite apparently had not been plunked down on God's green earth to sit crosslegged atop a tile floor and gyrate her head around her spinal column which she was not much flattered and improved by on account of her jowls that flapped and drooped and her chest that sagged and her stomach that bulged out and Mrs. Phillip J. King gave praise to the Lord in heaven that she had herself just lately grown taut and svelte and near about utterly wispy all over which the basement of the fellowship hall, situated like it was a mere stairwell from the house of God, seemed to her just the sort of place to give praise in.

Probably they would have the bunch of them gyrated their heads and hung limp elsewhere longer than they ended up gyrating and hanging limp if Mr. Estelle Singletary, that suffered with the vertigo, had not on a pass backwards opened his eyes and studied ever so briefly the acoustical ceiling like he suspected maybe he shouldn't have done even while he did it that he grew pretty thoroughly convinced about once he'd pitched over onto his shoulder blades with his crossed legs elevated above him that he told to Mr. Sleepy Pitts, who tilted him presently back upright, he would have surely gone ahead and uncrossed if his joints had been anymore near so spontaneous as one time they were that Mr. Sleepy Pitts confessed to him back was pretty much the case with his own personal joints any longer and him and Mr. Estelle Singletary shared with each other woeful expressions all of which Dr. Dewey Lunt in particular took some notice of and presently identified as a frank and candid exchange for the benefit of those people who had not taken themselves any notice of it. He was out, of course, to promote frank and candid exchanges like he'd found to be healthful and liberating which the Reverend Mr. Theodore J. Parnell, who was pretty much of a mind with his cousin Dr. Dewey Lunt, said a breathy Yes at and dangled as best he could over his kneecap his swirly pinky ring. In fact, Dr. Dewey Lunt insisted, they'd sat flush down on the tile floor and rolled their heads so as to get eased and uninhibited what way he'd found promoted sentiments all bald and forthright which Mrs. Phillip J. King had taken herself some notice of and in her eased and uninhibited state she went on ahead and spoke flatout of how Mrs. Cecil Dutton had surely not been made and manufactured to sit crosslegged on a tile floor due to her parts that were loose and droopy like wasn't precisely the manner of frank candid bald forthright sentiment Dr. Dewey Lunt had just lately told about that Dr. Dewey Lunt did not have truly the opportunity to say it was or say it wasn't either one before Mrs. Cecil Dutton herself made at Mrs. Phillip J. King a noise like a housecat that was part spit and part breath and part undiluted agitation and seemed most especially to Mrs. Phillip J. King fairly frank and candid and bald and forthright too.

Dr. Dewey Lunt, once he'd run his fingertips overtop his skimpy moustache and thrown his hair with a headjerk, undertook to calm most especially Mrs. Cecil Dutton and so said to her, "Joyce," in his altogether serenest tone and got told straightoff by Mrs. Cecil Dutton, "What?" back that Mrs. Cecil Dutton amended pretty directly once she'd seen who she'd snapped her What? at like she'd not meant to truly that she explained to Dr. Dewey Lunt she hadn't and told three times just precisely how sorry in fact she was for it that got her blessed and interrupted and waved a little at. It seemed to him they were all maybe ripe to vent a thing since they'd sat now a time together and rolled their heads around. It seemed to him they were all maybe set to go on and reveal a private manner of item about their own selves there at the first, exclusively about their own selves alone, Dr. Dewey Lunt suggested with some noticeable emphasis that Mrs. Phillip J. King displayed her bicuspids about so as to let on how she'd gone ahead and gleaned what he meant.

Judy Mrs. MacElrath's niece was anxious to reveal her own private manner of item firstoff and so extended her right arm, which she supported at the elbow, and wiggled her hand on the end of it while she wheezed and grunted and fairly much exclaimed, but Dr. Dewey Lunt passed her up for Mr. Luther Teague instead who'd been studying the strip of skin on his one leg between the trouser cuff and the sockend as a preface and a preamble to gauging it against the strip of skin on his other leg entirely like he was ever so slightly curious to see the difference in but like he was hoping chiefly would render him somehow moderately invisible, invisible enough anyway to get for a spell passed over until he'd landed just precisely on the manner of private item to tell that naturally he hadn't still when Dr. Dewey Lunt showed at Judy his pontifical fingers and said at Mr. Luther Teague opposite to her, "Luther," all breathy and soft.

Of course he was blank and empty there at the first and managed to be just breathy himself back for longer than Mrs. Luther Teague most especially figured he should be just breathy that she laid a pointy fingerend between his ribs about like prompted a discharge from Mr. Luther Teague that was still just air chiefly with some trifling noise to it, inadvertent trifling noise which Mr. Luther Teague set to working and shaping straightaway into a revelation that he guessed would have a thing to do with his recent intestinal blockage which he'd come lately to be cut open on account of. He figured he'd tell how they'd put him under and laid him wide and stitched him shut at last and had even commenced truly to tell it, had said anyway, "Well," and had dragged the tipend of his tongue across the roof of his mouth when he felt with it his partial plate that he decided just on the impulse of the moment he'd speak of instead and so spoke instead of it and popped it loose even onto the flat of his tongue that he displayed it atop of and wondered as best he could, with his tongue and his partial plate extended and exposed, had anybody previously known a thing in the world about it that only Mrs. Luther Teague intimated she had which was with her finger mostly that she poked and jabbed and her mouth somewhat that she said, "Luther!" with.

Judy Mrs. MacElrath's niece remained anxious to speak of her own private manner of item and oohed and puffed and grunted and wiggled her hand and would have probably been called on directly but for Mrs. Luther Teague who felt compelled to go on ahead and blurt a private thing herself, a private thing she'd only just the very minute she blurted it got inspired to blurt, and she told out to everybody around her how Mr. Luther Teague had been couth previously, had been when she met him couth a little bit, but had gotten lately shed of most every trace of couthness about him and so could lay out his tongue with his partial plate upon it right there in the basement of the fellowship hall among people who were decent and couth themselves like made her, she said, ashamed like she'd never previously had cause from Mr. Luther Teague to be and so was sorrowful with it, was probably even sorrowful chiefly that Mr. Luther Teague looked at his strip of naked legskin on account of and listened while Mrs. Estelle Singletary agreed that Mr. Luther Teague had just lately done a shameful thing which she told to Dr. Dewey Lunt was not her own particular private item but just a frank candid bald forthright item otherwise that she entertained some uplifted fingers about.

Naturally, talk of Mr. Luther Teague's general sorry state and evermore eroding couthness inspired all around him recollections of personal gaffs and the like that folks guessed maybe they could reveal and speak of if some other better private thing failed to come to them that way private things had in fact failed to come to most everybody but for Mrs. MacElrath's niece Judy who continued to flap her hand and grunt and puff and ooh and just sputter in general like a combustion engine until Dr. Dewey Lunt at long last jerked his head towards her in other than a hairthrowing sort of a way and let on how she might go ahead and tell her private thing that Judy inquired of him, "Me?" about, inquired of him two times Me? about as she laid her fingers upon her breastbone and waited to get jerked at another time like presently she did.

Judy had seen a boy at school in Chapel Hill that she liked and that she could tell by the way he looked sometimes sideways at her like her back, looked sometimes sideways at her when he figured she couldn't see him do it like every now and again she could which was part of how come she knew he liked her in conjunction with the way it was he ignored her altogether aside from the sideways looking which fairly completely confirmed for her his affection. He was a tall boy, a tall darkheaded boy from Charlotte that drove a red imported car and lived in a regular house off the campus with three other boys, a regular house east off Franklin Street that Judy's friend Denise from Moncure had followed him one day to, and he had this chin with a little creasy pocket in the tipend of it and teeth all white and straight and green eyes like a cat's, Judy told it. "Limpid," she said, "green eyes," and she studied briefly on her own the acoustical ceiling that she clutched her hands together and exhaled at.

She waited to get spoken to by him, put herself places she figured he might run up on her and so have the occasion right there before him to go on and say to her a thing, and he even did run up on her one time outside the library where she looked a little sideways at him and got looked at, as best as she could tell, a little sideways back but he didn't say to her even "Hey" or show her his white teeth truly that she grew for a time distraught on account of but had begun to improve and recover when she saw him that very afternoon in his red imported car, saw him that very afternoon at a light with the blond girl from her own biology class, the blond girl with the streaky hair who was getting shown to her his green eyes and his white teeth and was having likely, as best as Mrs. MacElrath's niece Judy could tell from the sidewalk, her kneecap touched too like Judy had gotten most especially crushed and done in by and so had dropped off into a funk, a deep and profound manner of funk that only her newfound Zenishness had brought her lately out of.

And Mrs. Phillip J. King felt moved and compelled to confirm for herself, which she indicated to Dr. Dewey Lunt was not hardly her private item, did Judy Mrs. MacElrath's niece mean to say she'd come to be Zenish and eat chicory and such on account of a darkheaded boy from Charlotte that looked every now and again sideways at her?

"Him," Judy told to her, "and her too. Them together."

"Well, child," Mrs. Phillip J. King said and humphed with her mouth shut and humphed with her mouth open and looked off beyond Mr. Phillip J. King to the widow Mrs. Askew who discharged a little herself prior to announcing outright how Judy's private item was the nearest nothing of a private item she'd ever yet heard. She guessed she'd rather look at partial plates from now on that Mrs. Phillip J. King went ahead and guessed with her while Judy showed to them her serene Zenish face that wasn't but a little twitchy and tight.

Mr. Estelle Singletary, inspired like he'd gotten to be by Mr. Luther Teague, selected for his secret innermost thing the time he'd slipped in the Big Apple on the wet linoleum and had undertaken to catch and right himself on the mayonnaise display that was just jars stacked and piled up at the end of the row like had not been fixed and situated truly to be grabbed onto and so pitched over with him and landed chiefly atop him where they busted against each other when they did not roll off him and bust against the linoleum instead like failed to seem, most especially to Mrs. Estelle Singletary, worth hearing about which Mr. Estelle Singletary guessed briefly it was until he got by Mrs. Estelle Singletary corrected altogether. Of course Mrs. Estelle Singletary was set to illustrate for Mr. Estelle Singletary with her own private item just how piddling and shabby his personal private item had in fact been when she got preempted entirely by Mrs. Phillip J. King who'd felt suddenly the urge to tell how she'd come lately to be wispy and svelte both. She hadn't needed to get up. Dr. Dewey Lunt and his cousin the Reverend Mr. Theodore J. Parnell both told her how, truly, she hadn't needed to once she'd gotten up already and turned slowly around in a circle so everybody could see, even if ever so briefly, Mrs. Phillip J. King's sleek comely profile that she fielded, from the reverend and the doctor and most especially Mr. Phillip J. King, compliments about prior to returning the pointiest part of her backside to her scant spread of napkins and speaking at some length of the tuna and the mixed greens and the brothy soups and the grapefruit halves and the hunger and the anguish and the dark nights of the stomach sac which her, she said, and P.J., she said, had suffered boldly through that she took up Mr. Phillip J. King's fingers on account of and paused to look on him like she meant for deep and soulful but that got taken by Miss Bernice Fay Frazier for punctuational instead which was how come she went on ahead and began to air her own private item that talk of anguish most especially had caused her to go on and begin to air.

She'd fallen over Bubbles her cat. She'd fallen full down atop the throwrug on account of her speckled cat Bubbles that Mrs. Phillip J. King said, "Hey!" at, or said Hey! after anyhow and set to informing Miss Bernice Fay Frazier and everybody otherwise how she'd not herself been done but had only paused and gapped like was temporary and dramatic that she got to look straightoff at three pontifical fingers on account of. She'd been in the front room in just her full slip, Miss Bernice Fay Frazier had, gone there to fetch a thing and had turned around to strike out in some particular direction when she stepped full onto the cat which naturally the cat objected to straightoff. She tried to hover briefly and levitate but as she'd not ever been much given to hovering and levitation she just went ahead and careened instead, just went ahead and lurched and stumbled and thumped at last flush down on the throwrug upon her backside that was not itself especially pointy, due to her sizeable bones, but was pointy enough to sting anyhow once it met the rug that didn't have hardly any nap at all to it. The trouble was she bumped and squeezed her nerves, bumped and squeezed the both of them that ran up her legs into her spinal column.

"Skyatic," Mr. Cecil Dutton told to her as he had those very nerves himself which kicked up every now and again a fuss for him.

"Them," Miss Bernice Fay Frazier told to him back, and she said how she plain lay on the floor all helpless and near about indecent and got looked at from under the settee by Bubbles her spotted cat that was peeved with her. And she feared she'd not likely get up, feared she'd lie all numb and disabled atop the throwrug until maybe she expired which she admitted was a sorrowful prospect but not hardly the worst prospect altogether on account of she'd probably not just come to be dead but would likely get found at it there in her full slip by somebody she didn't hardly know, would likely get plain gawked at all expired what way the bald Jeeter up the street had herself gotten pondered and perused and carted at last out the door and slid into the back of the hearse.

"And I wished I had somebody," Miss Bernice Fay Frazier said and grew a little weepy that she attended to with a wrinkly wad of Kleenex out from her pocketbook. "I wished I had somebody to heft me and take me up, and it came to me there on the throwrug that can't anybody feel so lonely as when he's dropped atop his sciatic nerves in his underclothes without any help for it. Can't anybody feel so lonely as when he's done that," and Miss Bernice Fay Frazier dabbed her eyes and then pulled at her tissue with her fingerends and looked fairly ponderously forlorn at the tile floor chiefly.

Miss Fay Dull, however, had read in the *Guidepost* of lonelier things altogether, black inky desperate sorts of lonely things that she spoke to Miss Bernice Fay Frazier about once she'd indicated to Dr. Dewey Lunt how wasn't a one of them her own personal private item. But the manner of black inky desperate sorts of lonely things from the *Guidepost* most times grew Jesusy at the end and came in a regular sort of way to get illuminated by your heavenly manner of light, mere talk of which stirred and set off Bob the Mormon who undertook to make mention another time of what light all radiant and golden he'd seen on the roadside in Vesuvius Virginia like had rendered him easeful and contented that he reminded most especially Judy Mrs. MacElrath's niece it had while he gazed on her with pieces of his cheeks clamped between his molars in an effort to look dimply as he could not somehow manage to look darkheaded and straighttoothed and limpid greeneyed instead.

But then Miss Bernice Fay Frazier was not so very anxious to have her personal black inky desperate forlorn episode made heavenly and bright as she was not truly done being weepy and being pitiful quite yet. So she dabbed and moaned and told as breathy as she was able how she did not sometimes know about things every now and again and grew on account of it sad and fearful and wanted just to get led and seen after, wanted to have sometimes her fingers taken up like she'd watched Mr. and Mrs. Phillip J. King take up fingers just lately which seemed to Mrs. Phillip J. King a variety of introduction and was how come she set back in with the brown squeaky crackers and the mixed silage and the niacin and such that she got punctuated another time at by Miss Bernice Fay Frazier who exhaled and lamented on account of her general state which Mrs. Dwight Mobley made a suggestion about, Mrs. Dwight Mobley whose momma's sister in Berkeley Springs West Virginia knew a woman that was looking to leave, knew a woman that was looking to be elsewhere entirely. And it probably wouldn't have advanced any further at all but for Mrs. Phillip J. King who'd grown ill and put out and so made plain to Miss Bernice Fay Frazier how she wouldn't herself take up with a woman from Berkeley Springs West Virginia if she was just lonesome and forlorn and fretful of stomping every now and again on her cat, how she hadn't run up on anybody ever from West Virginia that was worth anything much which Mrs. Dwight Mobley endeavored to take issue with but got prevented from it by Miss Bernice Fay Frazier who informed Mrs. Phillip J. King how she didn't likely know what it was to lay atop a throwrug in her full slip with her nerves pinched and wounded and no help anywhere roundabout for it, how she probably wasn't much acquainted with pain and anguishment other than the stomach sac sort, and how she didn't look anyhow near so svelte and slinky as she'd probably gone ahead and full well convinced herself she did that Mrs. Phillip J. King was particularly stung on account of and would have probably said a thing at if she'd not gotten of a sudden flashy, which was hot flashy and cold flashy both at the same time somehow and left chink enough in the general talk for Mr. Cecil Dutton to wonder at Miss Bernice Fay Frazier, "How'd you get up?"

"Climbed the settee," she told to him which Mr. Cecil Dutton tried to picture in his mind's eye and then tried, once he had, to leave off at it.

"Go on," Mrs. Phillip J. King said after a spell of not but taking air in and venting it back out again, "do what you want."

And Mrs. Dwight Mobley added back of it, "She will."

"Go on," Mrs. Phillip J. King said, and appreciable glaring ensued which Dr. Dewey Lunt moved to thwart with his upraised fingers that he poked and waved and worked with hardly any effect to speak of until Miss May Drumm, who felt she had a kind of a thing to say with some bearing on the things that had just lately been said, inquired might she go on and reveal her innermost item that Dr. Dewey Lunt with his upraised fingers indicated she could.

Miss May Drumm and Miss Halley Verna Drumm both together had driven in Miss May Drumm's Ford Customline to Roxboro to see the Beshears woman that lived most times up the road from Halley Verna but just lately had her hernia snipped at the hospital in Greensboro and was staying with her boy and his wife Gail until she felt able to go around like previously she had. They'd taken tea with her in the front room and cookies with nuts like did not May or Halley Verna either one much care for and they'd sat and they'd chatted and they'd watched the Beshears woman raise up her nightdress and show to them her incision and they'd headed at last back towards home where they'd almost in fact arrived when they decided to stop in at the Dairy Queen on the Lawsonville Road for a brazier burger with slaw and chili on it like you couldn't get at the Burger Chef in town where they were partial to just ketchup and just mustard and dill slices all papery thin. And May Drumm wondered could anybody tell to her who it was they saw at the Dairy Queen on the Lawsonville Road that Halley Verna said she could but got by May Drumm prevented from it for a brief spell until nobody otherwise had even so much as guessed truly when Halley Verna got allowed by May Drumm to point at Mr. Phillip J. King and got allowed to say to Mrs. Phillip J. King primarily, "Him."

They told of the brazier burger and the fries in the holster and the Pepsi-Cola and the turnover, like had been maybe apple or had been maybe cherry that they couldn't have known until he bit it which they never saw him do, and the quarter cantaloupe as well with the squirt of whipped cream on it like had not seemed to either one of them especially dietetic, not even so much as remotely and vaguely dietetic truly, and Mrs. Cecil Dutton, who had not been aware that the Dairy Queen served cantaloupe with whipped cream on it, set about to discuss the matter with May and Halley Verna Drumm together and had advanced so far along as to utter, "May?" and to utter, "Halley Verna?" with it when Mr. Phillip J. King interrupted her so as to lodge his protest with Dr. Dewey Lunt, so as to bring to light how May Drumm's own private personal item did not seem to him much at all about May Drumm what way he figured her private personal item should that May Drumm endeavored herself to say a thing about while Mr. Phillip J. King, who'd not gotten done, carried on further still and so provoked from Dr. Dewey Lunt some upraised fingers and a spate of breathy talk that Mr. Phillip J. King was set pretty much to say another thing after when he felt a little piece of his armskin get mashed and squeezed by Mrs. Phillip J. King next to him who told to him sweetly, "P.J." and grinned at him a toothy and carnivorous sort of a grin.

Dr. Dewey Lunt had expected maybe to get done altogether with private items after a solitary session or after just the bulk of a solitary session truly, but what with the friction and the conflict and the ill tempers and the heavenly light talk and the dietetic talk and the talk in particular from Miss Bernice Fay Frazier of her bedroom upstairs with the clutter in it that she figured would be a fit place for Mrs. Dwight Mobley's momma's sister's Berkeley Springs friend once the clutter got transported and relocated, they did not put their innermost revelations behind them until they'd squandered two full Thursday nights entirely when they did in fact move on to some deeper delving altogether and began to get in touch after a fashion with pretty much their own personal feelings like diminished the general agitation in a noticeable sort of a way. They advanced out of circlesitting on the tile floor due to how the napkins with the bells and the borders and the crinkly edges had all but given out and they set in to addressing their consciousnesses from folding metal chairs that they by turns stood up out of to say a thing, say a thing about whatever it might be they felt moved and inclined to say a thing about which was just regular local things there at the outset but inflated to altogether grander items presently like had not hardly any of them ever much felt inclined to speak of before.

Mr. H. Monroe Aycock got matters under way with a murky observation that was chiefly geopolitical which he explained most especially to Mrs. Estelle Singletary it was once she'd stood up out of her own folding chair so as to proclaim how she'd latched onto the murky pretty directly but could not somehow get much grip to speak of on the parts otherwise which was how come Mr. H. Monroe Aycock repeated his geopolitical observation fairly much precisely like he'd said it straightoff only slower and louder too which prompted at the culmination an "Oh" from Mrs. Estelle Singletary who felt, she insisted, edified. As long as they'd come to be on your large ponderous manner of things, the widow Mrs. Askew guessed she was curious to know why the earth had gotten pitched a little sideways and so did not spin straight up and down like seemed logical to her, and though nobody could say for certain why exactly they all agreed they were improved by thinking on it which they wouldn't have bothered with if Mrs. Askew hadn't stood up to inquire that Judy Mrs. MacElrath's niece and Bob the Mormon thanked her together for. Mr. Luther Teague had not ever figured out himself how birds manage to migrate like they do which he got explained to him by Mr. Cecil Dutton who in turn was himself explained at by Miss Bernice Fay Frazier and Mrs. Dwight Mobley both that contended they knew different from what it was Mr. Cecil Dutton had contended just previously that Mr. Cecil Dutton was set to object about when Dr. Dewey Lunt asked him all low and breathy if didn't he feel enriched for having been imparted to like he had which, after a time, he guessed he did feel maybe though he had not straightaway considered enriched was what he was getting chiefly.

Mr. Phillip J. King had a notion that it never anymore got so cold in the winter as it used to get and the winters weren't remotely so hard and foul as they used to be as best as he could tell that he got enriched over too partly by Miss Bernice Fay Frazier who had enriched Mr. Cecil Dutton just previously and partly by Halley Verna Drumm who begged to differ with him on account of the chinaberry tree in her sideyard that had been frozen and killed not the last winter but the winter before it which Mr. Phillip J. King guessed didn't tell him a thing on account of how chinaberry trees weren't any hardy manner of trees anyhow that Halley Verna Drumm begged to differ about which she got directly joined at by her sister May Drumm who begged to differ some with her. The widow Mrs. Askew, who'd moved off the poles of the earth, went ahead and let out in a gap she'd found for it an inquiry, went ahead and wondered how it was precisely organs worked that Miss Fay Dull undertook to explain to her commencing with your general airflow and the piping it traveled through and the slits and the holes it blew over that the widow Mrs. Askew interrupted Miss Fay Dull at so as to explain what manner of organs she'd meant just precisely which turned out to be the internal rather than the musical sort which Miss Fay Dull had not full well plumbed the mysteries of herself and consequently yielded to Mr. Sleepy Pitts who'd passed appreciable spiny stones and so felt kidney literate anyhow which he exhibited some of to the widow Mrs. Askew who was a little kidney literate herself and so naturally, once she found the chance for it, exhibited back.

By the middle of August Dr. Dewey Lunt with his breathy serene voice and his pontifical upraised fingers along with some ample sheer unmitigated perseverance had wrought a manner of fairly miraculous transformation that was maybe not altogether deep and innermost entirely but was noticeable anyhow since near about everybody had left off being short and irksome, or anyway had left off being short and irksome all plain and unadorned and were breathy anymore when they got ill, were easeful and polite, and so seemed sometimes fairly tolerant and unagitated, seemed sometimes even sublime and told to each other on that Thursday night that was but one Thursday night shy of the last one—what Mr. H. Monroe Aycock called penultimate as far as it was Thursday nights went that he got thanked for and breathed at on account of—not your private manner of items truly or your curious manner of items but your singularly soulful manner of items instead that the widow Mrs. Askew, who'd checked out a book from the bookbus out front of the Roses, set the tone for with a passage she cited once she'd rolled her eyes upwards towards the acoustical ceiling like was a habit with the widow Mrs. Askew whenever she bothered to cite. "Temperament," she said, "is the iron wire on which the beads are strung. The particolored wheel," she told behind it, "must revolve fast to appear white." And the widow Mrs. Askew said, "Ralph," and said, "Waldo," and said, "Emerson," too after which her and the Reverend Mr. Theodore J. Parnell quite plainly showed at each other their teeth like spoke and like communicated that everybody could tell it did as they'd had half of July and most of August to find out what precisely bare teeth meant.

So they talked ever so loose and vaguely that penultimate Thursday out of all the Thursdays they collected together, spoke of how it was they'd noticed their consciousnesses begin to raise up which is not truly anything a person can talk but loose and vaguely about. Judy, who'd been lately after all to the university at Chapel Hill, was coming up as best as she could tell on some outright serenity like she suspected everybody otherwise was coming up on too and she undertook to explain what sort of thing exactly her serenity seemed to her that Mr. Luther Teague, once she'd gotten done, guessed he related to and guessed he identified with that Mrs. Luther Teague in particular was doubtful about as she was not altogether certain a person could relate and identify both at the same time and was not hardly convinced Mr. Luther Teague could do either one alone that she made an announcement about so soft and easeful as to seem pleasant even and remotely complimentary and she got by Mr. Luther Teague thanked for it.

They were all OK, even Mrs. Estelle Singletary as best as Mrs. Sleepy Pitts could tell who'd not ever much cared for Mrs. Estelle Singletary that Mrs. Estelle Singletary appreciated the news of which she told she did to Mrs. Sleepy Pitts who figured that not only everybody otherwise was OK but she was OK her own self and she explained how exactly as she'd been out front of the Roses to the bookbus as well and come across a book about it. Bob the Mormon was grateful to have been taken in by Protestants that he told mostly at Judy Mrs. MacElrath's niece and bit his cheeks for her that way she'd grown fond of, and she forgave him altogether for being a Mormon in the first place anyhow like seemed to her pretty near to pagan if not pagan outright that Miss Fay Dull and Mrs. Cecil Dutton threw in sweetly with and inquired of the Reverend Mr. Theodore J. Parnell if wasn't his own opinion of Mormons fairly low and baleful as well that the Reverend Mr. Parnell swirled his ring about like Miss Fay Dull and Mrs. Cecil Dutton and Judy Mrs.

MacElrath's niece admitted to each other they'd known he would and that Bob the Mormon, once he'd been prodded and cajoled, guessed he'd pretty much counted on himself.

The ultimate Thursday there at the shankend of August they spent chiefly in deep ponderous meditation that had to it some fingerchewing and some eargouging and some throatdredging too but was just plain weighty thought primarily all still and unadorned right up to the bout of testifying that set out with Dr. Dewey Lunt who spoke of how just that very afternoon he'd eased his red Ventura into the Sunoco station shy of town for five dollars of high octane and had struck up some talk with the attendant who was troubled on account of his wife was suffering with a bladder ailment that gave her some pain and some worry, and Dr. Dewey Lunt told how he'd lifted up his pontifical fingers and laid them to that man's arm and said to him, "Go call that woman. Tell her you love her. Tell her she's on your mind," and he grabbed ahold himself of the gas nozzle and dismissed that man direct on into the station where he dialed his number and allowed the phone to ring and ring like gave his ailing wife the opportunity to leave the clothesline back of the house and run on across the yard and up the iron steps and along the hall to the phone table where she listened at her husband tell to her a thing she could not well make out on account of how poorly she most times heard when she had to hold to her knees like she found she had to. And maybe, Dr. Dewey Lunt figured, it would have been a sweet and a tender moment but for the running and the stairclimbing and the hard breathing in conjunction with the bladder complaint that the Sunoco man's wife found she'd run and climbed and breathed in the first place to hear of like failed to sit well with her that she informed her husband about who stepped shortly out to the pump island to tell Dr. Dewey Lunt of it.

And he wondered in a rhetorical sort of way at everybody roundabout him, Dr. Dewey Lunt did, why it was people felt obliged to be ill and be irksome when they might be warm and might be tender instead which gave rise to appreciable breathiness, inordinate windy widespread breathiness truly that swelled and rose up towards the acoustical ceiling and sounded there, most especially to Mr. Sleepy Pitts, a little typhoony which Mr. Luther Teague guessed he could fairly much get into and relate about himself that Mrs. Luther Teague assured him he couldn't. Miss Bernice Fay Frazier was looking forward to being warm and being tender with Mrs. Dwight Mobley's momma's sister's friend from Berkeley Springs West Virginia who she'd cleared the clutter out from her spare bedroom upstairs on account of that Mrs. Phillip J. King told to her she'd spoken already quite entirely too much about which Miss Bernice Fay Frazier and Mrs. Estelle Singletary together deciphered, they said, the bite in that Mrs. Phillip J. King disputed straightaway but with such grace and charm as to not get taken for contrary hardly like made in particular Dr. Dewey Lunt proud that he testified he was even though he'd just lately gotten done testifying once already.

They went entirely around the group and told each other what things seemed significant to them, trifling little things truly they'd heard themselves think and watched themselves do like surely they wouldn't have thought and done but for their newly upraised consciousnesses, and they hoped to celebrate their general elevation that Mrs. Estelle Singletary suggested the picnic for, or that Mrs. Estelle Singletary suggested somewhat the picnic for anyhow once the widow Mrs. Askew had undertaken already to suggest it a little herself along with Mrs. Cecil Dutton who'd eaten one time out by the reservoir with the Rotarians and so had the notion of a picnic at the Number 2 shelter fairly much embedded already in her upraised consciousness like she informed most especially Mrs. Estelle Singletary she did. And they all agreed they'd take the shelter and all agreed they'd invite heathens even and common regular people that could stand to be improved and rendered somehow sensitive like seemed worthwhile to Dr. Dewey Lunt who got made to promise outside in the church lot next to his momma's red Ventura that he'd come back and take supper with them under the Number 2 shelter at the reservoir which he told them a breathy Yes on account of, told them a breathy Yes, he most certainly would, and then slipped out from his suitjacket with the piping to it and laid it on the carseat prior to settling in beside it, and he started his Pontiac and dropped it into gear and lit out across the lot towards the road with such velocity just up and of a sudden as to fling rocks most all over.

They were all improved, sensed how it was they were all improved and uplifted, and once Mr. Phillip J. King and Mrs. Phillip J. King had settled in at home on their sofa before the TV they exchanged views and related together like had come to be a habit with them and Mrs. Phillip J. King sniffed, as was anymore her custom, Mr. Phillip J. King's breath to see could she find any coughdrop on it which lately she couldn't that they spoke of and related about as well. They shared a carrot that Mrs. Phillip J. King split longwise and a piece of an apple and watched a show on the cable about a tropical poisonous orange frog that a man didn't need but to touch to get killed by which prompted from Mrs. Phillip J. King some talk about life and how fragile and papery thin it seemed most times to be while Mr. Phillip J. King wondered how it was a man could up and die from just laying even to a poisonous orange frog his fingers that Mrs. Phillip J. King couldn't hardly tell him due to what a strange and wondrous world she guessed it was that her and that Mr. Phillip J. King related about some too before they got up together to retire and paused only briefly in front of the glass hutch doors where Mr. Phillip J. King admired Mrs. Phillip J. King headon and sideways both and told to her, "Like a pencil," as was anymore his custom.

He listened alone in the bathroom at his vapors once Mrs. Phillip J. King had finished with her grease and her ointment and her Scotchtape, and he contracted at last his duct and traveled with it roundabout the bedstead to the side by the window where he laid full down stomach upwards once he'd touched Mrs. Phillip J. King's shiny cheek with his lips, laid full down stomach upwards and pondered the overhead light as he groped and felt along the edge of the Posturepedic for the strap that he wrapped his fingers around and held grimly to.

iii.

IT had evermore been elsewhere, Nestor Tudor figured, had not anyway been so southernmost as he noticed straightoff it had come somehow to be like his own scant hairpart wasn't, like his hairpart never had been and like Dick Atwater's hairpart never, he recollected, had been itself previously which was how come he gazed a spell truly upon it, pondered how it ran pretty much the length of Dick Atwater's scalp just above his earpeak like struck Nestor Tudor as a curious place altogether for a hairpart to run on account of what niggling hair there was to comb downwards and what exceedingly inordinate hair there was to comb upwards and not just upwards all by itself but upwards and then flat level a ways and downwards beyond it so that the bulk of what hair grew on the one side of Dick Atwater's head had gotten combed and trained and Vitalised up across his bony ridge and down the far side altogether where it plain hung and laid when it did not get instead blown back to where it had started in the first place from. And Nestor Tudor and Wyatt Benbow stood together off towards the slab floor at the Number 2 shelter and watched Dick Atwater's vagrant hair lift off the naked patch atop his head that Dick Atwater undertook straightoff with his fingers to settle it back up onto again.

So it wasn't her he saw right there at the first on account of the hairpart all low and curious that him and that Wyatt Benbow exchanged between them some talk of which they got presently joined at by Tiny Aaron who Wyatt Benbow and Nestor Tudor together enlisted to comment himself upon the hairpart across the way like, after some gazing and some headshaking and some moderately articulate exhaling, he went ahead and did.

Nestor Tudor wasn't himself awfully well acquainted with anybody who'd been uplifted and so hadn't gotten personally invited to the picnic at the reservoir to view the elevated consciousnesses but had come instead in the company of Tiny Aaron, pretty much a fullblown and altogether lowslung heathen himself, who'd installed the stereo radio/tapedeck in the stunted blue Methodist activity bus and had won thereby the favor of the Methodists, or the favor of the bulk of the Methodists anyhow since Mr. Bill Covington's wife's brother Carl, who had the license to drive the thing, was partial himself to the collected recordings of the Harmonicats which he tended to play on the deck more often truly and with considerably more volume than a portion of the congregation found they could gracefully endure. But he got invited nonetheless and him and Nestor Tudor and Wyatt Benbow stood together and observed how it was Mr. Dick Atwater's long relatively wiry hair rose up from his lowslung hairpart and laid upon his otherwise slick and vacated topnotch like a steel wool hat.

And Mr. Wyatt Benbow told to Nestor Tudor and Tiny Aaron together, "I believe I'd just be bald."

"You are bald," Tiny Aaron informed him and jerked his nose at what particular place atop Mr. Wyatt Benbow's head he'd cultivated a cowlick previously that he did not any longer possess the means for.

"If I was him, I mean, I'd just be bald," Mr. Wyatt Benbow said with more breath truly than Tiny Aaron was accustomed to hearing from him, and Nestor Tudor confessed how he guessed he'd just be bald himself like provoked Tiny Aaron to inform him, "You are."

"I'm receding," Nestor Tudor said and thereby induced from Tiny Aaron a proclamation to the effect that the tide was indisputably already out after which Tiny Aaron himself, who had yet appreciable hair to him, raised up his loaf of Bunny bread in the sack that he'd carried to sop with and swung it a little at Dick Atwater but alongside him mostly and told to Wyatt Benbow and to Nestor Tudor both, "Her."

Now he'd not truly seen her before just that very instant. Nestor Tudor hadn't in fact but looked on her that way people most times look on people otherwise which is chiefly just partly and just somewhat so that he only had a notion she was there, but he hadn't truly seen her until

Tiny Aaron swung his loafbread and so pretty much made him look, and it wasn't straightoff but the back of her head and her black hair all thick and wavy and the breadth of her shoulders and of her waist and of her modest backside that Nestor Tudor and that Wyatt Benbow told to each other was modest, or raised up anyhow their eyebrows in a modest backside sort of a way like spoke of it for them, and they watched together Mr. Dick Atwater turn his face sideways on her and drop his chin and make what he seemed to intend for a diverting observation prior to laying his entire head backwards and snorting one time out his uplifted noseholes so as to enhance and punctuate what clever thing he'd just lately loosed that maybe the snort enhanced and punctuated both just before it served mostly to dislodge Dick Atwater's upswept hair which fell back down to where it surely would have already been if he'd not tried to put it elsewhere in the first place.

And she turned her own face sideways on him with her cheeks uplifted and her lips laid wide and said to him, "Oh you," and looked in fact genuinely diverted as she touched him flush on the forearm with the tipends of her fingers which seemed, most especially to Nestor Tudor, to loiter inordinately there.

Nobody appeared to know who she was or where she'd come from or how she'd ended up somehow with the Methodists at the reservoir that Nestor Tudor wandered around and inquired about what he figured for discreetly like it seemed to get construed until Halley Verna Drumm and Mrs. Cecil Dutton together fielded from him his discreet inquiry that they cut loose in back of like a pair of screech owls and told to Nestor Tudor, "You dog, you," not both together but one at the time so that it got said plainly twice for anybody that cared to hear it which was likely, as best as Nestor Tudor could tell, most everybody roundabout and which was certainly Halley Verna Drumm's sister May that asked after Nestor Tudor's inquiry most specifically and hooted and yowled herself once she'd had it told to her. So he left off inquiring a while and just plain wandered instead across the plot of grass down to the lake edge where Mr. Sleepy Pitts and Mr. Luther Teague were standing together with their hands in their trouser pockets watching a bug skate on the water like Mr. Sleepy Pitts told to Mr. Luther Teague he wished he could himself that he informed Nestor Tudor, once he'd full well arrived, he'd just told Mr. Luther Teague he wished he could. And they all three stood together and watched that bug a time and spat some and Mr. Luther Teague, as long as they'd gotten on the topic of things they wished they could do, went ahead and revealed to Mr. Sleepy Pitts and Nestor Tudor both how he'd always wanted to play the piano, how even if he could walk on the top of the water he'd probably give it over if he could play the piano in place of it like seemed to Mr. Sleepy Pitts foolhardy that he encouraged Nestor Tudor to go on and inform Luther Teague it was that Nestor Tudor appeared maybe about to do when he flung his arm instead back behind himself towards the shelter and wondered of Sleepy Pitts and Luther Teague if couldn't they tell him maybe who that woman he'd just lately flung at was, wondered it all flat and mumbly like he didn't care if he never found it out and couldn't truly comprehend why he'd bothered to wonder it in the first place at all.

Dr. Dewey Lunt eased his momma's red Ventura off the blacktop into the gravel lot alongside the Number 2 shelter and jumped on out of the driver's seat so as to circle around to the far door that he flung open for his woman friend whose fingers he held and whose elbow he took up as he brought her clean out from the Ventura entirely like the women in particular pinched up their faces about, pinched up their faces at most especially what men they could find hard by to pinch up their faces at. She was a leggy thing. Mrs. Dwight Mobley, who'd been one time a leggy thing herself, told back of her hand to Miss Fay Dull how a leggy thing was what she was like Mrs. Dwight Mobley did not seem to approve of now that she'd left off being a leggy thing too while Miss Fay Dull, who'd been born squat and never recovered from it, guessed she'd just as soon be Pentecostal as leggy which was such a pure and undiluted indictment as to strike Mrs. Dwight Mobley speechless, or pretty completely speechless anyhow, terse anyway for a time.

She had hair that lay down her back, thick brown hair with some wave to it and she'd worn a pair of fairly tiny pink shorts along with a knit top that had itself some pink around the armholes which picked up and complemented the pink of the shorts that Mr. Phillip J. King found himself pressed to tell to Mrs. Phillip J. King it did once she'd caught him with his face all slack and his eyes bulgy like she told him she'd never seen him stand before the clothescloset and get. Her sandals were pink even too with straps and buckles like Mr. Estelle Singletary admitted to Mr. Cecil Dutton made him all tingly which Mr. Cecil Dutton had not somehow figured Mr. Estelle Singletary could get unless maybe he jammed a butter knife into a wall socket that Mr. Estelle Singletary failed to find near so outright hilarious as Mr. Cecil Dutton apparently found it like he would have probably said a thing about but for Dr. Dewey Lunt's woman friend's red lacquered toenails which made him a little tingly themselves.

Dr. Dewey Lunt had on a pair of stretchy pants and a stretchy shirt with some appreciable sheen to it that lay open three entire buttons like would have seemed maybe immodest most especially to the widow Mrs. Askew who'd begun to gauge how far exactly Dr. Dewey Lunt's navel was from catching the light when she got put off from it by Dr. Dewey Lunt's shimmery gold chain with the radiant bejeweled pendant dangling from it which struck her as a purely stunning item most especially when it flopped and jumped like it did in the slanty evening sun every time Dr. Dewey Lunt tossed his hair.

His woman friend was a Sugg from East Gaffney South Carolina, was truly a Rock Hill Sugg who had early in life relocated to East Gaffney that Mr. H. Monroe Aycock recollected he'd one time sojourned in, or recollected he'd sojourned one time in regular Gaffney South Carolina which he reasoned was likely hard up on East Gaffney somehow.

"Just west of it," the East Gaffney Sugg told to him, "out eighty-five."

And Mr. H. Monroe Aycock told to her back, "Ah," and then bobbed his head and pressed his lips tight together so as to let on how he'd only lately reasoned as much.

She wished everybody would call her just Debbie that the men most especially were anxious to oblige her in and so went ahead and pretty unanimously said Debbie to her though they did not truly have anything between them to say Debbie about, or did not anyway have anything to say Debbie about until Mr. Estelle Singletary spoke of how he'd known one time a Debbie from somewhere which he failed to elaborate upon or contribute even the least bit further to that he got by everybody looked at on account of, got most especially by Mrs. Estelle Singletary looked at on account of like she persisted at until it was her alone looking at him which appeared to induce a little tingliness itself that Mr. Estelle Singletary admitted presently to Mr. Cecil Dutton was chiefly your butter knife sort.

They wanted to show to Dr. Dewey Lunt the buffet, wanted to show of course to Debbie Sugg and the Reverend Mr. Theodore J. Parnell the buffet too, but wanted most especially Dr. Dewey Lunt to lay eyes on it and so the women led him and led Debbie and led the Reverend Mr. Theodore J. Parnell who'd seen it already anyway up onto the slab under the Number 2 shelter where they'd laid out atop a cloth on the plank table their salads and their casseroles and their meat dishes and their Jell-O molds and their cakes and their pies and their one plate of outsized cookies with the pecan halves stuck in the middle of them that Halley Verna Drumm confessed she'd made herself before May Drumm, who'd concocted a manner of ambrosia with not just tangerine and grapefruit sections but leafy lettuce too, had managed to confess what it was exactly she'd made which she felt she had the right for most particularly in front of Halley Verna who'd not made an appetizer anyhow like struck May Drumm as a variety of food that should certainly get confessed to first, and Mrs. Sleepy Pitts, who'd brought her egg and chicken salad with the peas and the cocktail onions, couldn't imagine May Drumm had ever previously uttered a truer thing.

Consequently, then, they began to display their dishes for Dr. Dewey Lunt chiefly and Debbie and the reverend somewhat too, and they showed off first their assorted salads along with the solitary platter of tiny crustless sandwiches Mrs. Luther Teague had carried with her on account of how she'd been made to believe by Mrs. Cecil Dutton it was your tiny crustless sandwich sort of do that plainly it wasn't like she couldn't hardly help since she'd been led to believe already it would be, but Dr. Dewey Lunt told how he was partial himself to tiny crustless sandwiches and he took up a cream cheese one and bit it and then hummed at Mrs. Luther Teague in a breathy sort of way like rendered her near about easeful and serene although it did not much improve Mrs. Cecil Dutton truly who'd not told anything at all to Mrs. Luther Teague as best as she could recall which Mrs. Luther Teague disputed and got corrected by Mrs. Cecil Dutton about. The widow Mrs. Askew had passed the better part of the morning and a sizeable piece of the afternoon concocting her own personal entree which she uncovered and revealed with some extravagant show, or undertook anyway to uncover and reveal it in one altogether grand and florid gesture but her crinkly foil got caught on the lip of the roasting pan and so ripped and tore and thereby deflated the ceremony somewhat though did not deflate the ceremony altogether due to how the widow Mrs. Askew managed to sweep her arm and due to how the widow Mrs. Askew intoned as she did it, "Porkettes à la Barcelona," like was just the manner of thing to tolerate some intoning.

She'd gotten the recipe at her chiropractor's from a magazine where she probably wouldn't even have seen it but for the picture of all those upended porkchops arranged roundabout in a hub after a fashion that plain struck her like she was curious to know didn't it strike Dr. Dewey Lunt most especially too, and he glared down into the widow Mrs. Askew's pan and pondered her own loop of porkchops all vertical and boneupwards that he could not help but find intriguing like he told to Mrs. Askew he could not hardly help but find it. She was most especially proud of the sauce with the pineapple wedges and the peanuts in it that would be your Spanish peanuts with the red papery hulls like Mrs. Askew admitted did not truly stew near so well as she'd hoped but nonetheless enhanced, she told to Dr. Dewey Lunt, the bouquet that Dr. Dewey Lunt imagined they did just prior to getting by the widow Mrs. Askew instructed to dip his foremost finger right on down into the sauce like he dipped and licked it in advance of the humming he undertook behind it all which lacked, as best as Mrs. Luther Teague could tell, the appreciable zeal and passion of the humming she'd previously inspired him to.

Mrs. H. Monroe Aycock and Mrs. Dwight Mobley and Miss Fay Dull had all carried chicken though not the same manner of chicken truly as Mrs. Dwight Mobley's was baked with bacon and Velveeta and Miss Fay Dull's was fried while Mrs. H. Monroe Aycock's was casseroled and crusted over like struck Dr. Dewey Lunt as savory some way or another that he told Mrs. H. Monroe Aycock about prior to passing on down the table to Mrs. MacElrath's niece Judy's rice balls with spices and spring onions that he took up one of in his fingers so that him and Debbie Sugg and the Reverend Mr. Theodore J. Parnell could admire it all together and hum and rant pretty much at the same time.

Mrs. Phillip J. King had situated her stewpot lid back atop her stewpot so as to have it at a place she could whip it off from like she did in fact whip it off once the reverend and Debbie Sugg and most especially Dr. Dewey Lunt had arrived at last at her. Naturally, with the lid gone the aroma began straightaway to rise up and circulate which was truly how come Dr. Dewey Lunt, who appeared right there on the verge of exclaiming, failed for a time to exclaim as he'd not hardly anticipated he'd sniff most especially over a stewpot what it was he found himself sniffing like seemed a blend somehow of sweet scuppernong and ammonia vapors which Dr. Dewey Lunt raised up his head and looked a little tearyeyed at Mrs. Phillip J. King on account of and got told by her as she swept her arm in the widow Mrs. Askew vein of armsweeping, "Poached kidneys béarnaise," that Dr. Dewey Lunt appeared somewhat disposed to exclaim at too but got prevented from it by Mr. Sleepy Pitts who'd stepped up onto the slab so as to inquire what maybe it was had wet itself just before it expired.

She'd seen it on TV, Mrs. Phillip J. King had. She'd seen not the actual recipe on TV but had watched four Sundays in a row on the channel from the university in Chapel Hill a show about a pack of lordly people that ate with their forks upside down in the wrong hand but were otherwise purely elegant and cultured and they seemed to take oftentimes kidneys for supper when they did not take bangers instead.

And it was Debbie Sugg in her tiny pink shorts that said to Mrs. Phillip J. King, "Bangers?"

"You know, honey," Mrs. Phillip J. King told to her and raised up her hand so as to display a lengthsome gap between her thumbend and her fingertip. "Bangers," she said.

And she figured there were maybe twelve pigs' worth of organs all sunk down in the gravy though probably not twelve pigs' worth altogether as she'd eaten a piece of one to see was it near so succulent as it looked that she assured most especially Dr. Dewey Lunt it had in fact been, and she told him it was crunchy but not awful crunchy and chewy but not awful chewy and put her in mind, in a kind of a way, of a gizzard from a chicken. "Gizzard fillet," she told to him and presently heard it from Dr. Dewey Lunt back just prior to when it was Mr. Sleepy Pitts went on ahead and said into the air, "Gizzard fillet," twice himself, twice with some edge and whine to it like moved Mrs. Phillip J. King to inform him how he was presently invading her space, or actually how he was presently invading what particular patch of space she planned shortly to introduce her potlid into that Mr. Sleepy Pitts guessed he could relate about and so retreated to another piece of space entirely.

Miss Bernice Fay Frazier had carried the plates and the plastic forks and the napkins and the waxed cups for the iced tea which she showed off the bulk of to Dr. Dewey Lunt prior to giving an actual plate over to him, or truly two actual plates as she'd not bought the thick ones with the spines and the troughs but had settled for the thin ones instead that bent and seeped and grew linty after a time even stacked up two together. But Dr. Dewey Lunt laid his palm square under both of them like Miss Bernice Fay Frazier showed him he should and Mrs. Phillip J. King spooned up one entire kidney for him and doused it with creamy gravy and then admired it with Dr. Dewey Lunt in the dead middle of his plate where it looked like the manner of item that had passed through a horse to get there. All the ladies served him from their pots and dishes. All the ladies heaped him up with food that mixed and mingled and ran together like what food they heaped up for the Reverend Mr. Parnell as well while Debbie Sugg from East Gaffney, whom the ladies undertook to heap up some food for too, declined to take but assorted dibbles which was how precisely, she let it be understood, she could wear tiny pink shorts in the first place and look so exceedingly leggy in them like Mrs. Phillip J. King guessed she knew a thing about, said two times firm she guessed she knew a thing about it before Mr. Phillip J. King vented his observation, before Mr. Phillip J. King managed to see as how he was meant to proclaim, "Like a pencil," which he went ahead and proclaimed once southeasterly and once northwesterly too.

Most everybody else got to heap up their own food, or the men anyway heaped up food while the women helped themselves to just dibbles chiefly due to how leggy seemed to them a good thing to come to be like maybe they would have set out to come to be it even but for the awful many dishes they had before them to dibble from which caused their scant helpings to heap and pile up some themselves. So everybody but Debbie Sugg in her tiny shorts took a load of food truly and carried it off the slab towards the reservoir where they sat some of them just flush down on the grass and sat some of them in hinged chairs they'd carried particularly to take their supper in and sat some of them on quilts and blankets too which would be most especially Dick Atwater and her with him, her that held his heap of food and her heap of food together as Dick Atwater flung and flapped and laid out a brocaded gold bedspread with a fringe roundabout it and a tear in the corner of it and a brown unseemly stain up along about the pillow end that he went on ahead and apologized to her for once he'd laid his hair back up the side of his head where it had lately fallen off from.

Nestor Tudor sat in the grass next to Tiny Aaron, sat in the grass all turned and situated so that he needed only to lift up his head to see her and to see with her what trifling piece of Dick Atwater beyond her he was obliged to look at like was hardly enough Dick Atwater to put him off any at all. So he just gawked chiefly all plain and open, gawked through the blessing entirely while the Reverend Mr. Theodore J. Parnell let on to Jesus what it was they had presently to be grateful for like he seemed several times set to quit at but did not quit at it until it had begun to appear he never would, especially to Tiny Aaron who'd torn a breadslice and was poised to sop and bite a scrap of it. But he did in fact Amen presently and everybody otherwise Amened with him and got allowed to go on and eat by Dr. Dewey Lunt who rose up to say a thing, a thin airy breathy manner of thing about his own innermost self that he'd lately had some appreciable truck with like he hoped they'd all had some truck with their innermost selves lately too that his interdenominational uplifted consciousness group pretty unanimously exhaled a Yes on account of while just your regular people aside from them inquired of each other what all the thin airy breathy manner of talk was about anyhow which Tiny Aaron was a little anxious himself to know of from Nestor Tudor who watched her and watched Dick Atwater exchange gay toothsome looks and told to Tiny Aaron just, "What?" when at last he told to him anything at all.

As best as he could determine from where he was looking on her that he'd set and situated himself to do, she ate like a bird which Nestor Tudor sought from Tiny Aaron some confirmation about but Tiny Aaron, who ate himself like a buffalo chiefly, could not see much reason to still his fork so as to watch a woman poke and piddle with hers that he grunted to express and got spoken at back by Nestor Tudor who told to him, "Dainty," who told to him, "Dainty like a girl," that Tiny Aaron went on ahead and loosed a necknoise about.

And he didn't even know what it was mostly that made him gawk, that made him in the first place want to, didn't know it as he sat by the reservoir on the grassy patch or later once he'd arrived home either and had stood before the lavatory with his palms against the rim of it where he tried to recall just how it was she looked anyway, just how it was her hair lay and her eyes set and her lips swelled and pouted overtop her teeth like seemed to him straight and pearly there at the lavatory in front of the medicine chest which he could not be altogether certain of since what he knew of her at the sink was just the agitation mostly, maybe even the agitation by itself alone like seemed to have a thing to do with her though he could not tell what precise thing truly as he watched himself in the mirror, watched himself plain look for a time back prior to showing his own teeth and tossing his head in what he meant for a diverted sort of a way.

So he gawked and he pondered and did not undertake truly to so much as seem engaged otherwise not even once she'd gawked and pondered a little back, not even once she'd swung round her own head and looked on him and smiled and said with her lips primarily and maybe scant breath too, "Hey," like at home at the lavatory he went on and replied to with a manner of Hey himself like he'd meant at the reservoir to say it and had said it even a little, had said it somewhat and hardly at all as he'd dropped his chin and laid his mouth open which he'd left it to lay until Tiny Aaron suggested to him how maybe, on account of the gnats and the flies and the furry moths, he'd best go on and shut it instead. So it was mostly just looking all bald and flatout, looking while he ate his first heap of food and looking while he ate his second one and looking mostly still while he ate his poundcake with his fingers and his ambrosia with his plastic spoon that he had to pay some trifling attention to. And once he'd gotten done and finished he continued to gawk chiefly until him and Tiny Aaron spoke together to Judy Mrs. MacElrath's niece that had herself the pleasure of bringing to their notice her friend Bob from elsewhere that Mrs. Pipkin had near about squashed and done it after almost the very fashion she'd near about squashed and done in Tiny Aaron too that he shared with Bob the details of which Nestor Tudor got called in to confirm and to verify, or to say anyhow Yeah at, as he'd been with Tiny Aaron in his Impala back of the Big Apple that time Mrs. Pipkin had wheeled around the dumpster in her green Electra and rammed him.

"Full on," Tiny Aaron said, "like this here," and he butted his fingertips together that Nestor Tudor, who'd gotten invited, said Yeah at as well.

The bulk of the men had stood up and collected after supper down at the edge of the reservoir where they'd convened the opening session of the Debbie Sugg from East Gaffney pondering society due to how the light seemed to be propitious down at the reservoiredge where it fell from back of them onto most especially Debbie's leggy parts and so illuminated your dips and your bulges and your various contours which the Debbie Sugg from East Gaffney pondering society had convened in the first place to worship and revere. For their part, the women had mostly sought out Dr. Dewey Lunt and the Reverend Mr. Parnell so as to exhibit for them their refined consciousnesses that they'd honed ever since the end of August when the lessons quit and so were anxious to display, and they stood roundabout together up by the shelter slab and spoke one at the time of chiefly innermost sorts of things while the ladies otherwise and the reverend and Dr. Dewey Lunt too loosed air like assorted tire valves.

As for himself, Nestor Tudor undertook to edge over towards her or thought anyway how he'd best, if he was meaning to, go ahead and edge like he did in fact edge a little which he was pretty well set to persevere at when Mr. H. Monroe Aycock stepped on up to Dick Atwater and her too and said what seemed to Nestor Tudor likely a suave thing with some wit and some dash to it that her and that Dick Atwater and Mr. H. Monroe Aycock as well tossed their heads about after a fashion to stop Nestor Tudor entirely as he had not himself cultivated a clever sort of an item to tell like he guessed there was call for and so he left off edging to do it. He'd been intending to say a proper Hey, a Hey with considerably more volume and appreciably less adenoids than the initial Hey he'd said already, but after Mr. H. Monroe Aycock's clever item that everybody looked pretty completely diverted by, he did not suppose a Hey would much do at all even if he did in fact shut his mouth pretty close up behind it and look on her sweetly like he planned to look on her, so he left off edging and undertook to cultivate a time instead, undertook to land on the very thing she'd toss her head at like he guessed maybe he had in fact cultivated a little when Mr. H. Monroe Aycock's himself struck out for elsewhere and so left the way open for Nestor Tudor to edge some more, to edge right on up near about flush to her and say pretty much at her entirely, "Hey Dick."

"Nestor," Dick Atwater told to him back and still did not get looked on truly like probably he wouldn't have gotten looked on any at all but for his scent that Nestor Tudor, in the course of regular breathing, was obliged to inhale some of and so grew straightoff affected by it. He'd come to be, Mr. Dick Atwater had, pretty completely herbalized and maybe a little musked with it, but he was plainly herbal chiefly, herbal just everywhere all over, thick dank herbal, Nestor Tudor figured, like probably a mossy patch would smell to him if he got his nose laid in one and the back of his head stood on, and he could not somehow help but look on Dick Atwater and tell to him, "Whew!" which was not precisely his own personal suave item with wit and dash he'd left off edging to cultivate like he figured out directly it wasn't and so added back of it all lilty and bright, or as lilty and bright as he could manage to add it, "Aren't you fragrant this evening," like was a form of Whew! itself though with some almost measurable grace to it.

"A splash of cologne never drowned a man yet," Dick Atwater said back and appeared even a little jolly, appeared jolly exclusively at her alone who gazed a little jolly back at him.

"No," Nestor Tudor told Dick Atwater and her with him as best as he could make himself seem to be telling it to her with him too, "that's likely the truth of it," which was not hardly the clever item he'd left off edging to cultivate either.

And then they just stood a time and nobody told anybody anything much or did anything truly in place of talking but for how it was Nestor Tudor moved his front foot back some and his back foot up a little while Dick Atwater, who had suffered a gust of wind, collected up his hair from off his shoulder and drew it once more over his topnotch like was the extent of things altogether except for the plain standing and the uneasy grins until Nestor Tudor raised up his head and looked on her pretty much entirely by herself so as to loose at her a legitimate, "Hey," that didn't sound to him but a little pitched up and squeaky like he'd guessed it probably might.

Of course she said Hey to him back with again just her lips mostly like prompted Dick Atwater to go on and indicate her with his flat open hand as he told to Nestor Tudor, "Miss Mary Alice Celestine Lefler," and prompted Dick Atwater to ever so barely jerk his head as he told to her, "Nestor Tudor," that she laid out her own hand at the news of and so got her fingers straightaway taken up by Nestor Tudor himself who drew his feet together and ducked his head and bent a little at the waist, or bent as best at the waist as he was anymore able which was at the very outside a little, and said to her, "Charmed," like was in fact part of what he'd cultivated to say.

Naturally, she laid apart her lips and showed to him her teeth that way he'd hoped she would and he said to her a little deeper than he'd managed to say Hey or say Charmed either one, "Mary Alice Celestine Lefler. I had an aunt named that," like was the rest of what he'd cultivated, or was the bulk of the rest of what he'd cultivated anyhow on account of he'd figured he'd undertake some cheekbiting as well, the variety of cheekbiting he'd seen Mrs. MacElrath's niece Judy's friend Bob look so manly at and he was just there in the midst of clamping his molars shut when Dick Atwater informed him, "You did not either."

Of course Nestor Tudor could not quite figure how to clamp two folds of cheekskin between his molars so as to look drawn and gaunt and snap back at Dick Atwater at the same time which he'd not altogether left off puzzling about when Mary Alice Celestine Lefler swatted Dick Atwater ever so gently on the forearm and told to him, "Now Jerome, Nestor Tudor knows what aunts he had."

"He doesn't seem to," Dick Atwater said to her back by way of Nestor Tudor chiefly.

"Now Jerome," Miss Mary Alice Celestine Lefler told to him all over again and poked his scant belly with her foremost fingerend like prompted Dick Atwater to tell to her, "You," like prompted Dick Atwater to wrap his own fingers around her solitary extended one and tell to her, "You," another time that the two of them together shared a grin about which Nestor Tudor felt obliged to punctuate somehow and so looked off a little and away a little and said mostly into the empty air, "Yeah, I can see her like it wasn't but yesterday, see her up on the porch at Momma's house riding the glider," and he set about growing misty, endeavored anyhow to make for Mary Alice Celestine Lefler his tortured misty face that he sucked some breath on account of as it seemed to him fitting with a misty face to suck breath and even wheeze a little too like he went on ahead and wheezed prior to telling out into the empty air again, "Sweetest woman on God's earth," that he stuck his hands deep down into his trouser pockets in back of and undertook to look forlorn like near about got him touched on the forearm, like he could tell near about got him touched but did not in fact get him touched quite which was how come he drew out from his righthand trouser pocket his assorted keys and his solitary fob all slick and worn from time and use which would be rubbed chiefly and likely just discharged the once that was enough together to have made it smooth and lustrous, as lustrous anyhow as a walnut most times has cause to get, and Nestor Tudor raised it up to catch the light and said primarily at it, "She gave me this. It was her nut," that he grew a little misty and tortured and wheezy in the wake of.

And she touched him, Mary Alice Celestine Lefler did, touched him near about at the elbow with her fingertips and told to him, "Nestor," all sweet and low like he would have savored and held a spell to but for Dick Atwater that told to him, "Christ!" with it which was when they looked squarely upon each other, which was when they saw each other finally plain that Nestor Tudor recalled at home before the lavatory they had, at home before the lavatory once he'd checked the coatcloset for hoodlums and thrown the doorbolts and shut off the bulk of the lights but for the lamp by the bed and the naked bulb over the medicine chest. And they hadn't looked long truly but hadn't hardly needed to look long to see it on account of how it was the same one thing precisely that him and that Dick Atwater showed in their eyes to each other, the same exact solitary item all tinged and tainted with desperation and her just a piece and part of it, her just maybe the one last thing they'd resolved together to get desperate about, her that Nestor Tudor couldn't even call up once he'd gotten home, her that Nestor Tudor couldn't stand at the lavatory and see though he could feel, he figured, her fingertips along about his elbow and hear, he figured, her voice say Nestor to him with the Christ! hard up on it and hard up on that his own voice all deep and suave back as he told to Dick Atwater, "Now," and told to Dick Atwater, "Jerome."

Two

MRS. Dick Atwater hadn't herself ever called it at him but twice and one of them after the Reverend Mr. Cutwright had called it at him first thereby indicating how she could not help but call it at him too like she went on ahead and called it at him as she held his fingers and looked with her eyes as directly into his as she'd ever with her eyes looked but for maybe the other time she'd called it at him, the time she'd held to him by the elbow instead and made him to look on her, made him to pick up his head and show to her his face that he'd tried to render plain and regular but couldn't, not anyhow near so plain and so regular as to keep her from seeing in it what it was she'd caused him to pick up his head to see which she had not ever previously suspected she might and could not ever after forget she had either. And he didn't even know why like maybe she knew he wouldn't when she asked him. He couldn't even begin to say how come so much as partly like maybe she'd suspected he'd evermore fail at and so just squeezed him along about the elbow and watched him drop again his face that he'd not wanted to pick up and not wanted to show her at all.

It was just a Dillard and not so much even as a comely Dillard like he'd seen before himself comely Dillards along about Speedwell where there were considerable Dillards to choose from and the most of them comely and the rest of them altogether presentable and appealing like he guessed maybe she was both of sometimes but was sometimes too not either one of hardly which Speedwell Dillards, who lapsed themselves, never quite lapsed so far as. She'd not been blessed with proper ankles truly which was what he'd been struck by straightoff in spite of how he guessed he ought not to be struck since thick legs that were feet at the bottom and calves in the middle and ankles no perceptible where in between did not seem to him the manner of items that should be much entrancing, but he guessed he got taken with her anyhow on account of her legs that were smooth and white even where they should have been knobby instead and on account of her puffy feet with the toenails on them that she painted red chiefly but purple once like Mrs. Dick Atwater would not have approved of much at all and on account of her yellow hair and her gold dangly earrings and her sparkly eyelids that were blue sparkly sometimes and pink sparkly sometimes and green sparkly sometimes too. He had watched her through the glass wall at the rolling mill where she answered the phone and took the orders and sent the bills and figured the payroll and wrote the checks and sat every now and again just chewing on her fingerends and watching him through the glass wall back all full and outright like he was not much accustomed to getting watched, most especially by a yellowhaired woman with sparkly eyelids that called him whenever she spoke at him Dickey in that throaty voice that had sounded to him just congested there at the first but had come to seem presently otherwise instead, had come to seem presently otherwise altogether.

So he began to think on her places elsewhere than in his chair back of the glass wall, thought on her even in his own house with Mrs. Dick Atwater who wondered at him sometimes, "What?" and watched him tell to her, "Nothing," back and watched him after he'd told to her Nothing back even when he'd look to what place in the air he'd been looking and fix and hold again his face like Mrs. Dick Atwater had said in the first place What? about. And she was just a Dillard, not so much even as a comely Dillard but just a thick ordinary yellowhaired Dillard that he had occasion to watch and so had occasion to get watched by back and not hardly like he'd been watched lately, which was probably the most of it, not hardly like he'd guessed already he'd ever get watched again. So it wasn't even her much truly but was him almost entirely instead though he called it the white legs and the smooth knobless ankles and the puffy feet and the yellow hair and the gold earrings and the sparkly eyelids and the throaty voice too on account of he had to call it something and did not anyhow want it to be just him much, did not likely decipher how it had to be him near about wholly and altogether until he'd driven her what they'd told to each other too loud in front of everybody was home and was even home eventually but was not straightaway home at all and was out the Burlington Road instead and then off it down the track behind the cemetery where she slid across the seat to him and laid her lips to his neck like he had not lately had lips laid to it after which she raised on up and gnawed for a spell his fleshy earlobe like he'd never previously even contemplated getting in this lifetime his earlobe gnawed.

She told him she had a striped cat named Honey that slept in the hallcloset on a shelf and she told him how her and her brother hadn't ever gotten on hardly due to how he wasn't any different at all from her daddy that she hadn't ever gotten on hardly with either and she told him she'd made her hair yellow only after she'd made it red first like didn't suit her on account of what she called to him her milky skin that looked with yellow hair healthful like it hadn't looked much with red hair truly and she asked Mr. Dick Atwater if didn't her yellow hair seem to him to do a thing for her milky skin that maybe red hair wouldn't which Mr. Dick Atwater looked on her to see could he find out but did not find out exactly as he could not himself tell what red hair on the Dillard would have looked much like, could not himself, he discovered, tell hardly anything whatsoever about the Dillard at all but for that she was thick and ponderous and had on the back of her neck under her purely yellow hair some fine and wispy almost nearly purely yellow hair and had on the left of her mouth in the bottom of it a tooth turned entirely sideways and had on her right upper arm a big grainy mole and smelled all over somewhat like Mr. Dick Atwater's wife's sister's scent and somewhat like regular sweat with it and did not remotely strike Mr. Dick Atwater on the carseat much like previously through the glass wall she'd struck him.

And she said to him, "Sweet thing," and nipped his fleshy lobe while Mr. Dick Atwater lifted his head ever so slightly and saw in the mirror his right eye that he watched himself with.

So she'd taken him up by the elbow, Mrs. Dick Atwater had, and said to him, "Jerome," and then mashed and squeezed until he showed her his face he'd tried to make plain and tried to make regular and had in fact made a little plain and regular both that she saw he'd made it some of and that she saw he could not hardly make it all of entirely and so asked him how come without believing she'd get told it, without believing he even knew himself how come at all like Mr. Dick Atwater didn't know it and so couldn't say it and consequently lowered again his head and looked at the floor not plain and not regular either. And she didn't call it at him ever again, didn't call it at him even that last time she could have when she held him once more at the armjoint and looked him once more right square in the face and seemed as if she'd say it but failed to and only lay instead under the bedsheet and moved her legs both up and then both down and then both up again behind it before Mr. Dick Atwater leaned over to her from his chair and stilled her with the arm she'd not taken up the joint of to grip and to hold, and she wasn't by then but bone chiefly and droopy skin and eyes that sometimes roamed and shifted and she smelled of sickness and worse than sickness even too and she made every now and again mournful noises and moved every now and again her legs up and down and did not tell to him Jerome like he'd thought she might, did not tell to him anything for a time but just lay so she could look on him and told him only presently and only at last, "Oh Dick" all weak and quivery like was the thing anymore he thought about when he thought about her.

So he guessed he'd gotten done with women after the Dillard and Mrs. Dick Atwater and the Buffalo too who he'd carried to the fish house shy of Greensboro where she'd not much approved of the deviled crabs and had picked chiefly at her fishsteak and had eaten just a part of one of his shrimp that she'd let on had seemed a little rubbery to her, more rubbery anyhow than she cared most times for her shrimp to be. She'd told him about her boys, Evander Clark Buffalo and Vance Johnston Buffalo, that weren't either one any count as near as she could judge, and she informed Dick Atwater what a blessing it was he didn't have a daughter like her Martha Porter Buffalo that knew just every little thing there was to know, "Every little thing," she said and left some appreciable lipstick on her coffeecup like she wished she'd not even bothered to drink from due to what manner of beverage they'd seen fit to fill it with. He'd intended to take her to a show like he'd figured he'd suggest over supper until he grew persuaded to figure instead he wouldn't and so carried her directly home from the fish house and loitered a spell with her in her front room where she spoke further of the things she didn't much care for and the people she didn't much like and wished the world was a different place from the place it seemed to her it was like she guessed she'd do a thing about if she could do a thing about it that her and Dick Atwater figured together she plain never would and then humphed the both of them in a harmonious sort of a way just prior to when it was Mr. Dick Atwater said, "Well," and pushed against his knees so as to raise himself upright.

The still and the calm of his own empty house had not ever seemed so pure and wondrous to him as on that night he'd left the Buffalo for it and had just sat a time in his lounger with his shoes hanging off the toes of his feet and the *Chronicle* spread out before him which he didn't read truly much of as he was soaking up chiefly the still and the calm instead all pure and all wondrous like a woman would, he figured, fairly altogether do in and defeat that he'd sworn them off an account of and gotten, in the first place, done with them about like after the Buffalo he got done with them all over again and stayed even for a little while done with them too up until her that he hadn't needed but to see and gaze on even from as far off and away as that first time he saw and gazed on her when he tried to exclaim but couldn't and tried in place of it to make just a whistly noise that he lacked the spit for too. So instead he just stood where it was he'd come to be, stood chiefly anyway and leaned against the phonepost only a little bit, laid primarily his shoulderjoint and his cheek to it as he saw her and Miss Bernice Fay Frazier step down off the porch planking onto the front stairtreads and off them onto the flagstones and off them onto the walk where they struck out up the street towards him that he watched them at, or watched her at truly with his shoulder and his cheek leaned and canted until the creosote began to burn him when he stood just by himself upright like he stayed until they'd arrived at him and while they passed him and once they'd even gone on by him as well when he managed to turn a little and managed to pretty much intone, "Hey Bernice," like caused Miss Bernice Fay Frazier to turn a little herself and intone back, "I told you Hey. Didn't I tell him Hey?" she inquired of her who said, as best as Dick Atwater could make out, sweetly that she had, "and you didn't say nothing to me, did he?" she inquired of her again who said, as best as Dick Atwater could make out, sweetly that he hadn't.

"Well, Hey then," Dick Atwater fairly much proclaimed and laid open his jacketflaps with his hands that he put to his hips after the fashion he'd found appealing in the mirror over the sideboard back home where sometimes he held and twisted and pitched himself so as to see what poses struck him like his open jacketflap hipgripping pose near about always did. Miss Bernice Fay Frazier, who would have usually shrieked back at him one time more how she'd said Hey already the only occasion in this piece of the afternoon she intended to say it, told him instead all soft and breathy how she'd said Hey already the only occasion in this piece of the afternoon she intended to say it like seemed to Dick Atwater fairly queer and unforeseen and caused him to study Miss Bernice Fay Frazier a palpable while prior to telling to her, "Bernice?" on the incline like Miss Bernice Fay Frazier grinned and grew girlish at the sound of.

"I've been elevated," she said back and went on ahead and fairly smirked since she was not hardly seeking to hide her elevation under a bushel.

"Have you?" Dick Atwater wanted to know and studied Miss Bernice Fay Frazier further still as a preface and preamble to shifting his gaze onto her instead who looked ever so warmly on Miss Bernice Fay

Frazier and then ever so warmly on him and then ever so warmly on Miss Bernice Fay Frazier again who told to Dick Atwater, "I have. Been plain uplifted, transmogrified near about. Can't you tell it?" she inquired and swung her head around in profile for Dick Atwater to gaze upon as she had a notion she seemed a little more raised up from the side than she'd probably ever manage from fronton to seem it.

And Dick Atwater did in fact gaze upon and study the side of her head a scant while before he assured her, "I can. You don't hardly seem the same woman at all, does she?" he wanted to hear from her who admitted she couldn't possibly in the first place have known what manner of woman Miss Bernice Fay Frazier had previously seemed as she'd not herself been acquainted with the preelevated variety of her like appeared altogether intriguing news to Mr. Dick Atwater who weighed it briefly, or weighed it so long as seemed apt to him anyhow, and then told to her back fairly grave and earnest both, "Truly," that he made to look sober in the wake of but failed pretty much at it on account of her, on account of her who smiled on him and not just smiled on him all by itself alone but looked on him with it, looked on him like he was in fact maybe still somebody, still so much as a man even that way women in particular appeared to him lately to figure he'd left off being, appeared to him lately to guess he'd evermore quit at, and he felt moved and inspired of a sudden to give to her his fingers like he reached out his one hand for while he made to lift his hat with the other, his straw lacquered hat with the gray sateen band that he'd raised near about off his head entirely before he recollected the state of his scalp beneath it which was naked chiefly across the ridge of his head like he wore his hat in the first place for. So he lifted it up but did not lift it up awful much at all as he took hold of her at the knuckles and worked her whole entire arm. "Richard," he said, "Jerome Atwater," and she told to him just behind it all four of her own names back like seemed to Dick Atwater as comely a set of names as he'd had the pleasure lately to hear which he consulted Miss Bernice Fay Frazier about who figured they were all four together fairly comely names she guessed like sounded in her breathy voice pure ringing praise and sweetness.

She'd come the night previous on the Greyhound out of Danville, or had arrived truly at the depot beyond the icehouse along about suppertime but had been made to wait and linger into the full dark by, according to Miss Bernice Fay Frazier, Mr. Estelle Singletary and by, according to Mr. Estelle Singletary, Miss Bernice Fay Frazier who'd said she'd call him like she knew full well she'd never said she would. So nobody had come to meet and fetch her away that she found out once she'd climbed down off the bus nobody had, the bus she'd ridden from Berkeley Springs West Virginia which was not hardly a place at all anybody much would want to ride a bus from most especially clean to Danville and on past Danville even to the station at Neely alongside the icehouse where she looked roundabout for anybody that seemed disposed to look at her back which nobody much did but for black John Sykes who'd sucked enough lately on a bottleneck to have gotten rendered convivial like was a usual stop for him on his way to unconscious. So she sat by herself in the midst of a bank of plastic orange chairs against the depot wall and watched what people came in through the swinging glass doors which wasn't awful many people truly and listened at black John Sykes across the way from her say a loud indecipherable thing out into the air at nobody much in particular as best as she could tell and she spoke even one time to the Barefoot back of the ticket window, made at that Barefoot an inquiry about Miss Bernice Fay Frazier and had on that Barefoot an effect like was probably the first local effect she had. She stuck her one arm through the ticket window clear up to the elbow so as to poke that Barefoot's blue necktie with her fingerend, his blue necktie with the Econocruiseliner bilevel Greyhounds on it that she made out to be taken with and enchanted by and so touched that Barefoot on his breastbone right there in the depot and looked with her eyes directly into his own ones as she told to him, "Well, I never," like fairly transported the Barefoot who'd not ever previously had his Econocruiseliners poked and admired.

But it didn't seem there at the first that she'd get maybe much beyond the depot itself on account of Miss Bernice Fay Frazier, who would have come to fetch her, couldn't drive and Mr. Estelle Singletary, who'd gotten obligated to fetch her instead, had stopped even so much as anticipating a phone call and had carried his Swiss movement colon down the hall to his and Mrs. Estelle Singletary's bedroom and through it to the halfbath where he lowered and settled himself onto the ring and took up out from the wicker basket next to the bowl his personal copy of the *World Almanac* that he'd been reading in since 1971 without making truly much headway to speak of. So, naturally, like is the case with most people once they've lit upon the ring and taken up some reading matter, Mr. Estelle Singletary got all engaged with his almanac, got all engaged in particular with an arctic weather map that showed where it was the wind came from and where it was the wind went to and how it was the weather rode all roundabout the tip of the earth that Mr. Estelle Singletary figured, as he read and perused, would be of particular interest to the widow Mrs. Askew who'd exhibited previously in the basement of the fellowship hall an inclination for getting in touch with the ends of the earth and such as them like he guessed maybe he'd speak to her of the next time he came up on her and then found themselves of a mood to relate and identify, and he was meditating there upon the ring in just a general aimless sort of way, meditating about ice and wind and the widow Mrs. Askew's solitary black hair that grew somehow or another out the ridge of her nose when the telephone set to ringing which Mr. Estelle Singletary announced from the halfbath it had. The trouble was, Mrs. Estelle Singletary was almost at that very identical instant precisely announcing from down by the Maytag in the basement pretty much the same news to Mr. Estelle Singletary who sat on the toilet and waited for the receiver to get taken up by Mrs. Estelle Singletary who stood in the basement and waited for near about the same thing, waited in fact until the phone had quit of itself when she climbed the stairs and passed along the hallway and through the bedroom to the halfbath where her and Mr. Estelle Singletary exchanged some moderately breathy talk that was almost exclusively exhale breathy entirely on the part of Mrs. Estelle Singletary due to the funk Mr. Estelle Singletary had managed from upon the ring to manufacture like Mrs. Estelle Singletary had not when she married him hardly expected he nightly would.

So they didn't speak to Miss Bernice Fay Frazier there at the first who'd gotten no answer when she called and so had assumed they'd both gone together to the depot which she'd intended to dial the depot about to find out had they but was straightaway put off from it by Bubbles her cat that came spilling out from the front bedroom like she'd been dumped from a sack. Her ears were pitched and laid back that Miss Bernice Fay Frazier took some notice of and so slipped away from the phonetable in the backhall and sideways across the throwrug to the camelback loveseat that she settled herself down onto as she watched her cat Bubbles spin one time roundabout and then bolt like a shot back into the bedroom she'd just lately spilled out from that she went on ahead and left again shortly at a flatout gallop and swung around through the parlor into the dining room and on beyond it into the kitchen where she slipped and skidded across the linoleum and leapt at last up onto the countertop so as to sit ever so briefly in Miss Bernice Fay Frazier's colander. Of course she jumped straight up out of it when she left it so as to swing a time by her front feet from the draperies over the kitchen sink while with her back ones she knocked the Bufferin and the cherry Metamucil off from the windowsill like she grew inspired to run through the dish drainer on account of and leap from it onto the dinette where she slid across the Formica into the pepper mill and the green and orange Lake Waccamaw Boy's Home napkin rack that bounced together off the wall and made sufficient clamor between them to drive Bubbles on out from the kitchen entirely and up the backstairs into the spareroom and out again from it and down the stairs and along the hall and through the bathroom and into the front bedroom another time and onto the bed so as to chew and kick at the bedcovers and then off the bed of a sudden and into the clothescloset ever so briefly before she bolted once more across the bedroom and spilled out of it into the parlor again where she arrived with her ears still bent and laid.

Miss Bernice Fay Frazier had not when she took Bubbles from her cousin's girl Lucy been aware how rampaging was the manner of thing cats did, had not suspected truly housecats were prone to bolt and dart and careen roundabout like Bubbles was herself pretty regular at and had gotten stepped on one time already on account of. Miss Bernice Fay Frazier had simply figured cats slept mostly all balled up topside downwards on a sofa cushion and snug against whatever variety of throwpillow their loose cat hair would best darken and cling to, or slept mostly anyhow when they were not slapping their paws at pieces of dangly string or hunkering down to watch birds through the window lights, and she found in fact that even her cat Bubbles she'd gotten from Lucy her cousin's girl did sleep mostly all coiled and upturned against her quilted white throwpillows with the lacy frill but she'd simply found with it how mostly was not hardly enough. Since she'd fallen and lain with her legs numb mostly was, naturally, even less hardly enough anymore than previously she'd guessed it was which was how come she took to the settee midmorning and early afternoon and evening time too like seemed to be prime darting and bolting hours, or which was part of how come anyhow with the rest of how come being chiefly the lesson of her neighbor Mrs. Jane Sprinkle who'd lately suffered just precisely the manner of calamity to weigh heavy upon Miss Bernice Fay Frazier who was acutely prone herself to calamitous sorts of things.

Mrs. Jane Sprinkle's husband Jimmy sold Chevrolets out at the new lot on the bypass, sold Chevrolets anyway and OK used cars with them that were Chevrolets the bulk of the time but were vehicles otherwise too like Jimmy Sprinkle let on to Jane he evermore had to study up about which was how come he lingered all of the week and most of the weekend out on the bypass at his desk in the new corrugated showroom with the pointy roof and the sizeable sheetglass windows. Consequently, then, Jimmy did not find he had occasion much to cut his grass, or actually Jimmy's wife Jane went on ahead and discovered it for him once the yard had gotten ragged and shameful like she couldn't stand it to be that her and that Jimmy spoke of an evening about, that Jane Sprinkle anyway made some mention of while Jimmy studied up on his Skylark sedans as he'd lately taken one in a trade though truly he did not believe he'd be much disposed to own a Skylark sedan himself as he was not partial to the lines of it like he told to his wife Jane Sprinkle back once she'd asked him a shameful raggedy lawn sort of a question and had left him a gap to speak in.

She figured she'd hire a boy and she asked Jimmy if wouldn't it be all right if she went on and hired one like induced Jimmy to impart to her back how he did not himself have much use for just a six-cylinder engine that wouldn't hardly pull your factory air without heating and straining and such and guessed he just plain didn't know what some people were thinking sometimes that he spewed a breath about that way he spewed usually to let on what a foolish pack of folks there was loose on the landscape that Mrs. Jane Sprinkle told to him, "Jimmy!" in back of like Jimmy said presently What? at.

She took on Jack Vestal's boy Jack jr. that cut grass roundabout with his daddy's Toro, cut anyway Mrs. Darlene Montgomery's lawn across the road that did not have truly much grass to it on account of Mrs. Darlene Montgomery's maple trees either side of the front walk which shaded her grass purely to death and left her with chiefly black dirt instead that Jack Vestal smoothed and raked like Mrs. Jane Sprinkle across the street had watched him at and gotten taken with altogether. He said he'd mow and he'd clip and he'd edge and he'd sweep too which Jimmy Sprinkle never had, and so she went on and hired him and had him to come as shortly as he was able which was a Thursday in the midafternoon, a hot wilty Thursday that Mrs. Jane Sprinkle and Jack Vestal exchanged views on, or spoke that is ever so briefly about until Jack Vestal began to tell of the rash he'd been afflicted with just lately which prompted Mrs. Jane Sprinkle to recall suddenly the variety of things she could not afford to leave undone a moment more than she'd left them already.

Jack's daddy's Toro was a sluggish manner of Toro and was not usually somehow disposed to start up and run until whoever had undertaken to start it and run it both, like was anymore Jack Vestal jr. almost exclusively, had drawn on the starter cord a spell and then had advanced to yanking on it and had graduated beyond that even to jerking it instead and swearing the motor and kicking the cowl and lowering at last the handle so as to raise up the front tires high enough to drop them with some effect all of which, massed up and accumulated together, served some way or another as sufficient tribute for the Toro that would at last recoil and sputter and sound enough like it might actually run to keep Jack Vestal pulling at it until it did at last start. The trouble was, of course, Jack Vestal's daddy's Toro was not the manner of machine to start but one time a day, so once Jack Vestal got it going he could not hardly afford to shut it off and consequently mowed everything he could think to mow like proved to have some effect on Mrs. Jane Sprinkle once she'd gotten all heaped and piled up that way she came to be which, as best as Miss Bernice Fay Frazier could tell, was the chiefest calamitous part of the whole business like was of course colored by Miss Bernice Fay Frazier's acute personal fear of getting heaped and piled up herself, or actually getting discovered heaped and piled up truly.

So Jack Vestal set in with Mrs. Jane Sprinkle's frontyard that had in fact gone ragged and shameful and had sprouted pretty much all over with spindly weeds that lay down when he passed overtop them and fairly much rose up and resurrected once he'd gone on by which caused Jack Vestal to back up and mow again most everywhere he'd mowed once already like did not sit awfully well with him as mowing the same spot of ground frontwards and backwards both for one singular piece of money was not hardly, as best as he could tell, what he'd entered into the lawn care business for. So naturally he came to be irritated, irritated that is about the spindly weeds he had to cut twice and the singular piece of money he got for the trouble of it which he was obliged to take together with the additional patch of irritation along about where his legs met and joined that he'd arrived afflicted with. Jack Vestal jr. was, then, appreciably dissatisfied back of his daddy's Toro along with a trifle itchy at the inseam and so instead of considering like usual Marcia Satterwhite wholly buck naked who he'd not truly ever seen wholly buck naked entirely, had not truly ever seen even partly buck naked in fact though he'd prayed in a regular sort of way to the Lord in heaven he would, he considered instead his own pathetic self that did not ever any time get what was due him like was money chiefly for yards he had to cut backwards and forwards both and like was naked parts and pieces of girls somewhat too which he tried to leave off thinking on once he'd begun to think on them and so thought on them only twice so much as before he'd tried to leave off in the first place like was the trouble chiefly with naked parts and pieces that Jack Vestal got a little agitated about as well and went forwards and went backwards and went forwards some more as he told to himself what a sorry pitiful mess life sometimes was, most especially his own one.

He mowed the entire frontyard what amounted to twice over and idled the Toro a time while he raked up the weedy clippings and trimmed around the trees and edged the walk and the cement drive with his toothsome edging contraption that worked after a fashion though not hardly after what fashion it had likely been designed and manufactured to work as the little rubber wheel didn't turn and the spiked sprocket didn't spin round and the offending grass got loosed and uprooted by just sheer main force alone like Jack Vestal figured he hadn't probably needed to buy a toothsome edging contraption for which rendered him even more ill and sour somehow than he'd gotten already to be that Mrs. Jane Sprinkle herself found out about once she'd stepped through the front doorway onto the stoop with a tumbler of ice water for Jack Vestal, as it was after all hot and wilty, that Jack Vestal informed her he did not himself have the leisure just presently to drink.

The sideyard was full of sticks and trash from the treetops like Jack Vestal guessed he'd known it would be and he raked them into a pile and carried them down to the curb that way Mrs. Jane Sprinkle stuck her head out the frontdoor to wish he hadn't on account of the brick incinerator in the backyard that they burned the bulk of their sticks and trash in. So he carried them off from the curb and through the sideyard back to the incinerator that he dropped them in instead and thereby punctuated another thing he'd done twice over that he swore about just loud enough to get asked by Mrs. Jane Sprinkle, "What darling?" which he swore about too as he did not suppose he just presently needed some woman saying What darling? at him like were always the women anyway he didn't want to hear What darling? from.

"Nothing," he told to her and scratched his rash, stuck his entire hand up his shortsleg and made some relief for himself which Mrs. Jane Sprinkle did not appear much taken with the sight of that he could tell plain enough she wasn't like peeved him some itself as he did not suppose Mrs. Jane Sprinkle possessed even the manner of loose dangly pieces that would incite a rash or, as best as he'd ever heard and speculated, loose dangly pieces was what it was her sort of creature lacked though he could not say precisely what manner of pieces she probably had instead like he figured he should have seen already and known for himself as he guessed he was plenty old enough for it, had even earned already his learner's permit and had driven one time his daddy's Citation clean back from the Piggly Wiggly in Draper like seemed to him preamble and preparation enough for separating himself the dangly pieces from the flush ones that no woman yet had bothered to instruct him about, most especially Marcia Satterwhite who he was anxious to drink up a little knowledge from, Marcia Satterwhite who'd likely never gotten bumpy and chafed and probably never would get it, not anyhow like he got it which was regular and acutely, regular and acutely enough anyway to render him pathetic all over again which he went on ahead and swore about and so heard from Mrs. Jane Sprinkle an additional What darling? for it.

He mowed the sideyard two times over just like he'd mowed the frontyard prior to it and then swung on around to the opposite end of the house to cut the grass over there which there wasn't actually awful much of but for a strip alongside the drive and a thick bushy patch next to the porch steps, a thick bushy patch with the oil spout in it which Jack Vestal jr. managed to beat a while with his daddy's Toro blade like drew Mrs. Jane Sprinkle to the doorway where she informed him how her oil spout was down in precisely the very thick bushy patch of grass Jack Vestal had gone on ahead and just lately found for himself it was which he after a fashion apprised her of back. He guessed he'd best gas up his daddy's Toro before he set in on the backyard, and what with the thing hot and running it was a fairly delicate undertaking, or what with the thing hot and running in combination with his daddy's gas can that discharged fuel at the seams and the handle rivets and the threaded stopper and even out the neck a little where it was supposed to discharge fuel on into the tank hard up on the exhaust pipe that Jack Vestal slobbered onto so as to find out was it hot enough maybe to ignite and explode gasoline and blow his daddy's Toro up entirely like he figured was about all he needed what with the spindly weeds and the sticks and trash and the oil tank spout and his personal itchy rash that getting even exploded would likely not much improve.

But he survived, survived the refueling without so much as a minor fire and set in on Mrs. Jane Sprinkle's backyard that was fairly ripe itself with spindly weeds and riddled there at the first with sweetgum balls that Jack Vestal could not much stand the sensation of under his sneakerbottoms and so walked maybe faster than he should have and consequently left back of him more spindly weeds than he managed somehow to cut which meant he had to mow them even a third time after he'd mowed them twice already like he guessed was just the way things went sometimes, like he guessed was just the way things went most especially for pitiful afflicted people like himself. And he was ruminating upon his woes, which were general and farreaching, when he passed out from the sweetgum balls into a stretch of open grass where Mrs. Jane Sprinkle watched him from the kitchen window stride back and forth across the length of the yard and wipe himself every now and again with his forearm and scratch himself every now and again with his fingerends and beat sometimes at gnats and yellowjackets like she figured she could improve, figured she could make more tolerable anyhow and so set out towards the basement to do it.

Jane Sprinkle and her husband Jimmy had kept their white Coldspot with the chrome doorpull once they'd bought their coppertone Frigidaire that dumped its own little halfmoon ice slivers in the freezer bin, and they'd had the Coldspot set and situated off in a corner of the basement where they stored in the refrigerator part of it hardly anything but for a pair of hairy bluegreen oranges and a gallon pickle jar with just anymore the brine in it. In the freezer, however, they kept their sherbet and their icemilk and their Eskimo Pies too, most especially their Eskimo Pies that Jimmy Sprinkle had a fondness for, their Jumbo Eskimo Pies with the crinkly chocolate roundabout the edges that Mrs. Jane Sprinkle figured Jack Vestal jr. could probably stand one of like would cool and soothe him on such a hot and such a wilty day. So she crossed the basement floor to the Coldspot, flung open the door of it, reminded herself how she'd been lately intending to throw out her bluegreen oranges and empty and scour her pickle jar, and took from the freezer a pie for Jack Vestal and a pie for herself too like she guessed they could sit in the shade and eat together and chat maybe while they did it, and Mrs. Jane Sprinkle set to wondering what her and Jack Vestal jr. might exactly chat about that she was fairly completely engaged in altogether as she stepped out through the basement doorway into the stairwell which would be the block one with the slab floor and the clogged drain and the leaves and the beetles and the sizeable garden slugs that Mrs. Jane Sprinkle got a little engaged about as well, or watched anyhow where it was she laid her shoebottoms and pondered where it might be she'd lay them next.

The trouble was Jack Vestal had come to be a little engaged himself and so did not see Mrs. Jane Sprinkle's topnotch and then the side of her head rise up out from the stairwell or, more to the point truly, he did not see the side of her head and her topnotch drop off and disappear of a sudden back down into the stairwell they'd only just lately risen up from though he did in fact hear the thump that came like it did just midway between the rising up and the dropping back down, heard the thump enough to twitch and jump anyhow on account of it but not twitch and jump much actually as he was caught up with Marcia Satterwhite instead, Marcia Satterwhite that he'd rendered somehow grateful to him. They were sitting together under a tree, were in fact a little sprawled there he figured, sprawled there under a tree alongside a branch that was fairly rushing with water, was trilling and babbling and such that Marcia Satterwhite told to him she plain loved the sound of which he went ahead and assured her back was pretty much the case with himself as he couldn't hardly ever get enough trilling and babbling to suit him like Marcia Satterwhite let escape a tiny breath in back of, the variety precisely of tiny breath that indicated to Jack Vestal how talk from him of babbling and trilling had gone on and rendered her somehow fairly much set to get ravished.

Now, of course, Jack Vestal was not altogether acquainted with how it was a ravishment got under way, and as he passed back and forth across the breadth of Mrs. Jane Sprinkle's yard he reasoned where he might firstoff lay his fingers and saw himself even lay his fingers there without getting screeched and yowled at like emboldened him to go on and slide them south a little which inspired from Marcia Satterwhite a throaty sort of a noise that Jack Vestal grew all shivery at just the thought of back of his daddy's Toro where he did not generally grow shivery much. So he was occupied truly and fairly completely engaged and had just begun to think on what piece of his own self Marcia Satterwhite might come to feel obliged under the tree beside the trilling brook to lay her fingers upon which had commenced, behind his daddy's Toro, to be a sizeable unfurled piece of himself like he was trying to make lay some place other than where it had lately jabbed and unfurled into which was when it was he came upon Mrs. Jane Sprinkle's magnolia tree and heard the thump that he twitched and jumped about.

It was a seedpod, was anyway still the bulk of a seedpod once it had left the mower and shot across the yard and Mrs. Jane Sprinkle, who was just then climbing up out from the stairwell, heard it zip on by her head and heard it even strike the clapboard like was the last thing altogether she did hear before it bounced and careened and knocked her right square on a vessel like Dr. Shackleford guessed and speculated it did once later on he'd had the occasion for it. Naturally, she collapsed pretty much straightoff, just kind of sank down onto the steps and slid backwards atop the stairwell drain and joined there the leaves and the beetles and the iridescent slugs and the countless tiny black ants too that showed a fondness for Mrs. Jane Sprinkle's Eskimo Pies most especially once they began to run off her dressfront and puddle and pool up all creamy white alongside her. For his part, of course, Jack Vestal jr. was a little too shivery and unfurled to do much about what thump he'd heard lately except for twitch and jump both. He didn't in fact see what he'd shot and didn't at all see where he'd shot it and had truly no notion that he'd managed somehow to fell Mrs. Jane Sprinkle by her purply vessel as he was taken up otherwise with his branch that trilled and babbled and his fingers that roamed and traveled round and his altogether upright item that got at last laid bare by Marcia Satterwhite who quite plainly admired it and grew a little eeky on its behalf, exclaimed anyhow that way people sometimes exclaim once they've been led to a bluff to see the view. He told her how it wasn't anything hardly, told her how he'd been fairly much born with it though truly in a state otherwise than what state she'd promoted it to like he let on was rare for him, like he let on was near about utterly unheard of that he had back of the Toro to go ahead and let on a few times there together before he could make it seem a little accurate and truthful or so much as possible even since he'd not in fact been purely dangly for a half a decade or about it and so could not straightoff sound to have been chiefly dangly if not altogether exclusively dangly instead.

"Ain't no girl never touched me so," Jack Vestal said though appreciably more flatout than he'd meant to say it and so he said it again and rose up noticeably on the Never like seemed to improve the whole business that he confirmed for himself it did once he'd repeated it another time, and he heard in his head Marcia Satterwhite tell to him a fairly eeky thing back and grow pouty at the mouth what way was plainly invitation and preface both to some ravishment outright that her and Jack Vestal jr. together set in at under their tree by their ripply brook, or they began to roll anyway and tangle and he tugged at her blouse while she pulled at his trousers until the both of them were pretty completely naked entirely but for their wooly socks that Jack Vestal jr. back of his daddy's Toro could not think of a graceful way to get shed of.

He wasn't full well acquainted with how it was precisely men and women became, in the midst of a ravishment, connected and joined together but had heard from Bill Ed Myrick and Everet Little and Louis Benfield too assorted theories and speculations that he culled and picked through as he circled round back of Mrs. Jane Sprinkle's magnolia tree, and he just poked with his item everywhere he guessed he ought to until he'd found the place on Marcia Satterwhite she got eekiest about that seemed to him the spot he'd best dwell on and linger at like he dwelled and like he lingered both under the tree by the trilling branch and clear of the magnolia on back to the ligustrum bushes and behind them even to the aluminum fence at the end of the lot where Mrs. Jane Sprinkle's neighbor's sizeable brown dog with a head like a hamshank stuck her clammy nose far enough through the fencewire to touch Jack Vestal jr. on the forearm with it like incited a spell of twitching and jumping as well and furled briefly what item he lived mostly anymore unfurled with.

Of course, he couldn't find her once he'd gotten done. Of course, once he'd trimmed and raked and even blown the clippings off the drive he couldn't hunt her up anywhere, and he beat on the frontdoor and the sidedoor and called through an open window on the far end of the house but didn't raise her and didn't truly seek her out in the stairwell where she was just then presently in repose with the leaves and the beetles and the slugs and the countless black ants too that were wading on into the creamy puddle to drink and frolic. And he guessed that was just the way it went with pitiful sorts like himself, guessed they all just slaved and labored on hot wilty days that people gave out they'd pay money for when they did not hardly mean at all to pay money for it that Jack Vestal jr. swore on account of, swore two times loud and articulate on account of even so as to see would he get told a What darling? from somewhere maybe he hadn't thought yet to look.

Presently, he towed his daddy's Toro on across the road and figured at Mrs. Darlene Montgomery how, as long as he was close by, he'd cut her scant yard and rake her dirt and edge along her puny slip of a walk with his toothsome edger like Mrs. Darlene Montgomery was altogether skeptical at the need for until Jack Vestal took her out into her frontyard and her sideyard and her backyard too and indicated various wispy grass patches that appeared to him right there on the verge of getting entirely away from them like they could not hardly afford to let Mrs. Darlene Montgomery's wispy grass patches get. So he swayed her and moved her and requested from her payment in advance prior to endeavoring to start up his daddy's Toro that he wished he hadn't shut off at Mrs. Jane Sprinkle's like he'd gone on ahead and shut it off, and of course he yanked the cord and kicked the housing and dropped the front wheels as he loosed some potent invective but the Toro only clanked and rattled at him a little back and did not seem much disposed truly for combustion which was how come Jack Vestal clipped the wispy grass patches on his knees with his hand shears that Mrs. Darlene Montgomery raised up a windowsash to inquire about.

He hoped he'd see her once he set to raking the frontyard, hoped he'd look across the road and spy her maybe through a window or out on the drive waving money at him, but he smoothed and raked the dirt and ran his edging contraption along the walk without seeing but Mrs. Darlene Montgomery who led him around to the sideyard to display for him a grass patch he'd left somehow wispy by mistake. And he even dragged his Toro and his clippers and his gas can and his edging contraption back up to Mrs. Jane Sprinkle's house once he'd gotten done with the wispy grass and the black dirt altogether, and he banged on the frontdoor and the sidedoor and called in through an upraised window, said anyhow,

"Hey!" twice but did not get told back anything from it. Consequently, then, he went on home and left Mrs. Jane Sprinkle frontside upmost atop the stairwell drain that the Eskimo Pie puddle could not seep down through partly on account of Mrs. Jane Sprinkle who was lying frontside upmost atop it and partly on account of how the drainpipe was choked anyway with twigs and leaves and dirt and acorns and roly-poly bugs, and Mrs. Jane Sprinkle moved sometimes ever so slightly, moved at the neck chiefly and the feet every now and again, and grunted and grumbled and made just occasional assorted noises but primarily lay still and quiet and looked to be asleep if not maybe utterly expired instead.

And she had a dream, had a recollection truly that seemed to her there in the stairwell like a dream as it was gauzy and faint and quivery at the borders that way dreams sometimes are, but it was true too and actual and genuine from a while back when things had seemed to her dreamy mostly, just plain regular things like did not seem to her dreamy any longer. It was her. It was her and was Jimmy both together in Jimmy's brother's gray roadster with the rag top that they'd drawn and laid back so as to take the sun and the spring air, and she'd scooted on over to him what way she'd been prone to, had scooted on over beneath his arm he'd raised up for her to scoot under and then had squeezed and held her with while he drove with his opposite hand alone, or just his foremost finger truly that he'd curled overtop the wheel to steer by. They'd struck out north, north up 87 on into Virginia and then west a ways on 58 through Horse Pasture and Penn's Store and into Stuart and through Stuart even too and up the ridge beyond it where the air took a chill that she laid her nose to Jimmy's ear and spoke to him about and so got squeezed and held tighter even and closer in than she'd been squeezed and held already.

Church was letting out along the ridge and the Methodists and the Baptists and the Presbyterians too had spilled out from their sanctuaries and stood a little dazed in the bright afternoon and smoked and talked while their children ran around the churchyards and into the gravel lots among the cars and back out into the churchyards again that Jane Sprinkle frontside upmost atop the stairwell drain recalled along with the scraps of music she'd heard in Jimmy's brother's gray roadster, scraps of recessional music out from the sanctuaries just on the air like suited somehow the lively churchyards with the men in their white shirts and the women in their print dresses and the children that slipped and dodged there in the midst of them, and she told to Jimmy, "What a grand day," and he told to her, "Grand sure enough," himself which was back when she used to just up and say such things and he used to just up and hear her at it.

There was a spot he'd been to, a place he knew, a knoll he'd gotten previously acquainted with on a visit past Stuart up the mountain ridge that him and a buddy, who he said straightaway was a boy buddy before he could get asked was he, happened across and lingered awhile at to look south out over the valley like had laid, he told her, all flat and endless before them. And there'd been laurel bushes, he recalled, and hemlock trees and nappy grass to sit on and just the sky to see and the land beneath it that looked to sprawl and stretch that way from down in the valley land never seemed to look. Of course, he'd been taken and enchanted, admitted to Jane Sprinkle how taken and enchanted was what he'd been gazing off the mountain peak out over the flatlands that were washed places in the yellow sunlight and hidden places in the purply shade and were here and there settled and worked and cultivated and were here and there wild still and wooded too, and he'd been moved, him and his buddy both they'd been moved and they'd been affected along with it like they neither one hardly ever got much which was how come truly Jimmy had wanted to carry her up to the mountain peak and let her sit in the nappy grass at the very place he'd been taken and enchanted and moved and affected himself so as to see would she come to be maybe a little stirred up on her own like she told him in the roadster she knew she would, like she laid her nose flush up against his ear ridges and guessed at him she just had to come to be.

She'd brought a lunch in a box, Jane Sprinkle had, a lunch in a packing carton that was chiefly pieces of a bony chicken from the night previous and snap beans with gravy over them and boiled new potatoes and an assortment of greasy biscuits and some damson preserves to smear on them along with a hunk of resurrection cake that her momma had made and her daddy wouldn't eat on account of the shredded coconut topping that her daddy swore he could taste even once her momma had picked it off for him. They had tea in a vinegar jug and apply brandy in a milk of magnesia bottle in a sack in Jimmy's brother's brogan in the trunk due to how Jimmy was not looking, he told it, to get apprehended, and they'd carried with them a quilt too that Jimmy's momma's sister had made back before she'd come to be much educated about quilts truly and so it was a little inside out and backwards and square but for where it was oblong and stuffed and wadded what places it was not flat and vacant instead.

They turned off the highway at a shed that Jimmy told her was the shed he'd turned off at once already previously, and they followed a gravel road up a rise where it went to just hardpan, ribbed and rutted hardpan like a solitary finger could not hardly all by itself steer on, and the hardpan went shortly to a track in the brush and the treelimbs beat the fenders and the windshield and they rode all low and scrunched down on the seat until the brush and the track both gave out and quit together before a manner of house with some clapboards to it and some hammered tin and busted windowlights stuffed with rags and such and precious little paint all over and a piece of a drinkbox in the frontyard and a hound partway under the porch with ticks on his ears thick like berries on a bush. Up on the planking above him a redheaded man sat in an upholstered chair, a chair anyhow that was anymore upholstered somewhat, and he just plain watched the roadster swing on into his yard and back up across it and turn so as to head out again which was when he stood up and plain watched from his feet a spell that his hound joined him at, crawled full out from under the porch and looked set maybe to yelp and howl but only shivered a little instead.

"Taken," she told to him as they left the track for the hardpan. "Enchanted," she told to him as they left the hardpan for the gravel. "Moved," she said, "and affected," once they'd arrived again at the shed that Jimmy pondered and then admitted was maybe not the shed he'd turned at previously after all, news of which she absorbed and considered just ever so briefly prior to admitting to Jimmy back, "Dazzled altogether," that he poked and squeezed her at the ribcage on account of like caused her to lurch and squirm and brought her to lay at last flush up against him that way the poking and the squeezing used to evermore bring her to lay.

He found shortly the very shed he had turned at once previously in fact. She recollected from atop the drain in the stairwell how he had shortly found it and had swung his brother's roadster up the track alongside it that was just wheelruts chiefly with a hump between them for the oilpan to beat on and drag overtop of, and they climbed to a ridge and swung down in the saddle of it prior to climbing to another ridge beyond it and parking the roadster hard up on what Jimmy insisted was a trail through the undergrowth like Jane Sprinkle could not hardly be persuaded it actually was not even once Jimmy had waded on down it a stretch and turned round to her so as to throw wide his arms and say, "See?" that failed to inspire her to leap on out from the roadster and dart into the brush that she informed Jimmy about as she was not much anxious to tromp roundabout in such a weedy snaky place.

"Well," Jimmy told her, "all right then," and he waded on farther than he'd waded already, waded on down a dip and up a rise and out of sight beyond it that Jane Sprinkle sat high on the roadster seatback and watched him do and even lingered a scant while all by herself and listened at the birds call and the grass rustle and some manner of creature shriek and cry on back down the track where they'd come from like, all compounded and collected together, moved her to leap off the seatback entirely and do a little wading herself, wading with such vigor and velocity to it as to carry her not just shortly up on Jimmy but past Jimmy too and on out of the brush and the scrub and the trees into an open place that was lush and was grassy and was bathed all roundabout in pure unbroken light like stopped her and drew her up and allowed Jimmy to come up to her and hold her at the waist with his one arm while he pointed with his other, pointed and told to her, "Look there," by which he meant the valley that sprawled and lay before them both yellow and purply, peopled and wild.

It was altogether the vastest thing she'd ever seen. She admitted to him it was altogether the vastest thing entirely she'd ever had the pleasure to lay her eyes upon once her and once Jimmy had fetched their packing carton and their quilt and their jug of tea and their apply brandy in the trunk in the brogan in the sack in the milk of magnesia bottle and carried them to the grassy place where the two of them laid and sprawled a little themselves and admired the lone hemlock tree and the bank of laurel bushes with the buds just lately set on them and gazed out as well over the stretch of valley that Jane Sprinkle spied a lake in the midst of all flat and shiny which her and Jimmy decided together looked to them like a jewel, looked to them like a diamond shimmery and bright. They ate atop the quilt which Jimmy dripped some preserves onto that she'd warned him prior to it he probably would though she'd warned him that he'd probably drip some gravy first which he did not in fact drip any of until after he'd already dripped the preserves instead like seemed to Jimmy more nearly a manner of triumph than he could shape it somehow to seem to Jane Sprinkle with him, and she cleaned the quilt with spit and a napkin while Jimmy ate a chicken leg and tossed the bone from it out over the rock ledge before them and down towards the valley floor that Jane Sprinkle left off licking her napkin on account of so as to tell to Jimmy, "Jimmy!" and explain to him, like she had not figured she probably needed to or surely would have already, how a chicken bone tossed over a ledge to a valley floor was just the sort of item to knock a man on the head and kill him that Jimmy admitted he had not, when he tossed the chicken bone, thought much about, and he went ahead and seemed fairly sorrowful and contrite right up until she puckered her lips and made some gurgly talk at him when he flung a thighbone with some gristle and meat still on it and told to her how he'd evermore longed for a life of crime and danger that she presently grew even herself a littly jolly about.

They propped and lay fairly much atop and athwart each other on the oblong quilt once they'd eaten near about everything they'd carried to eat, even the entire hunk of resurrection cake that Jane Sprinkle hadn't herself wanted a piece of but had figured she'd just have a taste of Jimmy's piece like was how come Jimmy had what piece he had there at the first and what piece he had behind it and what piece he had behind that one too even which didn't leave but crumbs in the wax paper as they'd brought with them just a three-piece hunk Jane Sprinkle hadn't guessed she'd wanted but to taste and so had eaten only half of herself. Naturally, they gasped and sighed and lay still for a time once they'd done with their lunch altogether, and Jane Sprinkle propped her head on Jimmy's stomach as they watched the clouds slip on by above them, or watched the clouds primarily anyway and raised up every now and again to watch the valley some too which they assured each other by turns was truly a vast thing like they'd agreed already previously it was. Jimmy uncapped the milk of magnesia bottle and brought just so much as the neck of it out from the sack once he'd cut his eyes near about every direction he could manage to cut them and he took a draw and cut his eyes another time prior to offering up the exposed neck for Jane Sprinkle to drink from herself like Jane Sprinkle declined to do as she could not believe a lady should drink from a milk of magnesia bottleneck but for maybe in the case of acute indigestion and she told Jimmy how, if he served himself some apple brandy in a cup, she was liable to have a taste of it which she in fact did once he'd cut his eyes and poured a dram and cut his eyes some more.

They didn't talk for a time about anything hardly except to agree how the valley was vast and the sky was chiefly blue and the laurel blossoms would likely be exquisite once they opened in among the green leathery leaves, and Jane Sprinkle recalled all gauzy and faint and quivery from down in the stairwell atop the drain how lovely it had been just to lie and not say anything much that way they used to not say anything much sometimes like was hardly the same silence they knew anymore which never spoke itself of the manner of things they'd previously lain all quiet and somehow spoken of. And Jimmy, she recollected, began to tell how he meant to alter the house, that house they lived in firstoff down from the powerplant in with a row of houses like it. He aimed to bust out a wall and aimed to cut in a window that he'd told to her previously he would but hadn't yet though he seemed on the mountaintop truly disposed for it, seemed on the mountaintop capable somehow like he'd never seemed down home at the dinette where he'd spoken of it too. And that was the thing that came to her clear in amongst the faint and quivery items otherwise, was the manner of thing anyhow that prompted and spurred her to recollect in the stairwell with the leaves and the beetles and the slugs and the black ants what life she'd presently given up and didn't hardly have anymore like she'd one time had it back in that spring on the grassy knoll when they'd eaten and then lain together fairly into the darkness and talked and not talked and known between them how everything that was not maybe likely was probably merely possible instead which she made a noise on account of, loosed from along about her adenoids a manner of discharge with some edge and some whine to it due to what they'd had one time before it wore off and melted away like seemed to her worth being adenoidal about even in the stairwell atop the drain where she did not actually realize she was in fact being adenoidal until Jimmy up on the grassy knoll raised himself onto his elbows and told to her, "Great Christ!"

He'd been home from the carlot a time already. He'd stood in the kitchen and called to her and had looked out the frontdoor to see was she maybe across the road at Mrs. Darlene Montgomery's like he discovered, once he'd looked out the frontdoor, he couldn't truly know from just looking out it, and he stepped on down the hallway to the bedroom to find out was she maybe still bundled up in the bedclothes like sometimes of an afternoon she came to be, but she wasn't on the bed or in the fullbath or the halfbath either and wasn't as well in the linencloset at the end of the hall that Jimmy Sprinkle had guessed he'd go on and look in as long as he was right there at it. She just plainly was elsewhere as best as he could tell and he returned to the kitchen and stood a time upon the linoleum once more where his disposition began to alter and erode as he listened to the gurgling and whining and the general gastric uproar from his stomach that he'd not put a thing in since noon when he'd eaten just nabs and a Nu-grape and not so much as orange nabs with peanut butter like he'd had a yen for but brown speckledy nabs instead with a smear of cheese between them.

So he was getting to be put out, was getting to be fairly completely aggravated and he engaged with the kitchen light overhead in the manner of exchange he anticipated having with Mrs. Jane Sprinkle once she'd arrived in her own sweet time, the manner of exchange that was not really much in the way of a pure and actual conversation but was him mostly making pointed inquiries and her mostly dropping her eyes on account of them like an overhead light could suit well enough for until Mrs. Jane Sprinkle showed up herself to get inquired at. In the meantime, he guessed he might gnaw on a thing so as to keep from fainting into a heap from just general famishment mostly like he felt in some danger of and so opened the coppertone Frigidaire and stood there before it peeking into bowls and loosing dull crinkly foil from roundabout items which did not somehow turn out, once he'd laid them bare, to be much in the way of appealing to him like caused him presently to shut the coppertone Frigidaire and open the cabinet over the rangehood instead for a Cheez-it but weren't there any Cheez-its anymore in the cabinet over the rangehood except for the Cheez-it box and the Cheez-it residue in the bottom of it like somehow heightened the ill and heightened the peevish both.

The Milky Way did not come to him until after he'd fairly completely worked himself into a state there on the linoleum when of a sudden he recollected how he'd carried a Milky Way and a Heath Bar too home from the Handy Pantry back in May and had eaten the Heath Bar pretty much straightaway but had saved the Milky Way, had hidden it in the Coldspot downstairs back of the icemilk where he'd meant shortly to fetch it from once it got all frosty and hard but hadn't fetched it somehow like there before the rangehood he did in fact recall and so struck out across the linoleum and through the basement doorway and down the steps and along the length of the slab floor to the Coldspot that he flung open the doors of, which would be the main one and the freezer one beyond it, and he groped back of the sherbet and the Eskimo Pies and the icemilk too until he came at last across his actual Milky Way all stuck and frozen up in the prickly ice like he couldn't there at the first free it from and so beat it with his fist and pulled it with his fingers and tore the wrapper fairly much entirely off of it but failed to loose even the least little trifling scrap of the actual bar itself until he'd hunted up his tack hammer off the workbench out from under his chalkline and his assorted washer sack and beat the ice alongside his Milky Way with it.

Of course he broke the thing into pieces but freed it nonetheless and commenced straightoff to gnaw a chunk, commenced straightoff to gnaw the first chunk he could manage to fish out on account of how the beating and the busting loose together had truly carried him to the very brink of famishment like he'd been already pretty hard by just standing up in the kitchen doing nothing much. So he gnawed directly, or undertook anyhow to gnaw, clamped his teeth down on the hunk of Milky Way and tried to bite it, tried to bust it further still but couldn't somehow bite it and bust it just with regular jaw pressure which was how come he squatted, which was how come he hunkered down and concentrated what feeble pluck he had left into his jawhinges that he endeavored to shut and close together like the Milky Way kept them from even with Jimmy Sprinkle's feeble pluck all drawn up and concentrated, and he found himself obliged to wheeze and grunt in his hunkered squat and found himself inclined to pause from biting a time and just breathe deeply in and breathe deeply out which was when he noticed across the slab the outside door that had come to be left open and the item beyond it atop the drain in the stairwell that looked to him like some manner of sack that had gotten maybe dropped and had gotten maybe busted, or looked to him anyway like some manner of dropped and busted sack until he stood up out from his hunkered squat and stepped on over to the stairwell himself where he found cause to discharge his hunk of Milky Way and found cause to exclaim, "Great Christ!" like Mrs. Jane Sprinkle had not hardly anticipated up on the grassy knoll he'd raise himself onto his elbow and do.

She was seepy and oozy all across her dressfront from the Eskimo Pies like Mr. Jimmy Sprinkle did not take straightoff for Eskimo Pie seep and ooze but took for some manner of grave bodily fluid instead which was how come he wailed and cried out and said at Jane Sprinkle, "Jane!" and said at Jane Sprinkle, "Sugar!" and got told how he'd best lay on back down and hush a spell by Jane Sprinkle herself who did not open her eyes to tell it but just lay in the seep and the ooze with the bugs and such and moved her lips ever so hardly at all like seemed spooky to Jimmy Sprinkle who'd taken Jane Sprinkle already for expired and so naturally had not figured to get instructed and advised by her which prompted from him exclamations further still, inarticulate wheezy exclamations chiefly that Jane Sprinkle felt inclined from atop the drain to speak of as well. He took her up in his arms, had been intending to reach down and sweep her up in fact and had endeavored even to sweep her a little but found that Jane Sprinkle was not anymore hardly so willowy as she'd been once and found in addition to it that he no longer himself possessed truly the lumbar for sweeping, could not in fact but barely stoop and lift both together, and so he raised Jane Sprinkle but not with the flare and drama he'd intended to raise her, not maybe like Rhett would have taken up Scarlett unless of course he'd arrived at Tara riding the bumper of a pumptruck, but he got her anyhow up from the stairwell and off the drain and flicked what ants he could from her dressfront where they'd taken to wallowing in her grave bodily fluid, and he kind of flung her athwart him and draped her across him and toted her on up the steps like gave her cause somehow to lay her nose against his neck and giggle at him and coo even at him a little as well like she'd not hardly cooed at him lately, like he'd not anticipated she'd likely ever coo at him again.

He laid her on the bed upon the bedclothes and covered her with the green afghan his own dead momma had stitched together for him, covered her even though he was wholly doubtful grave bodily fluid would wash out of an afghan like he didn't guess mattered much even if his own dead momma had made the thing, and Jane Sprinkle wondered at him with her eyes shut and her lips moving hardly at all if hadn't it been just the best possible day, if hadn't it been just the best day possible altogether out of all the days they'd spent like Jimmy Sprinkle did not straightaway loose an opinion about but instead dialed on the telephone to Dr. Shackleford who guessed he'd leave the office and come right out as he didn't have left to see but Mrs. Estes from Pelham that had complaints about her organs and complaints about her joints and complaints about her white corpuscles and complaints about her red ones and complaints about her sugar that was low except when it was high instead and complaints even about her hairroots on the top of her head that hurt her when she woke up in the morning on account of how she was prone to bend and work them in the night, but she did not suffer truly from anything Dr. Shackleford could much tend to and remedy though he'd suggested one time a radical tonguectomy that Mrs. Estes from Pelham had not somehow found the mirth in.

So Dr. Shackleford drove directly on over to the house and him and Jimmy Sprinkle stood together alongside the bed and watched Mrs. Jane Sprinkle grin at them and coo even a little still with her eyes shut tight and her dressfront all seepy and oozy that Jimmy Sprinkle drew back the afghan about and indicated the fluid to Dr. Shackleford who he went ahead and consulted with so as to let on how he'd taken it to be grave and taken it to be bodily though he could not say for certain what organ might have leaked it that Dr. Shackleford, who consulted back, found he could not himself say either. They gauged her pulse at her wrist vessel and agreed it was not, for a pulse, inordinately low and lifeless and they hoisted Jane Sprinkle's eyelids so as to ponder her pupils that Dr. Shackleford most usually carried a tiny flashlight for though he'd come away from his office somehow without it and so made some use of the plain lamplight instead.

Presently, he probed and felt and groped a little with his fingers roundabout Mrs. Jane Sprinkle's neck and up the sides of her head and back of her hairline like Mrs. Jane Sprinkle grew fairly giddy about and he came at last upon a knotty lump behind her ear where he knew a vessel to be that Jimmy Sprinkle, once he'd gotten consulted, confessed he was not much surprised to hear of, which would be the vessel and the knotty lump in combination, as he'd suspected already how the probing and the feeling and the groping might turn up the manner of welt just precisely it had turned up in fact. Jimmy Sprinkle prescribed a cube of ice, maybe two cubes of ice even in a breadsack to hold the wet, and told Dr. Shackleford how their coppertone Frigidaire made its own ice slivers like seemed to him would best chill and shrink a knotty lump and he was set to explain his ice sliver theory when Dr. Shackleford took out from his medical bag a manner of capsule that he busted open under Mrs. Jane Sprinkle's noseholes.

She didn't know rightoff where she was. She didn't know rightoff how she'd come to be there and so asked to find out which Jimmy Sprinkle consulted straightaway with Dr. Shackleford about as he couldn't see that she needed to get told how she'd come to be where she'd ended up if she didn't know where she was in the first place that Jane Sprinkle heard Jimmy speak to Dr. Shackleford about and so looked at Jimmy for the first time she'd looked at him and saw precisely what Jimmy it was, saw precisely anyhow what Jimmy it anymore wasn't, and he reached out his fingers and touched her on the dressfront along about her grave bodily fluid as he inquired, "What happened, sugar?" that she didn't even draw breath to speak of but just watched him a time all still and quiet until she knew for certain where she was and who she was and how precisely she'd ended up when she closed her eyes once more and wheezed and sniffled and cried shortly straight down into her ears, and she said to her Jimmy, "Jimmy," all soft and sorrowful that he asked her What? about and got told another time just, "Jimmy," all soft and sorrowful again.

Surely it was a calamitous thing. Miss Bernice Fay Frazier, who'd heard of it from people that had heard of it themselves and had presently even found occasion to quiz Mrs. Jane Sprinkle about it, discovered calamity in every little aspect of the whole business by which she meant chiefly the falling and the heaping up attended by the bugs and the Eskimo Pie puddle like struck her as far worse than any variety of catstomping and sciatic complication. Prospective disaster just seemed to float and hover all roundabout, seemed anyhow to Miss Bernice Fay Frazier to float and to hover both like was how come she'd taken on a companion in the first place, a companion she figured she was due shortly to get, was past due to get in fact which was what alone incited her to sneak past her cat Bubbles and call Mr. Barefoot at the depot, Mr. Barefoot who informed her that her companion was, as best as he could tell from back of the ticket window, presently having a word with black John Sykes who was loitering there at the far boundary of conviviality all set to get crude and vile on his way to unconscious like Miss Bernice Fay Frazier could not help but suck air about as she'd not imported a woman clean from Berkeley Springs West Virginia to have her loiter at the depot with a man that imbibed so, and she instructed Mr. Barefoot to fetch her away from John Sykes like the Barefoot was reluctant to do on account of how he had the ticket window to watch and see to but then she'd just instructed him in her sweet breathy elevated voice there at the first which she altered and transformed with some pitch and some volume and so instructed the Barefoot all over again and after such a fashion as to leave him feeling considerably more imparted to than the first time he'd felt.

Straightaway, then, Miss Bernice Fay Frazier dialed up her sister's house another time and was fortunate enough to raise Mr. Estelle Singletary who managed to tell into the phone, "Hello," before he suffered himself to be reviled and abused without much preface and no introduction to speak of though, since his wife was in the basement by the Maytag, he guess he knew rightoff who it was had dialed up to revile and abuse him both. Of course he was able to glean precipitously where he was meant to go and how soon he was meant to be there and so departed directly in Mrs. Estelle Singletary's LeSabre with the coffee-cups on the floorboard under the frontseat that rolled roundabout and beat on occasion together, and he passed up the boulevard and by the square and down beyond the icehouse to the depot where he found Mr. Barefoot in an orange chair next to the ticket window with her alongside him, her who was touching Mr. Barefoot on the forearm with her fingerends and telling to him, "No!" in between what times he'd tell to her, "Yes!" and lay out his forearm to get touched.

From the far side of the depot in his own orange chair next to the water cooler, black John Sykes hailed Mr. Estelle Singletary, hollered to him anyhow a profane thing and raised up his papersack so as to suck on the bottleneck inside it prior to repeating the identical profane thing he'd only just lately hollered in the first place as it was presently the profane thing he had the most affection for, and Mr. Estelle Singletary loosed just a civil manner of hello back prior to stepping pretty much flush up to Mr. Barefoot and her with him that had her fingers raised and poised for some additional forearm touching once she exclaimed what No! she was intending in fact to exclaim and was pretty much set to come out with when she noticed Mr. Estelle Singletary and so lifted her face to him and consequently had an effect similar to the effect she'd had already previously on the Barefoot who was wondering how come her fingers just loitered all raised and poised in the air when she had obviously a No! to exclaim and a forearm to touch like the Barefoot was on the verge of making a playful inquiry about when Mr. Estelle Singletary went on ahead and blurted, went on ahead and uncorked a manner of "Hey there" that rang through the depot and was not maybe the loudest goofiest thing Mr. Estelle Singletary had ever before blurted at a woman but was probably, as best as he could tell, hard up on it like he was beginning to feel a little ill and wan on account of when she touched her raised and poised fingerends to his own personal forearm and told to him back, "Well, hey," herself like fairly much completed what effect she'd only with the lifted face commenced to have.

She was charmed and she was enchanted that she got up out from her orange chair to inform him she was and he stood before her all charmed and enchanted back like he was meaning to tell her of and set in even to telling her of it, made anyhow a squeaky noise in his neck that he followed with a raspy noise from the top of his mouth along with a manner of wheezy cough from down around his windpipe like he could not believe much communicated how charmed and enchanted he'd in fact come to be which was why precisely he undertook to speak to her another time and maybe even say a thing with some words to it though not in fact the words he ended up sharing shortly with her which was a "Hey" and which was a "There" back of it that the Barefoot with the necktie and the forearm stood up out from his orange chair to tell to Mr. Estelle Singletary he'd said already one time before that Mr. Estelle Singletary grew straightaway hot about as he didn't guess the Barefoot was anybody he needed just presently to hear from that the Barefoot disputed rightoff and put his own face as square up in Mr. Estelle Singletary's face as he could manage to get it that Miss Mary Alice Celestine Lefler interceded on account of, touched anyway two forearms together with her fingerends and told to the Barefoot and told to Mr. Estelle Singletary, "Now boys," after such a fashion as to melt them both a little.

Mr. Estelle Singletary carried her tiny square leathery case and her hanging bag while the Barefoot insisted he be allowed to tote her piece of Samsonite with the wheels to it like she guessed if it was her she'd go on and make some use of but the Barefoot, of course, hefted the thing straightaway and lugged it with just his one arm that Miss Mary Alice Celestine Lefler admired him at and wondered at Mr. Estelle Singletary if he'd ever previously seen such a strapping man as the Barefoot seemed to her to be, but Mr. Estelle Singletary did not appear to know if he had or if he hadn't either one and just opened the trunk of the LeSabre where he set the tiny leathery case and laid the hanging bag and then plain waited for the Barefoot to arrive with the piece of Samsonite that he tried at the bumper to relieve him of so as to illuminate for Miss Mary Alice Celestine Lefler how many strapping men exactly there were roundabout. The Barefoot, however, was not disposed to let loose of the piece of Samsonite until he'd laid it where he meant to, so him and Mr. Estelle Singletary together grappled it up past the taillights and fairly much flush down onto the hanging bag that Miss Mary Alice Celestine Lefler touched them another time on their forearms about and wished how they'd maybe grapple and lay her piece of Samsonite somewhere else entirely.

He struck out south by the square and down the boulevard and meant even to turn at the Heavenly Rest and drive Miss Mary Alice Celestine Lefler direct on over to Miss Bernice Fay Frazier's house, but Mr. Estelle Singletary did not turn somehow like he'd meant to and kept south a spell while him and her chatted, or while she anyway chatted chiefly that he heard her at and got every now and again his forearm touched on account of which he grew purely affected about and so stayed south until he swung east instead and then north for a stretch and back west so far as to take him south again by the depot and the square that didn't neither one of them notice they'd passed south again by due to how they'd come to be engaged there together in the LeSabre, engaged chiefly with talk of Berkeley Springs West Virginia that Mr. Estelle Singletary had driven through one time on his way to Pennsylvania though he could not recollect straightoff what it was he'd gone to Pennsylvania for like Miss Mary Alice Celestine Lefler undertook to remind him of by suggesting what things seemed to her cause for a man to travel clear through West Virginia and into Pennsylvania in the first place, but none of them struck a note with Mr. Estelle Singletary who humphed and beat the steering wheel and had shortly fingerends laid to him by her that wished he wouldn't fret and seethe so like was better somehow than getting by a woman reviled and abused both. And he pondered the road when it dipped and bent and he couldn't help but ponder it and gazed on her elsewise, her that was not stunning hardly that way women sometimes are, did not have hair all thick and shiny that cascaded and such or icy blue eyes and a scant slip of a nose and lips full and pouty but had a thing nonetheless, a thing that came off her like smoke and caused him to look and to ponder and to get by her fingerends affected and caused him in part and somewhat to drive Mrs. Estelle Singletary's LeSabre directly up onto the stretch of walk out front of Miss Bernice Fay Frazier's house like he'd meant only to park alongside that he admitted he had to Miss Mary Alice Celestine Lefler who reached across the seat and affected him another time still before he could climb on out the sidedoor and get perused by Mr. Wayne Fulp's speckled hound Bill that was most nights pleased to wet upon what tree Mr. Estelle Singletary had parked fairly flush up against.

Of course, Miss Bernice Fay Frazier had gotten to be near about frantic with worry and foreboding as she was disposed towards most especially foreboding even when she didn't have much truly to forebode about, and she shrieked straightaway at Mr. Estelle Singletary who she figured was pretty much why alone she'd had to forebode in the first place like was a thing lately she'd gleaned just sitting home all frantic and done in and she screeched at Mr. Estelle Singletary the news of how she'd gleaned it. Naturally, Miss Mary Alice Celestine Lefler sought to ease Miss Bernice Fay Frazier's agitation and reduce her down to regular talk so she laid her fingerends to her like soothed her somewhat but did not appear to affect her altogether after the fashion Mr. Estelle Singletary had himself been lately altogether affected, and Miss Bernice Fay Frazier just fell off from shrieking and fell off from screeching and stayed merely worked up and quivery in a quiet sort of a way until her cousin's girl Lucy's cat Bubbles sprang off the couch directly onto Miss Bernice Fay Frazier's velvety tufted chair and jumped from it onto Miss Bernice Fay Frazier's clawfooted table with the oval marble top that Bubbles could not grip much with her pointy claws and so slid and skated across the entire length of it and pushed Miss Bernice Fay Frazier's artificial fuzzy rose and her tin box with the glass jewels on the lid of it and her momma and daddy in their silvery frame clean onto the throwrug where Bubbles shortly joined them herself on her way to the backhall that she ran the length of once she'd managed to get entangled in the phone cord and bring the receiver down onto the floor like Miss Mary Alice Celestine Lefler found fairly delightful as she did not hardly care for but your spunky sorts of cats.

Once he'd been advised and directed and reminded back of them how he'd been advised and directed both, Mr. Estelle Singletary carried Miss Mary Alice Celestine Lefler's tiny leathery case and her hanging bag up the stairs to the room Miss Bernice Fay Frazier had near about made over where Miss Bernice Fay Frazier indicated the particular changes she'd wrought and Miss Mary Alice Celestine Lefler admired them inordinately until Mr. Estelle Singletary returned hauling her solitary piece of Samsonite that he got called strapping on account of what way he'd hoped along the backhall and up the stairs he would. They all returned together to the front room and Miss Bernice Fay Frazier settled onto the loveseat and patted the cushion next to her so as to bring Miss Mary Alice Celestine Lefler onto the loveseat with her like the patting managed to do though it somehow brought Bubbles onto the peak of the camelback as well and put Mr. Estelle Singletary into the velvety tufted chair that he plain dropped onto the cushion of that way he tended to like irked Miss Bernice Fay Frazier who was endeavoring to stay unirked on account of her company but failed to stay somehow unirked entirely and so wondered at Mr. Estelle Singletary could he have maybe dropped onto her chaircushion any harder than he'd already dropped onto it if he'd been taken up and pitched from the dining room that Mr. Estelle Singletary, from atop the tufted chaircushion, considered and pondered on prior to admitting to Miss Bernice Fay Frazier how, while he'd not sat so delicately as he might, that was generally just the way with your strapping sorts that Miss Mary Alice Celestine Lefler in particular and fairly much even all by herself grew amused on account of and said at Mr. Estelle Singletary, "Oh Eugene," like probably would have prefaced some armtouching if Mr. Estelle Singletary had not been so entirely out of armtouching range.

Miss Bernice Fay Frazier was anxious to hear of Miss Mary Alice Celestine Lefler's trip from Berkeley Springs West Virginia on the Greyhound bus and was curious to find out what manner of people Miss Mary Alice Celestine Lefler had in the first place come from as she didn't know anybody from West Virginia herself but for Mrs. Dwight Mobley who wasn't altogether from West Virginia precisely but had an aunt that had settled there.

"Eloise," Miss Mary Alice Celestine Lefler told her, "Mrs. Dwight Mobley's momma's sister."

"I know that, darling," Miss Bernice Fay Frazier said to her shortly back but not hardly so shortly and with barely the bite she likely would have said it to her before she got elevated and upraised that she wondered had Miss Mary Alice Celestine Lefler heard from Mr. Estelle Singletary talk yet of which Miss Mary Alice Celestine Lefler and Mr. Estelle Singletary both informed Miss Bernice Fay Frazier she hadn't like Miss Bernice Fay Frazier had not been looking truly to get from Mr. Estelle Singletary informed that she felt obliged to relate a spell with him about. So talk shifted a time from West Virginia and Miss Mary Alice Celestine Lefler's people there to Miss Bernice Fay Frazier's lately uplifted personal consciousness that had not itself, Miss Bernice Fay Frazier let on, been so awful lowly prior to when it got raised up but had had call for some tinkering and refinement as Miss Bernice Fay Frazier had come to be somehow mired up in trouble and woe and couldn't for a while there get back her grip like she'd one time had it which put her in mind of an item she'd heard lately from the widow Mrs. Askew, a pithy item she felt inspired to vent and air. "All things," she said, "have two handles. Beware of the wrong one." And she told it a second time to Miss Mary Alice Celestine Lefler who'd been so fond of it the first time through she'd wanted to hear it again, and her and Miss Bernice Fay Frazier and Mr. Estelle Singletary too decided between them how the widow Mrs. Askew was surely a singularly pithy sort of a woman though Miss Bernice Fay Frazier and Mr. Estelle Singletary both agreed that the widow Mrs. Askew had not always been so inordinately pithy as she'd lately come to be. She'd not in fact previously been known for her pith at all and had been known chiefly for her embroidery instead like was before she got upraised and before she got elevated.

And Miss Bernice Fay Frazier guessed she was herself serene anymore, guessed she was most especially serene now that Miss Mary Alice Celestine Lefler had come to stay with her, and she spoke briefly of her cousin's girl Lucy's cat Bubbles she'd stepped on and her own personal sciatic nerve she'd wrenched and twisted round and the throwrug she'd dropped atop of that all three together in combination constituted what she called her Incident which Miss Mary Alice Celestine Lefler straightaway oohed and lamented about. Naturally, Mr. Estelle Singletary guessed he would be pleased himself to be the object of some oohing and some lamenting as well and so endeavored to speak of a particular piece of his person he'd wrenched just lately like did not incite much of a discharge truly and so caused Mr. Estelle Singletary to shift afflictions and speak instead of a minor bit of surgery he'd undergone on an inflamed balky organ which Miss Bernice Fay Frazier was pretty well convinced herself Miss Mary Alice Celestine Lefler had not come clean from Berkeley Springs West Virginia to hear of. Consequently, then, she suggested to Mr. Estelle Singletary how he might best hush and how he might best go on home but suggested it with so much breath and so little articulation that Mr. Estelle Singletary, even for all his training, could not glean the gist of the thing and so continued to sit and continued to hold forth on the topic of most especially his incision which he appeared to Miss Bernice Fay Frazier to be threatening to display like she found she could not begin to stay breathy and unirked in the face of and so fairly wailed at him, "Hush!" and fairly wailed at him, "Go on!" and flung her arm by which she meant to indicate what direction precisely he ought maybe to go on it that she did with her flung arm indicate a little though she indicated primarily instead how a woman might inadvertently club her cousin's girl's cat and knock it back between the settee and the wall.

* * *

She'd not been there, then, but the one night and the piece of a day behind it when Mr. Dick Atwater saw her and saw Miss Bernice Fay Frazier with her step down off the porch planking onto the front stairtreads and off them onto the flagstones and off them onto the walk, and he watched her coming and watched her standing still for a spell close by and watched her leaving too after the fashion he'd not lately been inclined to watch a woman leave on account of what ponderous parts most leaving women showed to him. She wasn't, however, but a tiny slip of a woman herself like Mr. Dick Atwater could see she was most especially next to Miss Bernice Fay Frazier who had not been blessed with your tiny slip genes and chromosomes and so toted some appreciable meat like was especially plain to him once they'd begun to leave and begun to go away.

He watched them along the walk towards the boulevard and up by the Heavenly Rest and near about let them pass clean out of sight before he struck out himself along the walk and up by the Heavenly Rest too and followed along behind them towards town, stopping when they stopped and loitering when they loitered and proceeding only when they were proceeding themselves. Sleepy Pitts tried to speak at him, tried to engage him out front of the Gulf station in some fairly idle talk about a manner of squiggly rubber worm Sleepy Pitts had lately gotten a bass to take like he'd never thought truly he would due to how altogether inordinately squiggly the rubber worm had seemed to him, but Dick Atwater would not be engaged, hardly even stayed stopped long enough for Sleepy Pitts to lay apart his hands and show to him what length of bass exactly his squiggly worm had hooked, and as Dick Atwater turned abruptly and as Dick Atwater set to press on Sleepy Pitts shared with him a profoundly unpleasant manner of sentiment that Dick Atwater was himself fairly much the star of like Dick Atwater probably would in fact have deciphered but for the sweet breathy elevated tone of the thing.

They ducked on into the card emporium. Dick Atwater watched the two posteriors swing leftward and pass in profile through the glass doorway that still had the white paper Easter bunny dangling from it as Mrs. Sink who ran the store had gotten attached somehow to the paper bunny which wasn't but creased and baffled and puffed up with ears and teeth and eyes of cardboard along with an actual carrot that had been stapled and Scotchtaped and tied as well to the bunny's paw where maybe it had looked a little more succulent and carrotlike back around Easter when it had been in the first place stapled and Scotchtaped and tied too. Mrs. Sink sold all variety of cards for every possible occasion and sold cards even that weren't for anything in particular but just had flowers chiefly on the front and nothing on the inside and she carried tiny books in a rack about love, upholstered tiny books full of poems and gauzy pictures and she sold long elegant dinner candles and squat perfumy candles as well that did not even have to catch fire to stink. She had left over some plastic trolls with long silky hair from back when plastic trolls had been fairly much the rage but she didn't hardly move any trolls anymore and sold mostly instead little glass elves and little glass gnomes and the like painted to look real though with no silky hair to speak of. Trivets were a fairly big item and moved in a regular sort of way, most especially the tile ones with the flag on them and the president's face overtop it, and the wooden paper towel racks that stood upright on the countertop stayed usually bought up as well along with the Ladies' Garden Society wall calendar that had for every month a picture of some variety of leafy growth taken by Mr. Theodore Gill of Greensboro who'd been carried around by Mrs. Ira Penn and Mrs. Anna Victoria Hewitt-Sulley who had between them most especially preferred the shot of the rosebushes out at the sewage plant which had gotten cropped and enlarged and graced the calendar cover where it was rosebuds almost exclusively and not sewage plant but a trifle all blurred and fuzzy in the background.

Miss Bernice Fay Frazier was in some need of a squat perfumy candle for her mantelpiece like was part of how come she'd hauled her own posterior into the card shop in the first place but she wanted as well to display for Mrs. Sink Miss Mary Alice Celestine Lefler who'd come clean from elsewhere to be a comfort to her, so they passed up the squat perfumy candles there at the first and charged directly on back to the rear of the store where Mrs. Sink was attending to a manner of crisis in her sympathy card section as it seemed her deceased uncle cards had gotten somehow diluted with not just regular unrelated dead people cards but assorted vernal equinox cards as well that were supposed to be up front just shy of the Arbor Day cards but had moved and migrated somehow like Mrs. Sink could not puzzle out the cause for which she explained to Miss Bernice Fay Frazier was how come she was plain standing there at the dead uncle section sorting through her entire dead uncle display like was fairly solemn and grave up at the top of the rack but grew wry altogether on the descent and culminated at the rackbottom in your purely comical manner of items for uncles nobody gave a hoot in the first place about.

Mrs. Sink was of a mind that her vernal equinox cards had been relocated by ruffians and ne'er-do-wells on account of what boys she'd watched just poke roundabout, boys loose from school with nothing in the world to do but wreak havoc and such and Mrs. Sink waved what equinox cards she'd plucked from her dead uncle display so as to let on how it was havoc looked sometimes. Of course, while Miss Bernice Fay Frazier was as sorry and troubled as she could be on account of how the dead uncle cards had been diluted, she'd not dropped by truly to hear of it and consequently punctuated Mrs. Sink in that sweet breathy sort of way she could punctuate anymore, and she indicated whose posterior it was had joined her own one in the card shop and spoke ever so briefly of how come.

And Mrs. Sink said, "Ooohh," like was a habit with Mrs. Sink who was given to ooohhing and she slipped her eyeglasses down her noseridge and pondered Miss Mary Alice Celestine Lefler overtop of them while Miss Bernice Fay Frazier acquainted her with where precisely it was Miss Mary Alice Celestine Lefler had come from and why precisely it was she'd bothered in the first place to come from there and how pretty much she'd managed just in one night already to be a comfort and a blessing that Mrs. Sink could not hardly help but vent an ooohh about too.

For his part, Dick Atwater didn't think maybe they'd ever come out again except when he thought maybe they'd slipped out already and he'd not somehow seen them slip out even though he'd only looked at the doorway ever since they'd gone through it, or had pretty much entirely looked at the doorway anyhow but for when he'd looked at the fireplug briefly instead once he'd beaten it with his bony kneecap. He'd guessed he should hang back and so had hung back a ways, hung back so far as to seem to be maybe just lazing around, hung clean back at the shoeshop until the Privette that ran it stepped out onto the walk with a bootheel in his hand to speak to him and spit and whew and such when he'd excused himself and advanced so far as the Hair Lair that he guessed he could hang back in front of too. Debbie was giving Mrs. Phillip J. King a rinse in the chair by the window, not a regular rinse but a tinted inky sort of a rinse instead that was dripping and trickling down the side of Mrs. Phillip J. King's head like maybe she'd been dipped in a coffee urn, and naturally the sight of Mrs. Phillip J. King in the chair by the window with her hair fairly plastered to her skull and some manner of murky discharge leaking out from it captured and distracted Mr. Dick Atwater who'd not meant truly to lay his cupped hands to the windowglass and peer between them but could not seem to keep himself from it and so was looking fairly directly at Mrs. Phillip J. King once she got raised full up from the sink and swiveled round to where she could peer at Mr. Dick Atwater back like she did in fact peer at him an ever so scant while all by itself before she wailed and shrieked at him with it.

Of course he induced a flash in her that was a hot flash there at the first but straightaway fell and dropped off to a cold one in place of it, and as Mr. Dick Atwater had not truly seen a woman go flashy on him since Mrs. Dick Atwater had passed through her own personal spell of flashiness a considerable while back, he could not somehow draw off from the windowglass like he'd meant and intended to draw off from it but just stayed where he'd come to be, stayed where he'd gotten all taken and entranced and watched how the wet hair lay and the inky rinse dripped and the face flushed and then paled and then flushed again as Mrs. Phillip J. King warred with her hormones that were quite apparently kicking up an appreciable fuss. He just got plain fascinated and so gawked longer than was seemly, longer than was safe in fact too on account of Debbie who stepped out onto the walk so as to tell to Mr. Dick Atwater, "Shoo," and tell to Mr. Dick Atwater, "Get on from here," which wouldn't all by themselves have hardly budged him but got joined and augmented by the pointy handle end of Debbie's rattail comb that she jabbed Mr. Dick Atwater in the near haunch with.

"Shoo," she told to him another time but of course he could not shoo straightoff on account of how he had to leap first and lower his one cupped hand in particular to grab his affected haunch with and he could not shoo shortly even either due to how he had a Great Creeping Jesus to exclaim and a GodAlmighty to loose behind it, but he went on ahead and undertook to shoo there presently, spun around anyway and struck out only to see up the road at the card shop Miss Bernice Fay Frazier leaving with her squat perfumy candle in a sack and her too behind her with the tiny slip of a backside. Naturally, Mr. Dick Atwater spun back where he'd spun from in the first place so as not to get spied out but Debbie showed to him her pointy rattail combend in an ominous sort of a way and Mrs. Phillip J. King, who had recovered sufficiently to stand upright and walk and step even full out the doorway, commenced to explaining to him what ilk of creature he was exactly like she managed a little breathy there at the first, as she'd been after all elevated herself, but grew shrill about directly and so stood there on the sidewalk before the Hair Lair with her coif undone and her face streaky and a speckled plastic sheet dangling from her neck and screeched and hollered so at Mr. Dick Atwater as to mount and swell up to near about pure caterwaulian heights. So he spun around another time and saw how the posteriors were advancing together north away from him like allowed him to strike out and allowed him to flee up beyond the Hair Lair altogether and away from Debbie with her comb and Mrs. Phillip J. King with her hormones and past the real estate office and the Western Auto and Mrs. Sink's card emporium too where Mrs. Sink was herself at the rack by the door fishing out from her vernal equinox display assorted Negro anniversary cards with colored people on them like did not hardly have a thing in the world to do with the equinox at all and belonged, in fact, elsewhere altogether which was how come she plucked and collected them and waved them even at Mr. Dick Atwater so as to show him a little havoc on his way past the door.

They ducked in ever so briefly at the hardware store to tell Mr. Jack Eaton jr. Hey and looked in through the windowglass at the five-and-dime to see chiefly the notions that were located between the canvas rubbersoled shoes and the parakeets like Miss Bernice Fay Frazier figured Miss Mary Alice Celestine Lefler should know of as best as Mr. Dick Atwater could tell back of the barber pole where he'd undertaken to laze and loiter and look just shiftless primarily until the posteriors were towards him another time when he struck out himself. They passed the Baptist church and the Delmer C. Lloyd memorial building and pressed on across the sidestreet towards the Rexall that they entered into through the corner door and got followed shortly by Mr. Dick Atwater who guessed he could seem to be after a thing. Her and Miss Bernice Fay Frazier were not straightoff apparent to him on account of how they'd ventured up past the batteries and beyond the magazine rack and had advanced clean back to the pharmacy counter to speak to the pharmacist Mr. Donald Stone that Mr. Dick Atwater could not truly see but a piece of on account of Mrs. Ivy Jeeter Lynch who'd established a manner of encampment at the Russell Stover display and was hefting various of the boxed chocolates in an effort to discover the one box alone with not just tonnage to suit her but nutty turtles to suit her too as she was after mostly a two-pound box with near about half nutty turtles to it that she could not seem to find one of and so hollered out to Mr. Donald Stone's wife Lucinda back of the cosmetic counter if couldn't she tell to her please ma'm where the boxes with half nutty turtles to them might be as she hadn't found one yet that was more than a quarter nutty turtles altogether. So Mr. Donald Stone's wife Lucinda left the cosmetic counter for the Russell Stover display and said on her way to it Hey to Dick Atwater far louder entirely than he wished she'd said Hey to him as he did not want to seem to Miss Bernice Fay Frazier and her most especially with her to be lurking like he guessed he was in fact lurking after all and so determined to step around the magazine rack and make himself plain to them since he did not figure he could lurk and be plain all at the same time.

He was of a mind to charge on back to the pharmacy counter himself to hunt a thing once maybe he'd exclaimed just out in a general sort of way what an awful puny world it was after all, and he set to charging a little but loitered a bit along about the ointments before he managed to bring himself to press on back to the pharmacy counter proper and he made out to be studying the bunion pads briefly before he made out instead to be spying just up and of a sudden Miss Bernice Fay Frazier and her both together that he let out a little whoop about prior to observing with his voice fairly squeaky from wonderment how the world seemed sometimes to him such an awful puny place that her who he'd said it for mostly showed him some teeth on account of while Miss Bernice Fay Frazier, who grew a little toothsome herself, declared how sometimes the world was too awful puny to suit her that Mr. Dick Atwater vented an agreeable noise in back of as he'd determined previously already how once she'd gotten done he'd go on and vent an agreeable noise.

Miss Bernice Fay Frazier was hunting a sciatic pill and was not truly getting much help at it from the pharmacist Mr. Donald Stone that was partial himself to Ben-Gay deep heating rub which he'd gone off and fetched a tube of for Miss Bernice Fay Frazier who guessed if she'd wanted Ben-Gay she'd have gone off and fetched it herself. She was looking for a pill. She didn't have any use for an ointment. Her sciatic nerve was snug up to her legbone and surely wouldn't be much affected by even a deep heating rub that the pharmacist Mr. Donald Stone disputed as he guessed he would after all know a thing about sciatic nerves that Miss Bernice Fay Frazier went on ahead and disputed back.

Mr. Dick Atwater had grown fairly toothy himself and had thought to settle his hands to his hips and lay wide his jacketflaps but had not determined what exactly he'd speak of after the puny world and so did not speak of anything until he got moved to wonder at Miss Mary Alice Celestine Lefler how it was she found their fair city and he lifted a finger and jabbed it at the underside of his hatbrim like he'd seen men jab hatbrims previously though with maybe less force and velocity than he'd managed somehow to manufacture as his own fedora slipped and rode back so appreciably far on his head that he had to snatch and grab and jab another time at it just to keep it off the linoleum like drained and diminished the effect truly since hatjabbing seemed to him a singular sort of a thing that was best done one time alone. As far as Miss Mary Alice Celestine Lefler could tell she liked their fair city well enough though she'd not but walked a little ways through it that Dick Atwater told to her, "Oh?" on account of like he'd anticipated he might have occasion to tell Oh? to her, and he let on how fortunate he was himself to have a Toronado and how fortunate he was himself to have the wherewithal to drive it and guide it round and how fairly completely delighted he'd be to guide and drive it round too with her and him both in it and so show her every manner of thing she couldn't hardly walk to see that Miss Mary Alice Celestine Lefler let on to him back would be purely rapturous, or grew anyhow moderately eeky after what fashion seemed chiefly rapturous to him and then reached out and laid her fingerends to his forearm like left him fairly tingly even through his jacket and through his shirt and agitated and distracted him so that he did not hear her say to him sweetly, "Why Jerome, I'd be delighted," until him and Miss Bernice Fay Frazier together had asked her what it was precisely she'd said when she told it all over again.

Now of course Miss Bernice Fay Frazier had not imported Miss Mary Alice Celestine Lefler clean from West Virginia to be a comfort and a blessing to anybody but herself and so she displayed at Mr. Dick Atwater her best withering sidelong look like Dick Atwater might usually have been a little moved and impressed by but for how he'd come already to be tingly and so just grinned at Miss Bernice Fay Frazier back prior to shifting about and grinning a spell at Miss Mary Alice Celestine Lefler instead. Mr. Donald Stone had hunted up for Miss Bernice Fay Frazier some Doan's pills in the little vial that he guessed she could go on and take if wouldn't but a pill suit though he didn't know that Doan's pills would much soothe her sciatic nerve like she said she'd surely inform him about as she snatched the little vial of pills from him and set out for the front register, and Mr. Donald Stone wanted to know of Mr. Dick Atwater if he'd come after any particular item that Dick Atwater admitted in fact he had and reached out to lift a box from a rack before departing for the front register himself with her that escorted him down the digestive tract aisle and around the magazines and past Lucinda Stone and Ivy Jeeter Lynch at the Russell Stover display and up alongside Miss Bernice Fay Frazier at the front register where Mr. Donald Stone's brother's girl Julie Anne was speaking of what precisely Doan's pills had done one time for her daddy who'd wrenched himself lifting a coal scuttle. And they made arrangements between them, Dick Atwater and Mary Alice Celestine Lefler did, or he said anyhow he'd come sometime and she said anyhow he could while Miss Bernice Fay Frazier who was having her pills sacked aired out once more her withering glance that she spent chiefly on Mr. Dick Atwater himself but spent partly on the box Mr. Dick Atwater laid atop the counter before Julie Anne, the box that wasn't hardly much bigger than a soapbar and had a picture on the front of it of a man and woman walking all snug and clingy together along a beach in the orangy twilight.

It was a twelve-pack, the natural skin twelve-pack with the patented bumpy spots like were meant to be orgasmic. Mr. Dick Atwater had selected the pastel colors, or had selected anyhow the colors that were chiefly pastel except for the midnight black one that did not have much pastel to it and except for the striped one as well that was green striped somewhat and red striped somewhat and looked on the boxend like a manner of Italian flag, or more truly like a manner of Italian flagpole that Julie Anne saw on the boxend it did and that Miss Bernice Fay Frazier, with her withering sidelong look, took in as well just prior to snorting her "Good day" to Mr. Dick Atwater and hauling Miss Mary Alice Celestine Lefler on out the Rexall like left Dick Atwater to watch Julie Anne turn around the box to the back panel and to the far end panel and to the front panel another time and then raise it high up over her head and call out the length of the store to her uncle Mr. Donald Stone back of the pharmacy counter, "Price check."

And Mr. Donald Stone yelled to her, "What is it?"

"This here," she told him.

"What?" he said and made to squint at her.

And Julie Anne drew off a fairly hardy breath and informed her uncle how they were your natural skin Regency brand items in your princely size with the patented orgasmic bumps in your individually lubricated packets.

"Plain?" Mr. Donald Stone wanted to know.

"Pastel," she told to him and explained about the black one and explained about the striped one too like stopped the candy boxes from shaking and caused Mrs. Lucinda Stone and Ivy Jeeter Lynch to raise entirely up together and pull at Mr. Dick Atwater fairly extraordinary faces that they displayed every now and again for each other as well while Mr. Donald Stone, who was checking the price, asked to find out had it been ridges or had it been bumps as he couldn't recollect which he'd been told it was.

"Patented," Julie Anne hollered to him, "orgasmic bumps," and directly she heard from Mr. Donald Stone the price back that she rang up on the register and announced without looking much at him to Mr. Dick Atwater who was meaning to tell how he'd thought it was a bunion sort of a thing, who was meaning to tell how he'd figured it for an item otherwise entirely but Julie Anne just stuck out her hand and looked at her hand she'd stuck out like there were things maybe she didn't need to hear of, like there were things maybe she didn't so much as care to think on at all.

ii. HE'D almost squashed Stumpy Tate. According to Stumpy Tate anyhow he'd almost squashed him and would have likely squashed him too if Stumpy Tate hadn't leapt clear once he'd hooted already and whistled and called Nestor! three times as loud as he could call it like he figured he'd get heard at which he inquired of Harold Lister wouldn't he figure as well he'd have gotten heard at it, but Harold Lister went on ahead and just wished he'd gotten squashed as he didn't hardly have much use for Stumpy Tate and wouldn't have been so awful distraught if squashed was what he'd gotten like inspired Stumpy Tate to admit straightoff of even less use himself for Harold Lister whose nappy head he threatened to bust and crack open with just his bare naked hands that Harold Lister indulged in some chortling on account of and came shortly to be told by Stumpy Tate a wildly profane manner of thing. Nestor Tudor, who had in fact presently guessed he'd squashed something, climbed down from the cab and circled round to the back of the truck where he found Stumpy Tate's shovel handle sticking out from under the lefthand mudflap and found Stumpy Tate showing to Harold Lister five of his knuckles that Harold Lister seemed to Nestor Tudor inordinately diverted by.

And Stumpy Tate said to Nestor Tudor, "Can't you hear nothing?" and Stumpy Tate said to Harold Lister who'd gotten altogether too jolly to suit him, "Shut up," and Stumpy Tate said to Nestor Tudor, "Can't you hear nothing at all?" that Nestor Tudor just looked a little fretful about like he'd arrived looking at the top of the day and had not somehow given over to any way of looking otherwise even in the face of what Stumpy Tate informed him they'd just about together been in the face of but for how he'd leapt and jumped and sprung like he did sideways that Harold Lister wished he hadn't much bothered about and so got shown more knuckles that were some of them the same knuckles he'd been shown already and that were some of them other knuckles entirely.

They were filling a hole back of the bottling plant where the trucks left the yard and bounced anymore in it so that they broke sometimes their Sundrops and broke sometimes their Dr Peppers. They'd started the morning filling another hole west out 158 along about Monroeton where Stumpy Tate had gotten put upon to hoot and whistle and leap as well when Nestor Tudor had rolled this time forwards and near about dispatched him like Stumpy Tate had become already a little ill about which he'd seemed at the Tastee-Freez to recover from, but seeing his shovel crushed and run over and sticking pretty forlornly out from between the tandem wheels affected him all over again and so he swore and ranted and snorted a little as well like he probably would have persisted a spell at but for the silvery Cutlass that came at them out of the north and eased on by the hole and by the truck and by Harold Lister and Nestor Tudor and Stumpy Tate too who all entertained from it some upraised fingers on the hand of an actual verifiable woman like set Stumpy Tate off, like caused Stumpy Tate to shout and wail, "Beaver!" and draw on her a bead with his foremost finger that he fired and discharged, or made anyhow to recoil once he'd shouted, "Bang," like Nestor Tudor had suggested previously to him did not probably flatter and enchant most women after the fashion Stumpy Tate seemed convinced maybe it did.

Of course, the trouble for Nestor Tudor was her, or the trouble partly was her who Nestor Tudor tried to shut his eyes and call up and did in fact call up a little but did not call up awful much truly except for her shoes with the leathery bows and her dress with the speckles and her neck dimple down along about her collar with the veins either side of it that had seemed to him as graceful and shallow a neck dimple as he'd had lately the pleasure to watch. But he could not call up much of her otherwise, not even with his eyes shut and his face all squinty and his whole self a little hunkered and set low like was usually Nestor Tudor's best posture for calling up. He got chiefly for his trouble Dick Atwater instead, Dick Atwater from the hairpart down, or not just Dick Atwater truly from the hairpart down as there was anymore so appreciably much of Dick Atwater above the hairpart too like he got a little of as well. So naturally Nestor Tudor was fretful and Nestor Tudor was distracted and Nestor Tudor was a trifle acidic too an account of most every time he hunkered his stomach boiled and his tubes burned and he tasted in the back of his mouth what he'd taken when he ate them for gizzards though they'd not in fact seemed much in the way of gizzardly to him like when he hunkered they didn't still, and he wondered why he'd eaten them and he wondered what they were and he tried to recall her plain but couldn't and tried not to see Dick Atwater but did and made when he wasn't squinting and hunkering low to look just regular and ordinary that even Stumpy Tate, with all the native intuition of a treeroot, took for forlorn.

He didn't have call to want her. He didn't have call to need her at all like he'd not since Mrs. Nestor Tudor got lowered into the ground and covered over had much use for a woman though he'd been that one time a little captivated by the Draper Meecham that he'd carried to Danville for supper where he'd come to be over the chicken cutlets a little uncaptivated instead for no reason in particular as best as he could tell like he'd undertaken to explain to the Draper Meecham who'd hoped he'd stay captivated, who'd wished he'd linger a time wholly entranced and had grown pained at how he didn't, how he plain somehow could not like she'd guessed was a thing she'd done or a thing she'd said or a thing he'd thought she was that over the cutlets he'd figured out she wasn't after all like he told her it wasn't, assured her it hadn't been and explained that he didn't know why and couldn't say how come which the Meecham resisted and the Meecham defied as she'd never suspected uncaptivated was a thing people just up and got. So he did not go out again for supper any time shortly and stayed home evenings in his springy metal chair smoking his Old Gold filters and drinking his Ancient Age and watching the light fade like he probably would have remained a while uninterrupted at since he was not much of a mood to get recaptivated, had gained from the Draper Meecham a lesson on captivation truly and longed not to get caught up and entangled after the fashion he inadvertently had gotten shortly caught up and entangled both with the widow Mrs. MaySue Ludley whom he'd saved and rescued or whom he thought he was rescuing until he found how he wasn't when she went on ahead and began to believe he had like she felt obliged to be to him indebted about, indebted in fact in an altogether acute sort of a way.

Mrs. MaySue Ludley had gotten at the time only just lately bereaved, had mere months previously lost Mr. W. O. Ludley to a lingering affliction like she'd dropped off into a funk about though not a deep murky funk truly but a seemly sort of a funk anyway like appeared fairly ripe with sadness and woe. So people roundabout tended to her and sat with her and had her in and took her out and did not leave her much all alone to grow desperate and weepy, most especially the midget Miss Mottsinger who spent some considerable time with Mrs. MaySue Ludley, appreciably more time anyway than she'd spent with her ever before as Mr. W. O. Ludley had not much approved of midgets, had found them altogether too scant to suit him. She was in fact tiny all over, hadn't ever grown big anywhere and wore little frilly girl's dresses from the Hudson-Belk and little shiny girl's shoes with straps and buckles and carried usually a regular ladies' pocketbook that hung from her shoulder like a mailpouch. She drove a Bonneville, a green Bonneville that had been her momma's back when her momma drove and was not truly the sort of vehicle to have been manufactured with midgets in mind, was a little outsized for even regular people and handled like a frigate though Mrs. Mottsinger managed it well enough as she'd gotten her pedals extended and had gotten her seat upraised, or had gotten anyhow her own posterior lifted with the phonebook from Winston-Salem and both the A and the S encyclopedias from her 1963 World Book set along with the Sears and Roebuck spring catalog that she tended to replace yearly on account of the impression her backside most times made on it. Consequently, then, she could get around well enough in her momma's green Bonneville and took to carting Mrs. MaySue Ludley with her once Mrs. MaySue Ludley had come to be bereaved.

Of course they probably would have both just ridden around in the Bonneville together and not had occasion to be saved and rescued like they presently did but for Mrs. Russell Newberry who took from her husband a notion that the midget Miss Mottsinger got made to be party to. Mr. Russell Newberry was just at the time shy of a birthday and Mrs. Russell Newberry, for once alone, had an idea of what precisely he might care to receive due to how Mr. Russell Newberry, in a moment of mechanical despair over the blade flange on his Lawn Boy, had wished he owned a deep well socket set, had wished it in fact in the presence of Mrs. Russell Newberry who troubled herself to make a note. Straightaway she figured that Sears and Roebuck were likely the ones to carry a deep well socket set if anybody might and she set to hunting the catalog that she'd used previously to squash and assassinate a sizeable spider down in the basement alongside the oil burner, a spider she'd tossed the thing upon from the bottom step and had not bothered somehow to take it up like she failed to recall she hadn't. So she borrowed a catalog instead, borrowed the midget Miss Mottsinger's spring catalog, removed it out from under her on the occasion of a bridge luncheon at Mrs. Russell Newberry's house where the midget Miss Mottsinger had volunteered her spring catalog insisting she could make do a time well enough with just her phonebook and her encyclopedias to raise her, figured she could get along unuplifted for a spell until Mrs. Russell Newberry had called in her order and returned the catalog to her like Mrs. Russell Newberry for several days thereafter full well intended to do but neglected somehow and so left the midget Miss Mottsinger utterly catalogless and she peered and craned and perched as best she could until she came to be by Nestor Tudor interrupted at it.

Her and the widow Mrs. MaySue Ludley, only lately bereaved, had arranged to take lunch together at the Holiday Inn buffet on the bypass where they were both especially partial to the pepper steak and the fried okra and the spoonbread that was evermore moist and gummy after the fashion they couldn't either one of them seem to get their own spoonbread to be. Following lunch they intended to ride together out past Bethel and shy of Purley to where the midget Miss Mottsinger's momma's sister lived in a home with other people that had become like her fairly well dilapidated and had to be seen after and had to be tended to like was pitiful that Mrs. MaySue Ludley and the midget Miss Mottsinger agreed over the buffet it was but they guessed it was probably just precisely the variety of circumstance that couldn't be much helped either which prompted from Mrs. MaySue Ludley the observation that pitiful things by and large couldn't be much helped that the midget Miss Mottsinger mined some appreciable truth from which she told to Mrs. MaySue Ludley she had like Mrs. MaySue Ludley was pleased to know of since she'd not, ever since Mr. W. O. Ludley passed on, had anybody much roundabout to edify and enlighten like was presently seeming to her a little beyond help itself.

The midget Miss Mottsinger's momma's sister maintained usually a manner of yen for peanut butter cups, so they carried a sack of the tiny ones to her and Mrs. MaySue Ludley sat in the straight chair alongside the nightstand and the midget Miss Mottsinger sat on the bed with her legs dangling while her momma's sister inquired who she might be and got told by the midget Miss Mottsinger how she was in fact her own sister's child that the midget Miss Mottsinger's aunt begged to differ with her about since she'd not, as best as she could recollect, ever been blessed with a sister but had gotten a biddy hen one time at Easter that had presently turned out to be a goose, a wild vicious variety of goose in fact that had bit, she insisted, her foremost finger clean off, and she held up a foremost finger that did not look especially shorn away and told to Mrs. MaySue Ludley in particular, "See there," that Mrs. MaySue Ludley assured her from the straight chair she did.

The midget Miss Mottsinger's momma's sister ate from her sack of peanut butter cups all by herself there at the first until the midget Miss Mottsinger noticed from the foot of the bed how her aunt was not hardly troubling herself to peel off the crinkly paper when the midget Miss Mottsinger took the sack from her and so suffered a spell of her momma's sister's ire but not a lengthy spell truly since her momma's sister forgot shortly what she'd worked up her ire in the first place about. They offered to roll her outside in her wheelchair as it was, Mrs. MaySue Ludley informed her, a splendid afternoon but she was not much inclined to be rolled there at the first and stayed pretty completely uninclined altogether until she just up and decided how she was of a sudden inclined instead and wondered why they hadn't rolled her already. So they called on a nurse to load her and strap her in and they pushed her out back of the home onto the cement patio that was scattered about with patients otherwise who sat mostly with their heads a little laid over and told things just out into the air.

The patio and the scrawny flowerbed beyond it butted fairly flush up onto a field cultivated partly with soybeans and partly with tobacco and bordered on the far side by a half dozen bulk barns that the midget Miss Mottsinger's momma's sister insisted they all got carried to at night and shut up in like the midget Miss Mottsinger doubted straightaway though her momma's sister assured her they did and let on to her all low and sideways how as squat and puny as she was they'd probably plug her up in an oil drum and not think a thing of it like Mrs. MaySue Ludley could not hardly believe was what she'd deciphered once she deciphered it, and her and the midget Miss Mottsinger showed to each other their woeful faces and shared between them the news that they weren't hardly at all looking forward to getting decrepit like inspired the midget Miss Mottsinger's momma's sister to announce to them how she wasn't much looking forward to getting decrepit herself. "Dread the day," she told to them. "Dread it."

They didn't stay for supper as they were not of a mood for fruit cocktail and white bread and boiled chicken and as they'd only lately eaten from the buffet anyway, and they climbed together into the midget Miss Mottsinger's Bonneville and passed a prayerful few minutes venting what gratitude they could muster for their own personal uneroded faculties that they hadn't either one of them been prayerful lately about. Since her and the midget Miss Mottsinger had come to be close and had come to be friendly, the widow Mrs. MaySue Ludley wondered wouldn't she draw out a gun and shoot her like a dog if she saw her commence to lapse and fade that the midget Miss Mottsinger agreed straightoff she would as long as the widow Mrs. MaySue Ludley could see clear to draw out a gun and dispatch her too once her gears, she told it, went and together they swore a pact and took up each other by the fingers and looked a little moistly at each other in the face and then pondered together the antique manner of the gentleman who'd stepped out from the foyer onto the front landing in just his pajama top chiefly and his black wingtip shoes like did not somehow together render him decent and presentable which Mrs. MaySue Ludley and the midget Miss Mottsinger both seemed set to exclaim a little about when a stout colored nurse stepped out from the foyer herself and took him up at the elbow by which she induced him and his pajama top and his wingtip shoes and his wholly exposed and ventilated organ to wheel round and withdraw from the afternoon.

Now down off the lot and across the road Nestor Tudor was at pretty much that very moment studying a stretch of pavement that had heaved up and fairly completely busted open due to how the Watt boy that cultivated the field across from the nursing home had disced and plowed clean out to the roadedge thereby pretty entirely undoing the ditch and loosing the dirt to wash and shift out from under the asphalt like might have promoted some heaving and some busting open which Stumpy Tate could not much himself hold with as it seemed to him water had likely seeped instead and froze up what way would cause some heaving and some busting open itself that Nestor Tudor did not dispute it could though he was partial to the discing and the plowing like he wondered wasn't Harold Lister a little partial to as well that Harold Lister assured him he was since he couldn't hardly bring himself to be partial with Stumpy Tate instead. So they were all three eyeing the piece of the road that had cracked and heaved up when the midget Miss Mottsinger started her Bonneville and eased it back prior to nosing it down towards the street, nosing it ever so slowly there at the first that Nestor Tudor lifted up his head and watched the Bonneville briefly at before dropping it again to where the asphalt had split and laid wide that he'd studied only scantly and barely at all when he found himself compelled to raise up his head and look another time at the Bonneville easing towards him with the woman on the glovebox side of it, the woman with her mouth laid open like suggested to Nestor Tudor woe and dread most especially once he'd eyed the steering column side as well where he did not see any manner of creature truly, nothing anyhow but for a tiny lump that did not look from across the road and through the windowglass like a hairbun to him.

Naturally he yipped and exclaimed, could not help but yip and exclaim both once he'd grown of a sudden convinced how the woman on the glovebox side of the Bonneville had come to drop her chin and lay her mouth full open likely on account of the near about altogether vacant steering column side next to her with just the tiny lump in it that did not still hardly appear to Nestor Tudor a hairbun and did not come to appear a hairbun to him even after he'd struck out across the highway at what he intended for a dead run though he no longer possessed truly a dead run sort of physique and so bolted ever so hardly at all and lumbered chiefly while he beat his arms as best as he was able to maybe imply to the glovebox side woman how he meant to save and see to her.

And he did with his arms that he beat and his legs that he lumbered on imply a thing to the widow Mrs. MaySue Ludley who left off speaking of her own personal momma's sister who'd lately expired to inquire of the midget Miss Mottsinger, "Who is that?" that the midget Miss Mottsinger would probably have informed her about if it hadn't been but her phonebook and encyclopedias between her backside and the seatcushion like left her to see a strip of sky and a portion of upholstered dash and the whole entire odometer but not much roadway to speak of, not anyhow the piece of roadway Mr. Nestor Tudor was just presently lumbering across.

And the midget Miss Mottsinger wanted to know, "Who?"

"Him," Mrs. MaySue Ludley told to her, "there," and dropped her mouth open further still like seemed from the asphalt increasingly woeful and dreadful both.

Of course Nestor Tudor hadn't quite figured what he'd do with the Pontiac once he'd arrived at it, hadn't quite reasoned precisely how he might stop the thing and found how he was not hardly able at sort of a dead run to reason much at all like he decided later when he'd had the leisure for it was probably on account of his gray brain matter that he could not run with and oxygenate all at the same time, so the farther he ran the more feebleminded he came to be until he arrived at last at the far edge of the roadway where he was pretty completely idiotic which he guessed, when later he'd had the leisure to guess it, was why it did not seem much in the way of peculiar to him that a runaway driverless Bonneville Pontiac with just a tiny lump on the steering column side of it that still did not look a hairbun to him could swing west out the nursing home drive and accelerate even up the highway which if he'd not become unoxygenated and idiotic would have probably caused him to pull up and caused him to ponder.

So he leapt anyhow, or truly he endeavored to leap and even left the ground a little but did not stay awful long gone from it and likely would have missed the Bonneville entirely if he'd not managed to catch his fingers on the rear doorhandle like inspired him to travel west a ways himself at an actual verifiable dead run there straightaway but shortly caused him to travel all still and breathless atop the trunklid instead once he'd been flung onto it, and the widow Mrs. MaySue Ludley turned around a little before the glovebox and inquired of the midget Miss Mottsinger, "Who is that?" that the midget Miss Mottsinger looked behind herself at the vinyl upholstery about prior to wondering, "Where?" at the widow Mrs. MaySue Ludley back.

He guessed he'd climb up the backwindow to the roof and crawl the length of it and on down the frontwindow to the carhood where he figured the thing he'd do next would come to him as he was still even atop the trunklid quasi-idiotic and so did not yet notice how the Bonneville was traveling at a fairly steady speed along an altogether flat stretch of highway like most times would have probably suggested to Nestor Tudor eight cylinders full well combusted and a wheel all steered and held to had his gray matter been wholly aerated, but he was focusing the bulk of his feeble mind on climbing the backwindow that he edged up the width of and so gained the roof that he eased on his hands and knees across like even the midget Miss Mottsinger from down back of the dashboard heard him at and so felt herself moved to look roofwards as best she could and inquire, "Who is that?" of the widow Mrs. MaySue Ludley that told to her, "Him," and looked a little roofwards herself.

They meant to shriek, they both meant to shriek together once the hand plopped down on the windshield before them but they did not have time to shriek truly before the rest of Nestor Tudor slid across the windowglass and onto the hood and near about off of the hood as well but for the wiper arm that Nestor Tudor managed to hook his fingers around and hold to ever so barely at all like he was right there in the midst of congratulating himself about when he noticed through the windshield how the tiny lump he'd taken from the outset for a nameless impertinent brand of tiny lump was in fact an actual hairbun all swirled up and situated on the back of an actual head with some eyes to it and a nose to it and a mouth to it as well that told to him, "What in this world are you doing?" like Nestor Tudor would probably have been pleased to speak of and maybe would have in fact spoken of even had not the midget Miss Mottsinger found how, without her catalog from the Sears and Roebuck, she could stomp the brake harder altogether than she'd ever previously been able to stomp it.

So of course he departed from the carhood pretty straightaway, less straightaway than maybe he would have if he'd not felt inclined to take the wiper arm with him, but he departed nonetheless and traveled all by himself up the road a stretch just in the air there at the first but presently atop the pavement too, chiefly atop the pavement in fact like would be backwards a little and sideways a little as well until he came at last to a kind of a sliding stop and just laid still on the asphalt where his brain began to get reoxygenated and so gradually revealed to him what variety of idiocy precisely he'd lately engaged in. They hoped from the Bonneville he wasn't dead. The widow Mrs. MaySue Ludley hoped anyhow from the Bonneville he wasn't dead and encouraged the midget Miss Mottsinger to hope from it the same thing herself like she was reluctant about but managed to hope presently he was only maybe gravely injured since it seemed to her a man that rode unsolicited on her carhood needed to get at least gravely injured for it so as not to be led to believe he could just up and ride carhoods with impunity. She softened considerably, however, once they'd climbed out from the Bonneville and proceeded to the spot up the highway Nestor Tudor had flown and skidded to where he'd undertaken to sit upright and had in fact sat upright ever so hardly at all but had shortly retreated from it, had plain lain altogether back down as he could not with his freshly oxygenated gray matter discover much advantage in sitting even partly upright.

The midget Miss Mottsinger wondered was Nestor Tudor pleased with himself that Nestor Tudor, stretched full out on his backside atop the highway with just trifling elbow and kneecap skin left to him, employed briefly his gray matter about prior to assuring the midget Miss Mottsinger how he was not presently so taken with himself as on occasions previously he'd come to be like the midget Miss Mottsinger confessed to him she was hardly much surprised to hear of. Nestor Tudor, who did not wish to be impolite, told to Mrs. MaySue Ludley, "Ma'm," or told anyhow her underclothes Ma'm chiefly as she'd come to stand almost overtop him and showed to him her fretful expression except for when the breeze freshened and moved her billowy skirt after such a fashion as to reveal to him her rubberized corset and her pantyhose that it seemed to Nestor Tudor, from his backside upon the asphalt, the breeze was doing too awful much of, and she was anxious to know was he in terrible pain and squatted to find it out and touched even with her fingerend a skinned place like prompted truly a spell of terrible pain that he went on ahead and confessed he was presently in.

Being a reasonable woman, the midget Miss Mottsinger supposed at Nestor Tudor he'd been pressed some way to leap upon her Bonneville and crawl the length of it prior to getting discharged overtop the hood ornament, and she took up off from the roadway her wiper arm that her and that Nestor Tudor smiled a little sickly at each other about. Now of course he had been pressed after a fashion and meant to explain to the midget Miss Mottsinger why he'd arrived at what place he'd shortly gotten discharged from but with the jolt he'd taken lately and the skin he'd given up and the underclothes he had shown to him every now and again he could not straightoff focus his gray matter well enough to serve him in an explanatory sort of a way. Presently, though, he managed in fact to speak of how he'd stood there at the roadedge and watched the Bonneville nose and roll what way he'd thought it was loose at somehow though he could not say all skinned and jolted atop the asphalt why precisely he'd taken it for loose except to tell how the tiny lump had not seemed a hairbun to him.

And the midget Miss Mottsinger inquired, "Tiny lump?" and reached up her fingers to touch her hairbun with.

"Yes ma'm," Nestor Tudor told at the underclothes chiefly. "Tiny lump all by itself."

So she got some manner of grip on it, the midget Miss Mottsinger did, and set to explaining to Nestor Tudor what manner of grip precisely she'd gotten and she explained as well to Mrs. MaySue Ludley where it was Nestor Tudor had stood and how it was they'd together rolled at him and what thing precisely he'd seen the bulk of and what thing precisely he hadn't like Mrs. MaySue Ludley had just lately left off hearing from him herself, him that she'd pressed her skirt flat to watch and ponder, him that had seen her in peril and had run and leapt and crawled and slid and flown and, ultimately, skidded on account of it, him that had saved and had rescued her like she mashed her skirt and dropped her head about so as to study sweetly Nestor Tudor who failed straightoff from his back atop the asphalt to decipher in her expression how gravity was not anymore the primary force at work.

And she told to him, "Bless you, Nestor Tudor," and reached down to the roadway to help to raise and right him and did manage to set him on his feet from where he bent and touched his knees through his ripped twill trousers and so induced with his own fingerends some genuine anguishment. He walked even, didn't walk awfully well, but walked nonetheless back down the stretch of road he'd pretty completely sailed above to the midget Miss Mottsinger's Bonneville that he buffed the hood of with his pocket rag most especially where he figured his feet had laid that the midget Miss Mottsinger undertook to thank him about but got prevented from it by the widow Mrs. MaySue Ludley who fairly exuded appreciation and grabbed Nestor Tudor another time on a skinned place like Nestor Tudor made at Mrs. MaySue Ludley a toothsome expression about. He opened the doors for the ladies and entertained from them some fingers that beat the air as they left and departed and then he walked back alone to where he wished he'd never left from, back to the truck and the heaved pavement and Harold Lister and Stumpy Tate both that he raised up his head and looked for but didn't directly see, or saw truly but did not make out due to how they'd come some way to lay together on their backs along the roadside with their legs poking into the air like fenceposts, and they seemed the both of them to twitch and seemed the both of them to jiggle and made together wheezy noises which they persevered at until he'd arrived full up on them when Stumpy Tate and Harold Lister endeavored together to stand upright and did even stand a little upright briefly prior to pointing and prior to squinting and prior to squirting together appreciable breath as a preface to falling back over entirely and laying all jolly on the roadside.

She called him almost straightaway, not exactly the day he'd saved and rescued her but certainly the day beyond it when she rang up to find out had his weepy wounds scabbed and closed over like she let on to him she'd prayed personally to the Savior about. Two nights following she called again so as to remind him how he was much in her thoughts and reveries that she took him to be ever so grateful to hear of on account of the variety of noise he made over the phone line at her back that seemed to her in the course of the following afternoon to have been ripe with longing like was pretty much why she felt sufficiently emboldened to call him that very evening as well and inquire might he join her for a dinner party. Now Nestor Tudor, who most usually fried a cube steak once he'd tenderized it with a platerim, was attracted to the notion of a dinner party since it implied to him a legitimate and verifiable dinner in the company of assorted people which Mrs. MaySue Ludley could not possibly be but one of like was part of why exactly he told to Mrs. MaySue Ludley yes fairly directly, yes just all by itself like a man could not hardly begin to say no just all by itself which was the rest of why he'd gone ahead and said yes instead.

She wanted him for Friday evening at six-thirty and, consequently, he troubled himself come Friday afternoon to poke about in his clothes-closet and hunt up an ensemble. He guessed he'd wear his shirt with the horseheads on it, the purple horseheads that had been blue horseheads there at the outset before they met up in his washer with his red bandana that had rendered them purple instead. He meant to wear with it his brown trousers that appeared on the wire hanger to suit the horseheads well enough, but he found once he'd stuck his feet in the legholes and had endeavored to draw the things up that his brown trousers had come to be snug somehow, had in fact come to be too awful snug to button shut, or actually too awful snug to button shut the sort of way Nestor Tudor had to figure trousers were meant to button like would be without the breathholding and without the stomachsucking and the moderate leaping about which somehow in conjunction induced his button to in fact shut ever so briefly before it departed instead from his trousers entirely and beat against the far wall prior to dropping behind the bedstead to the floor.

He tried a pair of his green twill highway department trousers with his shirt with the horseheads on it, but the purple and the green did not appear to him to blend and to harmonize and did a thing together to his pupils which he failed to find soothing truly in a sartorial kind of a way, so he brought out from his closet his black suit pants that he'd lately carried to the laundry in town to get loosened and expanded since he could not afford for his black suit pants to grip and cling to him as people evermore sickened and died like called for black suit pants after a regular fashion. They complimented the horseheads well enough as best as he could tell and with his black suitcoat, that he'd not truly intended to wear but just took up since it was handy and put on, he looked near about as sharp and dashing as he guessed he'd lately managed to look, most especially sideways with his head swung around and his chin dropped low and his eyes a little shut and squinty like rendered him, he figured, moderately suave though he could not truly with his lids dropped low see how he'd been rendered precisely. Of course he figured he was getting suave and dashing for not just Mrs. MaySue Ludley alone but a gang of people otherwise as well like would have probably the midget Miss Mottsinger among them who'd tell her runaway tiny hairlump story on him that he practiced before the vanity being graceful about and made like to listen all sideways and squinty and made like to be quite thoroughly amused.

Although he aimed for half past, had calculated his route with arriving at half past in mind, he showed up closer to quarter past truly but did not knock there at the first near so hard as he'd intended like left him to beat another time on Mrs. MaySue Ludley's screendoor frame that Mrs. MaySue Ludley hooted at him on account of from partway down the backhall upon the commode that she'd calculated she'd have the leisure to settle briefly onto like it didn't seem to her she ever had the leisure to do once she'd already calculated she did. So Nestor Tudor hollered back as best he could suave and manly both how it was him Nestor Tudor that had arrived and was standing just presently on the front porch shy of the screendoor like was what he'd knocked in the first place about that he waited for a hoot on account of but got from the dining room just some inarticulate screeching instead that Zippy Mrs. MaySue Ludley's yellow bird with the leathery feet was partial to in place of singing and trilling and whistling and such.

And she said to him, "Nestor," before she'd even gotten out of the bathroom good and partway up the backhall, and maybe it would have struck him as inordinately low and treacly if she hadn't been scurrying like she was to lift the screenhook and so let him into the front room where just him and just her told to each other Hey alone though Nestor Tudor looked round for so much as a hairlump to say Hey at as well.

She admired his shirt almost straightaway, confessed how she'd evermore been partial to horseheads and had worked up suddenly a passion for his own horseheads in particular that she called to him, "Violet," and stepped briefly back to look on and hum about prior to taking up Nestor Tudor by an armjoint and studying most acutely his horseheads and his suitcoat in combination that she let on seemed swanky to her. She recollected how she'd not in fact seen such a swanky ensemble since Mr. W. O. Ludley wore that last July his stretchy pants with the maroon check and the navy shirt with the piping and the white belt with the gold buckle and the shiny white lace-up shoes too like had been, she figured, the pure picture of swank that Nestor Tudor bet at Mrs. MaySue Ludley it was though he could not truly fashion Mr. W. O. Ludley with any manner of swank roundabout him, Mr. W. O. Ludley who'd generally worn his trousers raised and hiked so that he likely had to lower his fly to roll on his deodorant.

"Swanky I bet," Nestor Tudor said and hummed briefly in his neck at Mrs. MaySue Ludley who squeezed him again at his armjoint and confirmed for him how it hadn't truly been hardly anything else but.

He figured everybody otherwise was back of the house maybe on the patio but for the one of them in the dining room that was cooing and screeching and scratching in what seemed to Nestor Tudor a midgety sort of a way until he'd loosed himself from Mrs. MaySue Ludley and stepped on across the parlor where he saw in the dining room Zippy that was clinging to his perch by his seedtrough engaged in some instantaneous digestion as he was eating and dripping both at the very same time, eating and dripping anyhow until he spied Nestor Tudor in the doorway when he undertook, maybe on account of the swank chiefly that he probably didn't anymore see much of, to dash himself into tiny yellow pieces against the cage walls like Mrs. MaySue Ludley, who'd followed Nestor Tudor to the dining room, reproved her bird Zippy about with no noticeable effect to speak of except for how the dripping that Zippy had temporarily left off at of a sudden commenced all over again.

And Mrs. MaySue Ludley wondered at Nestor Tudor, "Isn't he something?" which Nestor Tudor assured her, as far as yellow birds went, he purely was. "Evermore a comfort to me," Mrs. MaySue Ludley told him and admitted how sometimes when she got mournful and low she'd hear Zippy her yellow bird squawking or scratching around and be of a sudden improved just on account of how she knew in a cage in the dining room there was a thing that loved her, a thing that seemed to Nestor Tudor even with the dripping and beating about more dapper by a good ways than Mr. W. O. Ludley had ever somehow managed to seem to him like he almost communicated to Mrs. MaySue Ludley the news of but managed at the last second to keep from it.

He made to look all around, made to look somewhat at Zippy the yellow bird but made to look past him into the kitchen and on behind himself into the parlor as well like was preface to him inquiring where maybe the gang of people had gotten off to, the gay festive gang of people he'd driven over in his Fairlane to take supper with which straightoff Mrs. MaySue Ludley laughed in a headtossing sort of a way about and took up Nestor Tudor one time more at the armjoint so as to have a grip on him while she informed him what a caution he was, albeit an altogether swanky caution for certain, and she laughed another time still and got watched by Nestor Tudor at it, Nestor Tudor who paid some mind to the red lipstick and the pink rougey cheeks and the glittery green eyelids and the wavy silver hair she'd gone to the trouble to tie somehow a bow in like along with the armjoint and giddy laugh should probably have told to him a thing, a thing he'd not bothered yet to figure and bothered yet to guess about him that had dressed and preened for a gang and her holding to him that hadn't.

She was herself having a cocktail and wished to know from Nestor Tudor if wouldn't he join her and have maybe a cocktail too that Nestor Tudor didn't much mind if he did and followed the widow Mrs. MaySue Ludley through the dining room past Zippy her yellow bird into the kitchen where she'd taken out from somewhere already an altogether antique bottle of Wild Turkey. She was partial herself to 7-Up with her Wild Turkey and wondered what Nestor Tudor took usually his own Wild Turkey with like was most times the glass all by itself though Nestor Tudor was not entirely convinced that he wanted to get with Mrs. MaySue Ludley's Wild Turkey as gay and as festive as with Wild Turkey he usually got. So he guessed he'd take 7-Up himself and guessed he'd take cracked ice and guessed he'd take even a half a bottled cherry and an ever so scant shot of bottled cherry juice that Mrs. MaySue Ludley insisted was that one little thing in fact that set a Wild Turkey and 7-Up cocktail apart from most every kind of cocktail otherwise which she assured Nestor he'd find out himself it did like he did in fact manage to shortly to find it out.

They passed back through the dining room by Zippy that squawked and dripped for them and on into the parlor again where Mrs. MaySue Ludley swept her arm to indicate how Nestor Tudor should sit on the end of the settee like she allowed him to settle full well atop of before she slipped her own posterior right flush up next to him and made a kind of a giddy quasi-headtossing noise prior to showing to Nestor Tudor most especially her front teeth that had accumulated upon them some considerable lipstick which Nestor Tudor felt compelled to watch and ponder and so did not see straightoff how sweetly it was Mrs. MaySue Ludley looked on him and did not altogether take in what talk she loosed of being saved and being rescued on the highway by the convalescent home where she could have ended up some way entirely otherwise but for Nestor Tudor, some way entirely otherwise like she did not so much as imply would probably have been elsewhere and probably have been sooner that Nestor Tudor might have informed her about but for her red teeth that bobbed and worked and caused him to recall on Mrs. MaySue Ludley's settee how his dead wife Erlene hadn't ever let her own front teeth get red much like he guessed was part stewardship and part underbite with it.

And Mrs. MaySue Ludley assured him, "It was. It was for a fact," like prompted Nestor Tudor to ask her back, "Was it?" as he did not know precisely what variety of item he was getting presently assured about.

"It was," Mrs. MaySue Ludley told him, "I've never seen a braver thing and Nadine that's seen some things even hadn't never seen a braver thing herself. Told me she hadn't."

"Who?" Nestor Tudor wanted to know.

"Nadine," the widow Mrs. MaySue Ludley informed him. "Her with the hairlump."

And Nestor Tudor said, "Oh," though he'd meant to say more than just Oh truly but got put off briefly from it by the need to consider how maybe it was a man and a woman could together conceive of and give birth to an actual midget and then up and call her Nadine on top of it as if it wasn't enough already to be squat and puny.

"Never seen a thing braver," Mrs. MaySue Ludley insisted. "Not the both of us."

Naturally, Nestor Tudor explained what a trifling endeavor the running and the leaping and the crawling and the skidding had in fact been like Mrs. MaySue Ludley wagged a finger at him about, a finger which turned out presently to be among the group of them she grabbed once more his armjoint with. And it was just shortly beyond the armjoint grabbing that he began to see her for the first time plain, just shortly beyond the armjoint grabbing that he looked full on her and noticed at last how she'd been for a spell already looking full on him back and not just regular looking with a regular face but an acute variety of looking instead with a Draper Meecham sort of a face chiefly, a Draper Meecham sort of a face near about entirely altogether but for the eyes that were moist and dewy and but for the teeth that were red, and he meant to free his held arm, meant to make like to suffer from an itch and raise his arm to scratch himself with but she gripped it tighter than previously she'd gripped it and shut her dewy eyes of a sudden and drew in a ponderous breath that she told him just shortly, "Kismet," with like would be the once with her eyes shut and like would be the once just behind it with her eyes open.

He hated to wrench loose from a lady so but did not truly see any help for it. Consequently, he jerked and pulled and stood at last upright as he told to Mrs. MaySue Ludley, "No ma'm," as he told to Mrs. MaySue Ludley how they hadn't but lately just met and that on the highway under circumstances which seemed even to Nestor Tudor who'd made them that way peculiar. "No ma'm," he told to her another time and looked with palpable consternation upon Mrs. MaySue Ludley who said to him Kismet again even after he'd assured her twice already he wouldn't.

Consternation wasn't, however, anything Mrs. MaySue Ludley had presently any use for so she regripped Nestor Tudor at the identical armjoint she'd only lately gotten wrenched from her and spoke of how things got sometimes planned and fated by your forces and such that drove folks together and drove folks apart which she asked from Nestor Tudor a judgment about, said to him anyway, "Doesn't it seem so?" but Nestor Tudor was still altogether too consternated to speak and just stood where he'd raised up to watching somewhat Mrs. MaySue Ludley's upturned face and somewhat Mrs. MaySue Ludley's knobby fingers that she was gripping just presently an elbow scab with. She undertook to pull him back onto the settee. He felt her in his scab undertake to pull him, but he laid the bulk of himself into not being pulled just presently like knobby fingers weren't enough to undo so she rose up off the settee as well to stand alongside him and inquire if hadn't he ever felt driven together at least a little, if hadn't he ever just gotten by somebody wholly magnetized like induced Nestor Tudor, who could not somehow help but get induced, to recollect that night outside Lawsonville at the springhead which had been one time not just a seepy hole in the ground but had been a manner of spa instead on account of the water with sulfur to it and chalybeate to it and a trifle of dirt and grit to it too that people used to sit in and sprinkle and drink as well until they'd just gradually quit at it and so closed the hotel that fell in and the arcade that burned and the chapel that was taken plank by plant apart and transported entirely elsewhere leaving just all by itself the pavilion alone like was all even Nestor Tudor in his youth had known, the raised pavilion with the plank floor and the ornate stanchions and the rail roundabout worn slick and smooth from backends upon it. And come Saturday they'd hang paper lanterns, he recalled, along the ceiling and a string band would play and people would gather and collect and dance and drink and brawl even sometimes too like he'd gone himself that night for, which would be mostly the drinking and mostly the brawling, but he'd seen her instead who'd come in the company of a Pinkett and yet took a turn with him across the planking under the lanternlight and laid back her head as they spun and stomped round to watch him watch her, him who'd felt of a sudden driven and had felt of a sudden magnetized like he admitted to the widow Mrs. MaySue Ludley he previously had.

Of course, W.O. had gotten a grip on her, had gotten right from the start a grip on her, and Mrs. MaySue Ludley shut her eyes and told to Nestor Tudor how oh yes he had been a prize, how the women had just come to him like bees to a blossom. She drew Nestor by his elbow scab away from the settee and across the parlor to the mantelpiece with the beveled mirror above it that Nestor Tudor watched her and that Nestor Tudor watched himself briefly in before eyeing like he got instructed the pictures on the mantelpiece of MaySue as a lithe young thing and W.O. young with her, W.O. that looked scrawnier than Nestor Tudor had ever known him to be and with actual hair he'd had to go to the trouble even to grease and slick back and billowy trousers too up already then to his shirtpocket like in time they would cover and surpass.

"A prize," Mrs. MaySue Ludley said and took in and blew out a pre-kismet manner of breath prior to informing Nestor Tudor how there was some people a person didn't need but to see, didn't need but to lay from a distance eyes on to know most everything about and she wondered a little couldn't he tell what it was she meant but failed to allow him the occasion truly to assure her how he could or how he couldn't either one as she spoke directly instead of Mr. W. O. Ludley who long ago she'd laid eyes one time on in a parlor like her own parlor in a house like her own house where him and where her had been invited to a tea so as to be flung together by her momma and by his aunt who'd wanted to see would they stick and take. "W.O.," Mrs. MaySue Ludley said into the air and caught up with her free hand a picture of just him alone that she clutched tight against herself like Nestor Tudor watched a little square on and watched a little in the beveled mirror too.

And for a time she just stood holding tight the picture with one hand and holding tight the armjoint with the other and she began to look near about weepy in what Nestor Tudor took for a dead and gone W. O. Ludley kind of a way until she set again to speaking and he heard precisely what it was she was undertaking to say. "I knew," she told to him and looked sweetly full on his face with W.O. still clutched tight against her dressfront.

"Did you?" Nestor Tudor inquired as it seemed to him she'd left him a gap to inquire in.

"You knew too," she told to him and showed him briefly her red teeth after a fashion that Nestor Tudor might have one time taken for coy if it hadn't been him like he'd come to be and her like she'd gotten just standing in a parlor before a mantelpiece well past coy together.

"Did I?" Nestor Tudor inquired in what gap she'd left him to inquire in.

And Mrs. MaySue Ludley lifted her face towards the ceiling and looked off and looked away and said all soft and dreamy, "There's mysteries in this life, Nestor Tudor," and she heard from Nestor Tudor not truly in a gap at all, "Why you've said a thing there," that she fairly pinched his scab about and so punctuated him like allowed her to persevere the way she'd intended, like allowed her to tell pretty much at the ceiling still, "I knew. Didn't have but to see you slide down that windshield and slip on off that hood and I knew for certain even if I couldn't say why, even if I can't say why still," and she breathed in and she breathed out and she told pretty much at the ceiling, "Kismet."

He couldn't hardly get his No ma'm out, and he couldn't truly begin even to figure what he might say with it on account of how his Draper Meecham alarm had struck up suddenly, had swelled anyway and risen so that it was not any longer just dull and low but fairly shrieked and wailed at him both. "Forces," she said and squeezed W.O. in his frame and pinched again Nestor Tudor's elbow scab that Nestor Tudor vented a moderately profane thing about which was not truly what he'd landed on to tell her but was just an item he'd felt obliged to vent.

She was gone. He'd seen gone people before and she was pretty apparently one of them already from just the running and the leaping and the crawling and the sliding and the sailing and the skidding too which he wanted to tell her was not hardly even altogether worth getting gone about but Nestor Tudor, who'd seen gone people, knew how they'd watch you talking but would not even remotely hear what you said, so he did not tell her anything further than he'd told her already until Mrs. MaySue Ludley had dropped away from the walljoint entirely to look squarely on Nestor Tudor and say at him, "Saved," and say at him, "Rescued," when Nestor Tudor felt inclined to wonder if wouldn't she please proceed with him back across the parlor to the settee like she allowed she would and farther even, most anywhere in fact though Nestor Tudor assured her the settee would be plenty far enough for the time being and so drew her by his elbow scab to it, or to the endtable beyond it truly where he took up his glass off the cork coaster and ingested as precipitously as he was able to manage it his Wild Turkey and his 7-Up and his half a cherry and his scant cherry juice and a sliver or two of cracked ice with them that Mrs. MaySue Ludley watched him at after such a fashion as to suggest and as to imply how she could not hardly help but admire a man that was able to ingest so.

Naturally, Nestor Tudor was anxious to recall why in the world he'd gone to the trouble to get suave and dashing when he should have guessed it would be just him and would be just her except for Zippy that couldn't but screech and drip anyhow like wasn't worth getting suave and dashing for, and he wished he'd worn just his twill pants and his white shirt with the stain and his daddy's brother's shimmery red necktie like maybe would have forestalled the joint holding and the soft dreamy talk if not discouraged them altogether, and he laid back his head and shook a piece of ice off his glassbottom, a sizeable hunk that he cracked between his teeth after a fashion he hoped might render him a touch unsavory to the widow Mrs. MaySue Ludley who stood with him alongside the settee and regarded sweetly how he chomped and chewed like appeared to strike her as ever so swanky itself which she felt shortly moved and inspired to tell to him, "Oh Nestor," about.

She'd made appetizers even though she admitted she didn't truly make appetizers much but most nights set in directly with her entree like she most nights concluded with as well. They had before them, however, an occasion that she'd gone on ahead and made appetizers on account of and so drew Nestor Tudor by his elbow scab out from the parlor and into the dining room where she settled him onto the chair at the head of the table too altogether alongside Zippy to suit him much due to how it was Zippy's accumulated drips fairly emanated not to mention the seed that Zippy was prone to fling and the shrieking he was apt to partake of. So Nestor Tudor watched Zippy flap and beat and squeak every now and again and eat and drip too and clasped his hands before himself in a prayerful fashion and wished he'd not seen the hairlump, wished he'd not anyhow seen just the hairlump alone but had spied maybe some little piece of the midget beneath it like did not seem to him too awful much to be prayerful about. He just wished he'd stayed on the roadside with Harold Lister and Stumpy Tate where the asphalt had cracked and heaved up and had lifted maybe his head to watch the Bonneville roll and veer with the midget Miss Mottsinger to guide it, the midget Miss Mottsinger that could have at least raised up her fingers at him like he wished with his head bowed and his hands clasped together she had that Mrs. MaySue Ludley stepped out from the kitchen and caught him at and so straightaway grew impressed with how Nestor Tudor was not just swanky and brave but had as well some holiness to him which of course she'd already suspected on account of what feel she had for people most times.

It was a noodly sort of thing on a tiny saucer. Truly it was in fact a noodly sort of thing atop a lettuce leaf on a tiny saucer that she set one of before Nestor Tudor and the other of it at her own vacant place which stayed itself vacant until she'd lit with a match what she called at Nestor Tudor her tapers and then stepped over to the switch by the doorway to turn off the overhead light. Of course outside it was not quite yet dark entirely but was dusky enough anyhow to keep Nestor Tudor, with just the scant light through the windows and the low orangy taper glow, from seeing what precisely his noodly appetizer had to it aside from the noodles and the lettuce leaf. He did not, however, find himself much blinded to the widow Mrs. MaySue Ludley who settled just around the tableedge from him and watched overtop a taper as he poked his appetizer with his fork, or poked truly the tablecloth alongside his appetizer there at the first but shortly located the appetizer itself and poked it and ate even a crunchy piece of it that was plainly not noodle or lettuce either one like he made a kind of a noise about for Mrs. MaySue Ludley who he raised up his head and looked on just ever so briefly on account of what way he found himself getting pondered back like was bald and like was outright there in the taperlight which, while dim and flickery, was not somehow near so kind to Mrs. MaySue Ludley as her shaded incandescent bulbs in the parlor had been.

She did love to feed a man and recalled for Nestor Tudor the variety of vigor and enthusiasm Mr. W. O. Ludley had most times sopped his plate clean with that Nestor Tudor let on to be diverted about but was not in fact much diverted truly on account of Zippy that squawked and fluttered and Zippy's drips that emanated and the taper flames that flickered and danced and Mrs. MaySue Ludley that looked squarely on him like he'd not hardly anticipated he'd get looked squarely on. He'd just wanted to be suave for a night and dashing, had wanted to put on his black suit and his purple horsehead shirt and get of an evening engaged with items other than just his springy metal chair and his footstump and his daddy's nut that sometimes he dangled and rubbed, engaged with actual people maybe who would speak of things to him and hear from him things themselves. He'd not, however, much hoped to get mooned over, much hoped to get held at the armjoint, much hoped to get told of your forces that drive things together and told of your forces that drive things apart. He'd simply wanted to have a night with other than just the twilight and other than just his lone firecoal like did not at the table in the taperglow seem of a sudden such an altogether forlorn way to pass an evening, most especially once Mrs. MaySue Ludley had grabbed up with her fingers his forkholding hand and just for a spell gripped and clung to it while she told to him, "Nestor," told to him, "Nestor," lower and treaclier even than he'd ever previously suspected she might tell Nestor to him.

She didn't seem even to eat at all. She didn't seem but to look over the candletip at him and spoke only to tell of how in this life there were mysteries and such and various other of your kismety manner of things like Nestor Tudor undertook to steer her off of with some talk of the heat and some talk of the humidity and some talk of the bugs as well that had struck him lately as thick and troublesome. However, she was not much inclined to get steered and just sat back of her taper and looked on him but for when she went off to fetch the pork roast that she'd stuffed and decorated and garnished roundabout and the carrots she'd slivered and boiled and the greenbeans she'd sauteed in a nouvelle sort of a way like Nestor Tudor admitted he was not most times prone to take his greenbeans which Mrs. MaySue Ludley grew straightoff acutely distressed on account of but got shortly soothed and relieved once Nestor Tudor, who took up a bean and bit it, confessed what a rare experience it had proven to be.

So he ate all his sweet nutty beans and ate all his carrot slivers and finished off, but for the length of knotted string that he gnawed on a little, his slab of pork roast like got him straightaway gushed at by Mrs. MaySue Ludley from overtop her taper as she'd not had the pleasure to watch a man shovel and chew so since before Mr. W. O. Ludley stroked the way he had that Nestor Tudor made as best he could a grave face on account of and showed it over the taper to Mrs. MaySue Ludley who displayed her red teeth back and told how of a sudden there did not seem much point to her in lingering over her woes and troubles of the past, told how of a sudden she was not of a mood to be mournful and she reached like Nestor Tudor saw she was up to and groped like Nestor Tudor had feared a little she might and found at last Nestor Tudor's fingers another time and Nestor Tudor's fork with them that she squeezed and held while she inquired if didn't it seem sometimes to Nestor Tudor that people could say things back and forth without so much as raising a peep that Nestor Tudor had not ever truly cultivated an opinion about like he went ahead and raised a peep on account of and got shortly communicated at back by Mrs. MaySue Ludley who pitched her head the one way and pitched her head the other and flared ever so slightly her noseholes as she elevated both her eyebrows together like did speak in fact to Nestor Tudor, like told to him things he was not much inclined hardly to hear.

She'd made a cake and she'd made a pie both since she'd not somehow detected from him on the highway alongside the convalescent home a preference for the one or the other, and he tried firstoff the pie that was fruity and sweet and tried back of it the cake as well that seemed to him buttery, seemed to him ever so extravagantly buttery in fact which he made to speak of but did not, Mrs. MaySue Ludley informed him, need truly to speak of it like she let on was cause for additional fingergrabbing and so reached again and squeezed again and elevated another time her eyebrows together. Mrs. MaySue Ludley was of a mind to take coffee in the parlor that she told to Nestor Tudor in actual words she was of a mind about like Nestor Tudor, who guessed he'd been pondered and squeezed and emanated at enough already, allowed he was a little himself of a mind about too and so got by Mrs. MaySue Ludley escorted towards the settee where he lowered his backside and lounged a spell while she went off to fetch her china and to fetch her service that had been in fact her own dead momma's china and service both which she spoke of to Nestor Tudor as she poured the coffee and spooned the sugar and dolloped the cream and handed at last his saucer to him with his cup clinking and rattling upon it.

As broad and lengthsome as the settee seemed to him, Nestor Tudor did not find that Mrs. MaySue Ludley was much disposed to use the whole of it and took up for herself the cushion snug up next to his own cushion which she claimed a piece of too once she'd noticed how Nestor Tudor, who'd slid and scrunched and crowded the arm, was not using but half of it truly and he guessed she was communicating things to him with her head that she pitched and her face that she stretched and worked but he did not look to see what manner of things precisely and just studied instead his coffeecup and picked briefly at his trousers and admired across the way Mrs. MaySue Ludley's clawfooted table that he told her presently his daddy's people had owned one of which Mrs. MaySue Ludley grew inspired to air some actual talk about as it seemed coincidental to her in a purely extravagant sort of way that she her own self and his people both would be together in possession of pretty much the same identical clawfooted table like moved her to inquire yet another time of Nestor Tudor about the mysteries and the wonders of this life that was words just there at the first but was eyebrows presently and noseholes too.

Though he was not much of a mood for a liqueur, Mrs. MaySue Ludley poured a liqueur for him in a dainty liqueur glass and poured one for herself as well that she drank even some of, but he was not much of a mood for a liqueur and left his own one to sit while he began to make, as best as he was able, assorted stirring and leaving noises like caused presently his near hand to be gripped and clung to. And she chatted somewhat with him but sat chiefly just communicating, sat chiefly sideways looking on him in her lively print dress and her bejeweled necklace and with her lips red and glisteny and her cheeks rouged and her nose talced and her eyes shaded and her silver hair swept and curled and done up some way Nestor Tudor had yet to figure with a white hair ribbon like was all for him, like was all especially for him alone which was what he felt most acutely obliged to stir and leave about as he'd seen previously her corset even and not gotten much worked up about it. So he made what he figured to be a stirring and leaving sort of a face that he hoped might with his noises say a thing to her but she persevered at pondering him and gripping him and vented every now and again some trifling talk until the Wild Turkey and the iced tea at supper and the coffee and the liqueur conspired together to send her down the hallway and through the bedroom to the halfbath where she shut the door and opened the tap and sat upon the ring while Nestor Tudor stirred in fact and endeavored truly to leave, traveled anyhow so far as the screendoor and laid his hand flat upon the rail of it as he waited for Mrs. MaySue Ludley to return and exhibit for him her dismay like just shortly she did.

"No cause to run off," Mrs. MaySue Ludley told to him and took him up another time by the elbow scab which Nestor Tudor was hard pressed to yawn at her in the face of but had decided already how he would in fact yawn and so attempted to, dropped his jaw anyhow and managed not to seem but somewhat excruciated, and he told to her back of it, "Mrs. Ludley, I'm just plain beat."

"MaySue."

"Plain beat," he said to her and she laid all her fingers either side of his neck to his collarbone and set to poking and jabbing and squeezing him from behind like was soothing to him only because she'd had to let loose of his elbow scab to do it.

"Can't be easy to work the highway," Mrs. MaySue Ludley told him.

"No ma'm," Nestor Tudor confessed to her back.

"Most especially when there's women up and down it to save and rescue."

And Nestor Tudor admitted how he did not truly save and rescue awful many women, hadn't in fact ever chased down but Mrs. MaySue Ludley herself who, he refreshed her, there hadn't hardly been much call in the first place to chase like the widow Mrs. MaySue Ludley asked him, "Really?" on account of with some bend and some squeal to it.

"No ma'm," Nestor Tudor said.

"MaySue."

"No MaySue," Nestor Tudor said and reminded her how the midget Miss Mottsinger had been in fact attached to what he'd not even in the first place taken for a hairlump that he laughed about as best as he was able so as to let on how the entire business had been pretty completely a merry manner of mixup.

And Mrs. MaySue Ludley allowed all eight of her fingers and both of her thumbs to lie still a time while she pondered Nestor Tudor's thin swirly cowlick in a thoughtful sort of a way. "Just me?" she asked of him shortly. "Not anybody before?"

And Nestor Tudor had started even his No and had contemplated already his MaySue when he felt, that way people feel sometimes, the side somewhat and the back chiefly of his head getting admired what seemed to him unduly like drew him up short and induced from him a Well instead which had its own bend but not much squeal to speak of. He was intending to explain again about the hairlump. He was intending to mention another time the midget Miss Mottsinger beneath it. He was intending to air even his own view of sedans steered and guided by puny little catalogless women like seemed to him near as apt and seemed to him near as fitting as regular fullsized people that couldn't themselves hardly steer and guide sometimes, but he did not truly say anything much even after everything he'd intended to say on account of how he turned around and saw squarely before him the very face the widow Mrs. MaySue Ludley had been just lately studying his cowlick with like seemed to him altogether beyond talk entirely, like seemed to him more gone even than the face she'd shown to him by the mantelpiece already. So he meant to tell her all manner of things about midgets and hairlumps and Bonnevilles and such but he told her instead just another Well beyond the Well he'd lately aired and a wholly unadorned Yes ma'm in back of that which Mrs. MaySue Ludley imposed sufficiently upon her slack muscles to make a noise about.

And he pushed against the door rail and left even, began anyway to depart and got escorted across the porch and down the steps past the geraniums and along the walk to his Fairlane at the curb where he praised Mrs. MaySue Ludley's pork roast and Mrs. MaySue Ludley's crunchy green beans and most especially Mrs. MaySue Ludley's buttery cake like she let on she was grateful about, cooed at him anyhow in the throaty sort of way that Zippy himself might have cooed between drips and then just bobbed all of a sudden and bumped her lips right flush up against his, or right flush up against his own lips chiefly but flush up against his teeth a little as well like left them red and like left them perfumy and like prompted from Nestor Tudor an altogether wheezy discharge which struck Mrs. MaySue Ludley in her gone state as purely the pinnacle of romance that she touched him on his armjoint about.

"Bye," he said to her when he'd found again the spit to speak with.

"Night," she told to him back with such considerable breath and such scant volume that he could not be certain he'd heard the Sugar behind it like he thought he'd heard a Sugar as he watched to find out did she appear much inclined to bend and to pucker another time that she did in fact seem disposed for and so got backed shortly away from by Nestor Tudor who circled round his Fairlane and climbed in it and started it and dropped it into gear as if they were all three of them only one thing to do. He waved to her out the vent window and she managed even then to touch his fingerends briefly before he set off north up the road and then west on it and south on it too so far as the highway where he lingered a time on a tongue of gravel at the intersection and wrenched down his rearview mirror and wiped his red teeth and his red mouth and spoke briefly to himself of Jesus all sweet and creeping.

He came pretty rapidly in his bedroom at home to be unswanky entirely and retired fairly straightaway to his springy metal chair and his footstump with a jelly glass of Ancient Age and a pack of Old Gold filters, and he smoked and he drank and beat away the bugs from his face as he looked past the treetops to his piece of sky where presently he spied a star and wished about the running and the leaping and the crawling and the sliding and the sailing and the skidding upon it along with the lips he'd lately been bumped by that he hoped would in the future evermore stay off his face. When it rang the first time, he almost leapt up and ran to answer the phone but discovered, before he managed to stand full upright, that maybe people could in fact speak without so much as raising a peep like left him just to sit in his springy metal chair and drink and smoke and listen to the telephone ring and stop ringing and start shortly ringing again which he guessed told him more than he could ever take up the receiver and find out.

* * *

Along the roadside by the bottling plant, Nestor Tudor hunkered in the weeds and tasted from his tubes and byways the pungent gizzardy items he wished he'd left to lay on the potbottom. He conjured up the neck dimple with the veins either side of it and the dress with the speckles and the shoes with the leathery bows like came together with the hairpart that he could not somehow help but conjure as well. A truck rolled out from the plant lot and through the hole they'd not yet filled and smoothed over entirely like the driver hung briefly out the cab window and aired an opinion about to Stumpy Tate and Harold Lister and Nestor Tudor too who did not seem, just loitering along the roadside, up to much to him. He guessed he'd broken some Sundrops and guessed he'd broken some Dr Peppers that he spoke of as well and so fielded directly an inquiry back from Stumpy Tate who wanted to find out did he look to the truck driver the sort of fellow that might give a big goddam about the Sundrops or the Dr Peppers either one like was truly a rhetorical manner of inquiry and so did not in fact call for the variety of reply the driver saw fit to air.

He figured maybe he'd do a thing, Stumpy Tate did, figured maybe he'd pitch some tar if Nestor Tudor would roll the truck off his shovel like he'd hollered at him already about and hooted and whistled with it, and presently Nestor Tudor even did in fact stand and leave the roadside and climbed into the truckcab where he started the motor and sat for a time just listening to it run as he peered out the front windowglass conjuring up her in the clouds and seeing for his trouble Dick Atwater chiefly instead. For his part, Stumpy Tate watched the shovel handle and Stumpy Tate watched the tandem wheels and Stumpy Tate listened for the gearbox to ring like probably it would have had Nestor Tudor clutched and shifted in addition to the conjuring he was up to already, but he did not clutch and did not shift and merely laid his forehead against the steering wheel instead from where he recalled the lips and from where he recalled the fingerends pretty much exclusive of the hairpart altogether and he told at the steering column chiefly, "Forces," like inspired an inquiry from out by the doorpanel where Stumpy Tate and Harold Lister had united on the roadedge to stand and ruminate upon Nestor Tudor and to ask of him in the wake of his piece of talk, "What?" like by itself fairly revived Nestor Tudor who sat upright blinking on the truckseat and turned towards Harold Lister and Stumpy Tate long enough to wonder of them, "Isn't life strange sometimes?"

"Is today," Stumpy Tate told to him back.

iii.

WATER laid it over but water couldn't somehow keep it laid and presently the most of it grew unstuck and fell pretty much down to where it had come in the first place from like was, as best as Dick Atwater could tell, the trouble with water chiefly. He had in the medicine chest a dibble of hair balm left to him from back when he'd cultivated a manner of rowdy wave across the peak of his head but he was not in fact looking to get near so slick and greasy as he recalled hair balm would leave him, so he poked around in the depths of the cabinet under the lavatory and presently came across a Vitalis bottle with not truly awful much Vitalis in it but sufficient Vitalis anyway to splash pretty completely all over his scalp and saturate the bulk of what hair remained to him that he took straightaway a comb to and brought up and swept the strands he'd been trying with water alone to sweep previously.

Now, of course, Vitalis didn't appear straightoff much of an advancement over regular water since, out from the bottle, it was just thin like water and wet like water too. But once it had time to dry, once it had time to get pretty thoroughly dehydrated, the hairgrooming properties made themselves altogether apparent on account of how the Vitalis plating grew hard and crusty, sufficiently hard and sufficiently crusty in fact to hold even such hair as Dick Atwater's up from his altogether lowslung hairpart. And his upswept hair stayed even held and situated when he pitched his head a little sideways so as to see would it fall back to where he'd upswept it from, stayed even held and situated when he shook his head with what seemed to him more vigor than he'd likely in the course of an evening have cause to shake it, and he saw in the medicine chest mirror how the portion of his scalp that was naked skin just previously had anymore hair across it, hair that he laid ever so gently his fingerends to and thereby felt his Vitalis haircrust which seemed stout to him, struck him as pretty thoroughly joltproof that Dick Atwater found himself disposed to grin on account of, disposed to lay wide his entire mouth that caused most especially his upswept hair to crackle like wheat in a wind.

His fedora was a matter of some worry and debate to him, his straw fedora with the gray sateen band which, he was of a mind, rendered him chiseled on account of the shadows the brim of it threw, and while he guessed he could go unchiseled for an evening he didn't much care for the prospect of laying back his jacketflaps without his hatbrim to give him the illusion of scooped and give him the illusion of bony both. The trouble was, of course, that his straw fedora with the sateen band tended to muss his upswept hair whenever he lifted it before the mirror to be polite and courtly and he didn't figure his hair would probably stay Vitalised if he mussed it much, so he landed on how he might carry his straw fedora, might haul it around just in his hand and thereby have it with him if he ran up on a circumstance where it seemed maybe more worthwhile to be chiseled than upswept. He wore his favorite jacket with the tiny almost indecipherable stripe and his trousers with the pointy rear pocket flaps and his brown shoes with the buckles and his thin stretchy socks and just a regular white shirt otherwise with the collar laid open and his buttons undone farther down than usually he saw fit to undo his buttons, but he was feeling this night most especially stylish and inordinately hairypated and so displayed a sprig of wiry chesthair and a piece of undershirt with it like was not in the regular course of things a habit with Dick Atwater.

She'd said sevenish. She'd asked in fact if wouldn't sevenish suit him and he'd informed her sevenish would, shared with her even how he'd gone on ahead and contemplated previously sevenish himself like she'd seemed to him on the phone line pleased to know of. So he shot for sevenish, shot truly for six-thirtyish as didn't that seem but maybe a trifle sevenish to him itself, but he was groomed and primped and dressed in fact by fiveish and consequently had left to him a spell to loiter before the medicine chest and ponder himself sideways and ponder himself straight on and ponder himself somewhere between sideways and straight on as well, and he wished he was still taut all over like he'd been one time as a young man taut most everywhere and he wondered how come he'd gotten to be spotted and speckled when he'd not previously seemed much disposed towards freckledy even and he posed himself a trifle swung round and a trifle drawn back to where he seemed most taut and most unspeckled and intoned the thing he'd landed on to intone about the Regency brand pastel-colored items in the lubricated packets that he'd bought, he told the medicine chest, for Mr. Troutman the shut-in next door with the plastic hipsockets who put them, he figured, to some manner of therapeutic use, and he undertook to imply just posing and pitching ever so slightly how he was altogether too discreet a fellow himself to ask outright of Mr. Troutman what a shut-in with plastic hipsockets might find to do with a Regency brand pastel-colored item all orgasmic and bumpy and lubricated too like was in fact appreciably more than just posing and pitching could begin even to speak of.

He'd cleaned his Toronado, he'd taken the floormats out and beat off the grit from them and he'd wiped the seat with a rag and emptied from the ashtray the four cigarette butts somebody sometime had seen fit to squash there. He'd squirted the exterior with the hose and had endeavored with his seatrag to scrub the buggy residue off the front grill, and the entire vehicle had sparkled and shined right up until it dried when it looked to him almost precisely like it had previously looked. He stopped on his way at the Gulf for gas and got perused straightaway by Jump Garrison who'd come out from the station to ask what manner of octane he had just presently call for and stood alongside the doorpanel and said even, "Hightest?" before he saw where the hairpart had come to be, or before he saw truly where previously the hairpart had been like it wasn't any longer that he puzzled fairly deeply about and so did not hear the Good Gulf any of the three times it got told to him and heard only presently the particular invective which got loosed itself twice.

He sat in his Toronado out front of Miss Bernice Fay Frazier's house mashing his hair where it seemed to him to need mashing and puffing into his cupped hand so as to sniff his breath that smelled chiefly like his cupped hand to him. Presently, though, he got out from his car and situated his shirttail and tugged at his trouserlegs and inspected as best he was able his zipperslide to find out not just was it where it needed to be but would it maybe stay and cling there a spell like he came to be satisfied it might. He spoke briefly to Mr. Wayne Fulp's speckled hound Bill that had traveled to his treetrunk to urinate, told to him, "Don't you jump on me," like Bill had not remotely shown an inclination for and so lifted his head and rolled his eyes upwards at Dick Atwater prior to hunching back over to lick again his pink extended organ which was hardly the sort of undertaking he'd give over just to paw at a pair of trouser creases for a time.

There wasn't much call for Dick Atwater to knock once he'd gained the front porch and stood at the doorway, or there didn't seem anyway to him much call for it on account of how he could see through the doorscreen Miss Bernice Fay Frazier sitting upon the nearend of the settee reading in a book the widow Mrs. Askew had passed to her. It was a sort of a pith encyclopedia full of observations about most every little thing anybody might have ever seen fit to pronounce and observe on account of, and not just pronounce and observe after any regular sort of a fashion but pronounce and observe with altogether extravagant spunk and lilt both like seemed to Miss Bernice Fay Frazier to create somehow between them the pith though she could not say how precisely. So Miss Bernice Fay Frazier was just sitting on the settee reading pithy snatches aloud, pithy snatches she came across that struck her as worth hearing like were most all of the pithy snatches in fact which she fairly proclaimed with just so much volume as to irritate her cat Bubbles that was perched on the setteeback behind her with her head swiveling and her ears twitching and pivoting and her pupils growing slitty and round by turns which Mr. Dick Atwater watched briefly from the far side of the screendoor prior to offering Miss Bernice Fay Frazier a robust greeting, prior to fairly bellowing at her, "Evening," which she straightoff bellowed herself in back of.

Naturally she levitated though due to the girth of her sizeable bones she did not levitate awful much truly and plopped shortly back down where she'd departed briefly from like allowed the cat to near about clear her head entirely and careen off the settee arm to the floor and leap shortly up onto the boudoir chair that she bounced immediately off of, or bounced off of once she'd had occasion to puncture the upholstered chairback with all her claws together. Of course Miss Bernice Fay Frazier could not make out straightaway from the settee who'd bellowed the Evening at her and so asked was it Dick Atwater who she was expecting which Dick Atwater said robustly Yes about on account of his general agitation that would not let him talk just plain and low. So he got admitted once Miss Bernice Fay Frazier had unlatched both screenhooks and drawn back the barrelbolt too and she was meaning to air for him straightoff her opinion of a man that would be robust at her most especially through a doorscreen in the gathering dusk when she could hardly hope to see who precisely it was being robust in the first place like could jolt a woman, like could cause a woman's organs to seize up and such, that she'd cultivated on the settee just lately a moderately pithy pronouncement about which she'd almost begun to intone when she found herself suddenly inclined to ask of Dick Atwater instead, "What in God's name have you done to your hair?"

Now Dick Atwater had anticipated how he might get pressed, on account of his newly lowslung hairpart, to field inquiries and so had worked up in his Toronado a variety of slack utilitarian face that had seemed to say in the rearview mirror, "Huh?" to him. Naturally, he exhibited it straightaway at Miss Bernice Fay Frazier in hopes that it might say Huh? to her as well and it did in fact say Huh? a little but not Huh? much truly as it looked to her chiefly the face of a man that had maybe just swallowed a jarfly, did not look anyhow much in the way of an articulate sort of a face to her, a face that might tell her what she'd inquired about like prompted her to wonder again at Dick Atwater what in God's name he'd done to his hair precisely.

Of course, he made at her his bug-in-the-windpipe face all over again but spoke this time in conjunction with it, told to her, "Nothing," like Miss Bernice Fay Frazier disputed directly and informed Mr. Dick Atwater how he'd most undoubtedly done a thing to his hair, an altogether peculiar and unsavory variety of thing as best as she could tell that did not even begin to flatter and improve him like would have probably deflated Mr. Dick Atwater altogether but for the sweet breathy uplifted voice Miss Bernice Fay Frazier disclosed to him her opinion in, so he thanked her about it once she'd gotten done and heard from her back how it wasn't truly hardly much of anything at all.

Miss Mary Alice Celestine Lefler had landed on her yellow pantsuit out of all the skirts and pantsuits she'd carried from Berkeley Springs with her on account of she'd found herself just of a mood for yellow, and as she stepped out of the backhall into the parlor she twirled around on her shoebottoms so as to provide Dick Atwater and Miss Bernice Fay Frazier both the occasion to see what precisely it was yellow did for her like Mr. Dick Atwater in particular took some inordinate notice of and expressed at Miss Mary Alice Celestine Lefler a sentiment that came out near about in actual words. She happened to just love what it was he'd done to his hair, found herself fairly transported on account of it and praised his downswept portion and his upswept portion both and plumbed from Miss Bernice Fay Frazier her own utterly contrary opinion that Mr. Dick Atwater thanked her another time about. She smelled to him like a bouquet all sweet and fresh and flowery which he vented yet another vaguely articulate sentiment on account of prior to launching directly into talk of his neighbor Mr. Troutman with the plastic hipsockets and the therapeutic need for such as Regency brand bumpy lubricated items like he'd hoped they might the both of them infer a thing from but they did not appear to Mr. Dick Atwater much disposed for inferring as together they showed to him their own swallowed jarfly manner of faces, and probably he would have had to tell it all over again some way otherwise but for Miss Bernice Fay Frazier's sister's girl's cat Bubbles that found herself disposed of a sudden to dash and bolt, found herself disposed to streak on down the backhall and through the kitchen where she incited a racket which itself apparently inspired her to an altogether extravagant velocity that she maintained through the dining room and across the parlor and on into the bedroom as well where she leaped up onto the mattress and, from the nature of the uproar, seemed to undertake to devour the bedclothes like put everybody pretty completely off of Mr. Troutman and his plastic hipsockets and sent Miss Bernice Fay Frazier to the settee in a precipitous sort of a way.

She extracted assurances from him, Miss Bernice Fay Frazier did, that he'd not keep Miss Mary Alice Celestine Lefler late and that he'd not carry Miss Mary Alice Celestine Lefler far as they had yet a dish to prepare for the imminent upraised and elevated buffet at the reservoir, and Mr. Dick Atwater took up Miss Mary Alice Celestine Lefler lightly at the elbow and steered her across the porch and down the steps to the walk where him and where her together swung around to say bye to Miss Bernice Fay Frazier who from the doorway waved a little wanly with just her fingers alone.

As best as she could recollect, she'd not ever had yet the pleasure to ride in a Toronado like she let on was not hardly for the lack of wanting the pleasure of it as she'd admired, she said, Toronados from the getgo, and once she'd been steered by her elbow onto the seat she dragged her fingers slowly across the cushion of it and allowed her foremost one to linger at a hole Mr. Dick Atwater had punched one time with a screwdriver in his hip pocket like he spoke to her briefly about once he'd settled in himself, or told to her anyhow, "Hole," and told to her with it, "Screwdriver," and jabbed and poked his own foremost finger in a vaguely illuminating sort of a way that Miss Mary Alice Celestine Lefler took the gist of, made that is a manner of gisttaking noise like stirred Dick Atwater after a fashion as he'd not lately had roundabout a woman to illuminate. They spoke briefly together of the lines Mr. Dick Atwater's Toronado had to it that Mr. Dick Atwater knew a thing about since he'd gotten by Mr. Jimmy Sprinkle informed previously of the lines it had and Miss Mary Alice Celestine Lefler guessed wasn't but maybe a Cutlass sleeker like Dick Atwater felt inclined to allow though he shared with her news of what pistons he possessed and what liters and what cubic inches like sounded more potent than a Cutlass to her that he assured her it altogether was since he'd been by Mr. Jimmy Sprinkle assured about it one time himself.

They swung north onto the boulevard by the Heavenly Rest where Commander Tuttle had already switched on the lights back of the boxwoods that shone up the length of the chapel windows like seemed to Miss Mary Alice Celestine Lefler to produce an altogether ravishing effect and she wondered at Mr. Dick Atwater if didn't it seem to him fairly ravishing for an effect that Mr. Dick Atwater had near about looked to find out when he told to her it did. He spoke of how Commander Tuttle had buried for him his dead wife so as to communicate after a fashion how his wife was in fact dead and was in fact buried and he told of the blue dress she'd gotten laid out in and the black shoes nobody could see anyway and the clutchpurse even she held in her fingers that rendered him touched, that rendered him gripped ever so lightly at the forearm by her who spoke of her momma who'd passed on and who'd come shortly to be laid out on account of it. Mr. Dick Atwater was of a mind he'd as soon get incinerated. Miss Mary Alice Celestine Lefler didn't much care if she got incinerated herself and had, she supposed, just exactly the dress for it that was red, she said, with a bow in the front like Mr. Dick Atwater let on he could fashion her in.

Up the boulevard partway through town he slowed to point out the savings and loan where Mr. Dunford Hicks II, who'd been in fact incinerated, had come to get dead first, had just dropped over, or had grown actually inspired to drop over by a deposit slip in a canister in a pneumatic tube that got spat out into a wire basket right alongside him like he'd not that very moment been anticipating one might, and the canister beat against the basketbottom and bounced up into the air where it traded ends and dropped to the basketbottom again that Mr. Dunford Hicks II had jerked round to watch it do while he raised up his fingers and gripped his shirtfront with them as preface to pitching floorwards, as preamble to falling down dead. And Miss Mary Alice Celestine Lefler shook her head and lamented against the roof of her mouth and told to Mr. Dick Atwater, "You can't never know," which was itself the very notion precisely Mr. Dick Atwater had just been before airing on his own like seemed to him and Miss Mary Alice Celestine Lefler together a purely remarkable circumstance and indicated a thing, Mr. Dick Atwater insisted, a thing about the pair of them that he was fairly well set to speak of when he got somehow introduced into a crosswind that downswept his upswept hair and upswept his downswept hair and gave rise in Dick Atwater to a spell of such altogether undiluted consternation that he could not manage but to lament against the roof of his own mouth himself.

Talk of Mr. Dunford Hicks II dead of a sudden had fortunately inspired Miss Mary Alice Celestine Lefler to tell how her own momma had just up and all at once succumbed like kept her distracted and kept her engaged long enough for Mr. Dick Atwater to rake and mash and pull and just generally resweep his hair as best with his fingerends he was able, and some of it laid back down even and only most of it stood pretty much straight up, though not straight up truly for long on account of Miss Mary Alice Celestine Lefler who saw fit to leave off with her own dead momma to put some spit to Mr. Dick Atwater's locks, she called them, that she reraked and remashed and repulled and reswept after so gentle a fashion as to induce Mr. Dick Atwater to inadvertently slow his Toronado until it and him and her were sitting together still in the roadway that she asked him shortly were they and got admitted to her yes they were.

He'd not planned anywhere in particular to go but had thought he'd show to her their fair city in an aimless sort of a way and so continued north up the boulevard towards the square and pointed out the Hair Lair and the shoe shop and the Western Auto and Mrs. Sink's card emporium along with the Rexall where they'd just two days previous rendezvoused, he told her, and she made a noise to let on she recalled it herself. Once he'd arrived pretty much abreast of the square he stopped another time still in the roadway but with the purpose on this occasion of pointing out to her Colonel Byrd atop his pedestal with his saber drawn and his mouth dropped open and a drowsy pigeon upon the crown of his hat and he told her how he'd been a Bryd and told her how he'd been a colonel and told her how he'd said one time a thing that had been etched into his plaque though Dick Atwater could not recall what manner of thing precisely it was. He indicated the post office to her and suggested how there were boxes and such inside it and pointed out across the way the municipal building where nobody did hardly anything much at all. The benches in the flat grassy place between them mostly got lolled atop of, he told her, but for in the heat of the day when they did not usually get lolled atop of much that Miss Mary Alice Celestine Lefler managed a variety of exclamations about by which she suggested how she'd come just lately to be altogether sufficiently edified.

North down the hill she indicated to him the bus depot before he could manage to indicate it to her first so he indicated instead the town limit at the sign that said where the town limit was and the icehouse beyond it where they made, he told to her, ice. As he was going north already, he continued on north until he came to a place where he could go west instead that he turned onto so as to have before him the occasion to show to Miss Mary Alice Celestine Lefler some westerly things that was just chiefly houses and just chiefly barns along with a herd of ceramic deer and the lone ceramic Dutch girl with yellow hair in Mrs. Gilchrist's frontyard like seemed to Miss Mary Alice Celestine Lefler merry and consequently seemed merry as well to Dick Atwater who presently swung south on 87 and was meaning to drive straight back to town but came to be shortly prevented from it by Miss Mary Alice Celestine Lefler who saw the lights and who saw the people and told to Mr. Dick Atwater, "Look!" that Mr. Dick Atwater took straightaway the meaning of due to what wavelength precisely him and her together had come to be on and so he slowed to turn into the gravel lot even before she'd grabbed his arm and implored him with mostly her fingers themselves to slow and to turn both.

It was the golf range, Mr. Tadlock's golf range that Mr. Tadlock had purchased from the Swaim who'd owned it before him but had given it up primarily on account of insurance difficulties, insurance difficulties touched off and instigated by Mrs. Joan Crawford who was not the one with the lips and the eyebrows but was the one from Ruffin with the stomach instead. She'd carried her grandbabies out to play carpet golf and, in retrieving a ball for her least one, she'd managed somehow to get stuck up under Mr. Swaim's green spinybacked dinosaur where she claimed to have inflamed a muscle, claimed to have wrenched a joint, claimed it pretty directly to Mr. Swaim's insurance agent who expressed to Mr. Swaim his reservations about not just the green spinybacked dinosaur but the outsized fuzzy black gorilla as well as with the arms that moved and the windmill with the blades that turned round and the bowlegged cowboy with the pointy spurs in addition to the loop-the-loop cut from an old piece of barrel that seemed together a threat and a danger and, in combination with Mrs. Joan Crawford's claim, fairly cried out for an adjusted and heady premium, more adjusted and more heady in fact than Mr. Swaim found he was willing to tolerate and so he entertained and accepted instead an offer from Mr. Tadlock who owned a swimming pond beyond the trees alongside the driving range and guessed he would meet the heady premium and render the two enterprises together a recreational complex by virtue of a cinder path he did presently make between the pond and the golf range snack bar where bathers in transit were occasionally felled by duck hooks but could redeem the offending ball for a soda and a chopped barbecue sandwich.

Mr. Dick Atwater jumped out from his side and endeavored to bolt around the rear of the car so as to open Miss Mary Alice Celestine Lefler's door for her but his upswept hair could not stand so much velocity as even Dick Atwater managed at a bolt so he arrived at her door with his one hand pressed flat atop his head and his fedora in his other which did not leave his fingers truly to draw the door open with until he'd fixed and combed and situated his vagrant locks like Miss Mary Alice Celestine Lefler admired him at from beyond the upraised windowglass. He'd figured she'd want to putt but she wasn't truly much of a mind for it and guessed she'd just as soon hit balls on the range and she declared to Mr. Dick Atwater how he struck her as likely the type that could purely whale a ball and she told to him, "I bet you can," and poked him with her foremost finger as she told it, poked him pretty directly in his belly button so quick and unexpectedly that he did not get his loose droopy parts sucked in and firmed up until she'd fairly much gone on ahead and left off poking already, and she told him how she'd known a man one time that could purely whale a ball and she looked all dreamy off into the sky as she told it, looked all dreamy the sort of way that induced in Mr. Dick Atwater a thoroughgoing twinge as he did not much want to hear from Miss Mary Alice Celestine Lefler of what men she'd known that could whale balls and such, did not want to be but the only man alone who might deign to whale a ball for her.

Neither a tiny bucket nor a medium bucket either one hardly suited her as she preferred instead the gigantic bucket with the striped balls heaped up over the rim of it, and Mr. Dick Atwater selected for himself a metalheaded driver with a green rubber grip while Miss Mary Alice Celestine Lefler found an iron to please her that she carried with Mr. Dick Atwater's driver away from the booth and towards the range since Mr. Dick Atwater had come to be engaged otherwise with chasing the various heaped-up balls that managed to dribble out from the bucket and roll loose on the walkway like was hardly an upswept hair kind of an undertaking and called for some squatting at the knees and some blind groping with the fingers and not much bending at the spine to speak of. Miss Mary Alice Celestine Lefler found a lately vacated driving stall with a rubber tee and a strip of plush plastic grass to it that was separated from the stall to her left and the stall to her right by a pair of thigh-high plywood partitions which she discovered shortly to be useful items on account of the talent and inclination the gentleman to her left showed for cuing his own personal rangeballs off the toe of his club directly into the plywood like he did twice straightaway prior to telling to Miss Mary Alice Celestine Lefler by way of explanation, "Well shit."

Presently Mr. Dick Atwater arrived with pretty much the majority of the balls he'd left the booth with and he draped his jacket on a bench behind their particular stall and settled his fedora alongside it in preparation for the variety of whaling he intended, or somewhat anyhow in preparation to whale since he felt obliged to swing his metalheaded driver as well, felt obliged to whip it for practice back and forth after the fashion it appeared to him people up the mats and down the mats too were pretty much whipping their own clubs except maybe for Mr. Dale Gentry just right of them who was wearing a manner of contraption which appeared to extravagantly hinder his whipping altogether. His wife Judy Gentry had macraméd it for him as she'd learned at the community college to macramé and shape clay on a wheel and manufacture jewelry from dried beans too though she'd shown most readily a macraméing talent and so had undertaken Mr. Dale Gentry's contraption at the request of Mr. Dale Gentry himself who had gotten to the point where he could not any longer even so much as hope to hit a fairway due to how his balls bent and veered whenever anymore he struck them.

The trouble was he'd cultivated a slice that had started out as a kind of a fade but had grown lately acute, so acute in fact that his drives most especially seemed to almost come back to him, showed an irrefutable disposition for it anyway like had prompted him to visit the range and undertake a cure. Straightoff there, prior to his macraméd contraption, he'd managed to improve somewhat due partly to how he'd gotten at the range advised by whoever happened to be willing to advise him like was usually most everybody there since even the ones that couldn't much golf themselves felt most times gifted with powers of advisement and so informed Mr. Dale Gentry how he was raising up and how he was twisting round and how he was jerking and twitching and lunging, how he was just in a general sort of way pulling off the ball, they told him, though they could not between them decide precisely how he might keep from it except maybe to straighten his elbow and stiffen his wrist and bend at the knees and twist at the waist and lay his club on the backswing in the horizontal while he managed somehow to keep his head still and situated like would prevent him, they all supposed, from raising up and he didn't in fact raise up once he'd set and stilled and twisted himself back and twisted himself forwards too like left him to near about strike the ball with his clubhead that various of the ones who'd advised him told him he'd near about done.

Somehow, though, he could not manage to get cured with just advisement alone to aid him and had already, on number seven at the country club, broken his three wood against a hickory trunk in a fit of pique before he came across a picture in a magazine of pretty much precisely the item his wife Mrs. Judy Gentry macraméd for him. It was a sort of a harness designed most specifically for men like himself who had cultivated slices, had become somehow prone to pulling off the ball after a fashion that mere advisement alone could not right and rectify. A band of it fit around his head and was attached to straps that held him at the shoulders, straps that came together and joined at his belt buckle where they unified into a single strand that ran down the length of his fly and under his inseam and past his posterior and along his back on up to where it had gotten fixed and woven to the band around his head. The whole of it, of course, was soft cottony macramé string pretty much but for down along Mr. Dale Gentry's inseam where, per his instructions, Mrs. Judy Gentry had worked into the braid a manner of prickly item of Mr. Dale Gentry's own devising that looked for all the world like an outsized cocklebur. It was toothpicks chiefly stuck in a lump of wax, toothpicks meant to imply with their tipends how lifting and raising and lurching up were just precisely the variety of activities to cause a man's swing to suffer, by extension anyhow they were meant to imply it since what they implied right there at the first blush was how the lifting and the raising and the lurching up might torment a man's dangly apparatus instead.

Naturally, he'd developed a squeal. Mr. Dale Gentry had pretty much straightaway developed a squeal that came to be as much a part of his swing as his prefatory club waggling and his graceful looping followthrough, and there at the first he didn't truly but squeal chiefly, squealed that is and sliced with it when he was able at all to bring his clubhead and bring his ball together in the same place exactly. Presently, though, he got truly a grip upon what it was precisely the toothpick tipends by extension implied and he managed to curb his lifting and his raising and his lurching up to the point that he could begin even to construe his slice as a fade in place of it if he did not watch his ball land and bounce across the breadth of the range. And shortly even it was a fade mostly and he'd waggle and flex and set and rotate and cock and pause and uncoil and sweep and squeal and extend and then watch his ball fairly soar and only vaguely and hardly at all bend round from slightly to his left to slightly to his right but for the times he hit balls purely straight and but for the solitary occasion when he managed a verifiable hook into the trees that he became altogether too ecstatic on account of and yelped and leapt and fairly skewered his organ.

Mr. Dale Gentry was pretty much of a sight then, and if Mr. Dick Atwater had not been so thoroughly engaged with whipping his driver and endeavoring at the same time to appear the sort of man that knew in the first place why exactly he had cause to whip it he probably would have noticed what a sight Mr. Dale Gentry was like Miss Mary Alice Celestine Lefler noticed it pretty much at the outset. Straightoff, of course, she'd taken in the squeal like had led her to the headband and down the harness to the inseam strap with the outsized cocklebur fixed to it, and she'd been trying to grab hold of Mr. Dick Atwater so as to indicate most especially the cocklebur to him but the clubwhipping kept her back and once she finally found the opportunity to lay her fingers upon Mr. Dick Atwater and tell to him lowly, "Jerome," the gentleman to their left cued his teed up range ball directly into the partition like stunned and agitated the both of them together until, of course, the gentleman to their left had troubled himself to explain to them, "Well shit."

Presently, though, the both of them had a hoot. Presently she indicated the cocklebur to Mr. Dick Atwater who inadvertently invoked the Savior about it like he let on he could not help but invoke him due to what item chiefly Mr. Dale Gentry had seen fit to strap his cocklebur across. "I wouldn't wear such," Mr. Dick Atwater declared.

And Miss Mary Alice Celestine Lefler told ever so sweetly to him back, "I should surely hope not," or it seemed anyway ever so sweetly to Mr. Dick Atwater who found himself stilled and drawn up on account of how the talk struck him as their first truly intimate exchange since it was after all his own personal dangly parts they were speaking obliquely of.

He meant to exhibit a measure of prowess for her as he figured he had some prowess left, so he stepped up atop their rubber mat and settled a striped ball onto the tee. For a time he stood behind it and peered out across the range at the flags and the markers and most especially the target off two hundred yards with the bull's-eye on it, but eventually he stepped on around and addressed, he told to Miss Mary Alice Celestine Lefler, the ball. Back previously when he had in fact played some golf, addressing the ball had been a thing he'd excelled at due to how he'd evermore looked in his golfing stance capable of actually golfing, so once he'd addressed the ball for Miss Mary Alice Celestine Lefler he loitered at it since he could not help but believe his swing would thwart and undo the impression his stance had likely inspired. He was obliged, however, to swing at length and so drew back his metalheaded club as far as he could recollect he needed to draw it prior to shifting pretty much his entire weight forward and thrusting most especially his hipsocket towards the target with the bull's-eye on it like would have probably preceded a masterful stroke and an altogether lengthsome drive but for how it was Mr. Dale Gentry, who was not meaning to drive just presently on his own, accidentally poked himself in the cocklebur with his rubber grip and naturally exclaimed on account of it. Consequently, Mr. Dick Atwater grew distracted and did not find he could manage a masterful stroke like left him instead to loose across the range a fairly scorching dribble which he exhibited at Mr. Dale Gentry a hard look about like was nothing truly compared to the self-inflicted sensation Mr. Dale Gentry had lately endured.

Of course she soothed him, told to him, "Jerome," that way she had of telling Jerome to him that put him at peace and relieved entirely the shame the dribbling had brought about like Mrs. Dick Atwater with countless "Oh Dick"s probably could not hardly have managed since Mrs. Dick Atwater had not been the type who was prone to soothe. In fact, he felt shortly so easeful and unashamed that he teed up yet another striped ball and addressed it, addressed it with the notion it would be somehow dedicated to her who'd bothered to soothe him the wake of his dribble, her with the hair and the eyes and the lips and the fingerends, her that he thought on as he drew back and thought on as he swung and thought on as he watched his striped ball soar fairly straight up into the air and drop fairly straight back down out of it that she told him shortly a kind thing about.

On the range in their stall atop their rubber mat they were an item together and proved up the tees and down them to be near about as diverting as the buglight on the pole above them which was entertaining this particular evening a swarm of some manner of beetlebugs and so popped and sizzled like a skillet. Of course nobody much had previously seen Mr. Dick Atwater with a woman that wasn't Mrs. Dick Atwater and nobody much had previously seen Mr. Dick Atwater with such an altogether southerly hairpart like was two things worth looking at Dick Atwater about in addition to the variety of woman with him who seemed to the men up the tees and down them foreign and exotic and likely from out of the county entirely. She was even a trifle girlish as best as they could tell, girlish and sleek and comely too, girlish and sleek and comely enough that is to fairly indict Mr. Dick Atwater as a variety of old fool that George Lundee down the range a ways waggled his six iron and announced to anybody that cared to hear it. So he hit balls and she stood by to soothe him when she felt she had cause for it, and he aimed for a stretch at the target and aimed for a stretch at the flag shy of it but did not strike the target or so much as endanger the flag until a colored boy in Mr. Tadlock's employ took the tractor with the cage upon it and the ball scoop back of it out onto the range when most everybody that had been aiming previously at a thing otherwise undertook to hit him instead like Mr. Dick Atwater undertook to hit him himself and managed by it to hit once the target and strafe once the flag too.

Though she insisted she'd rather not, Mr. Dick Atwater could tell Miss Mary Alice Celestine Lefler was longing to beat a ball herself and he drew her up onto the mat with him where straightaway he showed her his addressing technique that she exhibited directly a knack for and she waggled like he'd waggled and whipped like he'd whipped and endured Mr. Dick Atwater snug up against her posterior from where he reached his arms around her and made as if to guide her backswing and made as if to guide her stroke and made as if to guide her followthrough beyond it for longer truly than her followthrough needed guiding which George Lundee had in particular a thing to say about, a loud unwholesome thing addressed just out to anybody that cared to hear it like might even have been Dick Atwater as well if he'd found himself of the moment disposed to hear, disposed to hear anyway other than his breath in his nose and his spit in his head and his blood that pounded all over. And she even hit the ball, hit it straight and solid and squealed on account of it in a Mr. Dale Gentry-homemade-cocklebur sort of a way prior to entertaining from Mr. Dick Atwater talk of how divine a stroke he'd taken hers to be which she endeavored to dispute and he endeavored to insist upon until just of a sudden they both together left off speaking and endeavoring even to speak and just gazed, it seemed to Mr. Dick Atwater when later atop his fitted sheet and beneath his flat one he'd undertaken to relive it, full on each other all charmed and transfixed both like would be him purely with her and would be her purely with him back.

It just seemed one of those snatches of time he'd previously heard tell of when people got caught up and people got stopped plain cold while life roundabout them still teemed and pulsated like life at the golf range continued to teem and to pulsate both, and Dick Atwater told to Miss Mary Alice Celestine Lefler three of her names together as he could not determine which name to tell to her alone and Miss Mary Alice Celestine Lefler told to him, "Jerome," in return, actually told to him, "What Jerome?" though atop the fitted sheet and beneath the flat one he did not have much use for the What and so heard just the names he'd called her and heard just the name she'd called him back while they'd gazed and stood oblivious together to the balls that whistled and the unharnessed golfers that grunted and swore and the sizeable beetlebugs that dropped from the lightpole like firecoals to the ground.

Three

TWO words. Mr. Phillip J. King said he had precisely just two words for him though he did not tell to him straightoff which two words they might be partly due to how it was he guessed he saw ahead of him a measure of drama to milk and partly due to how it was he could not truly find much place on his gnome to grip and grab to like drew him off the two words he'd spoken just lately about. He hadn't supposed a gnome would be so bulky and ponderous since he'd evermore figured gnomes for wispy and figured gnomes for spritelike and he wondered of Nestor Tudor if didn't their particular gnome seem to him fairly completely ungnomeish altogether that Nestor Tudor went ahead and let on he'd calculated already their gnome probably would.

"It's cement," he told to Mr. Phillip J. King who could not himself help but believe a gnome might be cement and puckish all at the same time, couldn't anyway see much reason why whoever it was made gnomes in the first place had to cast them so godawful heavy like wasn't, as best as Mr. Phillip J. King could figure, much in the spirit of the glade, and he wondered at Nestor Tudor would he tell to him please what could possibly be wry and waifish about a three-foot-high two-hundred-pound imp of the forest but Nestor Tudor found himself purely stymied by the inquiry and so could not muster a reply.

She'd guessed she'd be pleased with a gnome, Mrs. Phillip J. King had. She'd implied, that is, how she'd worked up lately an affection for lawn sculpture and so would likely take a frog and tolerate a speckled deer and endure even a pickaninny in among her begonias but a gnome, she suggested, was the item she had most especially a spot for back of the house alongside her camellia bush where her sweet William had lately given up the ghost. Of course, Mrs. Grady Floars's gnome two lots over had to a degree inspired her though she was not altogether taken with Mrs. Grady Floars's gnome entirely due chiefly to the lurid colors Mrs. Grady Floars had seen fit somehow to paint her gnome like left it to look a harlot, Mrs. Phillip J. King figured, like rendered it so thoroughly ungnomish as to pretty completely defeat in the first place the purpose of having a gnome at all. She'd leave her own gnome subdued, swore anyway to Mr. Phillip J. King that if she managed somehow to get blessed with a gnome she'd not hardly doll it up so but would touch it instead here and there with your muted sorts of colors and set it to lurk in the shrubbery like she'd been evermore convinced your gnomes were for. A gaudy gnome was hardly a thing she was looking to have. She assured Mr. Phillip J. King she couldn't see any use in a gaudy gnome at all.

Of course Mr. Phillip J. King did not himself have a thing in the world against gnomes and would have probably bought and hauled one for Mrs. Phillip J. King even if her hormones had not lately kicked up to torment her, but since she was suffering so with her condition he was willing to let her stick in the shrubbery anything at all she might see fit to stick in there and was just relieved she'd not selected a donkey with a cart back of it or a flock of painted chickens since, if he had to endure a thing, a gnome was what he figured he'd be most pleased to endure most especially if it soothed and diverted Mrs. Phillip J. King who'd suffered lately a setback at the Number 2 shelter on account of her stewed kidneys that had failed, she'd learned, to get taken for delectable like she'd hoped when she stewed them they would. Consequently, her elevated consciousness had in just the few days following the get-together lost some appreciable altitude and Mrs. Phillip J. King had begun to wallow in her stewed kidney misfortune, had begun to just mope roundabout in a pathetic sort of way there at first but had presently left off moping to grow aggravated instead like had shortly given way itself to a bout of pure peevishness which had culminated in the Irish potato and the Vadalia onion that together had served to communicate to Mr. Phillip J. King the manner of predicament precisely he'd come to be in.

Throughout the span of their marriage, throughout the stretches in particular of the span of their marriage that were not somehow all ripe with bliss, Mrs. Phillip J. King had only ever previously hurled one thing at him, had only ever hurled actually two things which were in truth four things together that came towards him pretty much like one thing by itself which was how most times he recalled it when he bothered to think on it at all. They'd been shoes. They'd been shoes with the socks stuck down in the toes of them and he'd left them, she'd told to him, in the middle of the floor for the ultimate time entirely she was willing to suffer in him the habit of it. In truth, of course, they'd not been just precisely in the middle of the floor exactly but had gotten dropped instead alongside Mr. Phillip J. King's upholstered chair just shy of his folding TV table that it seemed to him Mrs. Phillip J. King would have to be meaning to climb upon before she could enjoy the occasion to stumble on his shoes which he'd apprised presently Mrs. Phillip J. King of like she had not truly been looking to get apprised which she'd informed him sharply about prior to taking up his shoes together and hauling them out from the den into the backhall that she'd meant to carry them the length of to the bedroom where vacant shoes, she figured, most times belonged, and she'd even set out a little when Mr. Phillip J. King unaccountably found himself pressed with the urge to apprise Mrs. Phillip J. King further still than he'd apprised her already like stopped her and drew her around and moved her to inform him a little further herself, moved her to tell to Mr. Phillip J. King, "You just hush," like got punctuated with his black pebblegrained lace-up shoes that she flung and hurled both together so that they bounced off of him pretty much like one thing just by itself.

She'd not somehow been incited to fling much since and had subsequently only beaten him one time on the elbow with a skillet that had never truly departed from her hand and so could not be construed as flung truly like left just the shoes with the socks in the toes of them until the potato and until the onion too that he'd not either one anticipated. The carshed had beckoned to him. They'd been sitting together before the TV, him and Mrs. Phillip J. King, watching on the cable a show about your sexual variety of dysfunction like Mr. Phillip J. King could not straightaway identify as the topic due to how he'd arrived home in the middle of the thing and so found a few people perched upon a stage fielding inquiries from an audience in the studio who were, by and large, anxious to discover just what precisely had dysfuncted with them and how come. Naturally, Mr. Phillip J. King wondered of Mrs. Phillip J. King what in the hell it was they were the pack of them speaking of as he'd grown in his day wilty but had not, as best as he knew, dysfuncted even one time, and of course Mrs. Phillip J. King wondered with some moderately uplifted breathiness back how she was supposed to hear what in fact the pack of them were speaking of if he didn't shut his mouth so she might. Although he was tempted, Mr. Phillip J. King refrained from growing testy with Mrs. Phillip J.

King since he reasoned it was her hormones chiefly that had reared up and snapped at him, so he told her just, "Now sugar," and was meaning to be for a time sweet and smarmy when he caught sight on the TV of a woman in the audience with an altogether dysfuncted husband who she complained there over the airwaves about and told to anybody who cared to hear it what variety of undertakings that husband of hers evermore failed to consummate unless of course he did not so much as undertake to consummate them in the first place and instead drew up most all the bedclothes around him and slept on his back with his mouth open and his breath gurgling in his neck.

She was looking to find the cause of it all, that woman was, was hoping one of those previously dysfuncted people upon the stage could identify for her the cause of it so she could maybe go home to her man and heal him of his affliction which didn't appear to Mr. Phillip J. King there on the sofa probably much of her man's affliction at all since the woman on the TV hardly struck Mr. Phillip J. King as the sort he'd be himself even the least bit tempted to consummate with. She was a homely creature and there was so appreciably much of her to be homely that the homely and the appreciable together struck Mr. Phillip J. King as just precisely the variety of potent combination that could probably dysfunct a bull at fifty paces like left him to wonder how it was she could blame her man for dropping off into a slumber, left him to wonder it firstoff just at himself but left him to wonder it presently at Mrs. Phillip J. King too which would be the parts about the big and the homely and the neck gurgling and the livestock as well that he figured Mrs. Phillip J. King would likely share his view of and maybe, had her hormones not intervened, she would have, but what with her imbalance and what with her consequent state she found herself prompted to inform Mr. Phillip J. King how just because she'd come on her own to be slight and wiry and fetching she did not hardly feel obliged to join Mr. Phillip J. King in running down a woman who suffered quite apparently from a glandular disorder like seemed to her just precisely the sort of thing a man would evermore be up to. And Mrs. Phillip J. King grew on the sofa disgusted with Mr. Phillip J. King and inveighed there in the den against him until he sensed how the carshed was pretty stridently beckoning to him and so escaped to it through the kitchen and out the backdoor.

He'd taken up his sander and was working it across a piece of clapboard on the west carshed wall formulating while he did it the wry rejoinder he would have probably inflicted upon Mrs. Phillip J. King if he'd had previously occasion to formulate it, and he honed and refined it and told it just out into the air with some palpable bite to it though not hardly sufficient palpable bite to suit him like was how come he told it shortly just out into the air another time. For her part, Mrs. Phillip J. King managed to accumulate some moderate agitation on the sofa watching the previously dysfuncted people upon the stage advising what were, predominately, presently dysfuncted people in the audience, or wives chiefly anyhow of presently dysfuncted people who appeared to Mrs. Phillip J. King tormented due to just precisely the gender of creature Mr. Phillip J. King was himself one of like seemed on the sofa enough to her to be enraged with Mr. Phillip J. King about which was how come she got shortly enraged in fact and rose up herself to cross the kitchen to the backdoor and step out onto the landing from where she spoke of Mr. Phillip J. King's gender to him, from where she communicated down across the yard to the carshed her opinion just presently of the male of the species who seemed to her a shameful inconsiderate manner of beast, struck her as just the sort that would up and get dysfuncted once his woman had grown only the slightest bit poochy and thick. She could see in Mr. Phillip J. King the latent capacity for neck gurgling. She'd watched him sleep previously on his back with his mouth laid full open and his breath popping somewhere in among his molars like she had to figure was, doubtless, preamble to dysfunction itself, so she'd stepped out onto the landing intending to disclose to Mr. Phillip J. King down at the carshed how she'd come to be lately acquainted with what ilk precisely he was like she meant directly to reform him on account of but she could not from the landing truly disclose it all to him due to how his contraption whined and whirred like it seemed to her his contraption evermore did.

"P.J.," she hollered at him in just her regular hollering voice there at the first but presently in her excruciatingly highpitched squealy sort of a voice as well that she persisted at hollering at him with until the general tumult of her hormones sent her on back into the kitchen where she endured atop the linoleum a flashy spell that caused her head to swim and her knees to grow wobbly and thereby induced her to grab onto her doughbowl alongside the door, her doughbowl with the legs to it that she did not have much call to work and knead dough in like left her doughbowl free to hold potatoes and free to hold onions instead. Of course she was meaning to toss them, told herself how tossing was what she was truly meaning to do and, once her knees firmed a little and her head began to clear, she took up a sizeable Irish potato and a Vadalia onion with some inordinate heft to it and carried the both of them out onto the landing where she told herself yet another time how she was meaning chiefly just to toss the potato straightoff and only maybe the onion subsequently if the potato somehow did not manage to do what she tried to believe she hoped it might, if the potato somehow did not manage to rouse Mr. Phillip J. King off from his wall and away from his clapboard like she let on the tossing was for.

She didn't, however, toss truly and didn't purely fling either but chiefly hurled in fact, plain fired her Irish potato from the landing once she'd coiled and wound up, plain fired it directly at the back of Mr. Phillip J. King's bony head like she made to believe was tossing even once she'd gone on and commenced already to fire it. She'd simply found herself disposed to knock him over as she'd come to be in the midst of her froth and her agitation convinced altogether that even if the hormones were hers the blame was somehow his entirely like seemed to her to justify a fullblown potato-cranium collision, so she uncoiled and unwound pretty directly after she'd coiled and wound prior to them and loosed her potato with some extravagant velocity to it, pitched it down off the landing towards the carshed where Mr. Phillip J. King did not have occasion, naturally, to see it coming until it had sailed already past him and beat against the carshed wall that it bounced off of and fell shortly away from but for the piece that stuck which was a trifle of skin with a hunk of white tuber meat fixed to it. Of course the potato and the clapboard in combination straightaway stirred Mr. Phillip J. King who shut off his discsander and raised full upright to where he could peruse the scrap of skin and the hunk of white tuber meat which struck him together as so utterly unforeseen and exotic that he could not manage but to stand and but to gape upon them until he managed somehow to raise his head and look skyward as well so as to find out was there maybe above him a place a piece of potato could have come from.

He spoke even, said just out into the air, "Hey!" like was what he usually said in the face of a conundrum, and he left off studying the sky so as to swing around and tell towards the backdoor Hey! another time which he figured itself might draw Mrs. Phillip J. King out from the sitting room and into his conundrum with him but she was partaking just presently of a manner of mystery on her own and had set in to coiling and winding up so as to toss, she told to herself, her Vadalia onion and thereby gain, she told to herself, the attention of Mr. Phillip J. King who was turning already as she rared back and would have surely given his attention to her quite shortly all uninduced and thoroughly unprompted but for how he got prevented from it by the solitary piece of produce Mrs. Phillip J. King informed herself she was meaning just simply to stir him a little with. Likely, but for the turning and the swinging around, he would have entertained it full against his boniest cranial part which Mr. Phillip J. King, upon reflection, suspected would have been preferable probably to the patch of skin under his left ear where he took the onion instead like he'd not been truly anticipating taking an onion and so flopped on over from surprise as much as anything, fell into Mrs. Phillip J. King's leafy creeping groundcover and gazed up into a stretch of sky that seemed anymore fairly potatoless to him.

He raised shortly up on his elbows and spied atop the landing Mrs. Phillip J. King who just stood and just looked at him back until she set in briefly to railing at him on the topic of his ilk that he could not from down in the creeping groundcover make awful much sense of as it didn't seem to him he'd changed ilks lately but had been for a spell his ilk already like he was just before proclaiming with some heat and agitation himself when Mrs. Phillip J. King's hormones seemed to slosh and surge and thereby caused her to drop down upon the top step where she undertook to persist at railing but felt obliged to blubber a bit as well and so railed and blubbered both together at Mr. Phillip J. King who stretched again full out in the leafy creeping groundcover and endeavored to call up those pre-change-of-life days that seemed anymore so sweet and simple to him, those glorious times when Mrs. Phillip J. King could maintain somehow a mood all pure and undiluted, could stay peeved or stay unpeeved and did not ever seem so much as tempted to be both at once.

He brought himself upright and stepped on out from the groundcover and climbed the stairs up to Mrs. Phillip J. King who said a kind of a wet blubbery thing to him, a wet blubbery utterly incomprehensible variety of item that she waited there on the top step for an answer to, an answer other than just the "Now, sugar" that Mr. Phillip J. King saw fit to tell her prior to stroking her with his flat open hand on the top of her head just like he stroked every now and again their terrier Ittybit when Ittybit did not appear of a mood to chew on him for it.

"P.J.," Mrs. Phillip J. King fairly wailed from the top step after such a fashion as to leave Mr. Phillip J. King pretty remotely certain that P.J. was what she'd come out with. "P.J.," Mrs. Phillip J. King fairly wailed another time as a preface to an additional blubbery manner of thing that she loosed back of it, and Mr. Phillip J. King sat himself down alongside her and, with his arm full well roundabout her midsection, told to Mrs. Phillip J. King what a slinky pencil-thin creature she seemed to him to be which anymore was usually the sort of talk to pretty much still her hormones like her hormones began to seem to him on their way to being in fact pretty much stilled judging from how it was Mrs. Phillip J. King let up on her blubbering and drew in her knees so as to lay the side of her head down upon them from where she looked out across their yard and across the yard beyond it and so far as into Mrs. Grady Floars's backlot where Mrs. Grady Floars's painted gnome appeared to fairly caper in among the periwinkle which she said shortly another time, "P.J.," on account of though not near so mournful and blubbery as her P.J.'s just previously had seemed.

Stumpy Tate had agreed to help him haul it. Stumpy Tate had allowed how he'd be pleased for five dollars to get picked up at his room over the laundry and carried out the highway to the lawn sculpture yard so as to take up a gnome with Mr. Phillip J. King and load it in the car and ride it to the house and haul it even another time to the backyard, but come the Saturday two days past the onion and the blubbering when he'd agreed for five dollars to ride and tote and haul and carry Stumpy Tate found himself undisposed to so much as raise up off the mattress due to the vintage of mash he'd just the night previously ingested, or due truly to the vintage of mash in combination with the sheer unmitigated quantity of it like had caused him together to fall out and had rendered him near about deceased that all he had to do was wake up to wish it had. So Mr. Phillip J. King arrived at the laundry when they'd agreed together he should arrive and beat a manner of tattoo on his carhorn like was meant to signal Stumpy Tate and straightaway did signal him, floated him in fact clean up off the mattress which he'd only just settled back atop of when Mr. Phillip J. King lifted him another time and consequently brought him to the window where he hung out over the sill and appeared on the verge of discharging for Mr. Phillip J. King a portion of what mash precisely he'd ingested.

He sent him out to Nestor Tudor's, Stumpy Tate did, as he knew for certain Nestor Tudor to be the sort of man to haul a gnome without much notice to speak of, so Mr. Phillip J. King shortly pulled into Nestor Tudor's drive and launched into a carhorn serenade that brought Nestor Tudor around from the backyard where he'd lately been rearranging his assorted refuse, where he'd lately laid anyhow a piece of his dead wife Erlene's Maytag atop a heap that had been previously about half Buick and half Farmall Cub with just the grillwork from a Coldspot for a garnish. In the drive alongside Mr. Phillip J. King's green Mercury Monterey he listened to the gnome troubles Mr. Phillip J. King had lately been pressed to suffer and heard how, by extension, Mr. Phillip J. King's gnome troubles were chiefly hormonal truly that Nestor Tudor could not straightoff fathom on account of the appreciable gap he seemed to perceive even just on first blush in the driveway between gnomes and hormones like he thought briefly he might inquire about but didn't after all bother to inquire about it and just shut and latched his backdoor prior to climbing into Mr. Phillip J. King's green Monterey with him.

Together they spoke of Stumpy Tate who was ill, Mr. Phillip J. King called it, and appeared to have caught maybe a thing which Nestor Tudor assured Mr. Phillip J. King Stumpy Tate had, caught probably a bottleneck between his lips like was his habit come Friday night when he rendered himself most times afflicted and undone which Mr. Phillip J. King and Nestor Tudor both together wagged their heads about and humphed by turns until they'd grown again still and grown again quiet which they stayed for a time up the highway before Mr. Phillip J. King felt pressed and obliged to ask of Nestor Tudor if his dead wife Erlene had passed on her way into the everlasting through the change of life first that he let on he had grave and ponderous cause to know of or wouldn't in the first place have felt pressed and obliged to ask it.

"She suffered an edgy spell," Nestor Tudor admitted and then added back of it, "I think it was an edgy spell she suffered."

And Mr. Phillip J. King said himself, "An edgy spell," and grew squinty while he undertook to construe Mrs. Phillip J. King's own present personal spell as edgy somehow like even with his eyelids clapped near about full shut he could not manage to succeed at and shortly he confessed to Nestor Tudor how his own wife was pretty much past edgy, was in fact well beyond edgy altogether.

"Is she?" Nestor Tudor wanted to know.

And Mr. Phillip J. King jerked his head so as to indicate she was prior to wondering at Nestor Tudor if his dead wife Erlene had ever, back before she got dead and had been just edgy instead, shown much disposition to throw produce and such at him which Nestor Tudor could not recall even a solitary instance of though he told how she'd smacked him one time with her spongemop like Mr. Phillip J. King did not believe fell into the category of produce that got just plain hurled for no good reason at all. "Onion," Mr. Phillip J. King said and pointed towards the particular piece of his head the thing had bounced off of.

"Yellow onion?"

"Vadalia onion," Mr. Phillip J. King said, "like this," and he laid his hands together on the wheel so as to describe with the fingers of them an inordinately girthsome item of near about melonish proportions. "Fired it," Mr. Phillip J. King told to Nestor Tudor and could not help but boast of Mrs. Phillip J. King's arm that had seemed to him fine and strong for most especially a menopausal woman, and Nestor Tudor whewed and humphed and Mr. Phillip J. King whewed and humphed shortly with him prior to hearing from Nestor Tudor how he guessed maybe a cement gnome was in fact the item for her. "Bounce onions off one of them things all day," Nestor Tudor said and thereby inspired Mr. Phillip J. King to pretty dramatically alter his opinion of gnomes altogether.

The lawn ornament yard was north up 29 almost to Danville and Mr. Phillip J. King, who'd called to see did they stock gnomes, had been told about the two that sat and the three that stood and the one that hunkered which Mrs. Phillip J. King had informed him already she did not want him to bring home as she had no use whatsoever for a hunkering gnome. However, she couldn't truly know that a sitting gnome might not strike her and consequently had charged Mr. Phillip J. King to gauge the sitting gnomes and decide as best as he was able could maybe a plain cement sitting gnome get rendered somehow subdued though Mr. Phillip J. King was of a mind that a gnome sitting was pretty completely subdued already like he wanted to hear from Nestor Tudor about and so asked of him would he maybe himself take for subdued a sitting gnome that Nestor Tudor seemed in fact to be pondering and dwelling upon until he wondered at Mr. Phillip J. King if, as long as they'd gotten onto women anyhow, might he inquire a thing before they shifted off to gnomes entirely since he was curious just presently about women in a thoroughgoing sort of a way on account of a boy he knew who had come to get charmed, had come to get purely enchanted.

And Nestor Tudor heard from Mr. Phillip J. King, "All right then," and heard from Mr. Phillip J. King further still of the way he'd had one time with the ladies like he could not help but believe more than qualified him to field inquiries and he displayed for Nestor Tudor his sidelong look he'd been known to ever so routinely strike the women dead with like Nestor Tudor grew shortly obliged to admit was as fine a sidelong look as he'd seen lately and he displayed for Mr. Phillip J. King his own personal sidelong look back that Mr. Phillip J. King told to him was a start for a sidelong look though, like seemed to him the way with most things, he didn't guess a man could hope to just up and look sidelong all raw and unrehearsed.

As best as Nestor Tudor could recall, the boy he knew who'd gotten charmed and gotten enchanted hadn't ever somehow cultivated much of a sidelong look himself and so could not figure to just swivel his head and cut his eyes and thereby fell the women, thereby anyway fell the particular woman he'd come to be taken with, and Nestor Tudor wondered couldn't maybe that boy he knew do a thing otherwise than just look chiefly sidelong that he lacked in the first place the gift for. "Well," Mr. Phillip J. King said and freed his one arm to lay it along the seatback while he fairly sprawled with the rest of himself as best as he could sprawl and drive both prior to asking of Nestor Tudor, "Can't look sidelong?" that Nestor Tudor assured him about and so shortly learned from Mr. Phillip J. King of the manner of low whispery talk that felled women sometimes too.

"It's not the what," Mr. Phillip J. King disclosed. "It's the how primarily," and he treated Nestor Tudor to a spell of low whispery talk, low whispery municipal sewer bond talk that Nestor Tudor did not but vaguely take in the sewer bond part of due to the low and due to the whispery which conspired together to purely disguise the gist and laid full upon it like a mist on a stream. A rumination on the chance of rain all low and whispery as well impressed Nestor Tudor further still seeming like it did fairly saturated with tenderness, and Mr. Phillip J. King encouraged Nestor Tudor to undertake a snatch of such talk himself like shortly Nestor Tudor undertook one, said anyhow a thing about a hole in the boulevard he'd patched and smoothed but said it, Mr. Phillip J. King insisted, with inordinate hiss and hardly any lilt to speak of which prompted him to inform Nestor Tudor how he'd never even one time seen a woman felled by your liltless hissy sort of talk.

Shortly, however, Nestor Tudor had honed his delivery and he found he was fairly well capable of holding with Mr. Phillip J. King a low and whispery manner of confab about hardly anything at all. Of course he could not begin to look sidelong and talk both with what scintillating effect Mr. Phillip J. King looked sidelong and talked himself but, after some additional tutelage, Nestor Tudor discovered how he was able to work up at will a tender face with a palpable hint of fascination to it like seemed purely as good as a sidelong look to Mr. Phillip J. King who admitted there in the front seat of his Monterey to feeling a little swoony himself on account of it. "Show it to that boy you know," Mr. Phillip J. King advised. "A man might drop a whole pack of women with such as that," which Nestor Tudor admitted with his voice all low and whispery a man surely might.

Naturally they passed the ornament yard the first time they came up on it due partly to Mr. Phillip J. King's sidelong glance and partly to Nestor Tudor's fascinated face that they did not either one of them see straightoff the ornament yard with. But presently they grew regular again and turned around so as to pull shortly into the gravel lot where they climbed out from the Monterey and admired straightoff a puny armless woman, admired in fact three identical puny armless women together that weren't between them wearing a thing in the world but pensive expressions like caused Mr. Phillip J. King to admit how, if he had to look at an item in the shrubbery, a puny armless naked woman was just the manner of item he'd be pleased to see while, as for himself, Nestor Tudor got taken with an adjacent bird instead, a tall spindly sort of a bird alongside the northernmost puny armless woman that the Evers who'd come out from his shed back of the pickaninnies informed Nestor Tudor was an egret.

"A what?"

"An egret," the Evers told to him. "Stick one in a patch of monkey grass and you've plain got a sight."

"Do you?"

"Yes sir," the Evers insisted. "I can't keep them on the yard."

And Mr. Phillip J. King who'd drawn off briefly from the puny armless naked women to gaze on the egret himself figured how there wasn't probably an uglier pair of legs anywhere roundabout. "Bumpy sticks," he told to Nestor Tudor and told it to the Evers as well who told to him back, "You must not be acquainted with my wife's sister," that Mr. Phillip J. King had to admit he wasn't.

While they were in fact hunting a gnome, Mr. Phillip J. King felt disposed to price a puny armless naked woman as well since he guessed he might find room in his shrubbery for one, and on account of how the Evers was presently running a special on toads and chickens both he shared with Mr. Phillip J. King and Nestor Tudor news of the scant piece of money they could cart off a half dozen toads or a half dozen chickens for. "Mix them too," the Evers told them, "toads and chickens together," that Mr. Phillip J. King confessed was purely a temptation though he guessed since they were hunting chiefly a gnome, a gnome was what they'd probably best end up with. So the Evers led Mr. Phillip J. King and Nestor Tudor with him to his gnome section, led them past the lone egret and through the chickens and the toads and beyond the deer and the outsized sombrero planter boxes and the little Dutch boys and the little Dutch girls and the assorted birdbaths and sundials and the cement dogs and the cement lions and the two naked cement Grecian gentlemen with a set of cement testicles apiece back to his cache of assorted gnomes that were bunched up together by the cyclone fence looking fairly incarcerated. The sitting gnomes were perched upon cement stumps that the Evers was quick to announce were separate items altogether. The standing gnomes were just plain standing while the hunkering gnome was himself hunkering after such a fashion as to look to have been frozen up in the midst of a movement like Mr. Phillip J. King had to guess was apt in a horticultural sort of a way since the hunkering gnome would evermore appear right there on the verge of fertilizing whatever manner of greenery he'd been set in that the Evers let on was the beauty of a hunkering gnome in fact.

"What about these here?" Mr. Phillip J. King wanted to know and indicated the three upright gnomes that were two of them peering at each other while the third one stood snug up against the fence with his little stubby fingers partway through the wire of it like rendered him fairly forlorn, most especially for a creature that was supposed to be instead wily and gay.

"Them plain ones?" the Evers inquired and Mr. Phillip J. King indicated to him how yes it was the plain stumpless unhunkering gnomes he was singularly curious about. Consequently, then, the Evers announced to Mr. Phillip J. King and Nestor Tudor both his prime upright gnome price like seemed to Mr. Phillip J. King steep for a gnome, in particular a gnome that was stumpless and unhunkering and wasn't even wearing the sorts of shoes that curled up much at the toes like he'd figured was standard imp of the forest footwear. And the Evers said, "Well," and the Evers said, "all right," and retreated directly to a lesser prime upright gnome price which took into account, as best as he could tell, Mr. Phillip J. King's shoetoe distress.

"I don't know," Mr. Phillip J. King told to him and then looked a little sidelong, though not passionately sidelong truly, at Nestor Tudor who confessed back how he didn't himself know either. "That's a sizeable piece of money for a gnome," Mr. Phillip J. King said and the Evers threw directly in with him how yes in fact it was for a gnome a sizeable piece of money but he wondered at Mr. Phillip J. King could a fellow hope to put a price on the manner of joy a gnome in the shrubbery would bring to him and his loved ones that Mr. Phillip J. King couldn't say though he declared outright how the price on the actual gnome itself seemed sufficient to cover the joy as well that the Evers admitted to him it probably was.

Of course, there weren't in the county any gnomes otherwise to be had like the Evers did not need to up and tell plain to communicate as there hung about him the air of a man with the gnome market cornered, and once he'd spied a woman off across the yard perusing his birdbaths he excused himself from Mr. Phillip J. King and Nestor Tudor both so as to leave them to speak together of the gnome like they did in fact shortly speak together of it though straightaway the talk was chiefly of the Evers instead whom Mr. Phillip J. King felt obliged to issue assorted invectives about. For gnomes, most especially the three upright ones did not strike Mr. Phillip J. King as particularly elfin, though he could not say plain and for certain should he be struck elfin by a gnome like Nestor Tudor did not feel able himself to pass judgment on since he could not but suppose that maybe gnomes should seem just impish instead and possibly a trifle spritelike. The three upright gnomes against the fence were pretty completely identical except for the one of them turned roundabout with his fingers through the links that had a noticeable seam down the side of his head, a sloppy upraised seam which Mr. Phillip J. King could not himself much approve of, so he judged between the two remaining gnomes and undertook to figure which he preferred, or undertook truly to figure which of them Mrs. Phillip J. King might herself be partial to which proved to be a chore for him as he could fashion either of the two gnomes subdued in the plantbed alongside Mrs. Phillip J. King's camellia bush which left him to call on Nestor Tudor to pick a gnome for him that Nestor Tudor obliged him directly about and selected the near gnome which seemed to him as gnomy altogether as the far one and closer even too.

Naturally they both had to circle and study it and squat for a time before it while Mr. Phillip J. King recited into the air the Evers's gnome price, the Evers's adjusted-for-shoetoe-distress discounted gnome price which seemed itself still appreciable to Mr. Phillip J. King who spat northerly one time and spat easterly one time too prior to telling to Nestor Tudor, "Women," with what he meant for disdain though Nestor Tudor did not himself decipher the disdain truly on account of the sort of state he'd lately lapsed into.

He said in fact, "Women," to Mr. Phillip J. King back without any rue to speak of and wondered behind it if a gnome or some such lawn sculpture otherwise was the variety of item a woman might come to be impassioned about as he figured that boy he knew could possibly find himself disposed to make a gift maybe of a gnome or a gift maybe of an egret to that woman he'd gotten charmed by if a gnome or an egret might stir her, but Mr. Phillip J. King, who showed himself inclined to spit further still towards points otherwise than he'd spat at already, shortly informed Nestor Tudor, "Naw," and presently told to him behind it, "You don't catch them with gnomes and the like. Can't hardly hope to woo a woman with an egret. That's just how you soothe them once they're caught." And he said another time to Nestor Tudor, "Naw," and set to studying a plain patch of air, pondered it at some considerable length until he apparently grew from it moved and grew from it inspired and told, "Two words," to Nestor Tudor. "Ingot," he said, "Lounge."

Together between them they took up the gnome of preference and set to hauling it across the ornament yard towards Mr. Phillip J. King's Monterey, but they hadn't gone even halfway before they stopped in among some assorted cement wildlife and the two sets of cement Grecian testicles to recover their wind and ease their muscles and discuss between them the inordinate poundage of the gnome they'd endeavored to haul which Mr. Phillip J. King himself discussed primarily alone due to how Nestor Tudor mostly just said to him, "Ingot Lounge?" back. And they took up their gnome another time and toted it nearer still to the Monterey, so far anyhow as the toads and chickens where they rested again all but their tongues that inveighed on the one part and inquired on the other.

"At the Holiday Inn," Mr. Phillip J. King said once they'd set out another time with their gnome between them. "On the bypass."

And Nestor Tudor who was holding anyway the heavy end with the legs and the partly curled shoes and the lump of cement turf for the gnome to perch atop of managed with what spare and expendable breath he possessed to wonder at Mr. Phillip J. King one time more, "Ingot Lounge?"

"Downstairs," Mr. Phillip J. King told him, "under the restaurant."

"Better than a gnome?" Nestor Tudor wanted to know as they prepared to settle their own one upon the Monterey's backseat cushion.

"Hell," Mr. Phillip J. King said back and looked off again to a piece of air while he admitted how a puny armless naked woman was likely not so fine as the Ingot Lounge itself.

The Evers guessed they'd picked the very gnome he would have picked if he'd been looking for a regular upright gnome and he congratulated Mr. Phillip J. King and let on how pleased he'd be to receive cash money from him like shortly he did receive from him cash money and so returned to his accumulated birdbaths while Mr. Phillip J. King and Nestor Tudor together agreed that their gnome would probably not fall over upon the carseat which they told back and forth to each other it wouldn't until they'd rolled across the lot and swung round towards the highway when it did. So they allowed it to lay face downwards on the seat cushion and assured each other instead how it would probably not drop onto the floorboard that it didn't appear, once they'd pulled onto the highway, inclined to do and so left Mr. Phillip J. King in particular free enough from worry and woe to tell to Nestor Tudor, "Ah. The Ingot Lounge. Now there's a place to stir a woman."

Together they'd been there one time. Together they'd been there twice in fact though Mr. Phillip J. King was not disposed to count but the first time they'd gone which had been fraught, he told it, with romance unlike the second time they'd gone when their table had a sticky place atop it and Mrs. Phillip J. King found a hair in her old-fashioned. "But there at the outset," Mr. Phillip J. King turned to Nestor Tudor and informed him, "we had a night."

They'd not been planning even to go but had just up and gone anyway on the impulse of the moment as they'd been meaning for a while to take in the Ingot Lounge and simply found of a sudden they were ready to do it. She'd worn her blue dress, Mrs. Phillip J. King had, with the back that plunged and the front that plunged a little itself and her shoes with the straps that evermore did a thing to Mr. Phillip J. King who inquired of Nestor Tudor if he might fashion in his own mind what thing it was the straps evermore did since Mr. Phillip J. King could not discover the words for it. He'd himself worn his striped shirt and his blazer with the medallion on the front pocket along with his pleated gray trousers and his black cowhide loafers that he had to admit to Nestor Tudor rendered him probably too altogether spiffy for words like Nestor Tudor did not from beside him in the Monterey appear much to doubt. They'd gotten a table in the corner back in the dark shadowy recesses of the Ingot Lounge that was chiefly in fact dark and shadowy all over but was ever so deeply in the recesses dark and shadowy both like caused Mrs. Phillip J. King to sit there straightaway at the wrong table in the corner entirely, at the table in the corner alongside what table in the corner they'd been following the hostess to, the table in the corner that Mr. Ronny Spear and Mrs. Dwight Mobley's brother's girl Esmerelda had come already previously to be sitting at like Mrs. Phillip J. King, but for the dark and but for the shadowy, would likely have taken some notice of before she laid like she did her backside upon Mr. Ronny Spear's lap that Mr. Ronny Spear let on to be grateful about with such extravagant zeal and enthusiasm as to elevate Mrs. Dwight Mobley's brother's girl Esmerelda into a bout of pique not to mention the variety of elevating Mrs. Phillip J. King herself partook of.

Their evening, then, at the Ingot Lounge set out with noticeably more clamor and agitation than they'd between them anticipated, but they presently found their own vacant table with their own vacant chairseats beneath it that they lowered themselves upon without much incident to speak of. Shortly they received from their waitress the manner of setup they'd requested that was cracked ice and lime wedges and a quart of bubbly tonic which, thrown all together with a couple of shots of gin, fairly much becalmed most especially Mrs. Phillip J. King's nervy impulses and her and Mr. Phillip J. King admired from their dark and shadowy corner table the rest of the Ingot Lounge laid out before them.

It had, Mr. Phillip J. King admitted to Nestor Tudor, some palpable atmosphere to it like would be aside from the dark and would be aside from the shadowy and would be due chiefly to the decor that was your elegant sort of decor, Mr. Phillip J. King said, and he undertook there straightaway to express to Nestor Tudor what it was precisely that was elegant in fact about the decor but he got briefly put off from it by his recollection of their waitress's outfit that had been short and skimpy and pretty much hemmed, he told to Nestor Tudor, clean up to her fenders that Nestor Tudor, who'd not himself gazed upon any fenders lately, endeavored with his eyes shut to envision.

They'd had on the walls thick nappy wallpaper, Mr. Phillip J. King recalled, thick nappy maroon wallpaper with shields and swords and such mounted upon it all roundabout above the wainscoting that they'd had some of too, ponderous beveled wainscoting like had seemed itself to Mr. Phillip J. King fairly medieval though Mrs. Phillip J. King had been of a mind it was French instead and had not shown an inclination to consider how maybe it might be medieval and French both at the same time since she could not believe the French had ever somehow troubled themselves to be medieval at all. They'd gone in at the Ingot Lounge for flickery lights, Mr. Phillip J. King recollected, flickery electric wall torches with orange bulbs to them that were meant to look like fire and looked even like fire a little but did not look like fire much truly though the flickery and the orange together in combination manufactured an ambiance, Mr. Phillip J. King insisted, in addition to the flattering and enhancing they managed as well like Nestor Tudor, who'd lately witnessed an orange flickery ambiance play upon the widow Mrs. MaySue Ludley's jowly features, kept some way from disputing though he found himself precipitously inclined to dispute it.

But of course, Mr. Phillip J. King told at length, in addition to the fenders and the wallpaper and the shields and the swords and the wainscoting and the flickery torchlight what the Ingot Lounge had chiefly was live actual music from a bandstand and a parquet dancefloor before it to accommodate whoever it was the melodies might seduce, and he confided to Nestor Tudor, "Live music just slays a woman," that Nestor Tudor jerked his head about. "Live music and orange flickery light both," Mr. Phillip J. King said and studied Nestor Tudor a little sidelong as he said it prior to making in his neck the manner of noise meant to indicate how live music and orange flickery light in combination would doubtless just exterminate a woman altogether.

"We got seduced," Mr. Phillip J. King said meaning him and meaning Mrs. Phillip J. King who sat at their table in the corner drinking their cocktails and listened for a spell to Mrs. Otis Cribbs's girl, Holly Cribbs Dumont, croon like Holly Cribbs Dumont possessed a palpable talent for. She had back of her Mr. Harold Platt at the piano, Jumbo Hedley's boy Lancaster on the stand-up bass, and Mrs. Rachel Teeter at the drums which she struck with noticeably more authority than syncopation. But Mr. and Mrs. Phillip J. King found themselves seduced nonetheless in spite of the drumming and the bassplaying and the pianobeating too that were fairly sorry separately and managed to only rise up and blend into middling together, seduced partly on account of Holly Cribbs Dumont's purely angelic soprano and partly on account of Holly Cribbs Dumont's extraordinary trombone playing that she regularly interrupted her angelic soprano with.

"Trombone?" Nestor Tudor inquired with a noticeable measure of skepticism as he'd never himself been even the least bit titillated by a trombone much less seduced all fullblown and outright.

"Pure and sweet," Mr. Phillip J. King told to him back and dropped shortly into a manner of reverie that rendered him a little dewey roundabout the eyes like did not by itself serve much to convince Nestor Tudor of the pure or the sweet either one as he'd heard previously a trombone himself live and close in and it had sounded pretty much like a chatty heifer to him. "Ever so pure and sweet," Mr. Phillip J. King insisted and he told how he'd risen from the table and reached across it so as to take up Mrs. Phillip J. King's fingers and draw her by them out from the shadowy corner and onto the parquet floor where they began to step and twirl there together just at the shankend of "Little Brown Book" that gave way directly to a rendition of "Telstar" which Mr. Phillip J. King swung around sideways to admit to Nestor Tudor had been a rare and wondrous item. "I can't suppose a man's much tasted the joys of this life," Mr. Phillip J. King said, "until he's heard 'Telstar' on the trombone. We swayed," Mr. Phillip J. King admitted. "We twirled all roundabout and dipped even just up and of a sudden," dipped, Mr. Phillip J. King explained, once they'd both together come to be transported like they could not seem to help but come to be, and he told how Mrs. Phillip J. King in her blue dress with the back that plunged and the front that plunged a little itself and her shoes with the straps that evermore did a thing to him seemed that night a different creature altogether, seemed that night the woman he'd first laid eyes on at the S&W in Greensboro where he'd stood himself at the silverware bin and watched her up the line selecting a cobbler, watched her pitch a bit forward and reach past the pie slices and the molded Jell-O to the dish she'd most especially gotten struck by that she settled upon her tray like he watched her from the silverware bin do until just all at once she picked up her head and peered at him back.

"Right direct at me," Mr. Phillip J. King said. "It was spooky."

And Nestor Tudor told to Mr. Phillip J. King, "Forces," and added behind it a word on the ways they drove people that was every now and again together and was every now and again apart like was talk enough to induce Mr. Phillip J. King to announce just out in a general sort of way how life was in fact strange sometimes that Nestor Tudor with his own variety of throaty discharge undertook to confirm.

He'd never forget it, Mr. Phillip J. King admitted, would hold evermore in his mind to how it was they stepped and dipped and spun round and gripped each other but for when they plain sat instead at their table back in the shadowy corner and sipped on their cocktails and tapped their shoebottoms against the rug pile like was partly on account of Mrs. Rachel Teeter's forays into syncopation that Mr. Harold Platt and Lancaster Hedley endeavored as best they were able to join and augment but was chiefly on account of Holly Cribbs Dumont instead who crooned and blew by turns with such unmitigated elegance and grace that Mr. and Mrs. Phillip J. King could not but glance at each other and exhale about it that way people sometimes can manage only to glance and exhale.

"Yes sir," Mr. Phillip J. King told to Nestor Tudor, "we had us a night," and he said back of it, "Ingot," and said back of it, "Lounge," and then spied shortly in the rearview mirror Mrs. Phillip J. King's cement gnome face down atop the seatcushion looking for all the world like he'd just lately punctuated a binge.

And after riding a time in silence Mr. Phillip J. King told to Nestor Tudor, "I just don't know," that he followed with a spell of woeful headshaking prior to sharing with Nestor Tudor how out of all the things he didn't know the item he knew purely least about was why precisely it had to be that once he'd set to coming up on his twilight years his wife would begin to hurl produce at him. He'd all along anticipated his twilight years and even the scant years leading up to his twilight years would be together peaceful and serene and he'd not somehow ever gotten around to imagining that here in the shank of his days he'd find himself dispatched on account of a Vadalia onion chiefly to collect a cement gnome, and Mr. Phillip J. King inquired, "Who'd have thought it?" like Nestor Tudor could not truly tell to him beyond how it was Nestor Tudor had not remotely figured on it himself that Mr. Phillip J. King let on to take some solace from. And shortly he was anxious to discover from Nestor Tudor a thing further, asked anyhow of him in a vague and moderately hopeless sort of a way if he was perhaps acquainted with how precisely hormones worked that Nestor Tudor wished at Mr. Phillip J. King he was but felt compelled to admit how hormones were not the variety of items he'd ever cultivated much curiosity about which Mr. Phillip J. King appeared for a spell to mull on prior to dropping his chin and lamenting another time at Nestor Tudor, "I just don't know."

As they gained town Mr. Phillip J. King watched by turns the road before him and the gnome back of him and displayed on occasion his baleful expression for Nestor Tudor who was trying to recollect if he had about him any rhythm to speak of, sufficient rhythm anyhow to step and dip and spin round with like he feared he didn't but hoped possibly he might as he undertook to envision Miss Mary Alice Celestine Lefler's dainty fingers clutched in his own ones and Miss Mary Alice Celestine Lefler's comely face lifted and upraised sweetly towards him which he did in fact fairly much envision even before the whole business yielded and gave way to the lowslung hairpart mostly and the jowly cheeks somewhat with the gray stubble upon them like altogether undid the charm of the rumination.

Mrs. Phillip J. King met the Monterey as they pulled into the drive and coasted back towards the carshed that was itself so thoroughly naked of paint as to prompt Nestor Tudor to ask of Mr. Phillip J. King if wasn't it maybe a new carshed entirely like inspired Mr. Phillip J. King to grow ever so briefly animated which he would maybe have persevered at but for how Mrs. Phillip J. King had suffered in his absence a thoroughgoing hormonal reversal and had grown on account of it fairly completely anti-imp-of-the-forest and consequently hoped at Mr. Phillip J. King through the sidewindow he'd not after all bothered to carry home with him a gnome since a gnome seemed to her about the last thing in this life she wanted to look on just presently though she found herself compelled shortly to look on one, to look on anyhow the entire backside of an actual cement gnome laid out nose downwards upon the seatcushion like had on Mrs. Phillip J. King an effect.

Now Nestor Tudor had not lately had cause to see an affected woman, had not truly ever previously had cause to see a woman affected after what fashion Mrs. Phillip J. King grew at the sight of the cement gnome affected herself and she pulled a face at Mr. Phillip J. King and then pulled at Nestor Tudor the same face precisely prior to wondering in an ever so indelicate sort of a tone, "Where'd you get him?" like was at Nestor Tudor but was for Mr. Phillip J. King who figured himself it was about probably the gnome and so told to Mrs. Phillip J. King how he'd found him back of the cement testicles beyond the toads and the chickens which she worked up another face entirely about so as to let on what an altogether repulsive piece of news she'd just been pressed to endure.

Nestor Tudor and Mr. Phillip J. King lifted between them Mrs. Phillip J. King's gnome out from the back of the Monterey and settled it onto a spot of grass in the sideyard, a spot of grass Mrs. Phillip J. King had most especially not wished to see mashed and killed as she'd cultivated, she let on, a fondness for it like inspired Mr. Phillip J. King and Nestor Tudor both to snatch up the gnome yet again and shift it to a spot of grass Mrs. Phillip J. King had remained somehow less enthusiastic about. She walked entirely around the thing two times with her arms crossed over her chest and her head pitched and tilted after a fashion Mr. Phillip J. King had come to be lately quite thoroughly acquainted with like was how come he did not find himself much astounded when she left off circling her gnome so as to speak harshly of it to Mr. Phillip J. King, so as to tell what a homely little item it seemed to her to be and she declared how she did not most especially care for its silly pointy hat that appeared to her undignified even for an imp and could not begin to warm to its smock and its baggy kneebritches which did not together strike her hardly as spritelike. Of course she had to make an inquiry about the shoes as well, had to wonder at Mr. Phillip J. King chiefly and Nestor Tudor ever so hardly at all if they'd ever previously between them come across a gnome in oxfords like straightaway spurred Mr. Phillip J. King to recount for Mrs. Phillip J. King his inquiry to the Evers about the shoes most specifically that had not struck him right from the getgo as gnomy at all which Nester Tudor got called on to confirm and corroborate, got charged anyhow by Mr. Phillip J. King to speak of what shoetalk he'd heard and who most especially he'd heard it from like Nestor Tudor endeavored to do and had done even a little in fact before he got encouraged by Mrs. Phillip J. King to leave off please from confirming and corroborating both.

Mrs. Phillip J. King didn't know but that maybe she'd have been better off with a sitting gnome or a hunkering gnome likely instead of just a plain standing gnome in oxfords and a pointy cap. She didn't know in fact but that maybe she'd have been better off with even an item otherwise than a gnome entirely like inspired Nestor Tudor to wonder aloud at Mr. Phillip J. King if didn't he believe Mrs. Phillip J. King could help but be taken with the puny armless naked sort of women they'd seen just lately that Mr. Phillip J. King shook his head ever so vigorously on account of and set straightoff to speaking of the egret in an effort to forestall Nestor Tudor from wondering further on the topic of the women that had been puny and armless somewhat but had been naked chiefly all over like Mrs. Phillip J. King felt obliged to proclaim about, felt obliged to announce anyhow what a trifling surprise it was to discover that Mr. Phillip J. King had passed a piece of his morning rooting out and gawking at such women as were puny and armless somewhat but naked chiefly all over like suited, she told it, his ilk and his gender both that Nestor Tudor, in an effort to be agreeable, agreed with her it probably did and so enjoyed for his trouble a variety of wholly unromantic sidelong look which spoke itself of what ilk and gender Mrs. Phillip J. King found Nestor Tudor to be as well.

As long as they'd gone on and carried the thing home she guessed she'd try it out in the bushes and consequently directed Nestor Tudor and Mr. Phillip J. King in the hefting of the gnome, informed them of what parts they should grip and grab onto once they'd gripped and grabbed onto places otherwise already that people with sense would know better, she told it, than to take up. Straightaway they carried the thing along the sideyard and across the back one to the spot of ground beside the camellia bush where Mrs. Phillip J. King's sweet William had only lately expired but the upright gnome in just his regular oxford shoes didn't much suit Mrs. Phillip J. King alongside the camellia bush truly so she aired directly her desire to spy him in the creeping vines instead where Mr. Phillip J. King let on they'd be pleased to haul him and subsequently orchestrated the lifting and the toting and the settling as well that served together as preface to Mrs. Phillip J. King's distress since she'd hoped maybe the creeping vines would hide the shoes and obscure the kneebritches like the creeping vines failed somehow to do. She wished another time they'd brought maybe a gnome that sat or perhaps a gnome that hunkered a little which Mr. Phillip J. King took occasion to remind her he'd offered previously to carry her one of that Mrs. Phillip J. King had not in fact hardly needed to get reminded of which she straightaway educated Mr. Phillip J. King about prior to dispatching him and Nestor Tudor and dispatching the upright gnome between them down towards the rear of the lot to the apricot tree like did not, once they'd settled the gnome beside it, strike her as hardly the location for a gnome at all. So they hauled it back places they'd been already and hauled it as well places they'd just up and thought to go like did not seem, by and large, apt and suitable for most especially Mrs. Phillip J. King's variety of cement gnome until they'd arrived yet again at the piece of ground alongside the camellia bush where the sweet William had lately expired. Now of course Mrs. Phillip J. King hadn't herself found cause to alter her opinion of the place her sweet William had only lately been, but Mr. Phillip J. King and Nestor Tudor both had discovered between them, most especially down roundabout their kidneys, a passion for that particular sort of dirt due primarily to how Mrs. Phillip J. King's imp of the forest rested all by itself upon it. Consequently, they commenced to wax, Mr. Phillip J. King anyhow commenced to wax straightoff like shortly he compounded with a spell of ejaculation, your whooping and yelping manner of ejaculation chiefly, that Nestor Tudor presently saw fit to join him at and so ejaculated and waxed both himself about the gnome that just stood alone atop the dirt and did not somehow tax a spinal column while he did it.

He seemed to Mr. Phillip J. King to catch the light like prompted him to seem to Nestor Tudor to catch the light as well and get rendered, he told it, distinguished, more distinguished by far than all the great host of gnomes Nestor Tudor had previously laid eyes on and statelier even than an egret like Mr. Phillip J. King confirmed to be as true as the gospel itself. Naturally, however, Mrs. Phillip J. King, who was feeling on account of her hormones fairly contrary, did not directly come to be persuaded just because she'd been waxed and ejaculated at, but the whooping and the yelping along with the spells of earnest admiration served to erode Mrs. Phillip J. King's disposition until she noticed herself a shaft of light that it looked to her her gnome in fact caught.

And Mr. Phillip J. King confessed to her how that particular spot of ground alongside the camellia bush appeared to him to near about breathe some actual life into Mrs. Phillip J. King's gnome and he let on how he wouldn't be at all surprised if it just up and said a thing to him, albeit an altogether subdued and stately thing that Nestor Tudor found himself encouraged to throw in with and so ever so precipitously threw in with it like prompted Mrs. Phillip J. King to wonder at Nestor Tudor and wonder at Mr. Phillip J. King with him, "You think so?" which incited a pure explosion of waxing and ejaculating both. And she seemed swayed and seemed altered and appeared even moderately uplifted there alongside her gnome that she studied from near about every direction she could discover to study it from prior to climbing the backsteps and looking fairly set to study it from there as well before she grew all at once of a mood to sit and of a mood to lay her head upon her bony knees and of a mood to fairly wail, "P.J.!" as a preface to the blubbery manner of thing she loosed back of it like together induced Mr. Phillip J. King to address to Nestor Tudor a piece of advice that he might pass along to that boy he knew, to speak to Nestor Tudor of what two words seemed of a sudden ever so highly pertinent and he told to him, "Stay," and he told to him, "home," and then climbed the back steps so as to share with Mrs. Phillip J. King just where precisely she was wispy and where precisely she was taut.

ii.

IT wasn't like she needed another one since she had already two anyhow if you didn't count the Barefoot that she had as well, the Barefoot from the depot who'd gotten his necktie touched and admired like he'd come to be fairly charmed on account of, but she got another one nonetheless just by sheer and unmitigated happenstance chiefly and armtouching a little as well, tattootouching in fact though she'd not known when she said her ooooh and extended her fingers that a tattoo was what she might touch.

Tiny Aaron had been himself enduring lately a spell of snake trouble, not your vulgar human-dysfuncted-organ variety of snake trouble but your slick-scaly-slip-along-the-ground assortment of it instead. He had a reptile in his crawlspace and he could hear it of an evening sliding and twining in among the floorbraces like did not somehow render him sufficiently curious to crawl on under the joists himself and see what sort of snake precisely it was since they had between them plywood sheeting and oak flooring and gold speckledy pile carpet which, taken together, impressed Tiny Aaron as a fairly impenetrable snake blockade. His snake trouble had, however, recently undergone an alteration mostly on account of the snake, on account of the snake that is and the pipehole in combination that the snake, in the course of his travels roundabout the crawlspace, managed to discover. It wasn't any sizeable pipehole but was bigger by half than the ventpipe that went through it like wouldn't itself have been much of a problem truly if Tiny Aaron hadn't neglected to fit his ventpipe with a proper pipe collar and had decided instead to pack his pipehole with two pieces of the Greensboro *Daily News* from Sunday, November 12th, 1957, which had managed somehow to suit until they fell through the floor and into the crawlspace themselves which Tiny Aaron would probably have taken some notice of but for how his ventpipe and his ventpipe hole together were deep in the coatcloset behind his blue striped double-breasted suit that he hardly had cause anymore to extract and put on.

Consequently, then, Tiny Aaron's fairly impenetrable snake blockade had a manner of chink in it that his snake had the leisure to discover and so passed one evening tongue first out from the crawlspace entirely and in among the closet floor clutter like was shoes somewhat and paper sacks and jackets and sweaters that had long since dropped off the hangers onto the floor. It was, in short, the variety of clutter to suit a snake that found he preferred the closet floor to the crawlspace and so took up residence around a tassel loafer where he did not show an inclination to stray much from until the one night he did in fact just up and stray. Of course Tiny Aaron had come to figure his snake had migrated since he could not any longer hear it twining among the floor braces, but he was of a disposition to figure it had migrated out and did not even imagine it had migrated up chiefly instead like contributed to his profound amazement on the Tuesday evening his snake departed from the vicinity of the tassel loafer and ever so briefly joined Tiny Aaron before his Motorola.

He'd been watching on the news station a loop of news that had only just lately given way to the minute from Hollywood that was occupied almost entirely by a starlet from the breastbone up who was speaking directly into the camera lens of the projects she'd just lately gotten done with which she let on to be all tingly about, tingly after a fashion that Tiny Aaron found fairly hypnotizing and so did not straightoff notice what variety of creature had arrived to watch the starlet with him. Truly, he did not even shortly notice how he'd come to be in the company of a reptile until the headline sports, that had followed the minute from Hollywood, gave way to the business brief and subsequent talk of your assorted indicators which pretty completely unhypnotized Tiny Aaron altogether and so allowed him the occasion to see just barely and hardly at all a black slinky item on the throwrug. He caught it right there in the corner of his eye and so was not much alarmed when it appeared to him to move since things he caught in the corner of his eye often times had a way of appearing to move to him like the black slinky item appeared to him to move on out from the corner of his eye entirely to pretty much the center of his vision where things that appeared to slip and slide usually were in fact slipping and sliding both. Of course, he'd not anticipated getting joined before his Motorola by a reptile like was how come even once he'd seen the snake right there before him on the throwrug he could not full well take in that it was in fact an actual scaly creature though he hoisted his feet up onto the chaircushion nonetheless and went on ahead and exposed his molars to the lamplight just as if an actual scaly creature was what it was.

It didn't truly travel anywhere much but just slipped and slinked out between Tiny Aaron and the business brief prior to balling up in a manner of snaky knot which rendered Tiny Aaron a little tingly himself though not hardly in your Hollywood starlet sort of way. Naturally, he'd had some truck with snakes previously, had visited the snakehouse at the zoo in Asheboro and had even as a child taken up snakes in his very hands and allowed them to wrap their musky shankends around his forearms, but he found there with his feet drawn up atop his seatcushion that he was not much inclined to tolerate snakes any longer, had somehow lost the disposition for it and was more than a little fearful that perhaps his functions would get disturbed and interrupted in such a grave and acute fashion as to cause him to faint dead away and thereby provide the snake the opportunity to slither up the chairarm atop him and so surely punctuate what other of his functions had not come to be already punctuated. Consequently, then, he undertook to do a thing before he succumbed, undertook to do a thing that is other than back clean up the wall to the ceiling, undertook to drive that snake on out from the sitting room towards the frontdoor, made anyhow what he meant for a snakeherding kind of a noise that was a combination of whistling and tongueclicking and plain distraught puffing and blowing that the snake seemed to find moderately engaging and so raised up his flat black head and showed to Tiny Aaron the profile of it.

Of course, snakes drive almost as well as mules do which was how come Tiny Aaron's particular snake merely raised up his head and merely displayed his profile without offering to exert himself further like Tiny Aaron, from high upon his chair, took some notice of and so left off whistling and clicking and puffing and blowing and just persevered at palpitating alone while him and while his snake eyed each other so long as was required for the snake in particular to grow weary of it and determine how he'd rather slink and slither a spell across the throwrug which he uncoiled himself on account of and so incited from Tiny Aaron a new set of noises altogether along with a fresh bout of ever so vigorous chairback crawling. He looked to Tiny Aaron eight feet all stretched and laid out, looked to Tiny Aaron six feet anyhow and was in fact on the heavy end of two and a half feet and fairly slender for a blacksnake, girthsome no more than like a water hose but for where he'd eaten a thing and gotten lumpy that Tiny Aaron paid some considerable attention to from high upon his upholstered chair as he watched that snake slip and glide back across the floor towards the tableleg he'd come in the first place from. Naturally, a renewed bout of snakeherding noises seemed in order to Tiny Aaron once the snake had gotten on his own just up and under way and so the whistling and the clicking and the puffing and blowing ensued as Tiny Aaron ever so slowly crept towards his chairseat and then off it altogether onto the actual floor that he slinked a little himself across to the doorway from where he could watch that snake travel on its belly the length of the frontroom and beyond it into the backhall where Tiny Aaron arrived in time to see the last half foot of black scaly tail disappear under the coatcloset door which up and induced from him the variety of noise dogs sometimes make that was whiny and pathetic and hopeless all in the very same instant.

He meant to beat the thing to a snaky pulp, meant to swing wide the closet door and flail a spell once he'd figured what particular item might be best suited to beating a snake with which he studied ever so briefly about prior to landing upon a ballbat that he guessed maybe he could step up the street and get one of from Bill Ed Myrick who had ballbats and such, and he near about even stepped up the street to get one until he paused and wondered where in his absence that snake might go like could be all over and everywhere the mere thought of which gave rise in Tiny Aaron to a second whiny mongrel noise that he stood in the backhall and loosed. He didn't own himself anything good for flailing snakes but for a shovel at the bottom of the backsteps that he was not willing to leave the house to fetch and so retreated only so far as the kitchen where he reached in alongside the refrigerator and withdrew his spongemop with the springloaded aluminum wringer which seemed to him the sort of implement that might gouge and otherwise discourage a snake.

Needless to say he had to generate some nerve, couldn't somehow just throw open the closet door and set to banging about but felt obliged to grow all steely prior to it, felt obliged anyhow to undertake to grow as steely as he was able in the backhall to grow like was not truly purely steely and was not hardly mostly steely even but was a sufficiently detectable advancement over unsteely to inspire Tiny Aaron to tell at himself chiefly, "All right then," with what sounded to him palpable resolve most especially once he'd repeated it at the closet doorknob with precisely the variety of inflection it seemed to him a steely man would use.

He'd intended to fling open the door. When he'd reached and laid at last his fingers to the knob he'd guessed anyhow he would fling the thing open but the notion that he might startle his eight-foot snake and suffer it to leap up upon him stayed him a time from flinging like he'd meant to and caused him instead just to turn ever so slowly the knob and to draw back hardly at all the entire door itself so far as to allow him to reach his arm into the closet and tug on the lightcord which would have likely proven useful to him had he not just lately found occasion to empty the closet socket as a part of his general bulb migration scheme by which he replaced crucial spent bulbs with insignificant sound ones from elsewhere. He shut, then, the closet door that he'd only just lately opened so as to pitch his weight full against it and take the opportunity to grow moderately steely all over again that he was full in the middle of coming to be when he recollected the gap his eight-foot snake had entered the closet by like inspired him to leap and step after a wild and nimble fashion that pretty much undid his steeliness altogether.

It didn't seem to him he had much choice in the matter; he could stand against the shut closet door and wait to get devoured from the toenails up or he could throw the door open and get chewed instead from his cowlick the other way like left him to understand how plain standing all agitated and forlorn against the door panels was not truly the thing he needed to be just presently up to as snakes in the coatcloset called for a trifle of initiative instead and initiative was what precisely he undertook to generate a trifle of, breathed anyhow in and breathed anyhow out and told himself one time more, "All right then," prior to full well flinging in fact the closet door open and bludgeoning rightoff with his sponge-mop his dead momma's mangy fox stole that went pretty much to pieces straightaway and altogether. He pulverized a sweater sleeve and the bulk of a blue sock before he left off flailing long enough to vent an additional whiney mongrel noise as preface to the near about pure annihilation of a yellow straw porkpie hat with pipecleaner men and women roundabout the brim of it in skimpy swimsuits, a yellow straw porkpie hat his sister's boy had carried to him from the beach at Daytona and the disintegration of which revealed to him a length of electrical cord, a length in fact of Electrolux electrical cord from the canister model Tiny Aaron had long since replaced with an upright but had not entirely discarded and had only instead buried on his closet floor where he of a sudden uncovered the cord of it that did not somehow appear much in the way of electrical to him.

Of course he beat and flailed it pretty directly though not in fact hardly so directly as he undertook to beat and flail it due to how he could not straightoff seem to call upon his muscles to work for him after the fashion he'd hoped they might like led him to beat and flail just the doorframe there at the first and led him shortly to beat and flail a scant piece of the floor near about alongside where he'd been in fact aiming to beat and flail which was itself preamble to the actual fullblown thrashing of the Electrolux electrical cord that looked very much a snake to him most especially at the backend of the beating and flailing both when it came time for that cord to seem chiefly a dead snake that a cord alone could full well lay on the floor and do. Consequently, then, Tiny Aaron figured he'd killed it, figured he'd stunned it pretty thoroughly anyhow and poked and jabbed it with the mophead to see did that cord have much life left to it that it didn't appear to have truly any of which emboldened Tiny Aaron sufficiently to send him on into the closet itself where he freed an empty hanger from the rack and lifted the cord with the hook of it, lifted it clean up to the plugend that did not straightoff strike Tiny Aaron as a snaky sort of an item. Of course he undertook to leap, undertook to jump clean out from the closet altogether into the backhall once he'd loosed yet another whiny doleful mongrel noise prior to it, but he caught some way his shoetoe in an errant trouser cuff on a fallen and heaped up pair of trousers and consequently could not hardly leap and sail like he'd hoped he might but merely pitched instead, plunged fairly directly straight over onto the threshold and partway into the hall like left him plain ripe to get crawled and slinked atop of by his eight-foot snake he'd not but probably peeved and agitated and hardly beaten and flailed and pulverized at all.

Understandably, Tiny Aaron's palpitations were thunderous and precipitous together and all at once and he undertook to crawl and slink a little himself across the hallway and up the far wall beyond it where he managed to manufacture spit enough to whine another time while he brandished, as best as he was able, his wire coathanger and endeavored to look wild and lethal back of it which he shortly complimented with an assortment of snakeherding noises until he worked himself close enough to the closet door to kick it shut and escape up the backhall into the front room where he ventilated and palpitated and bent and squatted and stood and whined and felt altogether pitiful and forlorn and fairly utterly unsteely and told to himself, "Aw Tiny," in that quivery voice he sometimes told to himself Aw Tiny in.

He supposed he'd best trap and keep it if he could not somehow beat and flail it instead so he fetched out from the bureau in the front room his duct tape that was anymore his chief bonding agent around the house and held pretty much every little item that had come apart together. He closed the gap under the closet door with a length of it and ran a strand up the height of the jamb on the knob side and down it on the hinge one and across even the lintel as well since he did not know exactly how wily an eight-foot snake might be. Once he'd stepped back to where he'd brandished his coathanger just previously he was pleased to find his closet doorway fairly thoroughly sealed up altogether but for the keyhole that he laid a scrap of tape to as well and thereby grew straightaway satisfied that his eight-foot snake would stay where it was he'd slinked off to until such time as Tiny Aaron might discover how best to altogether eliminate a reptile, and he stepped fairly snug up to the closet door proper and almost laid his actual fleshy ear full upon it as he listened for any manner of snaky noise he could come across like he thought there after a spell he'd maybe even heard one of and subsequently squatted to run a second strand of tape along the doorsill since he figured a snake that was stirring might be of a mood to gnaw and chew.

He made to watch the television but did not watch the television truly and only watched mostly the seam where the wall met the ceiling and caught his breath as he listened for any slinking and sliding around that he went a full entire hour and near about a full entire half hour beyond it without hearing even the least little trace of before he heard what sounded to him a variety of slink though he could not straightaway tell where it was the slink had come from precisely and so drew off a fresh breath to catch and hold and cut his eyes floorwards to find out could he maybe see a ropy thing out the corner of one. It seemed to him he heard somewhat of a second slink beyond the first slink that he'd heard already but the television interfered with the sound of it, or the doctor with the pointy beard anyhow who'd come on the screen to snatch his glasses from his face and speak in an earnest sort of a way about where it was precisely piles came from like had obscured the slink fairly entirely for Tiny Aaron who'd found himself torn between his reptile and doctorly talk of piles as he felt he had cause to know of both and so deciphered somehow neither one like left him to sit all breathless one time more until he heard in fact a definite snaky noise in addition to a piece of a discourse on roughage and whole grains.

It wasn't much of a snaky noise truly and didn't seem positively to Tiny Aaron entirely the manner of noise that had to have come from a snake precisely. However, it was sufficient of a snaky noise to send Tiny Aaron to his Motorola where he shut off the volume on a piece of southerly vascular talk and breathed in alone without breathing out back of it until he'd heard in fact a sound among the floor joists, a low and undeniably slithery sort of a sound, a sound pretty much directly under his own feet before it wasn't in fact under his own feet any longer but had risen up from elsewhere altogether. Naturally he straightaway stepped on into the frontroom and through it to the backhall due to the impulse he'd entertained, due to the notion he'd gotten of a sudden taken with that maybe his snake in the closet had slipped somehow back under the floor and was twining again amongst the floorbraces, but once he'd arrived at the closet door he could not hardly begin to discover the nerve to loosen the tape and swing the door open like would possibly get him leapt upon and bit if the floorbrace snake was another snake entirely like maybe, he figured, the floorbrace snake was which conjured up for him a vision of snaky fornication and the subsequent tangly knot of little wormy snake babies that Tiny Aaron could not seem to help but shiver and whine about. He guessed he was likely inundated with serpents, concluded there in the hallway how he was hosting probably under his subfloor an entire clan of snakes like inspired him to step out from the hallway altogether and into the very middle of the front room where he figured he could spy a gang of snakes coming at him in time enough to expire and pitch over before they arrived.

He didn't know hardly what to do and so didn't do anything and didn't know hardly where to go and so didn't go anywhere at all but just stood a time there in the front room and listened for slithery noises and looked for snaky shapes like are together the sort of endeavors to erode a man's nerves near about past mending, and while he didn't hear much and saw even less he still somehow felt obliged to retire for a spell elsewhere, to step anyhow on out the door with a coverlet and a sofa bolster and his six-volt Ray-o-Vac green plastic flashlight and establish an encampment upon the glider on the porch that he'd never even one time discovered a snake atop of. And he slept even a little, drifted and started by turns, and leapt fully upright only once he'd come to be partly traversed by a granddaddy longlegs that had climbed up off his shirtcollar onto his ear and seemed disposed to tour the rest of his head. Otherwise he passed the night fairly unafflicted and had even dropped off into a manner of sleep outright when Ferguson Pike's boy that carried the paper bounced Tiny Aaron's own personal *Chronicle* off the clapboards by the righthand doorlight that Tiny Aaron rose up and fairly jitterbugged on account of and thereby induced from Ferguson Pike's boy a variety of ungodly shriek.

Tiny Aaron was eager to have his eight-foot snake exterminated, was anxious in fact to have it punished and annihilated but guessed he'd likely have to settle for plain exterminated instead and so called at eight A.M. precisely Mr. Slocum that killed bugs and beetles and ants primarily but guessed he might do in a snake if the snake was handy and roundabout to get done in that Tiny Aaron insisted his own personal snake was. So Mr. Slocum dropped by in his orange truck with the big green spotted bug atop it and Tiny Aaron led him to the backhall closet door that Mr. Slocum laid his ear to and listened through a time prior to hearing from Tiny Aaron of the visitation he'd been forced to endure and the violent mopplay that had followed it which Tiny Aaron let on to have been a fairly grand and epic struggle in your Biblical sort of way that the trouser cuff and the coathanger got together omitted from.

"Blacksnake?" Mr. Slocum wanted to hear again.

"Blacksnake," Tiny Aaron told to him.

"Eight foot long?" Mr. Slocum inquired and endured Tiny Aaron to lay wide his arms and altogether assure him, "Like this," after which he formed with his fingers a loop for the girth and eyed Mr. Slocum through it. Judging from the lump he'd observed, Tiny Aaron figured his eight-foot snake had probably lately dined on maybe a housecat and so was likely altogether satisfied to lay quietly upon the closet floor and digest which was why they didn't hear him slink and slither and such that Mr. Slocum discovered some sense in and so laid another time his ear to the doorpanel and humphed at Tiny Aaron once he'd heard in the closet what little or nothing he'd anticipated he might.

Together they ripped off the tape and not but some moderate part of the doorpaint with it, but they could not decide between them whether to ease or fling open the door until Tiny Aaron had conjured up for Mr. Slocum how it was precisely he knew for a fact eight-foot snakes could leap which was when they figured they might ease the door chiefly and so cracked it a little and undertook to peer on into the darkness like reminded Tiny Aaron of the tale he'd heard of a copperhead that sprang out from a corncrib to bite a woman on the nose. Seemed to him she'd been peering through a crack. Seemed to him the nosebite had plain knocked her over dead and he shared with the Slocum how it was the venom had gone straight to her brain that the Slocum pushed shut the door to hear. Consequently, they did not purely ease it or fling it either one but instead drew the door open with some palpable caution and dispatch both prior to pondering together the clothesheap which inspired the Slocum to inquire if Tiny Aaron was himself perhaps acquainted with an item called a coathanger that Tiny Aaron confessed he'd heard tell of once previously.

As the floormop was handy, the Slocum got encouraged to poke roundabout with it and so ever so gently deheaped Tiny Aaron's clothes an article at a time beginning with his offending trousers and the nappy cardigan beneath them that Tiny Aaron informed the Slocum he'd forgotten altogether he even owned one of. The Slocum took up with the mophandle a striped shirt at the sleeve end and whipped it into the hallway after what fashion Tiny Aaron had to figure might agitate a snake that he advised the Slocum about and so persuaded him to remove the powderblue shirt he took up next with considerably less velocity altogether that the Slocum was full in the middle of when he spied for himself a portion of Tiny Aaron's Electrolux electrical cord that he decided straightaway to go on ahead and exterminate once he'd yipped and howled prior to it. He reached in with his actual fingers and plucked out the shoes while Tiny Aaron, for his part, informed him what a foolhardy venture that seemed to him to be and spoke again of the corncrib and the lady with the nosebite that he had not entirely left off at when the Slocum inadvertently touched the otherwise unemployed mophandle to Tiny Aaron's shoetop and so prompted some additional yipping and howling on the part of Tiny Aaron who thereby induced the Slocum to throw in with him.

The emptier the closet floor got, the more utterly snakeless it appeared to be until the Slocum found himself down to the tassel loafers and two speckled neckties that an eight-foot snake plainly could not hide himself among which he shared the news of with Tiny Aaron who undertook with the mopend to poke around the closet shelf himself but did not turn up a snake there either and so decided along with the Slocum that the eight-foot snake had probably somehow gotten to be elsewhere instead though the Slocum could not figure where elsewhere just precisely once Tiny Aaron pressed to find out could be.

"Must have gotten out," the Slocum said and indicated the ventpipe to Tiny Aaron, indicated most especially the outsized ventpipe hole in the floor of the closet with not even a scrap of a pipe collar upon it that he indicated to Tiny Aaron as well and so earned for himself some ire back on account of the tone he'd indicated most especially the outsized pipehole with.

"I plugged it," Tiny Aaron told to him. "Come unplugged," which the Slocum grunted in back of as he dipped the mophandle pretty completely down into the crawlspace and then drew it back out again.

"Under the house, I guess," the Slocum said and so prompted Tiny Aaron to speak of what scraping and twining he'd heard among the floorbraces. "Won't stay there," the Slocum told back of it and Tiny Aaron demanded straightaway why it was the Slocum might insist a snake in the crawlspace would not stay where it had come to be.

"Too cold for a snake," the Slocum said and then eyed the closet floor and the hallway and gazed even out the hallway into the front room after such a fashion as to suggest to Tiny Aaron where it was a snake might be willing to loiter which was sufficient of a look altogether to bring out the duct tape that Tiny Aaron quite thoroughly obliterated the pipehole with and so felt some palpable measure of wellbeing until the Slocum suggested to him how there could likely be elsewhere other collarless pipeholes a snake would have the leisure to discover since leisure was the thing a snake probably had the most of.

"Well, let's kill it then," Tiny Aaron suggested though he did not know how precisely they might in fact do it in as he'd hoped maybe the Slocum was acquainted with some manner of snake poison that they could possibly manage to squirt on the snake from an altogether appreciable distance, hoped of course until the Slocum snorted a disdainful professional exterminator sort of a snort that by itself spoke to Tiny Aaron of the likelihood of getting his eight-foot snake squirted dead.

He took the Slocum out to the crawlspace door, led him off the porch and around the house to the squat piece of plywood with the strap hinges that had come to be rotted and eaten up at the bottom and sat evermore partway ajar which the Slocum loosed yet another professional exterminator variety of discharge at so as to suggest and imply how a crawlspace door eaten up and ajar both was not, in his estimation, much worth having at all. Together they squatted and peered into the musty darkness and saw most all over what they took for snakes until Tiny Aaron fetched his green Ray-o-Vac and played the beam of it on the wires and scraps of insulation that did not in the light look so inordinately snaky after all. Over time, Tiny Aaron had packed a fair assortment of items into the crawlspace, suggested anyway to the Slocum how they'd gotten other than just flung and tossed under the house that the Slocum generated a dubious species of exhalation about and cleared as best as he was able a passage through the boxes and sacks and buckets and lawn tools that he appeared to Tiny Aaron purely set to crawl along until he merely shone the light down it instead and announced to Tiny Aaron how his snake might be most anywhere, might be up in the joists, might be down upon the dirtfloor, might be coiled in a box or a sack that Tiny Aaron told to him, "Yeah," in back of and waited for the Slocum to crawl on in and find out for him where precisely his snake was that the Slocum seemed even a little disposed to do what with his purposeful crouch and the nervous play of the lightbeam, but he did not make to crawl, did not offer to move even but for how he shifted off his one haunch to his other that he squatted upon for a time prior to standing full upright and telling to Tiny Aaron, "Well," in an ever so palpable leavetaking fashion that Tiny Aaron made there straightaway just his whiny mongrel noise in back of.

"Where you going?" he managed presently to inquire of the Slocum who indicated with his flashlight-bearing hand his truck out front with the spotted bug atop it like inspired from Tiny Aaron an additional whiny mongrel noise in combination with a thoroughly lowslung and pathetic expression that together fairly goaded the Slocum into informing Tiny Aaron, "I ain't going under there. Ain't nobody can pay me enough to send me under there," which could not, of course, but one whiny mongrel noise further possibly suit.

"I can kill a bug," the Slocum said. "I can kill a whole swarm of them, but I can't do a thing in the world with an eight-foot snake but get wrapped up and bit by it."

Naturally, Tiny Aaron grunted and ventilated and twitched and shifted and made even as if to say an actual thing without truly succeeding at it and he undertook to appear disappointed and disgusted and afflicted and pathetic all at the same time like called for such considerable concentration that he did not straightoff hear the Slocum suggest to him how he might slip on under the house himself since it was after all his eight-foot black snake in the first place that the Slocum, upon request, repeated and so induced from Tiny Aaron a discharge so far beyond whiny and mongrel both as to scale fairly much the full heights of pathos.

As best as he was able, the Slocum instructed Tiny Aaron how a man might likely pluck up an eight-foot snake between his foremost finger and his thumb, and him and Tiny Aaron by turns snatched a discarded length of clothesline up from a grassy patch in the sideyard which the Slocum insisted was pretty much like plucking an actual snake though Tiny Aaron could not himself believe an actual snake would accommodate him in the sort of way a length of clothesline laid still and did. He felt, however, improved for having practiced his plucking and squatted with his Ray-o-Vac before the crawlspace doorway that the Slocum encouraged Tiny Aaron to slip on through like Tiny Aaron guessed he might if the Slocum would himself linger outside the crawlspace door so as to be available to haul Tiny Aaron's lifeless carcass into the sideyard if that eight-foot snake dropped on him and punctuated his functions that the Slocum and Tiny Aaron both together agreed was the very least thing the Slocum could manage to do. So he slipped on in among the boxes and the tools and the sacks and the power mower and then drew up and stilled himself to listen for any snaky variety of traveling noise but he heard just his own blood thumping and his own breath wheezing and his own personal exterminator reminding him from outside what fingers precisely would serve him best for plucking and so he slipped in farther than he'd slipped already and stopped another time to hear his blood and his breath and his exterminator as he played the Ray-o-Vac lightbeam most everywhere he could think to play it like he was beginning to repeat himself at when he heard that low and unmistakable scales-on-a-boardedge variety of noise off before him though not truly near so far off before him as he guessed straightaway he'd have liked which he communicated pretty much all of to the Slocum outside with just one throaty noise alone.

He meant to forge on ahead, Tiny Aaron did, meant to crawl and edge and slip towards the snaky noise with his plucking fingers at the ready but he could not somehow render himself mobile, could not somehow cultivate much of a disposition to forge and so stayed precisely where it was he'd ended up until the eight-foot snake moved itself yet another time when Tiny Aaron's pure and thoroughgoing immobility eroded sufficiently to allow him at last to forge in fact, forge exclusively back to where it was he'd come in the first place from that the Slocum out in the sideyard inquired about and so heard from Tiny Aaron, among the boxes and the sacks and the lawntools and the power mower, what tactical manner of forging he was up to just precisely. Of course, he presently left the crawlspace altogether, forged entirely out from it once he'd endured his third distinct snaky noise and the Slocum, who hadn't in the first place shown the nerve to crawl under the house at all, remarked to Tiny Aaron on the topic of his retreat with such noticeable disdain that Tiny Aaron felt obliged to exhibit at the Slocum not his foremost plucking finger precisely but the finger adjacent to it that he raised and displayed just upright by itself like served to propel the Slocum completely out from the sideyard and into his orange truck with the spotted bug atop it from where he bestowed upon Tiny Aaron an altogether novel and unseemly title prior to wheeling full into the roadway.

Though he figured and calculated, Tiny Aaron could not there in the sideyard discover in himself much of an inclination to return to the crawlspace with his Ray-o-Vac and his plucking fingers and so he undertook as best as he was able to render the sideyard inviting for a snake which he guessed he just chiefly had to leave it to do and so in fact left it. He wondered if he was a snake where it was he might go like he persevered at until he ended up coiled beneath the settee when he figured he'd best just retape his closet jamb instead and search roundabout for ventpipe holes and the like that he didn't truly discover any more of but for the slight one under the sink in the kitchen that he covered and closed up and the ever so trifling chink in the bathroom floor that he taped as well on his way to the toilet which he intended to light upon so as to maybe evacuate and ponder both and he did even light a little upon it until the notion of an eight-foot snake slinking somehow up the drainpipe and into the bowl inspired Tiny Aaron to elevate most especially his posterior well beyond evacuating range. Everywhere all over the house he went he saw what seemed to him straightoff a black lengthsome ropy manner of creature where no black lengthsome ropy manner of creature was truly like he'd presently discover once he'd jumped and sucked air already that Tiny Aaron could not help but believe was hardly the sort of pastime to do most especially his vital organs much good to speak of. So he came to be resolved, came to be anyhow pretty completely resolved for spells on end that he would shortly himself do in his snake once he'd allowed it the opportunity to evacuate the premises just up and of its own like he guessed straightoff an hour would suit before he'd worked it up into an afternoon and past an afternoon even into an entire day that seemed to Tiny Aaron interval enough to maybe get his snake gone and to allow him as well the occasion to hone and cultivate his plucking like it was altogether plain to him his plucking needed honing and cultivating both.

So Tiny Aaron resolved to leave his home for a piece of the day, resolved to drive around town in his white Impala and thereby soothe his own nervy impulses while he presented his snake the opportunity to get away altogether unscathed like shortly his snake would not anymore have the occasion for since Tiny Aaron meant in his Impala to formulate the various ways he might scathe his snake if he found when he got home he still had a snake to scathe. In fact, on his way north up the boulevard past the Hair Lair and the Rexall Tiny Aaron manufactured some fairly inordinate resolve to be firm and manly and get shortly shed of his snake entirely like would maybe be by plucking but would likely be by some means otherwise, a means all harsh and final like seemed to Tiny Aaron in the manly way of things. He slanted in briefly before the municipal building and lolled upon a bench where he spoke to Emmet Dabb of his snake troubles and let on how he was meaning himself shortly to get with that snake in a manly sort of a way that Emmet Dabb let on to him back would be just precisely how he himself would get with a snake if he had a snake to get with and he grunted at Tiny Aaron who had grunted at him first and they exchanged between them a moderately bloodthirsty variety of smirk prior to spitting and snorting that way the sort of men they guessed they were ought to. Tiny Aaron dropped by the FCX to see did they carry maybe a snake spray though he did not inquire outright about one but engaged instead in just some general reptilian talk, rough disdainful general reptilian talk truly that Tiny Aaron worked and bent as best as he was able towards a snake spray manner of discourse like the clerk Mr. Bolt did not take hardly the gist of and strayed off instead onto the topic of blood meal that his wife dusted her lilies with to thwart the rabbits and the groundhogs.

He'd tried, then, to come to be both manly and educated but he arrived home only a little more of each like was how come he lurked mostly behind his althaea bush at the corner of the house and undertook to see had his snake maybe slipped out into the sideyard but he couldn't find from back of the bush much evidence it had. Once he'd eased the front door open, he passed his head alone around the dooredge and looked for his snake upon the carpet, made even from the front porch chiefly what he meant for a snake call which was in fact a snakeherding sort of a noise but low and a little temptressy after what fashion Cleopatra likely spoke to her asps. His snake call, however, did not bring forth his eight-foot snake to get plucked and wrestled the way he'd prepared himself back of the dooredge to pluck and wrestle it, so Tiny Aaron stepped full into the frontroom and near about even shut the door back of him until his unmanly impulses kept him from it. He fairly completely scoured the house for his snake, managed anyway to pretty much squat in the middle of each room and peer briefly under the furniture of it where he could not find but matchpacks and inkpens and assorted dustballs like somehow indicated to him how he'd come in his absence to be pretty thoroughly snakeless altogether which he endeavored even to believe until he'd perched himself upon his upholstered chair before his Motorola when he began to grow edgy and pretty wholly unpersuaded about his snakelessness altogether.

In an effort to distract himself from his present dilemma, Tiny Aaron tuned in on his Motorola the syndicated show on the Greensboro station he'd come to be partial to, the syndicated quasi-educational show on the Greensboro station where he witnessed near about daily exchanges between the audience in the studio and the guests up on the raised stage and so came in a regular sort of way to be edified, had heard anyhow from a coalition of Baptist Nazis, three presidents' brothers' wives, a mixed assortment of wilty dysfuncted people on the mend, two women and three gentlemen who'd been dead but had come back from it, four illegitimate daughters of Elvis and one cousin of fairly questionable origins, a boxing nun, an accountant from Uranus by way of Fostoria Ohio, and, on this particular and only moderately snakeless afternoon, a half dozen transvestites for Christ who looked straightoff to Tiny Aaron perky nubile creatures with shimmery locks and rouge and lip gloss and only the merest hint of five o'clock shadow until he heard from the whitehaired host just what precisely a transvestite happened to be like induced Tiny Aaron to revise his impression. He managed somehow to pay even a piece of his attention to the TV and moved his eyes back and forth to the shadowy parts of the room only the bulk of the time while he heard how it was Jesus loved transvestites purely as much as he loved anybody otherwise if not more so like struck Tiny Aaron as a good thing since he could not for the life of him figure how anybody else might love a transvestite too, did not truly wish to think long and deeply upon it and so got up and changed the dial to the syndicated show on the Winston-Salem station with the black woman hostess who was quizzing, along with her audience, Liberace's sister's boy that Tiny Aaron was standing before the set to gauge and sample when he heard that low and lingering snake-on-a-boardedge variety of noise.

Rightoff he could not wholly determine just where precisely his eight-foot snake might be so he went on ahead and assumed it was fairly well set to slink and slither up his pantleg which he communicated to various of his organs so as to allow them to begin to palpitate that they all straightaway obliged him in. After a spell of just plain breathing and spit gathering, Tiny Aaron looked down towards his shoetops to see was his bony shin about to get crawled upon which was when he heard his eight-foot snake yet again dragging its entire length just precisely underneath him between the joists and across the braces that he watched the carpet on account of with his mouth a little open and his eyes a little bugged until he guessed he might endeavor instead to be manly and so snorted and grunted and said through the floor to that snake a provocative unflattering thing, a provocative unflattering thing that he felt obliged to repeat shortly prior to pointing with his foremost plucking finger straight down between his feet and advising his eight-foot snake, "All right then," with some pure and outright menace to it. For its part, Tiny Aaron's eight-foot snake just kept on heading wherever it had struck out in the first place to go and did not seem to Tiny Aaron somehow much attuned to his mood, did not strike him as affected by the threats and the hard talk like peeved Tiny Aaron further still and he sidestepped across the carpet to where he guessed his eight-foot snake had come to be and told to it, "All right then," another time and stomped even on the floor which stopped altogether his eight-foot snake that sounded to coil and bunch like Tiny Aaron grew a little shivery at the thought of.

He didn't know where it was going, meant straightoff to follow it across the floor and around the walls to discover where it might after all end up and he even near about set out but did not truly set out in fact and only sidestepped back to his upholstered chair that he dropped shortly upon and heard there a piece of the jolly recollection Liberace's sister's boy got induced to share with the audience in the studio and the folks at home as well which he had not arrived even at the jolly part of when

Tiny Aaron found himself agitated and found himself enraged and found himself impotent and forlorn all at the same time, not impotent and forlorn in your afternoon syndicated TV dysfuncted sort of a way but just stilled instead and punctuated by a snake he couldn't even so much as bring himself to pluck. And Tiny Aaron said at Liberace's sister's boy chiefly, "Ain't that pathetic," which he got told back a jolly thing on account of that did not in the least bit tickle him at all as he was not in the mood for a jolly thing truly and undertook to dredge and to snort and to grunt but could not somehow feel manly at it and so grew a trifle whiny instead and interrupted Liberace's sister's boy right there in the middle of the jolliest part of his recollection to bemoan his general spinelessness.

Wouldn't anybody pluck and pulverize his snake for him. Tiny Aaron just announced pretty much at his Motorola how he did not hardly anticipate anybody might, and he beat his chairarm and worked most especially his veiny neck muscles and endeavored even to generate some palpable resolve like he'd manufactured just a trace of when his eight-foot snake showed what seemed to Tiny Aaron the bald and colossal audacity to crawl another time among the floorbraces directly beneath him that Tiny Aaron didn't suppose even an impotent forlorn spineless whiny man could stand to endure. So he got after a fashion worked up, came to be even measurably steely and stalked out from the den into the kitchen after his Ray-o-Vac that he carried with him towards the frontdoor and almost out the frontdoor even before he grew of a sudden inspired with a notion, struck with an alternative to plucking and wrestling and pulverizing and so stopped briefly into the front bedroom and withdrew from the closet there the very item he guessed he'd needed all along which he laid upon his shoulder and toted out across the porch and around to the sideyard where he squatted before the crawlspace doorway and declared into the dark murky recesses how he was quite thoroughly prepared to send what eight-foot snake had seen fit to reside there pretty directly straight to hell that he'd heard a man one time say on the TV from atop a horse and behind a pistol.

Airsucking seemed to him to stir his juices so he passed a spell just ventilating and stoking his resolve prior to hunkering down onto his knees and the heel of his one hand and shining his lightbeam in upon the clutter and up upon the floorbraces where he could not straightaway discover his snake and so ventilated further and grunted and snorted and spat even as preamble to passing on in through the doorway where he felt disposed to whine but got by his juices kept from it. He crawled a little on his frontside and slid a little on his backside and loosed in a regular sort of a way profane bits of talk intended to be antagonizing to a snake while they bolstered and sustained Tiny Aaron's manly impulses, bolstered and sustained them for a spell anyhow until he'd arrived pretty well under the Motorola when his manly impulses up and ebbed on him like left Tiny Aaron to squirm chiefly and palpitate and vent just an occasional feeble snort. He was suspecting even his functions might just shortly dwindle and quit him and allowed himself to speculate as to who would possibly find him in with the boxes and the lawntools all dead and stiff and probably a little gnawed on that he hoped was maybe a comely woman who would wail and weep about him, and the notion of getting dead and getting stiff and most especially getting gnawed on was full well on its way to rendering Tiny Aaron forlorn and whiny all over again when he finally at last saw it, peered in his distraction off to the one side and saw it under the frontroom near about snug up against the chimney stack where it was holding to a brace with a piece of itself and allowing the rest of itself just to dangle chiefly and dart only every now and again in a thoroughgoing snaky sort of a way which Tiny Aaron felt obliged to shiver and twitch on account of.

He got a little fascinated, came to be moderately hypnotized by the dangling and the darting and just the general snakiness of his own black eight-foot specimen that he bathed briefly in his lightbeam until it showed to him its tongue when he felt obliged to shine his lightbeam elsewhere instead like was, Tiny Aaron figured, a direct result of his abject spinelessness that he came to feel another time impotent and forlorn on account of and arrived even right there at the verge of proclaiming how pathetic in fact his own present state seemed to him to be when his eight-foot snake undangled itself and departed across the braces towards the crawlspace door on a route that would presently bring it to pass, Tiny Aaron calculated, over what might be by then his lifeless carcass judging from what he took to be the state of his functions. Of course, he did manage to work up the spit sufficient to advise his snake how he was shortly intending to send it pretty directly straight to hell like did not appear to strike it as much in the way of bothersome since it did not stop or veer or slow even but merely persisted in dragging its length from boardedge to boardedge and advancing tonguetip foremost directly at Tiny Aaron who undertook to stoke his resolve with an inhalation and maybe even did stoke it a little, stoked it enough anyway to roll himself off his back onto his one side and raise with both his arms together what item he'd toted most especially to send that eight-foot snake pretty directly straight to hell with which would be his twenty-gauge Remington pump-action plugless shotgun loaded full up with five shells of number four shot that he'd intended for thieving hoodlums but guessed he could spend a few of if need be on a vagrant serpent instead.

Of course, he wouldn't have rolled over and raised up the gun if he wasn't meaning to shoot his snake like he shot it though in truth he was not hardly meaning to shoot his snake when precisely he shot it in fact, had meant to get set and aimed and leveled before he went on ahead and squeezed the trigger but due to his altogether agitated and fairly invertebrate state, he yanked off a shot before he'd spied along the barrel good and so beat his forehead with a length of the gunmetal and wrenched his shouldersocket with the butt of the hardwood stock and rolled inadvertently back to where he'd just shortly rolled over from like kept him from seeing the near about pure and outright obliteration of his eight-foot snake that departed from this life in scant and assorted pieces diluted like they were with a portion of iron wastepipe and the consequent effluvium that fairly rained out from it somewhat onto Tiny Aaron and somewhat onto Tiny Aaron's lawnmower and somewhat as well onto the ragged electrical cordends Tiny Aaron had with his number seven shot separated from each other. It didn't look to him but a puny hole he'd blown in the floor when at last Tiny Aaron managed to raise back up to see what in fact he'd sent to hell precisely which would be, aside from his eight-foot snake and his piece of iron elbow and his portion of electrical wire, a span of decking, a patch of carpet pad, and sufficient of the gold pile carpet itself to provide Tiny Aaron with a partial view of the walnut teatable in the frontroom that he had not truly ever hoped to see from flat out upon his backside atop the dirt crawlspace floor, and Tiny Aaron could not help but blow a breath and exclaim, "Aw shit," like he heard himself inside his head exclaim it without in fact realizing how he'd heard himself exclaim it inside his head alone.

Now out on the street before Tiny Aaron's house, actually out on the street across the road from Tiny Aaron's house in front of the widow Mrs. Boatwright's moderately trained creeping sweetpea Miss Mary Alice Celestine Lefler had interrupted her afternoon constitutional to remark to the widow Mrs. Boatwright on the topic of most especially her bushy wayward shoots that the widow Mrs. Boatwright, from up on her front porch where she was laying manure to her ferns, admitted she'd been meaning to prune. The wayward shoots, however, were the very shoots precisely Miss Mary Alice Celestine Lefler found herself to be altogether fondest of which she apprised the widow Mrs. Boatwright of and let on how her admiration for your bushy wayward sorts of shoots revealed a thing about her own spunky self, or undertook anyway to let it on without blurting it outright but did in fact presently blurt it pretty much outright after all due to how the widow Mrs. Boatwright squinted and pitched her head and failed to appear the sort that might just up and deduce a thing. Miss Mary Alice Celestine Lefler even stepped away from the sweetpea towards the front porch and had set out elaborating on the precise nature of her own personal spunk when she arrived at the outer rim of the widow Mrs. Boatwright's manure aroma which happened to have been manufactured, manure and aroma both, by Mr. Raeford Lynch's laying hens and consequently was thick and sour and so full well ammoniated as to cause Miss Mary Alice Celestine Lefler to squint and pitch her own head in an altogether unincisive sort of a way.

Of course she felt pressed to make herself understood on the topic of her personal spunk and had even begun to speak of it once further when her and the widow Mrs. Boatwright both came to be obliged to leap and start on account of Mr. Tiny Aaron's twenty-gauge explosion that they'd not either one of them had much cause to anticipate. Straightaway, the widow Mrs. Boatwright figured it to be the gasline as the gasline had evermore seemed to her the manner of item that might just up and of a sudden explode and she watched Mr. Tiny Aaron's house across the road for signs of combustion and traces of wispy smoke while she spoke to Miss Mary Alice Celestine Lefler of a gasline explosion she'd come to be acquainted with on the news, a gasline explosion that she seemed to recall had produced some inordinate carnage like led the widow Mrs. Boatwright to tell shortly of her own personal heatpump that was altogether unexplodable entirely.

There didn't seem to her any way she could help but traipse on across the street and find out what precisely had blown up. Miss Mary Alice Celestine Lefler guessed she just had to know it and so took her leave of the widow Mrs. Boatwright, who was not the sort to venture near a gasline herself, and crossed the road to Mr. Tiny Aaron's house where she mounted the porch and peered straightoff through the middle doorlight that gave on to Tiny Aaron's momma's marbletopped bureau chiefly and onto Tiny Aaron's momma's dropleaf endtable by the sofa arm as well along with what appeared to Miss Mary Alice Celestine Lefler a sizeable and altogether unseemly stain on the gold pile carpet that she was speculating there atop the front porch as to the cause of when four fingers and a thumb and a bony wrist along with an entire forearm clean up to the elbow plain sprouted up out from it and inspired from Miss Mary Alice Celestine Lefler an extravagant exclamation. She could not seem to help but watch the piece of arm wag briefly in the air prior to withdrawing entirely back down into the unseemly stain that she shortly swung around on the porch to speak of to the widow Mrs. Boatwright across the road but could not discover what words precisely to speak of it with and so communicated chiefly a snatch of generic consternation and alarm like seemed to the widow Mrs. Boatwright your basic gasline sort.

As he crawled and slid and scooted towards the doorway, Tiny Aaron made such appreciable noise kicking and grunting and beating on occasion the floorjoists with his gunbarrel and his Ray-o-Vac and his knobby head too that he sounded to Miss Mary Alice Celestine Lefler upon the front porch like some manner of outsized and inordinately aggravated vermin which she endeavored to squeal across the road about and did even squeal a little before she found herself drawn and baited by the racket to the very lip of the porch from where she peered around the corner of the house and saw presently Tiny Aaron's Ray-o-Vac and Tiny Aaron's twenty-gauge gunbarrel emerge through the crawlspace doorway with the bulk of Tiny Aaron himself back of them, everything that is but for his ankles and his feet that he left to lay across the threshold while he sprawled a time in the sideyard basking in the recollection of how it was precisely he'd obliterated his snake. Of course she yoo-hooed at him, did not feel it proper to stand there on the lip of his porch and watch him lay and sprawl without yoo-hooing to let him know she'd come to be where she'd ended up, but he did not appear to her much roused by her yoo-hoos and continued just to lay and just to recollect until he rolled up one time more like he'd rolled up previously and elevated his gunbarrel after the very fashion he'd elevated it and made with his breath chiefly and his spit a little a gunshot sort of noise that looked from the porchedge to please and divert him due to how it was he hooted and swore behind it prior to flopping back over and laying awhile further still.

Shortly, however, he did rise full upright and held with the fingers of his one hand his flashlight and his shotgun both while he brushed the dirt off his pants and attempted with his free fingerends, that he licked and moistened, to cleanse himself of what effluvium he'd accumulated from his busted four-inch effluvium pipe like just fingers and just spit could not hardly together even manage which Tiny Aaron was beginning to endure a revelation about when Miss Mary Alice Celestine Lefler, who'd left the porchlip for the sideyard, produced in her throat an ever so dainty phlegmdredging sort of a noise and waited for Tiny

Aaron to lift his head in the wake of it. Instead, however, Tiny Aaron mustered a wildly profane and copulatory variety of discharge himself due to the effluvia his spit and his fingers together could not loose, so wildly profane and copulatory in fact that Miss Mary Alice Celestine Lefler found herself obliged to inhale behind her knuckles for a time until she could collect herself sufficiently to dredge phlegm all over again. And she said to Tiny Aaron, "Pardon me," and she said to Tiny Aaron, "Pardon me sir but," and she said to Tiny Aaron, "Hey," and snapped her fingers and waved her one hand pretty much at the side of Tiny Aaron's head like was past even the corner of his eye where he saw things usually that weren't in the first place there to see. So she did not rouse him with her talking and her fingersnapping and had ventured near about snug up beside him so as to maybe poke him once when Tiny Aaron vented himself of such an extravagantly oathsome and exaltational sentiment that Miss Mary Alice Celestine Lefler came to be briefly staggered by the altogether robust vigor of it and consequently did not poke hardly like she set out to but instead just laid mostly her fingerends to Tiny Aaron's near forearm, laid in fact her fingerends flush upon Tiny Aaron's feathery eagle that was gripping a piece of the flag with his feet.

"Ooohh," she told to him and once he'd jerked his head he saw her lips go round and inside out like he probably would have watched more of had he not felt obliged to depart from the sideyard a time, had he not felt obliged to hover above it while he exhibited for Miss Mary Alice Celestine Lefler his boundless surprise along with the wrinkly roof of his mouth that she stood alone atop the ground and admired until Tiny Aaron deigned to light and join her there. And she said another time to him, "Ooohh," and touched him again not directly upon his eagle but primarily instead upon a rapidly encrusting patch of effluvium fairly close up against his eagle that she wondered at Tiny Aaron the origin of since she was not herself much acquainted with effluvium and the sundry travels of it, and Tiny Aaron for his part watched her lips work and her tongue move and her teeth show every now and again until she shut her mouth entirely a spell when he watched instead her eyes watch his eyes like indicated to him how the moment had arrived for him to tell to her, "WHAT?" in his best inquiring voice that the widow Mrs. Boatwright across the road left off with her manure on account of.

And then it was more of the lips and the tongue and the teeth somewhat along with the eyes that watched him watch her as a preface to Tiny Aaron apprising Miss Mary Alice Celestine Lefler in what sounded between his ears a moderate tone where it was he'd just lately been and how come.

And she wanted to know from him, "A snake?" that Tiny Aaron inquired of her in what he meant for his suave voice an additional WHAT? about.

"Did you say," she asked him, "you shot a snake?"

"NO, NO," Tiny Aaron informed her and exhibited briefly his own teeth. "IT WASN'T BUT A SNAKE," like induced Miss Mary Alice Celestine Lefler to plain lay her mouth open a time which appeared to Tiny Aaron sufficiently like talk to bring forth an additional WHAT? from him.

He knew it was her, hadn't known it was her straight from the outset but had come shortly to know it was her, her he'd spied just lately at the reservoir lolling upon the grass with Dick Atwater and Dick Atwater's lowslung hairpart, her Nestor Tudor had gone to the bother to indicate to him, her from elsewhere entirely who'd seen fit to lay her fingers to Tiny Aaron's tattoo and tell him a low murmurous thing with her lips turned inside out, vent what had looked to him a fairly amorous sort of an item like he guessed anymore he rated now that he'd stalked his snake and shot it which was the cause, he figured, which was undoubtedly the enticement since it seemed to him evermore the fellows with gumption and pluck that rendered the women low and murmurous both. He managed even a variety of swagger, Tiny Aaron did, laid his free and somewhat effluviated hand to his hip and twisted round and raised up his head after the fashion he figured was a snake conqueror's due that he augmented with a manner of sidelong look even Mr. Phillip J. King himself would have been pleased to cut his eyes and make.

"EIGHT FOOT," he told to Miss Mary Alice Celestine Lefler who worked her lips at him back and said to him what he took for a jolly adorational sort of a thing like seemed cause for mirth to Tiny Aaron who fairly yelped and yowled and so brought the widow Mrs. Boatwright off her own porch entirely and across the full breadth of her yard to the far boundary of it from where she could spy out the source of the yelping and the yowling both and call even to it, shriek a little herself, "Tiny Aaron what in this world is wrong with you?" that Miss Mary Alice Celestine Lefler straightaway swung full roundabout on account of and induced presently with her fingerend Tiny Aaron to swing roundabout a little himself to where he could spy back the widow Mrs. Boatwright and raise at her his unencumbered hand and tell to her, "HEY."

He guessed he wouldn't ever likely scale a chairback again as the rewards of manly pluck seemed to him even there in the sideyard at the first blush inordinately thoroughgoing and worthwhile and he struck for the widow Mrs. Boatwright what he figured for a suitable pose with his nose uplifted and his one foot settled atop his oiltank spout like he hoped would tell to her how he'd come to be bluff and come to be potent and done lately battle of a sort which the widow Mrs. Boatwright did not from across the road signify it had but only beat for a spell her lips together like brought forth from Tiny Aaron what sounded in his head a hale and robust sort of a discharge.

She touched his eagle another time, Miss Mary Alice Celestine Lefler touched one time more his bristly eagle with her fingerends and told him a thing he couldn't in the least bit make out but jerked most especially his nose at nonetheless as nosejerking seemed to him somehow to square with the posture he'd taken up and she showed to him her teeth and raised at him her entire open hand like brought forth from Tiny Aaron a fairly vigorous and lusty wink, more vigorous and lusty by far than he'd found occasion to ever wink previously, sufficiently vigorous and lusty anyhow to leave Miss Mary Alice Celestine Lefler what looked to Tiny Aaron palpably breathless and spent and able just barely to take her leave out the sideyard and across the road and back up the street where she'd come in the first place from while Tiny Aaron stepped out towards the road himself and admired various of Miss Mary Alice Celestine Lefler's retreating parts that the widow Mrs. Boatwright could not from alongside her ferns much approve of and so aired for Tiny Aaron her own particular view of men that gawked and slobbered at backsides and such which was a shrill and altogether fullblown opinion that she vented in fact two times complete at Tiny Aaron's bluff and potent profile which he showed alone to the widow Mrs. Boatwright as he watched the posterior leave from him and made with his tongue and his teeth and his spit in combination a snakeherding sort of a noise.

iii.

MR. Wayne Fulp's speckled hound Bill's favorite patch of treebark seemed to have accumulated from somewhere a vagrant bouquet that Mr. Wayne Fulp's speckled hound Bill sniffed at in a grave and sober sort of a way prior to dropping a time upon his backside and gazing ever so thoughtfully at an empty piece of air that a winged beetle undertook at length to pass through and so got by Bill bitten and gnawed on and, presently, ejected. In time, of course, Bill worked up sufficient liquid of his own to hose down his treetrunk all around its girth that he sat and lolled another spell in the wake of before the lure of his organ overcame him, inspired him anyhow to nose and lick it both like was just precisely the sort of endeavor he could not straightoff erode the charm of. Bill did, however, eventually get done, rose up and shook and stepped off the curb and around the rearend of the Toronado and on out into the middle of the road where he sampled the aroma of the yellow center line and examined a piece of a stick and, alongside it, a wrapper that proved especially tantalizing.

Presently, though, he did proceed to the Fairlane up snug to the far curb, the Fairlane with two tires most especially that had accumulated some vagrant bouquets of their own which Bill sampled and savored a time prior to wheeling and cocking like he had to to hose on what particular bouquet was his that he looked to be meaning to fairly much punctuate his evening with and so just sniffed briefly his own discharge and then made directly for Mr. Wayne Fulp's front porch where most nights he sat before the screendoor and grumbled and moaned until Mr. Wayne Fulp pushed the thing open. However, Bill got on this night distracted by a scent otherwise, a potent exotic variety of scent that wafted at him from down across the yard along about the crabapple tree in the corner of the lot and he followed his uplifted snout to discover what item might emanate a scent both potent and exotic together like brought him to Nestor Tudor's crinkled leather shoetops that were not themselves, Bill discovered, the precise source of the emanation.

Of course Nestor Tudor told what generally people told to Mr. Wayne Fulp's speckled hound Bill, Nestor Tudor told, "Go on," to him and kicked at him with what Bill had just lately found to be a potent but altogether unexotic black wingtip that he leaped and jumped and lurched on account of. Naturally, however, Bill didn't go on just precisely but only moderately went on for a time and lurked a couple of yards off from the shoetops where he felt obliged to drop upon his haunches and dig at an itch until he grew weary of it and got again intoxicated by Mr. Nestor Tudor's scent all potent and exotic that Bill advanced another time nose foremost on account of and managed to slip unseen up to Nestor Tudor's left kneejoint that he prodded once alone with his snoutend like fairly transported Nestor Tudor acutely and he exclaimed in such an altogether inarticulate sort of a way that Bill could not hardly begin to take much instruction from it which was how come he merely hunkered and sat and so was convenient to get swatted by Mr. Nestor Tudor's cornflower and gladiola nosegay which was not, Bill discovered, the source of the potent and exotic aroma either. The jerking and the armswinging did, however, stir up Mr. Nestor Tudor's scent afresh and it wafted and reeked on the air most especially from around his jowls where Nestor Tudor had figured, once he'd come across his eau de cologne, he'd best lay it, figured just there on the impulse of the moment as he'd not truly been hunting an eau de cologne when he'd found one in the cabinet back of the Mercurochrome and alongside the isopropyl alcohol, found his Hai Karate still in the bottle in the sack like it had come to him in the first place from his dead wife Erlene who'd bought it that Christmas she'd quite obviously been congested.

It was enough to make even a hound teary and Bill, that had retreated out of swatting range, turned his sad rheumy eyes on Nestor Tudor one time further like touched and affected Nestor Tudor sufficiently to inspire him to tell to Mr. Wayne Fulp's speckled hound Bill, "Go on," that he emphasized and augmented with the variety of highly animated nosegay brandishing that Bill could hardly mistake the intent of.

Consequently, then, Mr. Wayne Fulp's speckled hound gained shortly Mr. Wayne Fulp's front steps and Mr. Wayne Fulp's porch decking beyond it and planted himself before the screendoor where he commenced to grumble and moan while Nestor Tudor down by the crabapple tree undented his nosegay paper and refluffed, as best as he was able, his cornflowers and his gladiolas both that he'd not carried clean from Mr. T. Leslie Nathan's flower boutique just to beat a dog with which he was right there in the middle of advising himself about when the headlights that played briefly upon him sent him back into the branches and the leaves from where he watched the white Impala cruise east along the street and listened at the wheelbearings click and knock together. He'd intended to be cordial and neighborly, had come south down the highway into town with his scent and his nosegay and his swanky purple horseheaded shirt so as to rap upon Miss Bernice Fay Frazier's doorrail and get construed there on the threshold for cordial and neighborly both, but Mr. Dick Atwater had quite apparently arrived in his Toronado to get construed ahead of him like relegated Nestor Tudor to the murky gloom where it seemed to him he fairly much squandered his swank altogether.

There'd come to be a bit of a bite to the evening and Miss Bernice Fay Frazier had shut just previously her frontdoor on account of it like kept Nestor Tudor from spying any longer the portions and pieces he'd managed to spy of her with the teeth and the lips and the fingerends which he was left alongside the crabapple tree to ruminate pretty exclusively about but for the particular lowslung hairpart he mused briefly upon prior to touching off an Old Gold filter and retreating shortly with his firecoal back into the branches and the leaves once the lamplight had swept another time across him from the white Impala with the wheelbearings that beat and knocked together. And Nestor Tudor wondered what thing he'd seen fit to wonder ever since he'd raised up off the toilet ring back home and wondered it there the first time in the mirror over the sink. Wouldn't it, he wondered, be delightful for him and for her together to pass an evening at the Ingot Lounge where they might, if they pleased, dance like was not remotely the best wondering he'd done lately, hardly possessed the lilt and charm of the wondering he'd managed in his Fairlane on the way from the house that he undertook to manufacture anew, or had begun anyhow to undertaking it when Bill at last succeeded in inducing Mr. Wayne Fulp to push open the screendoor with the spring upon it that squeaked and twanged sufficiently to distract Nestor Tudor who looked up across the yard from the crabapple tree and watched Mr. Wayne Fulp admit Bill into the frontroom and turn as he did it so as to tell back into the house a thing about Gene Krupa that Nestor Tudor could not figure, even there in the throes of his present condition, Bill the speckled hound would be much curious to hear.

Understandably, Nestor Tudor felt obliged to step away from the crabapple and out towards the heart of the yard far enough to learn how it was a speckled hound might possibly entertain and respond to talk of Gene Krupa that he looked up through the screendoor on account of where he spied in place of the speckled hound near about all of Mr. Wayne Fulp and a length of trouserleg alongside him, a finely creased and altogether unwrinkled length of trouserleg with scant stripes to it, an elegant and tasteful length of trousering which by itself implied one whole entire refined individual who'd come for some reason to call upon Mr. Wayne Fulp and had gotten for some reason received like would not with most people have been worth leaving even a crabapple tree for but was with Mr. Wayne Fulp an occasion due to how Mr. Wayne Fulp had managed to become fairly celebrated for going unvisited and pretty completely uncalled upon but for his speckled hound Bill that nightly grumbled and moaned and so got allowed to join Wayne Fulp in the house he'd had to have an aunt die to get.

He hailed from elsewhere, Mr. Wayne Fulp did, came in fact from a pack of Tennessee Fulps on his daddy's side and an altogether thin and dwindling strain of Black Mountain Laytons on his momma's and he'd not ever visited his daddy's sister, who'd married and settled in with a local Puckett, until that Puckett had grown of a sudden compelled to be reposed in a blue suit atop a tufted satin liner when Mr. Wayne Fulp arrived in time to gaze upon him and speak to his aunt of how hardy he looked, more robust by far than most live people, which was just precisely the sort of talk to touch and affect his daddy's sister who'd not gotten even one time told of her Puckett's altogether palpable native vigor until her brother's boy Mr. Wayne Fulp arrived to tell her of it.

As Mr. Wayne Fulp's daddy's sister had no children of her own she fairly adopted Mr. Wayne Fulp and received occasional visits from him right up until the time of her own personal demise when Mr. Wayne Fulp arrived to admire her vigor and learned that she'd bequeathed him her house and goods that most everybody thought he'd sell but that he did not sell, did not even leave to sit empty but a scant time, not remotely a decent sort of an interval as best as most people could tell, people anyway who had need to see a house vacant and forlorn and relatively overgrown before the occupant could seem to them purely and irredeemably dead. He moved into it himself, hardly brought much with him beyond one piddling carload of boxes and bags along with his speckled hound Bill, and he never truly spoke of where he'd come from and what he'd done there in addition to the countless items otherwise he did not seem much prone to be chatty about and so was not, in fact, chatty about them no matter how he got probed and plumbed and plied as well there at the outset with casseroles and cakes and fruit salads and assorted chicken parts. Mr. Wayne Fulp was even privileged to receive from Miss Halley Verna Drumm a twig wreath she'd worked and twined herself of an evening at the middle school in her wreathweaving seminar and he'd stood, she told it, outside the house upon the porch decking where he'd held the thing long enough to seem to admire it prior to hanging it on a nail under his knocker, the very nail his daddy's dead sister had most usually dangled her holly from like Miss Halley Verna Drumm, who'd not felt her wreath had come to be sufficiently appreciated before it got hung and got dangled, grew palpably irritated about that Mr. Wayne Fulp and Mr. Wayne Fulp's dog Bill merely stood together upon the porch decking and watched her do.

And it wasn't that Mr. Wayne Fulp was some imported variety of ingrate all silent and rude and sour and incapable of much kindliness and grace. It wasn't that Mr. Wayne Fulp was even your local and indigenous surly sort of ingrate either that found himself pressed and moved to announce precisely what he thought in front of precisely who he thought it about. It was just that Mr. Wayne Fulp could not somehow muster up and exhibit much passion and enthusiasm for cakes or casseroles or fruit salads or chicken parts or twig wreaths either, or could that is muster it a little but did not possess at all the means to show it off. He could manage bereavement and consolation well enough but Mr. Wayne Fulp lacked somehow the talent to be just up and all at once conversational. As a result, he seemed odd to people, seemed to them queer and peculiar until they got persuaded by Mr. H. Monroe Aycock to take him for sullen and take him for churlish instead like was, Mr. H. Monroe Aycock implied, a refinement on queer and on peculiar and struck him as altogether closer to the nugget of the thing entirely which Mr. H. Monroe Aycock was fairly widely persuasive about on account of the considerable breadth and dimensions of his own personal sphere of opinion that pretty much smothered the county like a nappy blanket.

Of course the truth of the thing was something entirely otherwise altogether as Mr. Wayne Fulp was not sullen truly and was not even remotely churlish at all but was chiefly just pathetic instead like got found out almost straightaway by Mrs. Donnie Bunch at the dimestore who hired Mr. Wayne Fulp to see most especially after their gerbils and their skittery yellow and skittery limegreen birds and their guppies and tropical fish and lone boa constrictor that lived in a glass tank wrapped around a treelimb and smelled like a half dozen brogans dredged out of a ditch until Mr. Wayne Fulp, in his first official dimestore act, disinfected the tank and fairly thoroughly perfumed the snake with a subtle lilac scent that endured even for a brief spell before the brogan and ditchwater aroma insinuated itself once again. And it was plain from the first to Mrs. Donnie Bunch who managed and to Mrs. Cecil Dutton as well in notions that Mr. Wayne Fulp did not hardly have much churl to him but most closely resembled instead Mrs. Donnie Bunch's uncle and Mrs. Cecil Dutton's aunt's boy that had the both of them gotten somehow pathetic pretty much the very way exactly Mr. Wayne Fulp was quite plainly pathetic himself. He wasn't so much indifferent to social charms and graces as just flat without them and incapable most times of working up even the spit to venture into the world and speak with.

"Backwards," Mrs. Cecil Dutton had told directly to Mrs. Donnie Bunch who'd pressed her lips tight together and jerked her head ever so hardly at all like with her meant Precisely most times but meant this once more than just Precisely alone since Mr. Wayne Fulp was so far even past backwards as to make Mrs. Donnie Bunch's own personal pathetic uncle seem pretty much Dale Carnegie to her. He couldn't manage to look but at the floor except for when he watched instead assorted walljoints and lightboxes, anything truly but for whoever it was he was getting talked at by or whoever it was he was endeavoring somehow to speak at back, so Mrs. Donnie Bunch and Mrs. Cecil Dutton and most everybody otherwise that troubled themselves to undertake a confab with Mr. Wayne Fulp viewed primarily the top of his head where his hairline had lately begun to fairly bolt towards his cowlick unless of course they observed the underside of his jaw instead which was not truly near so engaging as his freckledy pate that was hardly itself the source of much delight and scintillation.

Mr. Wayne Fulp, then, did not exhibit inordinate or even truly detectable flair for customer relations and got on account of it pretty completely misapprehended after your sullen and churlish sort of a fashion since most people who endeavored to trade with him, people who undertook to buy a fish in a Baggie or a Day-Glo bird or a spotted gerbil or just your cedar gerbil chips or your fishflakes or your tiny round bird mirrors with the bells on them, had entered already into Mr. H. Monroe Aycock's sphere of opinion by virtue alone of the ears they owned to hear with and so they had to figure, once they'd initiated a confab and a confab somehow did not ensue, they were receiving from Mr. Wayne Fulp a snub since they'd learned previously what variety of churl Mr. Wayne Fulp was himself prone to be. So what with just the shiny topnotch and the bristly jowls and the vague occasional low murmurous indecipherable talk Mr. Wayne Fulp did not somehow seem much on the road to becoming a rousing sort of retail success and would have likely gotten himself discharged from the dimestore altogether if not for Mrs. Cecil Dutton's and Mrs. Donnie Bunch's individual pathetic relations that served, they told each other, as a reminder of their duty to pathetic people the world over which Mr. Wayne Fulp was quite plainly one of. They did not, as a result, trouble him to cultivate much charm on the sales floor and allowed Mr. Wayne Fulp to tend to his fishes and his birds and his gerbils and his lone musky snake while they took it upon themselves to intercede with what people stepped in off the boulevard and back to the pet department to make inquiries. So Mr. Wayne Fulp was left alone to flake his fishes and seed his birds and mulch his gerbils and fumigate his snake in addition to sweeping the linoleum and mopping it twice a week and assisting every now and again Mrs. Cecil Dutton in the dusting of her notions that seemed to collect, for notions, extravagant muck and debris from most all over.

Evenings he was generally left to be pathetic just all by himself alone but for Bill his speckled hound that most usually yapped and whined his way onto the throwrug before the TV where he loosed with some regularity that world-weary remotely exasperational canine sort of an exhalation that Bill had honed and perfected before he'd left even his puppyhood altogether. For his part Mr. Wayne Fulp sat sometimes back of Bill in his aunt's chintz wingchair and tuned in every now and again the Greensboro station like was often worth exhaling about which was how come Mr. Wayne Fulp did not loll in his aunt's chair before the TV with truly much frequency to speak of, or was a piece of how come anyway with the rest of how come being primarily Mr. Wayne Fulp's own personal passion that he chose most nights to indulge. Having come to get pathetic, of course, Mr. Wayne Fulp did not hardly seem the sort to harbor an enthusiasm but he possessed in fact the selfsame variety of juices most everybody otherwise was afflicted with as well and had cultivated on account of them a passion for record albums, or actually a passion for album sleeves and jackets almost exclusively and not the records themselves but ever so hardly at all due to Mr. Wayne Fulp's own personal sense of rhythm and beat which was sufficiently vague and murky as to be almost wholly undetectable. Mr. Wayne Fulp preferred to read the notes so as to get told what he might at the very same time precisely be listening to, so as to learn did it have to it much jump and sway and where exactly and how come or was it maybe a low and soulful ballady sort of an item instead that he had no call truly to stomp his foot about. Lacking such instruction and edification, Mr. Wayne Fulp simply possessed no means otherwise to gauge and evaluate what selection he set his needle upon and played, gauge and evaluate that is what selection he set his dead aunt's needle upon since Mr. Wayne Fulp had abandoned and discarded his own personal sound system prior to his move, had shut anyhow the lid and clasped anyhow the clasps and tossed the thing into the Dumpster back of the carlot once he'd discovered what all precisely he'd come to have bequeathed to him like was a moderately dilapidated frame house chiefly with appreciable frumpy furniture inside it along with one genuine and verifiable hi-fi console that had to it a speaker either side of the TV tube and appeared capable of some elevated fidelity if not pure and actual high fidelity outright.

But in fact the altitude of Mr. Wayne Fulp's fidelity was not truly of awful much consequence to him, and he was chiefly taken with the notion of a speaker for each ear, a potent and sizeable speaker for each ear that he could crank up, he'd told to his dog Bill, when he was of a mood for it like had gotten him significantly exhaled at. Of course Mr. Wayne Fulp didn't trouble himself much about a needle since he was too thoroughly pathetic to ask in the Radio Shack after one and too acutely tone deaf to much notice if he didn't like left him with his dead aunt's original console needle that was itself altogether as sharp and edgy as a six-penny nail and did not somehow come to be much honed and improved by Mr. Wayne Fulp's foremost fingerend that he dragged from time to time across it so as to find out had his tubes gotten sufficiently hot. Mr. Wayne Fulp had cultivated a personal preference for song stylists primarily and evermore kicked off an evening with a number from Mr. Frank Sinatra who, on his early albums, sang generally in a key Mr. Wayne Fulp could near about sing in himself and, on his later albums, hit the manner of notes Mr. Wayne Fulp possessed even the talent to hit as they were not in fact purely notes at all and were not on occasion snug up to notes even but lay sometimes partway beyond one note and halfway shy of another like Mr. Wayne Fulp could drop his chin and fairly approximate himself much to the outright consternation of his speckled hound that most usually gathered his bulk up off the rug and left the room once the "L. A. Is My Lady" trumpet preamble had begun to swell and bleat. The state of Mr. Wayne Fulp's dead aunt's needle, of course, did not much enhance the notes Mr. Frank Sinatra did manage to hit square and flush since Mr. Wayne Fulp's six-penny console fidelity left even the likes of Mr. Johnny Hartman sounding more than a little wheezy and consumptive, but Mr. Wayne Fulp didn't much care since he had his jackets and his sleeves to pore over, his lyrics to ponder, his notes to digest. And he retained even the most of it, knew who'd played the piano on Miss Bess Myerson's lone LP and who'd snapped the picture of Frank's girl Nancy in her clingy skirt and boots for her own personal album cover. He could tick off precisely who'd written what and when and who with and knew who all had sung it and arranged by whom and how. He could tell even which Ames brother was which and had the records they'd made together and had the records they'd made apart. He owned all variety of talking albums from Charleton Heston's Abraham Lincoln talking album to Jimmy Dean's *Big Bad John* talking album along with Mr. Rod McKuen's semipoetical album that was somewhere itself between talking and singing both and fared especially poorly under Mr. Wayne Fulp's dead aunt's needle due to Mr. Rod McKuen's natural congestive qualities.

He bought, in short, most everything he ran across that he did not already have one of and listened to even some of what he came home with and read and studied the rest prior to filing his acquisitions roundabout the frontroom on tabletops and shelves and floorboards as well, filing his acquisitions by catalog number in descending order from the front doorframe across the marble bureau top to the hutch and beyond it back of the settee along the far wall where Mr. Wayne Fulp had rigged planks and blocks together into a manner of item that appeared capable even of supporting record albums for a spell longer maybe. For each record he bought he filled out a three-by-five card that he kept the bulk of in his dead aunt's recipe card box with the rolling pin decoupaged atop it and kept the rest in a brown cardboard accordian file Mrs. Donnie Bunch had personally helped him to select at the dimestore, and naturally Mr. Wayne Fulp took measurable pleasure in consulting his cards alone when he was not of a mood to consult an album jacket instead or advance so far as to heat up his tubes and settle his six-penny needle upon an actual record.

Of course the trouble was that Mr. Wayne Fulp did not have but a speckled hound handy to share his enthusiasm with until by sheer and unanticipated happenstance he found himself late in the day in the dimestore at the fishflake display just up and of a sudden speaking to Mr. Dunford Hicks III, just up and of a sudden telling to him, "Tangerine," in near about plain discernible English.

Mr. Dunford Hicks kept fish. Mr. Dunford Hicks kept primarily red wag platies and blush angels along with an occasional yellow sword, or had kept previously platies and angels and yellow swords until Mrs. Dunford Hicks, whose hand he'd not but lately taken in holy matrimony, perched herself one evening upon his kneejoints, picked with her fingernails at his shirtbuttons, and told to him all low and treacly, "Sweetheart," as preamble to the revelation that she could not find much harmony in the red from the platies and the pink from the angels and the yellow from the swords that just plain did not blend and coordinate to suit her and clashed most especially with Mr. Dunford Hick's dead momma's valances which Mrs. Dunford Hicks III had gone to the trouble to have reupholstered that she tugged at a shirtbutton and reminded Mr. Dunford Hicks about. She wondered, if he had to keep fishes, couldn't he maybe get maroon ones and mix them, if he felt so inclined, with perhaps a dose of taupe fishes as well which Mr. Dunford Hicks considered briefly in silence prior to airing for his fairly new wife his own personal view that tropical fishes did not generally come in taupe, did not often come in maroon either like prompted Mrs. Dunford Hicks III to tell to her husband how she knew that he knew that she meant not pure maroon or pure taupe either one but just taupey and maroony sorts of colors which surely would not beat so against the ambiance like the red and the pink and the yellow seemed to beat. While she was on it, she guessed she might bring up Mr. Dunford Hicks's undersea castle as well that was chiefly aquamarine, she called it, and she indicated with just her crinkly nose alone how poorly in fact an undersea aquamarine castle sat with her like led her further still to Mr. Dunford Hicks's diver that blew the bubbles out his helmet and Mr. Dunford Hick's treasure chest all unhinged and flung open and heaped with jewels and doubloons and such. She pulled at a button and confessed how these were just precisely the sorts of items to up and confound her ambiance altogether as an ambiance was a delicate manner of thing which she drew on a button and communicated as well.

Naturally he was crushed. Well, in fact, he was just pinched chiefly at the kneejoints where his veins and vessels had gotten so completely closed up by his bride as to prevent rejuvenated blood with some oxygen to it from passing down towards his ankles and feet which had gone pretty thoroughly numb on him and, at the very moment he should have likely been pondering his offensive fishes and his new wife's hard-won ambiance, he was considering his circulation ever so deeply instead and managed even to let on a little to his bride how he was fixing to dump her off his lap before he stood fairly bolt upright and did pretty much fling her to the rug once the button she'd been holding to had given way.

She guessed that tore it, hurled first the shirtbutton into the firebox back of the gas logs and then announced from there atop the rug how what it was was torn chiefly and she made at Mr. Dunford Hicks the variety of afflicted face she'd hardly ever treated him to before he'd slipped the sparkly gold band upon her finger, a pouty afflicted face primarily with her lips turned pretty much inside out and her eyes focused on whatever convenient piece of air was presently uninhabited by him, Mr. Dunford Hicks III, the pure and unmitigated source of her torment. Of course, he was sorry he'd dumped her on the rug and undertook to explain how it was precisely blood traveled and through what like caused his bride to deduce, she told him, the implication that her manner of tonnage had plugged his bloodflow up which Mr. Dunford Hicks III felt obliged to grow straightaway gurgly about as growing gurgly seemed his only recourse to him and so he told to Mrs. Dunford Hicks, "Now doll," and endeavored to coo as he reached out his fingers before she could shrink so far as to go untouched. Subsequently, they began to make up after the fashion that had become customary for them and Mr. Dunford Hicks squatted low so as to squeeze and embrace Mrs. Dunford Hicks and assure her how she did not possess much tonnage to speak of and assure her as well how he had no intention whatsoever of confounding her ambiance like she cooed a little herself about and suggested to Mr. Dunford Hicks III an altogether new location for his fishtank, wondered if didn't it seem to him his fish could find a home in the basement off beyond the boiler between Mr. Dunford Hicks's dead daddy's workbench and Mr. Dunford Hicks's dead momma's halltree that had beaten a little against the ambiance itself.

"The basement?" Mr. Dunford Hicks inquired in a voice that had still a trifle of coo left to it.

"Other side of the boiler," Mrs. Dunford Hicks III told to him. "Shy of the halltree." And she took up and tugged between her fingerends an altogether fresh and previously untugged button like allowed Mr. Dunford Hicks the opportunity to grow moderate the sort of way the counselor had instructed him and his bride both to endeavor to grow moderate before they just dropped their chins and loosed a heated thing instead and presently he aired, like he'd been advised, a manner of fairly inarticulate exclamation that was meant itself to let on how he was weighing judiciously the notion she'd just lately up and shared with him that he was purely and unspeakably grateful she had which the counselor had told to them was a fine thing to seem to be. Of course she took him straightoff for an ally like was the trouble with seeming judicious and grateful and she schemed directly with him about where precisely they might put his fishtank and atop what that Mr. Dunford Hicks found himself pressed to coo another time ever so hardly at all about.

There wasn't truly much point in objecting, wasn't truly much point in getting injudicious and snide on account chiefly of Mrs. Dunford Hicks's arsenal of pouty expressions and blubbery laments that Mr. Dunford Hicks could not hardly hope to be contrary in the face of which he'd become already educated about due firstoff to his green plaid pants she'd banished and donated followed by his upholstered leatherette chair with the accompanying leatherette footstool that had been made to migrate out of the frontroom back deep into the house with stopoffs in the den and the downstairs guestroom before it departed from the property quite completely. The cracked and dreary oil portrait of Mr. Dunford Hicks's dead momma and daddy traveled a little itself once it yielded the spot above the mantelpiece to a variety of abstraction entitled Assemblage No. 37 that was part smeared paint, part shale, part newspaper, and what looked to Mr. Dunford Hicks a piece of a placemat. His daddy and his momma ended up in the hallway where you couldn't hope to step far enough away from them to see who it was. Naturally the walls got painted as Mrs. Dunford Hicks was not herself much partial to green and the wallpaper got torn off the stairwell and the foyer as Mrs. Dunford Hicks could work up no particular passion for hydrangea blossoms. What furniture did not come to be exiled and deported got recovered instead and so thoroughly rearranged that Mr. Dunford Hicks did not for a time feel much at home in the very house he'd not just lived in lately as a grown man but had gotten raised in as well, the house his own granddaddy had built and left to his daddy that expired on the bankfloor from his pneumatic coronary just months before Mr. Dunford Hicks's momma could no longer find reason to linger behind and so succumbed herself upstairs in the frontroom upon the bed with the turned posts and the leafy inlay, the bed that got eventually made to travel to the Junior League Bargain Box downtown where Mrs. Lawrence W. Ayers of Stacey bought it for her girl in Charlotte.

He'd just thought their union would have to it qualities otherwise. He'd seen married people previously and they'd not somehow appeared to him much like him and like her, most especially his own daddy and his own momma who had not precisely radiated contentment but had nonetheless struck together a harmonious sort of a chord and had seemed by marriage satisfied and improved the sort of way Mr. Dunford Hicks III had figured a man like him alone could not full well plumb and comprehend until he came himself to be wed like lately he'd come himself to be. And he'd waited to get harmonious and get contented, had prepared himself even to receive and entertain harmony and contentment both which he guessed he'd known a little of there at the first when all they did was coo and gurgle and hold to each other's fingers and press their nose ends snug up together like had presently eroded, like had presently given way to endeavors otherwise that did not truly have much coo and gurgle to them and hardly any call for fingers and nose ends to meet. It just grew different and Mr. Dunford Hicks discovered he'd passed entirely out from his moderately harmonious mildly contented chiefly oblivious state into another sort of predicament altogether that him and his bride had to hire and visit a counselor to discover was in fact the bliss of matrimony which Mr. Dunford Hicks had laid in the night on his back upon the bedsheet and never somehow figured it was.

Like most anybody might, then, Mr. Dunford Hicks grew distressed, not so much distressed in the particular with his own specific bride but distressed in a general and farreaching sort of a way with life as an item itself like he explained alone to the counselor he'd come to be and so learned directly back how what he'd dropped off into was a malaise which the counselor believed could be improved if not cured outright by an evening in Greensboro that began perhaps with a fine meal followed maybe by a show at the auditorium where they imported light and trifling sorts of musicals that evermore, the counselor insisted, undid his own malaises. So Mr. Dunford Hicks and his bride traveled to Greensboro and ate duck with a peppercorn sauce on it and sat through a show complete with wretched screechy songs and inordinate silvery hairpieces which, all taken together, suggested to Mr. Dunford Hicks III how him and his counselor did not suffer from the exact same strain of malaise precisely. As a consequence, his own personal state deepened and declined so he was up to near about his earlobes in a manner of funk already when his bride perched atop him, took up between her fingerends a shirtbutton, and commenced the banishment of his fishes, told to him anyhow, "Sweetheart," in that low falling voice that was evermore preamble to a migration.

Mr. Dunford Hicks III had come to be, then, fairly quasi-pathetic himself what with the deportation of his fishtank compounding like it did his thoroughgoing malaise, and while he took for a time some solace in visiting his fishes down between the boiler and the halltree, he was pressed shortly to grow more afflicted still once his platies began to roll and float followed by his blush angels and his yellow swords which he tossed by turns quite unceremoniously into the sump pump hole. Shortly enough there was not but a lone sword left to look at and him and Mr. Dunford Hicks pondered for a time each other while Mr. Dunford Hicks undertook to manufacture sufficient gumption to advise his wife how she'd best relent on the fishtank topic and allow him to return the thing upstairs to the very place where she'd seen fit lately to situate a tubular chrome serving cart that did not hardly appear to Mr. Dunford Hicks much of an improvement on a fishtank or an aquamarine castle either one that he was meaning to tell his lone sword about, as he'd taken to dropping his chin and being with his lone sword fairly injudicious altogether, when he found in the basement cause to toss his last remaining fish into the sump pump hole as well.

So anymore he didn't have even a yellow sword to talk at and could not hardly bear to be with his bride but gurgly and cooful since he was not much looking to speak of his malaise to her, was not much looking to speak even to his counselor of his malaise any longer but just suffered in silence with his affliction and moped roundabout the bank during the day and moped in a cooful and gurgly sort of a way roundabout the house at night and visited on occasion his fishtank with just anymore the castle and the diver and the chest and the doubloons and the milky water in it. And, due to what variety of malaise he'd contracted, he did not suppose he'd improve, did not but guess he'd decline like it seemed to him he'd already begun to do by the evening he stepped a little aimlessly into the dimestore and stood before the fishflake display whistling, without even knowing truly he was whistling it, the last selection he'd heard out the ceiling speakers at the bank which, like all the selections out the ceiling speakers, had set out as an electric organ and castinet sort of a ditty but had come to be shortly transformed by a marginally angelic variety of choir that oohed and hummed the melody which got by Mr. Wayne Fulp identified and announced two times right flush up together that sounded even nearly like talk a little, sounded enough anyway like talk to turn Mr. Dunford Hicks partway around where he looked inquisitively upon Mr. Wayne Fulp and so induced an additional discharge that was itself fairly much a proclamation.

" 'Tangerine,' " he told to him in outright articulate English that Mr. Dunford Hicks appeared to take in and digest prior to grinning at Mr. Wayne Fulp and telling him back, "Yeah," that way people grin and say Yeah sometimes when they have not full well comprehended the item they've lately taken in and endeavored to digest.

Now normally Mr. Wayne Fulp would not have pursued the topic further. Normally Mr. Wayne Fulp would not certainly have proclaimed in the first place, but there was somehow about Mr. Dunford Hicks a thing Mr. Wayne Fulp detected like was surely part malaise but was likely not pure malaise entirely, was probably instead Mr. Dunford Hicks's own personal ambiance that was itself just lately a blend of hope and despair with the latter enriched and the former diluted and the general proportions sufficiently ample and precise to induce Mr. Dunford Hicks to linger a little forlornly before the fishflake display where he could not somehow help but whistle like Mr. Wayne Fulp saw straightoff he could not somehow help but do as Mr. Wayne Fulp suffered as well from an ambiance all mixed and blended.

Mr. Wayne Fulp was exceedingly partial to "Tangerine" himself, assured anyway Mr. Dunford Hicks how he evermore got stirred by it that Mr. Dunford Hicks told him another time, "Yeah," about and so got shortly apprised of the virtues of the "Tangerine" melody as Mr. Wayne Fulp perceived them to be, or as he'd learned from an album jacket they likely were which was for Mr. Wayne Fulp an appreciable recitation, so appreciable in fact as to cause Mrs. Cecil Dutton to fetch Mrs. Donnie Bunch on back just shy of the fishflake display where they watched together Mr. Wayne Fulp look at a thing that was not a walljoint or floortiles either one and speak on a topic with some thoroughly palpable diction. After a time, Mr. Dunford Hicks even heard him plain and so told to Mr. Wayne Fulp other than just Yeah alone, told to him "Really?" every now and again too in the wake of the musical revelations Mr. Wayne Fulp disclosed that were chiefly at first moderately Tangeriney at least but came shortly to be fairly un-Tangeriney altogether, strayed to selections otherwise Mr. Wayne Fulp recited about, selections he let on he'd cultivated a passion for, and he spoke of the words and spoke of the beat and hummed every now and again a snatch of which particular refrains fairly transported him since he did not have himself much talent for whistling. And they sounded even, as he recited, like maybe his own passions in fact, sounded most especially to Mr. Dunford Hicks like genuine personal agitation and delight that Mr. Dunford Hicks had not lately himself known so awful much of and so found novel and found appealing both and admired how altogether worked up Mr. Wayne Fulp appeared to him to be.

He was fairly much of a mood, then, for an invitation when an invitation came to be extended to him, an invitation from Mr. Wayne Fulp to walk with him if he might over to Mr. Wayne Fulp's dead aunt's house where Mr. Wayne Fulp had collected, he told it, assorted "Tangerine"s that he would be ever so delighted to play for Mr. Dunford Hicks on what he called his sound system, and straightoff Mr. Dunford Hicks agreed that perhaps what he was presently in need of might in fact be a dose of "Tangerine"s like agitated and delighted Mr. Wayne Fulp even further still and he told to Mr. Dunford Hicks back, "Well, let's go then," and poked him even with his pointy elbow joint that Mrs. Donnie Bunch and Mrs. Cecil Dutton informed each other they could not hardly believe they'd just stood there together and seen.

So he excused himself from the dimestore, Mr. Wayne Fulp did, informed Mrs. Donnie Bunch how he'd come just lately to have an engagement which Mrs. Donnie Bunch made a wordless noise in the back of her neck about and watched with Mrs. Cecil Dutton Mr. Wayne Fulp and Mr. Dunford Hicks III fairly traipse together up through the ointments and the shampoos and past the reading glasses and down the length of the clutchpurse and keyfob aisle and on out the swinging doors into the dusk that Mrs. Donnie Bunch still could not manage but necknoises about while Mrs. Cecil Dutton admitted in actual words how it was far and away the damnedest thing she'd seen lately.

Mr. Wayne Fulp declaimed and recited down the boulevard and off around the Heavenly Rest, declaimed and recited on the topic of "Tangerine" primarily but strayed every now and again to matters otherwise and touched even a spell upon Mr. Frank Sinatra who Mr. Wayne Fulp did not have a "Tangerine" by though he had to suppose if anybody could croon a "Tangerine" Mr. Frank Sinatra could that Mr.

Dunford Hicks got encouraged to throw in with and so threw in with it, exhibited even a trifle of zeal himself as he spoke of what "Tangerine" it seemed to him likely Old Blue Eyes could muster, and he enthused a little at Mr. Wayne Fulp who enthused at him back prior to mounting a manner of recitation all purple and baroque, a purple and baroque recitation that had been penned in fact about Mel Torme but got applied by Mr. Wayne Fulp to the dusky night which was not truly the variety of dusky night to rate such twisted and purple talk since it had to it chiefly just haze and humidity and only the murkiest wash of orange off back of the treetops.

Due to how he'd hardly planned to receive a guest, Mr. Wayne Fulp could not offer Mr. Dunford Hicks but skim milk or tapwater or tomato juice from a can with a crust on it which Mr. Dunford Hicks made to ponder about prior to settling upon the water that he drank from a tumbler once he'd ever so surreptitiously scratched at the rim of it with his thumbnail. Mr. Wayne Fulp heaped a sleeve's worth of saltines onto a plate, opened a can of potted meat, and fetched from his dead aunt's silver case a blueblack butter knife for it, and before Mr. Dunford Hicks could discourage and prevent him Mr. Wayne Fulp loaded up a cracker that Mr. Dunford Hicks ate pretty much all of at one time and made, as best as he was able, an approving face about. They straightaway retired together to the music room which they'd passed through once already on their way to the kitchen when it had looked to Mr. Dunford Hicks your regular sort of parlor that he got shortly educated about by Mr. Wayne Fulp who lifted the lid on his dead aunt's console and threw the switch that set his tubes to glowing which he waited by the console for his tubes to do while with his foremost fingerend he stroked his dead aunt's six-penny needle until him and Mr. Dunford Hicks and Bill the speckled hound too got induced to listen to the ridges and declivities of Mr. Wayne Fulp's fingerprint in actual stereo.

Of course Mr. Wayne Fulp consulted his card box and consulted his accordian card file and toured shortly the parlor seeking "Tangerine"s while Mr. Dunford Hicks III got encouraged to settle upon the sofa and feast as best as he was able on the saltines and the potted meat and just the regular tepid tapwater that he made even to seem for a time to be up to before he took to touring the parlor a little himself admiring the geegaws in the corner geegaw cupboard and the whatnots on the mantelpiece and the altogether outsized oil portrait of Mr. Wayne Fulp's dead aunt's collie Ruth which Mr. Dunford Hicks and Mr. Wayne Fulp agreed was not likely the manner of thing they'd either of them call a collie if they had one. Mr. Dunford Hicks studied pictures otherwise as well, photographs chiefly of Mr. Wayne Fulp's dead aunt and photographs of the Puckett who'd expired on her and one lone picture of her and him together caught up in an embrace under a sweetgum tree, not a passionate but a warm and comely embrace that Mr. Dunford Hicks grew taken with the sight of and he watched how they clung each to the other in something undoubtedly other than rapture but plainly not worse than rapture at all, and he thought of his own bride who was handsome and who was sweet and who'd brought him no torment much past the banishments and the migrations and who sat still upon his lap so as to tug at his shirtbuttons like he did not suppose many women would. And confronted like he was up and all at once with your dead and affectionate people on the wall and your moderately pathetic sort in the flesh, Mr. Dunford Hicks could not help but feel a little blessed, feel a little smiled upon, and, much in the way of blessed and smiled upon people the world over, Mr. Dunford Hicks found himself inspired to issue a platitude, found himself moved to tell to Mr. Wayne Fulp, "Wayne," like Mr. Wayne Fulp had not been called so cordially Wayne in a very great while and so straightaway raised up and straightaway turned roundabout and heard from Mr. Dunford Hicks another time, "Wayne," which Mr. Dunford Hicks drew off a sizeable breath in back of and just generally inflated after the fashion that is evermore prologue to a platitude. "We don't often know how lucky we are, do we?"

And Mr. Wayne Fulp, who did not actually figure he was lucky at all and so could not know, if he was in fact lucky, how lucky precisely he was, agreed directly with Mr. Dunford Hicks by way of a variety of Nuhuh in conjunction with some lippressing and some headjerking and some thoroughly affirmative posture otherwise.

"No," Mr. Dunford Hicks said, "we're lucky and we don't often know it," which seemed to Mr. Wayne Fulp so altogether similar to the original platitude, lacking like it did much nuance to speak of, that he did not specifically press or jerk or stand or Nuhuh about it but just lingered beyond the settee with the album he'd selected and waited for Mr. Dunford Hicks to feel maybe a little less smiled upon.

"We don't," Mr. Dunford Hicks said. "No sir," and he eyed one time more the pictures of the aunt that was dead and the uncle that was dead along with the oil portrait of the collie Ruth that he had to figure was deceased herself.

"No," Mr. Dunford Hicks said. "No." And he engaged briefly in his own bout of lippressing that got shortly punctuated by Mr. Wayne Fulp who dropped his dead aunt's six-penny needle onto the altogether un-Tangeriney number he'd elected to set out with and the trumpets had not bleated but scantly when Bill the speckled hound rose up off the throwrug and bumped a little frantically against the doorrail like an outsized shorthaired droopyeared moth.

Over time Mr. Wayne Fulp had, of course, accumulated appreciable crooner talk that he aired a dose of at Mr. Dunford Hicks who was feeling sufficiently blessed and smiled upon to ever so pleasantly endure it and they waited together for the trumpets to lie down and the crooning to begin so Mr. Wayne Fulp could indicate various of the subtleties to Mr. Dunford Hicks who admitted how, without Mr. Wayne Fulp, the subtleties would probably have fairly completely escaped him. Presently they advanced to croooners otherwise and Mr. Wayne Fulp even inserted a solitary "Tangerine" so as to maintain the theme of the evening prior to bouncing his dead aunt's needle across the bulk of a Benny Goodman album to full well in the middle of "Swing, Swing, Swing" that Mr. Wayne Fulp took occasion to explicate most especially the beat of for Mr. Dunford Hicks as he stepped across the room to throw open the screendoor and readmit Bill his speckled hound that had arrived atop the porch planking to grumble and moan. And what with the dry and near about ceaseless liner recitations from Mr. Wayne Fulp and the murky congested fidelity from Mr. Wayne Fulp's dead aunt's console, Mr. Dunford Hicks's sense of relative personal woelessness was commencing to erode on him in a slight but palpable sort of a way due to how inordinately easier it is to come to feel blessed and smiled upon than to endure at it. He found himself shortly right flush up on the verge of maybe becoming malaised one time more and so took to repeating his platitude like a mantra and eyeing, when he was able to dodge Mr. Wayne Fulp long enough for it, the dead aunt and the dead uncle caught up together like forestalled his general erosion though he could not believe they would manage to forestall it for long. In fact, then, Mr. Dunford Hicks was beginning already to anticipate the outright revival of his funk when Mr. Wayne Fulp, who was hunting a second "Tangerine," inadvertently dropped his dead aunt's needle on another selection altogether, a variety of duet between Mr. Ben Webster on the one saxophone and Mr. Coleman Hawkins on the other, a duet Mr. Wayne Fulp was fairly well set to snatch his dead aunt's needle from when Mr. Dunford Hicks stopped him, merely held up his flat open hand and told to Mr. Wayne Fulp, "Wait."

Out in the yard before the house Nestor Tudor watched Mr. Wayne Fulp who watched Mr. Dunford Hicks show to him his wrinkly palm like altogether prevented Mr. Wayne Fulp from doing whatever it was he'd likely been up to that Nester Tudor could not well decipher from back of Mr. Wayne Fulp's dead aunt's bushy hollyhock where he'd arrived once he'd crept across the yard so as to have a place to lurk at and peer from. And Mr. Wayne Fulp just stood like the flat open hand had indicated he might ought to and studied how Mr. Dunford Hicks dropped shut his eyelids together and jabbed his previously upraised hand deep into his trouser pocket. As he felt obliged to, Mr. Wayne Fulp went on ahead and indicated which was Mr. Ben Webster and which was Mr. Coleman Hawkins instead that he let on was the lone thing he intended to indicate once it seemed to him he might get the wrinkly palm again though he did in fact shortly indicate further still, spoke that is in particular of Mr. Ben Webster's low breathy qualities, declaimed anyhow a piece of a thing he'd read before the hand came another time to be uplifted and the palm came another time to be exposed like punctuated Mr. Wayne Fulp after a fashion and caused him to allow Mr. Dunford Hicks to stand a time wholly unrecited at. And from out in the yard back of the hollyhock Nestor Tudor could not help but look and could not help most especially but listen, listen to the duet that was not in fact strictly a duet at all as Mr. Ben Webster gave way to Mr. Coleman Hawkins who gave way to Mr. Ben Webster back without the two of them playing somehow together at the same time but blowing only by themselves alone upon a melody that had some appreciable charm to it and sounded even out by the hollyhock, sounded probably most especially out by the hollyhock, as full well beautiful an item as Mr. Nestor Tudor had lately come across.

It was slow and rich and soulful all at the same time like Mr. Wayne Fulp, who'd read how it was slow and rich and soulful too, grew pressed to announce and did in fact announce it ahead of the wrinkly palm, told even the title as well, proclaimed, "It Never Entered My Mind" just out into the air in his favorite proclaiming posture and commenced to speak of the man who had written the music and the man who had written the words that he'd digested a tale about which he'd hoped he might speak of as well when he got thwarted once more by not just the palm but the voice too that told to him, "Wait," yet again. So Mr. Wayne Fulp just stood with his digested tale on his lips and watched Mr. Dunford Hicks who'd not so much as opened his eyes to tell Wait to him, watched Mr. Dunford Hicks weave and sway in an altogether slight but palpable sort of a fashion that Mr. Wayne Fulp's speckled hound Bill sat upon the throwrug and watched him at as well with more than just his usual vague and moderate canine regard, with thoroughgoing attention even as he seemed slightly struck and mystified by the swaying and by the weaving and by maybe even the reedy melody too that Mr. Ben Webster carried alone when Mr. Coleman Hawkins did not carry it in place of him.

Out in the yard back of his bush Nestor Tudor, who failed to consider himself the sort to lurk and peer in the first place, persevered at lurking and peering both and grew shortly affected which he had not hardly anticipated, when he'd crept up back of his bush, he'd come to be, affected chiefly by the hound and the music and the banker and his pathetic host even a little as well that formed together a manner of tableau, had struck as best as Nestor Tudor could tell a significant sort of a pose with a suitable piece of music to waft and circulate all roundabout them. The hound and the pathetic host both watched between them the banker who'd begun to look a little transported, did not anyhow appear to Nestor Tudor much malaised but just swayed and just wove with his eyes shut and his face uplifted and his whole self fairly carried off by the one saxophone that gave way shortly to the other. And like is the way with tableaus most times, just the speckled hound or just Mr. Wayne Fulp or just Mr. Dunford Hicks or just Mr. Ben Webster and Mr. Coleman Hawkins together on the night air alone could not have begun to render the moment near so significant and sorrowful as the moment seemed somehow to Nestor Tudor to have been rendered by the bunch of them together just standing and sitting and swaying and perusing and wafting too, not acutely sorrowful, not woeful outright, but just ever so vaguely sad and forlorn like comes of implying with a slow rich soulful melody how sweet life might be.

So he grew fairly enchanted, Nestor Tudor did, grew fascinated and purely caught up with the scene before him all tainted like it was with melancholy, fraught like it was with regret, and he lurked and he peered more intently surely than he could afford just presently to lurk and peer both from back of the bush alongside the walk that the headlights found him at and played even a time upon him before Nestor Tudor dodged and shifted roundabout and spied on the far sidestreet the white Impala that just sat and just idled and just shone its lights upon him for longer truly than struck Nestor Tudor as seemly, and he was growing there in the bushes moderately ill and aggravated at being so thoroughly imposed upon when the Impala eased at last out off the one road and onto the other and slipped up alongside the curbing back of the Toronado and stopped like Nestor Tudor felt obliged to lurk and peer on account of as well and he became shortly fascinated all over again though not truly much enchanted to speak of at the sight of Tiny Aaron stepping out onto the asphalt and drawing from the carseat his sportcoat behind him that he stood there under the mercury light and plucked a scrap of lint from.

And it wasn't so much the coat truly, which was Tiny Aaron's crinkly madras coat with the stripes and the blocks both, or the shirt he'd pressed pretty much the entire front of or the tie with the sheen to it and the elegant tiny dots or the shoes even with the purely ornamental buckles but was instead the pants almost entirely that struck Nestor Tudor straightaway, the skyblue pants with the back pocketflaps that had been in fact one time Nestor Tudor's own personal trousers received by him from his dead wife's sister, who could not well calculate girth, and passed by him to Tiny Aaron back when they'd been buddies which was just before the Impala door swung open and the first shoebottom hit the asphalt. And though he did not mean to speak, did not hardly intend to exclaim, Nestor Tudor spoke and exclaimed both, told into the tangly recesses of the hollyhock, "Sansabelt," like was chiefly just breath all touched and done in with consternation.

Tiny Aaron had cultivated his own personal jacketflap pose that he stood before the sidewindow and admired himself at fronton chiefly but sideways a little as well prior to circling around the car and advancing along Miss Bernice Fay Frazier's walk and up her steps to the door with the glass lights in it that Nestor Tudor watched him peek through one of in advance of how he smoothed and flattened his shirtfront, preened his tieknot, and assumed another time his jacketflap pose that he held and sustained in an altogether dapper sort of a way until he presently grew impressed with how he'd neglected somehow to knock. Off across the road back of his bush with his tableau behind him and vagrant soulful strains wafting roundabout him on the air, Nestor Tudor observed with some rising trepidation how a face at last arrived at the lowermost doorlight and admired, it seemed to him, Tiny Aaron's getup that Tiny Aaron showed off a little in profile and showed off a little straighton under the yellow buglight that did not somehow appear to render Tiny Aaron near so sallow as Nestor Tudor had hoped from across the road he'd get rendered, and he caught up his breath to hear what might transpire once the door got drawn open and the screen got unhooked but he'd not hardly needed to catch up his breath for it since Tiny Aaron pretty much wailed, "Hey there!" that Miss Bernice Fay Frazier appeared to tell to him a moderately civil and vaguely elevated variety of item in back of.

Tiny Aaron lowed and hollered about how he'd been meaning to slip on by but hadn't until this very evening found occasion for it, slip on by to welcome to town her with the lips and the locks and the roaming fingerends, her he called at Miss Bernice Fay Frazier that lovely young woman who Miss Bernice Fay Frazier had launched herself into some talk about when Bubbles her cat determined how she might just be of a mood to take the night air and so slinked that way cats can over a shoetop and out between the dooredge and the jamb and full well onto the front porch alongside Mr. Tiny Aaron who, in the spirit of his endeavor, felt obliged to tell to Miss Bernice Fay Frazier's cat, "Hey there!" with altogether more enthusiasm than cats can generally endure. Naturally Bubbles leapt direct on into the shrubbery, leapt down anyway off the porchedge among Miss Bernice Fay Frazier's azalea bushes that Miss Bernice Fay Frazier lowed and hollered a little about herself, lowed and hollered enough anyway to drive her cat through the monkey grass border and out into the red fescue where Bubbles squatted and cowered and appeared to Miss Bernice Fay Frazier right there on the verge of darting into the street and getting extinguished under a tiretread which she turned around and expressed after a fashion into the house, exclaimed a little anyway in undeniable anguishment like brought to the door her with the lips and the locks and the fingerends who Tiny Aaron turned a little sideways and struck his jacketflap pose for.

"Well," he intoned, "hey there!" which Nestor Tudor off across the road grew all agitated back of his bush about as he could not hardly stand to watch Tiny Aaron in his madras jacket and Sansabelt trousers intoning at her who he'd meant himself to intone just this very evening at, and then it was him with the hairpart as well, him up back of her that Tiny Aaron intoned at a little too but did not intone at much truly and Dick Atwater, that had cultivated a jacketflap pose of his own, struck it and so engaged through the screen with Mr. Tiny Aaron in a duel of the jacketflap poses.

Nestor Tudor had, of course, begun to grow profane back of his hollyhock, had set to wringing and wrenching the stemend of his nosegay and littering the ground with pieces of cornflower and bits of gladiola like did not come to be slowed and mitigated by the sight across the street of Mr. Dick Atwater and Mr. Tiny Aaron advancing together down the front steps into the yard so as to undertake the salvation of Miss Bernice Fay Frazier's cat, so as to rescue Bubbles from the threats and dangers of this world and win by it glory that they were not much anxious to share and dilute and so accelerated both together towards the cat that Mr. Tiny Aaron hoped to snatch from the grass before Mr. Dick Atwater might snatch it, but of course Bubbles could not just lie in the fescue and tolerate a two-jacket Sansabelt and hairpart charge across the lawn and consequently retreated out past the curbing under the Impala like Dick Atwater let on over his shoulder back towards the house was the fault somehow of the Impala itself that did not have much business being where it had ended up.

Other side of the road back of the hollyhock Nestor Tudor grew sufficiently inspired at the sight of Mr. Tiny Aaron and Mr. Dick Atwater circling the Impala and reaching occasionally up beneath it to figure he might join somehow the effort, circle and grope after Bubbles himself and so win perhaps a little glory on his own, accumulate a bit of gratitude anyway like was surely an improvement over what he might accumulate in the shrubbery which would be chiggers almost exclusively. Consequently, then, he undertook straightoff to calculate how he might spring out from the bushes and chase the cat without appearing to have just sprung out from the bushes to chase it like was a matter of some puzzlement to him most especially since he'd arrived in the first place set to wonder how delightful it might possibly be for him and for her to pass an evening at the Ingot Lounge which he'd honed and rehearsed and so thoroughly mastered that he could not directly transform it to a cat chasing sort of a thing and so honed and rehearsed back of the hollyhock an entirely new item altogether.

Meanwhile, across the road roundabout the Impala, Mr. Dick Atwater was suffering hairpart trouble due somewhat to the oncoming obsolescence of his dose of Vitalis, which had lost in the course of the evening its metallic qualities, in combination with the circling and the groping that served in consort to dislodge and downsweep Mr. Dick Atwater's previously upswept strands that he was evermore having to pause to tend to since there did not seem to him much use in winning glory if he had to become unswanky to do it. Mr. Tiny Aaron, then, was steadily gaining appreciable advantage in the catchasing derby and had scampered himself a little under the Impala in a moderately stylish and palpably swanky sort of a way and was reaching even for the actual cat with some prospect of latching onto it which Nestor Tudor from across the road back of his hollyhock gauged and comprehended and so determined how he'd best straightoff yield and give over his honing and rehearsing for some outright catchasing instead like he figured he'd have discovered an explanation for by the time he'd up and apprehended the cat and had commenced to get maybe admired on account of it.

So he pretty much charged out from the shrubbery and onto the walk and had hauled himself and his dilapidated nosegay near about down to the curbing when Tiny Aaron whooped and exclaimed from fairly directly under his universal joint and crawled shortly out from beneath the Impala so as to display Miss Bernice Fay Frazier's wayward cat aloft which was cause straightoff for jubilation, diluted and altogether segregated jubilation that is, confined like it was to Miss Bernice Fay Frazier and to her alongside her and to Tiny Aaron too who displayed the cat which Dick Atwater and Nestor Tudor and most especially Bubbles herself could not between them come to be much jubilant about. So the three of them that were of a mood for it whooped and hooted and praised the Maker while the cat just gaped and dangled and Mr. Nestor Tudor and Mr. Dick Atwater merely stood where they'd ended up seeming together measurably done in and downtrodden until Dick Atwater, in an effort to jerk and throw and just generally resituate a hairlock, spied Nestor Tudor across the road on the walk under the mercury light and loosed a noise about him sufficient to distract the entire jubilant faction and stir even the cat a little as well.

For his part, of course, Nestor Tudor just stood with his nosegay drooping alongside him as he'd not quite fully formulated the suitable piece of catchasing talk he'd undertaken to work up and had not even so much as started in on a snatch of congratulatory catcatching talk like left him just to stand and hold his nosegay which he got briefly watched at by Dick Atwater alone who persevered at pointing and exclaiming together and so came to be shortly joined by Miss Bernice Fay Frazier and her with the lips and the fingerends and Tiny Aaron too along with Bubbles the dangling cat who all watched Mr. Nestor Tudor plain stand with his nosegay atop the walk and enticed with their queries and exclamations Mr. Wayne Fulp and Mr. Dunford Hicks and Mr. Wayne Fulp's speckled hound Bill away from the stereo console and out onto the porch from where they studied Mr. Nestor Tudor too, Mr. Nestor Tudor who came to be transformed himself into a variety of tableau, came to be fairly thoroughly transfigured there on the walk under the mercury light where he stood in his purple horsehead shirt with his nosegay in his fingers and got pondered from the front and got pondered from the back and cut, he was certain, an altogether pitiful figure like Mr. Dunford Hicks set in to counting his own personal blessings about while, across the road beyond the Impala, Miss Bernice Fay Frazier relieved Mr. Tiny Aaron of her cat Bubbles that she pressed to her dressfront and embraced mightily while Dick Atwater in particular and Mr. Tiny Aaron a little and her somewhat too with the comely features and the enticements pondered Nestor Tudor with what seemed to him, from across the road and atop the walk, your regular variety of anticipation all mixed and mingled with more than a little surprise and less than a little delight most especially from him with the hairpart and him with the skyblue trousers who together watched Nestor Tudor raise up and wag his shabby nosegay and tell not hardly to them at all, "Hey."

Four

HE'D not ever previously murdered anybody even once but he guessed he would up and confound the regular course of things with a double homicide that he'd kick off with the grisly punctuation of Mr. Tiny Aaron whose limbs and pieces he'd detach and scatter but for maybe one sizeable appendage scrap he'd carry south out the highway so as to have handy an item to render Nestor Tudor a pulpy liquid with. Wasn't it him, he inquired on the air, who'd taken to her straightoff from the outset, who'd squired her roundabout, who'd spoken with her even of cremation and such intimate manner of things and had fairly much consummated their union, had gripped her anyhow out at the golfrange in such a fashion as to lay her consummating part in undeniable proximity to his own one? Wasn't that his very self? he wanted to know from the treelimbs and the undersides of the leaves out before his house where he stood in the shank of the morning and wondered. Surely it hadn't been him with the gaudy madras jacket. Surely it hadn't been him with the purple shirt and the nosegay. And Mr. Dick Atwater said in his throat chiefly, "Interlopers," with what seemed to him just precisely the variety of disdain he'd heard lately Walter Pidgeon say Interlopers on the TV with.

His intentions were to bless Tiny Aaron with some instruction and advice, to provide him with a manner of education about which consummating parts had already near about collided and which consummating parts certainly never would like he figured Tiny Aaron, who was not the sort to take instruction with much grace and gratitude, would grow to be contrary about and so bring on his annihilation and general dismemberment at the hands of Dick Atwater who was hardly a man to be trifled with as best as Dick Atwater himself could tell. Of course he hoped he might persuade and illuminate Nestor Tudor with talk of Tiny Aaron's recent misfortune once he'd gotten done befalling it on him though he anticipated he'd probably have to go on and annihilate Nestor Tudor as well like would undoubtedly eat up the bulk of his day. But Mr. Dick Atwater was intending to make a thorough job of it and supposed he could invest a piece of the morning and the most of the afternoon which he was stepping along the sidewalk undertaking to say pretty much like he figured Walter Pidgeon might say it when he came to be interrupted by a gentleman in a blueblack Lincoln sedan, a gentleman who'd drifted in his vehicle off to the curbing so as to hang out the sidewindow and make at Dick Atwater an inquiry, wonder where it was exactly Mrs. Dwight Mobley lived.

He was natty. Dick Atwater could tell it from just what piece of him hung out the window. He had a hairpart full well up atop his head and locks that dangled and locks that swept and swirled, thick silvery gray locks the identical shade exactly of his stubby moustache which did not rise to his noseholes but laid primarily upon his lip all thin and elegant and with no more nap to it than a pipecleaner like was just the sort of moustache Dick Atwater guessed he possessed himself the follicles for. His white shirt had worked into the pattern of it a kind of a stripe that was white itself and served somehow to set off his satiny maroon tie with the tiny dots which blended ever so harmoniously with his navy blazer that had upon the breastpocket of it a manner of crest that was bars and swords and horseheads primarily. There wasn't much of him otherwise Mr. Dick Atwater could see until he brought out his near arm to point and indicate where Mr. Dick Atwater had just himself left off pointing and indicating and to inquire, "Right is it and then back left?" which provided Mr. Dick Atwater the occasion to admire the gold ring and admire the gold watch with the gold mesh band and admire most especially the gold cufflink studded like it was with gems that caught the light.

And Mr. Dick Atwater told to that gentleman's sleeve end chiefly, "Right," and told most especially to the sparkly gems, "Then back left," which he got straightoff thanked most kindly about but did not hear himself get thanked most kindly due to the general panache he'd found to admire and persevered at admiring even once the blueblack Lincoln sedan had left from the curb and gained the road again. And he watched it go from him, pondered the back windowglass and the sleek shiny trunklid and the tirewell at the latch of it and the bright chrome bumper and even the license tag a little but not the license tag much truly, not the license tag enough anyhow to read the Wild and to read the Wonderful and to make out in yellow under the numbers the entire state of West Virginia like would have probably conjured a thing for him, would have surely called up her straightoff, her he'd taken to and squired and gripped and was set to maim and mutilate for the sake of, and then maybe him too, him of the thick hair and the moustache and the fine clothes and gold sparkly items who'd come some reason from the very same identical wild and wonderful state.

But he merely turned instead and struck back out to where he'd been heading already while that blueblack Lincoln sedan swung right on the first sidestreet and negotiated a full block of it prior to swinging left and advancing two full blocks and a piece of another one to the green frame house with the cement birdbath out front under a pinoak like he'd been advised to look for, a cement birdbath adorned full around with seahorses and capped by a water nymph that had been manufactured to spit and spew, had been made with its jowly face upturned and its lips puckered but had not ever come to be connected by Mrs. Dwight Mobley to the hose as she was under the impression an arching stream of water might render the thing tasteless somehow.

Mrs. Dwight Mobley herself watched the blueblack Lincoln settle up against her very own stretch of curbing, stood on the porch with her arms crossed before her and observed how the thing glided and stopped while the widow Mrs. Askew, who'd drawn her in the first place out from the house, repeated another time the item she'd dropped by to impart which Mrs. Dwight Mobley confessed yet again did not mean a thing in this world to her and she pitched her head and looked a little slantwise at the widow Mrs. Askew who explained one time further how if a man's reach outstripped his grasp then there wasn't much point in a heaven in the first place, now was there? that Mrs. Dwight Mobley could not manage but a paltry inarticulate noise in back of and so heard straightaway from the widow Mrs. Askew who set in to explaining the basic and fundamental difference between reaching and grasping like she guessed was the key to the pith of the thing in the first place. Shortly, however, Mrs. Dwight Mobley found herself induced to speak and wondered if wouldn't the widow Mrs. Askew please kindly shut up for a time as it seemed to her they had a guest. Of course, Mrs. Askew even pithy and elevated could not well endure getting hushed by the likes of Mrs. Dwight Mobley and so undertook to cite a suitable item in response but came to be straightaway prevented from it by him with the hair and the moustache and the blazer who climbed out from his sedan, shut his sedan door, and told what Mrs. Askew took for especially at her, "Ma'm," with an altogether distinguished sort of a headjerk back of it.

He was looking in particular for Mrs. Dwight Mobley that Mrs.

Dwight Mobley and Mrs. Askew both told to him Mrs. Dwight Mobley was though not with identical enthusiasm truly, and he made at Mrs. Dwight Mobley an undeniable bow with a manner of regal flourish which Mrs. Dwight Mobley grew a trifle flushed and giggly about even though flushed and giggly was the last things in this world she'd intended to grow. Notwithstanding how she'd entertained a headjerk just previously, the widow Mrs. Askew was fairly ravenous for a bow herself and consequently undertook to incite one with a curtsy that was more of an aborted squat than anything otherwise and so got her pondered and asked after in a solicitous sort of a way by him with the hair and the moustache and the gold sparkly baubles like turned out better than a bow in fact. He let on how he was pretty thoroughly enchanted to meet at last most especially Mrs. Dwight Mobley as he'd heard such extravagantly fine talk of her from her momma's sister in Berkeley Springs West Virginia who'd evermore seemed to him a woman of considerable charm and appeal, and he shared with Mrs. Dwight Mobley and the widow Mrs. Askew a variety of episode meant to illustrate the charm and the appeal together like it would have probably illustrated both of but for how Mrs. Dwight Mobley and the widow Mrs. Askew were not between them in much of a mood for an episode as they had the hair and the moustache and the fine square chin and the blazer and the crisp shirt and the satiny tie with the slender tieknot to admire, not to speak even of the gold baubles beyond the sleeve end that caught the light after such a fashion as to manufacture pure dazzlement.

Likely she would have ushered him into the frontroom if he'd not somehow managed to usher her instead, her and the widow Mrs. Askew both together that got herded and thoroughly transported by the arm he swept and the voice he told to them, "Ladies," with like they did not hardly ever between them get told Ladies anymore, so they fairly flew off the porch and onto the settee and admired how he lighted with ever so much grace and bearing upon Mrs. Dwight Mobley's upholstered boudoir chair where he laid his one kneejoint atop his other and tugged by turns at his shirtcuffs with such undeniable flair that Mrs. Dwight Mobley and the widow Mrs. Askew grew straightaway obliged to look at each other and suck air.

He found Mrs. Dwight Mobley's frontroom most handsome and selected for special praise Mrs. Dwight Mobley's geegaw cupboard in particular with the curved glass door that he let on was rare and extraordinary for a geegaw cupboard and so pretty completely set Mrs. Dwight Mobley's own personal one apart. The widow Mrs. Askew owned herself a china cabinet with a manner of curved door to it, and she indicted with her fingers in the empty air the variety of curve precisely that him with the hair and the moustache and the accoutrements and the lordly manners told to her, "Ah," about after such a fashion as to fairly set her juices boiling like was highly unusual for the widow Mrs. Askew who'd not ever been a woman of your saucy and tropical passions. Mrs. Dwight Mobley who guessed she could stand an Ah herself described an item she'd seen one time with some curves and some corners both which drew from him on the boudoir chair a variety of refined exclamation that Mrs. Dwight Mobley found a little stirring herself and so her and the widow Mrs. Askew sat together for a time upon the settee marshaling their juices in silence.

Most usually he was parched after a drive. He mentioned as just a general sort of an item how after a drive he was most usually parched that presently the widow Mrs. Askew deduced a thing from and so informed Mrs. Dwight Mobley how she might, if she pleased, serve a beverage that Mrs. Askew let on she would herself be grateful about and encouraged him upon the boudoir chair to throw in with her like rendered agitated Mrs. Dwight Mobley who'd been commencing to deduce herself and so did not hardly need the widow Mrs. Askew not just to deduce for her but to guide and instruct her in back of it like she communicated pretty much all of with a "Now, Doreen" that she turned her head and loosed so as to have occasion to exhibit most especially her incisors.

It seemed to Mrs. Dwight Mobley a spot of tea would suit which the widow Mrs. Askew was pretty well prepared to dispute, as she'd not had her mouth set for a spot of tea truly, when him with the satiny tie and the colorful coatpocket crest loosed his view of the sheer aptness of tea like swayed and altered Mrs. Askew who straightoff threw in with him. Naturally, Mrs. Dwight Mobley was not much anxious to leave him and leave her there together in her frontroom and undertook to draw the widow Mrs. Askew off the settee and in towards the kitchen with her pointy teeth primarily that she displayed and her head that she jerked like Mrs. Askew let on to be a puzzlement to her and so just stayed where she'd been and exhibited her own personal pointy teeth back like was sweet and like was venemous both at the same time together.

He said she could call him Raymond, instructed the widow Mrs. Askew to call him if she would Raymond please and so she did call him Raymond most every time thereafter she dropped her chin to say a thing like was straightoff, "Raymond, why don't you call me Doreen?" that Raymond insisted would be for him a pure delight which prompted from Mrs. Askew, "Oh," and hard up back of it, "Raymond," another time.

She sought to disclose with some tact and discretion how her husband Mr. Askew had been an appreciable spell dead and buried in the ground which she could not discover a tactful or discreet way to speak of and so fairly much blurted where he was and described how he'd come to be there which touched off a bout of sympathizing and commiserating between Raymond and Doreen who concluded together how life was sometimes rife with sorrow and woe. In the kitchen Mrs. Dwight Mobley could not manage somehow to unscrew the cap off her teaball even once she'd beaten it for a time on the counteredge, so she carried it into the frontroom and wondered would he with the hair and the moustache loosen it for her, he that told to her, "Raymond," he that told to her, "please," and straightaway freed up her teaball cap before she could tell to him, "Dot," back like shortly she told it to him and so endured from Doreen on the settee a dose of altogether exposed overbite.

He drank with his pinky extended like they'd both known together he would and held his saucer upon his palm in a princely sort of a way that Dot and Doreen admired from the settee and imitated as best they were able which would be the pinky chiefly and the saucerholding a little that they both managed well enough until the widow Mrs. Askew, who was polishing off her dregs, pinkied herself in the eye and started so on account of it as to lose her saucer down between the sofa cushions like Mrs. Dwight Mobley identified as a faux pas though not a grave and ponderous faux pas truly but just Mrs. Askew's usual sort of faux pas which Doreen herself was part irate and part consternated to hear of and so implied with her face muscles alone how Mrs. Dwight Mobley seemed just presently to her a vile sort of a creature. Matters would likely have escalated into some outright snitty talk between Doreen and Dot both who eyed each other across the breadth of the settee if not for him with the hair and the moustache and the baubles and the altogether impeccable demeanor who swallowed his Oreo, what Mrs. Dwight Mobley had called at him a biscuit, and was curious of a sudden to find out if they didn't all three of them have a common acquaintance, a Miss Mary Alice Celestine Lefler who'd traveled a few weeks previously to what very place he'd only himself just lately arrived at.

"Why yes, Raymond," Mrs. Dwight Mobley told to him.

"Raymond, yes," Mrs. Askew informed him as well, and they all three of them basked together in the sheer and unmitigated coincidence of it all like confirmed most especially for Mrs. Askew the mysteries of this life that she undertook to cite a pithy thing about but could not straightoff call up a mysteries-of-this-life variety of pithy thing.

He wanted to know where precisely she was but did not ask

straightout where she was precisely and so extracted by bits and scraps her location in Miss Bernice Fay Frazier's bedroom upstairs that was not in fact, Mrs. Askew let on, much fit to live in like Mrs. Dwight Mobley felt obliged to concede was true. And of course as long as they'd touched on the topic anyhow, the widow Mrs. Askew and Mrs. Dwight Mobley both together found themselves compelled to address with thoroughgoing frankness and palpable elevation Miss Bernice Fay Frazier's own personal assorted flaws and shortcomings which, Mrs. Askew confessed to him with the blazer and the baubles, were myriad.

"Take your breath," Mrs. Dwight Mobley confirmed to him, "Raymond."

And Mrs. Askew, who was not about to find herself up and out-Raymonded, contrived to say Yes and contrived to say Raymond on her own like Mrs. Dwight Mobley turned to her and announced she'd already gleaned she would.

Consequently, then, Raymond from West Virginia endured atop the boudoir chair a spate of talk about Miss Bernice Fay Frazier straightoff who was afflicted with some altogether unlovely qualities that Dot and Doreen were purely pained to reveal but revealed nonetheless pretty exhaustively and touched a time upon Miss Bernice Fay Frazier's cat Bubbles, that seemed to them a manner of quasi-domesticated beast, like gave on presently to Miss Bernice Fay Frazier's sister Estelle Singletary who was far too unsavory, they told him, for words. And he appeared even to take it in, looked even to hear and ponder and speculate along with Dot and along with Doreen how it was people managed sometimes to turn out the way they turned out, but he grew presently distracted once he'd settled his saucer and cup on the endtable and seemed for some reason anxious to skid and slide his chair across the carpet, not skid and slide his chair far truly but just skid it and slide it enough to put it somewhere it wasn't already like proved to be a troublesome endeavor. Naturally Mrs. Dwight Mobley and the widow Mrs. Askew inquired of him both together, "Raymond?" with fairly identical distress and concern that he made to deflect and undertook to ignore, undertook anyhow to seem for a time preoccupied, to appear to be fairly mired up in thought after such a fashion as to get him altogether acutely solicited by Dot and by Doreen who were keen to mine his distraction and arrive shortly at the source of it. So they troubled him for a revelation, prodded and petitioned him until at last Raymond told to Dot, "Dot," and told to Doreen, "Doreen," and loosed a grave and significant sort of an exhalation as prologue to confessing his worries and his woes.

For reasons he could not well name, Raymond from West Virginia with the hair and the moustache and the satiny speckled tie had of a sudden just up and cultivated a concern about how it was a fragile and delicate woman like Mrs. Dwight Mobley might shift and slide her furniture roundabout upon her pile carpet for purposes of vacuuming and such as it seemed to him her own particular carpet that was thick, he told her, and altogether luxurious was just the type to clutch and hold to a chairleg and grip a clawfoot and so inhibit thorough vacuuming and fairly completely thwart any impetuous furniture shifting Mrs. Dwight Mobley might find herself inspired to undertake. It was, Raymond from West Virginia let on, a sober and grave variety of revelation and he sat upon his boudoir chair appearing to mull and ponder just how precisely they might between them lubricate the feet of it like Dot and Doreen both together could not possibly say though they agreed and insisted that balky chairlegs and tablelegs were evermore a plague to them, evermore a plague most especially to the widow Mrs. Askew who told how her nappy beige wall-to-wall far surpassed Mrs. Dwight Mobley's in general luxuriousness which Dot and Doreen disputed briefly about without much detectable pith or elevation either.

Somehow, once he'd mulled and once he'd pondered, Raymond from West Virginia up and recollected how he was himself personally acquainted with a product that was undoubtedly just the very item to altogether unmire furniture feet. Why he believed he'd maybe even carried with him a set in the trunk of his sedan like Dot and Doreen both grew fairly eeky at the news of and endeavored straightaway to dispatch him with the hair and the moustache and the general panacea in his Lincoln out the door and along the walk to his trunklid which he appeared to them a little sluggish about and so got prodded further still by Dot and by Doreen together that had between them, they let on, a dire sort of a need and they blended their general eekiness with what pathetic pleading noises they could muster and so lifted shortly Raymond up off his boudoir chair and admired how he tugged at his shirtcuffs and drew at his coatsleeves and recoifed as best as he was able his thick silvery hair prior to begging briefly his leave from the ladies who fairly tittered as they gave it.

And of course he hadn't gotten even out the door good when the widow Mrs. Askew and Mrs. Dwight Mobley began to speak of him, wondered each at the other if wasn't he just the height of grace and charm, wasn't he purely dapper, wasn't he sweet and kind which they both together agreed after a fashion he was though with their enthusiasm measured and doled as they'd allowed themselves already more eeky outbursts than they guessed was seemly. For her part, Mrs. Dwight

Mobley informed the widow Mrs. Askew how she'd been herself searching just lately for the variety of item that might unmire and lubricate her furniture feet which the widow Mrs. Askew found herself dubious at the news of and so exhibited at Mrs. Dwight Mobley her toothy incredulous face that Mrs. Dwight Mobley straightoff interpolated the gist of and consequently assured the widow Mrs. Askew, "I was," and made in return a face of her own which had a trifle of gist itself that probably Mrs. Askew would have gone on and interpolated back had she not shut her eyes and lifted her chin so as to pronounce a thing about grain that got spread upon the water which Mrs. Dwight Mobley was not remotely of a mood to grope round for the pith in and so inquired straightoff of the widow Mrs. Askew if wouldn't she please one time just shut up.

They rose up off the settee and collected together before the doorlights where they watched Raymond lift out from his trunk a lacquered wooden box that he set upon the walk prior to adjusting his various sleeve ends and accoutrements in the wake of the effort. It was near about the size of a footlocker, deep as one anyhow but shorter and with a manner of leather lead out from one end of it, a leather lead Raymond from West Virginia squatted to take up and Mrs. Dwight Mobley and the widow Mrs. Askew had not begun even to recover from the grace and refinement of his squat when he struck out along the walk drawing behind him his lacquered box that appeared to plain float upon the concrete. Mrs. Dwight Mobley had never herself seen such a thing while the widow Mrs. Askew, in an effort to be contrary, proclaimed how she'd in fact seen such a thing once previously like prompted Mrs. Dwight Mobley to make chiefly at the doorlight an altogether indecipherable observation that she could not find the means somehow to repeat once the widow Mrs. Askew had inquired of her would she. Raymond hefted his box at the base of the steps and carried it up onto the porch decking where he treated the ladies to one squat further followed by a brief bout of preening and sleevetugging as a preamble to what knocking ensued, what graceful doorlight tapping with his foremost knuckle alone upon the pane opposite Mrs. Dwight Mobley's own particular nose end like meant she was handy to turn the knob and swing open the door and so admit him with the silver hair as she pressed her own self and the widow Mrs. Askew with her back up alongside the doorstop. Consequently, once Raymond had effected his entrance into the front room, once Raymond had stepped that is into the house himself and drawn behind him his lacquered box that clattered across the threshold, he could not discover who precisely he'd effected his entrance for until he turned around and spied Dot and Doreen both together peeking at him through the doorlights still like prompted Raymond to take hold of the knob himself and liberate them which they were grateful in a fairly eeky sort of way about and could not in their present state figure between them how they might have otherwise come to be liberated.

Words alone could not hardly begin to capture the widow Mrs. Askew's own personal impression of Raymond's lacquered box. She found it to be stunning of course but stunning just by itself did not seem to her apt and fitting and as she cast about for some suitable word otherwise Mrs. Dwight Mobley aired her own impression that was articulate English and necknoises in combination with what the widow Mrs. Askew identified for her as blathering plain and outright which Mrs. Dwight Mobley could not somehow shape to be an altogether edifying scrap of news. For his part, Raymond from West Virginia accepted the praise of his box with his native grace and elegance and tugged ever so lightly upon the leather lead so as to send the thing gliding first across the breadth of the carpet and then along the length of it and finally just around in a circle about himself which was just precisely the sort of stunt to prompt from the ladies additional frothy discharges that were part blather and part potent ineffable sentiments otherwise. Understandably, they were anxious to discover how it glided, how it floated—the widow Mrs. Askew told it—upon the pile and nap like a ship on a sea of turbulation and woe which Raymond insisted he'd be ever so pleased to reveal to them and subsequently squatted after his own particular fashion yet again and purely upended his lacquered box that clanked and rattled and dumped its burdensome contents from the boxbottom to the lid by way of exhibiting four shimmery gold casters upon its underside.

"Genuine," Raymond announced, "brass plating," and he dragged his foremost finger across his skimpy moustache in what seemed most especially to the widow Mrs. Askew an inordinately suave sort of a way and she intoned herself back of him, "Genuine brass plating," and swung around her head to look briefly upon Mrs. Dwight Mobley who intoned a little as well.

Raymond laid ever so lightly his fingerend to one particular caster and requested of the ladies their forbearance, he called it, that they gladly together bequeathed to him as they'd never before had their forbearance requested and so had accumulated some considerable of it. And he spun the thing, set it with his finger to twirling round and then encouraged the ladies to study with him how in fact it twirled precisely which was the part in particular he needed the forbearance for as the caster he'd laid his finger to and spun did not appear inclined at all to leave off spinning but just rolled roundabout in its socket at a regular sort of a clip that did not appear to diminish with time and forbearance both.

"Self-lubricating," Raymond explained to Dot and to Doreen who let on with their face muscles chiefly how charmed they were to hear of it prior to watching for a spell longer the way that caster spun round in its socket that especially Mrs. Dwight Mobley could not believe was on account of self-lubrication alone though she confessed straightoff she was not much up on your self-lubricational sorts of innovations since, when she was a child and had cause to know of it, lubrication was just spit chiefly and not much otherwise.

Talk of saliva, of course, grated straightaway on the widow Mrs. Askew who dispensed briefly with her forbearance so as to put herself at liberty to be fairly thoroughly appalled at Mrs. Dwight Mobley who'd found somehow cause to be indelicate in front of a guest, and the widow Mrs. Askew told to Mrs. Dwight Mobley, "Dot," pretty completely on the ascent and tried with her face alone to appear as if she'd just been privy to a gauche thing which looked unfortunately to Mrs. Dwight Mobley like a cross between gas and constipation and so inspired her to commiserate briefly with the widow Mrs. Askew who, Mrs. Dwight Mobley proclaimed, knew already where the toilet was as she'd had previously occasion to perch upon it which directly transformed the widow Mrs. Askew's expression into an inoperable bowel tract blockage sort of an item instead.

Raymond from West Virginia with the hair and the moustache felt obliged to explain for the ladies how the ball in the caster socket was not just lubricated alone but was as well finely balanced on its axis like aided and contributed to the lubrication and prompted, in consort with it, the variety of general rotation that called in the first place for forbearance to watch. He reminded the ladies, who remained moderately transfixed by the orb that spun and rotated, how he'd laid just his one finger to it to set it off and he exhibited what one finger precisely he'd spun the ball with which Mrs. Dwight Mobley and the widow Mrs. Askew let on they both recognized as the same exact finger in fact.

"The very one," Mrs. Askew told it and induced with a sidelong look a confirming headjerk from Mrs. Dwight Mobley who pondered and fairly adored the finger for a time until Raymond from West Virginia wondered might he employ that one finger and the remainder of his fingers otherwise in setting to rights his upended lacquered box which the ladies both together allowed he might.

So Raymond lifted the thing and situated it another time wheels downward upon the carpet like was sufficient of an exertion to call for a dash of hairsweeping and a bout of sleevetugging that the ladies had saved up some forbearance for and so watched and studied how he straightened and tended his parts that held for them an intrigue well past lubricational altogether. Raymond wondered would Mrs. Dwight Mobley fetch please her vacuum cleaner that struck Mrs. Dwight Mobley as a purely delightful notion and she fairly capered across the frontroom and partway down the backhall to the closet from where she wondered at Raymond did he have in mind any particular attachment that Raymond admitted he did as he'd cultivated hopes she'd sweep a patch of rug for him and so would likely need her ten-inch rugsweeping nozzle that she fairly whooped to reveal she had precisely one of.

Shortly, then, she reappeared with her nozzle and her coiled upholstered hose and her straight chrome pipe and her canister model Electrolux that she dragged behind herself by the cord of it like the widow Mrs. Askew was fairly well set to disapprove of when she took in how it was Mrs. Dwight Mobley's particular Electrolux wasn't the round type with the wheels but was the long tubular type with the runners that she disapproved of instead and told how she'd as soon drag a snowsled through her own house as a vacuum with skids to it that scored and marred the nap wherever it went which Mrs. Dwight Mobley did not much care to hear of further and so turned of a sudden roundabout and by sheer happenstance alone clubbed the widow Mrs. Askew on the side of the head with the straight chrome pipe that Mrs. Dwight Mobley wished aloud she could learn somehow to be more careful with. "I do," she informed the widow Mrs. Askew who rubbed her earlobe and exhibited a treacly sort of a grin back.

As for himself, Raymond from West Virginia was anxious for Mrs. Dwight Mobley to plug in her Electrolux and sweep for him if she would, sweep most especially in the vicinity of his lacquered box which she was, she told him, quite thoroughly pleased to oblige him in and so vacuumed in the vicinity of his lacquered box, swept right snug up to it though she could not, Raymond induced her to confess, sweep much beneath it on account of how lowslung a lacquered box it was. And consequently Raymond told to her and told to the widow Mrs. Askew as well, "Ah, ha," and produced out from what inconspicuous place he'd been holding to it the leather lead that he extended the loop of towards Mrs. Dwight Mobley, laid it anyhow across his forearm and purely intoned, "Madam," like seemed indisputably to Mrs. Dwight Mobley certainly at herself which she straightaway apprised the widow Mrs. Askew of once the widow Mrs. Askew, who'd recovered sufficiently from her blow to launch herself off the settee, had passed between Mrs. Dwight Mobley and the forearm and had intercepted the lead off of it. Raymond, however, mediated and supposed the widow Mrs. Askew could tug the lead while Mrs. Dwight Mobley vacuumed which he confided to the ladies was hardly a fair predicament due to the nature of the leadtugging and he had the widow Mrs. Askew undertake a practice tug which she managed with suitable zeal to wreck Raymond's lacquered box into Mrs. Dwight Mobley's cherrywood coffeetable legs like illustrated, Raymond insisted, his point since the leadtugging required hardly any effort or much zeal at all to speak of.

She took his meaning, the widow Mrs. Askew did, and gained shortly a touch for the thing like allowed her to draw the lacquered box clear of Mrs. Dwight Mobley's ten-inch rugsweeping nozzle once Mrs. Dwight Mobley had gotten as snug up to the lacquered box as she could get, and her and the widow Mrs. Askew performed together an utterly unchoreographed wholly improvised ballet across the frontroom wherein Mrs. Dwight Mobley pursued the lacquered box with her chrome pipe and her ten-inch nozzle and had evermore near about arrived at it when the widow Mrs. Askew pirouetted and yanked the thing out of the way. It was a delight to tug and draw on. The widow Mrs. Askew admitted to Raymond with the hair and the moustache how, for a lacquered box, it was pure heaven to pull and she allowed even Mrs. Dwight Mobley to pull it some herself, or did not anyway hardly contend for the leather lead once Mrs. Dwight Mobley had snatched it from her. There grew to be then a consensus between Mrs. Dwight Mobley and the widow Mrs. Askew who had never before between them so much as hoped to come across a lacquered box that rolled and glided like Raymond's lacquered box did that Raymond bowed briefly from near about his neck alone at the news of and allowed the ladies to carry on for a time with what was primarily your lubricational variety of talk before he ever so deftly shifted the emphasis by dropping off into a manner of funk, by coming presently to seem to both the ladies together enchanted with and fairly fixated upon the feet of Mrs. Dwight Mobley's settee.

They said to him by turns, "Raymond?" but got no rise to speak of like did not leave, Mrs. Askew insisted, much to do otherwise but poke him what way Mrs. Askew did in fact poke him between his middle ribs with her foremost finger that had all the effect of a gutternail and inspired him with the hair and the moustache and the fascination to rise up entirely out from his quandary and he took from the ladies inquiries as to why he'd in the first place drifted away from them like he did not straightaway seem disposed to speak of but got shortly encouraged and petitioned and consequently wondered aloud if casters caused his lacquered box to slip and glide what might they do to a settee or, better still, a geegaw cupboard with a curved glass door.

The effect on the ladies was immediate and full well galvanizing and they leapt and floated a little themselves from just the charge of the revelation alone prior to speaking by turns of what they envisioned a life with casters might hold for them which was furniture chiefly drifting across their carpets like leaves on a pond. For his part, Raymond encouraged them to imagine what hairballs and dustbunnies they could expunge once they'd shifted an item that had gone probably for years unshifted, and the widow Mrs. Askew most especially grew quivery at the notion of it as she was herself a manner of hairball and dustbunny fiend and had a hutch at home she desired in particular to get in back of and so sought from Raymond assurances that he could cause a hutch to roll and glide as well. In short, the air was fairly electrified with possibilities and by the time Raymond had squatted ever so gracefully alongside his lacquered box he hardly had but to throw the lid open and reveal the wealth of casters beneath it to receive from Dot and Doreen both together a manner of extravagant ovation.

They hoped he could install them, hoped he possessed somehow the wherewithal to fix the things to settee and sideboard and cupboard and table and hutchlegs himself as their need, they let on, was immediate and farreaching, and Raymond responded by drawing off from his lacquered boxbottom a highspeed three-quarter-inch electric drill that he held for a time aloft so as to get it admired by Dot and Doreen in consort. They all three together determined how likely he'd best start with the settee and move on beyond it to the geegaw cupboard with the curved glass door that Mrs. Dwight Mobley had to empty the geegaws from before they could pitch and lay the thing over. So the settee was what they commenced with and the three of them drew it off from the wall and turned it back downwards thereby revealing the cobwebby underside which Mrs. Dwight Mobley was fairly well set to be distressed about when the widow Mrs. Askew directed her attention instead to the newly vacant stretch of baseboard and quarter round that appeared to Mrs. Askew purely fuzzy from end to end like she wanted to discover from Mrs. Dwight Mobley didn't it appear to her as well but Mrs. Dwight Mobley's shame was so thoroughly acute as to thwart talk entirely.

Raymond from West Virginia with the hair and the moustache and the sparkly baubles desired a piece of newspaper to spread beneath his drill as he worked but Mrs. Askew took up the vacuum nozzle and insisted she'd see to his debris as it fell. Consequently, then, Raymond started to drill and Doreen started to sweep and Dot began to transport her geegaws to the sideboard top and the mantelpiece and the dining room table and whatever flat places otherwise seemed to her would tolerate a geegaw, so Mrs. Dwight Mobley did not herself observe precisely how it was Raymond bored his holes and introduced the stemends of the casters into them, but she had still geegaws left to transport when he was done already and required again Dot and Doreen's unanimous forbearance as he spun with his spinning finger the front left brassplated item which the widow Mrs. Askew identified straightaway as quite plainly altogether self-lubricational and balanced.

Once the widow Mrs. Askew, who harbored a passion, had been allowed to vacuum the cobwebs off the settee bottom, they lifted the thing upright and by turns wheeled it about the room one at the time with at first more leverage than the settee anymore called for but with presently just fingers alone, and Mrs. Dwight Mobley steered it back to what piece of wall it had previously sat against so as to have occasion to draw it out again and altogether unfuzz her baseboard like she assured most especially Raymond from West Virginia would evermore be her practice. The gewgaw cupboard itself got mobile immediately thereafter and the ladies drove it by turns roundabout the room until the widow Mrs. Askew, who apparently did not possess much talent for driving furniture and lacquered boxes and such, wrecked it into the dangly overhead light producing considerably more clamor than harm. The sideboard got emptied and upended next followed by the boudoir chair and Mrs. Dwight Mobley's secretary in the dining room after which she began to speak earnestly of having her bed bewheeled but the widow Mrs. Askew objected since it did not seem fair to her that Raymond, she called him sweetly, should squander his entire day in one house alone when there were houses otherwise—her own particular house for instance—where nothing much rolled and everything could stand to, and subsequently Mrs. Askew unleashed a pithy item that she implied by her manner was germane though Mrs. Dwight Mobley and Raymond with the hair and the moustache could not appear between them to figure germane how precisely.

Nonetheless, the widow Mrs. Askew persuaded Mrs. Dwight Mobley that there was need for Raymond elsewhere and Mrs. Dwight Mobley agreed to relinquish him once she'd blathered, the widow Mrs. Askew called it, a spell further in a grateful sort of a way which immediately preceded the presentation of the bill that Raymond had drawn up on a notepad with an inkpen utterly as dazzling as his sparkly items otherwise. And if not for the general mood, if not for Mrs. Dwight Mobley's own personal inordinate gratitude, that was part caster induced but part silvery hair and nappy moustache and sleek satiny tieknot induced as well, the charges might have struck Mrs. Dwight Mobley as steep and near about unseemly since they were steep and were unseemly near about, but in her present state she merely glanced at the total and informed Raymond how thoroughly delighted she was with it as a charge and a levy that Raymond bowed at the neck a little about in a Prussian sort of a way.

Once he'd folded and introduced her check into his blazer pocket, Raymond took his leave from Mrs. Dwight Mobley by laying ever so briefly his lips to her knuckles and intoning at her a Madam and a Good Day prior to ushering the widow Mrs. Askew out the doorway and drawing by the leather lead his lacquered box behind him. For her part, Mrs. Dwight Mobley found she could endure standing at the doorlight and watching him depart until he circled around his blueblack Lincoln sedan and threw open the passenger door of it for the widow Mrs. Askew who made as if she had to hold to him just to climb in and sit like set off Mrs. Dwight Mobley who left the doorlight, threw herself onto the settee in a snit, and so glanced off the wall and careened into an endtable.

The widow Mrs. Askew did not direct him straightoff to her own house, which was around the corner and up the road, but fairly paraded him through town instead and made for a while as if to be right there on the verge of arriving home beyond every turn until Raymond from West Virginia, who'd learned from the widow Mrs. Askew how she'd walked to Mrs. Dwight Mobley's, proclaimed her to be as robust a woman as he'd lately come across which the widow Mrs. Askew was ever so grateful to hear of and consequently directed Raymond with the baubles and the blueblack Lincoln out fairly much to the county line and back again so as to pretty completely cement her reputation. Presently they did in fact ease up out front of her own house which possessed, Raymond told it, more charm than he'd even imagined it might like naturally promoted a bout of altogether unsubdued eekiness in the widow Mrs. Askew who allowed herself to be fairly lifted out from the seat and settled upon the sidewalk. Of course she indicated straightoff the plantbeds she had herself laid out and cultivated and she entertained from Raymond a spell of praise for most especially her basket-of-gold border roundabout her snapdragons that had passed their peak but had lately been, Raymond suspected, exquisite like the widow Mrs. Askew could not hardly begin to dispute. As Raymond had only lately arrived from elsewhere, the widow Mrs. Askew felt obliged to indicate her neighbors' houses and discuss briefly her neighbors so as to place herself in a manner of context, and she commenced with the widow Mrs. Jennings W. Hayes up the road whom she did not much care for and who lived anymore alongside Mr. Wayne Fulp that was himself quite thoroughly pathetic. Down the road, the widow Mrs. Askew pointed out the bald Jeeter's house where the bald Jeeter had not too awful long ago perished like prevented the widow Mrs. Askew from indicting her so thoroughly as otherwise she might.

Other side of the street and up it lived Miss Bernice Fay Frazier who, Mrs. Askew reminded Raymond, they'd spoken of previously, and she pointed out in particular the windows of the room upstairs that was not hardly fit for Miss Mary Alice Celestine Lefler to sleep in, not that Miss Mary Alice Celestine Lefler was any special case since it seemed to the widow Mrs. Askew that Miss Mary Alice Celestine Lefler was in fact a manner of tramp like she hoped Raymond would not himself be offended to know of that Raymond shook his head and showed her straightaway some teeth about. And she herself turned to mount the stairs up the slope of her yard to her walk and anticipated how she might get squired at it but climbed a little alone instead with just the rail to aid her before she turned around to tell to the silvery back of Raymond's head, "Raymond?" and thereby drew him off the windows entirely.

As best as Raymond could determine, the widow Mrs. Askew had an enchanting touch for decor like was precisely the sort of talk to reduce the widow Mrs. Askew once again to eekiness, and she settled upon her loveseat to recover and encouraged Raymond to loose his leather lead and settle upon the loveseat with her where she guessed they could figure what might have call to get castered. Of course, her hutch was one item in particular she wished intently to roll but she was, she let on, open to persuasion if Raymond, in his wisdom, spied items otherwise that wheels might suit like prompted Raymond to cast round and land shortly on an altogether ponderous bureau which he could envision bewheeled along with a sizeable halltree and the vanity in the widow Mrs. Askew's bedroom that was weighted with three mirrors and assorted emollients and potions and swabs and such that the widow Mrs. Askew was so thoroughly embarrassed to have Raymond see that she almost failed to loose and intone what pithy item about the beauty of a woman she'd come across in a book which she did somehow manage at last to loose and intone both and accepted from Raymond congratulations on the aptness of the thing.

Mrs. Askew cleared and emptied the pieces she hoped to roll ahead of Raymond that drilled the feet of them and inserted the caster stems prior to illustrating with his foremost finger the lubricational qualities once the widow Mrs. Askew had worked up some suitable forbearance for it. She offered to Raymond refreshments which was tea again or Sundrop if he'd have it and biscuits as well that were in Mrs. Askew's own particular case

Fig Newtons, but Raymond wished only to get directed to where he might discharge what beverage he'd taken in already and refused to imbibe further no matter how sweetly Mrs. Askew beleaguered him about it. And it seemed to her, once he'd put wheels on most everything she could think of that might stand to have wheels on it and once he'd discharged what fluids he'd been of a mind to discharge, Raymond might just depart altogether leaving only plated casters and highly lubricated mobility and a trace of sweet leathery cologne on the air to remember him by like the widow Mrs. Askew could not hardly begin to contemplate the prospect of without anguishment settling upon her.

So she considered her predicament and was trying to come up somehow with another piece she might care to wheel round when Mrs. Sleepy Pitts rang her up on the telephone so as to apprise the widow Mrs. Askew of an extravagantly pithy thing she'd heard a man utter just lately on the TV, not a man from her story but a man from the story previous to her story that she usually caught the tailend of so as to have herself situated before the set when the organ music rose and swelled for the story she was in fact partial to. It had been a thing about a brief candle that went out, had been anyway on the face of it a thing about a brief candle but had seemed somehow to Mrs. Sleepy Pitts not actually about a brief candle truly due to the circumstances that had induced it to get uttered in the first place like was the death of a young comely woman who'd stolen away with her dentist only to die beside him in a fiery crash in his Jaguar, and it seemed to Mrs. Sleepy Pitts that the man left to grieve and be pithy at the close of the show was either that young comely woman's brother, her abandoned boyfriend, or a patient who'd lately enjoyed some altogether artful bridgework. Mrs. Sleepy Pitts simply could not be certain which.

Now Mrs. Sleepy Pitts was intending of course to undertake to reconstruct the entire pithy outburst that had, on the TV, gotten fairly screeched and declaimed which she was meaning to duplicate and so had drawn off a breath for it like had caused her for the moment to fall silent which allowed the widow Mrs. Askew to inquire after what dust and stray hair had accumulated back of most especially Mr. and Mrs. Sleepy Pitts's entertainment center which was a manner of knotty pine monstrosity Mr. and Mrs. Sleepy Pitts generally heaped things on they could not find a place elsewhere to heap. It was meant for a TV and so accommodated their Zenith but was meant as well for a hi-fi and a radio and a record collection and a tape collection and an assortment of books and such that Mr. and Mrs. Sleepy Pitts had not somehow ever accumulated any of but for the such chiefly along with three LPs Mrs.

Sleepy Pitts had felt compelled to order with her credit card over the phone as they'd seemed irresistible values to her notwithstanding how she did not own the means to play them.

Mrs. Sleepy Pitts had not, of course, anticipated fielding from the widow Mrs. Askew an inquiry about dust and stray hair back of her entertainment center and accordingly she squandered her entire screeching and declaiming breath on an inconsequential sort of a noise like allowed Mrs. Askew to persevere on the topic and speak of the casters and the brass plating and the lubrication and the forbearance and him with the hair and the moustache and the baubles who sold and installed the things, him the widow Mrs. Askew would be delighted to send to Mrs. Sleepy Pitts, him she'd be even willing to ride with so as to indicate the way like Mrs. Sleepy Pitts did not have time truly to consider and consent to before Mrs. Askew had informed her how they'd see her shortly and had hung up so as to turn around and tell to Raymond, "Raymond!" in a breathless sort of a fashion.

She only sent him one time in the opposite direction entirely like was off her street and around once more by Mrs. Dwight Mobley's and then east four blocks so far as to where the widow Mrs. Boatwright stood on her front walk and fairly wailed at them as they swung around the corner like Mrs. Askew let on to be the widow Mrs. Boatwright's usual variety of greeting. Otherwise they headed pretty directly out 29 beyond the plant toward Mrs. Sleepy Pitts's house that the widow Mrs. Askew informed Raymond was not near so grand and stately a dwelling as the dwellings he'd visited previously, but had to it furnishings with some measurable bulk and heft like could stand surely to get bewheeled. Mrs. Sleepy Pitts herself had undertaken to straighten and pick up once she'd gotten off the phone but she'd come to be distracted by her story on the TV that had to do this day with a woman who'd contracted some manner of disease that called, for one reason or another, that she be bandaged around her head clean down to her earchannels. Due to her affliction, she could not well remember most especially the devious and unseemly endeavors she'd lately partaken of but she was fortunately blessed with friends and relations who were willing to linger by her hospital bed and speak of them to her. Apparently, as best as Mrs. Sleepy Pitts could tell, she'd been in the bloom of health a vile woman with innumerable poor qualities which had gotten mysteriously eradicated by a feverish state she'd only lately woken out of. However, the scant virtues she'd harbored had come to be somehow eradicated as well like left her to sprawl upon the bedsheet as lively as a kumquat while she entertained talk of what a wretched creature she was.

The innate drama of the predicament was hardly squandered on Mrs. Sleepy Pitts who, without intending to at all, left off her straightening and her picking up and perched before the set upon the cushionedge of her armchair with an empty cracker box in her one hand and one of Mr. Sleepy Pitts's green socks in her other while she heard from a nephew talk of how his aunt with the affliction and the headwrap had one time previously taken his daddy, her brother-in-law, into her bed for purposes of fornication like could have possibly brought forth, as far as the nephew could tell, a sibling and a cousin both at the same time which was a notion of particular torment to him and he gnawed for a while on the scenery about it. Mrs. Sleepy Pitts came to be, of course, transfixed by the display since she was especially partial to scenery gnawing as a manner of thespian pursuit, came to be in fact so sufficiently transfixed that she did not hear the Lincoln arrive, did not hear the doors clap shut, and full well backed across the front room when a knock ensued so as to remain suitably oriented to watch the nephew lurch forlornly about the hospital room. She answered the door, then, with the sock in her one hand and the cracker box under her opposite arm and her attention fairly diverted and engaged like the widow Mrs. Askew remedied straightaway by being ever so pleased to present to Mrs. Sleepy Pitts Raymond from West Virginia who extended both his resplendent hands together so as to take up Mrs. Sleepy Pitts's sockless fingers and hold briefly to them like served to dislodge the cracker box that careened off Mrs. Sleepy Pitts's kneecap and skipped out the doorway onto the porch decking.

It almost went without saying that she was embarrassed, but Mrs. Sleepy Pitts went ahead and fairly broadcast the news of it like induced the widow Mrs. Askew to admit how if she was herself Mrs. Sleepy Pitts she'd be embarrassed as well, probably fairly mortified, like served for Mrs. Sleepy Pitts as consolation of a sort. Leaving Mrs. Askew and Raymond and Raymond's lacquered box in the doorway, Mrs. Sleepy Pitts fairly bolted across the room so as to switch off the TV set and to wonder just into the air how in the world it had come to be on in the first place in the middle of the afternoon like she could not hardly begin to say though she made as if to attempt it. For her part the widow Mrs. Askew, who was not one to be left lingering in a doorway, took up Raymond at the elbowjoint and escorted him on into the house, led him directly over to the sofa against the far wall where she settled herself upon a cushion and yanked him down alongside her.

They had some dazzling wares to display. The widow Mrs. Askew informed Mrs. Sleepy Pitts how they'd carried with them wares that were truly dazzling which Mrs. Sleepy Pitts was meaning to let loose the green sock and say, "Oh?" about but got stopped and drawn up altogether short by Mrs. Askew who inquired after Mrs. Sleepy Pitts's own personal forbearance. Was it, she wanted to find out, ample that Mrs. Sleepy Pitts assured her straightaway it most certainly was and admitted in particular to Raymond how she was known roundabout for her forbearance chiefly, that and her bean salad. So Raymond took it upon himself to upend his lacquered box and apply his foremost finger to a caster of it like did not seem to Mrs. Sleepy Pitts to have called for hardly any forbearance to speak of which she was fairly well set to utter a thing about when she got stilled and prevented by him with the hair and the moustache and the resplendent accoutrements who upraised a hand like brought with it a bejeweled shirtcuff which both together indicated to Mrs. Sleepy Pitts how she'd best just sit and forbear a while longer. So they all three together watched the caster spin round until shortly the widow Mrs. Askew poached from Raymond his brief self-lubricational remark that Mrs. Sleepy Pitts made merely a noise about prior to regarding the caster a spell further with the sort of concentration she guessed a forbearing woman might muster. The thing, however, just spun, just steadily rotated like did not hardly scintillate Mrs. Sleepy Pitts after the fashion the spinning and the rotating alone quite obviously stirred and agitated the widow Mrs. Askew who'd grown fairly frothy there on the sofa and was making out into the air various ejaculations meant to communicate what an indisputable thrill it was for her to sit before the caster and watch it roll around which was not, as a disposition, altogether infectious.

So the taxing of Mrs. Sleepy Pitts's storied forbearance did not in fact win her over to the plated casters, but once Raymond with the slender satiny tieknot and the sleek blue blazer wrested the presentation away from the widow Mrs. Askew and bore down on Mrs. Sleepy Pitts himself alone, she came to be affected and impressed with the charms a caster might hold. The charging vacuum and dodging lacquered box part of the thing most especially engaged her since she herself prodded with the nozzle while Raymond tugged the boxlead, drew at the thing in such a manly and elegant fashion both together that Mrs. Sleepy Pitts could not hardly keep her mind on her prodding, and when Raymond paused to draw for Mrs. Sleepy Pitts lessons from the vacuum and lacquered box engagement, his deep and lowly edifying tones fairly transported Mrs. Sleepy Pitts altogether. She did not of a sudden know how she'd gone wheelless and she purely blessed the widow Mrs. Askew for bringing to her Raymond from West Virginia that Mrs.

Askew informed her was truly not anything hardly at all, and both of the faithful plain looked upon Raymond for a time so as to adore him.

He began with the entertainment center which was itself outsized and rickety and pretty much fell to pieces once he laid it over but Raymond, demonstrating a strain of resourcefulness which the ladies could not help but adore as well, rigged the thing back together long enough for him to stand it upright, improved it anyhow to rickety once more and rolled it against the wall where he left it. Mrs. Sleepy Pitts had a highboy she'd been passionate to relocate and so removed the drawers of it for Raymond who pitched it over and drilled and becastered it and then advised Mrs. Sleepy Pitts how she might grip it to drive it around and she tried the thing against the far wall to the right of the window and against the far wall to the left of it and alongside the bed and then back pretty much where it had been in the first place though a bit closer to the corner like she would not, she insisted, have discovered to be such a fine location if she'd not been presented the occasion to see for herself how poorly the thing fared elsewhere.

She had a wardrobe she could stand to roll and a trunk at the foot of her guestbed that would undoubtedly be improved by wheels, so she loosed Raymond upon them and then stepped with Mrs. Askew back a ways to admire most especially Raymond's elegant squat that beat fairly much to pieces every squat otherwise they'd ever between them been witness to. Raymond let on to be rather extravagantly taken with what he called at Mrs. Sleepy Pitts her armoire like induced from her a variety of curtsy as she'd not ever previously suffered her armoire to be complimented and she told sweetly to Raymond as he drilled and castered, "You scoundrel you," and pretty much curtsied all over again.

Once he'd finished, Raymond tabulated and presented the bill which Mrs. Sleepy Pitts perused at length while she endeavored with a seemly expression to convince the widow Mrs. Askew and Raymond both that the total had not hardly drained off all the spit from her in fact. In an effort to appear magnanimous and altogether well to do, Mrs. Sleepy Pitts inquired if she could perhaps write out the check for a sum beyond the total even and thereby include a gratuity for Raymond who'd been so kind, she told it, and princely. Raymond, however, would not so much as hear of such a thing that Mrs. Sleepy Pitts made to be oh so distressed at the news of and so made out the check for just the original inordinate sum alone. She suggested that maybe if he had the time for it, Raymond might call upon Mrs. Wyatt Benbow as Mrs. Wyatt Benbow had in her music room an upright piano with just three wheels to it and one hardbound copy of *Magnificent Obsession* underneath the vacant wheelhole, and the widow Mrs. Askew apprised Raymond of how she herself knew precisely where it was Mrs. Wyatt Benbow lived like rendered her, she calculated, fairly indispensable which Raymond assured the widow Mrs. Askew was in countless ways the truth of the matter like near about caused her to puddle up on the carpet.

So they took their leave. Mrs. Askew locked onto the elbowjoint and fairly drove Raymond out of the house and down off the porch to the blueblack sedan where he opened her door and closed her door and paused midway around the car to wave at Mrs. Sleepy Pitts on the porch decking, wave in what appeared to her three-fingered papal fashion like induced her to raise up some fingers of her own. And then they were out of the driveway and gone down the road which left Mrs. Sleepy Pitts alone to reflect upon him with the hair and the moustache and the satiny tie and the white shirt with the white stripes worked into the pattern of it, and she stood for a time silent upon the decking before she mustered the breath to tell just out into the air, "Armoire."

Naturally the widow Mrs. Askew led him a chase for a spell and sent him due east and then southeast and then northeast and southwest at last to town and on through town and beyond it entirely like she'd not truly intended to send him but she'd come to be caught up with receiving from Raymond a compliment and so grew briefly too distracted to guide him. She presently recovered herself, however, and turned Raymond back around to the north and caused him to steer fairly directly for Mrs. Wyatt Benbow's house that he eased his blueblack Lincoln to a stop in front of prior to darting roundabout the backend so as to draw the widow Mrs. Askew off from the seat before he returned to the trunklid and liberated his lacquered box. For her part, Mrs. Wyatt Benbow had not been hardly pining for company as she'd come to be engaged polishing her set of three tiny ornamental silver bowls she'd won with Mr. Wyatt Benbow at the canasta round robin out at the country club. She'd not been intending truly to polish the things; she'd hoped to just dust them instead but had taken up one to wipe it without much good effect to speak of. She'd set, then, to work on her bowls in earnest with her soft fuzzy buffing rag and her jar of polish, set in once she'd donned her polishing uniform which was a pair of Mr. Wyatt Benbow's trousers that he'd bought once in a fit of optimism but had not ever actually raised much past his kneecaps and one of Mr. Wyatt Benbow's discarded twill shirts that he'd exhausted chiefly the elbows of along with a headrag which had been one time an ugly striped kerchief. All in all, Mrs. Wyatt Benbow looked to have just left off riveting a bomber and so when the front buzzer sounded she stopped her polishing and found herself straightaway torn between answering the door and slipping under the bed back of the dust ruffle.

She expected it was maybe Bill Ed Myrick jr. come to collect for the paper and eased out of the kitchen, through the dining room, and so far as the jamb of the music room door where she inquired sweetly, "Who is it?" and could have sworn an oath, she told it shortly, how she'd heard Bill Ed Myrick inform her it was him Bill Ed Myrick back like was how come she opened the door as she'd seen Bill Ed Myrick's mother out at the Big Apple in her housedress and pink hair rollers and so did not suppose she could herself startle him much to speak of which Mrs. Askew, alongside him with the hair and the moustache and the slim manly build, found to be an altogether quaint and jolly sort of an explanation and consequently engaged in the variety of headtossing that Mrs. Wyatt Benbow straightaway wanted to pick her up by the earlobes on account of.

She invited them both together into the house and wished they'd put themselves at ease in the frontroom while she retreated for a time so as to spiff up a little, and the widow Mrs. Askew took up Raymond at the elbow and drew him and, consequently, his lacquered box into the house and over to Mrs. Wyatt Benbow's tufted Naugahyde sofa that Mrs. Askew rubbed her hand on the arm of and identified for Raymond as Naugahyde in case he'd been deceived. They chatted briefly about Mrs. Wyatt Benbow's taste as reflected in her various knickknacks, and the widow Mrs. Askew identified for Raymond the items she did not much approve of and the items she failed to approve of at all prior to pointing out the piano with, as best as the widow Mrs. Askew could recollect, a lurid novel beneath a corner of it. The first sign of Mrs. Wyatt Benbow's imminent return wafted at them from the bathroom up the hallway and seemed, Mrs. Askew admitted, almost like a manner of perfume and a dose of Pine-Sol combined and she was speculating if maybe Mrs. Wyatt Benbow bought it by the gallon or by the vat instead when Mrs. Wyatt Benbow herself departed from the bathroom and struck out up the hallway with her shoeheels click-clacking on the hardwood.

What she'd undergone was pretty much a wholesale transformation as she'd given over her twill slacks and her ragged shirt and her ugly striped kerchief for a velvety green cocktail dress with lovely blue piping and, as best as the widow Mrs. Askew could tell, extravagant cleavage to it. The hem of it hardly fell to her kneecaps and the right side of the thing appeared to be slit open clean up to her hipsocket like Mrs. Askew found inexcusable for especially a woman as veiny as Mrs. Wyatt Benbow had come in her mature years to be. Of course the sheer black hose didn't even begin to improve matters any, the sheer black hose with the palpable seam up the back and the shiny black heels with the straps just by themselves fairly set the widow Mrs. Askew's teeth on edge. She could in fact barely work up the spit to inform Mrs. Wyatt Benbow how stunning it was she looked and then turn her incisors on Raymond from West Virginia with the hair and the moustache so as to inquire if didn't Mrs. Wyatt Benbow look in fact stunning to him that Raymond confirmed with ever so much grace and elegance she did.

The trouble was, however, that Mrs. Wyatt Benbow could not hardly sit down without her dressend advancing precipitously towards her navel like only the merest variety of chairedge perching could prevent, so Mrs. Wyatt Benbow lighted with a little piece of her backside on the front lip of her armchair like a big green bullfinch and made as if to be full well concentrated on what it was Mrs. Askew informed her Raymond himself had shortly to reveal out from his lacquered box like Mrs. Wyatt Benbow could not straightaway make terribly much sense of due to how taxing it was for her to perch and appear to be concentrated both at the very same time. She caught on shortly, though, once Raymond himself began to speak as she found herself taken in earnest with the graceful mellow tones that flowed out from beneath his nappy moustache, so she sat back a little and her dressend rose up but she did not herself care near so much about it as Mrs. Askew cared about it for her and consequently excavated phlegm on behalf of Mrs. Wyatt Benbow who herself had Raymond to admire and so was fairly completely immune to necknoises.

And shortly she intoned at him, "Self-lubricational?" that he confirmed and illustrated with his foremost finger once he'd petitioned another time for forbearance and received a promise of it. "Ah," she said and admired how steadily the brass plated caster rotated like she guessed was part grease and guessed as well was part balance too, guessed in advance of being informed how it was in fact part balance like Raymond fairly marveled about after such a fashion as to produce in the widow Mrs. Askew a touch of noticeable chagrin and she found herself moved and inspired to identify precisely for Mrs. Wyatt Benbow what piece of her corset was presently on view.

Mrs. Wyatt Benbow's vacant piano wheelhole had been, she let on, a constant plague and incessant worry to her, and she could not hardly begin to express to Raymond the vaulted heights her gratitude might reach were he to mend her upright for her, were he to fill her wheelhole with a self-lubricational brass plated caster, or were he to fill maybe all four of her wheelholes together with identical brassplated self-lubricational casters like would constitute, she figured, a matched set that Raymond confirmed for her they would and rose to take up Mrs. Benbow at the fingerjoints so as to help her unperch and stand in her brief slinky dress upright. Needless to say, the widow Mrs. Askew raised into the air her own fingerjoints to get gripped and drawn on but Raymond had already turned to squire Mrs. Wyatt Benbow into the music room like left Mrs. Askew to climb off the settee unaided which was just the variety of maneuver to foul her disposition altogether and send her with some velocity into the music room herself where she scanned for a piece of undergarment to speak of.

As best as he was able, Raymond examined the wheelhole and determined how he had in his lacquered box the stemend to fit it like served as cause for some inordinate jubilation on the part of Mrs. Wyatt Benbow who yelped and tittered and verily embraced him with the hair and the moustache which touched off an urge in the widow Mrs. Askew to go on ahead and embrace him a little herself like she endeavored to do but got fairly beat back by Mrs. Wyatt Benbow who assured Mrs. Askew how she'd not at all intended to pummel her about the head and shoulders with her bony elbowend which Mrs. Askew was a little too dazed and groggy to dispute. Once he'd helped her to tilt the thing, Mrs. Wyatt Benbow alone in her green velvety cocktail dress and her spiked heels managed to support the piano and keep it from falling completely over while Raymond filled the vacant wheelhole and extracted the remaining wheels otherwise that he replaced with shiny new brassplated casters as quickly as he could manage to replace them and shortly he backed off, threw his hands up in the air, and fairly bellowed at Mrs. Wyatt Benbow, "Clear," like induced her to let loose of the piano which righted itself with some considerable bump and clamor and had not hardly left off rattling and vibrating before Mrs. Wyatt Benbow was pushing it around the music room with as few fingers as before she could readily push it with. She proclaimed that the thing slid and shifted like a cloud in the heavens which she could not gather the breath to say all at one time and so said in scraps and pieces. She found herself inspired even to play for Raymond from West Virginia an étude, she called it, and so situated the piano and settled upon the bench like fairly indecently elevated her dressend which the widow Mrs. Askew was pretty well prepared to exclaim on account of when Mrs. Wyatt Benbow, who'd poised briefly her eight fingers and her two thumbs above the keyboard, beat just up and all at once what sounded about seventeen moderately harmonious notes like was the coda, she hollered, to the étude she'd chosen to play.

Mrs. Wyatt Benbow's own personal étude was not likely so soothing an item as most études otherwise due chiefly to Mrs. Wyatt Benbow's own personal fingering style which was fairly utterly approximate and only occasionally and accidentally precise. Being an étude, however, the thing did not truly have much velocity to it and so was endurable after a fashion since the various offenses did not arrive slam up on each other but issued off from the wires in a stately and near about dirgelike sort of a way that was suitable for a funeral or, more likely, a homicide. She ran through the thing twice over the objections of Raymond and the widow Mrs. Askew who assured her in consort they'd picked it up the first time but the man who'd composed it, Mrs. Wyatt Benbow insisted, had intended for it to be repeated like she'd have been pleased to show to them on the sheet music if she'd not already gotten the thing by heart and so tossed the sheet music away.

She wondered would they care for a nocturne once her étude had wound down and come to be hammered to a stop, but him with the hair and the moustache and the widow Mrs. Askew consulted together and arrived at the unanimous opinion that they were both of them, Raymond announced it, pretty well saturated and had likely soaked up all the music they could presently stand. Mrs. Wyatt Benbow, who had of course just lately delved down deep into her innermost self under the direction of Dr. Dewey Lunt, confessed how she'd discovered back in the nearly fathomless reaches of her person an acute sensitivity for music like kept her evermore unsaturated that the widow Mrs. Askew, who'd lately visited her own fathomless reaches, was pretty well set to be contrary about, was intending anyhow to illuminate her own particular sensitivities when she decided instead to merely indicate what piece of corset had come just lately to be on display. So Mrs. Wyatt Benbow raised shortly upright off the piano bench pretty much unaided though Raymond did attempt to draw her by what fingers she was meaning to lower her velvety green dressend with which she could not somehow help but forgive him about.

Together they retired back to the parlor they'd come out of and spoke a little of the harmonies they'd just lately all three of them been privy to prior to sitting for a time speechless like provided the widow Mrs. Askew the occasion to air a pithy sort of an observation that was chiefly about the waning of the days and the advent of general decrepitude though it was far too poetical an item to seem grim or to be but moderately comprehended. Presently, of course, talk turned again to casters and the widow Mrs. Ashew in particular suggested to Mrs. Wyatt Benbow what items she would, if she were Mrs. Wyatt Benbow, bewheel and how come that Raymond came to be every now and again encouraged to throw in with. Mrs. Wyatt Benbow, however, proved a sluggish customer and only after an extended spell did she guess she could tolerate maybe a bureau that rolled along with her knotty pine drysink that had come down to her from her grandmomma. So

Raymond slipped out from between the ladies and went on ahead and becastered the bureau and then set in on the drysink as well. Shortly, upon being pressed, Mrs. Wyatt Benbow determined she would probably go otherwise casterless like brought on the tallying of the bill which Raymond from West Virginia undertook once he'd licked his pencilend and he ciphered and carried while Mrs. Wyatt Benbow suggested to the widow Mrs. Askew that she might impose herself next upon Mrs. Estelle Singletary who was afflicted in her master bedroom with a whole suite of stout, ponderous, and altogether homely Mediterranean furniture that needed truly to be rolled off the edge of the earth but could stand maybe to travel around the bedroom first and, much to their mutual delight, Mrs. Wyatt Benbow and the widow Mrs. Askew discovered how they shared an antipathy for Mediterranean furniture and did not together care much for Mrs. Estelle Singletary either like served to cement them once more in a sisterly sort of a way.

Mrs. Wyatt Benbow did not even blanch much upon the presentation of the bill partly because she was a woman of appreciable resources, Mr. Wyatt Benbow's own personal accumulated resources chiefly, and partly because it did not seem the proper thing in a green velvety cocktail dress to do. Instead she merely proffered a check in her extended fingers and had them taken up and squeezed ever so slightly by him with the hair and the moustache who fairly beat together his heels and flapped his head at Mrs. Wyatt Benbow who was left moderately speechless by the general thrill Raymond's variety of etiquette inspired in her, and as he backed out the door with his lacquered box in tow he told to Mrs. Wyatt Benbow, "Au revoir," and flourished a sparkly hand at her with the steep shiny heels and the extravagant cleavage, her that—though she'd hardly meant to and could not even once she'd done it believe she had—told to him, "Happy trails," back.

The widow Mrs. Askew felt an obligation to tour Raymond roundabout the country club as they had to be out by the country club anyway and she did not know would he ever again have the opportunity to view for himself their verdant emerald fairways, their slick manicured greens, and their white glistening traps filled with sand imported clean from South Carolina. Mr. Wyatt Benbow himself was partly down the twelfth fairway and once the widow Mrs. Askew had identified for Raymond Mr. Wyatt Benbow with the cotton cap and the stomach she lowered her window by means of her button alone and hollered at him, "Wyatt," just as Mr. Wyatt Benbow had reached the top of his arc when he did not much need the distraction of having his name called to him from a car on the road since he had his left elbow to keep stiff and rigid and his head to hold dead still and his one knee to flex up and his one knee to flex back in anticipation of his ever so imminent general weight shift like would set him towards a timely impact and subsequent thoroughgoing followthrough which, all taken together, was plenty enough to engage a man without him having to suffer his name to be called to him from a car on the road like was how come, he told to Buford Needham who was himself already laying up in front of the green in two, he sliced into the branch that he wanted straightaway some unpenalized relief from once he'd found out just precisely which horse's ass it was that had hollered at him in the first place like he could not hardly determine with just the blueblack Lincoln to go by and the arm that waved out the window of it. His invective, consequently, was in many ways unspecified and general but for the part about the five iron and where he hoped to lodge it that seemed altogether plain and vivid enough to the widow Mrs. Askew who turned to Raymond from West Virginia so as to inform him what a pure and ceaseless caution Mr. Wyatt Benbow tended evermore to be.

Under regular circumstances, Mrs. Estelle Singletary could not bring herself to approve of the sorts of people that just up and dropped by, so once she'd peeked out from behind the drapes and spied a piece of the widow Mrs. Askew she began to work up a humor iller even than her normal native humor, a humor that was gaining a frothy head by the time she took up the doorknob and turned it and so brought herself face to face with the widow Mrs. Askew whom she was prepared to revile and face to face as well with Raymond of the hair and the moustache and the satiny tieknot and the sleek blue blazer, Raymond with his head set to flap and his heels set to collide.

"Oh," Mrs. Estelle Singletary said, "my," and the bulk of her agitation and peevishness drained off from her in a fullfledged eeky sort of a discharge as she reached discreetly back of her head so as to loose the curlers and clips she'd hoped to give herself a manner of wave with. Her grin, as best as the widow Mrs. Askew could tell, was inordinately toothsome most especially for Mrs. Estelle Singletary who was not given whatsoever to toothsome grins and once she'd closed up the curlers and the clips both in the fingers of her one hand she offered the fingers of her other to Raymond from West Virginia who gripped and squeezed them and drew them to him as he bent and lurched forward.

They made some insignificant talk together once they'd gained the foyer that itself came to be spoken of ever so extravagantly, and they toured shortly Mrs. Estelle Singletary's formal living room and her formal dining room and the breakfast nook where she and Mr. Estelle

Singletary most usually took their food when they were feeling casual instead. The runner up the back hallway induced most especially in the widow Mrs. Askew some noticeable rapture which she communicated a trace of to Raymond who aired shortly his own regard for most especially the maroon border and so brought forth from Mrs. Estelle Singletary a wholly unanticipated giddy sort of a necknoise. Like had been foretold by Mrs. Wyatt Benbow and the widow Mrs. Askew both, the bedroom was crowded with the variety of Mediterranean furniture that was not, unfortunately, just Mediterranean alone but had been as well distressed, had been in fact fairly thoroughly aggrieved and so did not look much in the way of ancient but just near about flogged to pieces chiefly.

Raymond adored it. Raymond was, he confessed, partial to Mrs. Estelle Singletary's own personal variety of bedroom suite like seemed to him Moorish and farflung and so seemed directly to the widow Mrs. Askew Moorish and farflung too which induced Mrs. Estelle Singletary to inquire of her Moorish how precisely but Moorishness, the widow Mrs. Askew insisted, was pretty much the sort of thing that defied explanation altogether. Raymond admired most especially the lines of the bureau and the chest of drawers and thereby incited the widow Mrs. Askew to admire the lines herself that had to them unspeakable Moorish qualities, she told it, along with the vanity and the night tables and the bedstead too that was itself most especially farflung.

She bet they were heavy and sluggish to move, bet a little at Mrs. Estelle Singletary but bet primarily at Raymond that the whole suite together would be a strain to shift and slide across the pile carpet, and Raymond told to her back, "Yes," told to her back, "I would surely imagine so," and then allowed Mrs. Estelle Singletary the occasion to own up to how acute a strain it in fact was to slip and slide her Moorish farflung suite that Mrs. Estelle Singletary did not at all hesitate to admit most especially to him with the hair and the slender nappy moustache who seemed to plumb her nooks and reaches and so could not likely be deceived anyhow. In her own defense, Mrs. Estelle Singletary pleaded general daintiness and supposed were she a woman like the widow Mrs. Askew with some girth and some bulk to her she could probably pitch and heave against her various pieces with immeasurably more success that the widow Mrs. Askew grew toothsome at the news of and supposed outright it was just the nature of Mrs. Estelle Singletary's customary smocks and jumpers that made her to look dumpy since Mrs. Askew took as a revelation Mrs. Estelle Singletary's general daintiness that she'd not suspected Mrs. Estelle Singletary possessed truly any of.

Raymond with just his fingers alone defused and undid what likely would have mounted to carnage shortly. He touched on the collarbone Mrs. Estelle Singletary and touched on the collarbone the widow Mrs. Askew and smiled warmly upon the both of them prior to inquiring, "Doreen, would you be so kind as to fetch my box?" that straightaway Mrs. Askew confessed would be a sheer delight for her. In her absence Raymond broached with Mrs. Estelle Singletary the topic of self-lubricational brassplated casters that seemed perhaps to him the antidote for Mrs. Estelle Singletary's general daintiness in the face of her Moorish and farflung suite that Mrs. Estelle Singletary, who'd not previously in her own personal recorded history been willing ever to yield and give way to opinions other than her own ones, straightaway yielded and gave way too and had worked up already inordinate enthusiasm for Raymond's particular manner of casters before the widow Mrs. Askew had even left the foyer and gained the hallway with his lacquered box that she could not rein and manage near so well as Raymond could rein and manage it and so beat the thing against Mrs. Estelle Singletary's fluted baseboard with all the rhythm and regularity of a drum tattoo that Mrs. Estelle Singletary stepped briefly out of the bedroom and into the hallway to admire her at.

Raymond bewheeled the bureau and the chest of drawers along with Mrs. Estelle Singletary's farflung poster bed and then followed Mrs. Estelle Singletary into her cozy den off the dining room where he worked his brassplated magic on the hide-a-bed settee in addition to Mr. Estelle Singletary's favorite upholstered chair with the greasespot in Mr. Estelle Singletary's favorite headlaying place. There was brief talk of a rolling halltree but it piddled out pretty quickly so Raymond came to be instructed yet again to work up his figures and present his bill that itself induced in Mrs. Estelle Singletary an additional variety of necknoise which was truly more gurgly than giddy, was in fact not much in the way of giddy at all. As she sorted through her bag in pursuit of her checkbook, Mrs. Estelle Singletary got interrupted by a phone call from her sister Miss Bernice Fay Frazier who was herself of a mind to revile Mr. Derwood Bridger who'd promised to stop off and replace a plank of her porch decking that had cracked at a knothole and become a hazard. Of course he'd not shown up like was pretty much what Miss Bernice Fay Frazier had expected of Mr. Derwood Bridger though, her expectations notwithstanding, she was able still somehow to work up the passion to revile him about it. Naturally, she was anticipating how her sister might kick in and revile him with her, anticipating how her sister would most surely have at least a solitary harsh thing to say but when even a moderately snide exclamation did not ensue Miss Bernice Fay Frazier grew sufficiently troubled to make an inquiry and so learned of Raymond with the hair and the moustache and the satiny tie and the sleek blue blazer and the casters that somehow lubricated themselves.

Miss Bernice Fay Frazier had a need for casters. Her need for a new length of porch decking was likely more pressing, but her need for casters was moderately acute. Consequently, she wondered would her sister please communicate to him with the hair and the moustache and the satiny tie and the sleek blue blazer how there was on the line a woman with some furniture to roll which Mrs. Estelle Singletary obliged her in without somehow giving warning of Raymond's altogether extravagant wages that renewed consideration of the hair and the moustache and the satiny tie and the blue blazer had fairly driven from her mind. For his part, Raymond pledged to Mrs. Estelle Singletary that he would in fact pay Miss Bernice Fay Frazier a call and Mrs. Estelle Singletary passed his pledge along over the line to Miss Bernice Fay Frazier without somehow capturing the sheer grace of it but imparting nonetheless enough of the elegance to apprise Miss Bernice Fay Frazier of how this was not remotely your Derwood Bridger sort of a pledge.

There were, then, shortly Au revoirs all around and, as best as the widow Mrs. Askew could tell, entirely too much fingersqueezing and heelbeating and headflapping not even to mention Mrs. Estelle Singletary's near about tearful testimony to Raymond's unmitigated prowess with a three-quarter-inch variable-speed reversible drill, but the widow Mrs. Askew did presently manage to guide Raymond by the elbowjoint down off the porch to the blueblack sedan in the drive where she turned briefly invalid and allowed herself to get placed and situated on the carseat after which she waved with her fingers to Mrs. Estelle Singletary who managed somehow to lift up her own fingers and just wave them back.

"Adieu," Mrs. Estelle Singletary called to Raymond who straightaway fished out his sparkly white handkerchief from his trouser pocket and rushed up the walk with it only to learn from Mrs. Estelle Singletary how her discharge had not been congestion but had been in fact French instead like gave rise to a gay moment which Raymond and Mrs. Estelle Singletary shared together until the widow Mrs. Askew reached across the seat and sounded the blueblack sedan horn.

Now that he'd traveled pretty widely roundabout, Raymond did not any longer require the widow Mrs. Askew to instruct him which meant that no matter how she pointed and indicated he would not be guided and drove altogether directly back to the widow Mrs. Askew's house where he eased up against the curbing and shut off the motor prior to informing the widow Mrs. Askew what extraordinary help she'd been to him. However, the widow Mrs. Askew was meaning to persist at being an extraordinary help and undertook to share with Raymond the news of it but got interrupted and prevented by Raymond himself who confessed how his conscience would not any longer allow him to impose upon the widow Mrs. Askew who'd shown, he told it, wholly extravagant native kindness which the widow Mrs. Askew endeavored to dispute but could not somehow work up the means to dispute it. Instead she said just, "Raymond," to him who'd circled round the car to draw open her door for her.

"Doreen," he told to her back and proffered an elbowjoint.

So she allowed herself to be deposited at her threshold and excused and she watched Raymond take his leave of her, watched him descend her front steps, lift his blueblack trunklid, and remove his lacquered box to the street. At the far curb he preened and tucked and straightened and situated his various parts and pieces, in particular his silvery hair that he swept and laid prior to striking on out up the walk towards Miss Bernice Fay Frazier's front porch with the hazardous length of decking somewhere upon it, the hazardous length of decking Miss Bernice Fay Frazier threw open the front door and the doorscreen both so as to issue a warning about like served to issue Bubbles the housecat as well who near about became loose and liberated one time more but got grabbed at the scruff of the neck and plucked up ever so deftly by Raymond who believed, he told it, this particular housecat to be Miss Bernice Fay Frazier's own one that Miss Bernice Fay Frazier straightaway confessed to him it was.

From across the road just back of her doorscreen the widow Mrs. Askew admired the deft piece of housecat plucking and ejaculated with just her breath chiefly, "Ah, Raymond," as she watched him take up Miss Bernice Fay Frazier at the fingers and just generally squander his various personal blessings and accoutrements upon her since she was not, as best as the widow Mrs. Askew had ever herself been able to determine, the sort to appreciate blessings and accoutrements and such like the widow Mrs. Askew left the doorway to have confirmed for her by Mrs. Dwight Mobley who she dialed up on the phone which was how come she did not personally witness the outset of the repercussions, which was how come she did not see for herself Miss Mary Alice Celestine Lefler step up back of Miss Bernice Fay Frazier in the doorway and tell, before she could even be presented and introduced, "Raymond!" to him with the hair and the moustache and the handful of catscruff who told to her softly, "Mary Alice," back while Miss Bernice Fay Frazier stood between them looking from him to her and from her to him and wondering even already how come the fingerends that had touched and laid upon most every man otherwise did not dart forth to light upon Raymond as well.

ii. "I got," he told it, "one word for you."

"I got for you," he told it, "three words."

"There's one thing alone," he proclaimed, "I want to say."

"I want to say to you," he insisted, "one thing alone."

And Nestor Tudor informed himself in the truck mirror, "Well hell," and endeavored to narrow his eyes that way he figured a man with violent passions might like served to send him over the center line and near about dispatch Mr. Wiley Gant to the everlasting, Mr. Wiley Gant who'd blown his horn and slowed his Pinto and was actively fearing annihilation when Nestor Tudor veered and swerved and managed only to spill a little loose and unheated asphalt on Mr. Wiley Gant's carroof. He couldn't decide how many words exactly Sansabelt was on account of it might have hyphens that would throw him and consequently he could not determine how best to announce to Tiny Aaron that Sansabelt was the lone item he wished to intone as introduction and preamble to what extravagant beating he was meaning to inflict like was hardly the variety of dilemma Nestor Tudor could hope to drive defensively and contemplate.

He'd left Harold Lister and Stumpy Tate out on a roadedge mending a crumbly shoulder, had spoken to them of an appointment he felt pressed to keep, or had intended anyhow to speak of it, had undertaken even to holler a thing out the cab before he dropped the truck into gear and struck out for the highway leaving Stumpy Tate to stand with his shovel and Harold Lister to stand with his steel rake and look from each other to the tailgate and back to each other again like they together persisted at in silence for so long as to render what Hey! they eventually harmonized about wholly inaudible to Nestor Tudor who was already around a bend in the road and gone. He was meaning to edify Tiny Aaron with an assortment of apt remarks, incisive apt remarks which he was planning to cultivate en route, remarks that is beyond the Sansabelt one, but Nestor Tudor was not in much mood truly to be apt and to be incisive and so chiefly just spewed in place of cultivating, chiefly just discharged into the truckcab whatever raw and unpolished observation came to mind like were most times merely vile and unsavory but were occasionally instructive after an anatomical sort of a fashion.

By the time he'd hit town proper and worked his way down the boulevard and off it past the Heavenly Rest, Nestor Tudor had achieved an outright lathery state and was expressing himself with pretty much inarticulate grumbly discharges alone which he vented a clutch of as he rolled up sufficiently snug to the curbing before Tiny Aaron's house so as to seem even a little bit parked there. He leapt from the cab with some measurable vigor and animation and paused on his way to the front steps only long enough to tuck his green twill shirt into his green twill trousers that he raised and elevated the waist of midway over his lowermost stomach roll which he took occasion to be briefly resolved to reduce prior to advancing up onto the porch proper and pounding the screenrail with the fleshy buttend of his fist. Tiny Aaron was, understandably, anxious to discover who precisely had come to dismantle his entranceway and so showed up ever so shortly opposite the screen from Nestor Tudor and conveyed to him a jolly greeting that culminated, as best as Nestor Tudor could tell, in a fullfledged and legitimate smirk which Nestor Tudor himself took for your purple horsehead shirt and dilapidated nosegay sort of a smirk but which was in fact a strain of smirk entirely otherwise.

Of course Nestor Tudor grew incited further and told straightoff to Tiny Aaron, "I got for you an item that I'm intending right now to say," and he added how it was three words that was one thing alone, or anyhow he meant to inform Tiny Aaron of the item he'd arrived to speak of and how many words precisely it was but found he could not engage in violent passions and talk with much suitable diction at the same time, so Tiny Aaron heard out Nestor Tudor and then pushed open the screen so as to step himself onto the porch and inquire, "What?" in a tone that Nestor Tudor could not hardly help but take for provocative coupled like it was with the smirk that Tiny Aaron had carried out from the house and into the open air.

Consequently, then, he went on ahead and hit him as there did not seem much use in debating the matter further. Nestor Tudor hollered a thing about the skyblue pants and his dead wife Erlene's generous soul but it all came out sounding pretty much like a dog chewing a sock, so Tiny Aaron did not hear from Nestor Tudor cause to anticipate the blow and did not in fact anticipate it but merely entertained it instead on the bony outcropping just behind his left ear. The cries and lamentations were immediate and altogether thoroughgoing, not just on the part of Tiny Aaron who had some noticeable cause to cry and lament but on the part of Nestor Tudor as well since Nestor Tudor had not been aiming for the bony outcropping truly and had been hoping instead to land his right hook on the unbony part of Tiny Aaron's face between his molars and his eyesocket. Nestor Tudor was not, however, much practiced at right hooking, had not in fact found cause to beat anybody senseless since back before he'd married Erlene his dead wife when he'd undertaken to pummel her least brother and had come to be himself beat senseless instead, so his experience was chiefly on the Tiny Aaron end of things like meant he was acquainted with how precisely to stoop and squat and hold to his beat places that way Tiny Aaron had seen fit himself to stoop and squat and hold in addition to exclaiming, "Shit Nestor!" in the variety of whiny voice beat people are most times prone to. For his part, Nestor Tudor did not find himself of a mood to exalt like he'd evermore suspected he might due chiefly to the fingers of his right hooking hand that had not hardly been made and manufactured to club bony outcroppings with and so had to be stooped about and squatted over and held a little themselves like prevented Nestor Tudor from poking his straight left flush against Tiny Aaron's noseholes, or was partly cause to stop him since Tiny Aaron's noseholes were not themselves just at the moment anywhere much they could get poked arriving like just lately they had in the general proximity of Tiny Aaron's kneecaps.

The fisticuffs, then, ceased for a time while Tiny Aaron stooped and held to his head and Nestor Tudor stooped and held to his fingers but the whiny plaintive moderately indecipherable talk persisted unchecked and Tiny Aaron made of Nestor Tudor wounded inquiries while Nestor Tudor intoned charges back, passably articulate charges about her with the hair and the lips and the fingerends and him with the madras jacket and the beltless trousers and the altogether monumental gall that Nestor Tudor spoke of at some considerable length with some appreciable passion and so grew all over again sufficiently incited to flail at Tiny Aaron who he caught with his straight left hand square upon the topnotch and so grew straightaway inclined to leap and holler and stoop and squat and whine another time and managed to induce in Tiny Aaron a similar disposition.

He'd been jolly, Tiny Aaron had. Just minutes prior to Nestor Tudor's arrival, he'd been inordinately jolly in fact due to how he'd enjoyed just lately an encounter, a scintillating encounter as best as he'd been able to tell at the moment when he'd had it and afterwards even once he'd set to reflecting and smirking both. And while it had been in fact a woman at the core of the thing, it hadn't been that particular woman with the hair and with the lips and with the fingerends, that particular woman Tiny Aaron had stepped out upon his porch and suffered blows to his head about, but had been instead a woman entirely otherwise with hair and with lips and with fingerends herself, a woman that seemed to know a manly sort of a fellow when she of a sudden came up on one. He'd traveled out to the bypass to dine at the Mr. Waffle as was his custom of a morning and had begun like usual with the pink grapefruit cocktail followed by a sticky bun that was itself prologue to the scrambled eggs and the sausage links and the orange fried potatoes and the silver dollar flapjacks on the side doused with maroon raspberry syrup that Tiny Aaron was most especially partial to. His Mr. Waffle coffeecup with the giddy pieface on it was, of course, bottomless so Tiny Aaron imbibed as much thirty-weight brew from the urn as his stomach lining could tolerate, more in fact than he could manage to purely defuse which meant he lingered over his plate sopping juices with a toastcrust and sipped his coffee and chatted with his waitress Marie back of the counter until his tracts and organs came to be quite full well saturated and of a sudden clenched on him so as to imply where he'd best just shortly perch.

Although not a man to usually pay much mind to portents, Tiny Aaron knew a grave omen when he came up on one and so pondered just ever so briefly his internal gastronomic twinge prior to leaving under his platerim his customary quarter and two dimes and departing fairly much at a trot from the restaurant. He did not believe he had before him the leisure to properly warm up his white Impala and so started the thing and dropped it into reverse in near about one motion alone and swung straightaway out from the lot and headed down the little piece of road towards the shopping center where he meant to take his usual imminent discharge shortcut between the Kroger and the Sears catalog showroom like would spill him out directly onto the bypass. Unfortunately, however, it happened that Mrs. MaySue Ludley was herself out and about in the late Mr. W. O. Ludley's gold New Yorker and had stopped briefly at the Hardees to pick up her customary chicken-fried steak biscuit that she was meaning to carry home directly before it grew more tepid even than it had started out. Now Mrs. MaySue Ludley was one to cut though the shopping center lot herself and pass between the Kroger and the Sears catalog showroom on her way to the bypass and as she entered at the southwest corner by the Fotomat Tiny Aaron turned in north of her and they advanced at pretty much identical velocities towards the far exit.

The trouble was, though, their conflicting styles of advancement chiefly. Tiny Aaron, being a lawful and responsible citizen of the community, took some heed of the white carlot lines and so did not drive wildly across the vacant spaces like he'd seen most especially some women drive wildly across them but proceeded instead in the direction of the arrow down a legitimate roadway that would presently bring him up alongside the Kroger. For her part, however, Mrs. MaySue Ludley traveled upon what appeared to be a purely southeasterly heading that sent her at a diagonal directly towards the Kroger–Sears showroom gap. She lurched and weaved every now and again to dodge lightpoles and shopping carts and your odd parked vehicle but she maintained pretty much her bead on the precise same stretch of asphalt Mr. Tiny Aaron was himself making towards at his habitual lubricated organ speed which was evermore something a little beyond stately. So they were closing fairly rapidly on each other but did not between them notice how a collision was perhaps in the offing partly on account of Tiny Aaron's astigmatism that prevented him from seeing sideways near so well as once he had and partly on account of Mrs. MaySue Ludley's general indifference to anybody who was not coming diagonally at her from the other direction. Consequently, Tiny Aaron closed on the Kroger as Mrs. MaySue Ludley closed on Tiny Aaron and had she not arrived at a Barracuda to swerve and accelerate around she would have likely bored flush in on the Impala headlamp to fender instead of slipping athwart it just beyond the chrome grillwork like Tiny Aaron found himself obliged to yelp and stomp his brake about and so could not help but jostle his tract and jostle his organs which were the last things on this earth he was looking just presently to jostle.

He blew his horn, leaned full well upon it as he loosed a spontaneous invective while, for her part, Mrs. MaySue Ludley merely proceeded in near about the proper driving lane to the bypass where she turned back towards town without so much as looking over her shoulder at Mr. Tiny Aaron who was by this time laying partly out the sidewindow apprising Mrs. MaySue Ludley of what particular deficiencies he'd had only lately cause to find her afflicted with. But laying out the sidewindow screaming just into the air did not somehow much soothe Tiny Aaron who guessed he might overtake the gold New Yorker, pull up alongside it, and be exceedingly profane and animated for the benefit of her who'd near about incited a grave mishap that Tiny Aaron wished to indicate he'd formulated an opinion about. So he sped and raced as responsibly as he was able out onto the bypass himself in pursuit of Mr. W. O. Ludley's gold New Yorker that was ahead of a Chevette ahead of him, a red indecisive Chevette that slowed and accelerated and made as if to turn but didn't turn and just generally aggravated Tiny Aaron further still and thereby induced in him a variety of heightened vehicular psychosis that came to be manifested in lengthsome bouts of hornblowing and oathmaking and some extravagant speeding up and some subsequent precipitous slowing down along with a variety of steering so thoroughly erratic as to be taken for lunatic.

So Mrs. MaySue Ludley hurried home her biscuit in Mr. W. O. Ludley's gold New Yorker while the red Chevette in back of her served exclusively to prompt Mr. Tiny Aaron into a fullfledged state which he managed to maintain the length of the bypass and on into town proper where the red Chevette came at last upon the very street it had been meaning all along to turn at and so did in fact turn and received from Tiny Aaron a fairly blistering sendoff that was part hornblowing coupled with an altogether manly and enthusiastic oath. Of course he accelerated straightaway and drew up snug behind the gold New Yorker from where he leered out through the windowglass and hoped to get taken for an imminent threat like he would have maybe gotten taken for one if Mrs. MaySue Ludley had been the sort to consult her mirror for purposes beyond rouge and eyeliner inspections. So she passed along the boulevard and he passed along the boulevard tight up back of her and turned when she turned and proceeded when she proceeded and followed her presently into her very own driveway where she caught at last sight of him once she looked to find out were her lips still ruby red pretty much all over.

He'd formulated an altogether ironic piece of talk, a cloying inquiry which he meant to air straightaway and which he meant to answer pretty shortly as well once he'd gotten done swaggering from his Impala door up to the front left gold New Yorker fender that he was intending to lay against with his arms crossed upon himself and thereby manufacture a mood and generate an effect. Unfortunately, however, Mrs. MaySue Ludley utterly undid Mr. Tiny Aaron's choreography when she flung open her door pretty directly into Mr. Tiny Aaron's inseam that the swaggering had left prominent and unprotected. Somehow Tiny Aaron found he could not managed to be anguished and irate both at the very same time precisely and so attended straightoff to his inseam to the detriment of his general irritation that waned and evaporated in the face of his discomfort, and he laid in fact against the front left fender but not with much pluck to speak of and told into the air an item that did not seem at all infested with irony.

Mrs. MaySue Ludley was quite understandably horrified at having flung open her door and beaten a man sharply upon the testicles with the edge of it and so leapt as best as she was able from Mr. W. O. Ludley's New Yorker and endeavored to attend to Tiny Aaron but did not know how precisely to attend to a man whose testicles she'd just lately flung open a door and beaten. Short of wailing and grabbing himself at the inseam, Tiny Aaron could not hardly figure how to attend to his injury either and so just laid against the fender watching Mrs. MaySue Ludley watch him and undertook to appear bluff and undertook to appear unafflicted and considered even a comment upon the quality of the morning air but did not wish to be taken for a contralto and so curbed the impulse quite completely. Not since the Nestor Tudor dinner party had Mrs. MaySue Ludley found occasion to entertain a gentleman, and she reached out and clutched Mr. Tiny Aaron by the very fingers he was struggling not to grab his inseam with so as to tell to him how she was in fact Mrs. MaySue Ludley and to seek to learn with a subsequent inquiring look who precisely he might be himself. Normally, of course, he was Tiny Aaron late of the manly disposition and he was considering even speaking to Mrs. MaySue Ludley of the eight-foot snake he'd annihilated when he grew shortly impressed with the notion of how he was likely this day the gentleman merely with the tract and with the organs instead, the tract and the organs that had previously come to be jostled once already prior to the dooredge-testicle collision when they'd clenched flatout on Tiny Aaron like he'd just lately discovered they'd clenched and so sought the words to disclose to Mrs. MaySue Ludley how he was chiefly the gentleman who'd traveled down the bypass and along the boulevard and steered into Mrs. MaySue Ludley's driveway back of her so as to bolt shortly into her house and light upon her toilet ring which he communicated chiefly with actual talk but communicated partly as well with a crop of sweatbeads upon his upper lip that Mrs. MaySue Ludley herself divined some meaning in.

He found, then, occasion to lift the fuzzy lid and hunker shortly down upon the seat that was fuzzy itself and he raised his voice in fairly clamorous praise to the variety of deity that people who've been saved from filling their trousers sometimes hunker down and raise their voices to like is part reverence and part distraction from the uproar otherwise. Mrs. MaySue Ludley kept matches from a hotel in her medicine cabinet where Mr. Tiny Aaron discovered them and shortly squandered pretty much an entire book, striking the matches and burning them down and pitching them at last into the bowl like pennies in a well all of which taken together served to alter the aroma so that it did not smell purely of evacuation and did not smell purely of conflagration but smelled chiefly instead like an outhouse afire. Meanwhile back in the kitchen, Mrs. MaySue Ludley was hoping to improve upon her good fortune by brewing a pot of coffee fresh and cutting her chicken-fried steak biscuit into quarters so as to make of it canapés for her and as well, she announced in the windowglass over the sink, for him, him that was being just presently noxious in the fullbath though Mrs. MaySue Ludley was exclusively mindful herself of just the swagger she'd noticed in the sidemirror and the feathery eagle she'd spied upon the forearm like seemed together potent and exotic to her.

Shortly Tiny Aaron emerged from the bathroom and arrived in the kitchen looking a little meek and sheepish and smelling a little charred and Mrs. MaySue Ludley ushered him towards the dinette where he got persuaded to sit and hear talk of the coffee he did not, he insisted, wish to drink and talk of the canapés he did not, he insisted, wish to eat but he came shortly to be made to drink and to be made to eat nonetheless by her who sat alongside him and endeavored to engage Tiny Aaron in a trifling and polite discourse that commenced with the beauty of the morning, proceeded on to the prospect of the weather ahead, and touched at last ever so briefly upon the circumstances of Mr. Tiny Aaron's own personal wife who Mrs. MaySue Ludley hoped at him with all her heart was not in fact stone cold dead.

"Never married," Tiny Aaron told to her and bit a canapé like masked for him the sound of Mrs. MaySue Ludley sucking air in a precipitous sort of way on account chiefly of her newfound delight.

"Couldn't find a woman to suit you, Mr. Aaron?" Mrs. MaySue Ludley inquired.

"Tiny," he insisted back and then grunted his profound approval of Mrs. MaySue Ludley's chicken-fried morsels like was, Mrs. MaySue Ludley let on, a fairly rapturous disclosure.

Tiny Aaron simply did not suppose he'd come up yet on the woman that could tame his sort which he was meaning to inform Mrs. MaySue Ludley about once he'd figured how to describe to her what sort precisely he was, but Mrs. MaySue Ludley announced it for him instead; Mrs. MaySue Ludley somehow just there at the dinette plumbed his depths and niches and informed Tiny Aaron how she did not suspect he'd yet met the woman that could tame him. She found him wild in his passions, found him fairly unbridled at heart and for his part Tiny Aaron, who guessed he knew when he'd been plumbed, went on ahead and confessed to Mrs. MaySue Ludley how there was not likely a tame and bridled thing about him.

"Tiny, why you're just a brute," Mrs. MaySue Ludley informed him sweetly. "Some things a woman knows," and she touched him lightly upon his feathery eagle tattoo, exceedingly lightly as if he were too altogether heated to linger with fingerends upon, and Tiny Aaron took up a second canapé and ate it at a bite.

They retired shortly to the dining room once Tiny Aaron had done in the remainder of the canapés and drained off even the dregs from the coffeepot, retired that is to the dining room so long as to visit with Mrs. MaySue Ludley's yellow bird Zippy who squawked and whistled and thrashed and dripped and bit at Tiny Aaron's extended finger with what Mrs. MaySue Ludley could not help but take for native affection. In the parlor they sat together on the sofa and, to Mrs. MaySue Ludley's profound delight, Tiny Aaron did not show a disposition to crowd the bolster once she'd begun to slide along the cushions towards him. Instead he hung firm where he'd ended up and laid even his arm along the sofaback like Mrs. MaySue Ludley construed for a species of embrace and so did not travel so far truly as Mr. Tiny Aaron's actual lap but came to rest just shy of his near thigh and endeavored with a tender expression to suggest to Tiny Aaron just how pleased she was to be there.

He admired what place she had and commented upon her dainty knickknacks and froufrous but explained how wild and unbridled sorts like himself were not usually the knickknack and froufrou type. "Nope," Tiny Aaron told to Mrs. MaySue Ludley and flexed and snorted and winked even too and thereby emboldened her to touch lightly his bony kneejoint and confess how her dead husband W.O. had been pretty much a brute himself and so had taught her a thing about men with passions.

"Did he now?" Tiny Aaron inquired as he worked his wiry arm muscles so as to animate his eagle.

"He did," Mrs. MaySue Ludley insisted with pretty much her breath alone and then listened at Tiny Aaron draw a spit dollop through his front toothgap.

She wondered might Tiny Aaron see fit to excuse her for the merest moment that Tiny Aaron supposed he might and then aided Mrs. MaySue Ludley in her attempt to stand by pushing against her backside like Mrs. Ludley found unforeseen but altogether invigorating as well, and she looked back behind herself as she departed so as to tell to Tiny Aaron, "Don't you slip off," that Tiny Aaron had a snort for and so snorted it.

He wandered a little roundabout in her absence, took up Mr. W. O. Ludley off the mantelpiece and studied how his pants rode up and how his hair laid back and looked to discover a wild and unbridled thing about him but could not truly discover one and consequently returned him where he'd come from and snatched up a dainty figurine instead that did not hardly hold much appeal for Tiny Aaron who intimated with his spit and his toothgap together his general disdain prior to passing along the wall to Mrs. MaySue Ludley's giltframed oval mirror that struck him as a far more intriguing item. He examined his swarthy features, turned and shifted so as to bathe them in a suitable light, and he pondered himself in profile for a time while he wondered how he might possibly look had he a chest that bulged and rippled. By the time Mrs. MaySue Ludley returned to join him, Tiny Aaron had embarked before the oval mirror upon a fullfledged nosehair expedition that Mrs. MaySue Ludley punctuated once she'd stepped out from the backhall and told softly, "Tiny," to him.

Of course he wheeled round that way wild and unbridled men are prone to and he was about to manufacture for Mrs. MaySue Ludley a fairly extravagant explanation as to why precisely he'd probably appeared to her to have his fingers just lately in an unseemly place when he caught full sight of her and so left off meaning even to talk. She'd changed out from her skirt and her blue blouse into a manner of relatively slinky dress, a dress anyhow with as much slink to it as Mrs. MaySue Ludley's shape could tolerate which was not in fact abundant slink truly but was inordinately more slink than her skirt and her blouse had managed, and she'd repowdered and rerouged and relipsticked herself pretty thoroughly in addition to what pool of scent she smelled to have dropped down and wallowed for a time in. Tiny Aaron could not of course manage an explanation and be bedazzled all at once and together and so he merely stood in silence and contemplated Mrs. MaySue Ludley's transformation, regarded how she'd come to get just lately more womanly even than she'd started out, and presently he undertook to advise her of his thoroughgoing approval, whistled that is and informed Mrs. MaySue Ludley, "Well shit," like was just the variety of observation to cause her blood to surge and rush and her parts most all over to tingle and she told to Tiny Aaron one time further, "Tiny," prior to displaying her red teeth for him.

He joined her directly at the sofa where his eyes did not sting him but a brief while and he laid another time his arm upon the sofaback that Mrs. MaySue Ludley construed again for an embrace and so loitered as best as she was able in the passion of it. They spoke of how lovely she'd come to look, or Tiny Aaron anyhow spoke of how lovely she'd come to look and did not get kept from it by Mrs. MaySue Ludley who was far too busy loitering to dispute him. Once they'd together fallen silent a time, Mrs. MaySue Ludley communicated to Tiny Aaron by way of her thoughts and urges and unspoken impulses alone and then shortly informed him how she'd just lately communicated with him and apprised him of what of her faculties precisely she'd communicated with like served as prologue to a piece of talk on how it seemed to her some people could, with just thoughts and urges and impulses, speak to each other, particular people who had come some way to get driven together by your forces and such.

"There's mysteries in this life, Tiny Aaron," Mrs. MaySue Ludley insisted, and she wondered could he tell her how come he'd selected her toilet to light upon out of all the toilets roundabout like conjured up for Tiny Aaron the diagonal lot driving which he did not deign to speak of and informed Mrs. MaySue Ludley instead, "When a man gets the call, he answers it," which Mrs. MaySue Ludley intimated with just one upraised finger by itself was not the case precisely.

"Forces," she told to him, and once she'd allowed herself the leisure to fairly bathe Tiny Aaron with a meaningful look she told to him as well, "Kismet," and drew up snug to gaze on him further still.

And Tiny Aaron, who figured he was a man of rash passions anyhow, almost straightaway informed Mrs. MaySue Ludley, "Well all right," and bent towards her sufficiently to press his lips ever so briefly to her forehead prior to drawing back so far as to get himself gazed upon further still by Mrs. MaySue Ludley who suggested to Tiny Aaron, "Kismet again."

Of course such a display of tempestuous emotions left most especially Mrs. MaySue Ludley palpably ravished and she exhaled and fairly wilted against Tiny Aaron where she laid in breathy silence until she found herself obliged to sweetly inform him, "I knew. You knew too. From the very instant you stepped out from your car and laid against my fender well, we both knew, didn't we?"

And Tiny Aaron, who was trying to recollect just what precisely he might have laid against her fender well and known told to Mrs. MaySue Ludley back, "We did?" that Mrs. MaySue Ludley confirmed for him with just her thoughts and urges and unspoken impulses alone and then tugged at her slinky dressend and resituated her entire person in the pit of Tiny Aaron's arm and thereby dispatched and wafted her scent in such a concentration as to momentarily blind Tiny Aaron who grew choked and teary and so appeared to Mrs. MaySue Ludley full well transported by the passions of the moment which suggested to her how she might best with her fingers squeeze Tiny Aaron's near kneejoint and so communicate further still like she did squeeze and like she did communicate though mostly she just pinched Tiny Aaron on what nerve precisely caused him to start up off the sofa and stand for a time before it.

There was scant talk further of forces and fate and your manner of things that get driven together and your manner of things that get driven apart but mostly Tiny Aaron just sat with his arm extended along the sofaback and suffered himself to be gazed upon by Mrs. MaySue Ludley who was endeavoring in fact to be chatty in a wordless sort of a way but got taken instead merely for wonderstruck at the sight and proximity of Tiny Aaron who, ever since his eight-foot snake, had begun to figure himself worth getting wonderstruck about. And those moments when his eyes were dry and temporarily unbeleaguered by the wafting scent, Tiny Aaron gazed upon Mrs. MaySue Ludley a little back and saw somewhat of the ribbons and the locks and the curls and the high powdered forehead and the sparkly eyelids and the rouged cheeks and the shiny red lips but saw chiefly just himself instead construed for manly and construed for bold and reflected in Mrs. MaySue Ludley's adoring face after a fashion he did not suppose he could ever hope to stand before a mirrorglass and see. Miss Mary Alice Celestine Lefler who'd touched first his eagle had seemed on her own a little stirred by him but not hardly to the extent Mrs. MaySue Ludley appeared to him stirred herself, appeared to him altogether fraught with adulation like he did not even know he'd been hoping for a woman to be until he discovered snug up against his armpit a woman who was already.

So she gazed upon him to admire his bold and his manly aspects and he gazed upon her to admire his bold and his manly aspects as well, and as she became moved and worked up he became moved and worked up himself and entertained from Mrs. MaySue Ludley a declaration of her affection for him and aired shortly on his own a declaration of his affection for him too which she bent and shaped to suit herself like Tiny Aaron did not much care if she did. So they fell both pretty precipitously in love with precisely the same individual exactly and sat together on the sofa quite thoroughly taken with him and communicated somewhat by way of thoughts and urges but spoke outright every now and again and managed even to make with each other an engagement for the following evening when Tiny Aaron supposed he could wear his madras jacket and his gold striped tie and most especially his skyblue Sansabelt trousers that had rendered him so extraordinarily becoming just the night previous when he'd squandered his splendor in catfetching. And naturally she did not wish him to scurry off but allowed him to scurry off nonetheless, allowed him anyhow to scurry off once she'd followed him out to his Impala and stood by the doorwell to tell him, "Until the morrow," and tell him, "Sugar," back of it like was so considerably more breath than volume that Tiny Aaron could not even be sure he heard it but only suspected maybe he had which got fairly completely confirmed for him by what lips shortly bumped against his lips and scented and stained them.

So he'd cultivated a smirk, figured he'd found cause to cultivate one and the mere recollection of her face as she gazed upon his incited Tiny

Aaron's lipends to turn up all by themselves in a smirky sort of a fashion like was not much trouble to refine truly. So he'd cultivated a smirk by the time he'd arrived home and employed it a spell in his bedroom where he'd laid out upon the spread his madras jacket and his skyblue Sansabelt trousers and his white shortsleeve shirt and his gold striped tie that appeared to him an altogether smashing array without even the benefit of his own personal form to fill and animate it. In fact, he'd after a fashion cultivated his smirk so completely that he could not even begin to get shed of it and so answered the doorknock with his smirk full upon him and heard vaguely from Nestor Tudor of the three things that was one word he intended to say like got followed shortly by the blow to Tiny Aaron's bony outcropping which came soon enough to be complimented by a sharp left to the topnotch. It was all certainly more than a bluff manly sort of a fellow could begin to endure unanswered, so Tiny Aaron reared up as best as he was able and embarked upon a right cross of his own that managed somehow to bypass Nestor Tudor entirely and collide instead with the wooden porch stanchion alongside the steps that was decidedly stouter even than a bony outcropping and so prompted from Tiny Aaron an altogether elaborate display of pure and unmitigated anguishment that was part leaping and was part squatting and was part wailing and moaning too.

Nestor Tudor retaliated to the right cross with a manner of left that had scant traces of jab and hook both to it but was in its essence an uppercut, not a species of uppercut with much prospect of success, due to how it was primarily an utterly vertical sort of an uppercut, but an uppercut nonetheless with sufficient force and velocity to it to strain and near about dislocate Nestor Tudor's shouldersocket once he'd missed Tiny Aaron's chin and proceeded on towards the porch ceiling. Tiny Aaron, in the wake of his errant right, unleashed shortly a moderately savage left of his own that was intended to reduce Nestor Tudor's nose to a pulpy mass but landed instead fairly flush upon Nestor Tudor's collarbone which did not straightoff strike Tiny Aaron as any measurable improvement over the porch stanchion. He was, then, pained and afflicted at eight of his ten knuckles all at the same time and was contemplating a further display of his pure and unmitigated anguishment when Nestor Tudor, whose own right hand had pretty fully recovered from the outcropping, attempted a vicious blow to Tiny Aaron's midsection like was intended to reduce him to breathlessness and did even reduce him to it though the blow itself failed to arrive at the midsection precisely and landed instead full upon the very inseam Tiny Aaron had only lately suffered a dooredge to beat. His sense of affliction was, understandably, immediate and altogether acute and he labored to breathe and labored to stand upright and failed pretty completely at the both of them like left him to stoop and wheeze and provided Nestor Tudor the opportunity to instruct and edify Tiny Aaron on the topic of her with the hair and with the lips and with the fingerends but Nestor Tudor could not work up much extraneous breath himself and so mainly just sustained life as best as he was able and hoped he might speak shortly.

So they together stooped and bent and wheezed atop the porch planking and Tiny Aaron, who was hardly so soft and misshapen as Nestor Tudor himself had managed to get, rallied his various faculties and functions sufficiently to apprise Nestor Tudor of what variety of asshole he'd come just lately to be like was thoroughgoing chiefly, was quite wholly undiluted as best as Tiny Aaron could tell from there atop the porch planking with one hand full of genitalia. Of course, Nestor Tudor was of a mind that if either of them was a thoroughgoing and quite wholly undiluted asshole it was surely Tiny Aaron who had slunk in low in the grass like a snake to poach and pilfer Nestor Tudor's woman that Tiny Aaron denied and disputed outright and then informed Nestor Tudor how he'd not himself slunk anywhere ever, didn't have cause to slink since he feared no man's wrath which he temporarily let loose of his testicles and stood pretty much upright to intone.

Straightaway Nestor Tudor communicated to Tiny Aaron back that he in fact slunk and that he was undeniably a thoroughgoing and quite wholly undiluted asshole which Tiny Aaron begged to differ about and informed Nestor Tudor how he was himself altogether full of palpable horseshit that Nestor Tudor took as an invitation to a right cross and so endeavored to throw one but faltered in the execution and struck Tiny Aaron obliquely upon the boniest part of his elbow like provided both him and Nestor Tudor the variety of sensation that left them together undisposed to speak further for a time.

His faculties and functions being what they were, Tiny Aaron told shortly to Nestor Tudor, "Shithead," before Nestor Tudor could discover the wind to tell to Tiny Aaron, "Son of a bitch," himself and to speak again of her with the hair and the lips and the fingerends that Nestor Tudor had laid claim to and that Tiny Aaron had known already Nestor Tudor had laid claim to before he'd slunk in like he did which Tiny Aaron went on ahead and denied again on the grounds this time that he had himself another woman like interrupted Nestor Tudor right in the middle of reviling Tiny Aaron further still.

"What woman's that?" Nestor Tudor wanted to know in a tone of voice fairly saturated with skepticism.

"Just a woman I know," Tiny Aaron told to him.

And Nestor Tudor insisted, "You don't know any women that'd have you. I don't even know any women that'd have you and I know a whole pack of women."

And Tiny Aaron expressed shortly the opinion that he did not believe Nestor Tudor knew in fact squat like would, he implied, include a whole pack of women.

"Who?" Nestor Tudor demanded of Tiny Aaron who still did not tell to him who precisely but revealed instead to Nestor Tudor how his woman saw him for bluff and for manly like left Nestor Tudor to conclude that Tiny Aaron had come up on somebody's blind idiot child which Tiny Aaron could not hardly begin to endure and tolerate and so straightoff cocked his right hand and slugged the ballister with it though the ballister had not hardly been the item he was hoping to slug.

"Who?" Nestor Tudor inquired one time further while Tiny Aaron hunkered low, held to his knuckes, and whined in a relatively bluff and manly sort of a way.

"Ain't hardly your business now is it," Tiny Aaron told to Nestor Tudor once he'd grown sufficiently unhunkered to tell it.

"Shit," Nestor Tudor said back, fairly disgusted. "Not a woman in this world but her. Get caught slinking and won't even own up to it, and wearing my pants. You are one lowly creature." And he contemplated a straight left hand and then a right that he guessed he might hook round wide and he'd even come to be a little drawn back and set for the left when Tiny Aaron told to him, "MaySue Ludley. You happy?"

Understandably, Nestor Tudor grew punctuated in his intentions straightoff, grew in fact fairly punctuated most every way possible and just stood a time before Tiny Aaron ventilating the inside of his mouth like Tiny Aaron took as occasion for him to explain about the Mr. Waffle and the subsequent organ and tract dilemma like led itself to the racing through the lot and the near miss with Mrs. MaySue Ludley coming crossways in her gold New Yorker. Of course the irate pursuit could not help but ensue; Tiny Aaron informed chiefly Nestor Tudor's bridgework and Nestor Tudor's gold teeth and Nestor Tudor's steely gray fillings how he could not discover at the time much alternative to irate pursuit and so set out behind her and followed her clear home where he was meaning to be ill after a peevish and relatively incensed sort of fashion but got ill instead in a purely digestive way like carried him on into the house and onto the toilet ring. He spoke of the coffee and the canapés as well as Mrs. MaySue Ludley's yellow bird Zippy that had seemed to him purely a winged delight, and he told to Nestor Tudor how Mrs. MaySue Ludley had settled him upon the settee prior to retiring to her bedroom for a change of outfit and returning shortly altogether ravishing.

"Ravishing," Nestor Tudor managed to shut his mouth briefly and say.

"Like a vision," Tiny Aaron told to him and thereby prompted Nestor Tudor to a sickly expression. "And right from the start we had a kind of a thing between us, right from the very outset."

"A thing," Nestor Tudor shut his mouth once further and managed to intone.

"You know how it is with people sometimes that don't hardly even have to talk to speak."

And Nestor Tudor admitted that he'd heard tell of it.

"That's me," Tiny Aaron informed him. "That's MaySue," which Nestor Tudor could work up just a meek and paltry sort of a noise about.

"I'll tell you a thing, Nestor," Tiny Aaron said and sucked a spit dollop as he made to seem wise and worldly and so commenced to grow, as best as Nestor Tudor could tell, pretty completely intolerable, "there's mysteries in this life, forces that drive folks together, drive folks apart. Seemed to me like just diarrhea at the outset but I guess the hand of God was in it all along. Her," he said, "MaySue. Nobody otherwise."

Nestor Tudor was ever so briefly too stunned to convey to Tiny Aaron his personal blessing and best possible wishes like Tiny Aaron was anticipating he might but he did not persevere at being too stunned for long as he felt shortly stirred by an obligation and a sober responsibility and so told to Tiny Aaron, "Great Christ Almighty!" which was not itself precisely the variety of blessing Tiny Aaron had anticipated. "What in this world is wrong with you?" Nestor Tudor wanted to know and as he paused to draw breath Tiny Aaron undertook to inform him how there were in fact mysteries and forces and such to this life that worked every now and again their magic on a fellow.

"Shut up," Nestor Tudor suggested to him, but Tiny Aaron was not remotely of a mood to shut up and endeavored to explain to Nestor Tudor, who he did not suppose had encountered your mysteries and forces and such before, how Mrs. MaySue Ludley with her hair ribbon and her sparkly eyeshade and her pink cheeks and her red lips and teeth and her thoroughly overwhelming treacly scent had come to pluck upon the strings of his very heart which called for talk further of mysteries and forces and the like that Nestor Tudor could not somehow help but interrupt with a straight left hand and a sharp right cross both together that he told to Tiny Aaron was purely for his own good once Tiny

Aaron had opened his eyes and raised up off the decking onto his elbows so as to inquire who precisely Nestor Tudor might be.

"Good God, Tiny," Nestor Tudor told to him, "you got no need for her."

And Tiny Aaron wanted to know, "Who?"

"Her. MaySue. Christ," Nestor Tudor said back. "She'll chase down anything comes her way."

"MaySue?" Tiny Aaron wanted to know.

And Nestor Tudor confirmed for him, "Yes, Tiny. MaySue," like gave to Tiny Aaron pause there atop the decking upon his elbows where he took time to work what jaw muscle had lately received a blow and to consider the nature of the conversation he'd come to be engaged in which prompted him to inform Nestor Tudor, "You know you're speaking of the woman I love," like straightaway hardened Nestor Tudor to the prospect of purely whaling the shit out of Tiny Aaron for Tiny Aaron's own personal benefit.

"First thing it's Mary Alice Celestine Lefler," Tiny Aaron said as he undertook to climb upright, "and now it's MaySue Ludley too. You looking a harem?"

"Get up," Nestor Tudor told to him and worked his fists before himself after such a fashion as to insinuate what precisely he was instructing Tiny Aaron to get up for.

"You can't have all of them, Nestor," Tiny Aaron said. "You can't probably even have any of them. Lurking in the bushes with a bouquet and that godawful purple shirt and here you're telling me about women. What do you know about them?"

"I've been with MaySue, buddy. I've seen for myself what she's like."

And once he'd risen pretty much to his full height Tiny Aaron worked his own fists as he reminded Nestor Tudor, "You're speaking of the woman I love."

"Idiot," Nestor Tudor told to him.

"Me? I haven't been in the shrubbery lately now have I?"

And Nestor Tudor jabbed with his left hand and caught Tiny Aaron slightly upon the breastbone that Tiny Aaron told to him, "Ha!" about and then danced and shuffled and circled around with as much grace and agility as a man of his mature years could muster which was not truly hardly any grace and agility at all.

"She's a princess," Tiny Aaron told to Nestor Tudor once he'd worked up the breath to tell it. "'She plucks upon the strings of my heart."

"How in the world did you get to be such a sap?" Nestor Tudor wanted to know as he drew back and cocked his potent right hand. "You'll thank me for this one day."

And Tiny Aaron, who had a right hand of his own, aimed it at the porchrail and consequently hit Nestor Tudor flush on the face instead like induced Nestor Tudor to weave and wobble and to sit at last, together with his potent right hand, down upon the porch decking where Tiny Aaron stepped up to loom above him and to tell to Nestor Tudor, "Thank you."

Once Nestor Tudor had managed to rise up to his feet, the engagement began in earnest and him and Tiny Aaron endeavored to beat each other senseless on account of two completely different women altogether but could not strike any clean blows and so at last fell into a clench and wrestled for a time upright before Tiny Aaron tripped Nestor Tudor and Nestor Tudor tripped Tiny Aaron back like sent the both of them sprawling onto the decking where they wrestled further still. On account of his superior bulk and general poundage, Nestor Tudor enjoyed a palpable advantage over Tiny Aaron like meant he sat upon him and undertook to crush and grind various of Tiny Aaron's parts and pieces into the wood floor. Tiny Aaron chiefly squirmed and swore and managed to find a way to slug Nestor Tudor in his own inseam one time as he'd learned already what a slug in the inseam could do, so Tiny Aaron got to sit high and crush and grind at Nestor Tudor for a spell until Nestor Tudor managed to throw him back over and, by mashing parts and tugging parts and plain beating the parts he couldn't see fit to mash or tug, endeavored to alter Tiny Aaron's opinion of Mrs. MaySue Ludley entirely and undertook to encourage Tiny Aaron to recite for him his altered opinion in a deep robust tone. As an alternative, however, Tiny Aaron recited in a deep robust tone his own personal estimation of Nestor Tudor which was chiefly quite thoroughly unflattering except for those portions that were only acutely unbecoming instead and, as a consequence, Nestor Tudor hunted up and shortly discovered a new and unafflicted piece of Tiny Aaron to mash and crush and grind and just generally afflict.

So they were the both of them pretty much preoccupied and engaged with the combat at hand and the attendant profanity, most especially Tiny Aaron that was suffering his various parts to be distressed and so had cause to be attendantly profane, and consequently they did not between them see Mr. Dick Atwater approaching from down the road and, since they were back of the pickets on the porch decking themselves, Mr. Dick Atwater did not straightoff see them either, did not in fact see them even presently until Tiny Aaron took upon himself the task of describing to Nestor Tudor just what variety of shithead he was precisely like proved to be an altogether exotic and thoroughgoing variety of shithead that Tiny Aaron spoke of with appreciable zeal and considerable volume, volume enough anyway to capture Mr. Dick Atwater's attention and suggest to him that Tiny Aaron had come somehow to be engaged and entangled on his porch with a fairly unsavory sort of a creature. Of course, quite shortly Dick Atwater's thoroughgoing and unforeseen good luck came to be revealed to him as he gained Tiny Aaron's sidesteps and spied at last Tiny Aaron who he was meaning to annihilate and generally dismember and spied atop him Nestor Tudor who he was meaning to beat and bludgeon with one of Tiny Aaron's dismembered parts. Fortune was surely smirking down upon him, and once he'd arrived atop the porch decking proper he paused only long enough to announce the variety of carnage he was meaning to wreak and to make a sort of a murky and incomprehensible reference to what consummating gland he'd been lately himself in proximity to with his own personal consummating organ, and then he removed his lacquered straw fedora and fairly flung himself hairpart foremost into the fray wailing like a banshee as he sailed and traveled, or intending anyhow to wail like a banshee though he lacked truly the wind for it and so wailed instead like a goat might if a goat found himself disposed to wail.

As Dick Atwater joined the fracas he directly dislodged Nestor Tudor who tumbled off of Tiny Aaron onto the decking and so provided Tiny Aaron the occasion to scramble atop him and crush and grind at Nestor Tudor a spell further, crush and grind that is until Dick Atwater resituated his hairpart and flung himself one time more full upon Tiny Aaron who he knocked over and flailed at for as long as it took Nestor Tudor to reach out with four of his fingers and one of his thumbs and close them around a clump of upswept hair that he yanked like a toilet chain and so induced straightoff from Dick Atwater a sort of a discharge that was in fact fairly completely bansheeish. Nestor Tudor, who took Dick Atwater for just precisely the variety of shithead that Tiny Aaron had lately taken Nestor Tudor for, explained to Dick Atwater his assorted exotic and thoroughgoing qualities and tugged for emphasis on the hairclump that Dick Atwater could not hardly help but object about and so objected about it and troubled himself as well to explain to Nestor Tudor how if he would be patient for a time he would presently beat him to a pulpy mass. Tiny Aaron, in the meanwhile, had regained his orientation and had fairly much caught his wind and had as well resolved to render Nestor Tudor thoroughly indisposed before he troubled himself with Dick Atwater, so when at last he leapt and lunged it was Nestor Tudor alone he leapt and lunged at though, on account of his grip, Nestor Tudor carried with him a goodly plug of Dick Atwater's upswept hair as he pitched over and suffered himself to be sat upon. For his part, Dick Atwater held briefly to his naked patch and wailed further still before priming himself to rejoin the fracas with Tiny Aaron as his objective since he had the parts and pieces to tear asunder before he could even hope to bludgeon with much good effect. So Dick Atwater grappled shortly with Tiny Aaron who grappled with Nestor Tudor who reached out his thumb and fingers together and found with them an additional hairclump that he tugged and yanked and drew on with sufficient force and enthusiasm to purely enrage Dick Atwater who rared back and slugged Tiny Aaron who himself grew inspired to find Nestor Tudor's inseam and beat it.

This was not, then, hardly a defensive encounter and each of the three of them endured pretty much the sort of drubbing they were simultaneously inflicting, so there was victory and there was defeat all at the same time together for everybody. Of course, there was considerable invective as well, a regular festival of profanation that a light southerly breeze served to carry off from the porch and across the road to where the widow Mrs. Boatwright was tending to her potted begonias that had begun to look to her fairly wispy and forlorn. Being a fine Christian woman, she straightaway came to be punctuated and drawn up by the spate of unseemly talk she detected on the air, and she squinted out across the road in an effort to discover the source of it though she suspected even before she squinted that Tiny Aaron was the source of it himself as he'd appeared to her moderately unbalanced ever since his recent explosion. She figured seepy gas had served to derange him and caught up her breath to see could she hear him rant further which she grew shortly satisfied about once the breeze had carried to her an enraged goat sort of a discharge. And the widow Mrs. Boatwright humphed once and guessed how she wouldn't herself have gas ever, and then she turned back to her potted begonias and wondered why they'd come to be wispy and wondered why they'd come to be forlorn.

Across the road on the porch decking Dick Atwater was purely getting the worst of it from Nestor Tudor who was threatening to snatch him bald and had already fairly much undone for good his lowslung hairpart which had depended most especially upon the particular clump that had come just lately to lay on the floor beside him. Next to Dick Atwater, Nestor Tudor was suffering pretty acutely as well on account of the ministrations of Tiny Aaron who was pounding Nestor Tudor's inseam with inexhaustible zeal and fervor while he himself was not truly much afflicted at all due to how Dick Atwater had not ever found cause to dismember and annihilate anybody previously and so could not quite determine how to go about it like left him to beat a little at Tiny Aaron and pull a little at Tiny Aaron and beat a little at Tiny Aaron further still when he did not find himself disposed to observe the passing of his hair with cries and lamentations instead. Needless to say, Nestor Tudor had a thing to tell to Dick Atwater about Miss Mary Alice Celestine Lefler and what sort of man it appeared to him she required that was not hardly Dick Atwater at all, and Dick Atwater had a thing to tell to Tiny Aaron about interlopers and what gruesome variety of fate they most usually met with while Tiny Aaron spoke further to Nestor Tudor of MaySue who he'd come already to decide he cherished and adored since she quite plainly was set to cherish and adore him back.

And Dick Atwater broke off his threats and ceased for the moment his cries and his lamentations so as to inquire of Tiny Aaron, "Who's MaySue?" since he'd alone of the three of them not come yet to be cherished and adored by her.

"Ah," said Tiny Aaron who'd left off pounding the inseam to say it, "MaySue." And he told how she was sweet and comely like the flowers of the field and ever so gentle like a balmy breath of air that stirred the leaves which was together more than Nestor Tudor could bring himself to endure and so he left off yanking at Dick Awater's hairclumps long enough to pummel Tiny Aaron about his upper torso for a spell that Tiny Aaron was far too transported by romance to even care about.

"She'll chase most anything with a dangly organ," Nestor Tudor said and let on how that included even such as Tiny Aaron.

And Dick Atwater inquired of him, "MaySue?"

"Yeah," Nestor Tudor told him back, "Her," which served pretty much to revive Tiny Aaron out from his poetical state and he informed Nestor Tudor how he was speaking of the woman Tiny Aaron had just lately declared he adored and cherished and he suggested to Nestor Tudor that he'd best prepare to defend his honor which meant in this particular case his inseam chiefly that Nestor Tudor endeavored to cover and Tiny Aaron endeavored to beat.

Dick Atwater, who'd been figuring on two rivals to pummel and annihilate, failed to recommence straightoff with the dismemberment of Tiny Aaron and instead inquired would Tiny Aaron please briefly confirm for him what woman it was he cherished and adored that Tiny Aaron was ever so delighted to oblige him in and so provided Nestor Tudor respite from his testicle distress as he spoke once further of his MaySue who was sweet and comely like the flowers afield and gentle as a balmy breath of air in the treetops that Dick Atwater considered for a moment in silence prior to wondering would Tiny Aaron tell to him please what precisely all that catchasing the night previous had been about.

And Tiny Aaron said to Dick Atwater, "B.M.," and watched Dick Atwater undertake to appear informed and apprised that presently he failed at and so heard from Tiny Aaron, "Before MaySue," which Dick Atwater grew genuinely illuminated in the wake of and he induced Tiny Aaron to swear an oath that he had no personal designs upon Miss Mary Alice Celestine Lefler now that he'd laid claim to her of the field and the treetops which was just precisely the sort of oath Tiny Aaron was pleased to swear with passion and resolve and so heard from Dick Atwater how he guessed he wouldn't annihilate and dismember Tiny Aaron after all that Tiny Aaron took as a welcome revelation.

So they forged between them a union and turned together on Nestor Tudor so as to beat the pure and unadulterated shit out of him that Dick Atwater and Tiny Aaron harmoniously proclaimed to be their purpose, beat the pure and unadulterated shit out of him on account of one woman he'd managed to escape and another woman he could not somehow begin even to catch and consequently had no cause truly to get the shit beat out of him about which he was fairly well prepared to share with Dick Atwater and Tiny Aaron both when they set together upon him and flailed pretty heartily at his assorted parts and pieces. Naturally Dick Atwater and Tiny Aaron were together of the opinion that Nestor Tudor was chiefly a devious and meddling son of a bitch who had sought to come between them and their women while Nestor Tudor himself advanced once more his personal theory that Tiny Aaron was a fullblown and multifaceted shithead and Dick Atwater was undoubtedly a fullblown and multifaceted shithead with him that Tiny Aaron and Dick Atwater felt obliged to object most stridently about and so screeched again their harmonious opinion of Nestor Tudor who wailed simultaneously his own singular opinion back which culminated in the variety of widespread and indiscriminate profanity that a good Christian woman like Mrs. Boatwright across the road could not hardly begin to ignore.

She did not even trouble herself to set down her watering can half full from the spigot with the Miracle-Gro mixed and diluted in it but carried the thing out to the front walk where she undertook to flag down a brown Capri and screeched and wailed at a blueblack Lincoln sedan without stopping the first or even slowing the second like left her to advance upon Tiny Aaron's front porch on her own as the slick bluegreen concoction slopped out from the tophole and splashed on her feet. She climbed the steps and stood even a time fairly much alongside where Tiny Aaron and Nestor Tudor and Dick Atwater moiled and rolled and profanated without discovering how they'd been lately joined and by whom, and she heard talk of MaySue of the fields and the treetops and Mary Alice of the lips and the fingerends in addition to the attendant claims and the counterclaims and the outright denials, and she watched the beating and she watched the pummeling and tolerated the invective until the widow Mrs. Boatwright, who was a woman herself and so guessed she was acquainted with a thing or two about women, upended her galvanized can overtop of Tiny Aaron and Dick Atwater and Nestor Tudor and thereby fairly bathed them in liquid fertilizer like served as preface to an opinion of her own, stilled and punctuated all three men together who heard shortly from the widow Mrs. Boatwright, "Fools!" that had to it some ire and had to it some disdain and had to it some palpable pity as well.

And they all of them lay back on the decking and sputtered and blew from the chill and the wet and the bluegreen stink and protested to the widow Mrs. Boatwright in a feeble sort of way with some measurable whine to it like incited her further still and so she disclosed to Tiny Aaron and to Dick Atwater and to Nestor Tudor too how her Jack Boatwright was a better man dead and in the ground than the three of them still breathing. "Look at yourselves," she told to them. "Shameful," and she puckered and scrunched and squinted and thereby embellished her thoroughgoing disapproval that Tiny Aaron whined further about and that Dick Atwater whined further about with him while Nestor Tudor merely lay upon the decking eyeing the slat ceiling overhead and casting back to when he'd himself been a better man too before the nosegay and the sidelong glancing and the low whispery talk along with the incessant fretfulness as well like had impressed him, all joined and combined, as love maybe and abiding affection until now that he'd been doused and instructed when he found himself growing somehow unimpressed instead. He climbed to his feet, Nestor Tudor did, and wrung himself out as best he was able prior to stepping past the widow Mrs. Boatwright and down the steps and along the walk and out to the truck and he drew off from the curb and swung through town and out from it while he watched the road some and while he watched himself in the mirror some as well, and as he rounded the bend to where he'd come from in the first place he found Stumpy Tate and Harold Lister engaged ever so earnestly in tossing gravel at a roadsign, Stumpy Tate and Harold Lister who watched Nestor Tudor ease the truck off the roadedge and studied him as he climbed from the cab thereby exhibiting his welts and contusions and his soppy blue shirtfront that they both together observed and took in in silence on the shoulder until Stumpy Tate found himself inclined to speak and so stepped up to Nestor Tudor and told to him, "For Christsakes, my Nabs was on the dash," like touched off Harold Lister who told to Nestor Tudor, "Mine too."

iii.

SHE'D seen on his finger the streak of white, had not seen it straightaway what with the grace and the charm and the princely demeanor to distract her, but she'd presently seen on his finger the streak that he'd cultivated a habit of reaching up across his palm with his thumbend and touching though Miss Bernice Fay Frazier could not imagine it was the streak truly he'd cultivated the habit to touch. And she'd studied how Miss Mary Alice Celestine Lefler sat primly in the boudoir chair with the heels of her hands to her kneetops and watched him speak of lubricational qualities and balance and such that he shared the talk of mostly with Miss Bernice Fay Frazier but shared the talk of every now and again with her too who he looked upon with a lingering and wholly undistracted gaze and who looked upon him with a lingering and wholly undistracted gaze back. She'd not been born just the day previous, Miss Bernice Fay Frazier hadn't, and she'd not lately dropped onto this earth from a planet otherwise either, so while they may have designed to deceive her they did not hardly begin to deceive her at all, most especially since she'd lately received instruction in plumbing and fathoming and such and so had delved from the outset to the very depths of the situation like did not hardly prevent her from taking casters for her loveseat and casters for her burled oak lowboy but kept her from taking them with much relish to speak of as it was sometimes a heavy burden to plumb and fathom so.

She called her sister Mrs. Estelle Singletary once they'd gone, once anyway he'd bid his good day and proclaimed how he was off directly for the Belvedere Hotel downtown where he meant to remain ensconced for a spell and once Miss Mary Alice Celestine Lefler had drummed up some cause to slip off shortly herself, had discovered suddenly a frightful dearth of hair gel like sent her fairly headlong out the door and up the walk towards town. So Miss Bernice Fay Frazier called her sister Mrs. Estelle Singletary and shared with her the recent events of the afternoon, explained about the lingering gazes and the white streak of skin where the ring had been along with, presently, the Belvedere Hotel and the hair gel both that, all taken together, appeared to her fairly condemning which she induced and persuaded Mrs. Estelle Singletary to throw in with.

As for herself, Miss Bernice Fay Frazier was pretty completely lathered up and felt fairly much on the verge of a conniption but managed somehow to forestall it a time while she expressed over the telephone to her sister her own personal impressions of living under the same roof with trash, most especially such trash as would meet a man at a hotel, a man with a streak on his finger where most probably his band had just lately been, and lay with him in the altogether, lay with him undoubtedly in the altogether contorted and twisted and maybe even upside down which Miss Bernice Fay Frazier, who'd been conjuring as she spoke, near about swooned at the sight of in her own mind's eye where a woman was free to contort and twist and upend her parts and pieces after a fashion no actual people had yet evolved the anatomy for. So Miss Bernice Fay Frazier was fairly much ascending to a state and had to hear from her sister Mrs. Estelle Singletary how perhaps she was being a bit hasty and rash in her judgment before she could find sufficient chink in the thing to announce her impending condition to Mrs. Estelle Singletary who detected in her sister's voice a frantic sort of a quiver and so inquired was she perhaps entering just presently into crisis.

Now of course Dr. Dewey Lunt had spent the bulk of a session on crises and how precisely to enter into one and he'd been himself partial to a frantic quiver at the outset followed by a variety of anguished discharge that was meant to be a kind of a shriek with some palpable torment to it, but when Miss Bernice Fay Frazier just quivered and failed to shriek back of it Mrs. Estelle Singletary found herself obliged to inquire of her sister was she or was she not entering into crisis since she could not hope to tell from just the frantic quiver by itself alone and could not afford to wait all the evening for a shriek most especially if a shriek was not in the least bit impending, and she asked of Miss Bernice Fay Frazier over the phone line, "Well?" like served to prod her into a shriek outright and so kicked off her crisis for certain. Naturally she blubbered soon enough as blubbering was to follow fairly hard up on shrieking in a crisis, and she registered her complaints about Miss Mary Alice Celestine Lefler and her complaints about Raymond the philandering salesman and her fears about the naked contortions along with a spattering of gurgly transactional suppositions that were full well as inarticulate and incomprehensible as the majority of the talk preceding them. Like was in keeping with the prescribed course of a crisis, Miss Bernice Fay Frazier's blubbering gave way to a round of forlorn self-pitying discharges that were intended to communicate to Mrs. Estelle Singletary over the phone line how Miss Bernice Fay Frazier did not hardly know what she would do, did not hardly know what she would do ever and felt pressed to wonder why she'd been plunked down on God's earth in the first place if she was only to see her kindness flung back upon her by faithless men and, as best as she could tell from her mind's eye, double-jointed women. It did not hardly seem a fit life to her, and she wondered in a rhetorical sort of a way if it was in fact a fit life and if she should even trouble herself to press on in her effort to live it that Mrs. Estelle Singletary, who'd never met a rhetorical question she didn't like, responded to at some appreciable length.

Mrs. Estelle Singletary was of a mind that life was fairly grand and should not be squandered or punctuated, life in general, that is, and not truly her very own particular life which was plagued by and afflicted with Mr. Estelle Singletary. But she guessed by and large life could be probably grand in fact for Miss Bernice Fay Frazier who'd not ever troubled herself to wed a plague and an affliction and so, in her declining years, would not likely stroke from aggravation that Mrs. Estelle Singletary gave out as an altogether resplendent blessing which was surely enhanced by Miss Bernice Fay Frazier's housecat Bubbles that Mrs. Estelle Singletary figured for a comfort chiefly and figured only partly for a source of abundant freefloating and altogether migratory cat hair. It seemed, then, to Mrs. Estelle Singletary that Miss Bernice Fay Frazier had before her some numerous blessings to count, but Miss Bernice Fay Frazier was not of a mood to count blessings and was not hardly gaining the mood for it either but had guessed she might wallow instead in her own forlorn circumstances that she endeavored to speak of but just primarily gurgled about.

So she'd gone from the frantic quiver to the anguished shriek to the inarticulate blubbering to the self-pitying discharges that had themselves deteriorated and given way to a bout of forlorn gurgly wallowing like fairly well served to ensconce Miss Bernice Fay Frazier so deep within her crisis that Mrs. Estelle Singletary could tell even over the phone line how there was not but a lone remaining remedy for it. She had call for an encounter with her elevated interdenominational group that would plumb and fathom her torment and then relate with it and identify about it and delve and testify on account of it sufficiently to drive Miss Bernice Fay Frazier up out from her morass and convince her how she was OK and they were OK and all of them pretty much together were likely about as OK as they could get. The trouble was, however, that Mrs. Estelle Singletary was meaning this very evening to serve dinner to the

Wishons from Greensboro and had plans the night following to dine at the club with Mr. Estelle Singletary so as to use up their meal fee before the new month came on like meant Mrs. Estelle Singletary could not possibly attend Miss Bernice Fay Frazier's encounter until Friday evening and she indicated to her sister how she would be quite thoroughly miffed if Miss Bernice Fay Frazier went ahead and had an encounter without her.

"Can't you just wallow for two days?" Mrs. Estelle Singletary wanted to know, and Miss Bernice Fay Frazier guessed she could maybe hold in a wallow if Mrs. Estelle Singletary would agree to have the encounter in her backyard alongside the fairway and would consider making it pot luck as well since Miss Bernice Fay Frazier could not help but believe she might emerge from her crisis with a craving for waxed bean salad and noodle casserole and the like.

Consequently, then, Mrs. Estelle Singletary agreed to play hostess to the encounter that Miss Bernice Fay Frazier agreed to put off until Friday while she maintained her woeful condition, and she took upon herself the task of calling up the encounterees and explaining to them how she'd come just presently to be in crisis and wondering would they maybe be free to collect Friday evening out by the fairway for purposes of relating and identifying and delving and plumbing and fathoming and might they each bring a dish. Now, of course, nobody much had found cause to relate and identify and delve and plumb and fathom after an organized fashion in the intervening couple of weeks since their gathering at the reservoir, so most everybody was anxious for the chance to hoist Miss Bernice Fay Frazier up out from her predicament as a preface to dining in the out of doors. Mrs. Phillip J. King most especially was anxious for a potluck encounter as she had designs already on an entree, a banger and turnip stew that she assured Miss Bernice Fay Frazier would prove inordinately savory like Miss Bernice Fay Frazier, who was after all in crisis already, was not of a mood to debate about. The widow Mrs. Askew tantalized Miss Bernice Fay Frazier with the promise of fresh and altogether incisive pith for the occasion which got her over the phone line a manner of frantic quiver in reply, and Mr. and Mrs. Luther Teague and Mr. and Mrs. Cecil Dutton agreed to bring some form of salad and frosted cake squares respectively while Miss Fay Dull inquired should she wear pants or simply carry a parka to perch upon. The Sleepy Pittses and the Wyatt Benbows looked forward between them to an evening alongside the fairway and Mr. H. Monroe Aycock expressed his unbounded delight at the prospect of a meal al fresco while the Reverend Mr. Theodore J. Parnell guessed he could stop in and delve and fathom and identify and relate for a spell but could not stay for the evening as he had some of God's work to see after which he seemed to suggest was more significant even than Miss Bernice Fay Frazier's personal crisis that got him his own frantic quiver back.

She'd saved Mrs. Dwight Mobley for last as she had an inquiry to make of Mrs. Dwight Mobley beyond the invitation, a delicate sort of an inquiry that she'd needed time to cultivate and shape to suit her, so finally she did in fact dial up Mrs. Dwight Mobley and chatted for a spell about her crisis and the upcoming encounter to cure it along with the need for one entree further like set Mrs. Dwight Mobley off on some talk of chicken drumettes in a sauce that she'd come across a recipe for, and she wanted to know from Miss Bernice Fay Frazier if didn't chicken drumettes in a sauce strike her as sublime which Miss Bernice Fay Frazier did not truly take time to consider and instead shifted topics of a sudden and entirely to him with the hair and the moustache and the gold sparkly watch and the white streak of fingerskin, him who Miss Bernice Fay Frazier and Mrs. Dwight Mobley agreed was dashing, him who they agreed possessed untold charms, him who Mrs. Dwight Mobley admitted set her heart aflutter. Miss Bernice Fay Frazier was anxious to discover had Raymond maybe one time passed through Berkeley Springs West Virginia that she guessed Mrs. Dwight Mobley might know or Mrs. Dwight Mobley's momma's sister might know instead, but Mrs. Dwight Mobley did not know for certain and could only tell to Miss Bernice Fay Frazier how Raymond had come to be acquainted somehow with Miss Mary Alice Celestine Lefler that he'd admitted to her and admitted to the widow Mrs. Askew he had.

"Acquainted?" Miss Bernice Fay Frazier wanted to know and so heard from Mrs. Dwight Mobley how she believed acquainted was what precisely she'd just finished saying though she did not know in what connection Raymond and Miss Mary Alice Celestine Lefler had come to be previously acquainted in like set off Miss Bernice Fay Frazier's mind's eye which envisioned a variety of connection that was pretty wholly unlikely and quite thoroughly antigravitational as well and so touched off a frantic quiver in combination with an anguished discharge that Mrs. Dwight Mobley took for a sneeze and so told to Miss Bernice Fay Frazier, "Bless you, honey," like caused her to be refreshed over the phone line as to the particular phases of the species of crisis Miss Bernice Fay Frazier had lately dropped off into, not one of which was sneezing.

"Might your momma's sister know acquainted how just exactly?" Miss Bernice Fay Frazier inquired and so heard from Mrs. Dwight Mobley that her momma's sister might like was sufficient to induce Miss Bernice Fay Frazier to take the number herself and to forestall Mrs.

Dwight Mobley as best as she was able from speaking further of the drumettes and from speaking most especially of the sauce as well that was meant to be piquant though Mrs. Dwight Mobley could not from the ingredients alone reason piquant how precisely and was set to ask after Miss Bernice Fay Frazier's own personal opinion of most especially the capers and the raisins in combination when she came to be interrupted by a gurgly discharge that was itself preamble to the thoroughgoing deadening of the line which freed Miss Bernice Fay Frazier to dial straightaway Mrs. Dwight Mobley's momma's sister who was sitting in her armchair with the crinkly beflowered ruffle endeavoring to untangle a word scramble from the newspaper, endeavoring anyway to see with her dead husband's eyeglasses the word scramble clue for the day which was for this Wednesday "insouciant" that Mrs. Dwight Mobley's momma's sister said into the air three different ways entirely prior to studying the word scramble cartoon picture of a man being, she supposed, insouciant himself, of a man striking what she had to take for an insouciant sort of a pose like appeared primarily slouchy to her though she could not hardly begin to make slouchy from the letters she'd been given to make slouchy from like caused her to pause in her ruminations and set herself to tell into the air, "Insouciant," one time further still which she came to be interrupted at and prevented from altogether by her telephone back of her that rang a piece of a ring and then a full ring and then a piece of another ring behind it before Mrs. Dwight Mobley's momma's sister had managed to push with her shoebottoms against the floor and thereby propel herself and her armchair together in a highly lubricational sort of a way across near about the entire breadth of the room to the far wall where she took up the handset and said sweetly into it her exchange and subsequent digits as well.

So Miss Bernice Fay Frazier came in fact to be edified and instructed, or had that is what she'd felt in her recesses confirmed for her by Mrs. Dwight Mobley's momma's sister who spoke of her with the lips and the fingerends who'd had a washstand bewheeled and him with the hair and the moustache who'd bewheeled it like did not appear to Mrs. Dwight Mobley's momma's sister much of a transgression until Miss Bernice Fay Frazier set forth her theory of how her with the lips and the fingerends and him with the silvery hair had touched off between themselves passionate sparks like had caused them to connive and conspire and to transport at last their mutual enchantment across state lines where they'd come lately to be joined and united in the altogether atop a queensize bed at the Belvedere Hotel, and Miss Bernice Fay

Frazier allowed her mind's eye to run momentarily amok so as to suggest to Mrs. Dwight Mobley's momma's sister the latent possibilities of the ball-and-socket joint. She guessed he had babies at home, Miss Bernice Fay Frazier did. She guessed he likely had an ailing wife gone too splayed in the hips to suit him, not near so svelte and willowy anyway as her with the lips and with the fingerends, her Miss Bernice Fay Frazier had taken to her very bosom and embraced.

"Like a sister," Miss Bernice Fay Frazier insisted and waited briefly for a sympathetic reply that Mrs. Dwight Mobley's aunt attempted one of but her clucking and her humphing got lost in and undone by the static on the line. Of course Miss Bernice Fay Frazier had suspected she was trash all along but had opened her heart and her home nonetheless until she might prove she was in fact a manner of harlot like it seemed to her this day she'd proved it, and Miss Bernice Fay Frazier bewailed briefly the lowly state of humanity and spoke of how dreadful it appeared to her people had come to be and then she left off talking so as to allow for assent from Mrs. Dwight Mobley's momma's sister who took the occasion to inquire of Miss Bernice Fay Frazier if the bugs this summer had been near so thick down her way as they'd been up in Berkeley Springs that Mrs. Dwight Mobley's momma's sister did not truly come to be satisfied about due to how Miss Bernice Fay Frazier made just a quivery sort of a noise at her before the line went dead, and Mrs. Dwight Mobley's momma's sister pondered briefly the receiver prior to launching herself with her shoebottoms back across the room where she raised up her piece of newspaper and sat a time quite apparently idle and unemployed until she drew off a breath to tell into the air, "Insouciant," quite emphatically in the wrong place altogether.

Miss Bernice Fay Frazier just stewed awhile on the settee and endeavored to soothe herself by stroking her cat Bubbles who'd lately nested upside down among the throwpillows like had left upended and exposed a piece of fluffy stomach that Miss Bernice Fay Frazier rubbed with her fingers until Bubbles roused herself sufficiently to sink her teeth into the meat of Miss Bernice Fay Frazier's hand and to scratch with her back claws down the length of Miss Bernice Fay Frazier's forearm which in combination suggested to Miss Bernice Fay Frazier how Bubbles was not presently of a mood to have her stomach scratched. Mr. Dick Atwater called on the phone after her of the acrobatic inclinations, spoke even three of her four names outright to Miss Bernice Fay Frazier who grew directly frantic and anguished both together and came to be shortly quite thoroughly inarticulate in a blubbery sort of a way and so did not truly tell to Mr. Dick Atwater anything much he had asked to know before she left him alone on the line and turned to seek solace once further from Bubbles her cat who'd laid and rotated her ears after such a fashion as to indicate that she was presently of an inflammatory and moderately lunatic disposition like presented Miss Bernice Fay Frazier with yet another circumstance to deepen and complicate her crisis further still as it struck her of a sudden that she'd made some sort of dreadful miscalculation to rely for companionship, here in the shank of her days, on a loose woman and a maniacal cat, and she was telling herself, "Sad, sad," as a commentary upon her very existence when she came to be obliged to answer the ring of the phone and inform Mr. Dick Atwater how life was a thing fraught with pitfalls that she left him directly alone on the line to absorb and consider.

She guessed she'd commence with her withering look that she'd train upon Miss Mary Alice Celestine Lefler once she'd stepped across the threshold and that she'd persevere with steadfastly until she found cause to shift instead to her altogether incredulous expression, the one of them with the wide eyes and the slack jaw and the thoroughgoing preponderance of bottom teeth, and she figured she might at this point in the encounter undertake a quip if a quip came to her or embark instead upon a piece of steely silence if steely silence struck her somehow as more apt. Consequently, then, Miss Bernice Fay Frazier rehearsed her withering look on the front doorlights and allowed herself a purely sardonic exchange with the switchplate alongside the jamb prior to growing slack and toothy and enduring at it a time until she heard in fact Miss Mary Alice Celestine Lefler herself on the steps and atop the decking and pitching finally against the door itself so as to swing it open like brought her squarely before Miss Bernice Fay Frazier who set about reducing her with a gaze.

And Miss Mary Alice Celestine Lefler told to Miss Bernice Fay Frazier, "Hey," and came right on in without even the first trace of hair gel about her while Miss Bernice Fay Frazier, who'd developed a twitchy nerve, endeavored to calm her look down from moderately psychotic to withering alone and so appeared just a little unbalanced and constipated in combination like was enough of an expression to cause Miss Mary Alice Celestine Lefler to linger at the doorway and inquire of Miss Bernice Fay Frazier, "What?"

She had a flush to her, a deep thoroughgoing flush along her neck and up the length of her face, such a deep and such a thoroughgoing and persistent sort of a flush that Miss Bernice Fay Frazier could not begin to suppose Raymond with the hair and the moustache had likely embarrassed her into it and so indulged again her mind's eye that revealed to her a variety of daring gymnastic stunts in the course of which Miss Mary Alice Celestine Lefler tumbled through the air, executed a near flawless twisting manuever with a partial somersault to it, and came at last to be fairly thoroughly impaled much to her unbounded delight which she expressed in a purely unanguished shriek along with a manner of creeping blush that climbed steadily upwards from her toenails to the roots of her, undoubtedly, tinted hair. The sight was certainly more than Miss Bernice Fay Frazier could hope to endure with an unbalanced and constipated expression, so her lips shortly developed a crinkle to them and she believed herself on the verge of a blubbery outburst when Miss Mary Alice Celestine Lefler advanced upon her, routed the cat out from the throwpillows, and sat among them herself from where she took up Miss Bernice Fay Frazier's fingers and looked so sympathetically upon her that Miss Bernice Fay Frazier's resolve to be harsh and withering began to erode but stopped shortly at it once she'd caught a whiff of Raymond's leathery scent on Miss Mary Alice Celestine Lefler in addition to a whiff of cigarette as well like called up another time the exploits that she guessed Miss Mary Alice Celestine Lefler and him with the hair and with the moustache had punctuated together with a smoke.

It was a matter of some debate to her whether she would call her straightoff a harlot or merely inquire instead if wasn't she in fact trash after all so as to allow Miss Mary Alice Celestine Lefler the opportunity for rebuttal which would undoubtedly provide Miss Bernice Fay Frazier occasion for her altogether incredulous expression, and she'd even begun to work her eyes wide and loosen up her jaw in preparation to slack it when Miss Mary Alice Celestine Lefler up and announced how she had a thing to say, confessed how she'd spent the bulk of her absence getting fetched or preparing anyway to get fetched that struck Miss Bernice Fay Frazier as unseemly in fact and very possibly taxing in an anatomical sort of a way since, in her present state, she took fetching for a sort of thing a man and a woman lay naked upon a bed together and did perhaps with the aid and assistance of a healthy dollop of hair gel.

So she said to her presently, "Fetched," with palpable distaste and entertained from Miss Mary Alice Celestine Lefler a spate of thoroughly giddy talk on the topic of Raymond with the hair and the moustache and the gold sparkly accoutrements not even to mention the princely deportment and the regal manners that she communicated her view of with a lengthsome exhalation alone.

"He rolled my washstand," Miss Mary Alice Celestine Lefler told partly to Miss Bernice Fay Frazier and partly to the walljoint at the hall doorway where she appeared to see Raymond once more before her washstand with his drill and his casters squatting upon his admirably skimpy posterior like induced from Miss Mary Alice Celestine Lefler an additional breathy discharge that sounded to have to it considerably more abandon than Miss Bernice Fay Frazier cared to hear of.

Being a lady of no trifling discretion, Miss Bernice Fay Frazier had resolved not to mention the streak of skin, not to throw up in Miss Mary Alice Celestine Lefler's face what appeared to Miss Bernice Fay Frazier the distasteful circumstances of the entire proceeding, and she did even manage not to speak of the streak of skin for a time and did even manage not but to hint obliquely about it for a spell as well before she just up and inquired of Miss Mary Alice Celestine Lefler if wasn't she in fact a home wrecker, if hadn't she in fact with her wiles and charms lured poor Raymond away from his wife and his babies and carried him full into iniquity like made her probably trash and like made her probably a harlot both together which Miss Bernice Fay Frazier let on to be a manner of query and so fell briefly silent in anticipation of a reply. For her part, Miss Mary Alice Celestine Lefler allowed Miss Bernice Fay Frazier to have her previously gripped and held fingers back prior to rising upright off the settee and flattening her dressfront with her open hands by which she prefaced a broad earwax sort of a smile for the benefit of Miss Bernice Fay Frazier who undertook to leer herself back before she grew quivery and anguished and agitated and so set to blubbering into her one hand while she raised the other to get the fingers of it gripped and held again by her who just stood before the settee and looked beyond the fingers that she did not move to grip or hold either one.

"I know where I'm welcome," Miss Mary Alice Celestine Lefler said, "and I know where I'm not. Pardon me, please, ma'm." And with that she spun round and left the front parlor for the backhall and the stairs to her room where she arrived shortly and quite apparently dragged her suitcase out from under the bed. Down on the settee Miss Bernice Fay Frazier could hear the rasp of it across the floor, and she told to the ceiling, "Well!" with measurable indignation and she told to her cat Bubbles who'd reclaimed the throwpillows, "Well!" too and guessed how she had not ever intended to open up a home for shiftless women to come wait for their married boyfriends to shed their various bonds and shackles and fetch them away, and she informed her cat Bubbles, "No we did not," and contemplated stroking the animal with the fingers she'd raised to get gripped but the lay of the ears prevented her from it.

"Go then," Miss Bernice Fay Frazier proclaimed and flung her arm with her indicating finger extended ever so dramatically towards the doorway. "Go then," she said and merely jerked her head instead like she guessed did not have near so much show and flair to it as the flung arm. "Go," she said and flung her arm another time, "then," which she liked well enough as a combination of flinging and speaking but guessed she might best fling and then speak or speak and then fling and not mingle the two of them together. She tried it sitting and she tried it standing and she tried it mostly upright but pitched a little against the sofa arm which seemed to her to have some icy style to it, and she flung and then spoke and she spoke and then flung and she laid her unemployed hand to her hip like seemed to purely coagulate the thing altogether and so left her merely to wait for Miss Mary Alice Celestine Lefler who collected and packed her belongings and then presently came bumping her luggage down the stairway and sliding it up the backhall floor.

"Go then," Miss Bernice Fay Frazier intoned and flung with excessive drama, but Miss Mary Alice Celestine Lefler was of a mind to use the telephone before she actually went so she'd have a way to go in fact which Miss Bernice Fay Frazier guessed she might allow her to do and so flung towards the phone as well though Miss Mary Alice Celestine Lefler assured her how she knew precisely where the phone was. She engaged in a whispery indecipherable conversation with him, no doubt, who Miss Bernice Fay Frazier endeavored to communicate her opinion about with just her posture against the sofa arm alone and she allowed Miss Mary Alice Celestine Lefler to cradle the receiver and arrive once more alongside her suitcase before she flung yet again and told to her, "Go then," but Miss Mary Alice Celestine Lefler preferred to wait inside the house if Miss Bernice Fay Frazier could see fit to endure it that Miss Bernice Fay Frazier figured from the sofa arm maybe she could.

Of course, she was not much accustomed to pitching and leaning and so had not anticipated how her various vessels and nerves, most especially her sciatic ones, would come to be pinched and constricted thereby benumbing Miss Bernice Fay Frazier's lower parts which she could not after a time determine she had any of unless she looked squarely at them. She was not, however, tempted at all to confess to Miss Mary Alice Celestine Lefler that she'd come to be pinched and constricted and benumbed and endeavored instead to surreptitiously stomp her feet and thereby incite her blood to circulate like was hardly a thoroughgoing success for Miss Bernice Fay Frazier who could not with her benumbed parts anticipate where the floor might be and so evermore encountered it before she'd figured she might which was just the sort of thing to cause her teeth to beat together and her head to jerk after such a fashion as to pretty much undo and fairly completely mitigate the icy style she'd hoped with the leaning to manufacture. So Miss Mary Alice Celestine Lefler stood alongside her baggage with her arms crossed before herself and her lips laid wide upon the breadth of her face in a sour, unamused sort of a way while Miss Bernice Fay Frazier engaged in a peculiar manner of hoedown alongside the sofa arm and looked baldly back as best as she was able when she was not stomping and inciting instead. They did not speak but by way of reasonably articulate exasperated breaths that told, it seemed, worlds more than actual words might, and Miss Mary Alice Celestine Lefler let on with her discharges how she was a woman in love and did not much care to be construed for a harlot while Miss Bernice Fay Frazier exhaled her own low opinion of men with newfound streaks of skin and the women that took up with them. And together they'd arrived at the verge of hyperventilation by the time Raymond slipped up against the curbing in his blueblack sedan and tooted upon the horn of it so as to announce how he'd come at last to actually fetch away Miss Mary Alice Celestine Lefler in fact.

Unfortunately, however, Raymond did not appear disposed there at the first but to toot and so busied himself tapping upon the padded wheel and did not offer to step into the house and carry off Miss Mary Alice Celestine Lefler's outsized piece of luggage and her overnight case and hanging bag until she arrived upon the porch herself so as to instruct Raymond how he had some items in the house to carry off and she meant truly straightaway. Now Raymond, who of course was acquainted with wifely tones, had not ever previously had occasion to hear one from Miss Mary Alice Celestine Lefler herself and so leapt out of the car from habit but lingered upon the sidewalk from surprise until he came to be shortly instructed again and climbed to the porch and passed through the doorway to the front room where he endured a glare from Miss Bernice Fay Frazier who cavorted with her feet but appeared content to lay and lean with the rest of herself.

"Ma'm," Raymond told to Miss Bernice Fay Frazier as he undertook to collect Miss Mary Alice Celestine Lefler's baggage that he managed to take up altogether and struggle with across the carpet to the doorway that Miss Bernice Fay Frazier watched him at and breathed at him about. She did not wish him to loose the cat into the yard and told him with disdain how she did not wish him to loose it like left Raymond to undertake to mind the baggage and to mind the door and to mind the cat all at the same time which was more truly than he could manage with much grace and princely charm and, consequently, he arrived on the porch a little ill and winded and attempted to rest atop the decking and collect himself, but Miss Mary Alice Celestine Lefler informed him how he'd probably best collect himself later and fairly drove him off the porch and down the steps to the backend of the blueblack sedan where he raised the trunklid and hefted the outsized suitcase into the trunk without hearing even one time of what strapping variety of specimen he was.

He tooted a bon voyage before she could keep him from tooting it and they eased away from the curb and out into the road that Miss Bernice Fay Frazier watched them at as best as she was able from the sofa arm that she'd raised off of but held to nonetheless as she was not, with her benumbed limbs, in any condition to walk even so far as the door. So she just stood alongside the camelback settee and looked out through the doorscreen to where the blueblack sedan had only lately been before him with the hair and the moustache and her with the lips and the fingerends had departed on their way to what Miss Bernice Fay Frazier could not help but figure for an illicit assignation in the altogether like called up for her the likelihood of gymnastics which she stood alongside the sofa arm and inadvertently conjured about before she came to be distracted by her twingy sciatic nerve like brought to mind for her her cat Bubbles with the ears and the attendant fur cloud, her cat Bubbles among the throwpillows that eyed Miss Bernice Fay Frazier with that wild, skewed out-from-the-asylum-on-a-daytrip sort of a cat look prior to leaping onto the carpet and charging headlong through the dining room into the kitchen where she jumped up upon the countertop and knocked from it in the process Miss Bernice Fay Frazier's salad spinner that in turn hit her broomhandle and so caused it to pitch over and slap against the linoleum like was just the sort of thing to terrify a cat and, consequently, terrified Bubbles who departed from the kitchen for the breakfast nook and out of it up the backhall and into the frontroom once more where she gained the settee yet again and hunkered upon it working most especially her back claws deep into the upholstery until Miss Bernice Fay Frazier reached out to soothe her with a touch and so incited Bubbles to depart another time straight out through the air like a nappy bullet.

Needless to say, a frantic quiver ensued, a thoroughly acute frantic quiver which served itself as a prologue to an anguished discharge like was preface to Miss Bernice Fay Frazier's fairly precipitous collapse atop the settee cushions where she lay with her knuckles upon her forehead and endeavored to bemoan her pitiful state that appeared to her just presently quite lowly and pretty completely irredeemable as far as pitiful states went. She guessed she needed somebody to relate briefly and identify on her behalf and to maybe help her delve and plumb for the time being down past her woes and recent reverses like she figured might hold her until her pot luck encounter. Accordingly, then, she struggled to the phone and dialed her sister Mrs. Estelle Singletary who she hoped would soothe her for the moment but Mrs. Estelle Singletary was right there in the middle of wine coolers and mixed nuts with the Wishons and had no time to speak to Miss Bernice Fay Frazier, so she thought she might call Miss Fay Dull instead but recollected in the midst of calling Miss Fay Dull how she did not truly much care for Miss Fay Dull and how she did believe she'd made lately a frank and candid disclosure to that effect like left her to figure that maybe she'd call the widow Mrs. Askew instead, the widow Mrs. Askew who was just across the road and so could arrive ever so shortly to delve and identify but would undoubtedly cart with her a thoroughgoing dose of unmitigated pith which Miss Bernice Fay Frazier did not believe she could presently endure with any detectable grace. She did not know then who she might enlist to calm and soothe her and was casting about for a candidate when she came to be startled by a rap upon her screendoor rail and looked up of a sudden to find Mr. Dick Atwater standing atop her porch decking with his lacquered hat in his hand. He appeared even through the screenwire to have gotten somehow altered, to have come to be swollen under his one eye and bruised alongside his mouth and it looked most especially to her that he had misplaced a sizeable sprig of hair, not that he'd laid it to the left when he should have laid it to the right or laid it to the right when he should have laid it to the left but that he'd lost it altogether somehow and just had anymore red prickly scalp where only lately a sprig of hair had been, red prickly scalp that was intensely red and prickly both even through the screenwire and so briefly distracted Miss Bernice Fay Frazier from her own personal woes and afflictions.

And she said to him, "Mr. Atwater?" and heard from him back, "Bernice," and then watched him look briefly down at his lacquered hat like revealed to her a second vacant patch of scalp that appeared to have lately entertained a sprig itself.

"I called," he told her. "Twice."

"Did you?" Miss Bernice Fay Frazier inquired and left the phone table to free herself to lurch pathetically towards the front doorway.

"Yes ma'm," Mr. Dick Atwater said and nodded so deeply as to display a third prickly patch where he'd come to be quite violently bald. "Two times."

"We've had here a situation," Miss Bernice Fay Frazier told to him and made what looked to Mr. Dick Atwater an altogether grave face, too altogether grave for him to endure on the porch and so he drew open the screendoor and thereby intercepted Miss Bernice Fay Frazier in the midst of her pitiful lurching, gripped to her at the elbow, and pressed her to tell him straightaway what situation precisely she meant.

Of course the sight of Mr. Dick Atwater newly illuminated by the lamplight and wholly unfiltered by the screenwire put Miss Bernice Fay Frazier off from speaking for a time and she looked from the scrapes and the bruises to the bald patches and then back to the scrapes and the bruises again prior to mustering up the means at last to speak and asking of Mr. Dick Atwater, "What on earth happened to you?"

"Fell down," Mr. Dick Atwater told to her and bore in contusions foremost on Miss Bernice Fay Frazier so as to maybe prompt her directly back to the situation he'd wanted in the first place to hear of.

"Fell down?" Miss Bernice Fay Frazier said to him and eyed the scrapes and the bruises and the patches and the wounds otherwise further still prior to inquiring, "Off what?"

"Just fell down," Mr. Dick Atwater told to her and fairly pinched off her circulation at her bony elbowjoint like Miss Bernice Fay Frazier felt shortly obliged to apprise him about and she wondered just out into the air if there was in this lifetime likely to be any end to her own personal acute suffering, by which she meant chiefly her own personal acute suffering in the general sense as she'd guessed already how she might pinch with her fingernails at Mr. Dick Atwater's forearm so as to relieve the acute suffering visited just presently upon her between her elbow and her fingerends. So they came the two of them to be shortly disengaged and Miss Bernice Fay Frazier veered off in her pathetic lurching away from the doorway and towards the settee where she settled shortly with Mr. Dick Atwater snug up behind her to settle at her side and press her to reveal to him what situation precisely she was suffering acutely about.

"You can't ever know people," Miss Bernice Fay Frazier informed him. "You can't ever know what it is people might do."

"What people?" Mr. Dick Atwater wished to discover and bore in another time on Miss Bernice Fay Frazier who sighed the deep resonant sigh of an acutely suffering woman.

"Oh, Mr. Atwater," she said and did not contribute any comment otherwise back of it but instead grew moved to indulge in a bout of forlorn wallowing that came to be shortly gurgly once it had left off being wheezy first.

For his part Mr. Dick Atwater, who'd peered into the kitchen and listened at the ceiling but had not seen anybody and had not heard anything except the drumming of tiny cat feet, figured for himself how she was not roundabout and figured of a sudden for himself as well who likely she was not roundabout with which incited him to an exclamation, which moved him to tell to Miss Bernice Fay Frazier, who was looking chiefly for a kind word, "That goddam Nestor Tudor. He come and took her off, didn't he? That son of a bitch. Just slipped on over here and snaked his way right in. I should have known it," Mr. Dick Atwater declared. "I should have seen it," and he sighed himself and wallowed a little on his own though not with much wheeze or gurgle to speak of.

Now Miss Bernice Fay Frazier possessed personally the constitution to be anguished and quivery and hotly indignant all at the same time and so she expressed straightaway at Mr. Dick Atwater her outright consternation, drew back anyhow and drew up both at the same time and fairly declaimed, "Mr. Atwater!" that she punctuated with a frantic sort of a tremor prior to persevering briefly with some talk on the moral perils of blasphemy and profanation. Furthermore, Miss Bernice Fay Frazier assured Mr. Dick Atwater that she had not herself laid eyes upon Nestor Tudor since the night previous when she'd spied him across the street in the lamplight with his rumpled nosegay in his hand, the news of which induced from Mr. Dick Atwater a variety of, "Oh," like was meant to express for him his regret on account of the goddam and on account of the son of a bitch though Miss Bernice Fay Frazier was herself hoping for something a trifle more apologetic and so waited in her best icy silence atop the settee until she had in fact induced from Mr. Dick Atwater a thoroughgoing statement of his sincere remorse like freed her to tell to him, "Raymond," that she allowed to sink and settle as best it might.

"Raymond?" Mr. Dick Atwater intoned on his own.

"Raymond," Miss Bernice Fay Frazier told him, "from West Virginia."

"Raymond," Mr. Dick Atwater intoned yet again but with this time a vagrant bend to it.

"Oh, Mr. Atwater," Miss Bernice Fay Frazier said and then fell for a brief spell upon the settee into her pensive silence which was not much like her icy silence at all as her pensive silence had to it relatively steady detectable nosebreathing which suggested, along with some scant and intermittent headshaking, how pensive in fact was what this silence was. So Mr. Dick Atwater did not feel then pressed to end this particular variety of silence with talk of his own personal shortcomings and regrets but just allowed it instead to culminate in a hardy exhalation followed by a brief and relatively pithy piece of talk on the part of Miss Bernice Fay Frazier who'd sat lately at the feet of the master of pith and so had troubled herself to glean some style from her. "When first we practice to deceive," she said, "it is truly a tangled web we weave," and as soon as she'd managed to look earnestly enough upon Mr. Dick Atwater to communicate to him how it was his occasion to snort and exhale he went straight on ahead and snorted and exhaled for her.

She was meaning to get to the particulars but she assured Mr. Dick Atwater, once he'd endeavored to press her, how he could not hardly hope to drive her to them though she did directly confirm for him that it was Raymond from West Virginia and Miss Mary Alice Celestine Lefler lately of the upstairs bedroom who were together an item like was truly the only particular Mr. Dick Atwater needed to hear, or was anyhow the only particular his stomach had cause to know of before it began to drain and empty off that way stomachs sometimes do leaving Mr. Dick Atwater increasingly hollow and ever so thoroughly vacant just up and all at once.

"He rolled her washstand," Miss Bernice Fay Frazier announced after she'd cast about and determined how undoubtedly the washstand itself was the original particular in fact.

But as he'd not quite yet cultivated the talent for gleaning Miss Bernice Fay Frazier had come to anticipate in people, Mr. Dick Atwater returned to the opening particular himself. "Raymond?" he said, "and Mary Alice."

"Them," Miss Bernice Fay Frazier told to him and returned to the washstand he'd rolled like was preface to the sparks and the passion and was prologue to the deceit as well. Of course she spoke of the streak of skin and moved from it to the fatherless children and the spavined wife left to shift for them and was meaning to touch upon the graceful bearing and the princely charm as the trappings of subterfuge like called, she believed, in this particular case for a pithy presentation that Miss Bernice Fay Frazier was endeavoring to work up when Mr. Dick Atwater interrupted her with an inquiry, asked of Miss Bernice Fay Frazier, "Raymond?," asked of Miss Bernice Fay Frazier, "Raymond who?"

Though truly not a woman to hunt up a tangent, Miss Bernice Fay Frazier was evermore willing to run with whatever one might get thrust upon her and consequently took up Raymond as a tangent himself and set to delving and plumbing and fathoming and, shortly, undertook to illuminate Mr. Dick Atwater as to what precisely Raymond had seemed to her to be. Of course she touched upon the baubles and the accoutrements as she had to delve past them to get anywhere much else and she spoke of the silvery hair and of the short prickly elegant moustache like contributed themselves to the regal bearing which she lingered upon as she was fondest personally of the regal bearing herself, and she'd just set to working her way ever so gradually through the subtleties of Raymond's technique, which would be his caster technique that she could not figure to be awful far removed from his romantic technique as well, when Mr. Dick Atwater horned in one time further so as to vent himself of an inquiry, an inquiry that had quite apparently come to seem to him excruciatingly germane judging chiefly from his pitched inquiring posture and his relatively tortured inquiring face.

"Blueblack sedan?" he wanted to know. "Long blueblack four-door sedan?"

Naturally Miss Bernice Fay Frazier, in the wake of her own semitortured expression, assured Mr. Dick Atwater how she would have presently arrived at the sedan herself as she was heading in fact in her systematical sort of way directly towards the blueblack sedan not so much as a vehicle but as primarily a variety of manifestation instead like would join and compliment the accoutrements and the baubles and the hair and the moustache and the princely bearing and thereby assist in the establishment of a general essence like anybody that delved and fathomed and related would have surely known she was up to which was meant, by implication, to fairly belittle and chastise Mr. Dick Atwater as to the general altitude of his own personal consciousness like might have ordinarily cultivated some umbrage if Mr. Dick Atwater had not just lately come to be too altogether emptied out for umbrage and such. Quite naturally he called up his particular encounter with the blueblack sedan and the gentleman inside it, the natty gentleman inside it with the northerly hairpart and the silvery locks that swept and laid and the white shirt with the white stripe worked into it and the satiny maroon tie that blended so with the blazer which had upon the breastpocket of it a manner of crest that was bars and swords and horseheads chiefly, and he called up as well the gold ring and the gold watch but most especially recollected the gem-studded cufflink that caught the light and sparkled and served by itself to remind Dick Atwater ever so acutely of his envy and of his admiration that seemed to coagulate somehow together and drop into his evacuated stomach so as to rattle roundabout like a ball bearing.

He felt of a sudden ill and sickly and could not work up the spit even to advise Miss Bernice Fay Frazier to please for a time shut up while he endeavored to keep from upchucking on her throwpillows, so he merely sat and endured extravagant insensible talk on the topic of vehicular manifestations and most especially of the long blueblack four-door variety and consequently he began to ebb and gurgle both together and was coming to believe he might shortly expire from the blow he'd endured, like appeared to him emotional and gastrointestinal joined and blended, when he complicated and worsened even his predicament by conjuring up in his own mind's eye Raymond with the hair and the moustache and her with the lips and the fingerends caught up together under the buglight at the golfrange in a back-to-front embrace that had been instigated, ostensibly, on account of an iron shot but had, quite apparently, considerably more to do with consummating parts instead and their general proximity each to the other. Mr. Dick Atwater could not seem to help but undertake to grow livid though he was not in much condition to be livid truly, and he interrupted Miss Bernice Fay Frazier with his own low and disdainful opinion of Raymond who he suspected, underneath his flair and glitter, was probably a kind of a heel.

"Paw at her all the evening, I'll bet," Mr. Dick Atwater said. "She won't long stand for that."

Of course Miss Bernice Fay Frazier pretty much straightaway plumbed and fathomed Mr. Dick Atwater's misapprehension and regarded herself bound to reveal to him the unseemly truth of the situation and so announced with all the drama she could muster short of armflinging, "She's not getting dated, Mr. Atwater. She's been fetched," and Miss Bernice Fay Frazier pitched her head and elevated her eyebrows after such a fashion as to intimate how fetching was chiefly an acrobatic endeavor with all variety of unevolved anatomical peculiarities to it like her eyebrows by themselves expressed in fact the bulk of.

"Fetched where?" Mr. Dick Atwater wanted to know.

"Off," Miss Bernice Fay Frazier told to him. "Away."

And Mr. Dick Atwater felt his blood rush and his skin prickle as he inquired of Miss Bernice Fay Frazier, "Off? Away?"

"Gone, Mr. Atwater. Gone."

He could not straightoff believe it and told to Miss Bernice Fay Frazier that straightoff he could not believe it at all on account of how him and on account of how Miss Mary Alice Celestine Lefler had cultivated between them a thing, had developed a species of attachment like would not allow the one or the other of them to just up and get fetched unannounced. "She would have told me," Mr. Dick Atwater insisted. "We had a thing. We were like this," and he showed to Miss Bernice Fay Frazier two fingers jammed up together which Miss Bernice Fay Frazier shook her head from side to side ever so forlornly about. "She wouldn't have just run off," Mr. Dick Atwater said. "She's too fine a woman for that."

"Mr. Atwater," Miss Bernice Fay Frazier replied in her best breathy elevated voice, "let me explain a thing to you," and she reached out and touched Mr. Dick Atwater's forearm with her own personal fingerends like did not produce near so galvanizing an effect as he'd known previously. "May I call you Jerome?" she wondered at him and so came shortly to be grunted at back. "Jerome, Miss Mary Alice Celestine Lefler is not in fact a fine woman. Miss Mary Alice Celestine Lefler is conniving trash."

Of course she was speaking of the woman Mr. Dick Atwater loved, or was speaking anyway of the woman who'd produced upon his consummating part the variety of sensation his consummating part had not lately been much acquainted with which Mr. Dick Atwater had guessed he might take for love as it had seemed pretty much like love to him. Consequently, then, he felt stirred and obliged to tell to Miss Bernice Fay Frazier, "Hey!" and attempted to draw off his arm so as to maybe exhibit his offense, but Miss Bernice Fay Frazier pinched up a tuft of armhair in her fingers and thereby forestalled Mr. Dick Atwater who heard from her talk further of Miss Mary Alice Celestine Lefler as an altogether loose and unscrupulous woman, as a harlot in fact with designs and intentions which came to be shortly explained and illuminated for Mr. Dick Atwater who mustered on Hey! further still but nonetheless got presently persuaded that Miss Mary Alice Celestine Lefler was perhaps wily and shrewd and deceitful too, persuaded by Miss Bernice Fay Frazier partly and persuaded partly as well by his own personal internal cavity where he felt, deeply within the pit of it, to have been connived in fact.

And Mr. Dick Atwater loosed a noise, told into the air, "Oh," with just breath primarily like maybe he would have told Oh into the air if he'd been clubbed upon his belt buckle, and he rose up off the settee once his hairtuft had been liberated and stepped over to the screendoor so as to look outside into the evening and feel openly pitiful both together, and he was set even to whine a little, was prepared to air a complaint about his own particular variety of fortune which did not hardly appear to him good fortune any longer but was evermore lamentable fortune instead, and he guessed his life was pretty much done and his usefulness was altogether exhausted along with his dangly consummating part that he supposed he might best just lop off which was truly worth whining on account of and so put him right there on the verge of a discharge which he'd drawn off the breath even to vent when Miss Bernice Fay Frazier whined herself ahead of him and proceeded from it directly into a frantic quiver that yielded shortly to a bout of outright anguishment as she guessed she'd neglected her own crisis long enough and so undertook to revive it with some zeal and some fervor and with a natural talent for whining that Mr. Dick Atwater himself did not hardly begin to possess.

She'd harbored trash. She'd opened her home to a harlot and told as much in her best gaspy tormented voice to Mr. Dick Atwater who guessed even though she was speaking still of the woman him and his dangly organ had been together fond of he'd allow her to persist at it a time since he did not much wish to contradict Miss Bernice Fay Frazier right there in the middle of her torment. So Mr. Dick Atwater lingered by the screendoor and listened at the whining that set out frantic and moderately anguished both together but came shortly to be moist and murky instead and was venturing into the realm of the outright indecipherable by the time Mr. Dick Atwater saw before him his duty and so carried his evacuated and altogether cavernous carcass across the room so as to settle it among the throwpillows alongside Miss Bernice Fay Frazier from where he could reach out with his fingers and take up hers that he simply held to while Miss Bernice Fay Frazier blubbered and moaned and continued to hold to after even she'd left off blubbering and moaning both and was down to just sniveling alone. Of course, he was of a mood to snivel with her but did not guess he would be much use sniveling since he did not suppose he could snivel and soothe at the same time together like left him just to hold the fingers and just to, every now and again, pat the arm while he assured Miss Bernice Fay Frazier how a woman could not begin to be blamed for having her sundry kindnesses turned against her by conniving trash, or while anyway he listened to Miss Bernice Fay Frazier speak to him of a woman and her kindnesses that some trash might connive about which he came to be allowed to confirm and assent to and so did in fact hold to the fingers and pat the arm as he confirmed and assented to it.

She had a balky sciatic nerve. She had a lunatic cat. She had excess blood sugar and tended to accumulate and retain fluid most especially roundabout her ankles and feet, and she wondered could Mr. Dick Atwater himself imagine the general discomfort of fluid retention in combination with the cat and the balky nerve that Miss Bernice Fay Frazier figured was more than any woman should be pressed to endure which seemed to Mr. Dick Atwater altogether likely though his own personal fluid failed ever to travel so far south as his ankles and feet. He did not, then, dispute that Miss Bernice Fay Frazier was in fact a pitiful and afflicted item and she continued to press her case upon him until talk of her woes with her parts and pieces and her pet cat and her live-in harlot lately of the Belvedere Hotel gave way to whimpering and sobbing and presently sniveling again that she persisted at until she grew too weary to snivel even and guessed she might stretch out on the settee under her afghan and nap a while if Mr. Dick Atwater would stay to soothe her once she awoke which Mr. Dick Atwater allowed he would and so helped to cover and situate Miss Bernice Fay Frazier upon the settee and watched as her cat Bubbles climbed up to join her, watched as her cat Bubbles burrowed and nested deep between Miss Bernice Fay Frazier's considerable thighs where she dropped almost entirely out of sight but for her snoutend and, shortly, the scant pink tonguetip that protruded from it.

So Mr. Dick Atwater observed a spinster and a spinster's cat sleep together upon a settee which was hardly what he'd hoped when he'd left his house he was in for. And he just sat a time feeling pathetic and evacuated and aired every now and again low, murmurous whiny sorts of noises that seemed to him in their essence to capture his predicament pretty completely. Miss Bernice Fay Frazier for her part was afflicted with not just a balky sciatic nerve and a lunatic cat and excess blood sugar and fluid that collected in her nether parts but snored as well with all the charm and whimsy of a tablesaw like presently drove Mr. Dick Atwater out from his whiny revery and into the dining room where he stooped to see himself in the scant slip of mirror above the sideboard, stooped to examine his contusions and his newly balded patches and discovered along with them a forlorn and abandoned expression that struck him as especially pitiful since it was his own one. He studied briefly Miss Bernice Fay Frazier's various knickknacks and geegaws after a distracted sort of a fashion and wandered presently back into the kitchen and out of it up the hallway where he stopped off in the bathroom so as to view in the medicine chest mirror his own thoroughgoing personal pathos one time further prior to entering again into the front room where Miss Bernice Fay Frazier was sleeping still by the board foot with Bubbles's pink tonguetip showing above her near thigh like a gaudy pinion. As there did not seem to him much profit in watching a woman and a cat sleep together on a settee, Mr. Dick Atwater proceeded on towards the doorscreen where he stood for a time peering out through the mesh into the gathering night without seeing straightoff any of the night at all since he was plagued with a mind's eye of his own that showed to him her with the consummating gland and him with the full head of silvery hair and the northerly hairpart, him who entertained five fingerends upon his forearm there in an elegant suite of rooms at the Belvedere Hotel which did not in fact rent out suites of rooms and had long since given over its elegance to general dilapidation and vague squalor instead which could be maintained without much fuss or effort. So he figured it straightoff for his mind's eye alone but watched nonetheless how the fingerends laid and listened at the suave piece of talk him with the hair and moustache and the gold accoutrements manufactured for the occasion prior to gazing in fact through the screenwire into the actual night that struck Dick Atwater this particular evening as most especially inky and deep.

iv.

HE found it savory and aromatic, had figured in fact even prior to arriving in the kitchen that savory and that aromatic was what he would likely find it and so he proclaimed how it was the one and how it was the other both together before Mrs. Phillip J. King had made yet to snatch away the potlid good and thereby reveal to him her stew with chiefly the bangers and the turnips to it. And he would have likely carried on past the savory and past the aromatic as well if he had not caught an actual whiff of the concoction which served by itself to pretty completely undo his fabricated enthusiasm and left him to linger a little queasily over the rangetop where he eyed the chopped bangers and turnip wedges and watched the juices gurgle and spit. He told to Mrs. Phillip J. King, "Mmmm," so as to be able to speak and keep his mouth shut both at the same time, but an Mmmm just by itself did not much appear to suit her and she pressed him to tell to her one admiring thing further still like he meant even to tell to her one of but somehow could not keep from announcing instead, "It's orange," since aside from unsavory and unaromatic orange was chiefly what it was.

She guessed she should have left it to him to illuminate a defect, guessed she might have anticipated how he would march straight into the kitchen to tell her that her stew was orange like wasn't even in the first place her fault since she couldn't hardly help it if she lived in a backwater, would not personally endure the blame if her grocer failed to carry a decent variety of banger like left her to make do with Jimmy Dean pork links which she'd sauteed, she told it, and drained on a paper towel before she'd dropped them in the pot to stew where they'd managed somehow to shed themselves of just barely enough additional orange grease to lubricate a Buick. "I can't help it," Mrs. Phillip J. King said. "There's not the first proper banger in this entire county."

Of course Mr. Phillip J. King moved straightoff to share with Mrs. Phillip J. King his own personal partiality for orange food, most especially soupy orange moderately iridescent sorts of food that he'd cultivated from somewhere an acute fondness for, and he bent a little over the stewpot and beat the air with his one hand so as to paddle the aroma up his noseholes and he made as best he was able to be transported by it, said anyhow, "Mmmm," one time further with inordinate conviction and altogether detectable enthusiasm. As fortune would have it, Mrs. Phillip J. King had just lately taken up her soup dipper off her soup dipper rest that had come to be moderately orange itself and she stirred and churned her stew with it prior to drawing up from down near the potbottom a ladleful of banger slices and turnip wedges that she dumped into a bowl along with some orange savory sauce and offered to Mr. Phillip J. King who'd hoped he could get by with just looking and sniffing and Mmmming at the pot and just looked and sniffed and Mmmmed in fact at his own personal bowl as well before he was presented with a spoon and encouraged by Mrs. Phillip J. King to go on ahead and eat as she hated to see a man kept from his orange food when he'd cultivated from somewhere an acute fondness for it.

It didn't taste to him nearly so dreadful as he'd feared it might which he shared, after a fashion, with Mrs. Phillip J. King who wondered if didn't the tang of the turnips complement and blend with the general banger seasoning in conjunction with the herbal bouquet of the sauce which struck Mr. Phillip J. King as a sheerly miraculous piece of talk since he'd been pretty much set to utter the identical sentiment himself. He even anticipated her query about the subtlety of the juices, told her anyhow once she'd mentioned a particular subtlety in fact that he'd been personally right there on the verge of speaking of it as it seemed to him an especially fine sort of a subtlety, and he smacked upon a scant dollop of sauce so as to appear to be relishing the qualities and even inquired what the item might be that seemed to him most especially piquant like led Mrs. Phillip J. King to explain to him how the recipe had called for a helping of tawny port but as she did not much herself care for tawny port she'd substituted a touch of cranapple juice instead.

"Oh?" Mr. Phillip J. King said to her and swallowed his dollop pretty straightaway while Mrs. Phillip J. King spoke to him of her own personal gift for culinary innovation like she guessed was an instinct with some people and then allowed Mr. Phillip J. King to guess back of her how with some people it was likely an instinct in fact.

She did not make him eat an entire helping on account of how the whole conglomeration of bangers and turnips and herbs and liquids and greases needed time to mix and meld together and thereby mingle their essences which Mr. Phillip J. King found to be cause for moderate jubilation since by his third spoonful of the banger and turnip stew he had begun to suspect that his arteries were just about to slam shut. So Mrs. Phillip J. King turned off the heat under her pot and allowed her stew to cool on the stovetop, left it the rest of the afternoon to stiffen and congeal prior to settling it for the night in the refrigerator where she expected the essences truly to mingle and so be quite thoroughly melded by morning like would be itself the Friday of the potluck encounter, and the essences did mingle and did meld pretty much by themselves alone but for momentarily deep in the night when Mr. Phillip J. King, who'd gotten up for a swallow of Wink out from the bottle in the door rack, stood in his undershorts in the white refrigerator light and contemplated the pot and the potlid and the potlid knob that he took up between his fingers and so uncovered the mingling stew which had developed a pumpkin-colored sludge on the top with an occasional piece of banger or turnip edge protruding out from it like scraps of land in an altogether unspeakable sea. He hoped she'd skim it, lay even awake a time under the pointy light fixture fearing she might not.

Mrs. Estelle Singletary had intended to devil a dozen eggs and pimento cheese maybe a few celery stalks since she was after all the hostess and had a spate of logistical matters to see to which she explained to her sister Miss Bernice Fay Frazier who'd never herself thrown an encounter and so could not possibly imagine the myriad details of one. Miss Bernice Fay Frazier, however, was not looking to imagine myriad details and had dialed her sister only to make what she figured for a meager request, only to wonder would please Mrs. Estelle Singletary cook for her ailing sister her special green bean casserole with the canned crusty onions and the cream of mushroom soup like she guessed, once she'd heard of the deviled eggs and the celery stalks and the regular spate of matters, was maybe more than one woman should ask of her own flesh and blood in a time of thoroughgoing crisis and she vented a frantic quiver and issued an anguished adieu prior to hanging up the phone and then lingering alongside it so as to be handy for what return call she'd known all along would ensure. Miss Bernice Fay Frazier insisted on making the iced tea herself and steeped the bags in a stockpot with a touch of mint from alongside the back doorstep where she'd planted one time a stand of it that Mr. Wayne Fulp's dog Bill was fond of in an irrigational sort of a way like Miss Bernice Fay Frazier had failed to discover he was until she'd already steeped her tea and had climbed up on a dinette chairseat to fish a jug out from the back of a cabinet when she saw through the window over the sink Bill the speckled hound go three-legged by the mint and then turn a circle and go three-legged by it again like was just the sort of thing to induce a tremor in Miss Bernice Fay Frazier who was coming to be already quite emotionally unraveled and so could not hardly stand the complication of urinational contamination. Naturally, she emptied her stockpot into the sink and discovered as well that she was altogether too shaken for additional teamaking that she called her sister about so as to issue to her a quivery report prior to retiring a time to her chamber where she lay sprawled atop the spread with the back of her hand upon her forehead and, shortly, her cat Bubbles snug up against her opposite armpit where she kneaded the gland most mercilessly with her sinewy feet and her pointy claws together.

Throughout the course of the afternoon Miss Bernice Fay Frazier entertained calls from well-wishers who asked after the state of her crisis and hoped she was improved but not healed entirely since they were all of them looking forward to the potluck encounter, most especially the widow Mrs. Askew from across the road who'd come to be a little distressed in the wake of her initial call on account of how Miss Bernice Fay Frazier had sounded to her inordinately chipper, had struck her as perhaps on the verge of a recovery that she called back to have dispelled for her by Miss Bernice Fay Frazier who assured the widow Mrs. Askew that she was not in fact much improved and anticipated she would maintain her funk for a while yet that the widow Mrs. Askew was grateful to hear of as she'd made already a curried fruit dish with an oatmeal crust which had been no little trouble to concoct like somehow put the widow Mrs. Askew in mind of a pithy thing that did not have much to do with curried fruit or oatmeal or lowslung funks either but was just incomprehensible after a totally irrelevant fashion.

Miss Bernice Fay Frazier could not determine what precisely to wear which proved of course to be an additional source of anguishment for her. She was hoping to discover an ensemble that would fairly harmoniously communicate and proclaim how she was afflicted yet stylish and reasonably svelte as well, but there was not certainly in Miss Bernice Fay Frazier's closet any ensemble so articulate and well spoken as that, so she tried her striped dress with the belt which was entirely too gay for the occasion and she slipped partway into her green suit that had come somehow to constrict her places it had never constricted her previously. Her beige outfit with the billowy skirt appealed to her until she discovered the brown stain upon the seat of it where she had not ever previously seen a brown stain and she cast back to when she'd last worn the thing and recalled where she'd been and supposed she had probably paraded all over the place with a stain on her backside like induced in

Miss Bernice Fay Frazier a bout of retroactive yet thoroughgoing humiliation and distress which was sufficient to send her another time to her bed where she sprawled atop the spread and came to be shortly a study in tragedy and armpit massage both together.

Her deep blue dress with the spots had not struck her straightoff as an appropriate item but once she'd come across it in the closet and drawn it out into the light she found it to hold some appeal for her on account of how it was solemn and grave of color but relatively tentlike of girth, what Miss Bernice Fay Frazier called to herself flowing, which implied elegance and style and room enough for a couple of Bedouins as well. The tiny white spots somehow helped to render Miss Bernice Fay Frazier moderately svelte before the mirror or anyhow enhanced and illuminated her native svelteness that she turned full around to admire the whole of, and she tried on her white shoes to match the spots but did not approve of how they forced her toes to lay and lap like prompted her to twirl and pose in her navy shoes with the slight leather bows instead which she'd spread already and expanded to suit her. Naturally, she was much taken with her aspect in the glass, informed herself what an altogether appropriate aspect it was since she managed to appear plagued and troubled but quite thoroughly dapper about it, and she vented a frantic quiver just to see what precisely a frantic quiver looked like and undertook an anguished discharge back of it which she found herself obliged to repeat and alter on account of how her initial anguished discharge did not much sound to have been induced by a grave emotional blow but maybe just fried onions instead. So she honed her particular symptoms and tinkered with her general aspect and, finally, proclaimed herself quite thoroughly fit for an encounter.

They were to gather at six alongside the fairway back of Mrs. Estelle Singletary's house like meant Mrs. Phillip J. King had cause to bring her banger and turnip stew out from the refrigerator in the vicinity of three o'clock and allow it to sit and warm of its own accord before she settled it upon the burner eye and raised it slowly to a simmer after what fashion she'd read somewhere promoted succulence. It was churning then already by the time Mr. Phillip J. King arrived home to stand upon the doorsill, like was anymore his custom, and announce himself into the house so as to maybe receive back some indication of Mrs. Phillip J. King's hormonal disposition. She sang out to him from the kitchen, sang out like she'd not lately been accustomed to singing out which would be with some noticeable spirit and good humor that kept Mr. Phillip J. King upon the doorsill a brief spell longer as he wondered might she be laying some variety of devious trap for him that he could not possibly ever discover from the doorsill he guessed and so ventured on into the house proper and made obliquely for the kitchen with pauses and sidetrips and aimless straggling along the way until he came to be beckoned, until he came to be charged to advance ever so straightaway onto the linoleum and over by the range where Mrs. Phillip J. King dipped her longhandled spoon into the pot and drew up for Mr. Phillip J. King a thick chunky helping of stew that was still entirely too orange to suit him.

She'd hauled out for the occasion her momma's fancy tureen with the scrolled handles on the sides and the lidgrip that was meant to look leafy and did look a little leafy in fact, and Mr. Phillip J. King saw fit to remark upon the extravagantly leafy and scrolled qualities of it prior to hoisting it off from the countertop and hauling it to the stove for Mrs. Phillip J. King who was put upon to hear in transit how Mr. Phillip J. King had not anticipated such a comely item would be so ponderous as well and he did not suspect he could carry that extravagantly leafy and scrolled tureen one step farther than the stovetop as it had to it more bulk than he'd ever anticipated a tureen could have which was just the sort of talk to briefly incite Mrs. Phillip J. King's hormones that caught fire and singed in the process Mr. Phillip J. King down the full length of his frontside. So he became, then, inestimably delighted to have a tureen to carry and settled it upon the stovetop with marked and profound regret like Mrs. Phillip J. King guessed she could not hardly begin to blame him for as it was such a charming and singularly ornate tureen to have in the first place the privilege to haul about.

As he'd plumbed already for the hormones and come up on them, Mr. Phillip J. King undertook to render himself ever so agreeable and admired the leafy lidgrip prior to informing Mrs. Phillip J. King how lovely he figured her momma's tureen would look full of orange stew that Mrs. Phillip J. King was fairly breathlessly anticipating the sight of on her own and so began to dip stew out from the pot with the matching white porcelain tureen ladle that was itself relatively leafless and more shallow truly than was useful even for her thick lumpy turnip and banger concoction. She was a while, then, filling the tureen but topped the thing off presently with the last of the scraps from the potbottom that served as a manner of charred and crusty garnish in conjunction with a palmful of dehydrated parsley flakes that Mrs. Phillip J. King flung and sprinkled to what Mr. Phillip J. King assured her was fairly extraordinary effect and they stood together and admired the orange stew that Mr. and Mrs. Phillip J. King both agreed was delectable and was exotic and was presented to the best possible advantage in the porcelain tureen with the scrolled handles and the leafy lidgrip that Mr. Phillip J. King wondered how he might raise up without the aid of a block and a winch.

Out alongside the fairway, Mr. Estelle Singletary had not hardly set up the tables to suit Mrs. Estelle Singletary who'd issued an explicit directive to him about where it was the redwood picnic table went and how it was the folding table should extend perpendicular from it like was itself the trouble chiefly since Mr. Estelle Singletary did not personally possess a pure and unclouded sense of the perpendicular and so had situated the folding table on a manner of relatively unperpendicular tangent in order to dodge a hole in the yard that he wished to put under the tabletop so as to keep people safe from it. Mrs. Estelle Singletary, however, had not requested a tangent of Mr. Estelle Singletary which she troubled herself to remind him about prior to repeating for him her explicit directive one time more that she punctuated with a wish to be heeded as it did not seem to her any longer she was ever heeded much which she spoke of presently as well while she crossed her arms over her frontside and glared from the backdoor at Mr. Estelle Singletary and then beyond him to the tangent he'd made.

Mrs. Estelle Singletary was herself in the midst of fabricating her special green bean casserole with the crusty onions and the cream of asparagus soup that she'd substituted for the cream of mushroom which Mr. Estelle Singletary had gone on ahead and helped himself to the last can of just the Saturday previous like was part of how come she was so excessively peeved with him in addition to his murky sense of the perpendicular that had helped together to raise her to a fairly rarified level of irritation along with the general unmitigated condition of her sister Miss Bernice Fay Frazier who let on to be too frazzled even to make tea. It was more than most women could likely have stood up under which Mrs. Estelle Singletary figured for small congratulations as she watched Mr. Estelle Singletary skid and slide the folding table as far beyond perpendicular as he'd been just lately shy of it which she screeched at him about and so heard from Mr. Estelle Singletary a brief snatch of low mumbly inarticulate justification back like probably would have set Mrs. Estelle Singletary off had she been a woman of regular lowslung inclinations but as she was elevated and as she was uplifted she told to Mr. Estelle Singletary merely, "Shut up!" instead which Mr. Estelle Singletary, who could plumb and fathom and delve a little himself, mined straightaway the gist of.

As the afternoon began to yield and give way to the evening, Miss Bernice Fay Frazier endeavored to maintain a relatively quivery state which she came to be assisted at by Mr. Dick Atwater who'd promised to pick her up and drive her in his Toronado to the encounter but who called late here on the day of it and begged off sighting an infirmity he did not wish to speak specifically of since they were not truly awfully well acquainted and their recent brush with intimacy consisted chiefly of her snoring and him watching her at it. So Miss Bernice Fay Frazier's crisis compounded, not so much because she could not any longer hope to ride with Mr. Dick Atwater but because she had probably to ride with the widow Mrs. Askew instead who was riding herself with Mrs. Dwight Mobley who was tolerable on her own but exhibited a pronounced tendency towards pith in the widow Mrs. Askew's presence. It was hardly a prospect Miss Bernice Fay Frazier could bring herself to savor, so she allowed it to complicate and deepen her crisis further still, laid anyhow upon the bedspread in a variety of tragic languishment and suffered shortly the vigorous attentions of her cat Bubbles upon her exposed gland.

Mr. Phillip J. King got charged to hold the tureen on his lap like seemed to him an altogether daunting proposition since he could not figure in the first place how to get the thing off the stovetop and through the house and out across the porch and down the steps to the Monterey where he could sit and have a lap to hold it on. He tried to lift it up by the scrolled handles and did even manage to raise it a little and venture a step or two off from the range before he felt himself growing a trifle herniated from the strain and so settled the tureen upon a convenient piece of countertop from where he turned back to peruse the full four feet he'd traveled. Mrs. Phillip J. King had hoped for a journey a scant more epic than four feet and she shared with Mr. Phillip J. King her thwarted expectations and suggested how he might, if he was able, better unthwart them and shortly. Of course, she meant to be helpful to him in his venture and so volunteered that the best way she could see for Mr. Phillip J. King to haul the thing out from the house to the car was to pick it up and plain go with it like did not, as a suggestion, have sufficient nuance to it to motivate Mr. Phillip J. King who straightaway took Mrs. Phillip J. King's proposal under advisement and left it there. He had the nature of the route to consider and looked for places he might settle a tureen if he came along the way to be strained and put upon, and he'd even set himself to embark on the second leg of his banger and turnip journey when Mrs. Phillip J. King cautioned him how he might best pull lightly upon the right scrolled handle which had broken once already and been Crazy Glued back together. Naturally, Mr. Phillip J. King could not determine how he might just pull lightly upon it and so induced from Mrs. Phillip J. King a second proposal that he took and left under advisement as well.

He wandered the house seeking a solution or a handtruck, whichever he happened upon first, and came presently across a kind of amalgamation of the two of them together in the TV cart from the bedroom which he lifted the TV off of so as to free the thing for tureen transport duty. Now Mrs. Phillip J. King was not enthusiastic about the enterprise at the outset since rolling an heirloom tureen upon a plastic and woodgrain TV cart did not much strike her as stylish and apt, but once Mr. Phillip J. King had hefted the vessel and settled it upon the cart top she revised her judgment due to how stately of a sudden the tureen looked to her and she determined that it was truly a dramatic and significant dish that had cause to be rolled out from the kitchen which she induced Mr. Phillip J. King to throw in with, Mr. Phillip J. King who did not know when last he'd seen a stewpot so proper and refined. They crossed the dining room together with Mr. Phillip J. King pushing the cart and Mrs. Phillip J. King steadying the lid by means of the leafy lidgrip which she pressed upon so as to prevent the variety of clatter that seemed to her might undo the tone of the procession, and they traveled the breadth of the frontroom as well and out across the threshold onto the porch where they paused before the steps so as to allow Mr. Phillip J. King the occasion to assure Mrs. Phillip J. King how he could not possibly hope to take up the tureen and haul it down to the walk which he shortly got persuaded to stand corrected about by Mrs. Phillip J. King who subscribed herself to positive thinking and so revealed to Mr. Phillip J. King how she meant positively for him to take up the tureen and depart from the porch with it and she was speaking of shortly, she told to him, speaking probably even of straightaway, and she smiled at him her toothsome elevated smile and indicated to Mr. Phillip J. King the waiting tureen that needed to get hefted and hauled like Mr. Phillip J. King undertook to heft and haul it and did even full well lift it clear of the cart and travel with it to the porchedge before he wondered might he set it down please for a moment that Mrs. Phillip J. King told to him sweetly, "No sir," about.

So he staggered down the steps holding heavily the good scrolled handle and holding lightly the Crazy Glued one and he did not burn and blister himself through his shirtfront but moderately though he managed with the hot stew to heat his belt buckle enough to brand himself across the belly button like served to distract him from the agony of his herniated muscles that tormented him all the way down the steps and across the little strip of sideyard to the Monterey where he moved to set the tureen upon the hood until Mrs. Phillip J. King, who was fearful for their green metallic finish, advised him sweetly against it and entertained back of it a request from Mr. Phillip J. King who wondered might she somehow bring herself to traipse on down the steps and throw open the sidedoor for him since he could not after all do every little thing alone. Of course, Mrs. Phillip J. King wanted shortly to know from him an item and so inquired, "Traipse?" and lingered at the porchedge watching Mr. Phillip J. King struggle to hold to the tureen which had begun to impart its appreciable heat to his trouser fly that was proving an altogether effective conductor which Mr. Phillip J. King came directly to discover and so attempted to shift and resituate the tureen and his nether parts both but could not somehow manage to separate them like inspired Mr. Phillip J. King to reveal to his wife how what he'd meant by traipse was would she please haul her butt straightaway down the stairs and open the goddam door before his organ got quite utterly scarred and melted and he added back of it a variety of Argh! that Mrs. Phillip J. King had not ever expected to come across but in the funny papers. She grew, understandably, sufficiently impressed to actually haul her butt down the steps and open in fact the goddam door for Mr. Phillip J. King who fairly tumbled onto the carseat with the tureen but managed to stay righted and to get settled and to separate his organ from his whitehot zipper track which Mrs. Phillip J. King learned from him he'd done before she abused and berated him and repeated for him everything he'd just lately told her that she could not find altogether much charm in.

She wanted to carry the TV cart with them as well but guessed since she could not count on Mr. Phillip J. King to climb out from the car to get it she'd fetch it herself and load it onto the backseat which she undertook to do while she simultaneously protested about it and once she'd situated the thing she climbed in under the wheel and apprised Mr. Phillip J. King of how the tureen was surely not nearly so hot or so heavy as he'd made it out to be that Mr. Phillip J. King was set to dispute and would have undoubtedly disputed but for the streak of orange stew he'd allowed somehow to seep out from under the tureen lid and drip down the side of the vessel that Mrs. Phillip J. King found ghastly and endeavored to clean with some spit on a tissue while she informed Mr. Phillip J. King how he did not but have to lay his fingers to a thing to muck it up which Mr. Phillip J. King decided to dispute instead and had begun even to dispute it, had begun already to catalog for Mrs. Phillip J. King his own personal unmucked successes when she turned the key to start the Monterey, turned the key to start the

Monterey twice in fact like would be once while it had call to get started and once after it was running already that served to produce a variety of uproar, truly two varieties of uproar like would be the one from under the hood and would be as well the one from alongside the tureen that was chiefly itself an Argh!

It did not seem fitting to Miss Bernice Fay Frazier that she get made to ride in the backseat of Mrs. Dwight Mobley's Caprice Classic which did not even have to it but front doors in the first place like would leave her to clamber past the upflung seatback and drop fairly irretrievably onto the rear cushion from where she could not possibly hope to raise and remove herself that Mrs. Dwight Mobley commiserated with Miss Bernice Fay Frazier about since she guessed she had not considered how troublesome a backseat might sometimes be for a girthsome woman which precipitously moved Miss Bernice Fay Frazier to explain for the benefit of Mrs. Dwight Mobley chiefly the staggering difference between a girthsome woman and a svelte creature with merely girthsome bones. The widow Mrs. Askew, who arrived from across the road in the midst of Miss Bernice Fay Frazier's illuminating piece of talk on girth and how to gauge it offered straightaway to give over the front seat to her though neither Miss Bernice Fay Frazier nor Mrs. Dwight Mobley could tell it for certain due to how the widow Mrs. Askew had cloaked her largess in some appreciable pith and so had rendered it altogether inscrutable like left Miss Bernice Fay Frazier, on behalf of Mrs. Dwight Mobley, to wonder at the widow Mrs. Askew, "What now?" which got her told another time the same identical inscrutable thing only louder and with remarkably crisper diction. The widow Mrs. Askew did directly make good, however, on her indecipherable offer by clambering herself into the backseat which effectively closed off the inquiry and allowed Miss Bernice Fay Frazier the occasion to observe for the benefit of Mrs. Dwight Mobley how the widow Mrs. Askew, who possessed herself little spindly bones with some fleshy girth roundabout them, could clamber well enough on account of how fleshy girth was not near so troublesome as bony girth could be which the widow Mrs. Askew heard and comprehended enough of to feel pressed of a sudden to air a sentiment that Miss Bernice Fay Frazier most especially did not have to labor at all to decipher.

They rode towards the country club by a route Miss Bernice Fay Frazier would not personally have selected had she been charged herself to select a route, but she guessed some people could go just any old way they wanted to like brought to mind for the widow Mrs. Askew a scrap of pith that she leaned up towards the seatback to impart, a scrap of pith about how it is we all of us travel through this vale of woe and strife that had in fact a thing to do with routes but was concerned truly more with woe and with strife instead that Miss Bernice Fay Frazier detected it was and felt obliged to share the news of it with the widow Mrs. Askew like she was pretty well set to do when she looked briefly out the windowglass to gain her bearings and found herself inclined to speak directly to Mrs. Dwight Mobley, to inquire of her, "Where in the world are you going?" that Mrs. Dwight Mobley responded to exclusively with the ball of her right foot that she raised off of the accelerator so as to beat one time upon the brake pedal and thereby dislodge Miss Bernice Fay Frazier who bounced off the glovebox girthsome bones foremost like Mrs. Dwight Mobley had hoped she might.

Mrs. Phillip J. King was closing herself on the country club from another direction entirely alongside Mr. Phillip J. King who was diverting her with talk of how he did not figure he would probably ever stand full upright again which would partly be due to lifting the tureen but would partly be due to sitting beneath it as well since he did not guess his organ and sack had been manufactured with tureen support in mind. He claimed to be presently in the throes of some genuine agony but Mrs. Phillip J. King, who guessed she knew better, assured him he wasn't and wondered would he please for a time quit whining at her. Since she was hoping to make a variety of splash, Mrs. Phillip J. King did not wish to arrive at the country club too awful early on and so induced Mrs. Phillip J. King to loiter in the throes of his agony for a spell further while she passed on by Mrs. Estelle Singletary's street and struck out along the old Burlington Road so far as the Sertoma Park where she pulled into the gravel lot and idled beside the pool for longer truly than Mr. Phillip J. King guessed he was fit to endure and so he whined in earnest another time at Mrs. Phillip J. King and explained how the bottom lip of the tureen was mashing his housekey into his thighskin with surely sufficient force to make an indelible impression like seemed to him an altogether frightful circumstance and he undertook to communicate the pure frightfulness of it with a woeful look and necknoise both together which served only to touch off Mrs. Phillip J. King who did not suppose she'd had a moment's peace since they'd left the house and wondered why in the first place Mr. Phillip J. King would fret so over chiefly an organ he didn't seem much disposed but to sluice into the bowl with anyhow like straightoff stung Mr. Phillip J. King who was pained and anguished already and did not need to be stung as well.

"Me?" he wanted to know. "My organ?"

And Mrs. Phillip J. King told him yes him and yes his organ and reminded Mr. Phillip J. King how they'd last shared between them an amorous moment in the late spring of the year. "Twenty-fourth of May," Mrs. Phillip J. King said. "I recall I had to waylay you."

"Me?" Mr. Phillip J. King wanted to know still even after he'd gotten told yes him already, and he provided Mrs. Phillip J. King with one of his fairly undiluted exasperated expressions that came replete with a whiny breathy discharge like served as preface to his inquiry of Mrs. Phillip J. King if he had personally to remind her how she'd gone lately quite thoroughly hormonal in the wake of which Mrs. Phillip J. King told to him, "Oh," and told to him, "that," like induced one whiny breathy discharge further.

Mr. Phillip J. King confessed from under the tureen how lately he would have as likely caught up a groundhog in a tender embrace as Mrs. Phillip J. King that Mrs. Phillip J. King found diverting and so snorted about it prior to admitting how certainly she'd suffered through a bout of hormonal turbulation but had settled recently into a state of relative flashlessness like left her neither hot nor cold but pretty much room temperature all the time. She allowed how certainly her juices had flowed in the past weeks but insisted how they'd ebbed already pretty dramatically and were evermore ebbing further still.

"Ebbing," Mr. Phillip J. King said.

And Mrs. Phillip J. King told to him, "Yes baby," and slid partway along the seatcushion leaving her left foot pretty much on the brake pedal though not truly sufficiently on the brake pedal to prevent the Monterey from edging ever so gradually across the gravel lot and crunching stone beneath its tires after such a fashion as to distract Mr. Phillip J. King who said, "Sugar?" said Sugar in fact twice like would be once while Mrs. Phillip J. King was still in the middle of sidling and once after she'd already arrived snug up next to him where she laid her foremost finger to most especially the soft dangly portion of his near ear and then dragged it tipend foremost down his neck and along his collar and under his T-shirt so as to gain his solar plexi and touch at last his special place which unerringly rendered him tingly and so rendered him in fact tingly on this occasion as well, tingly even in his unguided mobile Monterey and with a ponderous tureen of unspecified but doubtless considerable weight upon his lap, and he could have under the circumstances probably stood to be tingly alone but grew aware shortly of his own juices flowing and felt his personal item begin to unfurl and stiffen and Mr. Phillip J. King in his stirred and anguished state looked out the windshield and saw how they would likely meet shortly with a trash barrel that he was hoping to speak of when he opened his mouth but what with his Monterey unguided and his juices flowing and his lone organ undertaking to levitate a tureen he managed to turn his head and tell to Mrs. Phillip J. King just "Argh!" alone.

Naturally Miss Bernice Fay Frazier explained as best as she was able how precisely she'd lapsed into crisis in the first place like came complete with a disclaimer for the benefit of Mrs. Dwight Mobley who Miss Bernice Fay Frazier did not hold personally responsible for her own present tragic circumstances since most probably Mrs. Dwight Mobley had not known her momma's sister's friend from Berkeley Springs was trash which Mrs. Dwight Mobley insisted was in fact the truth of the thing. Of course news had already circulated as to Raymond and Miss Mary Alice Celestine Lefler's intimate attachment like would be partly on account of Miss Bernice Fay Frazier, who'd fairly thoroughly broadcast her circumstances, and partly on account of Mr. H. Monroe Aycock as well who'd learned from Mr. Bethune at the Belvedere Hotel how Raymond and Miss Mary Alice Celestine Lefler together had holed up and then absconded which managed to touch off in Mr. H. Monroe Aycock a bout of moral indignation and served as the inspiration for his weekly murky geopolitical editorial in the *Chronicle* which was not, for one of his geopolitical editorials, most especially murky but was chiefly just moderately opaque instead like rendered it near about intelligible, particularly the part concerning Raymond ("a gentleman from distant climes") and the part concerning Miss Mary Alice Celestine Lefler ("an import of late with charms and wiles"). Even the passage about their dalliance at a local inn of repute and tradition would yield up its nugget in the face of acute analysis. At heart, of course, Mr. H. Monroe Aycock's primary concern was Godless communism and he'd touched on Raymond and Miss Mary Alice Celestine Lefler's illicit union only as an illustration of how lately the national moral fabric was getting pretty thoroughly rent that Mr. H. Monroe Aycock found to be a wholly woeful circumstance and he prognosticated that we were surely as a people well on our way to calling each other comrade and wearing those gray slouchy hats with the tiny bills that communists seem so inordinately fond of which struck Mr. H. Monroe Aycock as sufficient of a danger to fill any God-fearing soul with mortal dread.

The widow Mrs. Askew who, with her recently cultivated powers of plumbing and delving and fathoming, had read Mr. H. Monroe Aycock's column and had managed to come to a relatively lucid understanding of Mr. H. Monroe Aycock's personal opinion of the state of the nation's moral fabric informed Miss Bernice Fay Frazier and Mrs. Dwight Mobley both how she'd heard somewhere that communists were prone to rape and pillage, that rape in fact and pillage along with general and thoroughgoing Godlessness was what pretty much communism was all about. With various democratic principles at risk, then, the widow Mrs. Askew could not quite understand how a man and a woman might bring themselves together in a hotel to rend the national moral fabric in the first place, and she wondered at Mrs. Dwight Mobley and Miss Bernice Fay Frazier if she'd spoken to them previously of the variety of tangled web people wove when they practiced there at the outset to deceive which Mrs. Dwight Mobley and Miss Bernice Fay Frazier said harmoniously together, "Yes," about.

Since it was after all her encounter in the first place they'd near about already arrived at, Miss Bernice Fay Frazier wondered might she speak freely of her present state without the inconvenience of interjected pith which the widow Mrs. Askew allowed she might though she could not resist appending to it a statement on the topic of friends together in all kinds of weather which struck Miss Bernice Fay Frazier as suspiciously pithy after its own fashion. Nevertheless, she proceeded and provided the ladies with her personal version of events and spoke of Raymond with his hair and his moustache and his accoutrements and his blazer and his general princely charm and spoke as well of whom she called That Woman, That Woman with the raven locks and the lips and the fingerends and the thoroughgoing indecent streak as well, That Woman who was undoubtedly trash to the core which inspired the widow Mrs. Askew to throw in with one comment further on the topic of the national moral fabric which Miss Bernice Fay Frazier allowed since she was pleased to find her ramifications broad and farreaching. Mrs. Dwight Mobley was especially curious as to the nature of the encounter upon Miss Mary Alice Celestine Lefler's return from her foray which Miss Bernice Fay Frazier was briefly forestalled from speaking of by the widow Mrs. Askew who found foray most apt and invigorating and took occasion to congratulate Mrs. Dwight Mobley about it which Miss Bernice Fay Frazier allowed as well though she communicated chiefly with a sidelong leer how her native generosity was fairly precipitously eroding.

"She was flushed," Miss Bernice Fay Frazier said, "from the toes up," and she added how she'd viewed well enough in her own mind's eye the means by which a woman with Miss Mary Alice Celestine Lefler's rubbery joints might come to get flushed atop a bed in an inn of repute and tradition. "Talk about rending your moral fabric," Miss Bernice

Fay Frazier told most especially to the widow Mrs. Askew and then humphed back of it after such a fashion as to speak worlds of her personal pain and indignation at least according to the widow Mrs. Askew who fathomed in the breathy discharge the acutest emotional consequences of That Woman's thoughtless and altogether selfish carnal foray, she called it.

"It was surely a blow," Miss Bernice Fay Frazier admitted and cast a wounded look at the rubber floormat before her.

Mrs. Dwight Mobley wanted to know had sparks flown because she figured if she'd been the one waiting for her own houseguest to return from a foray sparks surely would have, and Miss Bernice Fay Frazier confessed that sparks did in fact presently fly but did not fly straightoff due to how Miss Bernice Fay Frazier, being a Christian woman, had provided Miss Mary Alice Celestine Lefler with the occasion to explain her absence, had greeted her in fact sweetly upon her return but could not afford truly to ignore the incriminating flush and, most especially, the rank cigarette smell and the leathery scent with it like together had inspired Miss Bernice Fay Frazier to an inquiring and altogether arch expression that she demonstrated for the benefit of Mrs. Dwight Mobley and the widow Mrs. Askew as well who found it in fact appreciably more inquiring than arch but allowed how it was certainly some of both and suspected between them it was precisely the sort of expression that would draw a response from a plagued and guilty conscience that Miss Bernice Fay Frazier assured them it had.

"She told me he'd come to fetch her," Miss Bernice Fay Frazier said. "Told me he'd rolled her washstand, gushed like a girl and her having just left from a hotel bed, having just engaged with a man in unseemly gyrations and the like, a man with a wife, a man with babies."

"A wife," Mrs. Dwight Mobley said and the widow Mrs. Askew added back of it, "Babies."

"You just can't know what some people will do," Miss Bernice Fay Frazier told earnestly to the widow Mrs. Askew back of her prior to shifting round to tell to Mrs. Dwight Mobley, "You can't. Not hardly a scrap of shame left in this world," and the widow Mrs. Askew and Mrs. Dwight Mobley could not believe between them they'd ever before heard a truer thing and congratulated Miss Bernice Fay Frazier on how she'd cut just like a knife to the heart of the predicament.

"She had to go," Miss Bernice Fay Frazier said like inspired the widow Mrs. Askew and Mrs. Dwight Mobley to purely ejaculate together how they guessed she most certainly did. "Couldn't stay under my roof," Miss Bernice Fay Frazier added and so rendered the ladies ejaculatory one time further that together they persevered at for longer truly than Miss Bernice Fay Frazier found proper most especially since she was intending to speak directly of the icy style with which she'd propped and flung as she expelled Miss Mary Alice Celestine Lefler out from the house to the waiting arms of him with the hair and the moustache who got charged with the luggage, and she re-created the entire episode once the clamor had dwindled and died, approximated for the ladies how she'd pitched and then she flung for them and spoke and spoke for them and flung and managed even one time simultaneously to speak and fling together that Mrs. Dwight Mobley and the widow Mrs. Askew were most especially partial to as a means of eviction and so requested an additional display of it from Miss Bernice Fay Frazier who obliged them with an altogether chilling rendition.

"I guess she went then?" Mrs. Dwight Mobley said and heard from Miss Bernice Fay Frazier that she did in fact go and straightaway like was the intention but touched off as well Miss Bernice Fay Frazier's present difficulties which would be chiefly her balky nerve, her mischievous cat, and the ever present threat of ne'er-do-wells like singly or together could leave her dead or afflicted atop the rug in her underclothes for just any old body to find. "Any old body," Miss Bernice Fay Frazier said and laid her one hand flat out upon her breastbone as she set to quivering in what the widow Mrs. Askew determined straightoff for a frantic sort of a way which the subsequent anguished discharge served to confirm resolutely for her.

Fortunately, however, they'd gained at last the country club, had driven already through the rail gateway and were drawing up on Mrs. Estelle Singletary's house where the driveway was thoroughly choked with cars and the curbing out front was entertaining a Pontiac as well like proved to be sufficient of a vehicular inducement to elevate Miss Bernice Fay Frazier to performance pitch and she quivered and wailed and raised a pitiful lamentation that worsened once Mrs. Dwight Mobley had run her front radial up onto the curb and then bounced it back down into the gutter like induced Miss Bernice Fay Frazier to wonder had she not yet suffered quite enough jolts already thank you very much which itself touched off the widow Mrs. Askew who'd not found lately occasion to speak of the sea of turbulation and woe we all float upon but discovered in Miss Bernice Fay Frazier's renewed suffering cause to speak of it which failed somehow to improve Miss Bernice Fay Frazier's general humor. She emerged, then, ill from the Caprice Classic and peevish and sufficiently weak as well at her nether joints to call for support from Mrs. Dwight Mobley who gripped her at her one elbow and the widow Mrs. Askew who squeezed her at her tender armpit and so helped to heighten Miss Bernice Fay Frazier's general disposition down the drive and around back of the house to the strip of yard alongside the fairway where she arrived in an altogether churlish state and straightaway removed Mr. Sleepy Pitts from his webbed lawnchair, fairly dumped him out of it as she asked him would he get up like she guessed any gentleman might before he had in the first place to be asked.

She dropped onto the seat of the thing herself and the plastic webbing stretched and whined while the aluminum frame popped at the joints and creaked everywhere otherwise as reminder of how they were after all just plastic and aluminum and had not been manufactured truly but for bones of a regular sort of a girth. Mr. Wyatt Benbow bet Mr. Cecil Dutton that the entire item would collapse in a heap before Miss Bernice Fay Frazier loosed even her first frantic quiver, but Miss Bernice Fay Frazier had come to be so extravagantly quick on the quiver by now that she was out with a spate of them before the chair could even set up much of an additional fuss.

They'd all arrived there before her, they'd almost all arrived there before her anyhow, and the Reverend Mr. Theodore J. Parnell stepped forward to take up Miss Bernice Fay Frazier's fingers and to offer to her his actual fullsized elegant silky handkerchief out from his breastpocket in the event that distraught blubbering ensued which seemed to the reverend likely and imminent. Miss Bernice Fay Frazier, however, decided to forestall her blubbering briefly for the benefit of a pitiful lamentation which she engaged in instead, a pitiful lamentation which was in truth fairly moist and rheumy but did not have to it the blubbery sort of heaving and gasping the reverend had anticipated since the heaving and the gasping would have surely undone the pathetic inquiry Miss Bernice Fay Frazier had decided in the first place to set up her lamentation about. She was anxious to discover how it was she'd come to deserve such treatment as she'd lately received at the hands of trash when she'd evermore endeavored to be a goodly woman, but she did not wait to hear from the reverend a response and did in fact blubber after all, quaked and heaved and laid her face into the Reverend Mr. Parnell's silky handkerchief which proved about as absorbent as Saran Wrap and so served to smear her various emanations which diluted and mingled with her rouge and her fleshtone powder and her sparkly bluegreen eyeshade as well after such a fashion as to fairly transform her visage which she raised up her head and exhibited primarily in the direction of Mr. Luther Teague who told to her straightaway, "Good

God" and entertained a tattoo played upon his ribs by Mrs. Luther Teague with both her foremost fingerends together.

Miss Bernice Fay Frazier might likely have incited additional exclamations on the topic of her transformed visage if most everybody had not come already to be distracted from the blubbering by the arrival of Mr. Phillip J. King, or more accurately by the arrival in fact of Mr. Phillip J. King's TV cart with Mrs. Phillip J. King's momma's tureen upon it, Mr. Phillip J. King's TV cart and Mrs. Phillip J. King's momma's tureen that had together effected somehow an escape from Mr. Phillip J. King who was pursuing the cart and the tureen both down the edge of the driveway alongside the vehicles and was receiving from up at the head of the drive strident encouragement from Mrs. Phillip J. King who apparently had told him already previously how he was in some danger of losing the cart before he in fact lost it which she seemed excessively anxious to remind him about. They were the three of them, like would be the cart and the tureen and Mr. Phillip J. King as well, heading pretty directly towards Mrs. Estelle Singletary's bushy peonies at the bottom of the drive, or heading anyhow for Mrs. Estelle Singletary's rustic roughhewn timber bushy peony border that Mrs. Phillip J. King up by the Monterey informed Mr. Phillip J. King about prior to taking occasion to lavish him with threats and imprecations and to speak briefly of what life for Mr. Phillip J. King in the wake of a TV cart/roughhewn timber collision might resemble which sounded most especially to Mr. Wyatt Benbow and Sleepy Pitts together like nothing a man could look forward to with much fervor.

It didn't at all appear that he'd catch the thing, not even to Miss Bernice Fay Frazier who'd interrupted her blubbering and had lifted her visage to see what the fuss was about, and he didn't in fact catch the cart at all but only gained upon it there at the last and reached the bushy peony bed himself so close after the crash that he managed by dent of extraordinary good fortune and impeccable timing to grab up the tureen in both his arms and clutch it tight to his shirtfront once it had risen off the cart and floated briefly free on the air. Of course the cart itself took flight and traded ends prior to landing top foremost in Mrs. Estelle Singletary's bushiest peony with the withering papery pink blossoms upon it, but nobody much noticed how the cart had upended and sailed on the air as they had instead Mr. Phillip J. King to watch and admire, Mr. Phillip J. King who dashed through the peony bed himself, cleared the far border of it with a graceful leap and fairly bolted across the yard with the tureen lid clattering and the banger and turnip stew sloshing and dripping and his shirtbuttons hot like firecoals against his ever so tender stomach skin which, all taken together, served just precisely as the variety of inducement to propel Mr. Phillip J. King to a purely astounding velocity that he managed to maintain clean across the yard to the perpendicular part of the buffet where he unburdened himself of the tureen and jumped and beat his arms and rubbed his shirtfront and did not generally appear awfully much relieved.

The ovation, however, seemed to soothe him a bit, most especially as it grew and swelled and came to be a fairly thoroughgoing and widespread ovation that had initially been confined to Mr. Wyatt Benbow and Mr. Sleepy Pitts alone who had instigated the hooting and the stomping and the clapping too. Of course Mrs. Estelle Singletary herself did not join in the merriment as she'd stepped across the peony bed and seen with her own eyes the carnage. "My prized *Edulis superba,*" Mrs. Estelle Singletary said as she flung her arm peonyward with the sort of flair Miss Bernice Fay Frazier was pleased to have raised up her visage and witnessed. "Crushed. Beat back altogether." And she induced Mr. Phillip J. King to gaze himself across the yard to the peony bed like was anymore four regular leafy moderately beflowered peony bushes and one bush otherwise among them that was partly stems and leaves and withering blossoms as well but was chiefly anymore plastic wheels and brassy wheel collars on the tipends of four upraised woodgrain legs with a brassy wire shelf between.

"Edulis," Mrs. Estelle Singletary said, *"superba,"* and Mr. Phillip J. King, who was growing genuinely contrite on account of the horticultural havoc he had quite apparently wreaked, was fairly well set to offer a consoling sentiment to Mrs. Estelle Singletary but got to be prevented from it by Mrs. Phillip J. King who'd circled around the peony bed herself and had pretty much stormed across the yard so as to arrive at where precisely Mr. Phillip J. King was presently growing contrite and grab him up by a particular piece of shirtfront that assured her not just a handful of polyester blend dress shirt and cotton undershirt beneath it but a representative sample as well of Mr. Phillip J. King's remaining chesthair like was primarily what altered Mr. Phillip J. King's contrition and transformed it of a sudden to acute distress.

And Mr. Phillip J. King told to Mrs. Phillip J. King, "Argh!" one time further and heard straightaway back every little thing Mrs. Phillip J. King had troubled herself to speak of previously up at the top of the drive which concerned chiefly the cart and Mr. Phillip J. King's grip upon it that had appeared to her insubstantial which she refreshed Mr. Phillip J. King she'd told him it had and Mr. Phillip J. King made to cast back to see if he could not himself remember such a conversation and

Mrs. Phillip J. King didn't have to twist her handful of shirt and follicles but the merest bit to produce from Mr. Phillip J. King a miraculous snatch of verbatim recall. Mrs. Phillip J. King wondered why he'd not bothered to heed her which naturally incited Mr. Phillip J. King to wonder pretty much the same identical thing on his own, and it seemed to him she might rare back and punch him on his breastbone like she'd been known in fits of pique to punch him on his breastbone previously, but Mrs. Phillip J. King had her tureen and her banger and turnip concoction to see after so she merely twisted and tweaked his chesthair one time further prior to letting loose of him altogether and attending to her concoction.

She licked a tissue and cleaned the outside of her tureen with it in the company of Mr. and Mrs. Luther Teague who'd not between them had call to identify and relate with Mrs. Phillip J. King lately and so had stepped over to inquire was she in fact still OK like they were OK themselves and Mrs. Phillip J. King was explaining as she wiped the ways precisely she was OK and the ways precisely she was not OK at all, was not even middling truly, which Mr. Phillip J. King managed to suffer the brunt of the blame for most especially once he'd assured Mr. and Mrs. Luther Teague how he was himself pretty completely OK all over. As soon, however, as Mrs. Phillip J. King had laid the blame and Mr. Phillip J. King had agreed to absorb it, circumstances improved remarkably and the Kings and the Teagues related and identified and delved and fathomed in the gayest sort of way right up to the very instant Mrs. Phillip J. King took hold of the leafy grip and lifted the tureen lid so as to dip her porcelain ladle into the stew and stir it which struck Mr. Luther Teague as reason enough to gape into the dish where he watched Mrs. Phillip J. King churn up the banger bits, which he could not personally identify as banger bits, along with the turnip wedges, which did not themselves look truly to be turnip wedges to him, not even to mention the near about Day-Glo orange sauce which she beat and folded into a frothy mass like pretty much by itself alone induced Mr. Luther Teague to inform Mrs. Phillip J. King along with most anybody else who cared to know it, "Good God" that nobody anywhere had fingerends pointy enough to punctuate.

Off from the table over by Mrs. Estelle Singletary's ornamental pear tree, Miss Bernice Fay Frazier was coming to feel neglected and she wondered aloud to nobody in particular why it was she'd bothered to cart her crisis clean across town in the first place when she could have been ignored altogether in the comfort of her own home like appeared to strike a chord with the Reverend Mr. Parnell who stepped over to join Miss Bernice Fay Frazier, laid even his fingerends upon the knobby bone along the back of her neck which seemed undoubtedly prelude to commiseration, and the reverend leaned down close and asked softly of Miss Bernice Fay Frazier, "You done with my handkerchief?" that Miss Bernice Fay Frazier had not anticipated at all as the nature of the reverend's intentions and she held up for the reverend his silky handkerchief which had gone lately fairly technicolored and as she trained her sullen visage upon him she told to him, "Here then," with no lilt to speak of and she crossed her arms over herself and laid against her folding chairback with what Mr. H. Monroe Aycock shortly insisted had been undue alacrity like would be after her rear legs had begun to plunge and sink into the ground and she'd shrieked and hollered and thereby induced the reverend and induced Mr. H. Monroe Aycock to hoist and right her by chiefly her tender armpit glands.

And if it wasn't enough already that she'd blubbered and wiped and so altered her visage and had not even found occasion yet to delve and plumb and fathom and relate and identify but had only sunk a little through the turf instead, she shortly spied at the top of the drive not just Miss Fay Dull with her parka over her arm and her bowl of mandarin salad clutched tight against her dressfront but Mr. Tiny Aaron and Mrs. MaySue Ludley as well, Mr. Tiny Aaron and Mrs. MaySue Ludley together as an item judging from how Mrs. MaySue Ludley gripped Mr. Tiny Aaron at his elbowjoint and Mr. Tiny Aaron did not thrash about to free himself of her. She'd seen his ensemble just lately, Miss Bernice Fay Frazier had, his madras jacket with the stripes and the checks and the white shirt and the skyblue Sansabelt pants so she pondered primarily instead Mrs. MaySue Ludley's flowing green skirt that she did not think truly awful much of most especially in combination with Mrs. MaySue Ludley's speckled blouse that appeared to Miss Bernice Fay Frazier just plain crawling with spots. Apparently Mrs. MaySue Ludley was anymore a woman of conspicuous visage herself, conspicuous even unblubbered on and unwiped since she appeared from a distance pretty much all lips and eyelids and not just to Miss Bernice Fay Frazier but to Mrs. Dwight Mobley and Mrs. Cecil Dutton as well who suspected together that Mrs. MaySue Ludley applied her ointments and glosses and powders with a basting brush. Of course Mrs. MaySue Ludley's scent ensued, wafted clean down the drive and across the yard and tainted the general atmosphere with its thoroughgoing treacle that thickened and compounded as Tiny Aaron and Mrs. MaySue Ludley advanced on the encounter group somewhat in the company of Miss Fay Dull and her green parka, Miss Fay Dull who managed presently to outstrip the pair of them so as to arrive firstoff in the backyard and proclaim how she'd met them at the curb and should not be construed to have come with them at all.

Mr. Tiny Aaron was carrying a thing in his free hand. Mrs. Estelle Singletary noticed straightaway how Mr. Tiny Aaron was carrying in his free hand a thing that she was at first too misty from the wafting treacly scent to make out but determined shortly to be a breadloaf in a sack, a brown whole wheat breadloaf which did not strike Mrs. Estelle Singletary as awful much of a contribution most especially from the likes of Mr. Tiny Aaron who'd not in the first place been invited anyhow which Mrs. Estelle Singletary, being a woman of extravagant social grace, determined she'd not speak directly of but would only maybe imply snidely. Consequently, then, she offered Mr. Tiny Aaron and Mrs. MaySue Ludley a fairly sour greeting and embarked straightaway on an implication concerning Mr. Tiny Aaron's breadsack that did not seem to provoke in Tiny Aaron detectable offense and he informed Mrs. Estelle Singletary how MaySue—and he shifted to look sweetly upon MaySue as he uttered her name, MaySue who fairly beat up a wind with her eyelids back at him—had encouraged him to give over white flour for whole grains instead on account of the general healthful effects of whole grains that anymore he sopped with exclusively, and Tiny Aaron braved the treacly scent so as to lean in and exhibit his appreciation to Mrs. MaySue Ludley by means of a peck on the check which induced Mrs. MaySue Ludley to turn and admire Tiny Aaron back like, out of all Mrs. MaySue Ludley's traits and habits, was the one he was truly fondest of since she managed evermore to turn and admire him just precisely like he guessed, were he able, he'd turn and admire himself.

So Mrs. MaySue Ludley watched Tiny Aaron and Tiny Aaron watched Mrs. MaySue Ludley watch him and together they proved impervious to Mrs. Estelle Singletary's ongoing implications even once they'd surpassed snide altogether and had grown quite thoroughly testy and sharp. Worse yet, Mrs. MaySue Ludley continued to cling to Mr. Tiny Aaron's elbowjoint as Mr. Tiny Aaron squired her about and presented her after a courtly sort of a fashion to whoever it was they came up on to present her to, so most everybody got wafted and treacled at up close and had to suffer through what Mr. H. Monroe Aycock identified as Mr. Tiny Aaron's blandishments not even to mention the visage and the fluttery eyelids as well. And Mr. Tiny Aaron spoke with open affection of Mrs. MaySue Ludley and deferred every now and again to her so as to allow Mrs. MaySue Ludley to speak with open affection of him back which the women in particular took some notice of since they could not many of them say when last they'd been warmly deferred to or had heard their men blandish even a little on their accounts. Even Miss Bernice Fay Frazier admitted to the widow Mrs. Askew that they seemed to her a cute couple once they'd stopped by her chair to pay their respects and to condemn and vilify Miss Mary Alice Celestine Lefler who Mr. Tiny Aaron in particular had suspected was trash all along which he insisted at Miss Bernice Fay Frazier he had, insisted it twice in fact with altogether palpable conviction and so was not reminded of the catsnatching by Miss Bernice Fay Frazier who did not wish to undo a couple so cute.

Needless to say, Miss Bernice Fay Frazier was growing fairly anxious to delve and relate and fathom and plumb and identify now that everybody who was meant to come and two people who weren't had all arrived, but the tide of opinion was running stiffly against her since most everybody otherwise was of a mind to eat before they encountered. Were she pressed, however, Miss Bernice Fay Frazier guessed she might relent and ingest an altogether minuscule portion of Mrs. Estelle Singletary's bean casserole if someone would be so kind as to spoon it up for her and carry it to her like got delegated to Mr. Estelle Singletary pretty much by thoroughgoing default and he brought to Miss Bernice Fay Frazier a plate with not a thing in the world on it but an ever so puny dollop of bean casserole as well as some attendant bean casserole juices like appeared to Miss Bernice Fay Frazier a waste of a perfectly good excursion since Mr. Estelle Singletary could certainly have stood to spoon up a few other puny dollops for Miss Bernice Fay Frazier's perusal as long as he was coming her way in the first place. So she presently got her food heaped and piled and mounded up on the plate just like most everybody otherwise except for Mr. Tiny Aaron who did not want to seem in the presence of Mrs. MaySue Ludley a glutton and so spooned up only those items Mrs. MaySue Ludley saw fit to spoon up herself and in portions smaller even than Mrs. MaySue Ludley's own personal portions like were slight and, as best as Mr. Tiny Aaron could tell, altogether dainty. Nevertheless, he was succeeding down the length of the buffet to seem a man of moderation until he turned the perpendicular corner and arrived at last at the porcelain tureen with the scrolled handles and the leafy lidgrip and Mrs. Phillip J. King herself in attendance for purposes of ladling and elucidation. Now Tiny Aaron, being a man in the company of his own absorbent breadloaf, was partial to greases and sauces not even to mention the iridescent union of the two, so he bent and gaped into the tureen with some considerable interest and not a little enthusiasm, and he pointed at a turnip and inquired of Mrs. Phillip J. King, "What's that?" which she spoke of straightaway in addition to the bangers that he did not even have to inquire about to hear of as well along with the herbal bouquet that had served in conjunction with the low cooking heat to extract the essences from the turnips and the hangers both which Mr. Phillip J. King got enlisted to confirm and so rested his own fork long enough to confirm it.

He had to have him a taste of it, but Mrs. Phillip J. King was not meaning to ladle up mere tastes and so deposited a sizeable helping between Mr. Tiny Aaron's dollop of mandarin salad and his lone chicken drumette, and straightaway he sampled a banger which met with his giddy approval and he nibbled as well at a scrap of turnip which he proclaimed to be as savory a scrap of turnip as he'd ever had occasion to nibble like touched off Mr. Phillip J. King who stilled his fork and told into the air, "Savory," as he could not somehow seem to keep himself from it. Naturally, Mr. Tiny Aaron was anxious to baptize a breadslice and he opened the neck of his sack and drew one out, a brown breadslice fairly riddled with hulls and chaff and various lumpy healthful inedible items otherwise. He tore the thing in half and dipped with the crustless part direct into the orange sauce, swirled and sopped it about until it looked to him as saturated as a lumpy halfslice could get when he folded it expertly with his fingers like only an inveterate sopper might and raised it dripless to his mouth where he took in the entire item.

He was quite directly overcome with delight and Mmmmed like Mr. Phillip J. King could never in this lifetime hope to, Mmmmed with infectious passion and assured Mrs. Phillip J. King how her banger and turnip concoction was purely ambrosia to his palate, assured her once Mr. H. Monroe Aycock had suggested ambrosia and had suggested palate both in the wake of Mr. Tiny Aaron's infectious discharge. He could not speak too highly of the orange turnip and banger stew. It possessed the items he most adored in a dish like would be grease and salt and pork and herbs simmered and reduced together to their succulent essences, and Mr. Tiny Aaron proclaimed so everybody might know it how the essences were in fact succulent, broadcast his approval of the orange stew and invited those people who'd been put off by the orange chiefly and the iridescence somewhat to step forward and sop up a puddle of it with brown lumpy bread he would gladly supply from his own personal sack. And they came forward, men exclusively, and sopped sauce at the recommendation of Mr. Tiny Aaron who spoke of how they might savor upon their palates the grease and the salt and the pork and the turnips in addition to the herbal bouquet which the men that bothered to sop did in fact savor all of, even Mr. Luther Teague who'd been previously reluctant to so much as look upon the orange juices which he had not suspected were the least bit ambrosial as far as orange juices went.

The Mmmming was riotous and near about deafening and Mrs. Phillip J. King could not help somehow but grow flashy in the face of it, not especially hot flashy or especially cold flashy either but just prickly flashy instead, goosepimply flashy from the general reception her stew had inspired like expunged altogether from her recollection the kidneys she'd attempted previously. She accepted the accolades and the various culinary discharges with almost measurable modesty and proclaimed ever so briefly that her stew was hardly the triumph it was presently getting taken for though she managed soon enough to be convinced otherwise by a coalition of Mr. Wyatt Benbow and Mr. Sleepy Pitts and Mr. Tiny Aaron too who insisted on discovering the ingredients but got charged to guess them instead by Mr. Phillip J. King who bet they could not name the one most piquant which the three of them together failed in fact at.

"She's got an instinct," Mr. Phillip J. King announced in the wake of the disclosure and he caught up Mrs. Phillip J. King across the shoulders and squeezed her to him.

"I've got an instinct," Mrs. Phillip J. King announced herself in the direction chiefly of the widow Mrs. Askew whose own personal curried fruit dish had gone so far relatively untouched and altogether unsopped in like probably was what induced her to tell to Mrs. Phillip J. King back, "I'll bet you do," with so remarkably little pith as to be fairly arresting.

"She's got an instinct," the widow Mrs. Askew told to Mrs. Cecil Dutton as preface to a thoroughgoing exchange of smirks between them. "An instinct," she said to Miss Bernice Fay Frazier once she'd arrived at her folding chair. "She's got one." But Miss Bernice Fay Frazier for her part could not even muster a proper smirk to display and only sneered weakly at the widow Mrs. Askew prior to informing her how she might as well have just stayed home for all the attention her crisis was getting which was not, as best as Miss Bernice Fay Frazier could tell, any attention at all, and she quivered frantically and discharged in an anguished sort of a way and turned at last her besmeared visage on the widow Mrs. Askew so as to speak of Bubbles her cat who evermore grew forlorn in her absence. "She misses me so," Miss

Bernice Fay Frazier said. "I hate to go off and leave her for no more call than this," like touched off the widow Mrs. Askew who wondered had she ever previously shared with Miss Bernice Fay Frazier how it was the fog sometimes came in on little cat feet.

Bubbles, in fact, was being presently forlorn. She was dangling from the sheer draperies back of the settee fairly much in the throes of despondency judging from her expression since she could not appear to decide how she might, now that she'd managed to dangle from the draperies, come to undangle from them. Out on the strip of grass between the walk and the curb alongside the phonepole Mr. Dick Atwater watched Miss Bernice Fay Frazier's cat Bubbles swing in silhouette and thought her as well to appear quite thoroughly forlorn at it though Mr. Dick Atwater had dropped off lately into such a mood that no matter where he looked he found desolation, even in a cat dangling from sheer draperies which struck him as a source of grief. He'd been two days now and one full night hollow and cavernous and relatively done in by her chiefly with the hair and with the lips and with the fingerends and he saw her face most all over and heard her dainty laugh on the breeze, or strenuously undertook anyhow to see her face and to hear her dainty laugh like he figured maybe he ought to to be truly forsaken. She'd sent him a card. She'd not just up and left after all but had taken the time to explain to him her motives and inclinations in as much as she could explain her motives and inclinations to him on the back of a Belvedere Hotel postcard with, on the front of it, an artist's rendering of the Belvedere Hotel itself which the artist who'd rendered it had quite obviously not ever laid eyes on since he'd fashioned the place to look pretty much like the palace at Versailles but with potted geraniums and a green canvas awning out front, just the sort of a spot where a man and a woman could throw in together on a fullblown assignation like Mr. Dick Atwater could not, along with the face and the dainty laugh, help but undertake to conjure up as well.

It was pretty much your typical Dear Jerome sort of a card. She saluted him there at the outset with a Hey! prior to sharing with him the news of how she'd found him to be nice, found him in fact to be awfully nice and would evermore cherish the evenings they'd passed together though she preferred, she guessed, to be diddled by somebody else entirely which of course she'd not come flat out and said though Mr. Dick Atwater, who'd read that card every way but edgewise, had assumed it almost straightoff as an implication. She wished him much success in his pursuits and went to the trouble even to bless him prior to signing off with Xs over top of a happy face and Mr. Dick Atwater caught onto the Xs chiefly and invested them with undue passion, passion enough anyway to leave him to wonder how she could give him over and X him so both at the same time.

"Aw Mary Alice," Dick Atwater said from the strip of grass between the walk and the curb and extracted the card from his coatpocket so as to study it one time further like would be the sentiments on the back and like would be the grand and preposterous rendition on the front as well.

He'd taken to wandering about, had anyway for two days and one evening now wandered about as he'd not known otherwise what in the world to do with himself and his troublesome vacant cavity and so had figured he might as well be afoot, figured he'd just as soon drift and roam loose from his moorings, so he'd walked and loitered and walked some more like had made him most especially difficult for Mr. Nestor Tudor to find, Mr. Nestor Tudor who'd been seeking Mr. Dick Atwater in his Fairlane, had been trolling around for him on account of how it seemed to him he had a thing likely to say to Mr. Dick Atwater, Mr. Dick Atwater who he'd beaten and balded for the sake of a woman who'd run off to rend the national moral fabric with somebody else altogether. He didn't truly know what thing precisely it was he had to say, but he felt sure it would come to him once he'd found Mr. Dick Atwater to say it to. So he rode round this evening like he'd ridden round the evening previous and headed south down the boulevard and headed north back up it and swung east towards Mr. Dick Atwater's house where Mr. Dick Atwater did not appear to be and headed then southwest where he eased up before Mr. Wayne Fulp's and spied at last Mr. Dick Atwater alongside the phonepole on the strip of grass.

For his part, Mr. Dick Atwater was not at all aware he was being joined until he'd been in fact joined already by Mr. Nestor Tudor who Mr. Dick Atwater turned briefly and glared at prior to standing again like he'd stood and watching again what he'd been watching. Nestor Tudor just stood as well for a time but did presently manage to speak, looked where it was Mr. Dick Atwater was looking and worked up an inquiry on account of it, asked of Mr. Dick Atwater, "What is that?"

"Cat," Mr. Dick Atwater told to him, and together they studied how Bubbles clung to the sheer drapery which itself twitched and swayed in the windowbox.

"He hung up?" Nestor Tudor wanted to know.

And Mr. Dick Atwater told to him, "She seems to be."

Nestor Tudor confessed how he did not suppose he would ever have a cat himself since he'd never worked up somehow a partiality for cats that Dick Atwater confessed back he did not hardly give a happy shit about like would usually have touched off some turmoil but Nestor Tudor supposed he'd had with Mr. Dick Atwater turmoil enough already so he allowed Mr. Dick Atwater not to give a happy shit unscathed and just stood for a time alongside him watching the draperies sway and lurch before wondering was Mr. Dick Atwater meaning to stand against the phonepole on the strip of grass all the night.

"I might be," Dick Atwater told to him.

And Nestor Tudor said, "Well," and then turned and indicated his Fairlane, "I got my car there. Thought I'd go riding."

"Go riding," Dick Atwater told to him and then laid his fingers to a contusion like had come over the past couple of days to be a habit with him.

"Why don't you come on?" Nestor Tudor said. "Why don't you come on and ride with me?"

And Dick Atwater did not guess he would and did not guess he wouldn't either one but just laid against the phonepole watching the outline of Bubbles the dangling cat endeavoring somehow to come to be undangled.

"Come on, Dick," Nestor Tudor told to him, "ain't nobody here," and Dick Atwater looked from the windows to the ground before him and from the ground before him to the windowbox again and he said presently to Nestor Tudor, "Ain't nobody here, is there?"

"Nobody," Nestor Tudor assured him and then stood watching Dick Atwater alongside him and continued just to stand watching Dick Atwater even once he'd raised off the pole and stepped into the gutter and struck out across the road to the Fairlane where he situated himself on the seat and cranked down the window and inquired of Nestor Tudor, "You coming?" that Nestor Tudor from atop the grass strip between the walk and the curbing jerked his head yes about.

And they just rode there at the outset, south down the boulevard so far as the bypass and north back up it beyond the square and the colonel with his sword unsheathed and near about to the power plant where Nestor Tudor swung west so as to show to Dick Atwater a house he'd come across previously, a white frame house with gaudy turquoise shutters and an altogether inexplicable barn red door like were sufficient in combination to induce Nestor Tudor and Dick Atwater to agree how they did not know precisely what was wrong with some people. They passed a place Dick Atwater used to live as a child before it had come to be a thicket chiefly with a chimney in it somewhere and a splintery elm stump out front in a swale where the tree had succumbed to the beetle and the blight, and Dick Atwater recalled his momma had grown roses in the sideyard and they stopped dead in the road to look for the remnants of a bush but could not see much past the milkweed and the brambles. "She had a touch with roses," Mr. Dick Atwater said. "It's not everybody that does," which Nestor Tudor straightaway agreed about and sat in his Fairlane in the road looking with Mr. Dick Atwater at the chimney and the thicket and the splintery stump, Mr. Dick Atwater who reached up with his fingers and laid them to a contusion on his cheek that he left shortly for a red prickly bald patch instead which he touched and loitered upon and discharged a breath about, a breath fairly ripe with longing and regret like served itself as preface to an observation, an observation Mr. Dick Atwater turned towards Nestor Tudor and made. "I wish," he said, "you hadn't pulled out these here. I won't ever get them back."

And Nestor Tudor and Dick Atwater looked for a moment square across the Fairlane at each other like seemed to Nestor Tudor a suitable occasion for him to tell Dick Atwater the thing he'd gone to the trouble to hunt him up in the first place to tell to him which he still had not cultivated exactly the words for and so merely snorted instead, snorted and shook his head back of it like prompted from Dick Atwater an identical display and turned out after all to be the thing Nestor Tudor had meant all along to say.

"I think I could use a soda," Dick Atwater told to Nestor Tudor. "Got a few things to wash down," and Nestor Tudor, who confessed he was pining a little for a soda himself, proceeded west to the junction at 87 and north up it past a Sunoco that was shut already for the night and so far as Mr. Tadlock's sports complex that Nestor Tudor turned into the gravel lot of under the bluewhite vapor lights and eased on up to the rail fence short of the carpet links where a child was lingering alongside number twelve attempting to fracture the concrete slab with his putterhead alone notwithstanding how he was being ever so passionately advised over the loudspeaker that fracturing the slab was just the variety of thing they discouraged out on the carpet links. And as they got out of the car Nestor Tudor looked from the links to the range to the illuminated cinder path off towards the pond and told to Dick Atwater, "Some place. Can't say I've ever been here."

"I have," Dick Atwater told him back. "Once."

"Didn't know you golfed."

"Oh yeah," Dick Atwater said. "Send that ball screaming."

Nestor Tudor bought Sundrops from the machine and him and Dick Atwater together strolled out between the range and the links where they sat on a bench and watched Mr. Dale Gentry hit with a long iron,

Mr. Dale Gentry who had on shiny white golf shoes and red trousers and a white shirt with tiny blue horizontal stripes to it and a bird on the breastpocket not even to mention his skyblue golfing glove and his skyblue golfing hat and his slender embossed green towel dangling from his beltloop, his slender embossed green towel that he wiped his clubheads with most especially in the wake of a shank like was for Mr. Dale Gentry rare since he tended to hit the ball square and true, had established what Mr. Dick Atwater called at Nestor Tudor his personal rhythm and thereby induced Nestor Tudor, who'd been watching previously just the red pants chiefly that struck him as uglier even than his own purple horsehead shirt, to study pretty much the rest of Mr. Dale Gentry as well, Mr. Dale Gentry who hunkered and waggled and flexed and set and rotated and cocked and paused and uncoiled and swept and squealed and extended which was just itself for practice and served as preamble to the ensuing legitimate hunkering and waggling and flexing and setting and rotating and cocking and pausing and uncoiling and sweeping and squealing and extending that put the actual ball in flight.

Now Nestor Tudor was not himself a student of the game and he turned straightoff to Dick Atwater and confessed how he was not himself a student of the game at all, "but I've seen those boys on TV," Nestor Tudor said, "and I don't recall that they do much squealing," which prompted and inspired Dick Atwater to spit Sundrop in a sparkly mist all over the both of them.

If Miss Fay Dull had gone to the trouble in the first place to carry her parka with her she was meaning to perch upon it and announced as much most especially to the Reverend Mr. Theodore J. Parnell who she guessed would know that they could not the bunch of them encounter with any good effect from patio furniture since they had cause to get down low with their karmas if they hoped to delve and plumb with measurable success. The Reverend Mr. Parnell, however, had worn this evening his buffcolored suit that would undoubtedly show off grass stains like neon which induced him to differ with Miss Fay Dull along with most everybody otherwise who differed with Miss Fay Dull as well except for Tiny Aaron and except for Mrs. MaySue Ludley, Tiny Aaron who sat directly on the grass and Mrs. MaySue Ludley who sat on Tiny Aaron's madras jacket that he'd flung and laid for her with extravagant ceremony. Miss Bernice Fay Frazier retained her folding chair with the addition of a plank beneath the backlegs which Mr. Estelle Singletary assured her she would surely not under regular circumstances require but the ground had come to be somehow so spongy and soft that even the merest wisp of a woman like Miss Bernice Fay Frazier might sink in it up to the fenders. Everybody else went pretty much plankless and as there were not sufficient chairs to go around Mr. Phillip J. King and Mr. Wyatt Benbow and Mr. H. Monroe Aycock sat on the picnic bench while Mr. Cecil Dutton, who went off to the garage after a crate to upend, discovered instead Mrs. Estelle Singletary's folding lounger that he carried out and unfolded and lounged shortly upon.

The Reverend Mr. Parnell, who had duties and obligations that would soon call him away, guessed he might for his part touch off the proceedings with a variety of invocation, and as it was his custom to stand and invoke he did stand and did begin invoking in his deepest preacherly tones. He sought to bless their gathering and to give thanks to the Maker for the bounty they'd just enjoyed and called out even a few of the dishes by name like would be Mrs. Estelle Singletary's bean casserole, Mrs. Luther Teague's chicken in a pot with the feathery crust, and most especially Mrs. Phillip J. King's iridescent banger and turnip stew which the reverend had found unique among the dishes. Of course, Mrs. Phillip J. King rose directly up out from her own seat and gave thanks herself, interrupted the invocation so as to tell how the banger and turnip stew had been in fact nothing truly. She spoke as well of her joy at seeing it sopped and devoured after what fashion it had been sopped and devoured in fact, and she grew fairly rapturous at the prospect of other unique dishes she might carry to encounters in the future convinced like she was that there were people roundabout with the palates to relish fine cuisine.

"Ambrosia to mine," Tiny Aaron fairly hollered at her from down alongside Mrs. MaySue Ludley who clutched at his elbowjoint and admired how he'd just lately hollered.

"Aw," Mrs. Phillip J. King told to him in such a tone as to invite Mr. Tiny Aaron to repeat and confirm what he'd only just lately finished hollering, so he did in fact repeat and confirm it.

As best as Miss Bernice Fay Frazier could tell, her personal encounter was ever so rapidly degenerating into a manner of testimonial to Mrs. Phillip J. King's covered dish and she sought to regain the purpose of the affair in the first place by manufacturing a plaintive sort of a wail that did not in fact regain the purpose straightaway but managed to rouse Mr. Luther Teague who'd dozed off in the midst of the invocation atop Mrs. Estelle Singletary's lounger and grew sufficiently stirred on account of the plaintive wail to raise up and inquire of everybody, "What?" like punctuated Mrs. Phillip J. King and Mr. Tiny Aaron both and allowed the Reverend Mr. Parnell to take up one time more the reins of the invocation which he gripped and held to as he spoke just generally of Miss Bernice Fay Frazier's recent tribulation and strife.

"A whole sea of it," the widow Mrs. Askew could not help somehow but interject though she suffered herself to be forestalled by the reverend from interjecting further, the reverend who invoked mostly at her, "Yes, a sea of tribulation, a sea of strife, an entire world of pain suffered at the hands of a stranger in our midsts, a faithless woman," which Miss Bernice Fay Frazier, who'd not personally intended to interject herself, could not truly help but interject in back of due to how she felt inclined to suggest to the reverend conniving trash as a substitute for faithless woman since faithless woman did not seem to Miss Bernice Fay Frazier to travel awful close to the heart of the thing.

"Conniving trash?" the reverend said.

And Miss Bernice Fay Frazier told to him, "Please, if you will," like the reverend supposed he might though he found conniving trash quite thoroughly irregular in an invocational sort of a way. He made it, however, fit in nonetheless and sound even a little prayerful as he invoked it and he concluded with the hope that Miss Bernice Fay Frazier might go for a while pretty completely unconnived that most everybody otherwise saw fit to throw in with and interject about.

Once he'd left off the invocation and suffered himself to be congratulated about it, the Reverend Mr. Parnell departed almost straightaway, after that is he'd taken up Miss Bernice Fay Frazier at the fingers and shared with her a low preacherly sentiment meant just for her alone and intended not at all for Mrs. Cecil Dutton who leaned in only to learn from Miss Bernice Fay Frazier of her wishes that Mrs. Cecil Dutton would lean back out again. Of course in the absence of the reverend, the widow Mrs. Askew felt duty bound to step forward and take charge of the encounter herself and she provided fair cause in the form of an elaborate and quite incomprehensible declaration partly on the topic of how uneasy it is the head lies that wears the crown but partly as well on a topic otherwise that sounded to Mr. Tiny Aaron to have a thing to do with a verdant copse like was not a sort of copse he knew personally anything about and so sought illumination from Mr. H. Monroe Aycock who was evermore prepared to illuminate.

The widow Mrs. Askew did not truly stir much ardor as a candidate for encounter leader and Mr. Estelle Singletary, who'd deciphered a pointed glance, nominated Mrs. Estelle Singletary in her stead, Mrs. Estelle Singletary who demurred so convincingly that Mr. Estelle Singletary moved to unnominate her and so entertained one glance further still. The ensuing vote left Mrs. Estelle Singletary the altogether decisive victor which the widow Mrs. Askew muttered a moderately gracious sort of a pithy thing about before retiring to the far reaches of the encounter circle between Mr. Luther Teague, who'd lately sought the position of Worshipful Master at the Masonic hall but had lost it in a runoff and so guessed he could purely relate to and identify with the widow Mrs. Askew's present plight which he insisted at her in breathy elevated tones he could, and Mr. Cecil Dutton sprawled flat out again atop the lounger with his eyes shut and his head laid over sideways and a streak of drool trailing out the corner of his mouth. Mrs. Estelle Singletary who'd had, she insisted, no designs on encounter leadership accepted boldly the challenge of the position and swore as her oath to be as sensitive to as many needs and vibes as she could possibly be sensitive to like prompted Mr. Estelle Singletary to endeavor to incite a huzzah but he could not manage somehow to incite one.

Naturally, it seemed to Mrs. Estelle Singletary that Miss Bernice Fay Frazier's vibes and needs were the ones they all should straightaway pay some heed to which Mrs. Dwight Mobley seconded and Miss Fay Dull seconded with her and so together carried the motion which Mrs. Estelle Singletary took as a mandate and consequently turned the floor directly over to her afflicted sister who received an ovation at the instigation of Mr. Estelle Singletary as recompense for the huzzah he'd lately failed to incite. Miss Bernice Fay Frazier, of course, hardly knew exactly where to start and so set out with a frantic quiver that gave way to a scant bout of blubbering which brought forth a tissue from Mrs. Phillip J. King, a tissue she'd licked to wipe her tureen with but had not truly made any use of otherwise like had left it only a little orange in places. As a suggestion, Mrs. Wyatt Benbow wondered if wouldn't Miss Bernice Fay Frazier sketch out for them all her recent plagues and torments which Miss Bernice Fay Frazier did in fact attempt and got so far as her cat Bubbles and her troublesome sciatic nerves before she fell into the throes of some relatively inarticulate puling and whining on the topic, as best as anybody could tell, of the taint that had come to Miss Bernice Fay Frazier from her with the hair and the lips and the fingerends, her who'd lately rended the national moral fabric which prompted Mr. H. Monroe Aycock to interject at Miss Bernice Fay Frazier, "Rent," and he used it for her in an utterly unrelated sentence about the national moral fabric and then repeated for the benefit of most everybody, "Rent," and expressed behind it his own personal belief that it was not such a stretch to be distraught and correct at the same time.

The effect upon Miss Bernice Fay Frazier's personal psyche was palpable and immediate and she puled and whined and blubbered with renewed zeal and spoke ever so damply of how she was not just anymore plagued and tormented but was grammatically culpable on top of it, chastised and humiliated and kicked surely when she was down like brought to bear upon Mr. H. Monroe Aycock what he himself identified as thoroughgoing opprobrium. He guessed he was in some danger of becoming a veritable pariah, which he spoke of as well, when Mr. Tiny Aaron wondered might Mr. H. Monroe Aycock, as long as he was making sentences, devise one for verdant copse on account of how, Tiny Aaron confessed, he did not have much grip on verdant copse truly. Needless to say, the opprobrium shifted to Tiny Aaron almost straightaway since he was quite plainly unelevated himself and had not even been invited to the encounter in the first place that Miss Bernice Fay Frazier and Mrs. Estelle Singletary and the widow Mrs. Askew as well took turns insinuating before Mrs. Phillip J. King, who'd been gratified previously by Tiny Aaron's enthusiasm for her turnip and banger stew, rose to his defense, or said anyhow to the ladies in question, "Just hush," like served to shift the opprobrium one time further still.

Miss Bernice Fay Frazier found herself shortly pressed to wonder if couldn't they please get back to her plagues and torments as she had not by a long stretch exhausted her puling and her whining like inspired the widow Mrs. Askew to air a pithy sort of a sentiment about the wonders of this world and how they did not ever seem to her to cease, a sentiment however not near in fact so pithy as to remain incomprehensible even to Miss Bernice Fay Frazier who was in chiefly her puling and her whining mode but possessed the personal resources to fathom and plumb simultaneously and so grew sufficiently offended to inform the widow Mrs. Askew how if she did not personally care for the tenor of the proceedings she could pack up her pith and just haul it on out of there.

"I believe I might," the widow Mrs. Askew declared and then sought straightaway to revise her declaration to the effect that what she believed she might do was step on over to the buffet and enjoy a helping of her exotic curried fruit dish with the altogether extraordinary oatmeal crust that she'd not seen anybody much have the decency to taste even like was cause yet for another pithy item about her own personal culinary nonconformity and how the world whipped her with its displeasure on account of it which prompted her as she rose to suppose straightoff how if she always scorned appearances she always could which itself inspired her to an additional item about the hobgoblin of little minds which she was pretty much in the midst of when she stepped full into the hole in the yard Mr. Estelle Singletary had attempted with the semiperpendicular buffet to cover before he'd come to be prevented from it. For a hole it was not awfully deep but was spacious enough to accommodate the widow Mrs. Askew's right leg well up the shinbone past the ankle like seriously impeded and punctuated her pith entirely which itself gave way to what amounted to some puling and some whining of her own and she cried out and pitched over after such a fashion as to seem to Miss Bernice Fay Frazier pretty much a ruse and Miss Bernice Fay Frazier turned far enough around in her folding chair to tell to the widow Mrs. Askew, "Get up," but the widow Mrs. Askew just laid upon the ground in a heap and puled and whined and whimpered until Mr. Wyatt Benbow stepped over to her to inquire about her predicament when she gurgled a little as well.

He meant to raise her to her feet, extract her from the hole and set her once more upright upon the yard but did not presently possess the strength of ten men like Mr. Wyatt Benbow discovered, once he'd caught up a piece of the widow Mrs. Askew and pulled at it, he'd have some call for if he meant to lift her even a little. So he enlisted the assistance of Mr. Sleepy Pitts and Mr. Luther Teague and Mr. Estelle Singletary and Mr. Phillip J. King and Tiny Aaron as well who assured them all he'd hoisted women previously and so knew precisely just how to go about it, and they each grabbed onto a piece of the widow Mrs. Askew and puled and whined and whimpered themselves as they brought her out from the hole and righted her onto her feet and then came to be persuaded by the widow Mrs. Askew, who felt weak and who felt wobbly, to carry her back to the encounter circle where they settled her upon Mrs. Estelle Singletary's reclining lounger once Mr. Wyatt Benbow had managed, by the application of his shoetoe chiefly, to dislodge Mr. Cecil Dutton who jumped to his feet and stood of a sudden blinking before the widow Mrs. Askew and her entourage and felt compelled to inquire of them, "What?"

Mr. H. Monroe Aycock, who was not of course a doctor himself, was acquainted nonetheless with medical dictates, he called them, and so assumed the task of feeling with his fingerends the widow Mrs. Askew's ankle and telling to her, "Hmmm," just precisely like an actual doctor might. He pronounced it a sprain though he did not speak of what sort of sprain exactly it was and so heard straightaway from the widow Mrs. Askew who campaigned for a severe sprain while Miss Bernice Fay Frazier inquired of Mr. H. Monroe Aycock if wasn't it likely a scant and altogether niggling sort of a sprain instead that Mr. H. Monroe Aycock guessed he could not from just his fingerends say, and he was set to enlarge upon the medical uses and limitations of fingerends when Mrs. Estelle Singletary got up out from her own chair and crossed through the heart of the encounter circle to the lounger where she took occasion to berate Mr. Estelle Singletary on account of the hole in the yard that he certainly should have seen to previously already which touched off from Mr. Estelle Singletary talk of the moderately perpendicular buffet table with which he'd intended to cover the hole before he'd come to be prevented from it. Naturally, Mrs. Estelle Singletary wondered was he implying it was all primarily her fault then, and Mr. Estelle Singletary told to her after a fashion yes, or did not anyway tell to her no like she could not help but take for yes and so she grew induced to berate Mr. Estelle Singletary further still and was intending to speak of his various poor qualities when Miss Bernice Fay Frazier wondered might the blame lie elsewhere instead, might the blame lie maybe with the inedible curried fruit dish that the widow Mrs. Askew had been drawn to eat since nobody else could.

Understandably, the widow Mrs. Askew rose as best as she was able to the defense of most especially her elaborate oatmeal crust and had begun to tell of the particular ingredients when Miss Fay Dull, who hardly intended to perch upon her parka all the evening, interrupted the widow Mrs. Askew so as to inquire in a general sort of a way if they meant to delve and relate and plumb and fathom and identify further still since she had better things to do than loll upon the ground and the widow Mrs. Askew, who was not truly of a mood to bear interrupting, told to Miss Fay Dull, "Well get up then," and Miss Fay Dull guessed she just might and so raised her fingers in the direction of Mr. Wyatt Benbow, Mr. Wyatt Benbow who had not suspected he'd pass the evening hoisting sizeable women and made a face that pretty thoroughly informed Miss Fay Dull of it.

Mrs. Cecil Dutton guessed at Mrs. Luther Teague that a capable encounter leader would have long since brought some order to the proceedings and Mrs. Luther Teague could not possibly have agreed with her more and suggested that they make a frank and candid disclosure on the topic to Mrs. Estelle Singletary herself, Mrs. Estelle Singletary who was still berating Mr. Estelle Singletary with apparently inexhaustible energy and enthusiasm, Mrs. Estelle Singletary who heard out even the bulk of the frank and candid disclosure on the topic of her meager powers as encounter leader before she shared with Mrs. Cecil Dutton and Mrs. Luther Teague how she did not personally give a big goddam what they thought like was simply grist, the ladies agreed, for the mill.

Most everybody, then, was growing offended by stages and the men in particular who'd savored and sopped the orange stew were coming to be palpably dyspeptic as well and so stood roundabout with their hands upon their bellies and paid some appreciable heed to their juices and gases that mingled and that surged, so much heed in fact that they could not hardly hope to delve and plumb and relate and fathom and identify not even to mention quarrel and bicker and seethe and so just stood by instead marshaling their ducts and sweating under their noses and wondering of their wives in frail little voices if couldn't they possibly head on out towards home. Mrs. Luther Teague and Mrs. Cecil Dutton themselves touched off the exodus since they'd suffered already a staggering affront at the hands of their hostess and they gathered up their dishes and simply departed, or truly got driven and herded up out of the backyard and past the house to the curb by Mr. Luther Teague and Mr. Cecil Dutton who were both together dancing to the tune of the banger and turnip two-step and were feeling between them far more lubricated than they guessed they had any right or inclination even to feel. Miss Fay Dull, who'd lolled upon her parka quite long enough, went off shortly herself in a fit of pique and was followed fairly precipitously by Mr. and Mrs. Wyatt Benbow and Mr. and Mrs. Sleepy Pitts together that wished they'd not ever agreed to encounter in the first place, most especially Mrs. Sleepy Pitts who was missing at that very moment the show on the cable about the mysteries of the universe, the show on the cable that was this evening to have focused upon an altogether inexplicable sinkhole in Cincinnati that she wished she'd stayed home for.

Even Mr. H. Monroe Aycock, who'd hoped to find occasion in the course of the evening to rail against Godless communism, could not foresee any longer the prospect of it and so took his leave of Miss Bernice Fay Frazier and Mr. and Mrs. Estelle Singletary along with the widow Mrs. Askew and her indeterminate sprain and was about even to make off clean before he came to be enlisted by Mr. Tiny Aaron and Mr. Phillip J. King and on behalf of Mr. Estelle Singletary, who was too busy getting berated to speak, to help them to haul the widow Mrs. Askew across the backyard and up the drive to the curb since they did not want to get left alone to haul her notwithstanding how she'd failed yet to request to get hauled like they suspected shortly she would request it. So they hauled her preemptively, the four of them at first but the three of them presently since Mr. Estelle Singletary could manage to suffer hardship and abuse on only one front at a time, and they carried her across the grass to the drive where they set her down by mutual consent flat upon the asphalt or explained anyhow that by mutual consent they'd set her down once they'd all three of them together in fact dropped her instead. It was Tiny Aaron who suggested the TV cart, though Mr. H. Monroe Aycock disclosed how he'd been ruminating himself upon the matter, and they fetched the thing out from alongside the peony bed and endeavored to entice the widow Mrs. Askew to climb upon it, the widow Mrs. Askew who was looking to get raised and lifted and so did not in fact offer to climb but merely stayed where she'd ended up until they plucked her together up off the drive and settled her upon the cart that flexed and creaked but did not somehow splinter into countless little woodgrained slivers like Mr. Phillip J. King in particular had suspected it might.

Mr. H. Monroe Aycock offered to navigate, offered exclusively to navigate alone but came shortly to be charged to push as well on account of how the little plastic wheels were not themselves even half so well lubricated as the indigenous digestive tracts, so they all three together heaved and groaned and advanced up the drive after a slow and stately sort of a fashion while the widow Mrs. Askew held as best as she was able to the cart edges and thereby completed the spectacle which looked most especially from down in the backyard like some variety of parade float gone horribly wrong. Mrs. Estelle Singletary could not even manage to rail and berate much in the face of such a display and so abused Mr. Estelle Singletary in only a wan and feeble sort of a way while she watched the TV cart advance up the drive, watched in the company of Mr. Estelle Singletary and Mrs. Dwight Mobley and Mrs. Phillip J. King and Mrs. MaySue Ludley as well, Mrs. MaySue Ludley who removed a lacy handkerchief from her pocketbook and waved it in the air as she shouted encouragement to most especially Mr. Tiny Aaron who was quite obviously, she told it, bearing the bulk of the weight.

They accumulated even some velocity as the driveway peaked and flattened and they gained the road at what seemed particularly to the widow Mrs. Askew an altogether reckless speed which she was entirely too busy shrieking and wailing to speak of, most especially once they'd swung out into the middle of the street and wheeled round to make for the passenger door of Mrs. Dwight Mobley's Caprice Classic where it appeared to the widow Mrs. Askew she would surely come to be wrecked and mangled. However, Mr. Phillip J. King and Mr. Tiny Aaron and Mr. H. Monroe Aycock managed in fact to slow the cart sufficiently so that they did not find call but to bounce the widow Mrs. Askew off the fender well just the one time which she proved to be inordinately grateful about and she lifted her arms so as to allow herself to get raised and hefted once further, raised and hefted and deposited altogether abruptly upon the carseat which she came to be informed had been in fact the product of mutual consent as well.

Mrs. Dwight Mobley, who'd walked up the drive herself in the wake of the procession, could not quite figure how she might offload the widow Mrs. Askew once she'd gotten her home and she endeavored with a look alone to entreat Mr. Phillip J. King and Mr. Tiny Aaron and Mr. H. Monroe Aycock too who would not somehow stand to be entreated and so joined Mrs. Dwight Mobley in her general bafflement and did not guess they could much themselves figure the thing either. Mrs. Dwight Mobley returned partway down the drive to yell into the backyard at Miss Bernice Fay Frazier and inquire was she intending to ride home with her but Miss Bernice Fay Frazier only sat in her folding chair upon her plank and gazed out before herself at the encounter circle like was anymore just chairs and a bench and a lounger along with some vacant grassy places, her encounter circle where she'd anticipated she would likely manage to come to be improved if not healed outright, would likely plumb and fathom and delve and relate and identify and get sufficiently at last in touch with her own feelings to discover that she was probably OK after all like she'd not in fact done truly any of but had only instead stained her dressfront with ambrosia juice and pretty dramatically smeared her visage.

"Bernice," Mrs. Dwight Mobley called to her one time further and managed even to turn her partway around. "You coming?"

And Miss Bernice Fay Frazier told her back a breathy Yes like was hardly enough of a Yes to suit Mrs. Dwight Mobley who inquired another time further still which served to raise and animate Miss Bernice Fay Frazier who pushed out from her chair and crossed past the buffet to the drive where she endured a rendezvous with Mrs. Phillip J. King whose tureen was so near to empty that she could pick it up herself like she'd picked it up herself which she showed to Miss Bernice Fay Frazier she had and carried it even up the drive alongside Miss Bernice Fay Frazier and so far as the curbing where she issued some altogether frantic instructions to Mr. Phillip J. King whom she wished would come and take the tureen as merely a convenience to her and not hardly because it was burdened any longer with much stew at all to speak of.

Miss Bernice Fay Frazier bid everybody good evening, told anyhow, "Night then," to Mr. and Mrs. Phillip J. King and Mr. and Mrs. Estelle Singletary and MaySue Ludley and Tiny Aaron and Mr. H. Monroe Aycock as well before she moved towards Mrs. Dwight Mobley's Caprice Classic where she discovered the widow Mrs. Askew nursing her indiscriminate sprain in the front seat and so climbed herself past the seatback Mrs. Dwight Mobley had upraised for her and settled her girthsome bones upon the rear cushion where she allowed herself to be consoled by the notion that she had at home to comfort her Bubbles her fluffy cat who'd managed in fact only lately to disengage herself from the sheer drapery by rendering the entire item into a manner of gauzy wadding.

North out the highway at the golf range, Nestor Tudor and Dick Atwater found they had together wearied of Mr. Dale Gentry's assorted antics and were not much taken any longer with the buglight as well and its intermittent shower of ignited moths and beetlebugs, and it was Nestor Tudor who suggested that perhaps they should ride further still and he had in mind the place precisely they should ride to which Mr. Dick Atwater was agreeable about and so proceeded with Nestor Tudor to the Fairlane and rode with him out from the lot and east to 14 and north up it to Nestor Tudor's own house where Nestor Tudor slipped into his drive and around back to the shed he'd built to put a car in but could not hope to get a car in any longer as he'd seen fit to fill it instead with flotsam and detritus, just any old thing he felt inclined to heave in through the doorway. He had an item to show to Dick Atwater and situated him in a springy metal chair in the backyard so as to prepare him to view it while he himself retired briefly to the house and returned with his bottle of Ancient Age and a bowl of ice cubes along with a squat and legitimate liquor glass for Mr. Dick Atwater and a Yosemite Sam jelly tumbler for himself. He poured the both of them pretty much full, too full but for a solitary cube apiece and insisted that they bang their glassrims together before they sipped and exhaled, so they did in fact bang their glassrims and then did sip and did exhale both.

Nestor Tudor instructed Dick Atwater in how precisely to sit in his springy metal chair with his feet upon the upended log before him which Dick Atwater was relatively quick to master and so rocked and sprung with Nestor Tudor who waited for the circumstances to get just precisely propitious before he pointed west out over the tops of the slash pines and the loblollies alongside his lot, pointed precisely at his own personal streak of gaudy sky which was fading presently from orange to pink as preamble to how it would shortly drain past the horizon altogether and so leave just the stars and the wispy clouds along with what piece of moon had been up a time already. And Dick Atwater was of a mind that it might perhaps be the most resplendent streak of gaudy sky he'd ever had the pleasure to see except for maybe a similar streak he and Mrs. Dick Atwater had shared together the sight of down at Salter Path sometime back. They'd sat on a piece of treetrunk by the sound and had watched the sun dip and fade off beyond the Coratan Forest.

"It was purely a sight," Dick Atwater confessed and looked from the present streak of gaudy sky to Nestor Tudor prior to gazing for a time into his squat legitimate liquor glass as he drew in a breath and discharged it. "Purely a sight," he told to his lone cube, and Nestor Tudor, who had a dead wife himself, took occasion to gaze into his own tumbler and breathe a little as well.

And the light gave way and the jarflies set in and with every new dram the glassrims beat together. Nestor Tudor smoked his Old Gold filters and Dick Atwater, who did not smoke, smoked Nestor Tudor's Old Gold filters too and, as they drew and inhaled, their cigarette coals illuminated their faces and a faint breeze carried their sparks and ashes off across the yard into the darkness which was anymore complete and thoroughgoing but for the ever so scant glow from the piece of moon that had climbed to the south of them and hung what appeared directly over town where it threw its paltry light down on the boulevard and the square and rooftops roundabout with the people beneath them who slept already and the people beneath them who didn't yet, the ones with cats to chastise and pitiful states to lament, the ones with ankles to elevate and icepacks to apply, the ones with almanacs to read upon the ring and wives to berate them as they did it, the ones with women to admire them like they would if they possibly could admire themselves, and the ones as well like Mr. and Mrs. Phillip J. King, Mr. and Mrs. Phillip J. King who had retired together to the bedroom where Mrs. Phillip J. King had slipped off to the halfbath to apply her unctions and ointments and various beauty creams while Mr. Phillip J. King had disrobed pretty much entirely but for his fuzzy blue socks and was sitting in the altogether atop the bedclothes awaiting Mrs. Phillip J. King who did in fact presently swing open the bathroom door and had embarked even upon a bit of talk further about her triumphant stew when she spied Mr. Phillip J. King, or spied anyway the moderately prominent token of his enthusiasm which fairly completely punctuated her and allowed Mr. Phillip J. King the occasion to slap at the mattress, cut his eyes sidelong like a variety of devious and sophisticated mackerel, and tell to her, "Babydoll," which in conjunction with the token itself induced Mrs. Phillip J. King to un-Scotchtape her hair and ungirdle her blue quilted housecoat and utterly spook and unnerve her terrier Ittybit that she drove before her as she charged across the room with as near as she could get anymore to abandon.

About the Author

T. R. Pearson is the author of three other novels, ***A Short History of a Small Place, Off for the Sweet Hereafter,*** and ***The Last of How It Was.***